PROLOGUE

The dead ship was a thing of obscene beauty.

Skade looped around it in a helical pseudo-orbit, her corvette's thrusters drumming a rapid tattoo of corrective bursts. The starscape wheeled behind the ship, the system's sun eclipsed and revealed with each loop of the helix. Skade's attention had lingered on the sun for a moment too long. She felt an ominous tightening in her throat, the onset of motion sickness.

It was not what she needed.

Irritated, Skade visualised her own brain in glassy three-dimensional complexity. As if peeling a fruit, she stripped away layers of neocortex and cortex, flinging aside the parts of her own mind that did not immediately interest her. The silvery loom of her implant web, topologically identical with her native synaptic network, shimmered with neural traffic, packets of information racing from neuron to neuron at a kilometre per second, ten times faster than the crawl of biological nerve signals. She could not actually perceive those signals moving—that would have required an accelerated rate of consciousness, which would have required even faster neural traffic—but the abstraction nonetheless revealed which parts of her augmented brain were the most active.

Skade zoomed in on a specific locus of brain function called the *Area Postrema,* an ancient tangle of neural circuitry that handled conflicts between vision and balance. Her inner ear felt only the steady pressure of her shuttle's acceleration, but her eyes saw a cyclically changing view as the background wheeled behind the ship. The ancient part of her brain could only reconcile that mismatch by assuming that Skade was hallucinating. It therefore sent a signal to another part of her brain that had evolved to protect the body from ingesting poisons.

Skade knew there was no point blaming her brain for making her feel nauseous. The hallucination/poison connection had worked very well for millions of years, allowing her ancestors to experiment with a wider diet than would otherwise have been possible. It just had no place here and now, on the chill, dangerous edge of another solar system. She supposed it would have made sense to erase such features by deftly rewiring the basic topology, but that was a lot easier said than done. The brain was holographic and messy, like a hopelessly overcomplicated computer program. Skade knew, therefore, that by "switching off" the part of her brain that was making her feel nauseous, she was almost certainly affecting other areas of brain function that shared some of the same neural circuitry. But she could live with that; she had done something similar a thousand times before, and she had seldom experienced any cognitive side effects.

There. The culprit region pulsed pink and dropped off the network. The nausea vanished; she felt a great deal better.

What remained was anger at her own carelessness. When she had been a field operative, making frequent incursions into enemy territory, she would never have left it until now to make such a modest neural adjustment. She had become sloppy, and that was unforgivable. Especially now that the ship had returned: an event that might prove to be as significant to the Mother Nest as any of the war's recent campaigns.

She felt sharper now. The old Skade was still there; she just needed to be dusted off and honed now and then.

[Skade, you will be careful, won't you? It's clear that something very peculiar has happened to this ship.]

The voice she heard was quiet, feminine and confined entirely to her own skull. She answered it subvocally.

I know.

[Have you identified it? Do you know which of the two it is, or was?]

It's Galiana's.

Now that she had swept around it, a three-dimensional image of the ship formed in her visual cortex, bracketed in a loom of shifting eidetic annotation as more information was teased out of the hulk.

[Galiana's? *The* Galiana's? You're sure of that?]

Yes. There were some small design differences between the three that left together, and in as much as this matches either of the two that haven't come back yet, it matches hers.

The presence took a moment to respond, as it sometimes did. [That was our conclusion as well. But something has clearly happened to this ship since it left the Mother Nest, wouldn't you say?]

A lot of somethings, if you ask me.

[Let's begin at the front and work backwards. There is evidence of damage—considerable damage: lacerations and gouges, whole portions of the hull that appear to have been removed and discarded, like diseased tissue. Plague, do you think?]

Skade shook her head, remembering her recent trip to Chasm City. *I've seen the effects of the Melding Plague up close. This doesn't look like quite the same thing.*

[We agree. This is something different. Nonetheless, full plague quarantine precautions should be enforced; we might still be dealing with an infectious agent. Focus your attention towards the rear, will you?]

The voice, which was never quite like any of the other voices she heard from other Conjoiners, took on a needling, tutorial quality, as if it already knew the answers to the questions it posed. [What do you make of the regular structures embedded in the hull, Skade?]

Here and there, situated randomly, were clusters of black cubes of varying size and orientation. They appeared to have been pressed into the hull as if into wet clay, so that their faces were half-concealed by the hulk's hull material. They radiated curving tails of smaller cubes, whipping out in elegant fractal arcs.

I'd say those are what they were trying to cut out elsewhere. Obviously they weren't fast enough to get them all.

[We concur. Whatever they are, they should certainly be treated with the utmost caution, although they may very well be inactive now. Perhaps Galiana was able to stop them spreading. Her ship was able to make it this far, even if it returned home on autopilot. You are sure that no one is alive aboard it, Skade?]

No, and I won't be until we open her up. But it doesn't look promising. No movement inside, no obvious hot spots. The hull's too cold for any life-support processes to be operational unless they're carrying a cryo-arithmetic engine.

Skade hesitated, running a few more simulations in her head as background processes.

[Skade . . . ?]

There could be a small number of survivors, I admit—but the bulk of the crew can't be anything other than frozen corpses. We might be able to trawl a few memories, but even that's probably being optimistic.

[We're really only interested in one corpse, Skade.]

I don't even know if Galiana's aboard it. And even if she is . . . even if we directed all our efforts into bringing her back to the living . . . we might not succeed.

[We understand. These are difficult times, after all. While it would be glorious to succeed, failure would be worse than never having attempted it. At least in the eyes of the Mother Nest.]

Is that the Night Council's considered opinion?

[All our opinions are considered, Skade. Visible failure cannot be tolerated. But that doesn't mean we won't do our best. If Galiana is aboard, we will do what we can to bring her back to us. But it must be done in absolute secrecy.]

How absolute, precisely?

[Knowledge of the ship's return will be impossible to conceal from the rest of the Mother Nest. But we can spare them the torment of hope, Skade. It will be reported that she is dead, beyond hope of revival. Let our compatriots' grief be quick and bright, like a nova. It will only make their efforts against the enemy more strenuous. But in the meantime we will work on her with diligence and love. If we bring her back to the living, her return will be a miracle. We will be forgiven our bending of the truth here and now.]

Skade caught herself before she laughed aloud. *Bending of the truth? It sounds like an outright lie to me. And how are you going to ensure that Clavain sticks to your story?*

[Why do you imagine Clavain will be a problem, Skade?]

She answered the question with a question of her own. *Don't tell me you're planning on not telling him either?*

[This is war, Skade. There is an old aphorism concerning truth and casualty with which we will not presently detain you, but we're certain you grasp the point. Clavain is a major asset in our tactical armoury. His thinking is unlike any other Conjoiner's, and for that reason he gives us a constant edge against the enemy. He will grieve and grieve quickly, like the others, and it will be painful. But then he will be his old self again, just when we need him the most. Better that, don't you think, than to inflict upon him some protracted period of hope and—likely—crushing disappointment?]

The voice shifted its tone, perhaps sensing that it still needed to make its point convincingly. [Clavain is an emotional man, Skade—more so than the rest of us. He was old when he came to us, older in neurological terms than any other recruit we have ever gained. His mind is still mired in old ways of thinking. We mustn't ever forget that. He is fragile and needs our care, like a delicate hothouse flower.]

But lying to him about Galiana . . .

[It may never come to that. We're getting ahead of ourselves. First we have to examine the ship—Galiana may not be aboard after all.]

Skade nodded. *That would be the best thing, wouldn't it? Then we'd know that she's still out there, somewhere.*

[Yes. But then we'd have to address the small matter of whatever happened to the third ship.]

In the ninety-five years since the onset of the Melding Plague, the Conjoiners had learned a great deal about contamination management. As one of the last human factions to retain an appreciable pre-plague technology, they took quarantine very seriously indeed. In peacetime the safest and easiest option would have been to examine the ship *in situ,* as it drifted through space on the system's edge. But there was too much risk of the Demarchists noticing such activity, so the investigations had to be conducted under cover of camouflage. The Mother Nest was already equipped to take contaminated craft, so it was the perfect destination.

But precautions still had to be taken, and that entailed a certain amount of work out in open space. First, servitors removed the engines, lasering through the spars that braced them on either side of the lighthugger's tapering conic hull. An engine malfunction could have destroyed the Mother Nest, and while such a thing was nearly unthinkable, Skade was determined to take no chances while the nature of what had happened to the ship remained mysterious. While that was going on, she ordered tractor rockets to haul slugs of black unsublimated cometary ice out to the drifter, which servitors then slathered on to the hull in a metre-thick caulk. The servitors completed their work quickly, without ever coming into direct contact with the hull. The ship had been dark to begin with; now it became impossibly black.

Once that was done, Skade fired grapples into the ice, anchoring tractor rockets all around the hulk. Since the ice would be bearing all the structural stress of moving the ship, she had to attach a thousand tractors to avoid fracturing any one part of the caulk. It was exquisitely beautiful when they all ignited: a thousand pinpricks of cold blue flame stabbing out from the black spirelike core of the drifter. She kept the acceleration slow, and her calculations had been so accurate that she needed only one small corrective burst before the final approach to the Mother Nest. Such bursts were timed to coincide with blind spots in the Demarchist's sensor coverage, blind spots which the Demarchists thought the Conjoiners knew nothing about.

Inside the Mother Nest, the hulk was hauled into a five-kilometre-wide ceramic-lined docking bay. The bay had been designed specifically for handling plague ships and was just large enough to accommodate a lighthugger with its engines removed. The ceramic walls were thirty metres thick and every item of machinery inside the bay was hardened against known plague strains. The chamber was sealed once the ship was inside it, along with Skade's hand-picked examination team. Because the bay had only the most meagre data connections with the rest of the Mother Nest, the team had to be primed to deal with isolation from the million other Conjoiners in the Nest. That requirement made for operatives who were not always the most stable—but Skade could hardly complain. She was the rarest of all: a Conjoiner who could operate entirely alone, deep in enemy territory.

Once the ship was secured, the chamber was pressurised with argon at two atmospheres. All but a fine layer of ice was removed from the ship by delicate ablation, with the final layer melted away over a period of six days. A flock of sensors hovered around the ship like gulls, sniffing the argon for any traces of foreign matter. But apart from chips of hull material nothing unusual was detected.

Skade bided her time, taking every possible precaution. She did not touch the ship until it was absolutely necessary. A hoop-shaped imaging gravitometer whirred along the ship, probing its internal structure, hinting at fuzzy interior details. Much of what Skade saw matched what she expected to see from the blueprints, but there were strange things that should not have been there: elongated black masses which corkscrewed and bifurcated through the ship's interior. They reminded her of bullet trails in forensic images, or the patterns sub-atomic particles made when they passed through cloud chambers. Where the black masses reached the outer hull, Skade always found one of the half-buried cubic structures.

But there was still room in the ship for humans to have survived, even though all the indications were that none still lived. Neutrino radar and gamma-ray scans elucidated more of the structure, but still Skade could not see the crucial details. Reluctantly, she moved to the next phase of her investigation: physical contact. She attached dozens of mechanical jackhammers around the hull, along with hundreds of paste-on microphones. The hammers started up, thudding against the hull. She heard the din in her spacesuit, transmitted through the argon. It sounded like an army of metalsmiths working overtime in a distant foundry. The microphones listened for the metallic echoes as the acoustic waves propagated through the ship. One of Skade's older neural routines unravelled the information buried in the arrival times of the echoes, assembling a tomographic density profile of the ship.

Skade saw it all in ghostly grey-greens. It did not contradict anything that she had already learned, and improved her knowledge in several areas. But she could glean nothing further without going inside, and that would not be easy. All the airlocks had been sealed from inside with plugs of molten metal. She cut through them, slowly and nervously, with lasers and hyperdiamond-tipped drills, feeling the crew's fear and desperation. When she had the first lock open she sent in an exploratory detachment of hardened servitors, ceramic-shelled crabs equipped with just enough intelligence to get the job done. They fed images back into her skull.

What they found horrified Skade.

The crew had been butchered. Some had been ripped apart, squashed, dismembered, pulped, sliced, fragmented. Others had been burned or suffocated or frozen. The carnage had evidently not happened quickly. As Skade absorbed the details, she began to picture how it must have happened: a series of pitched battles and last stands in various parts of the ship, with the crew raising makeshift barricades against the invaders. The ship itself had done its desperate best to protect its human charges, rearranging interior partitions to keep the enemy at bay. It had tried to flood certain areas with coolant or high-pressure atmosphere, and in those cells Skade found the corpses of strange, ungainly machines—conglomerations of thousands of black geometric shapes.

She formed a hypothesis. It was not difficult. The cubes had glued themselves on to the outside of Galiana's ship. They had multiplied, growing as they absorbed and reprocessed the ship's integument. In that respect it was indeed a little plaguelike. But the plague was microscopic; one never saw the individual elements of the spore with the naked eye. This was more brutal and mechanistic, almost fascistic, in the way it replicated. The plague at least imbued transformed matter with something of its earlier characteristics, yielding chimeric phantasms of machine and flesh.

No, Skade told herself. She was certainly not dealing with the Melding Plague, as comforting as that might now have been.

The cubes had wormed into the ship and then formed attacking units—soldier conglomerations. These soldiers had done the killing, advancing slowly away from each infection point. Judging by the remains they were lumpy and asymmetric, more like dense swarms of hornets than individual entities. They must have been able to squirm through the tiniest opening, reassembling on the other side. Nonetheless, the battle had taken time. By Skade's estimate, it might have taken many days for the whole ship to fall. Many weeks, even.

She shivered at the thought of it.

A day after they had first entered, her servitors found some human bodies that were nearly intact, except that their heads had been swallowed by black helmets of surrounding cubes. The alien machinery appeared inert. The servitors removed parts of the helmets and found that prongs of machine-growth reached into the corpses' skulls, through the eye sockets or the ears or the nasal cavity. Further study showed that the prongs had bifurcated many times, until they reached microscopic scale. They extended deep into the brains of the dead, establishing connections with their native Conjoiner implants.

But the machines, and their hosts, were now very much dead.

Skade tried to work out what had happened; the ship's records were thoroughly scrambled. It was obvious that Galiana had encountered something hostile, but why hadn't the cubes simply destroyed her ship in one go? The infiltration had been slow and painstaking, and it only made sense if the cubes wanted to keep the ship intact for as long as possible.

There had been another ship: two had gone on—what had happened to that one?

[Ideas, Skade?]

Yes. But nothing I like.

[You think the cubes wanted to learn as much as possible, don't you?]

I can't think of any other reason. They put taps into their minds, reading their neural machinery. They were intelligence-gathering.

[Yes. We agree. The cubes must have learned a great deal about us. We have to consider them a threat, even if we don't yet know where Galiana was when they found her. But there is a glimmer of hope, wouldn't you say?]

Skade failed to see what that glimmer could possibly be. Humanity had been searching for an unambiguous alien intelligence for centuries. All they had found so far had been tantalising leads—the Pattern Jugglers, the Shrouders, the archaeological remains of another eight or nine dead cultures. They had never encountered another extant machine-using intelligence, nothing to measure themselves against.

Until now.

And what this machine-using intelligence did, so it seemed, was stalk, infiltrate and slaughter, and then invade skulls.

It was not, Skade conceded, the most fruitful of first encounters.

Hope? Are you serious?

[Yes, Skade, because we don't know that the cubes were ever able to transmit that knowledge back to whatever it was that sent them. Galiana's ship made it back home, after all. She must have steered it here, and she would not have done that if she thought there was any danger of leading the enemy back to us. Clavain would be proud, I think. She was still thinking of us; still thinking of the Mother Nest.]

But she ran the risk . . .

The voice of the Night Council cut her off sharply. [The ship is a warning, Skade. That is what Galiana intended and that is how we must read it.]

A warning?

[That we must be ready. They are still out there, and one way or another we will meet them again.]

You almost sound as if you were expecting them to arrive.

But the Night Council said nothing.

It was another week before they found Galiana, for the ship was vast and there had been many changes to its interior that prohibited a rapid search. Skade had gone inside it herself, along with other sweep teams. They wore heavy ceramic armour over their pressure suits, oiled carapacial plaques that made movement awkward unless one exercised great care and forethought. After several minutes of fumbling and locking herself into postures that could only be got out of by laborious back-tracking, Skade wrote a hasty body image/motion patch and assigned it to run on a clump of idle neural circuits. Things became easier then, though she had the unpleasant feeling that a shadowy counterpart of herself was driving her. Skade made a mental note to revise the script later, so that the movement routines would feel totally voluntary no matter how illusory that might be.

By then the servitors had done about all they were able. They had secured large volumes of the ship, spraying diamond-fibred epoxy over the ruins of the alien machines, and they had DNA-sampled most of the corpses in the explored zones. Every individual sample of genetic material had been identified against the crew manifests in the Mother Nest, preserved since the departure of the exploratory fleet, but there were many names on the list that had yet to be matched to DNA samples.

There were bound to be names Skade would never match. When the first ship had returned home, the one carrying Clavain, the Mother Nest had learned that there had been a decision in deep space, dozens of light-years out, to split the expedition. One party wanted to come back home, having heard rumours of war against the Demarchists. They also felt that it was time to deliver the data they had already accrued—far too much to be transmitted home.

The separation had not been acrimonious. There had been regret, and sadness, but no real sense of disunity. After the usual period of debate typical of any Conjoiner decision-making process, the split came to be viewed as the most logical course of action. It allowed the expedition to continue, while safeguarding the return of what had already been learned. But while Skade knew exactly who had chosen to stay out there in deep space, she had no way of knowing what had happened subsequently. She could only guess at the exchanges that had taken place between the remaining two ships. The fact that this was Galiana's ship did not mean that she had to be on it, so Skade readied herself for the inevitable disappointment should that prove to be the case.

More than that, it would be a disappointment for the entire Mother Nest. Galiana was their figurehead, after all. She was the woman who had created the Conjoiners in the first place, four hundred years ago and eleven light-years away, in a huddle of labs beneath the surface of Mars. She had been away for nearly two centuries; long enough to assume the mythic stature that she had always resisted during her time amongst them. And she had returned—if she was indeed aboard this ship—on Skade's watch. It hardly mattered that she was very likely dead, along with all the others. For Skade, it would be enough to bring home her remains.

But she found more than remains.

Galiana's resting place, if it could be called that, was a long way from the central core of the ship. She had secured herself behind armoured barricades, well away from the others. Careful forensic study showed that the data links between Galiana's resting place and the remainder of the ship had been deliberately severed from within. She had obviously tried to isolate herself, cutting her mind off from the other Conjoiners on the ship.

Self-sacrifice or self-preservation? Skade wondered.

Galiana was in reefersleep, cooled down to a point where all metabolic processes were arrested. But the black machines had still reached her. They had smashed through the armour of the reefersleep casket, cramming themselves into the space between Galiana and the casket's interior surface. When the casket was dismantled, the machines formed a mummylike shell of pure black around Galiana. There was no doubt that it was she: scans peering through the cocoon picked out bone structure, which matched Galiana's perfectly. The body within appeared to have suffered no damage or decay during the flight, and the sensors were even able to pick up weak signals from Galiana's implant web. Although the signals were too faint to allow mind-to-mind linkage, it was clear that something inside the cocoon was still capable of thought, and was still reaching out.

Attention shifted to the cocoon itself. Chemical analysis of the cubes drew a blank: they appeared not to be "made" of anything, or to possess any kind of atomic granularity. The faces of the cubes were simply blank walls of sheer force, transparent to certain forms of radiation. They were very cold—still active in a way that none of the other machines had been so far. But the individual cubes did not resist being prised away from the larger mass, and once they were separated they shrunk rapidly, dwindling down to microscopic size. Skade's team attempted to focus scanners on the cubes themselves, trying to glimpse anything buried beneath the facets, but they were never quick enough. Where the cubes had been they found only a few micrograms of smouldering ashes. Presumably there were mechanisms at the heart of the cubes that were programmed to self-destruct under certain circumstances.

Once Skade's team had removed most of the surrounding plaque, they took Galiana to a dedicated room nestling in one wall of the spacecraft bay. They worked in extreme cold, determined not to inflict more damage than had already been done. Then, with immense care and patience, they began to peel away the final layer of alien machinery.

Now that they had less obstructive matter to peer through, they began to get a clearer impression of what had happened to Galiana. The black machines had indeed forced their way into her head, but the accommodation appeared more benign than had been the case with any of her crew. Her own implants had been partly dismantled to make way for the invading machines, but there was no sign that any major brain structures had been harmed. Skade had the impression that the cubes had been learning how to invade skulls until then, but that with Galiana they had finally found out how to do it without hurting the host.

And now Skade felt an optimistic rush. The black structures were concentrated and inert. With the right medichines it would be possible—trivial, even—to dismantle them, ripping them out cube by cube.

We can do it. We can bring her back, as she was.

[Be careful, Skade. We're not home and dry just yet.]

The Night Council, as it transpired, was right to be cautious. Skade's team began removing the final layer of cubes, beginning at Galiana's feet; they were pleased when they found that the underlying tissue was largely undamaged, and continued to work upwards until they reached her neck. They were confident that she could be warmed back to body temperature, even if it would be a more difficult exercise than a normal reefersleep revival. But when they began to expose her face, they learned that their work was far from over.

The cubes moved, slithering without warning. Sliding and tumbling over each other, contracting in nauseating waves, the final part of the cocoon oozed into Galiana like a living oil slick. The black tide sucked itself into her mouth, her nose, her ears and her eye-sockets, flowing around her eyeballs.

She looked the way Skade had hoped she would: a radiant homecoming queen. Even her long black hair was intact, frozen and fragile now, but exactly as it had been when she had left them. But the black machinery had reestablished itself inside her head, augmenting the formations that were already present. Scans showed that there was still little displacement of her own brain tissue, but more of her implant loom had been dismantled to make way for the invader. The black parasite had a crablike aspect, extending clawed filaments into different parts of her brain.

Slowly, over many days, they brought Galiana back to just below normal body temperature. All the while Skade's team monitored the invader, but it never changed, not even as Galiana's remaining implants began to warm and re-interface with her thawing brain tissue.

Perhaps, Skade dared to wonder, they might still win?

She was, it turned out, almost right.

She heard a voice. It was a human voice, feminine, lacking the timbre—or the strange Godlike absence of timbre—that ordinarily meant that the voice was originating inside her skull. This was a voice that had been shaped in a human larynx and propagated through metres of air before being decoded by a human auditory system, accumulating all manner of subtle imperfections along the way. It was the sort of voice that she had not heard in a very long time.

The voice said, "Hello, Galiana."

Where am I?

There was no answer. After a few moments the voice added kindly, "You'll have to speak as well, if you can. It's not necessary to do more than attempt to make the sound shapes; the trawl will do the rest, picking up the intention to send electrical signals to your larynx. But simply thinking your response won't work, I'm afraid—there are no direct links between your mind and mine."

The words seemed to take an eternity to arrive. Spoken language was horridly slow and linear after centuries of neural linkage, even if the syntax and grammar were familiar.

She made the intention to speak, and heard her own amplified voice ring out. "Why?"

"We'll come to that."

"Where am I? Who are you?"

"You're safe and sound. You're home; back in the Mother Nest. We recovered your ship and revived you. My name's Skade."

Galiana had been aware only of dim shapes looming around her, but now the room brightened. She was lying on her back, canted at an angle to the horizontal. She was inside a casket very much like a reefersleep casket but with no lid, so that she was exposed to the air. She saw things in her peripheral vision, but she could not move any part of her body, not even her eyes. A blurred figure came into focus before her, leaning over the open maw of the casket.

"Skade? I don't remember you."

"You wouldn't," the stranger replied. "I didn't become one of the Conjoined until after your departure."

There were questions—thousands of questions—that needed to be asked. But she could not ask all of them at once, most especially not via this clumsy old way of communicating. So she had to begin somewhere. "How long have I been away?"

"One hundred and ninety years, almost to the month. You left in . . . "

"2415," Galiana said promptly.

" . . . Yes. And the present date is 2605."

There was much that Galiana did not properly remember, and much that she did not think she wanted to remember. But the essentials were clear enough. She had led a trio of ships away from the Mother Nest, into deep space. The intention was to probe beyond the well-mapped frontier of human space, exploring previously unvisited worlds, looking for complex alien life. When rumours of war reached the three vessels, one ship had turned back home. But the other two had carried on, looping through many more solar systems.

As much as she wanted to, she could not quite recall what had happened to the other ship that had continued the search. She felt only a shocking sense of loss, a screaming vacuum inside her head that should have been filled with voices.

"My crew?"

"We'll come to that," Skade said again.

"And Clavain and Felka? Did they make it back, after all? We said goodbye to them in deep space; they were supposed to return to the Mother Nest."

There was a terrible, terrible pause before Skade answered. "They made it back."

Galiana would have sighed if sighing were possible. The feeling of relief was startling; she had not realised how tense she had been until she learned that her loved ones were safe.

In the calm, blissful moments that followed, Galiana looked more closely at Skade. In certain respects she looked exactly like a Conjoiner from Galiana's era. She wore a plain outfit of pyjamalike black trousers and loosely cinched black jacket, fashioned from something like silk and devoid of either ornamentation or any indication of allegiance. She was ascetically thin and pale, to the point where she looked on the ravenous edge of starvation. Her facial tone was waxy and smooth—not unattractive, but lacking the lines and creases of habitual expression. And she had no hair on either her scalp or her face, lending her the look of an unfinished doll. So far, at least, she was indistinguishable from thousands of other Conjoiners: without mind-to-mind linkage, and devoid of the usual cloud of projected phantasms that lent them individuality, they could be difficult to tell apart.

But Galiana had never seen a Conjoiner who looked anything like Skade. Skade had a crest—a stiff, narrow structure that began to emerge from her brow an inch above her nose, before curving back along the midline of her scalp. The narrow upper surface of the crest was hard and bony, but the sides were rilled with beautifully fine vertical striations. They shimmered with diffraction patterns: electric blues and sparkling oranges, a cascade of rainbow shades that shifted with the tiniest movement of Skade's head. There was more to it than that, however: Galiana saw fluidlike waves of different colours pump along the crest even when there was no change in its angle.

She asked, "Were you always like that, Skade?"

Skade touched her crest gently. "No. This is a Conjoiner augmentation, Galiana. Things have changed since you left us. The best of us think faster than you imagined possible."

"The best of you?"

"I didn't mean to put it quite that way. It's just that some of us have hit the limitations of the basic human bodyplan. The implants in our heads enable us to think ten or fifteen times faster than normal, all the time, but at the cost of increased thermal dissipation requirements. My blood is pumped through my crest, and then into the network of rills, where it throws off heat. The rills are optimised for maximum surface area, and they ripple to circulate air currents. The effect is visually pleasing, I'm told, but that's entirely accidental. We learned the trick from the dinosaurs, actually. They weren't as stupid as you'd think." Skade stroked her crest again. "It shouldn't alarm you, Galiana. Not everything has changed."

"We heard there'd been a war," Galiana said. "We were fifteen light-years out when we picked up the reports. First there was the plague, of course . . . and then the war. The reports didn't make any sense. They said we were going to war against the Demarchists, our old allies."

"The reports were true," Skade said, with a trace of regret.

"In God's name, why?"

"It was the plague. It demolished Demarchist society, throwing open a massive power vacuum around Yellowstone. At their request, we moved in to establish an interim government, running Chasm City and its satellite communities. Better us than another faction, was the reasoning. Can you imagine the mess that the Ultras or the Skyjacks would have made? Well, it worked for a few years, but then the Demarchists started regaining some of their old power. They didn't like the way we'd usurped control of the system, and they weren't prepared to negotiate a peaceful return to Demarchist control. So we went to war. They started it; everyone agrees about that."

Galiana felt some of her elation slipping away. She had

hoped that the rumours would turn out to be exaggerations. "But we won, evidently," she said.

" . . . No. Not as such. The war's still happening, you see."

"But it's been . . . "

"Fifty-four years." Skade nodded. "Yes. I know. Of course, there've been lapses and lulls, cease-fires and brief interludes of détente. But they haven't lasted. The old ideological schisms have opened up again, like raw wounds. At heart they've never trusted us, and we've always regarded them as reactionary Luddites, unwilling to face the next phase of human transcendence."

Galiana felt, for the first time since waking, an odd migrainous pressure somewhere behind her eyes. With the pressure came a squall of primal emotions, howling up from the oldest part of her mammalian brain. It was the awful fear of being pursued, of sensing a host of dark predators coming closer.

Machines, said a memory. *Machines like wolves, which came out of interstellar space and locked on to your exhaust flame.*

You called them wolves, Galiana.

Them.

Us.

The odd moment abated.

"But we worked together so well, for so long," Galiana said. "Surely we can find common ground again. There are more things to worry about than some petty power struggle over who gets to run a single system."

Skade shook her head. "It's too late, I'm afraid. There have been too many deaths, too many broken promises, too many atrocities. The conflict has spread to other systems, wherever there are Conjoiners and Demarchists." She smiled, though the smile looked forced, as if her face would instantly spring back to its neutral state the moment she relaxed her muscles. "Things aren't quite as desperate as you'd imagine. The war is turning in our favour, slowly but surely. Clavain returned twenty-two years ago, and immediately began to make a difference. Until his return we had been on the defensive, falling into the trap of acting like a true hive mind. That made our movements very easy for the enemy to predict. Clavain snapped us out of that prison."

Galiana tried to force the memory of the wolves from her mind, thinking back to the time she had first met Clavain. It had been on Mars, when he had been fighting against her, a soldier in the Coalition for Neural Purity. The Coalition opposed her mind-augmenting experiments and saw the utter annihilation of the Conjoiners as the only tolerable outcome.

But Clavain had seen the larger picture. First, as her prisoner, he had made her realise how terrifying her experiments had seemed to the rest of the system. She had never really grasped that until Clavain patiently explained it to her, over many months of incarceration. Later, when he had been freed and terms of cease-fire were being negotiated, it was Clavain who had brought in the Demarchists to act as a neutral third party. The Demarchists had drawn up the cease-fire document and Clavain had pushed Galiana until she signed it. It had been a masterstroke, cementing an alliance between the Demarchists and the Conjoiners that would endure for centuries, until the Coalition for Neural Purity barely merited a footnote in history. Conjoiners continued with their neurological experiments, which were tolerated and even encouraged provided they made no attempts to absorb other cultures. Demarchists made use of their technologies, brokering them to other human factions.

Everyone was happy.

But at heart, Skade was right: the union had always been an uneasy one. A war, at some point, was almost inevitable—especially when something like the Melding Plague came along.

But fifty-four damned years? Clavain would never have tolerated that, she thought. He would have seen the terrible waste in human effort that such a war entailed. He would either have found a way to end it decisively, or he would have sought a permanent cease-fire.

The migrainelike pressure was still with her, now a little more intense than before. Galiana had the disturbing sense that something was peering through her eyes from inside her skull, as if she was not its only tenant.

We narrowed the distance to your two ships, with the unhurried lope of ancient killers who had no racial memory of failure. You sensed our minds: bleak intellects poised on the dangerous verge of intelligence, as old and cold as the dust between the stars.

You sensed our hunger.

"But Clavain . . . " she said.

"What about Clavain?"

"He would have found a way to end this, Skade, one way or another. Why hasn't he?"

Skade looked away for an instant, so that her crest was a narrow ridge turned edge-on. When she turned back she was attempting to shape a very odd expression on to her face.

You saw us take your first ship, smothering it in a caulk of inquisitive black machines. The machines gnawed the ship apart. You saw it detonate: the explosion etched a pink swan-shape on to your retina, and you felt a net of minds being ripped away, like the loss of a thousand children.

You tried to get farther away, but by then it was too late.

When we reached your ship we were more careful.

"This isn't easy, Galiana."

"What isn't?"

"It's about Clavain."

"You said he returned."

"He did. And so did Felka. But I'm sorry to tell you that they both died." The words arrived one after another, slow as breaths. "It was eleven years ago. There was a Demarchist attack, a lucky strike against the Nest, and they both died."

There was only one rational response: denial. "No!"

"I'm sorry. I wish there was some other way . . . " Skade's crest flashed ultramarine. "I wish it had never happened. They were valuable assets to us . . . "

" 'Assets'?"

Skade must have sensed Galiana's fury. "I mean they were loved. We grieved their loss, Galiana. All of us."

"Then show me. Open your mind. Drop the barricades. I want to see into it."

Skade lingered near the side of the casket. "Why, Galiana?"

"Because until I can see into it, I won't know whether you're telling the truth."

"I'm not lying," Skade said softly. "But I can't allow our minds to talk. There is something inside your head, you see. Something we don't understand, other than that it is probably alien and probably hostile."

"I don't believe . . . "

But the pressure behind her eyes suddenly became acute. Galiana experienced a vile sense of being shoved aside, usurped, crushed into a small ineffectual corner of her own skull. Something inexpressibly sinister and ancient now had immediate tenancy, squatting behind her eyes.

She heard herself speak again.

"Me, do you mean?"

Skade seemed only mildly taken aback. Galiana admired the other Conjoiner her nerve.

"Perhaps. Who would you be, exactly?"

"I don't have a name other than the one she gave me."

" 'She'?" Skade asked amusedly. But her crest was flickering with nervous pale greens, showing terror even though her voice was calm.

"Galiana," the entity replied. "Before I took her over. She called us—my mind—the wolves. We reached and infiltrated her ship, after we had destroyed the other. We didn't understand much of what they were at first. But then we opened their skulls and absorbed their central nervous systems. We learned much more then. How they thought; how they communicated; what they had done to their minds."

Galiana tried to move, even though Skade had already placed her in a state of paralysis. She tried to scream, but the Wolf—for that was exactly what she had called it—had complete control of her voice.

It was all coming back now.

"Why didn't you kill her?" Skade said.

"It wasn't like that," the Wolf chided. "The question you should be asking is a different one: why didn't she kill herself before it came to this? She could have, you know; it was within her power to destroy her entire ship and everyone inside it simply by willing it."

"So why didn't she?"

"We came to an arrangement, after we had killed her crew and left her alone. She would not kill herself provided we allowed her to return home. She knew what it meant: I would invade her skull, rummage through her memories."

"Why her?"

"She was your queen, Skade. As soon as we read the minds of her crew, we knew she was the one we really needed."

Skade was silent. Aquamarines and jades chased each other in slow waves from brow to nape. "She would never have risked leading you here."

"She would, provided she thought the risk was outweighed by the benefit of an early warning. It was an accommodation, you see. She gave us time to learn, and the hope of learning more. Which we have, Skade."

Skade touched a finger to her upper lip and then held it before her as if testing the direction of the wind. "If you truly are a superior alien intelligence, and you knew where we were, you'd already have come to us."

"Very good, Skade. And you're right, in a sense. We don't know exactly where Galiana has brought us. I know, but I can't communicate that knowledge to my fellows. But that won't matter. You are a starfaring culture—fragmented into different factions, it is true—but from our perspective those distinctions do not matter. From the memories we drank, and the memories in which we still swim, we know the approximate locus of space that you inhabit. You are expanding, and the surface area of your expansion envelope grows geometrically, always increasing the likelihood of an encounter between us. It has already happened once, and it may have happened elsewhere, at other points on the sphere's boundary."

"Why are you telling me this?" Skade asked.

"To frighten you. Why else?"

But Skade was too clever for that. "No. There's got to be another reason. You want to make me think you might be useful, don't you?"

"How so?" the voice of the Wolf purred amusedly.

"I could kill you here and now. After all, the warning has already been delivered."

Had Galiana been able to move, or even just blink, she would have signalled an emphatic "yes." She did want to die. What else had she to live for, now? Clavain was gone. Felka was gone. She was sure of that, as sure as she was that no amount of Conjoiner ingenuity would ever free her of the thing inside her head.

Skade was right. She had served her purpose, performed her final duty to the Mother Nest. It knew that the wolves were out there, were, in all likelihood, creeping closer, scenting human blood.

There was no reason to keep her alive a moment longer. The Wolf would always be looking for a chance to escape her head, no matter how vigilant Skade was. The Mother Nest might learn something from it, some marginal hint of a motive or a weakness, but against that had to be set the awful consequences of its escape.

Galiana knew. Just as the Wolf had access to her memories,

so, by some faint and perhaps deliberate process of back-contamination, she sensed some of its own history. There was nothing concrete; almost nothing that she could actually put into words. But what she sensed was an aeons-old litany of surgical xenocide; of a dreadful process of cleansing waged upon emergent sentient species. The memories had been preserved with grim bureaucratic exactitude across hundreds of millions of years of Galactic time, each new extinction merely an entry in the ledger. She sensed the occasional frenzied cleansing—a cull that had been initiated later than was desirable. She even sensed the rare instance of brutal intercession where an earlier cull had not been performed satisfactorily.

But what she did not sense, ever, was ultimate failure.

Suddenly, shockingly, the Wolf eased aside. It was letting her speak.

"Skade," Galiana said.

"What is it?"

"Kill me, please. Kill me now."

ONE

Antoinette Bax watched the police proxy unfold itself from the airlock. The machine was all planar black armour and sharp articulated limbs, like a sculpture made from many pairs of scissors. It was deathly cold, for it had been clamped to the outside of one of the three police cutters which now pinned her ship. A rime of urine-coloured propellant frost boiled off it in pretty little whorls and helices.

"Please stand back," the proxy said. "Physical contact is not advised."

The propellant cloud smelt toxic. She slammed down her visor as the proxy scuttled by.

"I don't know what you're hoping to find," she said, following at a discreet distance.

"I won't know until I find it," the proxy said. It had already identified the frequency for her suit radio.

"Hey, look. I'm not into smuggling. I like not being dead too much."

"That's what they all say."

"Why would anyone smuggle something to Hospice Idlewild? They're a bunch of ascetic religious nuts, not contraband fiends."

"Know a thing or two about contraband, do you?"

"I never said . . . "

"Never mind. The point is, Miss Bax, this is war. I'd say nothing's ruled out."

The proxy halted and flexed, large flakes of yellow ice cracking away from its articulation points. The machine's body was a flanged black egg from which sprouted numerous limbs, manipulators and weapons. There was no room for the pilot in there, just enough space for the machinery needed to keep the proxy in contact with the pilot. The pilot was still inside one of the three cutters, stripped of nonessential organs and jammed into a life-support canister.

"You can check with the Hospice, if you like," she said.

"I've already queried the Hospice. But in matters such as this, one likes to be absolutely certain that things are above board—wouldn't you agree?"

"I'll agree to anything you like if it gets you off my ship."

"Mm. And why would you be in such a hurry?"

"Because I've got a slush . . . sorry, a cryogenic passenger. One I don't want thawing on me."

"I'd like to see this passenger very much. Is that possible?"

"I'm hardly likely to refuse, am I?" She had expected as much, and had already donned her vacuum suit while waiting for the proxy to arrive.

"Good. It won't take a minute, and then you can be on your way." The machine paused a moment before adding, "Provided, of course, that there aren't any irregularities."

"It's this way."

Antoinette thumbed back a panel next to her, exposing a crawlway that led back to *Storm Bird*'s main freight bay. She let the proxy take the lead, determined to say little and volunteer even less. Her attitude might have struck some as obstinate, but she would have engendered far more suspicion had she started to be helpful. The Ferrisville Convention's militia were not well liked, a fact which they had long since factored into their dealings with civilians.

"This is quite a ship you have, Antoinette."

"That's Miss Bax to you. I don't remember us being on first-name terms."

"Miss Bax, then. But my point stands: your ship is outwardly unremarkable, but betrays all the signs of being mechanically sound and spaceworthy. A ship with such a capacity could run at a profit on any number of perfectly legal trade routes, even in these benighted times."

"Then I'd have no incentive to take up smuggling, would I?"

"No, but it makes me wonder why you'd waste such an opportunity by running a peculiar errand for the Hospice. They have influence, but not, so far as we can gather, very much in the way of actual wealth." The machine halted again. "You have to admit, it's a bit of a puzzler. The usual route is for the frozen to come down from the Hospice, not go up to it. And even moving a frozen body around is unusual—most are thawed before they ever leave Idlewild."

"It's not my job to ask questions."

"Well, it does rather happen to be mine. Are we nearly there yet?"

The freight bay was not currently pressurised, so they had to cycle through an internal airlock to reach it. Antoinette turned the lights on. The enormous space was empty of cargo but filled with a storage lattice, a three-dimensional framework into which cargo pallets and pods were normally latched. They began to clamber their way through it, the proxy picking its way with the fastidious care of a tarantula.

"It's true, then. You are flying with an empty hold. There's not a single container in here."

"It's not a crime."

"I never said it was. It is, however, exceedingly odd. The Mendicants must be paying you extremely good money if you can justify a trip like this."

"They set the terms, not me."

"Curioser and curioser."

The proxy was right, of course. Everyone knew that the Hospice cared for the frozen who had just been off-loaded from recently arrived starships: the poor, the injured, the terminally amnesiac. They would be thawed, revived and rehabilitated in the Hospice's surroundings, tended by the Mendicants until they were well enough to leave, or at least able to complete a minimum set of basic human functions. Some, never regaining their memories, decided to stay on in the Hospice, training to become Mendicants themselves. But the one thing the Hospice did not routinely do was take in frozen who had not arrived on an interstellar ship.

"All right," she said. "What they told me was this: there was a mistake. The man's documentation was mixed up during the off-loading process. He was confused with another puppy who was only meant to be checked over by the Hospice, not actually revived. The other man was supposed to be kept cold until he was in Chasm City, then warmed up."

"Unusual," the proxy said.

"Seems the guy didn't like space travel. Well, there was a fuck-up. By the time the error was discovered, the wrong frozen body was halfway to CC. A serious screw-up and one that the Hospice wanted to get sorted out before the mess got worse. So they called me in. I picked up the body in the Rust Belt and now I'm rushing it back to Idlewild."

"But why the hurry? If the body's frozen, surely . . . "

"The casket's a museum piece, and it's received a lot of rough handling in the last few days. Plus, there are two sets of families starting to ask awkward questions. The sooner the pups are switched back, the better."

"I appreciate that the Mendicants would wish to keep the matter discreet. The Hospice's reputation for excellence would be tarnished if this got out."

"Yeah." She allowed herself to feel the tiniest hint of relief, and for a dangerous instant was tempted to throttle back on the studied obstinacy. Instead she said, "So now that you can see the whole picture, how about letting me get on my way? You wouldn't want to piss off the Hospice, would you?"

"Most certainly not. But having come this far, it would be a shame not to check out the passenger, wouldn't it?"

"Yeah," she intoned. "A real shame."

They reached the casket. It was an unremarkable-looking reefersleep unit, tucked near the back of the freight bay. It was matte-silver, with a smoked-glass rectangular viewing window set into the top surface. Beneath that, covered by its own smoked-glass shield, was a recessed panel containing controls and status displays. Indistinct coloured traces flickered and moved beneath the glass.

"Strange place to put it, this far back," said the proxy.

"Not from my point of view. It's close to my belly door—it was quick to load and it'll be even quicker to off-load."

"Fair enough. You don't mind if I take a closer look, do you?"

"Be my guest."

The proxy scuttled to within a metre of the casket, extending sensor-tipped limbs but not actually touching any part of it. It was being ultra-cautious, unwilling to run the risk of damaging Hospice property or doing anything that might endanger the casket's occupant.

"You said this man came in to Idlewild recently?"

"I only know what the Hospice told me."

The proxy tapped a limb against its own body, thoughtfully. "It's odd, because there haven't been any big ships coming in lately. Now that knowledge of the war's had time to reach the furthest systems, Yellowstone isn't quite the popular destination it used to be."

She shrugged. "Have a word with the Hospice then, if it bothers you. All I know is I've got a puppy and they want it back."

The proxy extended what she took to be a camera, probing close to the viewing window set into the casket's upper surface.

"Well, it's definitely a man," it said, as if this would be news to her. "Deep in reefersleep, too. Mind if I pop back that status window and take a look at the read-outs, while I'm here? If there's a problem, I can probably arrange an escort to get you to the Hospice in double-quick time . . . "

Before she could answer or frame a plausible objection, the proxy had flipped back the smoked-glass panel covering the matrix of controls and status displays. The proxy leant closer, steadying itself against the spars of the storage lattice, and swept the scanning eye back and forth across the display, dithering here and there.

Antoinette looked on, sweating. The displays appeared convincing enough, but anyone who knew their way around a reefersleep casket would have been instantly suspicious. They were not quite as they should have been had the occupant been in a state of normal cryogenic hibernation. Once that suspicion had been aroused, all it would take would be a few more enquiries, a little burrowing into some of the hidden display modes, and the truth would be laid bare.

The proxy scrutinised the read-outs and then pulled back, apparently satisfied. Antoinette closed her eyes for an instant, and then regretted it. The proxy approached the display again, extending a fine manipulator.

"I wouldn't touch that if I were . . . "

The proxy tapped commands into the read-out panel. Different traces appeared—squirming electric-blue waveforms and trembling histograms.

"This doesn't look right," the proxy said.

"What?"

"It's almost as if the occupant's already dea—"

A new voice boomed out. "Begging your pardon, Little Miss . . . "

Under her breath she swore. She had told Beast to shut up while she was dealing with the proxy. But perhaps she should be relieved that Beast had decided to ignore that particular order.

"What is it, Beast?"

"An incoming transmission, Little Miss—beamed directly at us. Point of origin: Hospice Idlewild."

The proxy jerked back. "What's that voice? I thought you said you were alone."

"I am," she replied. "That's just Beast, my ship's subpersona."

"Well, tell it to shut up. And the transmission from the Hospice isn't intended for you. It's a reply to a query I transmitted earlier . . . "

The ship's disembodied voice boomed, "The transmission, Little Miss . . . ?"

She smiled. "Play the damned thing."

The proxy's attention jerked away from the casket. Beast was relaying the transmission on to her helmet faceplate, making it seem as if the Mendicant was standing in the middle of the freight bay. She assumed the pilot was accessing its own telemetry feed from the one of the cutters.

The Mendicant was a woman, one of the New Elderly. As always, Antoinette found it slightly shocking to see a genuinely old person. She wore the starched wimple and vestment of her order, emblazoned with the Hospice's snowflake motif, and her marvellously veined and aged hands were linked beneath her chest.

"My apologies for the delay in responding," she said. "Problems with our network routing again, wouldn't you know. Well, formalities. My name is Sister Amelia, and I wish to confirm that the body . . . the frozen individual . . . in the care of Miss Bax is the temporary and beloved property of Hospice Idlewild and the Holy Order of Ice Mendicants, and that Miss Bax is kindly expediting its immediate return . . . "

"But the body's dead," the proxy said.

The Mendicant continued, ". . . and as such, we would be grateful for the absolute minimum of interference from the authorities. We have employed Miss Bax's services on several previous occasions and we have experienced nothing less than total satisfaction with her handling of our affairs." The Mendicant smiled. "I'm sure the Ferrisville Convention appreciates the need for discretion in such a matter . . . after all, we do have something of a reputation to uphold."

The message ended; the Mendicant blinked out of reality.

Antoinette shrugged. "See—I was telling the truth all along."

The proxy eyed her with one of its cowled sensors. "There's something going on here. The body inside that casket is medically dead."

"Look, I told you the casket was an old one. The read-out's

faulty, that's all. It'd be pretty stupid to carry a dead body around in a reefersleep casket, wouldn't it?"

"I'm not done with you."

"Maybe not, but you're done with me *now,* aren't you? You heard what the nice Mendicant lady said. *Expediting its immediate return,* I think that was the phrase she used. Sounds pretty official and important, doesn't it?" She reached across and flipped the cover back over the status panel.

"I don't know what you're up to," the proxy told her, "but rest assured, I'll get to the bottom of it."

She smiled. "Fine. Thanks. Have a nice day. And now get the fuck off my ship."

Antoinette held the same heading for an hour after the police had left, maintaining the illusion that her destination was Hospice Idlewild. Then she veered sharply, burning fuel at a rate that made her wince. An hour later she had passed beyond the official jurisdiction of the Ferrisville Convention, leaving Yellowstone and its girdle of satellite communities. The police made no effort to catch up with her again, but that did not surprise her. It would have cost them too much fuel, she was outside their technical sphere of influence and, since she had just entered the war zone, there was every chance that she was going to end up dead anyway. It was simply not worth their bother.

On that cheering note, Antoinette composed and transmitted a veiled message of thanks to the Hospice. She was grateful for their assistance and, as her father had always done under similar circumstances, promised to reciprocate should the Hospice ever need her help.

A message came back from Sister Amelia. *Godspeed and good luck with your mission, Antoinette. Jim would be very proud.*

I hope so, Antoinette thought.

The next ten days passed relatively uneventfully. The ship performed perfectly, without even offering her the kind of minor technical faults that would have been satisfying to repair. Once, at extreme radar range, she thought she was being shadowed by a couple of banshees—faint, stealthed signatures hovering on the limit of her detection capability. Just to be on the safe side she readied the deterrents, but after she had executed an evasive pattern, showing the banshees just how difficult it would be to make a hard-docking against *Storm Bird,* the two ships fell back into the shadows, off to look for another victim to plunder. She never saw them again.

After that brief excitement, there was not an awful lot to do on the ship except eat and sleep, and she tried to do as little of the latter as she could reasonably get away with. Her dreams were repetitious and disturbing: night after night she was taken prisoner by spiders, snatched from a liner making a burn between Rust Belt carousels. The spiders carried her off to one of their cometary bases on the edge of the system, where they cracked open her skull and plunged glistening interrogation devices into the soft grey porridge of her brain. Then, just when she had almost been turned into a spider, had almost had her own memories erased and been pumped full of the implants that would bind her into their hive mind, the zombies arrived. They smashed into the comet in droves of wedge-shaped attack ships, firing corkscrewing penetration capsules into the ice, which melted through it until they reached the central warrens. There they spewed forth valiant red-armoured troops who tore through the maze of cometary tunnels, killing spiders with the humane precision of soldiers trained never to waste a single flèchette, bullet or ammocell charge.

A handsome zombie conscript pulled her from the spider interrogation/indoctrination room, applied emergency procedures to flush the invading machines from her brain, then replaced and sutured her skull and finally put her into a recuperative coma for the long trip back to the civilian hospitals in the inner system. He held her hand while she was taken into the cold ward.

It was nearly always the same fucking thing. The zombies had infected her with a propaganda dream, and although she had taken the usual recommended regimen of flushing agents, she could never clear it out completely. Not that she even wanted to, particularly.

The one night when she had slept untroubled by Demarchist propaganda, she had spent the entire time dreaming sad dreams of her father instead.

She knew that the zombie propaganda was, to some extent, an exaggeration. But only in the details: no one argued about what the Conjoiners did to anyone unfortunate enough to become their prisoner. Equally, Antoinette was certain, it would not exactly be a picnic to be taken prisoner by the Demarchists.

But the conflict was a long way away, even though she was

technically in the war zone. She had chosen her trajectory to avoid the main battlefronts. Now and then Antoinette saw distant flashes of light, signifying some titanic engagement taking place light-hours from her present position. But the silent flashes had an unreal quality about them, allowing her to pretend that the war was over that she was merely on some routine interplanetary haul. That was not too far from the truth, either. All the neutral observers said that the war was in its dying days, with the zombies losing ground on all fronts. The spiders, by contrast, were gaining by the month, pushing towards Yellowstone.

But even if its outcome was now clear, the war was not yet over, and she could still become a casualty if she was careless. And then she might find out exactly how accurate that propaganda dream was.

She was mindful of this as she backed in towards Tangerine Dream, the largest Jovian-type planet in the entire Epsilon Eridani system. She was coming in hard at three gees, *Storm Bird*'s engines straining at maximum output. The gas-giant world was an ominous pale orange mass that bulged towards her, heavily pregnant with gravity. Counter-intrusion satellites were sewn around the Jovian, and these beacons had already latched on to her ship and had started bombarding it with increasingly threatening messages.

This is a Contested Volume. You are in violation of . . .

"Little Miss . . . are you certain about this? One must respectfully point out that this is completely the wrong trajectory for an orbital insertion."

She grimaced. It was about all she could manage at three gees. "I know, Beast, but there's an excellent reason for that. We're not actually going into orbit. We're going into the atmosphere instead."

"*Into* the atmosphere, Little Miss?"

"Yes. In."

She could almost hear the cogs churning away as antiquated subroutines were dusted off for the first time in decades.

Beast's subpersona lay in a cooled cylindrical housing about the size of a space helmet. She had seen it only twice, both times during major stripdowns of the ship's nose assembly. Wearing heavy gloves, her father had eased it from its storage well and they had both looked at it with something close to awe.

"In, did you say?" Beast repeated.

"I know it's not exactly normal operational procedure," Antoinette said.

"Are you absolutely certain of this, Little Miss?"

Antoinette reached into her shirt pocket and removed a shred of printed paper. It was oval, frayed and torn at the edges, with a complex design marked in lambent gold and silver inks. She fingered the scrap as if it were a talisman. "Yes, Beast," she said. "More certain than I've ever been of anything, ever."

"Very well, Little Miss."

Beast, obviously sensing that argument would get it nowhere, began to prepare for atmospheric flight.

The schematics on the command board showed spines and clamps being hauled in, hatches irising and sliding shut to maintain hull integrity. The process took several minutes, but when it was done *Storm Bird* looked only slightly more airworthy than it had before. Some of the remaining bulges and protrusions would survive the trip, but there were still a few spines and docking latches that would probably get ripped off when it hit air. *Storm Bird* would just have to manage without them.

"Now listen," she said. "Somewhere in that brain of yours are the routines for in-atmosphere handling. Dad told me about them once, so don't go pretending you've never heard of them."

"One shall attempt to locate the relevant procedures with all haste."

"Good," she said, encouraged.

"But might one nonetheless enquire why the need for these routines was not mentioned earlier?"

"Because if you'd had any idea what I had in mind, you'd have had all the more time to talk me out of it."

"One sees."

"Don't sound hurt about it. I was just being pragmatic."

"As you wish, Little Miss." Beast paused just long enough to make her feel guilty and hurtful. "One has located the routines. One respectfully points out that they were last used sixty-three years ago, and that there have been a number of changes to the hull profile since then which may limit the efficacy of . . . "

"Fine. I'm sure you'll improvise."

But it was no simple thing to persuade a ship of vacuum to skim an atmosphere, even the upper atmospheric layer of a gas giant—even a ship as generously armoured and rounded as hers. At best, *Storm Bird* would come through this with some heavy hull damage that would still allow her to limp home to the Rust Belt. At worst, the ship would never see open space again.

And nor, in all likelihood, would Antoinette.

Well, she thought, at least there was one consolation: if she trashed the ship, she would never have to break the bad news to Xavier.

So much for small mercies.

There was a muted chime from the panel.

"Beast . . . " Antoinette said, "was that what I thought it was?"

"Very possibly, Little Miss. Radar contact, eighteen thousand klicks distant, three degrees off dead ahead; two degrees off ecliptic north."

"Fuck. Are you certain it isn't a beacon or weapons platform?"

"Too large to be either, Little Miss."

She did not need to do any mental arithmetic to work out what that meant. There was another ship between them and the top of the gas giant; another ship close to the atmosphere.

"What can you tell me about it?"

"It's moving slowly, Little Miss, on a direct course for the atmosphere. Looks rather as if it's planning to execute a similar manoeuvre to the one you have in mind, although they're moving several klicks per second faster and their approach angle is considerably steeper."

"Sounds like a zombie—you don't think it is, do you?" she said quickly, hoping to convince herself otherwise.

"No need to speculate, Little Miss. The ship has just locked a tight-beam on to us. The message protocol is indeed Demarchist."

"Why the fuck are they bothering to tight-beam us?"

"One respectfully suggests you find out."

A tight-beam was a needlessly finicky means of communication when two ships were so close. A simple radio broadcast would have worked just as well, removing the need for the zombie ship to point its message laser exactly at the moving target of *Storm Bird*.

"Acknowledge whoever it is," she ordered. "Can we tight-beam them back?"

"Not without redeploying something one just went to rather a lot of trouble to retract, Little Miss."

"Then do it, but don't forget to haul it back in afterwards."

She heard the machinery push one of the spines back into vacuum. There was a rapid chirp of message protocols between the two ships and then suddenly Antoinette was looking at the face of another woman. She looked, if such a thing were possible, more tired, drawn and edgy than Antoinette felt.

"Hello," Antoinette said. "Can you see me as well?"

The woman's nod was barely perceptible. Her tight-lipped face suggested vast reserves of pent-up fury, like water straining behind a dam. "Yes. I can see you."

"I wasn't expecting to meet anyone out here," Antoinette offered. "I thought it might not be a bad idea to respond by tightbeam as well."

"You may as well not have bothered."

"Not have bothered?" Antoinette echoed.

"Not after your radar already illuminated us." The woman's shaven scalp gleamed blue as she looked down at something. She did not appear to be very much older than Antoinette, but with zombies you could never be sure.

"Um . . . and that's a problem, is it?"

"It is when we're trying to hide from something. I don't know why you're out here, and frankly I don't much care. I suggest that you abort whatever you're planning. The Jovian is a Contested Volume, which means that I'd be fully within my rights to blast you out of the sky right now."

"I don't have a problem with zom . . . with Demarchists," Antoinette said.

"I'm delighted to hear it. Now turn around."

Antoinette glanced down again at the piece of paper she had removed from her shirt pocket. The design on it showed a man wearing an antique spacesuit, the kind with accordioned joints, holding a bottle up to his gaze. The neck ring where his helmet should have been latched was a broken ellipse of gleaming silver. He was smiling as he looked at the bottle, which shone with gold fluid. No, Antoinette thought. It was time to be resolute.

"I'm not turning around," she said. "But I promise I don't want to steal anything from the planet. I'm not going anywhere near any of your refineries, or anything like that. I won't even open my intakes. I'm just going in and out, and then I won't bother you again."

"Fine," the woman said. "I'm very glad to hear that. The trouble is it's not really me that you need to be worried about."

"It isn't?"

"No." The woman smiled sympathetically. "It's the ship behind you, the one I don't think you've even noticed yet."

"Behind me?"

The woman nodded. "You have spiders on your tail."

That was when Antoinette knew she was in real trouble.

TWO

Skade was wedged between two curving black masses of machinery when the alert came in. One of her feelers had detected a change in the ship's attack posture, an escalation in the state of battle readiness. It was not necessarily a crisis, but it certainly demanded her immediate attention.

Skade unplugged her compad from the machinery, the fibre-optic umbilical whisking back into the compad's housing. She pressed the blank slate of the compad against her stomach, where it flexed and bonded with the padded black fabric of her vest. Almost immediately the compad began backing up its cache of data, feeding it into a secure partition in Skade's long-term memory.

Skade crawled through the narrow space between the machine components, arching and corkscrewing through the tightest spaces. After twenty metres she reached the exit point and eased herself partway through a narrow circular aperture that had just opened in one wall. Then Skade froze, falling perfectly silent and still; even the colour waves in her crest subsided. The loom of implants in her head detected no other Conjoiners within fifty metres, and confirmed that all monitoring systems in this corridor were turning a blind eye to her emergence. But still she was cautious, and when she moved—looking up and down the corridor—she did so with exquisite calm and caution, like a cat venturing into unfamiliar territory.

There was no one in sight.

Skade pulled herself entirely free of the aperture, then issued a mental command that made it sphincter tight, forming an invisibly fine seal. Only Skade knew where these entry apertures were, and the apertures would only show themselves to her. Even if Clavain detected the presence of the hidden machinery, he would never find a way to reach it without using the brute force that would trigger the machinery to self-destruct.

The ship was in free fall, still, so Skade presumed, sidling closer to the enemy ship they had been chasing. Weightlessness suited Skade. She scampered along the corridor, springing from contact point to contact point on all fours. Her movements were so precise and economical that she sometimes seemed to travel within her own personal bubble of gravity.

[Report, Skade?]

She never knew precisely when the Night Council was going to pop into her head, but she had long since stopped being fazed by its sudden apparitions.

Nothing untoward. We haven't even scratched the surface of what the machinery's capable of doing, but so far everything's working just the way we thought it would.

[Good. Of course, a more extensive test would be desirable . . .]

Skade felt a flush of irritation. *I already told you. At the moment it takes careful measurement to detect the influence of the machinery. That means we can perform clandestine tests under the cover of routine military operations.*

Skade pounced into a junction, kicking off towards the bridge. Forcing calm, tuning her blood chemistry, she continued, *I agree that we need to do more before we can equip the fleet, but the instant we increase testing we risk widespread knowledge of our breakthrough. And I don't just mean within the Mother Nest.*

[Your point is well made, Skade. There is no need to remind us. We were merely stating the facts. Inconvenient or otherwise, more extensive tests must take place, and they must take place soon.]

She passed another Conjoiner on his way to a different part of the ship. Skade peered into his mind, glimpsing a surface slurry of recent experiences and emotions. None of it interested her or was of tactical relevance. Beneath the slurry were deeper layers of memory, mnemonic structures plunging down into opaque darkness like great drowned monuments. All of it was hers to sift and scrutinise, but again none of it interested her. Down at the very deepest level Skade detected a few partitioned private memories that he did not think she could read. For a thrilling instant she was tempted to reach in and edit the man's own blockades, screening one or two tiny cherished memories from their owner. Skade resisted; it was enough to know that she could.

By way of return she felt the man's mind send enquiring probes into her own, and then flinch away at the stinging denial of access. She felt the man's curiosity, doubtless wondering why someone from the Closed Council had come aboard the ship.

This amused her. The man knew of the Closed Council, and might even have some inkling of the Council's super-secret core, the Inner Sanctum. But Skade was certain that he had never even imagined the existence of the Night Council.

He passed her by; she continued on her way.

[Reservations, Skade?]

Of course I have reservations. We're playing with God's own fire. It's not something you rush into.

[The wolves won't wait for us, Skade.]

Skade bristled, hardly needing to be reminded of the wolves. Fear was a useful spur, she admitted that, but it could only make so much difference. As the old saying went, the Manhattan Project wasn't built in a day. Or was that Rome? Something to do with Earth, anyway.

I haven't forgotten about the wolves.

[Good, Skade. We haven't, either. And we very much doubt that the wolves have forgotten about us.]

She felt the Night Council withdraw, retreating to some tiny unlocatable pocket in her head where it would wait until next time.

Skade arrived at the bridge of *Nightshade,* conscious that her crest was pulsing livid shades of rose and scarlet. The bridge was a windowless spherical room deep inside the ship, large enough to contain five or six Conjoiners without seeming cramped. But for now only Clavain and Remontoire were present, just as they had been when she left. They were both lying in acceleration hammocks, suspended in the middle of the sphere, their eyes closed as they tapped into the wider sensory environment of *Nightshade*. They looked absurdly restful, with their arms neatly folded across their chests.

Skade waited while the room threw a separate hammock

around her, wrapping her in a protective mesh of lianalike vines. Idly, she skimmed their minds. Remontoire's was fully open to her, even his Closed Council partitions appearing as mere demarcations rather than absolute barriers. His mind was like a city made of glass, smoked here and there, but never entirely opaque. Seeing through Closed Council screens had been one of the first tricks that the Night Council had taught her, and it had proven useful even after she had joined the Closed Council. Not all Closed Council members were privy to exactly the same secrets—there was the Inner Sanctum, for a start—but nothing was hidden from Skade.

Clavain was frustratingly harder to read, which was why he both fascinated and disturbed her. His neural implants were of a much older configuration than anyone else's, and Clavain had never allowed them to be upgraded. Large parts of his brain were not subsumed by the loom at all, and the neural bondings between these regions and the Conjoiner parts were sparse and inefficiently distributed. Skade's search-and-retrieve algorithms could extract neural patterns from any part of Clavain's brain that had been subsumed by the loom, but even that was a lot easier said than done. Searching Clavain's mind was like being given the keys to a fabulous library that had just been swept through by a whirlwind. By the time she located what she was looking for, it was usually no longer relevant.

Nonetheless, Skade had learned a great deal about Clavain. It was ten years since Galiana's return, but if her reading of his mind was accurate—and she had no reason to doubt that it was otherwise—Clavain still had no real idea about what had happened.

In common with the whole of the Mother Nest, Clavain knew that Galiana's ship had encountered hostile alien entities in deep space, machines that had come to be called the wolves. The wolves had infiltrated the ship, ripping open the minds of her crew. Clavain knew that Galiana had been spared and that her body was still preserved; he knew also that there was a structure of evident wolf origin lodged in her skull. What he did not know, and to the best of Skade's knowledge had never suspected, was that Galiana had returned to consciousness; that there had been a brief window of lucidity before the Wolf had spoken through her. More than one, in fact.

Skade recalled lying to Galiana, telling her that Clavain and Felka were already dead. It had not been easy at first. Like any

Conjoiner, Skade viewed Galiana with awe. She was the mother of them all, the queen of the Conjoined faction. Equally, the Night Council had reminded Skade that she had a duty to the Mother Nest that superseded her reverence towards Galiana. It was her duty to make maximum use of the windows of lucidity to learn what could be learned of the wolves, and that meant unburdening Galiana of any superfluous concerns. Hurtful as it had felt at the time, the Night Council had assured her it was better in the long run.

And gradually Skade had come to see the sense of it. It was not really Galiana she was lying to, after all, but a shadow of what Galiana had been. And one lie naturally demanded another, which was why Clavain and Felka had never learned of the conversations.

Skade withdrew her mental probes, settling for a routine level of intimacy. She allowed Clavain access to her surface memories, sensory modalities and emotions, or rather to a subtly doctored version of them. At the same time Remontoire saw precisely as much as he expected to see—but again, doctored and modified to suit Skade's purposes.

The acceleration hammock tugged Skade into the centre of the sphere, next to the other two. Skade folded her arms under her breasts, settling them over the curved plate of the compad, which was still whispering its findings into her long-term memory.

Clavain's presence asserted itself. [Skade. Nice of you to join us.]

I sensed a change in our attack readiness, Clavain. I imagine it has something to do with the Demarchist ship?

[Actually, it's a little more interesting than that. Take a look.]

Clavain offered her one end of a data feed from the ship's sensor net. Skade accepted the feed, instructing her implants to map it into her sensorium with her usual filters and preferences.

She experienced a pleasing instant of dislocation. Her body, the bodies of her companions, the room in which they floated, the great sleek carbon-black needle of *Nightshade*—all these things shifted to insubstantiality.

The Jovian was a massive presence ahead, wrapped in an ever-moving geometrically complex cloud of interdicted zones and safe passages. An angry swarm of platforms and sentries whipped around the world in tight precessional orbits. Closer, but not much closer, was the Demarchist ship that *Nightshade* had been chasing. It was already touching the top of Tangerine Dream's atmosphere, beginning to glow hotter. The shipmaster was taking a risk with the atmospheric dive, hoping to gain concealment beneath a few hundred kilometres of overlying cloud.

It was, Skade reflected, a move born of desperation.

Transatmospheric insertions were risky, even for ships built to make skimming passes into the upper layers of Jovians. The shipmaster would have had to slow down before attempting the plunge, and would be moving slowly again upon return to space. Aside from the camouflaging effect of the overlying air—the benefits of which depended on the armoury of sensors that the pursuing ship carried, and on what could be detected by low-orbit satellites or floating drones—the only advantage in making a skim was to replenish fuel reserves.

In the early years of the war, both sides had used antimatter as their main energy source. The Conjoiners, with their camouflaged manufactories on the edge of the system, were still able to produce and store antimatter in militarily useful quantities. Even if they could not, it was common knowledge that they had access to even more prodigious energy sources. But handling antimatter was something that the Demarchists had not been able to do for more than a decade. They had fallen back on fusion power, for which they needed hydrogen, ideally dredged from the oceans within gas giants where it was already compressed into its metallic state. The shipmaster would open the ship's fuel scoops, sucking in and compressing atmospheric hydrogen, or might even attempt a plunge into the "merely" liquid hydrogen sea overlaying the metallic-state hydrogen wrapped around the Jovian's rocky nugget of a core. But that would be a hazardous thing to attempt in a ship that had already sustained battle damage. Very probably the shipmaster would be hoping that the scoops would not be necessary; that it might instead manage to rendezvous with one of the whale-brained tankers circling endlessly through the atmosphere, singing sad, mournful songs of turbulence and hydrocarbon chemistry. The tanker would inject slugs of pre-processed metallic hydrogen into the ship, some to use as fuel and some to use as warheads.

Atmospheric insertion was a gamble, and a desperate one, but one that had paid off enough times to be slightly preferable to a suicidal scuttling operation.

Skade composed a thought and popped it into her companions' heads. *I admire the shipmaster's determination. But it won't help him.*

Clavain's response was immediate. [It's a she, Skade. We picked up her signal when she tight-beamed the other ship; they were passing through the edge of a debris ring, so there was enough ambient dust to scatter a small fraction of the laser light in our direction.]

And the interloper?

Remontoire answered her. [We always suspected it was a freighter from the moment we had a clean lock on its exhaust signature. That turns out to be the case, and we know a little more now.]

Remontoire offered her a feed, which she accepted.

A fuzzy image of the freighter sharpened in her mind's eye, accreting detail like a sketch being worked to completion. The freighter was half the size of *Nightshade,* a typical in-system hauler built one or two centuries ago; definitely pre-plague. The hull was vaguely rounded; the ship might once have been designed to land on Yellowstone or one of the other atmosphere-bound bodies in the system, but it had gained so many bulges and spines since then that it made Skade think of a fish afflicted with some rare recessive mutation. Cryptic machine-readable symbols flickered on its skin, some of which were interrupted by blank acres of repaired hull cladding.

Remontoire anticipated her question. [The ship's *Storm Bird,* a freighter registered out of Carousel New Copenhagen in the Rust Belt. The ship's commander and owner is Antoinette Bax, although she hasn't been either for more than a month. The previous owner was a James Bax, presumably a relative. We don't know what happened to him. Records show, however, that the Bax family has been running *Storm Bird* since long before the war, possibly even before the plague. Their activities seem to be the usual mixture of the legal and the marginally legal; a few infringements here and there, and one or two run-ins with the Ferrisville Convention, but nothing serious enough to warrant arrest, even under the emergency legislation.]

Skade felt her distant body acknowledge this with a nod. The girdle of habitats orbiting Yellowstone had long supported a spectrum of transportation ventures, ranging from prestigious high-burn operations to much slower—and commensurately cheaper, fewer-questions-asked—fusion and ion-drive haulers. Even after the plague, which had turned the once-glorious Glitter Band into the far less than glorious Rust Belt, there had still been commercial niches for those prepared to fill them. There were quarantines to be dodged, and a host of new clients rising from the smouldering rubble of Demarchist rule, not all of who were the kinds of clients one would wish to do business with twice.

Skade knew nothing about the Bax family, but she could imagine them thriving under these conditions, and perhaps thriving even more vigorously during wartime. Now there were blockades to be run and opportunities to aid and abet the deep-penetration agents of either faction in their espionage missions. No matter that the Ferrisville Convention, the caretaker administration that was running circum-Yellowstone affairs, was just about the most intolerant regime in history. Where there were harsh penalties, there would always be those who would pay handsomely for others to take risks on their behalf.

Skade's mental picture of Antoinette Bax was almost complete. There was just one thing she did not understand: what was Antoinette Bax doing this far inside a war zone? And, now that she thought about it, why was she still alive?

The shipmaster spoke to her? Skade asked.

Clavain answered. [It was a warning, Skade, telling her to back off or face the consequences.]

And did she?

Remontoire fed her the freighter's vector. It was headed straight into the atmosphere of the Jovian, just like the Demarchist ship ahead of it.

That doesn't make any sense. The shipmaster should have destroyed her for violating a Contested Volume.

Clavain responded. [The shipmaster threatened to do just that, but Bax ignored her. She promised the shipmaster she wasn't going to steal hydrogen, but made it pretty clear she wasn't about to turn around either.]

Either very brave or very stupid.

[Or very lucky,] Clavain countered. [Clearly the shipmaster didn't have the ammunition to back up her threat. She must have used up her last missile during some earlier engagement.]

Skade considered this, anticipating Clavain's reasoning. If the shipmaster really had fired her last missile, she would be desperately keen to keep that information from *Nightshade*. An unarmed ship was ripe for boarding. Even this late in the war, there were still useful intelligence gains to be made from the capture of an enemy ship, quite apart from the prospect of recruiting her crew.

You think the shipmaster was hoping the freighter would do as she said. She detected Clavain's assent before his answer formed in her head.

[Yes. Once Bax shone her radar on to the Demarchist ship, the shipmaster had no choice but to make some kind of response. Firing a missile would have been the usual course of action—she'd have been fully within her rights—but at the very least she had to warn the freighter to back off. That didn't work—for whatever reason Bax wasn't sufficiently intimidated. That immediately put the shipmaster in a compromised position. She'd barked, but she sure as hell couldn't bite.]

Remontoire completed his line of thinking. [Clavain's right. She has no missiles. And now we know.]

Skade knew what they had in mind. Even though it had already begun to dive into the atmosphere, the Demarchist ship was still within easy range of *Nightshade*'s missiles. A kill could not be guaranteed, but the odds were a lot better than even. Yet Remontoire and Clavain did not want to shoot the enemy down. They wanted to wait until it had emerged from the atmosphere, slow and heavy with fuel, but still no better armed than it had been before. They wanted to board it, suck data from its memory banks and turn its crew into recruits for the Mother Nest.

I can't consent to a boarding operation. The risks to Nightshade *outweigh any possible benefits.*

She sensed Clavain trying to probe her mind. [Why, Skade? Is there something that makes this ship unusually precious? If so, isn't it a little odd that no one told me?]

That's a matter for the Closed Council, Clavain. You had your chance to join us.

[But even if he had, he wouldn't know everything, would he?]

Her attention flicked angrily to Remontoire. *You know that I'm here on Closed Council business, Remontoire. That is all that matters.*

[But I'm Closed Council and even I don't know exactly what

you're doing here. What is it, Skade—a secret operation for the Inner Sanctum?]

Skade seethed, thinking how much simpler things would be if she never had to deal with old Conjoiners. *This ship is precious, yes. It's a prototype, and prototypes are always valuable. But you knew that anyway. Of course we don't want to lose it in a petty engagement.*

[There's clearly more to it than that, though.]

Perhaps, Clavain, but now isn't the time to discuss it. Allocate a spread of missiles for the Demarchist ship, and spare another for the freighter.

[No. We'll wait for both ships to come out the other side. Assuming either survives, then we'll act.]

I can't allow that. So be it, then. She had hoped it would not come to this, but Clavain was forcing her hand. Skade concentrated, issuing a complex series of neural commands. She felt the distant acknowledgement of the weapons systems recognising her authority and submitting to her will. Her control was imprecise, lacking the finesse and immediacy with which she addressed her own machines, but it would suffice; all she had to do was launch a few missiles.

[Skade . . . ?]

It was Clavain; he must have sensed that she was overriding his control of the weapons. She felt his surprise at the fact that she could do it at all. Skade assigned the spread, the hunter-seeker missiles quivering in their launch racks.

Then another voice spoke quietly in her head. [No, Skade.]

It was the Night Council.

What?

[Release control of the weapons. Do as Clavain wishes. It will serve us better in the long run.]

No, I . . .

The Night Council's tone became more strident. [Release the weapons, Skade.]

Furious, feeling the sting of reprimand, Skade did as she was told.

Antoinette reached her father's coffin. It was lashed to the cargo-bay storage lattice, precisely as it had been when she had shown it to the proxy.

She placed one gloved hand on the upper surface of the casket. Through the glass of the viewing window she could see his profile. The family resemblance was quite evident, though age and gravity had shaped his features into an exaggerated masculine caricature of her own. His eyes were closed and the expression on his face, what she could see of it, was almost one of bored calm. It would have been typical of her father to snooze through all the excitement, she thought. She remembered the sound of his snoring filling the flight deck. Once she had even caught him peering at her through nearly closed eyelids, just pretending to be asleep. Watching to see how she handled whatever crisis was in progress; knowing that one day she would have to do it all herself.

Antoinette checked the rigging that bound the coffin to the lattice. It was secure; nothing had come adrift during the recent manoeuvres.

"Beast . . . " she said.

"Little Miss?"

"I'm down in the hold."

"One is uncomfortably aware of that, Little Miss."

"I'd like you to take us subsonic. Call me when we're there, will you?"

She had steeled herself for a protest, but none came. She felt the ship pitch, her inner ear struggling to differentiate between deceleration and descent. *Storm Bird* was not really flying now. Its shape generated very little aerodynamic lift, so it had to support itself by vectoring thrust downwards. The vacuum-filled hold had provided some buoyant lift until now, but she had never planned on going deep with a depressurised hold.

Antoinette was acutely aware that she really should have been dead by now. The Demarchist shipmaster should have shot her out of the sky. And the pursuing spider ship should have attacked before she had time to dive into the atmosphere. Even the dive should have killed her. It had not been the gentle, controlled insertion she had always planned, but more of a furious scramble to get beneath the clouds, riding the vortex that the Demarchist ship had already carved. She had appraised the damage as soon as level flight had been restored, and the news was not good. If she made it back to the Rust Belt, and that was a big "if"—the spiders were still out there, after all—then Xavier was going to be very, very busy for the next few months.

Well, at least it would keep him out of trouble.

"Subsonic now, Little Miss," Beast reported.

"Good." For the third time, Antoinette made sure that she was bound to the lattice as securely as the coffin, and then checked her suit settings again. "Open the number one bay door, will you?"

"Just a moment, Little Miss."

A brilliant sliver of light cracked open at her end of the lattice. She squinted against it, then reached up and tugged down the bottle-green glare visor of her suit.

The crack of light enlarged, and then the force of the inrushing air hit her, slamming her against the lattice's strut. Air filled the chamber in a few seconds, roaring and swirling around her. The suit's sensor analysed it immediately and sternly advised against opening her helmet. The air pressure had exceeded one atmosphere, but it was both lung-crackingly cold and utterly toxic.

An atmosphere of choking poisons and shocking temperature gradients was, Antoinette reflected, the price you paid for such exquisite coloration when seen from space.

"Take us twenty klicks deeper," she said.

"Are you certain, Little Miss?"

"Fuck, yes."

The floor pitched. She watched as the suit's barometer ticked off the increments in atmospheric pressure. Two atmospheres; three. Four atmospheres and rising. Trusting that the rest of *Storm Bird*, which was now under negative pressure, would not fold open around her like a wet paper bag.

Whatever else happens, Antoinette thought, *I've probably blown the warranty on the ship by now . . .*

When her confidence had risen, or rather when her pulse had dropped to something like a normal level, Antoinette began to inch along towards the open door, dragging the coffin with her. It was a laborious process, since now she had to fasten and unfasten the coffin's moorings every couple of metres. But the last thing she felt was impatience.

Looking ahead, now that her eyes had adapted she saw that the light had an overcast silver-grey quality. Gradually it became duller, taking on an iron or dull bronze pall. Epsilon Eridani was not a bright star to begin with, and much of its light was now being filtered out by the layers of atmosphere above them. If they went deeper it would get darker and darker, until it was like being at the bottom of an ocean.

But this was what her father had wanted.

"All right, Beast, hold her nice and steady. I'm about to do the deed."

"Take care now, Little Miss."

There were cargo-bay entrance ports all over *Storm Bird,* but the one that had been opened was in the ship's belly, facing backwards along the direction of flight. Antoinette had reached the lip now, the toes of her boots hanging an inch over the edge. It felt precarious, but she was still safely anchored. Her view above was obstructed by the dark underside of the hull, curving gently up towards the tail; but to either side, and down, nothing impeded her vision.

"You were right, Dad," she breathed, quietly enough that she hoped Beast would not pick up her words. "It is a pretty amazing place. I think you made a good choice, all things told."

"Little Miss?"

"Nothing, Beast."

She began to undo the coffin's fastenings. The ship lurched and swayed once or twice, making her stomach twist and the coffin knock against the lattice's spars, but by and large Beast was doing an excellent job of holding altitude. The speed was now highly subsonic relative to the current airstream, so that Beast was doing little more than hover, but that was good. The wind's ferocity had died down except for the odd squall, as she had hoped it would.

The coffin was almost loose now, almost ready to be tipped over the side. Her father looked like a man catching up on forty winks. The embalmers had done a superlative job, and the coffin's faltering refrigeration mechanism had done the rest. It was impossible to believe that her father had been dead for a month.

"Well, Dad," Antoinette said, "this is it, I guess. We've made it now. Not much more needs to be said, I think."

The ship did her the courtesy of saying nothing.

"I still don't know whether I'm really doing the right thing," Antoinette continued. "I mean, I know this is what you once said you wanted, but . . . " *Stop it,* she told herself. *Stop going over that again.*

"Little Miss?"

"Yes?"

"One would strongly advise against taking too much longer."

Antoinette remembered the label of the beer bottle. She did not have it with her now, but there was no detail of it that she could not call immediately to mind. The brilliance of the silver and gold inks had faded a little since the day when she had lovingly peeled the label from the bottle, but in her mind's eye they still shone with a fabulous rare lustre. It was a cheap, mass-produced item, but in her hands, and in her mind, the label had assumed the significance of a religious icon. She had been much younger when she had removed the label, only twelve or thirteen years old, and, flush from a lucrative haul, her father had taken her to one of the drinking dens that the traders sometimes frequented. Though her experience was limited, it had seemed to be a good night, with much laughter and telling of stories. Then, somewhere towards the end of the evening, the talk had turned to the various ways in which the remains of spacefarers were dealt with, whether by tradition or personal preference. Her father had kept quiet during most of the discussion, smiling to himself as the conversation veered from the serious to the jocular and back again, laughing at the jokes and insults. Then, much to Antoinette's surprise, he had stated his own preference, which was to be buried inside the atmosphere of a gas-giant planet. At any other time she might have assumed him to be mocking his comrades' proposals, but there was something about his tone that had told her that he was absolutely earnest, and that although he had never spoken of the matter before, it was not something he had just conjured out of thin air. And so she had made a small, private vow to herself. She had peeled the label from the bottle as a memento, swearing that if her father should ever die, and should she ever be in a position to do anything about it, she would not forget his wish.

And for all the years that had followed it had been easy to imagine that she would hold to her vow, so easy, in fact, that she had seldom thought of it at all. But now he was dead, and she had to face up to what she had promised herself, no matter that the vow now struck her as faintly ridiculous and childlike. What did matter was the utter conviction that she believed she had heard in his voice that night. Though she had been only twelve or thirteen, and might even have imagined it, or been fooled by his poker-face facade of seriousness, she had made the vow, and however embarrassing or inconvenient, she had to stick to it, even if it meant placing her own life in jeopardy.

She undid the final restraints, and then budged the coffin forwards until a third of its length projected over the edge. One good shove and her father would get the burial he had wanted.

It was madness. In all the years after that one drunken conversation in the spacer's bar he had never again mentioned the idea of being buried in the Jovian. But did that necessarily mean it had not been a heartfelt wish? He had not known when he was going to die, after all. There had been no time to put his affairs in order before the accident; no reason for him to explain patiently to her what he wanted doing with his mortal remains.

Madness, yes . . . but heartfelt madness.

Antoinette pushed the coffin over the edge.

For a moment it seemed to hang in the air behind the ship, as if unwilling to begin the long fall into oblivion. Then, slowly, it did begin to fall. She watched it tumble, dropping behind the ship as the wind retarded it. Quickly it diminished: now a thing the size of her outstretched thumb; now a tiny, tumbling hyphen at the limit of vision; now a dot that only intermittently caught the weakly transmitted starlight, glinting and fading as it fell through billowing pastel cloud layers.

She saw it one more time, and then it was gone.

Antoinette leant back against the rig. She had not expected it, but now that the deed was done, now that she had buried her father, exhaustion came crushing down on her. She felt suddenly the entire leaden weight of all the air pressing down from above. There was no actual sadness, no tears; she had cried enough already. There would be more, in time. She was sure of that. But for now all she felt was utter exhaustion.

Antoinette closed her eyes. Several minutes passed.

Then she told Beast to close the bay door, and began the long journey back to the flight deck.

THREE

From his vantage point in an airlock, Nevil Clavain watched a circular part of *Nightshade*'s hull iris open. The armoured proxies that bustled out resembled albino lice, carapaced and segmented and sprouting many specialised limbs, sensors and weapons. They quickly crossed the open space to the enemy ship, sticking to her claw-shaped hull with adhesive-tipped legs. Then they scuttled across the damaged surface, hunting for entry locks and the known weak spots of that type of ship.

The proxies moved with the random questing motion of bugs. The scarabs could have swept through the ship very quickly, but only at the risk of killing any survivors who might have been sheltering in pressurised zones. So Clavain insisted that the machines use the airlocks, even if that meant a delay while each robot passed through.

He need hardly have worried. As soon as the first scarab made its way through, it became clear that he was going to encounter neither resistance nor armed survivors. The ship was dark, cold and silent. He could almost smell death aboard her. The proxy edged its way through the enemy craft, the faces of the dead coming into view as it passed their duty stations. Similar reports came back from the other machines as they scuttled through the rest of the ship.

He withdrew most of the scarabs and then sent a small detachment of Conjoiners into the ship via the same route the machines had used. Through the eyes of a scarab, he watched his squad emerge from the lock one at a time: bulbous white shapes like hard-edged ghosts.

The squad swept the ship, moving through the same cramped spaces that the proxies had explored, but with the additional watchfulness of humans. Gun muzzles were poked into hideaways, equipment hatches opened and checked for cower-ing survivors. None were found. The dead were discreetly prodded, but none of them showed the slightest signs of faking it. Their bodies were beginning to cool, and the thermal patterns around their faces showed that death had already occurred, albeit recently. There was no sign of violent death or injury.

He composed a thought and passed it back to Skade and Remontoire, who were still on the bridge. *I'm going inside. No ifs, no buts. I'll be quick and I won't take any unnecessary risks.*

[No, Clavain.]

Sorry, Skade, but you can't have it both ways. I'm not a member of your cosy little club, which means I can go where the hell I like. Like it or lump it, but that's part of the deal.

[You're still a valued asset, Clavain.]

I'll be careful. I promise.

He felt Skade's irritation bleeding into his own emotional state. Remontoire was not exactly thrilled either.

As Closed Council members, it would have been unthinkable for either of them to do anything as dangerous as board a captured enemy ship. They were taking enough of a risk by leaving the Mother Nest. Many of the other Conjoiners, Skade included, wanted him to join the Closed Council, where they could tap his wisdom more efficiently and keep him out of harm's way. With her authority in the Council, Skade could make life awkward for him if he persisted in remaining outside, relegating him to token duties or even some kind of miserable forced retirement. There were other avenues of punishment and Clavain took none of them lightly. He had even begun to consider the possibility that perhaps he should join the Closed Council after all. At least he would learn some answers that way, and perhaps begin to exert influence over the aggressors.

But until he took a bite of that apple he was still a soldier. No restrictions applied to him, and he was damned if he was going to act as if they did.

He continued with the business of readying his suit. For a time, a good two or three centuries, that process had been much easier and quicker. You donned a mask and some communications gear and then stepped through a membrane of smart matter stretched over a door that was otherwise open to vacuum. As you went through it, a layer of the membrane slithered around you, forming an instant skintight suit. Upon your return, you stepped through the same membrane and your suit returned to it, oozing off like enchanted slime. It made the act of stepping outside a ship about as complex as slipping on a pair of sunglasses. Of course, such technologies had never made much sense in wartime—too vulnerable to attack—and they made even less sense in the post-plague era, when only the hardiest forms of nanotechnology could be deployed in sensitive applications.

Clavain supposed that he should have been irritated at the extra effort that was now needed. But in many ways he found the act of suiting-up—the martial donning of armour plating, the rigorous subsystem criticality checks, the buckling-on of weapons and sensors—to be strangely reassuring. Perhaps it was because the ritualistic nature of the exercise felt like a series of superstitious gestures against ill fortune. Or perhaps it was because it reminded him of what things had been like during his youth.

He left the airlock, kicking off towards the enemy ship. The claw-shaped craft was bright against one dark limb of the gas giant. It was damaged, certainly, but there had been no outgassing to suggest a loss of hull integrity. There had even been a chance of a survivor. Although the infra-red scans had been inconclusive, laser-ranging devices had detected slight back-and-forth movement of the entire ship. There could be any number of explanations for that movement, but the most obvious was the presence of at least one person still moving around inside, kicking off from the hull now and then. But the scarabs hadn't found any survivors, and neither had his sweep team.

Something caught his eye: a writhing pale green filament of lightning in the dark crescent of the gas giant. He had barely given the freighter a second thought since the Demarchist vessel had emerged, but Antoinette Bax's ship had never emerged from the atmosphere. In all likelihood she was dead, killed in one of the several thousand ways it was possible to die in an atmosphere. He had no idea what she had been doing, and doubted that it would have been anything he would have approved of. But she had been alone—hadn't she?—and that was no way to die in space. Clavain remembered the way she had ignored the shipmaster's warning and realised that he rather admired her for it. Whatever else she had been, he could not deny that she had been brave.

He thudded into contact with the enemy ship, absorbing the

impact by bending his knees. Clavain stood up, his soles adhering to the hull. Holding a hand against his visor to cut down sun glare, he turned back to look at *Nightshade,* relishing the rare opportunity to see his ship from the outside. *Nightshade* was so dark that at first he had trouble making it out. Then his implants boxed it in with a pulsing green overlay, scale and distance annotated by red gradations and numerals. The ship was a lighthugger, with interstellar capability. *Nightshade*'s slender hull tapered to a needle-sharp prow, streamlined for maximum near-light cruise efficiency. Braced near the thickest point of the hull, just before it retapered to a blunt tail, was a pair of engines, thrown out from the hull on slender spars. They were what the other human factions called Conjoiner drives, for the simple reason that the Conjoiners had a monopoly on their construction and distribution. For centuries the Conjoiners had allowed the Demarchists, Ultras and other starfaring factions to use the technology, while never once hinting at the mysterious physical processes that allowed the tamperproof engines to function in the first place.

But all that had changed a century ago. Practically overnight, the Conjoiners had ceased production of their engines. No explanation had been given, nor any promise that production would ever be resumed.

From that moment on, the existing Conjoiner drives became astonishingly valuable. Terrible acts of piracy were waged over issues of ownership. The event had certainly been one of the contributing causes of the current war.

Clavain knew there were rumours that the Conjoiners had continued building the engines for their own uses. He also knew, as far as he could be certain of anything, that these rumours were false. The edict to cease production had been immediate and universal. More than that, there had been a sharp decline in the use of existing ships, even by his own faction. But what Clavain did not know was why the edict had been issued in the first place. He guessed that it had originated in the Closed Council, but beyond that he had no idea why it had been deemed necessary.

And yet now the Closed Council had made *Nightshade*. Clavain had been entrusted with the prototype on this proving mission, but the Closed Council had revealed few of its secrets. Remontoire and Skade evidently knew more than he did, and he was willing to bet that Skade knew even more than Remontoire. Skade had spent most of the trip hidden away somewhere, presumably tending some ultra-secret military hardware. Clavain's efforts to find out what she was up to had all drawn a blank.

And he still had no idea why the Closed Council had sanctioned the building of a new starship. This late in the war, against an enemy that was already in retreat, what sense did it make? If he joined the Council he might not get all the answers he wanted—he would still not have penetrated the Inner Sanctum—but he would be a lot closer than he was now.

It almost sounded tempting.

Disgusted at the ease with which he had been manipulated by Skade and the others, Clavain turned from the view, the overlay vanishing as he made his cautious way to the entry point.

Soon he was inside the bowels of the Demarchist vessel, passing along ducts and tubes that would not normally have held air. Clavain requested an intelligence upload on the design of the ship and imagined a faint tickle as the knowledge appeared in his head. There was an instant eerie sense of familiarity, like a sustained episode of *déjà vu*. He arrived at an airlock, finding it a tight fit in his cumbersome armoured suit. Clavain sealed the hatch behind him, air roared in, and then the inner door allowed him to pass through into the pressurised part of the ship. His overwhelming impression was of darkness, but then his helmet clicked into high-sensitivity mode, dropping infra-red and sonar overlays across his normal visual field.

[Clavain.]

One of the sweep-team members was waiting for him. Clavain angled himself so that his face was aligned with the woman's and then hitched himself against the interior wall.

What have you found?

[Not much. All dead.]

Every last one of them?

The woman's thoughts arrived in his head like bullets, clipped and precise. [Recently. No sign of injury. Appears deliberate.]

No sign of a single survivor? We thought there might be one, at least.

[No survivors, Clavain.] She offered him a feed into her

memories. He accepted it, steeling himself for what he was about to see.

It was every bit bad as he had feared. It was like uncovering the scene of an atrocious mass suicide. There were no signs of struggle or coercion; no signs even of hesitation. The crew had died at their respective duty stations, as if someone had been delegated to tour the ship with suicide pills. An even more horrific possibility was that the crew had convened at some central location, been handed the means of euthanasia and had then returned to their assigned niches. Perhaps they had continued to perform their tasks until the shipmaster ordered the mass suicide.

In zero gravity, heads did not loll lifelessly. Even mouths did not drop open. Dead bodies continued to assume more or less lifelike postures, whether restrained by webbing or allowed to drift untethered from wall to wall. It was one of the earliest and most chilling lessons of space warfare: in space, the dead were often difficult to tell from the living.

The crew were all thin and starved-looking, as if they had been living on emergency rations for many months. Some of them had skin sores or the bruised evidence of earlier wounds that had not healed properly. Perhaps some had even died before now, and had been dumped from the ship so that the mass of their bodies could be traded against fuel savings. Beneath their caps and headsets none of them had more than a greyish fuzz of scalp stubble. They were clothed uniformly, carrying only insignia of technical specialisation rather than rank. Under the bleak emergency lights their skin hues merged into some grey-green average.

Through his own eyes now Clavain saw a corpse drift into view. The man appeared to paw himself through the air, his mouth barely open, his eyes fixed on an indeterminate spot several metres ahead of him. The man thudded into one wall, and Clavain felt the faint reverberation where he was hitched.

Clavain projected a request into the woman's head. *Secure that corpse, will you?*

The woman did as she was asked. Then Clavain ordered all the sweep-team members to tether themselves and hold still. There were no other corpses drifting around, so there should not have been any other objects to impart any motion to the ship itself. Clavain waited a moment for an update from *Nightshade,* which was still spotting the enemy with range-finding lasers.

At first he doubted what he was being shown.

It made no sense, but something was still moving around inside the enemy ship.

"Little Miss?"

Antoinette knew that tone of voice very well, and the omens were not auspicious. Pressed back into her acceleration couch, she grunted a reply that would have been incomprehensible to anyone or anything other than Beast.

"Something's up, isn't it?"

"Regrettably so, Little Miss. One cannot be certain, but there appears to be a problem with the main fusion core."

Beast threw a head-up-display schematic of the fusion system on to the bridge window, superimposed against the cloud layers *Storm Bird* was punching through as it climbed back to space. Elements of the fusion motor were blocked in ominous pulsing red.

"Holy shit. Tokamak, is it?"

"That would appear to be the case, Little Miss."

"Fuck. I knew we should have swapped it during the last heavy-general."

"Language, Little Miss. And a polite reminder that what's done is done."

Antoinette cycled through some of the other diagnostic feeds, but the news did not get any better. "It's Xavier's fault," she said.

"Xavier, Little Miss? In what way is Mr. Liu culpable?"

"Xave swore the tok was at least three trips away from life-expiry."

"Perhaps, Little Miss. But before you ascribe too much blame to Mr. Liu, perhaps you should keep in mind the enforced main-engine cut-off that the police demanded of us as we were departing the Rust Belt. The hard shutdown did the tokamak no favours at all. Then there was the additional matter of the vibrational damage sustained during the atmospheric insertion."

Antoinette scowled. Sometimes she wondered whose side Beast was really on. "All right," she said. "Xave's off the hook. For now. But that doesn't help me much, does it?"

"A failure is predicted, Little Miss, but not guaranteed."

Antoinette checked the read-outs. "We'll need another ten klicks per second just to make orbit. Can you manage that, Beast?"

"One is doing one's utmost, Little Miss."

She nodded, accepting that this was all that could be asked of her ship. Above, the clouds were beginning to thin out, the sky darkening to a deep midnight blue. Space looked close enough to touch.

But she still had a long way to go.

Clavain watched while the last layer of concealment was removed from the survivor's hiding place. One of his soldiers shone a torch into the gloomy enclosure. The survivor was huddled in a corner, cocooned in a stained grey thermal blanket. Clavain felt relief; now that this minor detail was attended to, the enemy ship could be safely destroyed and *Nightshade* could return to the Mother Nest.

Finding the survivor had been much easier than Clavain had expected. It had only taken thirty minutes to pinpoint the location, narrowing down the search with acoustic and biosensor scanners. Thereafter, it had simply been a question of stripping away panels and equipment until they found the concealed niche, a volume about the size of two cupboards placed back to back. It was in a part of the ship that the human crew would have avoided visiting too often, bathed as it was in elevated radiation from the fusion engines.

The hideaway, Clavain quickly decided, looked like a hastily arranged brig; a place of confinement in a ship never designed to carry prisoners. The captive must have been placed in the hole and the panelling and equipment bolted and glued back into place around him, leaving only a conduit along which to pass air, water and food. The hole was filthy. Clavain had his suit sample the air and pass a little through to his nose: it reeked of human waste. He wondered if the prisoner had been neglected all the while, or only since the crew's attention had been diverted by *Nightshade*'s arrival.

In other respects, the prisoner seemed to have been well looked after. The walls of the hole were padded, with a couple of restraining hoops that could have been used to avoid injury during combat manoeuvres. There was a microphone rigged through for communication, though as far as Clavain could tell it only worked one way, allowing the prisoner to be talked to. There were blankets and the remains of a meal. Clavain had seen worse places of confinement. He had even been a guest in some of them.

He pushed a thought into the head of the soldier with the torch. *Get that blanket off him, will you? I want to see who we've found.*

The soldier reached into the hole. Clavain wondered who the prisoner would turn out to be, his mind flashing through the possibilities. He was not aware of any Conjoiners having been taken prisoner lately, and doubted that the enemy would have gone to this much trouble to keep one alive. A prisoner from the enemy's own ranks was the next most likely thing: a traitor or deserter, perhaps.

The soldier whipped the blanket away from the huddled figure.

The prisoner, crouched into a small foetal shape, squealed against the sudden intrusion of light, hiding its dark-adapted eyes.

Clavain stared. The prisoner was nothing that he had been expecting. At first glance it might have been taken for an adolescent human, for the proportions and size were roughly analogous. A naked human at that—unclothed pink human-looking flesh folded away into the hole. There was a horrid expanse of burned skin around its upper arm, all ridges and whorls of pink and deathly white.

Clavain was looking at a hyperpig: a genetic chimera of pig and human.

"Hello," Clavain said aloud, his amplified voice booming out of his suit speaker.

The pig moved. The motion was sudden and springlike and none of them were expecting it. The pig lashed out with something long and metallic clutched in one fist. The object gleamed, its edge reverberating like a tuning fork. The pig daggered it hard into Clavain's chest. The tip of the blade shivered across the armour, leaving only a narrow shining furrow, but found the point near Clavain's shoulder where two plaques slid across each other. The blade slipped into the gap, Clavain's suit registering the intrusion with a shrill pulsing alarm in his helmet. He jerked back before the blade was able to penetrate his inner suit layer and reach his skin, and then collided with a sharp crack against the wall behind him. The weapon tumbled from the pig's grip, spinning away like a ship that had lost gyroscopic control. Clavain recognised it as a piezoknife; he carried something similar on his own suit's utility belt. The pig must have stolen it from one of the Demarchists.

Clavain got his breath back. "Let's start again, shall we?"

The other Conjoiners had the pig pinned down. Clavain inspected his suit, calling up damage schematics. There was a mild loss of pressure integrity near the shoulder. He was in no danger of suffocating to death, but he was still mindful of the possibility of undiscovered contaminants aboard the enemy ship. Almost as a reflex action he unhitched a sealant spray from his belt, selected nozzle diameter and pasted the rapidly hardening epoxy around the general area of the knife wound, where it solidified in the form of a sinuous grey cyst.

Somewhere before the dawn of the Demarchist era, in the twenty-first or twenty-second century, not far from the time of Clavain's own birth, a spectrum of human genes had been spliced into those of the domestic pig. The intention had been to optimise the ease with which organs could be transplanted between the two species, enabling pigs to grow body parts that could be harvested later for human utilisation. There were better ways to repair or replace damaged tissue now, had been for centuries, but the legacy of the pig experiments remained. The genetic intervention had gone too far, achieving not just cross-species compatibility but something entirely unexpected: intelligence.

But no one, not even the pigs, really knew what had happened. There might not have been deliberate tinkering to bring their cognitive faculties up to human level, but the pigs had certainly not gained language by accident. Not all of them had it—there were distinct subgroups of pigs with various mental and vocal capacities—but those that could speak had been engineered that way by someone who had known exactly what they were doing. It was not simply that their brains had the right grammatical machinery wired in. They had also had their throats, lungs and jaws adapted so that they could form human speech sounds.

Clavain eased forwards to speak to the prisoner. "Can you

understand me?" he asked, first in Norte and then in Canasian, the Demarchists' main language. My name is Nevil Clavain. You're in the custody of Conjoiners.'

The pig answered, his remodelled jaw and throat anatomy enabling him to form perfect human sounds. "I don't care who I'm in the custody of. You can fuck off and die."

"Neither happens to be on my agenda for the day."

The pig warily uncovered one pink-red eye. "Who the fuck are you anyway? Where are the rest of them?"

"The shipmaster's crew? I'm afraid they're all dead."

The pig showed no detectable gratitude at this news. "You killed them?"

"No. They were already dead when we got aboard."

"And you are?"

"As I said, Conjoiners."

"Spiders . . . " The pig contorted its almost human mouth into a semblance of disgust. "You know what I do to spiders? I piss them off toilet seats."

"Very nice."

Clavain could see this was going nowhere fast; subvocally he asked one of the nearby troops to get the prisoner sedated and ferried back to *Nightshade*. He had no idea who or what the pig represented, how it slotted into the spiralling endgame of the war, but he would know a great deal more once the pig had been trawled. And a dose of Conjoiner medichines would do wonders for the pig's reticence.

Clavain remained on the enemy ship while the sweep teams completed the last of their checks, ensuring that the enemy had left behind no tactically useful information. But there was nothing; the ship's data stores had been wiped clean. A parallel search revealed no technologies that were not already well understood by the Conjoiners, and no weapons systems that were worth appropriating. The standard procedure at this point was to destroy the searched vessel, to prevent it falling back into enemy possession.

Clavain was thinking about the best way to scuttle the ship—a missile or a demolition charge?—when he felt Remontoire's presence invade his head.

[Clavain?]

What is it?

[We're picking up a general distress message from the freighter.]

Antoinette Bax? I thought she was dead.

[She isn't, but she might soon be. Her ship has engine problems—a tokamak failure, it seems. She hasn't made escape velocity, and she hasn't managed an orbital injection either.]

Clavain nodded, more for his benefit than Remontoire's. He imagined the kind of parabolic trajectory *Storm Bird* had to be on. She might not have reached the apex of that parabola yet, but sooner or later Antoinette Bax was going to start sliding back towards the cloud deck. He imagined, too, the kind of desperation that would have led her to issue a general distress signal when the only ship within answering distance was a Conjoiner vessel. In Clavain's experience, the majority of pilots would have chosen death rather than capture by the spiders.

[Clavain . . . you realise we can't possibly acknowledge her call.]

I realise.

[That would set a precedent. We'd be endorsing illegal activity. At the very least, we'd have no choice but to recruit her.]

Clavain nodded again, thinking of the times he had seen prisoners scream and thrash as they were led to the recruitment theatres, where their heads would be pumped full of Conjoiner neural machinery. They were wrong to fear it; he knew that better than anyone, since he had once resisted it himself. But he understood how they felt.

And he wondered if he wanted to inflict that terror upon Antoinette Bax.

A little while later Clavain saw the bright blue spark as the enemy ship hit the gas giant's atmosphere. The timing had been accidental, but she had hit on the dark side, illuminating stacked cloud layers in purple strobe flashes as she plummeted deeper. It was impressive, beautiful, even, and Clavain momentarily wanted to show it to Galiana, for it was exactly the kind of visual spectacle that would have delighted her. She would have approved of his scuttling method, too: nothing as wasteful as a missile or a demolition charge. Instead, he had attached three tractor rockets from *Nightshade,* tiny drones which had glued themselves to the enemy's hull like remora. The tractors had whisked the enemy ship towards the gas giant, only detaching when she was minutes from re-entry. The angle of attack had been steep, and the enemy craft had incinerated impressively.

The tractors were haring home now, accelerating at high burn to catch up with *Nightshade,* which had already turned back towards the Mother Nest. Once the tractors had returned the operation could be considered closed; there would only be the matter of the prisoner to attend to, but the pig's fate was of no great urgency. Of Antoinette Bax . . . well, irrespective of her motives, Clavain admired her bravery; not just because she had come so far into a war zone, but also because of the way she had so brazenly ignored the shipmaster's warning and, when it became necessary, the way she had summoned the courage to ask the Conjoiners for help. She must have known that it was an unreasonable request; that by the illegality of her trespass into the war zone she had forfeited any right to assistance, and that a military ship was hardly likely to waste time or fuel helping her out. She must also have known that even if the Conjoiners did save her life, the penalty she would pay for that would be conscription into their ranks, a fate that the Demarchist propaganda machine had made to seem hellish in the extreme.

No. She could not have reasonably expected rescue. But it had been brave of her to ask.

Clavain sighed, teetering on the edge of self-disgust. He issued a neural command instructing *Nightshade* to tight-beam the stricken freighter. When the link was established, he spoke aloud. "Antoinette Bax . . . this is Nevil Clavain. I am aboard the Conjoiner vessel. Can you hear me?"

There was some timelag now, and the return signal was poorly focused. Her voice sounded as if it was coming from somewhere beyond the furthest quasar.

"Why are you answering me now, you bastard? I can see you've left me to die."

"I'm curious, that's all." He held his breath, half-expecting that she would not reply.

"About what?"

"About what made you ask for our help. Aren't you terrified of what we'll do to you?"

"Why should I be terrified?"

She sounded nonchalant but Clavain wasn't fooled. "It's generally our policy to assimilate captured prisoners, Bax.

We'd bring you aboard and feed our machines into your brain. Doesn't that concern you?"

"Yes, but I'll tell you what concerns me a fuck of a lot more right now, and that's hitting this fucking planet."

Clavain smiled. "That's a very pragmatic attitude, Bax. I admire it."

"Good. Now will you fuck off and let me die in peace?"

"Antoinette, listen to me carefully. There's something I need you to do for me, with some urgency."

She must have detected the change of tone in his voice, although she still sounded suspicious. "What?"

"Have your ship transmit a blueprint of itself to me. I want a complete map of your hull's structural integrity profile. Hardpoints, that kind of thing. If you can persuade your hull to colour itself to reveal maximum stress contours, all the better. I want to know where I can safely put a load without having your ship fold under the strain."

"There's no way you can save me. You're too far away. Even if you turned around now, it'd be too late."

"There's a way, trust me. Now, that data, please, or I'll have to trust my instincts, and that may not be for the best."

She did not answer for a moment. He waited, scratching his beard, and only breathed again when he felt *Nightshade*'s acknowledgement that the data had been uploaded. He filtered the transmission for neuropathic viruses and then allowed it into his skull. Everything he needed to know about the freighter bloomed in his head, crammed into short-term memory.

"Thank you very much, Antoinette. That will do nicely."

Clavain sent an order to one of the returning tractor rockets. The tractor peeled away from its brethren at whiplash acceleration, executing a hairpin reversal that would have reduced an organic passenger to paste. Clavain authorised the tractor to ignore all its internal safety limits, removing the need for it to conserve enough fuel for a safe return to *Nightshade*.

"What are you going to do?" Bax asked.

"I'm sending a drone back. It will latch on to your hull and drag you to clear space, out of the Jovian's gravity well. I'll have the tractor give you a modest nudge in the direction of Yellowstone, but I'm afraid you'll be on your own from then. I hope you can fix your tokamak, or else you'll be in for a very long fall home."

It seemed to take an eternity for his words to sink in. "You're not going to take me prisoner?"

"Not today, Antoinette. But if you ever cross my path again, I promise one thing: I'll kill you."

He had not enjoyed delivering the threat, but hoped it might knock some sense into her. Clavain closed the link before she could answer.

FOUR

In a building in Cuvier, on the planet Resurgam, a woman stood at a window, facing away from the door with her hands clasped tightly behind her back.

"Next," she said.

While she waited for the suspect to be dragged in, the woman remained at the window, admiring the tremendous and sobering view that it presented. The raked windows reached from floor to ceiling, leaning outwards at the top. Structures of utilitarian aspect marched away in all directions, cubes and rectangles piled atop one another. The ruthlessly rectilinear buildings inspired a sense of crushing conformity and subjugation; mental waveguides designed to exclude the slightest joyful or uplifting thought.

Her office, which was merely one slot in the much larger Inquisition House itself, was situated in the rebuilt portion of Cuvier. Historical records—the Inquisitor had not been there herself during the events—established that the building lay more or less directly above the ground-zero point where the True Path Inundationists had detonated the first of their terrorist devices. With a yield in the two-kilotonne range, the pinhead-sized antimatter bombs had not been the most impressive destructive devices in her experience. But, she supposed, it was not how big your weapon was that mattered, but what you did with it.

The terrorists could not have picked a softer target, and the results had been appropriately calamitous.

"Next . . . " the Inquisitor repeated, a little louder this time.

The door creaked open a hand's width. She heard the voice of the guard who stood outside. "That's it for today, ma'am."

Of course—Ibert's file had been the last in the pile.

"Thank you," the Inquisitor replied. "I don't suppose you've heard any news on the Thorn inquiry?"

The guard answered with a trace of unease, as well he might given that he was passing information between two rival government departments. "They've released a man after questioning, I gather. He had a watertight alibi, though it took a little persuasion to get it out of him. Something about being with a woman other than his wife." He shrugged. "The usual story . . . "

"And the usual persuasion, I imagine—a few unfortunate trips down the stairs. So they've no additional leads on Thorn?"

"They're no closer to catching him than you are to catching the Triumvir. Sorry. You know what I mean, ma'am."

"Yes . . . " She prolonged the word tortuously.

"Will that be all, ma'am?"

"For now."

The door creaked shut.

The woman whose official title was Inquisitor Vuilleumier returned her attention to the city. Delta Pavonis was low in the sky, beginning to shade the sides of the buildings in various faint permutations of rust and orange. She looked at the view until dusk fell, comparing it in her mind's eye with her memories of Chasm City and, before that, Sky's Edge. It was always at dusk that she decided whether she liked a place or not. She remembered once, not long after her arrival in Chasm City, asking a man named Mirabel whether there had ever come a point when he had decided he liked the city. Mirabel had, like her, been a native of Sky's Edge. He had told her that he had found ways of getting used to it. She had doubted him, but in the end he had been proven right. But it was only when she was wrenched away from Chasm City that she had begun to look back on it with anything resembling fondness.

She had never reached that state on Resurgam.

The lights of government-issue electric cars stirred silver rivers between the buildings. She turned from the window and walked across the room to her private chamber. She closed the door behind her.

Security considerations dictated that the chamber was windowless. She eased herself into a padded seat behind a vast horseshoe-shaped desk. It was an old escritoire whose dead cybernetic innards had been reamed out and replaced by much cruder systems. A pot of stale, tepid coffee sat on a heated coil at one end of the desk. A buzzing electric fan gave off the tang of ozone.

Three walls, including most of the wall she had stepped through, were lined with shelves containing bound reports detailing fifteen years' worth of effort. It would have been an absurdity for an entire department of government to be dedicated to the capture of a single individual: a woman who could not with certainty be said to be still alive, much less on Resurgam. Therefore the remit of the Inquisitor's office extended to the gathering of intelligence on a range of external threats to the colony. But it was a fact that the Triumvir had become the most celebrated of the still-open cases, in the same way that the apprehension of Thorn, and the dismantling of the movement he fronted, dominated the work of the neighbouring department, Internal Threats. Though it was more than sixty years since she committed her crimes, high-ranking officials continued to bray for the Triumvir's arrest and trial, using her as a focus for public sentiments that might otherwise have been directed at the government. It was one of the oldest tricks of mob-management: give them a hate figure. The Inquisitor had a great many other things she would rather be doing than pursuing the war criminal. But if her department failed to show the necessary enthusiasm for the task, another would surely take its place, and that could not be tolerated. There was the faintest of possibilities that a new department might succeed.

So the Inquisitor maintained the pretence. The Triumvir case remained legitimately open because the Triumvir was an Ultra, and could therefore be assumed to be still alive despite the time that had passed since her criminal activities. On her case alone there were lists of tens of thousands of potential suspects, transcriptions of thousands of interviews. There were hundreds of biographies and case summaries. Some individuals, around a dozen, each merited a good portion of a shelf. And this was just a fraction of the office's archive; just the paperwork that had to be immediately on hand. Down in the basement, and at other sites around the city, were many more miles of documentation. A marvellous and largely secret network of pneumatic tubes enabled files to be whisked from office to office in seconds.

On her desk were a few opened files. Various names had been ringed, underscored or connected by spidery lines. Photographs were stapled to summary cards, blurry long-lens acquisitions of faces moving through crowds. She leafed through them, aware that she had to give a convincing impression of actually following up these apparent leads. She had to listen to her field agents and digest the snippets of information passed on by informers. She had to give every indication that she was actually interested in finding the Triumvir.

Something caught her eye. Something on the fourth wall.

The wall displayed a Mercator projection of Resurgam. The map had kept up with the terraforming program, showing small blotches of blue or green in addition to the unrelenting shades of grey, tan and white that would have been the case a century earlier. Cuvier was still the largest settlement, but there were now a dozen or so outposts that were large enough to be considered small cities in their own right. Slev lines connected most of them; others were linked by canals, roads or freight pipelines. There were a handful of landing strips, but there were not enough aircraft to permit routine journeys for anyone other than key government officials. Smaller settlements—weather stations and the few remaining archaeological digs—could be reached by airship or all-terrain crawler, but not usually in less than weeks of travel time.

Now a red light was winking up in the northeastern corner of the map, hundreds of kilometres away from anywhere most people had heard of. A field agent was calling in. Operatives were identified by their code numbers, winking next to the spot of light that denoted their position.

Operative Four.

The Inquisitor felt the short dark hairs on the back of her neck prickle. It had been a long, long time since she had heard from Operative Four.

She tapped a query into the desk, hunting and pecking for the stiff black keys. She asked the desk to verify that Operative Four was currently reachable. The desk's readout confirmed that the red light had only come on in the last two hours. The operative was still on the air, awaiting the Inquisitor's response.

The Inquisitor picked up the telephone handset from her desk, squeezing its sluglike black bulk against the side of her head.

"Communications," she said.

"Comms."

"Put me through to Field Operative Four. Repeat, Field Operative Four. Audio only. Protocol three."

"Hold the line, please. Establishing. Connected."

"Go secure."

She heard the pitch of the line modulate slightly as the comms officer dropped out of the loop. She listened, hearing nothing but hiss.

"Four . . . ?" she breathed.

There was an agonising delay before the reply came back. "Speaking." The voice was faint, skirling in and out of static.

"It's been a long time, Four."

"I know." It was a woman's voice, one the Inquisitor knew very well. "How are you keeping, Inquisitor Vuilleumier?"

"Work has its ups and downs."

"I know the feeling. We need to meet, urgently and in person. Does your Office still have its little privileges?"

"Within limits."

"Then I suggest you abuse them to the fullest extent. You know my current location. There is a small settlement seventy-five klicks to the southwest of me by the name of Solnhofen. I can be there within one day, at the following . . . " and then she gave the Inquisitor the details of a hostelry that she had already located.

The Inquisitor did her usual mental arithmetic. Via slev and road it would take in the region of two to three days to reach Solnhofen. Slev and airship would be quicker but more conspicuous: Solnhofen was not on any of the normal dirigible routes. An aircraft would be faster, of course, easily capable of reaching the meeting point within a day and a half, even if she had to take the long way around to avoid weather fronts. Normally, given an urgent request from a field agent, she would not have hesitated to fly. But this was Operative Four. She could not afford to draw undue attention to the meeting. But, she reflected, not flying would do precisely that.

It was not easy.

"Is it really so urgent?" the Inquisitor asked, knowing what the answer would be.

"Of course." The woman made an odd henlike clucking sound. "I wouldn't have called otherwise, would I?"

"And it concerns her . . . the Triumvir?" Perhaps she imagined it, but she thought she could hear a smile in the field agent's reply.

"Who else?"

FIVE

The comet had no name. It might once have been classified and catalogued, but not in living memory, and certainly no information relating to it was to be found in any public database. No transponder had ever been anchored to its surface; no Skyjacks had ever grappled themselves in and extracted a core sample. To all intents and purposes it was completely unremarkable, simply one member of a much larger swarm of cold drifters. There were billions of them, each following a slow and stately orbit around Epsilon Eridani. For the most part they had been undisturbed since the system's formation. Very occasionally, a resonant perturbation of the system's larger worlds might unshackle a few members of the swarm and send them falling in on sun-grazing orbits, but for the vast majority of comets the future would consist only of more orbits around Eridani, until the sun itself swelled up. Until then they would remain dormant, insufferably cold and still.

The comet was large, as swarm members went, but not unusually so: there were at least a million that were larger. From edge to edge it was a twenty-kilometre frozen mudball of nearly black ice; a lightly compacted meringue of methane, carbon monoxide, nitrogen and oxygen, laced with silicates, sooty hydrocarbons and a few glistening veins of purple or emerald organic macromolecules. They had crystallised into beautiful refractive crystal seams several billion years earlier, when the galaxy was a younger and quieter place. Mostly, though, it was pitifully dark. Epsilon Eridani was merely a hard glint of light at this distance, thirteen light-hours away. It looked scarcely less remote than the brighter stars.

But humans had come, once.

They had arrived in a squadron of dark spacecraft, their holds bursting with transforming machines. They had covered the comet in a caul of transparent plastic, enveloping it like a froth of digestive spit. The plastic had given the comet structural rigidity it would otherwise have lacked, but from a distance it was all but undetectable. The backscatter from radar or spectroscopic scans was only slightly compromised, and remained well within the anticipated error of Demarchist measurements.

With the comet held stiff by its plastic shell, the humans had set about sapping its spin. Ion rockets, emplaced cunningly across its face, slowly bled it of angular momentum. Only when there was a small residual spin, enough to ward off suspicion, were the ion rockets quietened and the installations removed from the surface.

But by then the humans had already been busy inside. They had cored out the comet, tamping eighty per cent of its interior volume into a thin, hard shell that was used to line the outer shell. The resultant chamber was fifteen kilometres wide and perfectly spherical. Concealed shafts permitted entry into the chamber from outside space, wide enough to accept a moderately large spacecraft provided the ship moved nimbly. Berthing and repair yards festered across the inner surface of the chamber like the dense grid of a cityscape, interrupted here and there by the cryo-arithmetic engines, squat black domes which studded the grid like volcanic cinder plugs. The huge engines were quantum refrigerators, sucking heat out of the local universe by computational cooling.

Clavain had made the entrance transition enough times not to be alarmed by the sudden whiplash course adjustments necessary to avoid collisions with the comet's rotating husk. At least, that was what he told himself. But the truth was he never drew breath until he was safely inside or out. It was too much like diving through the narrowing gap in a lowering portcullis.

And with a ship as large as *Nightshade,* the adjustments were even more brutal.

He entrusted the operation to *Nightshade*'s computers. They knew exactly what needed to be done, and the insertion was precisely the kind of well-specified problem that computers handled better than people, even Conjoined people.

Then it was over, and he was in. Not for the first time, Clavain felt a dizzying sense of vertigo as the comet's interior space came into view. The husk had not stayed hollow for long. Its cored-out volume was filled with moving machinery: a great nested clockwork of rushing circles, resembling nothing so much as a fantastically complex armillary sphere.

He was looking at the military stronghold of his people: the Mother Nest.

There were five layers to the Mother Nest. The outer four were all engineered to simulate gravity, in half-gee increments. Each layer consisted of three rings of nearly equal diameter, the plane of each ring tilted by sixty degrees from its neighbour. There were two nodes where the three rings passed close to each other, and at each of these nodes the rings vanished into a hexagonal structure. The nodal structures functioned both as an interchange between rings and a means of guiding them. Each ring slid through sleeves in the nodal structures, constrained by frictionless magnetic fields. The rings themselves were dark bands studded with myriad tiny windows and the occasional larger illuminated space.

The outermost triplet of rings was ten kilometres across and simulated gravity at two gees. One kilometre of empty space inwards, a smaller triplet of rings spun within the outermost shell, simulating gravity at one and a half gees. One kilometre in from that was the one-gee ring triplet, consisting of by far the thickest and most densely populated set of rings, where the majority of the Conjoiners spent the bulk of their time. Nestling within that was the half-gee triplet, which in turn encased a transparent central sphere that did not rotate. That was the null-gee core, a pressurised bubble three kilometres wide stuffed with greenery, sunlamps and various microhabitat niches. It was where children played and elderly Conjoiners came to die. It was also where Felka spent most of her time.

Nightshade decelerated and came to a stop relative to the outermost triplet. Already, servicing craft were emerging from the whirling rings. Clavain felt the jolts as the tugs latched on to *Nightshade*'s hull. When he had disembarked, his vessel would be hauled towards the shipyards quilting the chamber's wall. There were many ships already berthed there: various elongated black shapes hooked into a labyrinth of support machines and repair systems. Most were smaller than Clavain's ship, however, and there were no genuinely large vessels.

Clavain left the ship with his usual slight feeling of unease, of a job not properly finished. It had been many years before he realised quite what caused this: it was the way that his fellow Conjoiners said nothing to each other as they left the craft, despite the fact that they might have spent months together on a mission, and encountered many risks.

A robot tender collected him from one of the hull airlocks. The tender was an upright box with generous windows, squatting on a rectangular base studded with rockets and impeller fans. Clavain boarded it, watching a larger tender depart from the next airlock along. In the other tender he saw Remontoire with two other Conjoiners and the prisoner they had captured on the Demarchist ship. From a distance, the pig, slouched and docile, could easily have been mistaken for a human prisoner. For a moment Clavain thought that the pig was being pleasingly co-operative, until he recognised the glint of a pacification coronet wrapped around the prisoner's scalp.

They had trawled the pig on the way back to the Mother Nest, but had learned nothing specific. The pig's memories were highly blockaded; not in the Conjoiner fashion, but in the crude black-market style that was common amongst the Chasm City criminal underworld, and which was usually implemented to shield incriminating memories from the various branches of the Ferrisville constabulary: the sirens, scythes, skulltappers and eraserheads. With the kind of interrogation techniques that were possible in the Mother Nest, Clavain had no doubt that the blockades could be dismantled, but until then he could discover nothing other than that they had recovered a small-time pig criminal with violent tendencies, probably affiliated to one of the larger pig gangs operating in and around Yellowstone and the Rust Belt. Clearly the pig had been up to no good when he was captured by the Demarchists, but that was hardly unusual for pigs.

Clavain neither liked nor disliked hyperpigs. He had met

enough to know that they were as morally complex as the humans they had been engineered to serve, and that every pig should be judged on its own terms. A pig from the Ganesh industrial moon had saved his life three times during the Shiva-Parvati cordon crisis of 2358. Twenty years later, on Irravel's Moon, orbiting Fand, a group of pig brigands had taken eight of Clavain's soldiers hostage and had then begun to eat them alive when they refused to divulge Conjoiner secrets. Only one Conjoiner had escaped, and Clavain had taken his pain-saturated memories as his own. He carried them now, locked away in the most secure kind of mental partition, so that they could not be unlocked accidentally. But even this had not made him hate pigs as a species.

He was not sure whether the same could be said for Remontoire. Deep in Remontoire's past lay an even more horrific and protracted episode, when he had been taken prisoner by the pig pirate Run Seven. Run Seven had been one of the earliest hyperpigs, and his mind had been riddled with the psychotic scars of flawed neuro-genetic augmentation. He had captured Remontoire and isolated him from the mental communion of other Conjoiners. That had been enough of a torture, but Run Seven had not stinted on the other, older kind. And he had been very good at it.

Remontoire had escaped, finally, and the pig had died. But Clavain knew that his friend still carried profound mental wounds that now and then broke through to the surface. Clavain had watched very carefully when Remontoire made the preliminary trawls of the pig, fully aware of how easily that procedure could become a kind of torture in its own right. And while nothing that Remontoire had done had been improper—indeed, he had been almost too reticent in his enquiries—Clavain admitted to feeling a sense of misgiving. If only it had not been a pig, he thought, and if only Remontoire had not had to be associated with the prisoner's questioning . . .

Clavain watched the other tender fall away from *Nightshade,* convinced that he had not heard the last of the pig and that the repercussions of the capture would be with them for some time. Then he smiled and told himself he was being silly. It was only a pig, after all.

Clavain issued a neural command to the simple subpersona of the tender, and with a lurch they detached from the dark whale-like hull of *Nightshade*. The tender whisked him inwards, through the great rushing clockwork of the centrifugal wheels, towards the green heart of the null-gee core.

This stronghold, this particular Mother Nest, was only the latest to be built. Though there had always been a Mother Nest of sorts, in the war's early stages it had only been the largest of many camouflaged encampments. Two-thirds of the Conjoined had been spread throughout the system in smaller bases. But separation brought its own problems. The individual groups had been light-hours apart, and the lines of communication between them had been vulnerable to interception. Strategies could not be evolved in real time, nor could the group-mind state be extended to encompass two or more nests. The Conjoiners had become fragmented and nervous. Reluctantly, the decision had been taken to absorb the smaller nests into one vast Mother Nest, hoping that the advantage gained through centralisation would outweigh the danger involved in placing all their eggs in one basket.

With hindsight, the decision had been massively successful.

The tender slowed as it neared the membrane of the null-gee core. Clavain felt utterly dwarfed by the green sphere. It glowed with its own soft radiance, like a verdant miniature planet. The tender squelched through the membrane, into air.

Clavain dropped a window, allowing the core's atmosphere to mingle with the tender's own. His nose prickled at the vegetative assault. The air was cool and fresh and moist, its smell that of a forest after an intense midmorning thunderstorm. Though he had visited the core on countless occasions, the scent nonetheless made Clavain think not of those previous visits but of his childhood. He could not say when or where, but he had certainly walked through a forest that had this quality. It had been somewhere on Earth—Scotland, perhaps.

There was no gravity in the core, but the vegetation that filled it was not a free-floating mass. Threading the sphere from side to side were spars of oak up to three kilometres long. The spars branched and merged randomly, forming a wooden cytoskeleton of pleasing complexity. Here and there the spars bulged sufficiently to accommodate enclosed spaces, hollows that glowed with pastel lantern-light. Elsewhere, a cobweb of smaller strands provided a structural mesh to which most of the greenery was anchored. The whole assemblage was festooned with irrigation pipes and nutrient feedlines, threading back into the support machinery lurking at the very heart of the core. Sun lamps studded the membrane at irregular intervals, and were distributed throughout the green masses themselves. Now they shone with the hard blue light of high noon, but as the day progressed—they were slaved to twenty-six-hour Yellowstone time—the lamps would slide down through the spectrum towards the bronze and russet reds of evening.

Eventually night would fall. The spherical forest would come alive with the chirrups and calls of a thousand weirdly evolved nocturnal animals. Squatting on a spar near its heart during nightfall, it would be easy to believe that the forest reached away in all directions for thousands of kilometres. The distant centrifugal wheels were only visible from the last hundred metres of greenery beneath the membrane, and they were, of course, utterly silent.

The tender dodged through the mass, knowing precisely where it had to take Clavain. Now and then he saw other Conjoiners, but they were mostly children or the elderly. The children were born and raised in the one-gee triplet, but when they were six months old they were brought here at regular intervals. Supervised by the elderly, they learned the muscle and orientation skills necessary for weightlessness. For most of them it was a game, but the very best would be earmarked for duty in the arena of space war. A few, a very few, showed such heightened spatial skills that they would be steered towards battle planning.

The elderly were too frail to spend much time in the high-gee rings. Once they had come to the core, they often never left. Clavain passed a couple now. They both wore support rigs, medical harnesses that doubled as propulsion packs. Their legs trailed behind them like afterthoughts. They were coaxing a quintet of children into kicking off from one side of a woody hollow into open space.

Seen without augmented vision, the scene had a tangibly sinister quality. The children were garbed in black suits and helmets that protected their skin against sharp branches. Their eyes were hidden behind black goggles, making it difficult to interpret their expressions. The elderly were equally drab, though they wore no helmets. But their fully visible faces betrayed nothing resembling enjoyment. To Clavain they looked like undertakers engaged in some solemn burial duty that would be ruined by the slightest hint of levity.

Clavain willed his implants to reveal the truth. There was a moment of florid growth as bright structures blossomed into existence out of thin air. The children wore filmy clothes now, marked with tribal swirls and zigzags of lurid colour. Their heads were bare, unencumbered by helmets. Two were boys; three were girls. He judged their ages to lie between five and seven. Their expressions were not entirely joyous, but neither were they miserable or neutral. Instead, they all looked slightly scared and slightly exhilarated. No doubt there was some rivalry going on, each child weighing the benefits and risks of being the first to take the aerial plunge.

The elderly couple still looked much the same, but now Clavain was attuned to the thoughts they were radiating. Bathed in an aura of encouragement, their faces now looked serene and patient rather than dour. They were quite prepared to wait hours for the children.

The environment itself had also changed. The air was full of jewel-bright butterflies and dragonflies, darting to and fro on busy trajectories. Neon caterpillars worked their way through the greenery. Hummingbirds hovered and translated from flower to flower, moving like precisely programmed clockwork toys. Monkeys, lemurs and flying squirrels jumped into free space with abandon, their eyes gleaming like marbles.

This was what the children perceived, and what Clavain was tuned into. They had known no other world but this storybook abstraction. Subtly, as they aged, the data reaching their brains would be manipulated. They would never notice the change from day to day, but the creatures haunting the forest's spaces would gradually grow more realistic, their colours dimming to naturalistic greens and browns, blacks and whites. The creatures would become smaller and more elusive. Eventually, only the real animals would remain. Then—the children would be ten or eleven at this point—they would be gently educated about the machines that had doctored their view of the world so far. They would learn of their implants, and how they enabled a second layer to be draped over reality, one that could be shaped into any form imaginable.

For Clavain the educational process had been somewhat

more brutal. It had been during his second visit to Galiana's nest on Mars. She had shown him the nursery where the young Conjoiners were being instructed, but at that point he had not possessed any implants of his own. Then he had been injured, and Galiana had filled his head with medichines. He still remembered the heart-stopping moment when he had first experienced his subjective reality being manipulated. The feeling of his own skull being gate-crashed by numerous other minds had only been part of it, but perhaps the most shocking element had been his first glimpse of the realm the Conjoiners walked through. The psychologists had a term for it—cognitive breakthrough—but few of them could have experienced it for themselves.

Suddenly he drew the attention of the children.

[Clavain!] One of the boys had pushed a thought into his head.

Clavain made the tender come to a halt in the middle of the space the children were using for flying lessons. He orientated the tender so that he was more or less level with them.

Hello. Clavain gripped the handrail in front of him like a preacher at a pulpit.

A girl looked at him intently. [Where have you been, Clavain?]

Outside. He eyed the tutors carefully.

[Outside? Beyond the Mother Nest?] the girl persisted.

He was unsure how to answer. He did not remember how much knowledge the children possessed at this age. Certainly, they knew nothing of the war. But it was difficult to discuss one thing without it leading to another. *Beyond the Mother Nest, yes.*

[In a spaceship?]

Yes. In a very big spaceship.

[Can I see it?] the girl asked.

One day, I expect. Not today, though. He felt the tutors' disquiet, though neither had placed a concrete thought in his head. *You've got other things to take care of, I think.*

[What did you do in the spaceship, Clavain?]

Clavain scratched his beard. He did not enjoy misleading children and had never quite got the hang of white lies. A mild distillation of the truth seemed the best approach. *I helped someone.*

[Whom did you help?]

A lady . . . a woman.

[Why did she need your help?]

Her ship—her spaceship—had got into trouble. She needed some assistance and I just happened to be passing by.

[What was the lady called?]

Bax. Antoinette Bax. I gave her a nudge with a rocket, to stop her falling back into a gas giant.

[Why was she coming out of the gas giant?]

I don't really know, to tell the truth.

[Why did she have two names, Clavain?]

Because . . . This was going to get very messy, he realised. *Look, um, I shouldn't interrupt you, I really shouldn't.* He felt a palpable relaxation in the tutors' emotional aura. *So—um—who's going to show me what a good flier they are, then?*

It was all the spur that the children needed. A welter of voices crowded his skull, competing for his attention. [Me, Clavain, me!]

He watched them kick off into the void, barely able to contain themselves.

There was a moment when he was still peering into green infinity, and then the tender burst through a shimmer of leaves into a clearing. It had navigated the forest for another three or four minutes after leaving the children, knowing exactly where to find Felka.

The clearing was a spherical space enclosed on all sides by dense growth. One of the structural spars thrust its way clean through the volume, bulging with residential spaces. The tender whirred closer to the spar and then held station with its impellers while Clavain disembarked. Ladders and vines provided hand- and footholds, allowing him to work his way along the spar until he found the entrance to its hollow interior. There was some sense of vertigo, but it was slight. Part of his mind would probably always quail at the thought of clambering recklessly through what felt like a forest's elevated canopy, but the years had diminished that nagging primate anxiety to the point where it was barely noticeable.

"Felka . . . " he called ahead. "It's Clavain."

There was no immediate answer. He burrowed deeper, descending—or ascending?—headfirst. "Felka . . . "

"Hello, Clavain." Her voice boomed from the middle distance, echoed and amplified by the spar's peculiar acoustics.

He followed the voice; he could not feel her thoughts. Felka did not participate routinely in the Conjoined mind-state, although that had not always been the case. But even if she had, Clavain would have maintained a certain distance. Long ago, by mutual consent, they had elected to exclude themselves from each other's minds, except at the most trivial level. Anything else would have been an unwanted intimacy.

The shaft ended in a womblike interior space. This was where Felka spent most of her time these days, in her laboratory and atelier. The walls were a beguiling swirl of wooden growth patterns. To Clavain's eye, the ellipses and knots resembled geodesic contours of highly stressed space-time. Lanterns glowed in sconces, throwing his shadow across the wood in threatening ogre-like shapes. He helped himself along by his fingertips, brushing past ornate wooden contraptions that floated untethered through the spar. Clavain recognised most of the objects well enough, but one or two looked new to him.

He snatched one from the air for closer examination. It rattled in his grasp. It was a human head fashioned from a single helix of wood; through the gaps in the spiral he could see another head inside, and another inside that one. Possibly there were more. He let the object go and seized another. This one was a sphere bristling with sticks, projecting out to various distances from the surface. Clavain adjusted one of the sticks and felt something click and move within the sphere, like the tumbler of a lock.

"I see you've been busy, Felka," he said.

"I gather I wasn't the only one," she replied. "I heard reports. Some business about a prisoner?"

Clavain pawed past another barrage of wooden objects and rounded a corner in the spar. He squeezed through a connecting aperture into a small windowless chamber lit only by lanterns. Their light threw pinks and emeralds across the ochre and tan shades of the walls. One wall consisted entirely of numerous wooden faces, carved with mildly exaggerated features. Those on the periphery were barely half-formed, like acid-etched gargoyles. The air was pungent with the resin of worked woods.

"I don't think the prisoner will amount to much," Clavain said. "His identity isn't apparent yet, but he seems to be some kind of pig criminal. We trawled him, retrieved clear and recent memory patterns that show him murdering people. I'll spare you the details, but he's creative, I'll give him that. It's not true what they say about pigs having no imagination."

"I never thought it was, Clavain. What about the other matter, the woman I hear you saved?"

"Ah. Funny how word gets around." Then he recalled that it had been he who had told the children about Antoinette Bax.

"Was she surprised?"

"I don't know. Should she have been?"

Felka snorted. She floated in the middle of the chamber, a bloated planet attended by many delicate wooden moons. She wore baggy brown work clothes. At least a dozen partially worked objects were guyed to her waist by nylon filaments. Other lines were hooked into woodworking tools, which ranged from broaches and files to lasers and tiny tethered burrowing robots.

"I imagine she expected to die," Clavain said. "Or at the very least to be assimilated."

"You seem upset by the fact that we're hated and feared."

"It does give one pause for thought."

Felka sighed, as if they had been over this a dozen times already. "How long have we known each other, Clavain?"

"Longer than most people, I suppose."

"Yes. And for most of that time you were a soldier. Not always fighting, I'll grant you that. But you were always a soldier a heart." Still with one eye on him, she hauled in one of her creations and peered through its latticed wooden interstices. "It strikes me that it might be a little late in the day for moral qualms, don't you agree?"

"You're probably right."

Felka bit her lower lip and, using a thicker line, propelled herself towards one wall of the chamber. Her entourage of wooden creations and tools clattered against each other as she moved. She set about making tea for Clavain.

"You didn't need to touch my face when I came in," Clavain remarked. "Should I take that as a good sign?"

"In what way?"

"It occurred to me that you might be getting better at discriminating faces."

"I'm not. Didn't you notice the wall of faces on your way in?"

"You must have done that recently," Clavain said.

"When someone comes in here that I'm not sure about, I touch their face, mapping its contours with my fingers. Then I compare what I've mapped with the faces I've carved in the wall until I find a match. Then I read off the name. Of course, I have to add new faces now and then, and some need less detail than others . . . "

"But me . . . ?"

"You have a beard, Clavain, and a great many lines. You have thin white hair. I could hardly fail to recognise you, could I? You're not like any of the others."

She passed him his bulb. He squeezed a stream of scalding tea into his throat. "I don't suppose there's much point denying it."

He looked at her with as much detachment as he could muster, comparing the way she was now with his memory of her before he had left on *Nightshade.* It was only a matter of weeks, but in his estimation Felka had become more withdrawn, less a part of the world than at any time in recent memory. She spoke of visitors, but he had the strong suspicion that there had not been very many.

"Clavain?"

"Promise me something, Felka." He waited until she had turned to look at him. Her black hair, which she wore as long as Galiana had, was matted and greasy. Nodes of sleep dust nestled in the corners of her eyes. Her eyes were pale green, almost jade, the irises jarring against bloodshot pale pink. The skin beneath them was swollen and faintly blue, as if bruised. Like Clavain, Felka had a need for sleep that marked her as unusual amongst the Conjoined.

"Promise you what, Clavain?"

"If—when—it gets too bad, you'll let me know, won't you?"

"What good would it do?"

"You know I'd always try to do my best for you, don't you? Especially now that Galiana isn't here for us."

Her raw-rubbed eyes studied him. "You always did your best, Clavain. But you can't help what I am. You can't work miracles."

He nodded sadly. It was true, but knowing it hardly helped.

Felka was not like the other Conjoiners. He had met her for the first time during his second trip to Galiana's nest on Mars.

The product of an aborted experiment in foetal brain manipulation, she had been a tiny damaged child, not merely unable to recognise faces, but unable to interact with other people at all. Her entire world revolved around a single endlessly absorbing game. Galiana's nest had been encircled by a giant structure known as the Great Wall of Mars. The Wall was a failed terraforming project that had been damaged in an earlier war. Yet it had never collapsed, for Felka's game involved coaxing the Wall's self-repair mechanisms into activity, an endless, intricate process of identifying flaws and allocating precious repair resources. The two-hundred-kilometre-high Wall was at least as complex as a human body, and it was as if Felka controlled every single aspect of its healing mechanisms, from the tiniest cell upwards. Felka turned out to be much better at holding the Wall together than a mere machine. Though her mind was damaged to the point where she could not relate to people at all, she had an astonishing ability for complex tasks.

When the Wall had collapsed in the final assault by Clavain's old comrades, the Coalition for Neural Purity, Galiana, Felka and he had made a last-ditch escape from the nest. Galiana had tried to dissuade him from taking Felka, warning him that without the Wall she would experience a state of deprivation far crueller than death itself. But Clavain had taken her anyway, convinced that there had to be some hope for the girl; that there had to be something else her mind could latch on to as a surrogate for the Wall.

He had been right, but it had taken many years to prove the point.

Through the years that followed—four hundred of them, although neither of them had experienced more than a century of subjective time—Felka had been coaxed and guided towards her current fragile state of mind. Subtle and delicate neural manipulation gave her back some of the brain functions that had been destroyed in the foetal intervention: language, and a growing sense that other people were more than mere automata. There were setbacks and failures—she had never learned to distinguish faces, for instance—but the triumphs outweighed them. Felka found other things to snare her mind, and during the long interstellar expedition she was happier than she had ever been. Every new world offered the prospect of a shatteringly difficult puzzle.

Eventually, however, she had decided to return home. There had been no rancour between her and Galiana, merely a sense that it was time to begin collating the knowledge that she had helped gather so far, and that the best place to do so was the Mother Nest, with its vast analytic resources.

But she returned to find the Mother Nest embroiled in war. Clavain was soon off fighting the Demarchists, and Felka found that interpreting the data from the expedition was no longer viewed as a high-priority task.

Slowly, so slowly that it was barely evident from year to year, Clavain had watched her retreat back into her own private world. She had begun to play a less and less active role in Mother Nest affairs, isolating her mind from the other Conjoiners except on rare occasions. Things had only worsened when Galiana had come back, neither dead nor alive, but in some horrible intermediate state.

The wooden toys Felka surrounded herself with were symptoms of a desperate need to engage her mind with a problem worthy of her cognitive abilities. But for all that they held her interest, they were doomed to fail in the long run. Clavain had seen it happen already. He knew that what Felka needed was beyond his powers to give.

"Perhaps when the war's over . . . " he said lamely. "If starflight becomes routine once more, and we start exploring again . . . "

"Don't make promises you can't fulfil, Clavain."

Felka took her own drinking bulb and cast off into the midst of her chamber. Absently, she began to chisel away at one of her solid compositions. The thing she was working on looked like a cube made from smaller cubes, with square gaps in some of the faces. She poked the chisel into one of these gaps and rasped back and forth, barely looking at the thing.

"I'm not promising anything," he said. "I'm just saying I'll do what I can."

"The jugglers might not even be able to help me."

"Well, we won't know until we try, will we?"

"I suppose not."

"That's the spirit," Clavain said.

Something clunked inside the object she was working on. Felka hissed like a scalded cat and flung the ruined contraption at the nearest wall. It shattered into a hundred blocky pieces.

Almost without hesitation she hauled in another piece and began working on that instead.

"And if the Pattern Jugglers don't help, we could try the Shrouders."

Clavain smiled. "Let's not get ahead of ourselves. If the Jugglers don't work, then we can think about other possibilities. But we'll cross that bridge when we come to it. There's the small matter of winning a war first."

"But they say it will soon be over."

"They do, don't they?"

Felka slipped with the tool she was using and gouged a little flap of skin from the side of her finger. She pressed the finger against her mouth and sucked on it hard, like someone working the last drop of juice from a lemon. "What makes you think otherwise?"

He felt an absurd urge to lower his voice, even though it made no practical difference. "I don't know. Perhaps I'm just being a silly old fool. But what are silly old fools for, if not to have the occasional doubt now and then?"

Felka smiled tolerantly. "Stop speaking in riddles, Clavain."

"It's Skade and the Closed Council. Something's going on and I don't know what it is."

"Such as?"

Clavain chose his words carefully. As much as he trusted Felka, he knew that he was dealing with a member of the Closed Council. The fact that she had not participated in the Council for some time, and was presumably out of the loop on its latest secrets, did not count for much.

"We stopped building ships a century ago. No one ever told me why, and I quickly realised it wasn't much use asking. In the meantime I heard the odd rumour of mysterious goings-on: secret initiatives, secret technology-acquisition programmes, secret experiments. Then suddenly, just when the Demarchists are about to cave in and admit defeat, the Closed Council unveils a brand-new starship design. *Nightshade* is nothing if it isn't a weapon, Felka, but who the hell are they planning to use it against if it isn't the Demarchists?"

" 'They,' Clavain?"

"I mean us."

Felka nodded. "But you occasionally wonder if the Closed Council isn't planning something behind the scenes."

Clavain sipped at his tea. "I'm entitled to wonder, aren't I?"

Felka was quiet for several long moments, the silence interrupted only by the rasp of her file against wood. "I could answer some of your questions here and now, Clavain. You know that. You also know that I won't ever reveal what I learned in the Closed Council, just as you wouldn't if you were in my position."

He shrugged. "I wouldn't expect anything less."

"But even if I wanted to tell you, I don't think I know everything. Not any more. There are layers within layers. I was never privy to Inner Sanctum secrets, and I haven't been allowed near Closed Council data for years." Felka tapped the file against her temple. "Some of the Closed Council members even want me to have my memories permanently scrubbed, so that I'll forget what I learned during my active Council years. The only thing that's stopping them is my odd brain anatomy. They can't swear they wouldn't scrub the wrong memories."

"Every cloud has a silver lining."

She nodded. "But there is a solution, Clavain. A pretty simple one, when you think about it."

"Which is?"

"You could always join the Closed Council."

Clavain sighed, grasping for an objection and knowing that even if he found one it would be unlikely to satisfy Felka. "I'll have some more of that tea, if you don't mind."

Skade strode through the curving grey corridors of the Mother Nest, her crest flaming with the scarlet of intense concentration and anger. She was on her way to the privy chamber, where she had arranged to meet Remontoire and a quorum of corporeal Closed Council members.

Her mind was running near its maximum processing rate. She was contemplating how she would handle what was sure to be a delicate meeting, perhaps the most crucial in her campaign to recruit Clavain to her side. Most of the Closed Council were putty in her hands, but there were a few that worried her, a few that would need more than the usual amount of convincing.

Skade was also reviewing the digested final performance data from the secret systems inside *Nightshade,* which were feeding into her skull via the compad now resting across her abdomen like a piece of armour. The numbers were encouraging;

there was nothing, other than the problem of keeping the breakthrough secret, to prevent a more extensive test of the machinery. She had already informed the Master of Works of the good news, so that the final technical refinements could be incorporated into the exodus fleet.

Although she had assigned a large fraction of herself to these issues, Skade was also replaying and processing a recording, a transmission that had recently arrived from the Ferrisville Convention.

It was not good.

The spokesperson hovered ahead of Skade, his back to the direction of her travel, his feet sliding ineffectually above the flooring. Skade was replaying the transmission at ten times normal speed, lending the man's gestures a manic quality.

"This is a formal request to any representative of the Conjoined faction," said the Convention spokesman. "It is known to the Ferrisville Convention that a Conjoiner vessel was involved in the interception and boarding of a Demarchist ship in the neighbourhood of the Contested Volume around gas-giant . . . "

Skade fast-forwarded. She had already played the message eighteen times, searching for nuance or deception. She knew that what followed was a supremely tedious list of legal strictures and Convention statutes, all of which she had checked and found to be watertight.

" . . . Unknown to the Conjoined faction, Maruska Chung, the shipmaster of the Demarchist vessel, had already made formal contact with officers of the Ferrisville Convention regarding the transfer into our custody of a prisoner. The prisoner in question had been detained aboard the Demarchist vessel after his arrest on a military asteroid under Demarchist jurisdiction, in accordance with . . . "

More boiler-plate. Fast-forward again.

" . . . prisoner in question, a hyperpig known to the Ferrisville Convention as 'Scorpio,' is already sought for the following crimes in contravention of emergency powers general statute number . . . "

She allowed the message to cycle over again, but detected nothing that had not already been clear. The bureaucratic gnome of the Convention seemed too obsessed with the minutiae of treaties and sub-clauses to be capable of real deception. He was almost certainly telling the truth about the pig.

Scorpio was a criminal known to the authorities, a vicious murderer with a predilection for killing humans. Chung had told the Convention that she was bringing him back into their care, presumably tight-beaming ahead before *Nightshade* had been close enough to snoop on her transmissions.

And Clavain, damn him again, had not done what he should have done, which was wipe the Demarchists out of existence the first chance he got. The Convention would have grumbled at that, but he would have been entirely within his rights. He could not have been expected to know about the ship-master's prisoner of war, and he was not obliged to ask questions before opening fire. Instead, he had rescued the pig.

". . . request the immediate return of the prisoner into our custody, unharmed and uncontaminated by Conjoiner neural-infiltration systems, within twenty-six standard days. Failure to comply with this request . . ." The Convention spokesman paused, wringing his hands in miserly anticipation. ". . . Failure to comply would be greatly to the detriment of relations between the Conjoined faction and the Convention, as I need hardly stress."

Skade understood perfectly. It was not that the prisoner was of any tangible value to the Convention. But as a coup—as a trophy—the prisoner's value was incalculable. Law and order were already in a state of extreme collapse in Convention airspace, and the pigs were a powerful, and not always lawful, group in their own right. It had been bad enough when Skade had gone to Chasm City herself on covert Council business and had almost ended up dead. Matters had certainly not improved since. The pig's recapture and execution would send a powerful signal to other miscreants, especially the more criminally inclined pig factions. Had Skade been in the spokesman's position, she would have made much the same demand.

But that didn't make the pig any less of a problem. On the face of it, knowing what Skade knew, there was no need to comply. It would not be long now before the Convention was of no consequence at all. The Master of Works had assured her that the exodus fleet would be ready in seventy days, and she had no reason to doubt the accuracy of the Master's estimate.

Seventy days.

In eighty or ninety it would be done. In barely three months nothing else would matter. But there was the problem. The fleet's existence, and the *reason* for its existence, had to remain a matter of total secrecy. The impression had to be given that the Conjoiners were pressing ahead towards the military victory that every neutral observer expected. Anything else would invite suspicion both from within and without the Mother Nest. And if the Demarchists discovered the truth, there was a chance—a slim one, but not something she could dismiss—that they might rally, using the information to gain allies that had previously remained neutral. Right now they were a spent force, but if they combined with the Ultras, they might present a real obstacle to Skade's ultimate objective.

No. The charade of coming victory demanded a degree of obeisance to the Convention. Skade would have to find a way of returning the pig, and it would have to happen before suspicion was roused.

Her fury reached a crescendo. She made the spokesman freeze ahead of her. His body blackened to a silhouette. She strode through him, scattering him like a flock of startled ravens.

SIX

The Inquisitor's private aircraft could have made extremely short shrift of the journey to Solnhofen, but she decided to make the final leg of the trip by surface transport, having the plane drop her off at the nearest reasonably sized community to her destination.

The place was called Audubon, a sprawl of depots, shacks and domes pierced by slev rails, cargo pipelines and highways. From the perimeter, the finefiligreed fingers of dirigible docking masts poked into the slate-grey northern sky. But there were no airships moored today and no sign that any had come in lately.

The plane had dropped her off on a patch of concreted

ground between two depots. The concrete was scabbed and rutted. She walked across it swiftly, her booted feet scuffing the bristlelike tufts of Resurgam-tolerant grass that ripped through the concrete here and there. With some trepidation she watched the plane arc back towards Cuvier, ready to serve some other government official until she requested that it take her back home.

"Get in, get out fast," she muttered under her breath.

She had been observed by workers going about their business, but this far from Cuvier the activities of the Inquisition were not the subject of intense speculation. Most people would correctly assume she was from the government, even though she wore plain clothes, but they would not immediately guess that she was on the trail of a war criminal. She could equally well be a police officer, or she might be an inspector from one of the government's many bureaucratic arms, come to check that funds were not being misappropriated. Had she arrived with armed assistance—a servitor or a squad of guards—her appearance would definitely have attracted more comment. As it was most people did their best not to meet her eye, and she was able to make her way to the roadhouse without incident.

She wore dark, unostentatious clothes covered by a long coat of the kind people used to wear when the razorstorms were more common, with a fold-down pouch beneath the chin for a breather mask. Black gloves completed the outfit, and she carried a few personal items in a small knapsack. Her hair was a glossy black bowl-cut which she occasionally had to flick out of her eyes. It effectively concealed a radio transmitter with throat-mike and earpiece, which she would only use to retrieve the aircraft. She carried a small Ultramanufactured boser-pistol, aided by a targeting contact lens covering one eye. But the gun was there for her sanity only. She did not anticipate using it.

The roadhouse was a two-storey structure slung across the main route to Solnhofen. Big balloon-wheeled freight transports rumbled up and down the road at irregular intervals, with ribbed cargo containers tucked beneath their elevated spines like overripe fruit. The drivers sat inside pressurised pods mounted near the fronts of the machines, each pod articulated on a double-hinged arm so that it could be lowered to ground level or raised higher for boarding from one of the roadhouse's overhead access gates. Typically, three or four transports trundled in robot-mode behind a crewed rig. No one trusted the machines to make the journey totally unsupervised.

The roadhouse's faded decor had a permanent greasy ambience that made the Inquisitor anxious to keep her gloves on. She approached a huddle of drivers sitting around a table, bitching about their working conditions. Snacks and coffee lay on the table in various states of consumption. A poorly printed newspaper contained the latest artist's impression of the terrorist Thorn, alongside a catalogue of his most recent crimes against the people. A ring-shaped coffee stain surrounded Thorn's head, like a halo.

She stood by the drivers for what felt like several minutes until one of them deigned to look at her and nod.

"My name is Vuilleumier," she said. "I need a lift to Solnhofen."

"Vuilleumier?" said one of the drivers. "As in . . . ?"

"Draw your own conclusions. It's not *that* unusual a name on Resurgam."

The driver coughed. "Solnhofen," he said dubiously, as if it was a place he had barely heard of.

"Yes, Solnhofen. It's a small settlement up that road. In fact it's the first one you're going to hit if you head in that direction for more than about five minutes. Who knows, you may even have passed through it once or twice."

"Solnhofen's a bit off my route, love."

"Is it? That's funny. I was under the impression that the route, as you put it, pretty much consisted of a straight line right through Solnhofen. Difficult to imagine how anything could be 'off' it, unless we've abandoned the idea of being on a road at all." She fished out some money and was about to lay it on the food-strewn table when she thought better of it. Instead she just waved it in front of the drivers, the notes crisp in her leather-gloved hand. "Here's the deal: half of this now to any driver who can promise me a trip to Solnhofen; a quarter more if we leave within the next thirty minutes; the remainder if we arrive in Solnhofen before sun-up."

"I could take you," one the drivers said. "But it's difficult at this time of year. I think I'd . . . "

"The offer's non-negotiable." She had made a decision not to try to ingratiate herself with them. She had known before she took a step into the roadhouse that none of them would like her. They could smell government a mile off and none of them, financial incentives aside, really wanted to share a cabin with her all the way to Solnhofen. Frankly, she could not blame them for that. Government officials of any stripe made the average person's skin crawl.

If she had not been the Inquisitor she would have been terrified of herself.

The money worked wonders, however, and within twenty minutes she was sitting in the elevated cab of a cargo hauler, watching the lights of Audubon fall back into the dusk. The rig was only carrying one container, and the combination of light lading and the cushioning effect of the house-sized road wheels leant the motion a soporific yawing. The cabin was well heated and silent, and the driver preferred to play music rather than engage her in pointless conversation. For the first few minutes she had watched as he drove, observing the way the rig needed only occasional human intervention to stay locked on the road. Doubtless it could have managed with none at all, were it not for local union laws. Very rarely another rig or string of rigs whipped past in the night, but for the most part the journey felt like a trek into endless uninhabited darkness.

On her lap was the newspaper containing the story about Thorn, and she read the article several times as she grew more fatigued, her eyes stumbling over the same leaden paragraphs. The article portrayed Thorn's movement as a gang of violent terrorists obsessed with bringing down the government for no other reason than to plunge the colony into anarchy. It made only passing mention of the fact that Thorn's avowed aim was to find a way to evacuate Resurgam, using the Triumvir's ship. But the Inquisitor had read enough of Thorn's statements to know his position on the matter. Ever since the days of Sylveste, successive governments had downplayed any suggestions that the colony might be unsafe, liable to suffer the same extinction event that had wiped out the Amarantin nearly a million years earlier. Over time, and especially in the dark, desperate years that had followed the collapse of the Girardieau regime, the idea of the colony being destroyed in some sudden cataclysmic episode had been quietly erased from public debate. Even mentioning the Amarantin, let alone what had happened to them, was the sort of thing that got one branded a troublemaker. Yet Thorn was right. The threat might not be imminent, but it had certainly not gone away.

It was true that he struck against government targets, but usually the strikes were surgical and considered, with the minimum of civilian casualties. Sometimes they were intended to publicise his movement, but more often than not their function was the theft of government property or funds. Bringing the administration down was a necessary part of Thorn's plan, but not the primary goal.

Thorn believed that the Triumvir's ship was still in the system; he also believed that the government knew where it was and how to reach it. His movement claimed that the government had two functioning shuttles with the capability to make repeated flights between Resurgam and *Nostalgia for Infinity.*

Thorn's plan, therefore, was simple enough. He would first locate the shuttles, something he claimed he was close to doing. Then he would bring down the government, or at least enough of it to enable the shuttles to be seized. Then it would be up to the people to make their way to the agreed exodus point, where the shuttles would make round trips between surface and orbit. The last part would presumably involve the complete overthrow of the existing regime, but Thorn repeatedly stated that he wished his goal to be achieved as bloodlessly as possible.

Very little of that desire came through in the government-sanctioned article. Thorn's goal was glossed over, the idea of a threat to Resurgam made to seem faintly ludicrous. Thorn was portrayed as deranged and egotistical, while the numbers of civilian deaths associated with his activities were greatly exaggerated.

The Inquisitor studied the portrait. She had never met Thorn, though she knew a great deal about him. The picture bore only a very vague likeness to the real man, but Internal Threats had accepted its plausibility all the same. She was pleased with that.

"I wouldn't waste your time with that rubbish," the driver said, when she had just nodded off properly. "The sod's dead."

She blinked awake. "What?"

"Thorn." He poked a thick finger into the paper spread across her lap. "The one in the picture."

She wondered if the driver had deliberately kept silent until she was asleep, whether this was a little game he played with his passengers to amuse himself through the journey. "I don't know that Thorn's dead," she answered. "I mean, I haven't read anything in the papers or heard anything on the news that says so . . . "

"The government shot him. He didn't call himself Thorn for nothing, you know."

"How could they have shot him if they don't even know where he is?"

"They do, though. That's the point. They just don't want us to know that he's dead yet."

" 'They'?"

"The government, love. Keep up."

He was toying with her, she suspected. He might have guessed that she was from the government, but he might also have guessed that she had no time to report minor instances of wayward thought.

"So if they've shot him," she said, "why don't they announce the fact? Thousands of people think Thorn's going to lead them into the Promised Land."

"Yes, but the only thing worse than a martyr is a dead martyr. There'd be a lot more trouble if word got around that he was really dead."

She shrugged and folded the paper. "Well, I'm not really sure that he ever existed. Maybe it suited the government to create a fictitious hope figure, just so that they could clamp down on the population even more effectively. You don't really believe all the stories, do you?"

"About him finding a way to lead us off Resurgam? No. Nice if it happened, I suppose. Get rid of all the whiners, for a start."

"Is that really your attitude? That the only people who want to leave Resurgam are whiners?"

"Sorry, love. I can tell which side of the fence you'd come down on. But some of us actually like it on this planet. No offence."

"None taken." Then she leant back in the seat and placed the folded paper across her eyes, so that it served as a mask. If that message failed to get through to the driver, she decided, there was really no hope for him.

Fortunately it did.

This time when she nodded off it was into deep sleep. She

dreamed about the past, memories flashing back now that the voice of Operative Four had unlocked them. It was not that she had been able to stop thinking about Four completely, but in all that time she had managed to avoid thinking of Four as a person. It was too painful. To remember Four was to think about how she had arrived on Resurgam, and that in turn meant thinking about her other life, the one that, compared with the bleak reality of the present, seemed like a distant and improbable fiction.

But Four's voice had been like a trapdoor into the past. There were now certain things that could not be ignored.

Why the hell had Four called her now?

She woke when the motion of the vehicle changed. The driver was backing them into an unloading bay.

"Are we there yet?"

"Solnhofen it is. Not exactly bright lights, big city, but this is where you wanted to go."

Through a gap in the slats of the depot wall she could see a sky the colour of anaemic blood. Dawn, or near enough.

"We're a bit on the late side," she commented.

"We arrived in Solnhofen a quarter of an hour ago, love. You were sleeping like a log. I didn't want to wake you."

"Of course you didn't." Grudgingly, she handed over the rest of the driver's fee.

Remontoire watched the last few members of the Closed Council take their seats around the tiered inner surface of the privy chamber. A number of the very old were still able to make their own way to their seats, but the majority were aided by servitors, exoskeletons or black clouds of thumb-sized drones. A few were so near the end of physical life that they had nearly abandoned the flesh entirely. They came in as heads, hooked up to spiderlike mobility prostheses. One or two were massively swollen brains so full of machinery that they could no longer be housed in skulls. The brains rode inside transparent fluid-filled domes dense with throbbing support machinery. They were the most extreme Conjoined, and by this stage most of their conscious activity would have devolved into the distributed web of greater Conjoiner thought. Each retained their brain like a family unwilling to demolish a crumbling mansion even though they hardly ever lived in it.

Remontoire tasted the thoughts of each newcomer. There

were people in this room he had long assumed dead, individuals who had never attended any of the Closed Council sessions in which he had participated.

It was the matter of Clavain. He brought everyone out of retirement.

Remontoire felt the sudden presence of Skade as she entered the privy chamber. She had emerged on a ring-shaped balcony halfway up the side of the spherical room. The chamber was opaque to all neural transmissions; those within it could communicate freely, but they were totally isolated from the other minds in the Mother Nest. It enabled the Closed Council to meet in session and communicate more freely than through the usual restricted neural channels.

Remontoire shaped a thought and assigned it high priority, so that it immediately cut across the general wash of gossip and gained everyone's attention. *Does Clavain know about this meeting?*

Skade snapped around to address him. [Why should he know about it, Remontoire?]

Remontoire shrugged. *Isn't it him we've come to talk about, behind his back?*

Skade smiled sweetly. [If Clavain consented to join us, there'd be no need to talk about him behind his back, would there? The problem's his, not mine.]

Remontoire stood up, now that everyone was looking at him or directing some sort of sensory apparatus in his direction. *Who said anything about a problem, Skade? What I'm objecting to is the hidden agenda behind this meeting.*

[Hidden agenda? We only want what's best for Clavain, Remontoire. As his friend I would have imagined that you'd have grasped that.]

Remontoire looked around. There was no sign of Felka, which did not surprise him in the slightest. She had every right to be present, but he doubted that she would have been on Skade's list of invitees.

I am his friend, I admit that. He's saved my life enough times, but even if he hadn't . . . well, Clavain and I have been through more than enough together. If that means I don't have an objective view on the matter, so be it. But I'll tell you something. Remontoire glanced around the room, nodding as he made eye or sensor contact. *All of you—or those of you who need reminding—no matter what Skade would like to make you think, Clavain owes us nothing. Without him, none of us would be here. He's been as important to us as Galiana, and I don't say that lightly. I knew her before anyone in this room.*

Skade nodded. [Remontoire is right, of course, but you'll note his use of the past tense. Clavain's great deeds all lie in the past—the distant past. I don't deny that since his return from deep space he has continued to serve us well. But then so have we all. Clavain has done no more and no less than any senior Conjoiner. But don't we expect more of him than that?]

More than what, Skade?

[His tired devotion to mere soldiery, constantly putting himself at risk.]

Remontoire realised that, like it or not, he had become Clavain's advocate. He felt a mild contempt for the other Council members. He knew that many of them owed their lives to Clavain, and would have admitted it under other circumstances. But Skade had them cowed.

It was down to him to speak up for his friend. *Someone has to patrol the border.*

[Yes. But we have younger, faster and, let us be frank here, more expendable individuals who can do precisely that. We need Clavain's expertise here, in the Mother Nest, where we can tap it. I don't believe that he clings to the fringes out of any sense of duty to the Nest. He does it out of pure self-interest. He gets to play at being one of us, being on the winning side, without accepting the full implications of what it means to be Conjoined. It hints at complacency, self-interest—everything that is inimical to our way. It even begins to hint at disloyalty.]

Disloyalty? No one's shown more loyalty to the Conjoined faction than Nevil Clavain. Maybe some of you need to brush up on your history.

One of the detached heads spidered on to a seat-back. [I agree with Remontoire. Clavain doesn't owe us anything. He's proven himself a thousand times over. If he wants to stay outside the Council, that's his right.]

Across the auditorium a brain lit up, its lights pulsing in synchronisation with its voice patterns. [Yes; no one doubts that, but it is equally the case that Clavain has a moral obligation to join us. He cannot continue to waste his talents outside the Council.]

The brain paused while fluid pumps throbbed and gurgled. The knotted mass of neural tissue swelled and contracted for several lethargic cycles, like some horrible lump of dough. [I cannot endorse Skade's inflammatory rhetoric. But there is no escaping the essential truth of what she says. Clavain's continued refusal to join us is tantamount to disloyalty.]

Oh, shut up, Remontoire interjected. *If you're anything to go by, I'm not surprised Clavain has second thoughts . . .*

[The insult!] the brain spluttered.

But Remontoire detected a suppressed wave of amusement at his barb. The swollen brain was clearly not as universally respected as it liked to imagine. Sensing his moment, Remontoire leant forward, hands clasped tight around the railings of the balcony. *What is this about, Skade? Why now, after all the years when the Closed Council has managed without him?*

[What do you mean, why now?]

I mean, what exactly has precipitated this move? Something's afoot, isn't it?

Skade's crest blushed maroon. Her jaw was clenched rigid. She stepped back and arched her spine like a cornered cat.

Remontoire pressed on. *First we have a renewal of the starship-building programme, a century after we stopped building them for reasons so secret even the Closed Council isn't allowed to know them. Then we have a prototype crammed with hidden machinery of unknown origin and function, the nature of which again can't be revealed to the Closed Council. Then there's a fleet of similar ships being put together in a comet not far from here—but again, that's as much as we're allowed to know. Of course, I'm sure the Inner Sanctum might have something to say on the matter . . .*

[Be very careful, Remontoire.]

Why—because I might be in danger of harmless speculation?

Another Conjoiner, a man with a crest a little like Skade's, stood up tentatively. Remontoire knew the man well, and was certain that he was not a member of the Inner Sanctum.

[Remontoire's right. Something *is* happening, and Clavain's just one part of it. The cessation of the shipbuilding programme, the strange circumstances surrounding Galiana's return, the new fleet, the disturbing rumours I hear about the hell-class weapons—these things are all connected. The present war is just a distraction, and the Inner Sanctum knows it. Perhaps the true picture is simply too disturbing for we mere Closed Council members to grasp. In which case, like Remontoire, I will indulge in a little speculation and see where it takes me.]

The man looked intently at Skade before continuing. [There's another rumour, Skade, concerning something called Exordium. I'm sure I don't need to remind you that that was the codeword Galiana gave to her final series of experiments on Mars—the ones she swore she would never repeat.]

Remontoire might have been imagining it, but he thought he saw a visible change of colour sweep through Skade's crest at the mere mention of the word. *What about Exordium?* he asked.

The man turned to Remontoire. [I don't know, but I can guess. Galiana never wanted the experiments to be repeated; the results were useful, incredibly useful, but they were also too disturbing. But once Galiana was away from the Mother Nest, off on her interstellar expedition, what was to stop the Inner Sanctum from re-running Exordium? She need never have found out about it.]

The codeword meant something to Remontoire; he had definitely heard it before. But if it referred to experiments Galiana had performed on Mars, it was something that had happened more than four hundred years earlier. It would require delicate mnemonic archaeology to dig through the strata of overlying memories, especially if the subject itself was shrouded in secrecy.

It seemed simpler to ask. *What was Exordium?*

"I'll tell you what it was, Remontoire."

The sound of a real human voice cutting through the chamber's silence was as shocking as a scream.

Remontoire followed the sound until he saw the speaker, sitting on her own near one of the entry points. It was Felka; she must have arrived since the session had commenced.

Skade slammed a furious thought into his head. [Who invited her?]

"I did," Remontoire said mildly, speaking aloud for Felka's benefit, "on the assumption that you didn't seem very likely to, and since the matter under discussion happened to be Clavain . . . it seemed the right thing to do."

"It was," Felka said. Remontoire saw something move in her hand and realised that she had brought a mouse into the privy chamber. "Wasn't it, Skade?"

Skade sneered. [There's no need to talk aloud. It takes too long. She can hear our thoughts as well as any of us.]

"But if you were to hear *my* thoughts, you'd probably all go mad," Felka said. The way she smiled was all the more chilling, Remontoire thought, because what she said was probably true. "So rather than risk that . . . " She looked down, the mouse chasing its tail around her hand.

[You have no right to be here.]

"But I do, Skade. If I wasn't recognised as a Closed Council member, the privy chamber wouldn't have admitted me. And if I wasn't a Closed Council member, I'd hardly be in a position to talk about Exordium, would I?"

The man who had first mentioned the codeword spoke aloud, his voice high and trembling. "So my guess was correct, was it, Skade?"

[Ignore anything she says. She knows nothing about the programme.]

"Then I can say what I like, can't I, and none of it will matter. Exordium was an experiment, Remontoire, an attempt to achieve unification between consciousness and quantum superposition. It happened on Mars; you can verify that much for yourself. But Galiana got far more than she bargained for. She curtailed the experiments, frightened at what she had invoked. And that should have been the end of it." Felka looked directly at Skade, tauntingly. "But it wasn't, was it? The experiments were begun again, about a century ago. It was an Exordium message that made us stop making ships."

"A message?" Remontoire said, perplexed.

"From the future," Felka said, as if this should have been obvious from the start.

"You're not serious."

"I'm perfectly serious, Remontoire. I should know—I took part in one of the experiments."

Skade's thoughts scythed across the room. [We're here to discuss Clavain, not this.]

Felka continued to speak calmly. She was, Remontoire thought, the only one in the room who was unfazed by Skade, including himself. Felka's head already held worse horrors than Skade could imagine. "But we can't discuss one without discussing the other, Skade. The experiments have continued, haven't they? And they have something to do with what's happening now. The Inner Sanctum's learned something, and they'd rather the rest of us didn't know anything about it."

Skade clenched her jaw again. [The inner Sanctum has identified a coming crisis.]

"What kind of crisis?" asked Felka.

[A bad one.]

Felka nodded sagely and pushed a strand of lank black hair from her eyes. "And Clavain's role in all this—where does he come in?"

Skade's pain was almost tangible. Her thoughts arrived in clipped packets, as if, between her utterances, she was waiting for a silent speaker to offer her guidance. [We need Clavain to help us. The crisis can be . . . lessened . . . with Clavain's assistance.]

"What kind of assistance did you have in mind, exactly?" Felka persisted.

A tiny vein twitched in Skade's brow. Jarring colour waves chased each other along her crest, like the patterns in a dragonfly's wing. [A long time ago, we lost some objects of value. Now we know exactly where they are. We want Clavain to help us get them back.]

"And these 'objects,'" Felka said. "They wouldn't by any chance be weapons, would they?"

The Inquisitor said farewell to the driver who had brought her to Solnhofen. She had slept for five or six hours clean through on the drive, offering the driver ample opportunity to rifle her belongings or strand her in the middle of nowhere. But everything was intact, including her gun. The driver had even left her with the newspaper clipping, the one about Thorn.

Solnhofen itself was every bit as miserable and squalid as she had suspected it would be. She only had to wander around the centre for a few minutes before she found what passed for the settlement's heart: an apron of ground surrounded by two slovenly-looking hostels, a couple of drab administrative structures and a motley assortment of drinking establishments. Looming beyond the centre were the hulking repair sheds that were Solnhofen's reason for existence. Far to the north, vast terraforming machines worked to speed the conversion of Resurgam's atmosphere into a fully human-breathable form. These atmospheric refineries had functioned perfectly for a few decades, but not they were becoming old and unreliable. Keeping them working was a major drain on the planet's centrally managed economy. Communities like Solnhofen made a precarious living from servicing and crewing the terraforming rigs, but the work was hard and unforgiving, and required—demanded—a certain breed of worker.

The Inquisitor remembered that as she stepped into the hostel. She had expected it to be quiet at this time of day, but when she shoved open the door it was like stepping into a party that had only just passed its peak. There was music and shouting and laughter, hard, boisterous laughter that reminded her of barracks rooms on Sky's Edge. A few drinkers had already passed out, huddled over their mugs like pupils guarding homework. The air was clotted with chemicals that made her eyes sting. She clenched her teeth against the noise and swore softly. Trust Four to pick a dump like this. She remembered the first time they had met. It had been in a bar in a carousel orbiting Yellowstone, probably the worst dive she had ever been in. Four had many talents, but selecting salubrious meeting places was not one of them.

Fortunately no one had noticed the Inquisitor's arrival. She pushed past some semi-comatose bodies to what passed for the bar: a hole punched through one wall, ragged brickwork at the edges. A surly woman pushed drinks through like prison rations, snatching back money and spent glasses with almost indecent haste.

"Give me a coffee," the Inquisitor said.

"There isn't any coffee."

"Then give me the nearest fucking equivalent."

"You shouldn't speak like that."

"I'll speak any fucking way I want to. Especially until I get a coffee." She leant on the plastic lip of the serving hatch. "You can get me one, can't you? I mean, it's not like I'm asking for the world."

"You government?"

"No, just thirsty. And a tiny bit irritable. It's morning, you see, and I really don't do mornings."

A hand landed on her shoulder. She twisted around sharply, her own hand instinctively reaching for the haft of the boser-pistol.

"Causing trouble again, Ana?" said the woman behind her.

The Inquisitor blinked. She had rehearsed this moment many times since she had left Cuvier, but still it felt unreal and melodramatic. Then Triumvir Ilia Volyova nodded at the woman behind the hatch.

"This is my friend. She wants a coffee. I suggest you give her one."

The serving woman squinted at her, then grunted something and vanished from view. She reappeared a few moments later with a cup of something that looked as if it had just been drained from the main axle bearing of an overland cargo hauler.

"Take it, Ana," Volyova said. "It's about as good as it gets."

The Inquisitor took the coffee, her hand trembling faintly. "You shouldn't call me that," she whispered.

Volyova steered her towards a table. "Call you what?"

"Ana."

"But it's your name."

"Not any more, it isn't. Not here. Not now."

The table that Volyova had found was tucked into a corner, half-hidden by several stacked beer crates. Volyova swept her sleeve across the surface, brushing detritus on to the floor. Then she sat, placing both elbows on the table's edge and locking her fingers under her chin. "I don't think we need worry about anyone recognising you, Ana. No one's given me more than a second glance and, with the possible exception of Thorn, I'm the most wanted person on the planet."

The Inquisitor, who had once called herself Ana Khouri, sipped experimentally at the treaclelike concoction that passed for coffee. "You've had the benefit of some expert misdirection, Ilia . . . " She paused and looked around, realising as she did so how suspicious and theatrical she must look. "Can I call you Ilia?"

"That's what I call myself. Best leave off the Volyova part for the time being, though. No sense in pushing our luck."

"None at all. I suppose I should say . . . " Again, she looked around. She could not help herself. "It's good to see you again, Ilia. I'd be lying if I said otherwise."

"I've missed your company, too. Odd to think we once started out almost killing each other. All water under the bridge now, of course."

"I began to worry. You hadn't been in touch for so long . . . "

"I had good reasons to keep a low profile, didn't I?"

"I suppose so."

For several minutes neither of them said anything. Khouri, for that was how she was daring to think of herself again, found herself recalling the origin of the audacious game the two of them were playing. They had devised it themselves, amazing each other with their nerve and ingenuity. Together, they made a very resourceful pair indeed. But for maximum usefulness they found that they had to work alone.

Khouri broke the silence, unable to wait any longer. "What is it, Ilia? Good news or bad?"

"Knowing my track record, what do you think?"

"A wild stab in the dark? Bad news. Very bad news indeed."

"Got it in one."

"It's the Inhibitors, isn't it?"

"Sorry to be so predictable, but there you are."

"They're here?"

"I think so." Volyova's voice had dropped low now. "*Something* is happening, anyway. I've seen it myself."

"Tell me about it."

Volyova's voice, if anything, became quieter still. Khouri had to strain to hear it. "Machines, Ana, huge black machines. They've entered the system. I never saw them actually arrive. They were just . . . here."

Khouri had tasted the minds of those machines briefly, feeling the furious predatory chill of ancient recordings. They were like the minds of pack animals, ancient and patient and drawn to the dark. Their minds were mazes of instinct and hungry intelligence, utterly unencumbered by sympathy or emotion. They howled across the silent steppes of the galaxy to each other, summoning themselves in great numbers when the bloody stench of life again troubled their wintry sleep.

"Dear God."

"We can't say we weren't expecting them, Ana. From the

moment Sylveste started fiddling around with things he didn't understand, it was only a matter of when and where."

Khouri stared at her friend, wondering why the temperature in the room appeared to have dropped ten or fifteen degrees. The feared and hated Triumvir looked small and faintly grubby, like a bag lady. Volyova's hair was a close-cropped greying thatch above a round, hard-eyed face which betrayed remote Mongol ancestry. She did not look like a very convincing herald of doom.

"I'm scared, Ilia."

"I think you have excellent reason to be scared. But try not to show it, will you? We don't want to terrify the locals just yet."

"What can we do?"

"Against the Inhibitors?" Volyova squinted through her glass, frowning slightly, as if this was the first time she had given the subject any serious consideration. "I don't know. The Amarantin didn't have a lot of success in that department."

"We're not flightless birds."

"No, we're humans—the scourge of the galaxy . . . or something like that. I don't know, Ana. I really don't. If it was just you and I, and if we could persuade the ship, the Captain, to come out of his shell, we could at least consider running away. We could even contemplate using the weapons, if that would help matters."

Khouri shuddered. "But even if it did, and even if we could make a getaway, it wouldn't help Resurgam much, would it?"

"No. And I don't know about you, Ana, but my conscience isn't exactly whiter-than-white as it is."

"How long do we have?"

"That's the odd thing. The Inhibitors could have destroyed Resurgam already, if that was all they intended to do—it's within even our technology to do that much, so I very much doubt that it would trouble them particularly."

"So maybe they haven't come to kill us after all."

Volyova tipped back her drink. "Or maybe . . . just maybe . . . they have."

In the swarming heart of the black machines, processors that were not themselves sentient determined that an overseer mind mus t be quickened to consciousness.

The decision was not taken lightly; most cleansings could be performed without raising the spectre of the very thing that the machines had been made to suppress. But this system was prob-

lematic. Records showed that an earlier cleansing had been performed here, a mere four and half thousandths of a Galactic Turn ago. The fact that the machines had been called back showed that additional measures were clearly necessary.

The overseer's task was to deal with the specifics of this particular infestation. No two cleansings were ever quite the same, and it was a regrettable fact of life that the best way to annihilate intelligence was with a dose of intelligence itself. But once the cleansing was over, the immediate outbreak traced back to source and its daughter spores sanitised—which might take another two-thousandths of a Galactic Turn, half a million years—the overseer would be dumbed down, its self-awareness packed away until it needed it again.

Which might be never.

The overseer never questioned its work. It knew only that it was acting for the ultimate good of sentient life. It was not at all concerned that the crisis it was acting to avert, the crisis that would become an unmanageable cosmic disaster if intelligent life was permitted to spread, lay a total of thirteen Turns—three billion years—in the future.

It did not matter.

Time meant nothing to the Inhibitors.

SEVEN

[Skade? I'm afraid there's been another accident.]

What kind of accident?

[A state-two excursion.]

How long did it last?

[Only a few milliseconds. It was enough, though.]

The two of them—Skade and her senior propulsion technician—were crouched in a black-walled space near *Nightshade*'s stern, while the prototype was berthed in the Mother Nest. They were squeezed into the space with their backs arched and their knees pressed against their chests. It was unpleasant, but after her first few visits Skade had blanked out the sensation of postural comfort, replacing it with a cool Zenlike calm. She could endure days squashed into inhumanly small hideaways—and she had. Beyond the walls, secluded in numerous cramped openings, were the intricate and perplexing elements of the machinery. Direct control and fine-tuning of the device was only possible here, where there were only the most rudimentary links to the normal control network of the ship.

Is the body still here?

[Yes.]

I'd like to see it.

[There isn't an awful lot left to see.]

But the man unplugged his compad and led the way, shuffling sideways in a crablike manner. Skade followed him. They moved from one hideaway to another, occasionally having to inch through constrictions caused by protruding elements of the machinery. It was all around them, exerting its subtle but undeniable effect on the very space-time in which they were embedded.

No one, not even Skade, really understood quite how the machinery worked. There were guesses, some of them very scholarly and plausible, but at heart there remained a gaping chasm of conceptual ignorance. Much of what Skade knew about the machinery consisted only of documented cause and effect, with little understanding of the physical mechanisms underpinning its behaviour. She knew that when the machinery was functioning it tended to settle into several discrete states, each of which was associated with a measurable change in the local metric . . . but the states were not rigidly isolated, and it had been known for the device to oscillate wildly between them. Then there was the associated problem of the various field geometries, and the tortuously complex way they fed back into the state stability . . .

State two, you said? Exactly what mode were you in before the accident?

[State one, as per instructions. We were exploring some of the nonlinear field geometries.]

What was it this time? Heart failure, like the last one?

[No, at least, I don't think heart failure was the main cause of death. Like I said, there isn't much left to go on.]

Skade and the technician pushed ahead, wriggling through a tight elbow between adjoining chunks of the machinery. The field was in state zero at the moment, for which there were no measurable physiological effects, but Skade could not entirely shake a feeling of wrongness, a nagging sense that the world had been skewed minutely away from normality. It was illusory; she would have needed highly sensitive quantum-vacuum probes to detect the device's influence. But the feeling was there all the same.

[Here we are.]

Skade looked around. They had emerged into one of the larger open spaces in the bowels of the device. It was a scalloped black-walled chamber just large enough to stand up in. Numerous compad input sockets woodwormed the walls.

This is where it happened?

[Yes. The field shear was at its highest here.]

I'm not seeing a body.

[You're just not looking closely enough.]

She followed his gaze. He was focusing on a particular part of the wall. Skade moved over and touched the wall with the gloved tips of her fingers. What had looked like the same gloss-black as the rest of the chamber revealed itself to be scarlet and cloying. There was perhaps a quarter of an inch of something glued to most of the wall on one side of the chamber.

Please tell me this isn't what I think it is.

[I'm afraid it's exactly what you think it is.]

Skade stirred her hand through the red substance. The covering had enough adhesion to form a single sticky mass, even in zero gravity. Now and then she felt something harder—a shard of bone or machinery—but nothing larger than a thumbnail had remained in one piece.

Tell me what happened.

[He was near the field focus. The excursion to state two was only momentary, but it was enough to make a difference. Any movement would have been fatal, even an involuntary twitch. Maybe he was already dead before he hit the wall.]

How fast was he moving?

[Kilometres per second, easily.]

It would have been painless, I suppose. Did you feel him hit?

[Throughout the ship. It was like a small bomb going off.]

Skade willed her gloves to clean themselves. The residue

flowed back on to the wall. She thought of Clavain, wishing that she had some of his tolerance for sights like this. Clavain had seen horrid things during his time as a soldier, enough that he had developed the necessary mental armour to cope. With one or two exceptions, Skade had fought all her battles at a distance.

[Skade . . . ?]

Her crest must have reflected her discomposure. *Don't worry about me. Just try to find out what went wrong, and make sure it doesn't happen again.*

[And the testing programme?]

The programme continues, of course. Now get this mess cleaned up.

Felka floated in another chamber of her quiet residential spar. Where tools had been tethered to her waist earlier many small metal cages now orbited her, clacking gently against each other when she moved. Each cage contained a clutch of white mice, scratching and sniffing at their constraints. Felka paid them no attention; they had not been caged for long, they were well fed and shortly they would all enjoy a sort of freedom.

She squinted into gloom. The only source of light was the faint radiance of the adjacent room, separated from this one by a twisting throat of highly polished wood the colour of burned caramel. She found the UV lamp attached to one wall and flicked it on.

One side of the chamber—Felka had never bothered deciding which way was up—was sheeted over with bottle-green glass. Behind the glass was something that at first glance resembled a convoluted wooden plumbing system, a palimpsest of pipes and channels, gaskets and valves and pumps. Diagonals and doglegs of wood spanned the maze, bridging different regions, their function initially unclear. The pipes and channels had only three wooden sides, with the glass forming the fourth wall so that whatever flowed or scurried along them would be visible.

Felka had already introduced about a dozen mice to the system via one-way doors near the edge of the glass. They had quickly taken divergent paths at the first few junctions and were now metres apart, nosing through their own regions of the labyrinth. The lack of gravity did not bother them at all; they could obtain enough traction against the wood to scamper freely in any direction. The more experienced mice, in fact, eventually learned the art of coasting down pipes, minimising the frictional area they exposed to the wood or glass. But they seldom learned that trick until they had been in the maze for several hours and through several reward cycles.

Felka reached for one of the cages attached to her waist, flipping open the catch so that the contents—three white mice—spilled into the maze. Away they went, momentarily gleeful to have escaped the metal prisons.

Felka waited. Sooner or later one of the mice would run into a trapdoor or flap that was connected to a delicate system of spring-loaded wooden levers. When the mouse pushed past the flap, the movement caused the levers to shift. The movement would often be transmitted across the maze, causing a shutter to open or close one or two metres away from the original trigger point. Another mouse, working its way through a remote stretch of the maze, might suddenly find its way blocked where previously it had been clear. Or the mouse might be forced to make a decision where previously none had been required, anxieties of possibility momentarily clouding its tiny rodent brain. It was quite probable that the choices of the second mouse would activate another trigger system, causing a distant reconfiguration of another part of the maze. Floating in the middle, Felka would watch it happen, the wood shifting through endless permutations, running a blind program whose agents were the mice themselves. It was fascinating enough to watch, after a fashion.

But Felka was easily bored. The maze, for her, was just the start of things. She would run the maze in semi-darkness, with the UV lamp burning. The mice had genes that expressed a set of proteins that caused them to fluoresce under ultraviolet illumination. She could see them clearly through the glass, moving smudges of bright purple. Felka watched them with ardent, but perceptibly waning, fascination.

The maze was entirely her invention. She had designed it and fashioned its wooden mechanisms herself. She had even tinkered with the mice to make them glow, though that had been the easy bit compared with all the fettling and filing that had been needed to get the traps and levers to work properly. For a while she even thought it had been worth it.

One of the few things that could still interest Felka was

emergence. On Diadem, the first world they had visited after leaving Mars in the very first near-light ship, Clavain, Galiana and she had studied a vast crystalline organism which took years to express anything resembling a single "thought." Its synaptic messengers were mindless black worms, burrowing through a shifting neural network of capillary ice channels threading an ageless glacier.

Clavain and Galiana had wrenched her away from the proper study of the Diadem glacier, and she had never quite forgiven them for it. Ever since, she had been drawn to similar systems, anything in which complexity emerged in an unpredictable fashion from simple elements. She had assembled countless simulations in software, but had never convinced herself that she was really capturing the essence of the problem. If complexity sprung from her systems—and it often had—she could never quite shake the sense that she had unwittingly built it in from the outset. The mice were a different approach. She had discarded the digital and embraced the analogue.

The first machine she had tried building had run on water. She had been inspired by details of a prototype that she had discovered in the Mother Nest's cybernetics archive. Centuries earlier, long before the Transenlightenment, someone had made an analogue computer which was designed to model the flow of money within an economy. The machine was all glass retorts and valves and delicately balanced see-saws. Tinted fluids represented different market pressures and financial parameters: interest rates, inflation, trade deficits. The machine sloshed and gurgled, computing ferociously difficult integral equations by the power of applied fluid mechanics.

It had enchanted her. She had remade the prototype, adding a few sly refinements of her own. But though the machine had provided some amusement, she had seen only glimpses of emergent behaviour. The machine was too ruthlessly deterministic to throw up any genuine surprises.

Hence the mice. They were random agents, chaos on legs. She had concocted the new machine to exploit them, using their unpredictable scurrying to nudge it from state to state. The complex systems of levers and switches, trapdoors and junctions ensured that the maze was constantly mutating, squirming through phase-space—the mind-wrenching higher-dimensional mathematical space of all possible configurations that the maze could be in. There were attractors in that phase-space, like planets and stars dimpling a sheet of space-time. When the maze fell towards one of them it would often go into a kind of orbit, oscillating around one state until something, either a build-up of instability or an external kick, sent it careering elsewhere. Usually all that was needed was to tip a new mouse into the maze.

Occasionally, the maze would fall towards an attractor that caused the mice to be rewarded with more than the usual amount of food. She had been curious as to whether the mice—acting blindly, unable to knowingly co-operate with each other—would nonetheless find a way to steer the maze into the vicinity of one of those attractors. That, if it happened, would surely be a sign of emergence.

It had happened, once. But that batch of mice had never repeated the trick since. Felka had tipped more mice into the system, but they had only clogged up the maze, locking it near another attractor where nothing very interesting happened.

She had not completely given up on it. There were still subtleties of the maze that she did not fully understand, and until she did it would not begin to bore her. But at the back of her mind the fear was already there. She knew, beyond any doubt, that the maze could not fascinate her for very much longer.

The maze clicked and clunked, like a grandfather clock winding up to strike the hour. She heard the shutterlike clicking of doors opening and closing. The details of the maze were difficult to see behind the glass, but the flow of the mice betrayed its shifting geometry well enough.

"Felka?"

A man forced his way through the connecting throat. He floated into the room, arresting his drift with a press of fingertips against polished wood. She could see his face faintly. His bald skull was not quite the right shape. It seemed even odder in the gloom, like an elongated grey egg. She stared at it, knowing that, by rights, she should always have been able to associate that face with Remontoire. But had six or seven men of about the same physiological age entered the room, possessing the same childlike or neotenous facial features, she would not have been able to pick Remontoire out from them. It was only the fact that he had visited her recently that made her so certain it was him.

"Hello, Remontoire."

"Could we have some light, please? Or shall we talk in the other chamber?"

"Here will do nicely. I'm in the middle of running an experiment."

He glanced at the glass wall. "Will light spoil it?"

"No, but then I wouldn't be able to see the mice, would I?"

"I suppose not," Remontoire said thoughtfully. "Clavain's with me. He'll be here in a moment."

"Oh." She fumbled one of the lanterns on. Turquoise light wavered uncertainly and then settled down.

She studied Remontoire's expression, doing her best to read it. Even now that she knew his identity, it was not as if his face had become a model of clarity. Its text remained hazy, full of shifting ambiguities. Even reading the commonest of expressions required an intense effort of will, like picking out constellations in a sprinkling of faint stars. Now and then, admittedly, there were occasions when her odd neural machinery managed to grasp patterns that normal people missed entirely. But for the most part she could never trust her own judgement when it came to faces.

She bore this in mind when she looked at Remontoire's face, deciding, provisionally, that he looked concerned. "Why isn't he here now?"

"He wanted to give us time to discuss Closed Council matters."

"Does he know anything about what happened in the chamber today?"

"Nothing."

Felka drifted to the top of the maze and popped another mouse into the entrance, hoping to unblock a stalemate in the lower-left quadrant. "That's the way it will have to continue, unless Clavain assents to join. Even then he may be disappointed at what he doesn't get to know."

"I understand why you wouldn't want him to know about Exordium," Remontoire said.

"What exactly is that supposed to mean?"

"You went against Galiana's wishes, didn't you? After what she discovered on Mars she discontinued Exordium. Yet when you returned from deep space—when she was still out there—you happily participated."

"You've become quite an expert all of a sudden, Remontoire."

"It's all there in the Mother Nest's archives, if you know where to look. The fact that the experiments took place isn't much of a secret at all." Remontoire paused, watching the maze with mild interest. "Of course, what actually happened in Exordium—why Galiana called it off—that's another matter entirely. There's no mention in the archives of any messages from the future. What was so disturbing about those messages that their very existence couldn't be acknowledged?"

"You're just as curious as I was."

"Of course. But was it just curiosity that made you go against her wishes, Felka? Or was there something more? An instinct to rebel against your own mother, perhaps?"

Felka held back her anger. "She wasn't my mother, Remontoire. We shared some genetic material. That's all we had in common. And no, it wasn't rebellion either. I was looking for something else to engage my mind. Exordium was supposed to be about a new state of consciousness."

"So you didn't know about the messages either?"

"I had heard rumours, but I didn't believe them. The easiest way to find out for myself seemed to be to participate. But I didn't start Exordium again. The programme had already been resurrected before our return. Skade wanted me to join it—I think she thought the uniqueness of my mind might be of value to the programme. But I only played a small part in it, and I left almost as soon as I had begun."

"Why—because it didn't work the way you'd hoped?"

"No. As a matter of fact it worked very well. It was also the most terrifying thing I've ever experienced in my life."

He smiled at her for a moment; then his smile slowly vanished. "Why, exactly?"

"I didn't believe in the existence of evil before, Remontoire. Now I'm not so certain."

He spoke as if he had misheard her. "Evil?"

"Yes," she said softly.

Now that the subject had been raised she found herself remembering the smell and texture of the Exordium chamber as if it had been only yesterday, even though she had done all she could to steer her thoughts away from that sterile white room, unwilling to accept what she had learned within it.

The experiments had been the logical conclusion to the work Galiana had initiated in her earliest days in the Martian labs. She had set out to enhance the human brain, believing that her work could only be for the greater good of humanity. As her model, Galiana used the development of the digital computer from its simple, slow infancy. Her first step had been to increase the computational power and speed of the human mind, just as the early computer engineers had traded clockwork for electromechanical switches; switches for valves; valves for transistors; transistors for microscopic solid-state devices; solid-state devices for quantum-level processing gates which hovered on the fuzzy edge of the Heisenberg uncertainty principle. She invaded the brains of her subjects, including herself, with tiny machines that laid down connections between brain cells which exactly paralleled those already in place, but which were capable of transmitting nerve signals much more rapidly. With the normal neurotransmitter and nerve-signal events inhibited by drugs or more machines, Galiana's secondary loom took over neural processing. The subjective effect was normal consciousness, but at an accelerated rate. It was as if the brain had been supercharged, able to process thoughts at a rate ten or fifteen times faster than an unaugmented mind. There were problems, enough to ensure that accelerated consciousness could not usually be sustained for more than a few seconds, but in most respects the experiments had been successful. Someone in the accelerated state could watch an apple fall from a table and compose a commemorative haiku before it reached the ground. They could watch the depressor and elevator muscles flex and twist in a hummingbird's wing, or marvel at the crownlike impact pattern caused by a splashing drop of milk. They also, needless to say, made excellent soldiers.

So Galiana had moved on to the next phase. The early computer engineers had discovered that certain classes of problem were best tackled by armies of computers locked together in parallel, sharing data between nodes. Galiana pursued this aim with her neurally enhanced subjects, establishing data-corridors between their minds. She allowed them to share memories, experiences, even the processing of certain mental tasks such as pattern recognition.

It was this experiment running amok—jumping uncontrolled from mind to mind, subverting neural machines which were already in place—that led to the event known as the Transenlightenment and, not inconsequentially, to the first war against the Conjoiners. The Coalition for Neural Purity had wiped out Galiana's allies, forcing her back into the seclusion of a small fortified huddle of labs tucked inside the Great Wall of Mars.

It was there, in 2190, that she had met Clavain for the first time, when he had been her prisoner. It was there that Felka had been born, a few years later. And it was there that Galiana pushed on to the third phase of her experimentation. Still following the model of the early computer engineers, she now wished to explore what could be gained from a quantum-mechanical approach.

The computer engineers in the late twentieth and early twenty-first centuries—barely out of the clockwork era, as far as Galiana was concerned—had used quantum principles to crack problems that would otherwise have been insoluble, such as the task of finding the prime factors of very large numbers. A conventional computer, even an army of conventional computers sharing the task, stood no chance of being able to find the prime factors before the effective end of the universe. And yet with the right equipment—an ungainly lash-up of prisms, lenses, lasers and optical processors on a lab bench—it was possible to do it in a few milliseconds.

There had been fierce debate as to exactly what was happening, but not that the primes *were* being found. The simplest explanation, which Galiana had never seen any reason to doubt, was that the quantum computers were sharing the task between infinite copies of themselves, spread across parallel universes. It was conceptually staggering, but it was the only reasonable explanation. And it was not something they had plucked out of thin air to justify a perplexing result; the idea of parallel worlds had long been at least one conceptual underpinning of quantum theory.

And so Galiana had tried to do something similar with human minds. The Exordium chamber was a device for coupling one or more augmented brains to a coherent quantum system: a bar of magnetically suspended rubidium that was being continually pumped into cycles of quantum coherence and collapse. During each episode of coherence the bar was in a state of superposition with infinite counterparts of itself, and it was at this moment that a neural coupling was attempted. The act itself always forced the bar to collapse down to one macroscopic state, but the collapse was not instantaneous. There was a moment when some of the bar's coherence bled back into the linked minds, putting them into weak superposition with their own parallel-world counterparts.

In that moment, Galiana hoped that there might be some perceptible change in the experienced consciousness state of the participant. Her theories, however, did not say what that change might be.

It was, in the end, nothing like she had expected.

Galiana had never spoken to Felka about her detailed impressions, but Felka had learned enough to know that her own experience must have been broadly similar. When the experiment began, with the subject or subjects lying on couches in the chamber, their heads swallowed in the gaping white maws of high-resolution neural interfacing trawls, there was a presentiment, like the aura that warned of an impending epileptic seizure.

Then there would come a sensation that Felka had never been adequately able to describe outside of the experiment. All she could say was that her thoughts suddenly became plural, as if behind every thought she detected the faint choral echo of others that almost perfectly shadowed it. She did not sense an infinity of such thoughts, but she did sense, faintly, that they receded into *something,* diverging at the same time. She was, in that moment, in touch with counterparts of herself.

Then something far stranger would begin to happen. Impressions would gather and solidify, like the phantoms that take shape after hours of sensory deprivation. She became aware of something stretching ahead of her, into a dimension she could not quite visualise but which nonetheless conveyed a tremendous sense of distance and remoteness.

Her mind would grasp at the vague sensory clues and throw some kind of familiar framework over them. She would see a long white corridor stretching towards infinity, washed out in bleak colourless light, and she would know, without being able to articulate quite how she knew, that what she was seeing was a corridor into the future. Numerous pale doors or apertures, each of which opened into some more remote future epoch, lined the corridor. Galiana had never intended to open a door into that corridor, but it seemed that she had made it possible.

Felka sensed that the corridor could not be traversed; one could only stand at its end and listen for messages that came down it.

And there *would* be messages.

Like the corridor itself they were filtered through her own perceptions. It was impossible to say from how far in the future they had come, or what exactly the future that had sent them looked like. Was it even possible for a particular future to communicate with the past without causing paradoxes? In trying to answer this, Felka had come across the nearly forgotten work of a physicist named Deutsch, a man who had published his thoughts two hundred years before Galiana's experiments. Deutsch had argued that the way to view time was not as a flowing river but as a series of static snapshots stacked together to form space-times in which the flow of time was only a subjective illusion. Deutsch's picture explicitly permitted past-directed time travel with the preservation of free will and yet without paradoxes. The catch was that a particular "future" could only communicate with the "past" of another universe. Wherever these messages were coming from, they were not from Galiana's future. They might be from one that was very close to it, but it would never be one she could reach. No matter. The exact nature of the future was less important than the content of the messages themselves.

Felka had never learned the precise content of the messages Galiana had received, but she could guess. They had probably been along the same lines as the ones that came through during Felka's brief period of participation.

They would be instructions for making things, clues or signposts that pointed them in the right direction rather than detailed blueprints. Or there would be edicts or warnings. But by the time those distant transmissions had reached the participants in the Exordium experiments, they had been reduced to half-heard echoes, corrupted like Chinese whispers, intermingled and threaded with dozens of intervening messages. It was as if there was only one open conduit between the present and the future, with a finite bandwidth. Every message sent reduced the potential capacity for future messages. But it was not the actual content of the messages that was alarming, rather the thing that Felka had glimpsed behind them.

She had sensed a mind.

"We touched something," she told Remontoire. "Or rather something touched *us*. It reached down the corridor and grazed against our minds, coming through at the same time as we received the instructions."

"And that was the evil thing?"

"I can't think of any other way to describe it. Merely encountering it, merely sharing its thoughts for an instant, drove most of us insane, or left us dead." She looked at their reflections in the glass wall. "But I survived."

"You were lucky."

"No. It wasn't luck. Not entirely. Just that I recognised the thing, so the shock of encountering it wasn't so absolute. And because it recognised me, too. It withdrew as soon it touched my mind, and concentrated on the others."

"What was it?" Remontoire asked. "If you recognised it . . . "

"I wish I hadn't. I've had to live with that moment of recognition ever since, and it hasn't been easy."

"So what was it?" he persisted.

"I think it was Galiana," Felka said. "I think it was her mind."

"In the future?"

"In *a* future. Not ours, or at least not precisely."

Remontoire smiled uneasily. "Galiana's dead. We both know that. How could her mind have spoken to you from the future, even if it was a slightly different one from ours? It can't have been *that* different."

"I don't know. I wonder. And I keep wondering how she became like that."

"And that's why you left?"

"You'd have done the same thing." Felka watched the mouse take a wrong turning; not the one she had hoped it would take. "You're angry with me, aren't you? You feel that I betrayed her."

"Irrespective of what you've just told me, yes. I suppose I do." His tone had softened.

"I don't blame you. But I had to do it, Remontoire. I had to do it once. I don't regret that at all, even though I wish I hadn't learned what I did."

Remontoire whispered, "And Clavain . . . does he know any of this?"

"Of course not. It would kill him."

There was a rap of knuckle against wood. Clavain pushed his way into the space, glancing at the maze before speaking. "Talking about me behind my back again, are you?"

"Actually, we weren't really talking about you at all," Felka said.

"That's a disappointment."

"Have some tea, Clavain. It should still be drinkable."

Clavain took the bulb she offered him. "Is there anything you want to share with me about what happened in the Closed Council meeting?"

"We can't discuss specifics," Remontoire said. "All I can say is that there is considerable pressure for you to join. Some of that pressure comes from Conjoiners who feel that your loyalty to the Mother Nest will always be questionable until you come in from the cold."

"They've got a bloody cheek."

Remontoire and Felka exchanged glances. "Perhaps," Remontoire said. "There are also those—your allies, I suppose—who feel that you have more than demonstrated your loyalty over the years."

"That's more like it."

"But they'd also like you in the Closed Council," Felka said. "The way they see it, once you're in the Council, you won't be able to go around putting yourself in dangerous situations. They view it as a way of safeguarding a valuable asset."

Clavain scratched his beard. "So what you're saying is I can't win either way, is that it?"

"There's a minority that would be quite happy to see you remain out of the Closed Council," Remontoire said. "Some are your staunchest allies. Some, however, think that letting you continue to play soldier is the easiest way to get you killed."

"Nice to know I'm appreciated. And what do you two think?"

Remontoire spoke softly. "The Closed Council needs you, Clavain. Now more than ever."

Something unspoken passed between them then, Felka sensed. It was not neural communication but something far older, something that could only be understood by friends who had known and trusted each other for a very long time.

Clavain nodded gravely and then looked at Felka.

"You know my position," she said. "I've known you and Remontoire since my childhood on Mars. You were there for me, Clavain. You went back into Galiana's nest and saved me when she said it was hopeless. You never gave up on me, through all the years that followed. You made me into something other than what I was. You made me into a person."

"And now?"

"Galiana isn't here," she said. "That's one less link to my past, Clavain. I don't think I could stand to lose another."

In a repair berth on the rim of Carousel New Copenhagen, in the outer habitat lane of the circum-Yellowstone Rust Belt, Xavier Liu was having considerable difficulty with monkeys. The shop steward, who was not a monkey at all but an enhanced orang-utan, had pulled all of Xavier's squirrel monkeys out of the workshop at short notice. It was not Xavier's fault—his own labour relations had always been good—but the orang-utan had ordered the workers to down tools in sympathy with a party of striking colobus monkeys halfway around the rim. As far as Xavier could tell, the dispute had something to do with lemurs who were working at below-union rates and thereby taking work away from higher primates.

It was the sort of thing that might have been mildly interesting, even amusing, had it not impacted his latest job. But, Xavier reflected, it very much came with the territory. If he did not like working with monkeys, or apes, or prosimians, or even the occasional group of pygmy sloths, he should not have chosen to set up business in Carousel New Copenhagen.

The outer habitat lane was a bristling grey torus spinning within the Rust Belt, the ramshackle procession of habitats and the gutted remains of habitats that, despite all that had happened, still orbited Yellowstone. Habitats came in all shapes and sizes even before they began to suffer age, sabotage and collision. Some were enormous air-filled cylinders or spheres, adorned with mirrors and delicate gold sunshades. Others had been constructed on small asteroids or comet fragments, eased into orbit around Yellowstone by armies of Skyjacks. Sometimes the habitats wormed deep within these solid foundations, transforming their rocky hearts into a confusion of vertiginous plazas and air-filled public spaces. Others were built mainly on the surface, for ease of access to and from local space. These domed low-grav communities were clumped together like frogspawn, shot through with the iridescent green and blue of miniature biomes. Typically, the domes showed evidence of hasty repair work: scars and spider webs of emergency epoxy sealant or foam-diamond. Some had not been resealed, and what lay within was dark and lifeless, like the ashes of a fire.

Other habitats conformed to less pragmatic designs. There were wild spirals and helices, like blown glass or nautilus shells. There were enormous concatenations of spheres and tubes resembling organic molecules. There were habitats that reshaped themselves continually, slow symphonic movements of pure architecture. There were others that had clung to an outmoded design through stubborn centuries, resisting all innovation and frippery. A few others had cloaked themselves in fogs of pulverised matter, concealing their true design.

Then there were the derelicts. Some had been evacuated during the plague and had suffered no major catastrophes afterwards, but the majority had been struck by collision fragments from other habitats that had already crashed and burned. A few had been scuttled, blown apart by nuclear charges; not much remained of those. Some had been reclaimed and re-fitted during the years of reconstruction. A few were still held by aggressive squatters, despite the best efforts of the Ferrisville Convention to evict them.

Carousel New Copenhagen had weathered the plague years more successfully than some, but it had not come through totally unscathed. In the current era it was a single fat ring, rotating slowly. The rim of the ring was a kilometre wide. Seen from a distance, it was a festering blur of intricate structures, as if a strip of industrial cityscape had been wound on the outside of a wheel. Closer, it resolved into a coral-like mass of gantries and cranes and docking bays, service towers and recessed parking bays, spindly latticework exfoliating into vacuum, studded with a million stuttering lights of welding torches, advertising slogans and winking landing beacons. Arriving and departing ships, even in wartime, formed a haze of insect motion around the rim. Traffic management around Copenhagen was a headache.

At one time the wheel had rotated at twice its current rate: sufficient to generate a gee of centrifugal gravity at the rim. Ships had docked in the de-spun hub, still in free fall. Then, at the height of the plague, when the former Glitter Band was being downgraded to the Rust Belt, a rogue chunk of another habitat had taken out the entire central hub. The rim had been left spinning alone, spokeless.

There had been deaths, inevitably, many hundreds of them. Emergency ships had been parked where the hub had been, loading evacuees to ferry down to Chasm City. The precision of the impact had looked suspicious, but subsequent examination showed that it had been caused by exceptional bad luck.

Yet Copenhagen had survived. The carousel was an old one and not especially reliant on the microscopic technologies that the plague had subverted. For the millions who lived within it, life continued almost as it had before. With no easy location for new ships to dock, evacuation was painstaking at best. By the time the plague's worst months were over, Copenhagen was still mostly inhabited. The citizenry had kept their carousel running where others had been abandoned to the care of faltering machines. They had steered it out of the way of further collisions and taken ruthless measures to stamp out plague outbreaks within their own habitats. Barring the odd subsequent accident—like the time Lyle Merrick had slammed a chemical-drive freighter into the rim, gouging the crater that the tourist ghouls still came to drool over—the carousel had survived major catastrophe pretty much intact.

In the years of the reconstruction, the carousel had tried time and again to raise the funds for rebuilding the central hub. They had never succeeded. The merchants and ship owners complained that they were losing commerce because it was so hard to land on the moving rim. But the citizenry refused to allow the wheel to be spun-down, since they had grown accustomed to gravity. Eventually they reached a compromise that pleased neither side. The spin rate was sapped by fifty per cent, dropping rim gravity by one-half. It was still tricky to berth a ship, but not quite as tricky as it had been before. Besides, the citizenry argued, departing ships were given a free kick by the carousel, flung away at a tangent; they shouldn't complain. The pilots were not impressed. They pointed out that they had already burned the fuel that would have given them that kick during the approach itself.

But the unusual arrangement turned out to have strange benefits. During the occasionally lawless years that followed, their carousel was immune to most kinds of piracy. Squatters went elsewhere. And some pilots deliberately berthed their ships on Copenhagen's rim because they preferred to make certain repairs under gravity, rather than in the usual free-fall docks that the other habitats offered. Things had even begun to perk up before the outbreak of war. Tentative scaffolding pointed inwards from the wheel, hinting at the spokes that would come later, followed by a new hub.

There were thousands of dry-docks on the rim. They came in many sizes and shapes, to accommodate all major classes of in-system ship. They were mostly recessed back into the rim, with the lower side open to space. Ships had to be eased up into a dock, usually aided by robot tug, before being anchored securely into place with heavy-duty docking clamps. Anything not anchored fell back out into space, usually for good. It made working on berthed ships interesting, and it was work that required a head for heights; but there were always takers.

The ship that Xavier Liu was working on, alone now that his monkeys had gone on strike, was not one he had serviced before, but he had worked on many of the same basic type. She was a Rust Belt runner; a small semi-automated cargo hauler designed to nip between habitats. Her hull was a skeletal frame on to which many storage pods could be hung like Christmas-tree ornaments. The hauler had been running between the Swift-Augustine cylinder and a carousel controlled by the House of Correction, a shadowy firm that specialised in the discreet reversal of cosmetic surgical procedures.

There were passengers aboard the hauler, each packed into a single customised storage pod. When the hauler had detected a technical fault in its navigation system it had located the nearest carousel capable of offering immediate repairs, and had made an offer of work. Xavier's firm had returned a competitive bid, and the hauler had steered towards Copenhagen. Xavier had made sure there were robot tugs to assist the hauler towards its berth, and was now clambering around the frame of the ship, adhesive patches on his soles and palms gripping him to ticking cold metal. Tools of varying complexity hung from his spacesuit belt, and a compad of recent vintage gripped his left sleeve. Periodically he spooled out a line and plugged it into a data port in the hauler's chassis, biting his tongue as he made sense of the numbers.

He knew that the fault in the nav system, whatever it was, would turn out to be relatively simple to fix. Once you found the fault, it was usually just a matter of ordering a replacement component from stores; a monkey would normally have brought it to him within a few minutes. The trouble was he had been climbing around this hauler for forty-five minutes, and the precise source of the error was still eluding him.

This was a problem, since the terms of the bid guaranteed that he would have the hauler back on its journey within six hours. He had used up most of the first hour already, including the time it had taken to park the ship. Five hours was normally plenty of time, but he was beginning to have the nasty feeling that this was going to be one of those jobs that ended with his firm paying out penalty money.

Xavier clambered past one of the storage pods. "Give me a fucking clue, you bastard . . . "

The hauler's subpersona was shrill in his earpiece. "Have you found the fault in me? I am most anxious to continue my mission."

"No. Shut up. I need to think."

"I repeat, I am most anxious . . . "

"Shut the fuck up."

There was a clear patch near the front of the pod. He had so far avoided paying too much attention to any of the recipients, but this time he saw more than he intended to. There was a thing inside like a winged horse, except horses, even winged horses, did not have perfectly human female faces. Xavier looked away as the face's eyes met his own.

He spooled his line into another plug, hoping that this time he would nail the problem. Maybe there was nothing actually wrong with the nav system, just with the fault-diagnostics web . . . hadn't that happened once before, with that hauler that came in on a slush-puppy run from Hotel Amnesia? He glanced at the time display in the bottom-right corner of his faceplate. Five hours, ten minutes left, including the time he would need to run health checks and slide the hauler back out into empty space. It was not looking good.

"Have you found the fault in me? I am most . . . "

But at least it kept his mind off the other thing, he supposed. Up against the clock, with a knotty technical problem to solve, he did not think about Antoinette with quite the usual frequency. It had not become any easier to deal with her absence. He had not agreed with her little errand, but had known that the last thing she needed was him trying to argue her out of it. Her own doubts must have been strong enough.

So he had done what he could. He had traded favours with another repair shop that had some spare capacity, and they had pulled *Storm Bird* into their service bay, the second largest in all of Copenhagen. Antoinette had looked on nervously, convinced that the docking clamps could not possibly hold the freighter in place against its hundred thousand tonnes of centripetal weight. But the ship had held, and Xavier's monkeys had given it a thorough service.

Later, when the work was done, Xavier and Antoinette had made love for the last time before she went away. Antoinette had stepped back behind the airlock bulkhead and a few minutes after that, on the edge of tears, Xavier had watched *Storm Bird* depart, falling away until it looked impossibly small and fragile.

A little while after that, the shop had received a visit from a nastily inquisitive proxy of the Ferrisville Convention: a frightening sharp-edged contraption that crawled around for several hours, seemingly just to intimidate Xavier, before finding nothing and losing interest.

Nothing else had happened.

Antoinette had told him that she would maintain radio silence when she was in the war zone, so he was not surprised at first when he did not hear from her. Then the general news-nets had carried vague reports of some kind of military activity near Tangerine Dream, the gas giant where Antoinette was planning to bury her father. That was not supposed to have happened. Antoinette had planned her trip to coincide with a lull in military manoeuvres in that part of the system. The reports had not mentioned a civilian vessel being caught up in the struggle, but that meant nothing. Perhaps she had been hit by cross fire, her death unknown to anyone but Xavier. Or perhaps they knew she had died but did not want to advertise the fact that a civilian ship had strayed so far into a Contested Volume.

As the days turned into weeks and still there had been no report from her, he had forced himself to accept that she was dead. She had died nobly, doing something courageous, if pointless, in the middle of a war. She had not allowed herself to be sucked into cynical abnegation. He was proud to have known her, and quietly tormented that he would not see her again.

"I must ask again. Have you found the fault . . . "

Xavier tapped commands into his sleeve, disconnecting his comms from the subpersona. *Let the bastard thing stew a bit,* he thought.

He glanced at the clock. Four hours, fifty-five minutes, and he was still no closer to identifying the problem. In fact, one or two lines of enquiry that had looked quite promising a few minutes earlier had turned out to be resolute dead ends.

"Fuck this bastard piece of . . . "

Something pulsed green on his sleeve. Xavier studied it through a fog of irritation and mild panic. How ironic it would be, he thought, if the shop went out of business anyway, even though he had stayed behind . . .

His sleeve was telling him that he was receiving an urgent signal from outside Carousel New Copenhagen. It was coming in right at that moment, routed through to the shop via the carousel's general comms net. The message was talk-only, and there was no option to respond in real time, since whoever was transmitting was too far downstream. Which meant that whoever was sending was well outside the Rust Belt. Xavier told his sleeve to route the message through to his helmet, spooling back to the start of the transmission.

"Xavier . . . I hope you get this. I hope that the shop is still in business, and that you haven't called in too many favours recently. Because I'm going to have to ask you to call in a hell of a lot more."

"Antoinette," he said aloud despite himself, grinning like an idiot.

"All you need to know is what I'm about to tell you. The rest we can go over later, in person. I'm on my way back now, but I've got way too much delta-vee to make the Rust Belt. You need to get a salvage tug up to my speed, and pretty damn quickly. Haven't they got a couple of Taurus IVs over at the Lazlo dock? One of those can handle *Storm Bird* easily. I'm sure they owe us for that job down to Dax-Autrichiem last year."

She gave him coordinates and a vector and told him to be alert for banshee activity in the sector she had specified. Antoinette was right: she was moving very quickly indeed. Xavier wondered what had happened, but figured that he would find out soon enough. The timing *was* tight, too. She had left it to the last minute to transmit the message, which only gave him a narrow window to sort out the deal with the Taurus IVs. No more than half a day, or the tugs would not be able to reach her. Then the problem would be ten times harder to solve, and would require the calling-in of favours far outside Xavier's range.

Antoinette liked to live dangerously, he reflected.

He turned his attention back to the hauler. He was no closer to solving the problem with the nav system, but somehow it no longer weighed on his mind with quite the same sense of extreme urgency.

Xavier prodded his sleeve again, reconnecting with the subpersona. It buzzed immediately in his ear. It was as if it had been talking to him all along, even when he was no longer listening. " . . . fault yet? It is most strenuously urged that you remedy this error within the promised time period. Failure to comply with the terms of the repair bid will render you liable to penalty charges of not more than sixty thousand Ferris units, or not more than one hundred and twenty thousand if the failure to comply is . . . "

He unplugged his sleeve again. Blissful silence descended.

Nimbly, Xavier climbed off the chassis of the hauler. He hopped the short distance back on to one of the bay's repair ledges, landing amid tools and spooled cable. He turned off the grip in his palm and steadied himself, taking one last look at the hauler to make sure he had left no valuable tools lying around on it. He had not.

Xavier flipped open a panel in the oil-smeared wall of the bay. There were many controls behind the wall, huge toylike, grease-smeared buttons and levers. Some controlled electrical power and lighting; others governed pressurisation and temperature. He ignored all these, his palm coming to rest above a very prominent lever marked in scarlet: the control that undid the docking clamps.

Xavier looked back towards the hauler. It was silly, really, what he was going to do. A little more work, an hour or so, perhaps, and he might stand a very good chance of tracking down the fault. Then the hauler could go on its way, there would be no penalty fees and the repair shop's slide into insolvency would have been arrested, if only for the next couple of weeks.

Set against that, however, was the possibility that he would continue working for the next five hours and still not find the problem. Then there would be penalty charges, not more than one hundred and twenty thousand Ferris, as the hauler had helpfully informed him, as if knowing the upper limit in some way lessened the sting, and the fact that he would be five hours late in arranging Antoinette's rescue.

It was no contest, really.

Xavier tugged down the scarlet lever. He felt it lock into its new position with a satisfyingly old-fashioned mechanical clunk. Immediately, orange warning lights started flashing all around the bay. An alarm sounded in his helmet, telling him to keep well away from moving metal.

The clamps retracted in a rapid flurry, like telegraphic relays. For a moment the hauler hung suspended, magically. Then centrifugal gravity took over, and with something close to majesty the skeletal spacecraft descended out of the repair bay as smoothly and elegantly as a falling chandelier. Xavier was denied a view of the hauler dwindling into the distance—the carousel's rotation snatched it out of his line of sight. He could wait until the next pass, but he had work to do.

The hauler was unharmed, he knew. Once it was clear of Copenhagen another repair specialist would undoubtedly pick it up. In a few hours it would probably be back on its way to the House of Correction with its load of unfashionably mutated passengers.

Of course, there would still be hell to pay from a number of quarters: the passengers themselves, if they ever got wind; Swift-Augustine, the habitat that had sent them; the cartel that owned the hauler; maybe even the House of Correction itself, for endangering its clients.

They could all go fuck themselves. He had heard from Antoinette, and that was all that mattered.

EIGHT

Clavain looked at the stars.

He was outside the Mother Nest, alone, perched head-up or head-down—he could not decide which—on the practically weightless surface of the hollowed-out comet. There was no other human being visible in any direction, no evidence, in fact, of any kind of human presence at all. A passing observer, spying Clavain, would have assumed that he had been cruelly marooned on the surface of the comet without ship, supplies or shelter. There was no evidence whatsoever of the vast clockwork which spun at the comet's heart.

The comet spun slowly, periodically lifting the pale jewel of Epsilon Eridani above Clavain's horizon. The star was brighter than all the others in the sky, but it still looked like a star rather than a sun. He felt the immense chill of the empty space between himself and the star. It was a mere 100 AU distant—not even a scratch compared with interstellar distances, but it still caused him to shiver. He had never lost that mingled combination of awe and terror that welled up in him when confronted by the routinely huge distances of space.

Light caught his eye. It was an impossibly faint flicker somewhere in the plane of the ecliptic, a hand's width from Eridani. There it was again: a sharp, sudden spark at the limit of detectability. He was not imagining it. Another flash followed, a tiny distance away from the first two. Clavain ordered his helmet visor to screen out the light of the sun, so that his eyes did not have to deal with such a large dynamic range in brightness. The visor obliged, occluding the star with a precise black mask, exactly as if he had stared at the sun for too long.

He knew what he was looking at. It was a space battle dozens of light-hours away. The ships involved were probably spread through a volume of space several light-minutes from side to side, firing at each other with heavy relativistic weapons. Had he been in the Mother Nest he could have tapped into the general tactics database and retrieved information on the assets known to be patrolling that sector of the solar system. But it would have told him nothing he could not deduce for himself.

The flashes were mostly dying ships. Now and then one would be the triggering pulse of a Demarchist railgun—cumbersome, thousand-kilometre-long linear accelerator barrels. They had to be energised by detonating a string of cobalt-fusion bombs. The blast would rip the railgun to atoms, but not before it had accelerated a tank-sized slug of stabilised metallic hydrogen up to seventy per cent of light-speed, surfing just ahead of the annihilation wave.

The Conjoiners had weapons of similar effectiveness, but which drew their energising pulse from space-time itself. They could be fired more than once, and steered more quickly. They did not flash when they were fired.

Clavain knew that a spectroscopic analysis of the light in each of those flashes would have confirmed their origin. But he would not have been surprised to learn that most of them were caused by direct hits to Demarchist cruisers.

The enemy were dying out there. They were dying instantly, in explosions so bright and fast that there could be no pain, no realisation that death had come. But a painless death was only a small consolation. There would be many ships in that squadron; the survivors would be witnessing the destruction of their compatriots' vessels and wondering who would be next. They would never know when a slug was on its way towards them, and they would never know when it arrived.

From where Clavain stood, it was like watching fireworks above a remote town. From the colours of Agincourt to the flames of Guernica, to the pure shining light of Nagasaki like a cleansing sword blade catching the sun, to the contrails etched above the skies of the Tharsis Bulge, to the distant flash of heavy relativistic weapons against a starscape of sable-black in the early years of the twenty-seventh century: Clavain did not need to be reminded that war was horrific, but from a distance it could also have a terrible searing beauty.

The battle sunk towards the horizon. Presently it would be gone, leaving a sky unsullied by human affairs.

He thought of what he had learned about the Closed Council. Remontoire, with, Clavain assumed, Skade's tacit approval, had told him a little about the role Clavain would be expected to play. It was not merely that they wanted him within the Closed Council so that he could be kept out of harm's way. No. Clavain was needed to assist in a delicate operation. It would be a military action and it would take place beyond the Epsilon Eridani system. It would concern the recovery of a number of items that had fallen into the wrong hands.

Remontoire would not say what those items were; only that their recovery—which implied that they had at some point been lost—would be vital to the future security of the Mother Nest. If he wanted to learn more, and he would *have* to learn more if he was to be of any use to the Mother Nest, he would have to join the Closed Council. It sounded breathtakingly simple. Now that he considered it, alone on the surface of the comet, he had to admit that it probably was. His qualms were out of all proportion to the facts.

And yet he could not bring himself to trust Skade fully. She knew more than he did, and that would continue to be the case even if he agreed to join the Closed Council. He would be one layer closer to the Inner Sanctum then, but he would still not be within it—and what was to say that there were not additional layers behind that?

The battle rose again, over the opposite horizon. Clavain watched it dutifully, noting that the flashes were far less frequent now. The engagement was drawing to a close. It was practically certain that the Demarchists would have sustained the heaviest losses. There might even have been zero casualties on his own side. The enemy's survivors would soon be limping back to their respective bases, struggling to avoid further engagements on the way. Before very long the battle would figure in a propaganda transmission, the facts wrung to squeeze some tiny drop of optimism out of the overwhelming Demarchist defeat. He had seen it happen a thousand times; there would be more such battles, but not many. The enemy were losing. They had been on the losing side for years. So why was anyone worried about the future security of the Mother Nest?

There was, he knew, only one way to find out.

* * *

The tender found its slot on the rim, edging home with unerring machine precision. Clavain disembarked into standard gravity, puffing for the first few minutes until he adjusted to the effort.

He made his way through a circuitous route of corridors and ramps. There were other Conjoiners about, but they spared him no particular attention. When he felt the wash of their thoughts, sensing their impressions of him, he detected only quiet respect and admiration, with perhaps the tiniest tempering of pity. The general populace knew nothing of Skade's efforts to bring him into the Closed Council.

The corridors grew darker and smaller. Spartan grey walls became festooned with conduits, panels and the occasional grilled duct through which warm air blasted. Machines thrummed beneath his feet and behind the walls. The lighting was intermittent and meagre. At no point had Clavain stepped through any kind of prohibited door, but the general impression now to anyone unfamiliar with this part of the wheel would have been that they had strayed into some slightly forbidding maintenance section. A few made it this far, but most would have turned back and kept walking until they found themselves in more welcoming territory.

Clavain continued. He had reached a part of the wheel that was unrecorded on any blueprints or maps. Most of the citizens of the Mother Nest knew nothing of its existence. He approached a bronze-green bulkhead. It was unguarded and unmarked. Next to it was a thick-rimmed metal wheel with three spokes. Clavain grasped the wheel by two of the spokes and tugged it. For a moment it was stiff—no one had been down here in some time—but then it oozed into mobility. Clavain yanked it round until it spun freely. The bulkhead door eased out like a stopper, dripping condensation and lubricant. As he turned the wheel further the stopper hinged aside, allowing entry. The stopper was like a huge squat piston, its sides polished to a brilliant hermetic gleam.

Beyond was an even darker space. Clavain stepped over the half-metre lip of the bulkhead, ducking to avoid grazing his scalp against the transom. The metal was cold against his fingers. He blew on them until they felt less numb.

Once he was inside, Clavain spun a second wheel until the bulkhead was again tightly sealed, tugging his sleeves down over his fingers as he worked. Then he took a few steps farther into the gloom. Pale green lights came on in steps, stammering back into the darkness.

The chamber was immense, low and long like a gunpowder store. The curve of the wheel's rim was just visible, the walls arcing upwards and the floor bending with them. Into the distance stretched row after row of reefersleep caskets.

Clavain knew precisely how many there were: one hundred and seventeen. One hundred and seventeen people had returned from deep space aboard Galiana's ship, but all had been beyond any reasonable hope of revival. In many cases, the violence inflicted on her crew had been so extreme that the remains could only be segregated by genetic profiling. Nonetheless, however sparse the remains had been, each identified individual had been allocated a single reefersleep casket.

Clavain made his way down the aisles between the rows of caskets, the grilled flooring clattering beneath his feet. The caskets hummed quietly. They were all still operational, but that was only because it was considered wise to keep the remains frozen, not because there was any realistic hope of reviving most of them. There was no sign of any active wolf machinery embedded in any of the remains—except, of course, for one—but that did not mean that there were no dormant microscopic wolf parasites lurking just below the detection threshold. The bodies could have been cremated, but that would have removed the possibility of ever learning anything about the wolves. The Mother Nest was nothing if not prudent.

Clavain reached Galiana's reefersleep casket. It stood apart from the others, raised fractionally on a sloping plinth. Exposed intricacies of corroded machinery suggested ornate stonework carving. It called to mind the coffin of a fairy queen, a much-loved and courageous monarch who had defended her people until the end and who now slept in death, surrounded by her most trusted knights, advisers and ladies-in-waiting. The upper portion of the casket was transparent, so that something of Galiana's form was visible in silhouette long before one stood by the casket itself. She looked serenely accepting of her fate, with her arms folded across her chest, her head raised to the ceiling, accentuating the strong, noble line of her jaw. Her eyes were closed and her brow smooth. Long grey-streaked hair lay in dark pools on either side of her face. A billion ice particles glittered across her skin, twinkling in pastel flickers of blue and pink and pale green as Clavain's angle of view changed. She looked exquisitely beautiful and delicate in death, as if she had been carved from sugar.

He wanted to weep.

Clavain touched the cold lid of the casket, skating his fingers across the surface, leaving four faint trails. He had imagined a thousand times the things he might say to her should she ever emerge from the Wolf's clasp. She had never been thawed again after that one time shortly after her return, but that did not mean that it might not happen again, years or centuries from now. Time and again Clavain had wondered what he would say, were Galiana to shine through the mask even for the briefest of moments. He wondered if she would remember him and the things they had shared. Would she even remember Felka, who was as close to being her daughter as made no difference?

There was no point thinking about it. He knew he would never speak to her again.

"I've made my mind up," he said, the fog of his breath visible before him. "I'm not sure you'd approve, since you would never have agreed to something like the Closed Council existing in the first place. They say the war made it inevitable, that the demands for operational secrecy forced us to compartmentalise our thinking. But the Council was already there before the war broke out, in a nascent form. We've always had secrets, even from ourselves."

His fingers were very cold. "I'm doing it because I think something bad is going to happen. If it's something that has to be stopped, I will do my best to make sure it is. If it can't be helped, I will do my best to guide the Mother Nest through whatever crisis is awaiting it. But I can't do either on the outside.

"I've never felt so uneasy about a victory as I do about this one, Galiana. I've a sense you'd feel much the same way. You always used to be suspicious of anything that looked too simple, anything that looked like a ruse. I should know. I fell for one of your tricks once."

He shivered. It was suddenly very cold and he had the prickly feeling that he was being watched. All around him the reefersleep caskets hummed, their banks of status lights and read-outs unchanging.

Clavain suddenly knew that he did not want to spend much

longer in the vault. "Galiana," he said, too hastily for comfort, "I have to do it. I have to accede to Skade's request, for good or ill. I just hope you understand."

"She will, Clavain."

He turned around sharply, but even in the act of turning he realised that he knew the voice and it was nothing to be alarmed by. "Felka." His relief was total. "How did you find me?"

"I assumed you'd be down here, Clavain. I knew Galiana would always be the one you spoke to last of all."

She had entered the vault unheard. He could see now that the door at the end was ajar. What had made him shiver was the shift in air currents as the vault was opened.

"I don't know why I'm here," Clavain said. "I know she's dead."

"She's your conscience, Clavain."

"That's why I loved her."

"We all did. That's why she still seems to be alive, to be guiding us." Felka was by his side now. "It's all right to come down here. It doesn't make me think less of you, or respect you less."

"I think I know what I have to do."

She nodded, as if he had merely told her the time of day. "Come on, let's get out of here. It's too cold for the living. Galiana won't mind."

Clavain followed her to the door leading out of the vault.

Once they were on the other side he worked the wheel, sealing the great piston-like stopper back into place, sealing memories and ghosts away where they belonged.

Clavain was ushered into the privy chamber. As he crossed the threshold he felt the million background thoughts of the Mother Nest drop from his mind like a single dying sigh. He imagined that the transition would have been traumatic for many of the Conjoined, but even if he had not just come from Galiana's place of rest, where the same kind of exclusion applied, he would not have found it more than a little jarring. Clavain had spent too much time on the fringes of Conjoiner society to be troubled by the absence of other thoughts in his head.

He was not entirely alone, of course. He sensed the minds of those in the chamber, although the usual Closed Council restrictions still only allowed him to skim the surfaces of their thoughts. The chamber itself was unremarkable: a large sphere with many seats arranged in encircling balconies reaching almost to the chamber's zenith. The floor was flat and gleaming-grey, with a single austere chair positioned in the chamber's centre. The chair was solid, curving seamlessly into the floor as if it had been pushed through from beneath.

[Clavain.] It was Skade. She was standing on the tip of a protruding tongue jutting from one side of the chamber.

Yes?

[Sit in the seat, Clavain.]

He walked across the glittering floor, his soles clicking against the material. The atmosphere could not help but feel judicial; he might as well have been walking towards a place of execution.

Clavain eased himself into the seat, which was as comfortable as it had appeared. He crossed his legs and scratched his beard. *Let's get this over with, Skade.*

[All in good time, Clavain. Do you appreciate that with the burden of knowledge comes the additional burden of holding that knowledge secure? That once you have learned Closed Council secrets, you cannot jeopardise them by risking enemy capture? That even communicating these secrets to other Conjoiners cannot be tolerated?]

I know what I'm letting myself in for, Skade.

[We just want to be certain, Clavain. You cannot begrudge us that.]

Remontoire rose from his seat. [He's said he's ready, Skade. That's enough.] She regarded Remontoire with an absence of emotion that Clavain found far more chilling than mere anger. [Thank you, Remontoire.]

He's right. I am ready. And willing.

Skade nodded. [Then prepare yourself. Your mind is about to be allowed access to previously excluded data.]

Clavain could not help gripping the armrests of his chair, knowing as he did so how ridiculous the instinct was. This was how he had felt four hundred years earlier, when Galiana had first introduced him to Transenlightenment. It had been in her nest on Mars, and she had infected his mind with droves of machines after he had been injured. She had given him a glimpse then, no more than that, but in the moments before it arrived he had felt like a man standing before the rushing wall of a tsunami, counting down the seconds until he was engulfed. He felt like that now, even though he was anticipating no actual change in consciousness. It was enough to know that he was about to be granted access to secrets so shattering that they merited layers of hierarchy within an otherwise omniscient hive mind.

He waited . . . but nothing happened.

[It's done.]

He relaxed his grip on the seat. *I feel exactly the same.*

[You're not.]

Clavain looked around him at the ringed walls of the chamber. Nothing had altered; nothing felt different. He examined his memory and there seemed to be nothing lurking there that had not been present a minute earlier. *I don't . . .*

[Before you came here, before you made this decision, we permitted you to know that the reason for our seeking your assistance was a matter of recovering lost property. Isn't that true, Clavain?]

You wouldn't tell me what you were looking for. I still don't know.

[That's because you haven't asked yourself the right question.]

And what question would you like me to ask, Skade?

[Ask yourself what you know about the hell-class weapons, Clavain. I'm sure you'll find the answer very interesting.]

I don't know anything about any hell-class . . .

But he faltered, fell silent. He knew exactly what the hell-class weapons were.

Now that the information was available to him, Clavain realised that he had heard rumours of the weapons on many occasions during his time amongst the Conjoined. Their bitterest enemies told cautionary tales of the Conjoiners' hidden stockpile of ultimate weapons, doomsday devices so ferocious in their destructive capability that they had hardly been tested, and had certainly never been used in any actual engagements. The weapons were supposedly very old, manufactured during the very earliest phase of Conjoiner history. The rumours varied in detail, but all the stories agreed on one thing: there had been forty weapons, and none of them were precisely alike.

Clavain had never taken the rumours seriously, assuming that they must have originated with some forgotten piece of fear-mongering by one of the Mother Nest's counter-intelligence units. It was unthinkable that the weapons could ever have been real. In all the time he had been amongst the Conjoined, no official hint of the existence of such weapons had ever come his way. Galiana had never spoken of them, and yet if the weapons were truly old—dating back to the Mars era—she could not possibly have been unaware of their existence.

But the weapons *had* existed.

Clavain sifted through his bright new memories with grim fascination. He had always known there were secrets within the Mother Nest, but he had never suspected that something so momentous could have been concealed for so long. He felt as if he had just discovered a vast, hidden room in a house he had lived in nearly all his life. The feeling of dislocation—and betrayal—was acute.

There were forty weapons, just like in the old tales. Each was a prototype, exploiting some uniquely subtle and nastily inventive principle of breakthrough physics. And Galiana did indeed know about them. She had authorised the construction of the weapons in the first place, at the height of the Conjoiner persecution. At the time, her enemies had been effective only by weight of numbers rather than technical superiority. With the forty new weapons she could have wiped the slate clean, but at the eleventh hour she had chosen not to: better to be erased from existence than have genocide on her hands.

But that had not been the end. There had been blunders by the enemy, lucky breaks and contingencies. Galiana's people had been pushed to the brink, but they had never quite been excised from history.

Afterwards, Clavain learned that the weapons had been locked away for safekeeping, stockpiled inside an armoured asteroid in another system. Murky images flickered through his mind's eye: barricaded vaults, fierce cybernetic watchdogs, perilous traps and deadfalls. Galiana had clearly feared the weapons as much as she feared her enemies, and though she was not willing to dismantle the weapons, she had done her best to put them beyond immediate use. The data that had allowed them to be made in the first place was erased, and apparently this had been sufficient to prevent any further attempts at duplication. Should the weapons ever be needed again—should another time of mass persecution arise—the weapons were still there to be used; but distance—years of flight-time—meant there was a generous cooling-off period built into the arrangement. Her forty hell-class weapons could only ever be used in cold blood, and that was the way it should be.

But the weapons had been stolen. The impregnable asteroid had been breached and by the time a Conjoiner investigative team arrived there was no trace of the thieves. Whoever had done it had been clever enough both to break through the defences and to avoid waking the weapons themselves. In their dormant condition the forty weapons could not be tracked, remotely destroyed or pacified.

There had been many attempts to locate the lost weapons, Clavain learned, but so far all had failed. Knowledge of the cache had been a closely guarded secret to begin with; the theft was kept even more hush-hush, with only a few very senior Conjoiners knowing what had happened. As the decades passed, they held their collective breaths: in the wrong hands, the weapons could shatter worlds like glass. Their only hope was that the thieves did not realise the potency of what they had stolen.

Decades became a century, then two centuries. There had been a great many disasters and crises in human space, but never any indication that the weapons had been awakened. The few Conjoiners in the know began to dare to believe that the matter could be quietly forgotten: perhaps the weapons had been abandoned in deep space, or tossed into the searing face of a star.

But the weapons had not been lost.

Completely unexpectedly, not long before Clavain's return from deep space, activation signatures had been detected in the vicinity of Delta Pavonis, a sunlike star slightly more than fifteen light-years from the Mother Nest. The neutrino signals were weak; it was possible that earlier flickers of awakening had been missed entirely. But the most recent signals were quite unambiguous: a number of the weapons had been awakened from dormancy.

The Delta Pavonis system was not on the main trade routes. It did have a single colony world, Resurgam, a settlement established by an archaeological expedition from Yellowstone that had been led by Dan Sylveste, the son of the cyberneticist Calvin Sylveste and scion of one of the wealthiest families within Demarchist society. Sylveste's archaeologists had been picking through the remains of a birdlike race that had lived on the planet barely a million years earlier. The colony had gradually severed formal ties with Yellowstone, and a series of regimes had seen the original scientific agenda replaced by a conflicting policy of terraforming and widescale settlement. There had been coups and violence, but it was nonetheless highly unlikely that the settlers were the ones who now possessed the weapons. Scrutiny of outbound traffic records from Yellowstone showed the departure of another ship en route to Resurgam: a lighthugger, *Nostalgia for Infinity,* that had arrived around the system at approximately the time that the activation signatures were detected. There was scant information on the ship's crew and history, but Clavain learned from Rust Belt immigration records that a woman named Ilia Volyova had been scouting for new crewmembers immediately before the ship's departure. The name might or might not have been genuine—in those confused post-plague days, ships could get away with whatever identities suited them—but Volyova had reappeared. Although very few transmissions made it back to Yellowstone, one of those, panicked and fragmentary, had mentioned Volyova's ship terrorising the colony into surrendering its former leader. For some reason, Volyova's Ultranaut crew wanted Dan Sylveste aboard their ship.

This did not mean that Volyova was definitely in charge of the weapons, but Clavain agreed with Skade's assessment that she was the most likely suspect. She had a ship large enough to have held the weapons, she had used violence against the colony and she had arrived on the scene at the same time as the weapons had been revived from dormancy. It was impossible to guess what Volyova wanted with the weapons, but her association with them appeared beyond question.

She was the thief they had been looking for.

Skade's crest pulsed with ripples of jade and bronze. New memories unpacked into his head: video clips and still-frame grabs of Volyova. Clavain was not quite sure what he had been expecting, but it was not the crop-haired, round-faced, shrewlike woman that Skade revealed to him. Had he walked into a room of suspects, Volyova would have been one of the last people he would have turned to.

Skade smiled at him. She had his full attention. [Now you understand why we need your help. The location and status of the thirty-nine remaining weapons . . .]

Thirty-nine, Skade? I thought there were forty.

[Didn't I mention that one of the weapons has already been destroyed?]

You missed that part out, I think.

[We can't be certain at this range. The weapons slip in and out of hibernation, like restless monsters. Certainly one weapon hasn't been detected since 2565, local Resurgam time. We presume it lost, or damaged at the very least. And six of the remaining thirty-nine weapons have become detached from the main grouping. We still have intermittent signals from those weapons, but they are much closer to the neutron star on the system's edge. The other thirty-three weapons are within an AU of Delta Pavonis, at the trailing Lagrange point of the Resurgam—Delta Pavonis system. In all likelihood they are within the hull of the Triumvir's lighthugger.]

Clavain raised a hand. *Wait. You detected some of these signals as long ago as 2565?*

[Local Resurgam time, Clavain.]

Nonetheless, you'd still have detected the signals here around . . . when, 2580? Thirty-three years ago, Skade. Why the hell didn't you act sooner?

[This is wartime, Clavain. We've hardly been in a position to mount an extensive, logistically complex recovery operation.]

Until now, that is.

Skade conceded his point with the slightest of nods. [Now the tide is turning in our favour. Finally we can afford to divert some resources. Make no mistake, Clavain, recovering these weapons will not be easy. We will be attempting to repossess items that were stolen from a stronghold that we would even now have grave difficulty breaking into ourselves. Volyova has her own weapons, quite apart from those she has stolen from us. And the evidence of her crimes on Resurgam suggests that she has the nerve to use them. But we simply must have the weapons back, no matter the cost in assets and time.]

Assets? You mean lives?

[You have never flinched from accepting the costs of war, Clavain. That is why we want you to co-ordinate this recovery operation. Peruse these memories if you doubt your own suitability.]

She did not give him the dignity of a warning. Chunks of his past crashed into his immediate consciousness, jolting him back to past campaigns and past actions. War movies, Clavain thought, remembering the old two-dimensional, monochrome recordings he had watched during his earliest days in the Coalition for Neural Purity, sifting them—usually in vain—for any hint of a lesson that he might use against real enemies. But now the war movies that Skade showed him, slamming past in accelerated bursts, were ones in which *he* was the protagonist. And for the most part they were historically accurate, too: a parade of actions he had participated in. There was a hostage release in the warrens of Gilgamesh Isis, during which Clavain had lost a hand to a sulphur burn, an injury that took a year to heal. There was the time Clavain and a female Conjoiner had smuggled the brain of a Demarchist scientist out of the custody of a faction of renegade Mixmasters around Marco's Eye. Clavain's partner had been surgically modified so that she could keep the brain alive in her womb, following simple reverse Caesarean surgery that Clavain had administered. They had left the man's body behind for his captors to discover. Afterwards, the Conjoiners had cloned the man a new body and packed the traumatised brain back into it.

Then there was Clavain's recovery of a stolen Conjoiner drive from dissident Skyjacks camped in one of the outer nodes of the Bloater agrarian hive, and the liberation of an entire Pattern Juggler world from Ultra profiteers who wanted to charge for access to the mind-altering alien ocean. There were more, many more. Clavain always survived and nearly always triumphed. There were other universes, he knew, where he had died much earlier: he hadn't been any less skilled in those histories, but his luck had just played out differently. He could not extrapolate from this run of successes and assume that he was bound to succeed at the next hurdle.

Even though he was not guaranteed to succeed, it was clear that Clavain stood a better chance than anyone else in the Closed Council.

He smiled ruefully. *You seem to know me better than I know myself.*

[I know that you will help us, Clavain, or I would not have brought you this far. I'm right, of course, aren't I? You will help us, won't you?]

Clavain looked around the room, taking in the gruesome menagerie of wraithlike seniors, wizened elders and obscene glass-bottled end-state Conjoiners. They were all hanging on his answer, even the visible brains seeming to hesitate in their wheezing pulsations. Skade was right, of course. There was no one Clavain would have trusted to do the job other than himself, even now, at this late hour in both his career and his life. It would take decades, nearly twenty years just to reach Resurgam, and another twenty to come back with the prize. But forty years was really not a very long time when set against four or five centuries. And for most of that time he would be frozen, anyway.

Forty years; maybe five years at this end to prepare for it, and perhaps as much as a year for the operation itself . . . altogether, something close to half a century. He looked at Skade, observing the expectant way the ripples on her crest slowed to a halt. He knew that Skade had trouble reading his mind at the deepest level—it was his very opacity which made him both fascinating and infuriating to her—but he suspected that she could read his assent well enough.

I'll do it. But there are conditions.

[Conditions, Clavain?]

I pick my team. And I say who travels with me. If I ask for Felka and Remontoire, and if they agree to come with me to Resurgam, then you'll allow it.

Skade considered, then nodded with the precise delicacy of a shadow puppet. [Of course. Forty years is a long time to be away. Is that all?]

No, of course not. I won't go against Volyova unless I have a crushing tactical superiority from the word go. That's how I've always worked, Skade: full-spectrum dominance. That means more than one ship. Two at the very least, three ideally, and I'll take more if the Mother Nest can manufacture them in time. I don't care about the edict, either. We need lighthuggers, heavily armed with the nastiest weapons we've got. One prototype isn't enough, and given the time it takes to build anything these days, we'd better start work immediately. You can't just click your fingers at an asteroid and have a starship pop out of the end four days later.

Skade touched a finger to her lower lip. Her eyes closed for an instant longer than a blink. For that moment Clavain had the intense feeling that she was in heated dialogue with another. He thought that he saw her eyelids quiver, like a fever-racked dreamer.

[You're right, Clavain. We will need ships; new ones, incorporating the refinements built into *Nightshade*. But you don't have to worry. We've already started making them. As a matter of fact, they're coming on nicely.]

Clavain narrowed his eyes. *New ships? Where?*

[A little way from here, Clavain.]

He nodded. *Good. Then it won't hurt to take me to see them, will it? I'd like to have a look over them before it's too late to change anything.*

[Clavain . . .]

That isn't open to negotiation either, Skade. If I want to get the job done, I'll need to see the tools of my trade.

NINE

The Inquisitor relaxed her seat restraints and sketched a window for herself in the opaque hull material of the Triumvir's shuttle. The hull obligingly opened a transparent rectangle, offering the Inquisitor her first view of Resurgam from space in fifteen years.

Much had changed even in that relatively brief span of planetary time. Clouds which had previously been vapid streaks of high-altitude moisture now billowed in thick creamy masses, whipped into spiral patterns by the blind artistry of Coriolis force. Sunlight glared back at her from the enamelled surfaces of lakes and miniature seas. There were hard-edged expanses of green and gold stitched across the planet in geometric clusters, threaded by silver-blue irrigation channels deep enough to carry barges. There were the faint grey scratches of slev lines and highways. Cities and settlements were smears of crosshatched streets and buildings, barely resolved even when the Inquisitor asked the window to flex into magnification mode. Near the hubs of the oldest settlements, like Cuvier, were the remnants of the old habitat domes or their foundation rings. Now and then she saw the bright moving bead of a transport dirigible high in the stratosphere, or the much smaller speck of an aircraft on government duty. But on this scale most human activity was invisible. She might as well have been studying surface features on some hugely magnified virus.

The Inquisitor, who after years of suppressing that part of her personality was again beginning to think of herself as Ana Khouri, did not have any particularly strong feelings of attachment to Resurgam, even after all the years she had spent incognito on its surface. But what she saw from orbit was sobering. The planet was more than the temporary colony it had been when she had first arrived in the system. It was a home to many people, all they had known. In the course of her investigations she had met many of them and she knew that there were still good people on Resurgam. They could not all be blamed for the present government or the injustices of the past. They at least deserved the chance to live and die on the world they had come to call their home. And by dying she meant by natural causes. That, unfortunately, was the part that could no longer be guaranteed.

The shuttle was tiny and fast. The Triumvir, Ilia Volyova, was snoozing in the other seat, with the peak of a nondescript grey cap tugged down over her brow. It was the shuttle that had brought her down to Resurgam in the first place, before she contacted the Inquisitor. The shuttle's avionics program knew how to dodge between the government radar sweeps, but it had always seemed prudent to keep such excursions to a minimum. If they were caught, if there was even a suspicion that a spacecraft was routinely entering and leaving Resurgam's atmosphere, heads would roll at every level of government. Even if Inquisition House was not directly implicated, Khouri's position would become extremely unsafe. The backgrounds of key government personnel would be subjected to a deep and probing scrutiny. Despite her precautions, her origins might be revealed.

The stealthy ascent had necessitated a shallow acceleration profile, but once it was clear of atmosphere and outside the effective range of the radar sweeps the shuttle's engines revved up to three gees, pressing the two of them back into their seats. Khouri began to feel drowsy and realised, just as she slid into sleep, that the shuttle was pumping a perfumed narcotic into the air. She slept dreamlessly, and awoke with the same mild sense of objection.

They were somewhere else.

"How long were we under?" she asked Volyova, who was smoking.

"Just under a day. I hope that alibi you cooked up was good, Ana; you're going to need it when you get back to Cuvier."

"I said I had to go into the wilderness to interview a deep-cover agent. Don't worry; I established the background for this a long time ago. I always knew I might have to be away for a while." Khouri undid her seat restraints—the shuttle was no longer accelerating—and attempted to scratch an itch somewhere near the small of her back. "Any chance of a shower, whenever we get where we're going?"

"That depends. Where exactly do you think we're headed?"

"Let's just say I have a horrible feeling I've already been there."

Volyova stubbed out her cigarette and made the front of the hull turn glassy. They were in deep interplanetary space, still in the ecliptic, but good light-minutes from any world, yet something was blocking the view of the starfield ahead of them.

"There she is, Ana. The good ship *Nostalgia for Infinity*. Still very much as you left her."

"Thanks. Any other cheering sentiments, while you're at it?"

"The last time I checked the showers were out of order."

"The last time you checked?"

Volyova paused and made a clucking sound with her tongue. "Buckle up. I'm taking us in."

They swooped in close to the dark misshapen mass of the lighthugger. Khouri remembered her first approach to this same ship, back when she had been tricked aboard it in the Epsilon Eridani system. It had looked just about normal then, about what one would expect of a large, moderately old trade lighthugger. There had been a distinct absence of odd excrescences and protuberances, a marked lack of daggerlike jutting appendages or elbowed turretlike growths. The hull had been more or less smooth—worn and weathered here and there, interrupted by machines, sensor-pods and entry bays in other places—but there had been nothing about it that would have invited particular comment or disquiet. There had been no acres of lizardskin texturing or dried-mudplain expanses of interlocked platelets; no suggestion that buried biological imperatives had finally erupted to the surface in an orgy of biomechanical transformation.

But now the ship did not look much like a ship at all. What it did resemble, if Khouri had to associate it with anything, was a fairytale palace gone sick, a once-glittering assemblage of towers and oubliettes and spires that had been perverted by the vilest of magics. The basic shape of the starship was still evident: she could pick out the main hull and its two jutting engine nacelles, each larger than a freight-dirigible hangar; but that functional core was almost lost under the baroque growth layers that had lately stormed the ship. Various organising principles had been at work, ensuring that the growths, which had been mediated by the ship's repair and redesign subsystems, had a mad artistry about them, a foul flamboyance which both awed and revolted. There were spirals like the growth patterns in ammonites. There were whorls and knots like vastly magnified wood grain. There were spars and filaments and netlike meshes, bristling hairlike spines and blocky chancrous masses of interlocked crystals. There were places where some major structure had been echoed and re-echoed in a fractal diminuendo, vanishing down to the limit of vision. The crawling intricacies of the transformations operated on all scales. If one looked for too long, one started seeing faces or parts of faces in the juxtapositions of warped armour. Look longer and one started seeing one's own horrified reflection. But under all that, Khouri thought, it was still a ship.

"Well," she said, "I see it hasn't got a fuck of a lot better since I was away."

Volyova smiled beneath the brim of her cap. "I'm encouraged. That sounds a lot less like the Inquisitor and a lot more like the old Ana Khouri."

"Yeah? Pity it took a fucking nightmare like that to bring me back."

"Oh, this is nothing," Volyova said cheerfully. "Wait until we're inside."

The shuttle had to swerve through a wrinkled eyelike gap in the hull growth to reach the docking bay. But the interior of the bay was still more or less rectangular, and the major servicing systems, which had never much depended on nanotechnology, were still in place and recognisable. An assortment of other in-system craft was packed into the chamber, ranging from blunt-nosed vacuum tugs to major shuttles.

They docked. This part of the ship was not spun for gravity, so they disembarked under weightless conditions, pulling themselves along via grab rails. Khouri was more than willing to let Volyova go ahead of her. Both of them carried torches and emergency oxygen masks, and Khouri was very tempted to start using her supply. The air in the ship was horribly warm and humid, with a rotten taste to it. It was like breathing someone else's stomach gas.

Khouri covered her mouth with her sleeve, fighting the urge to retch. "Ilia . . . "

"You'll get used to it. It isn't harmful." She extracted something from her pocket. "Cigarette?"

"Have you ever known me to say yes to one of those damned things before?"

"There's always a first time."

Khouri waited while Volyova lit the cigarette for her and then drew on it experimentally. It was bad, but still a marked improvement on unfiltered ship air.

"Filthy habit, really," Volyova said, with a smile. "But then filthy times call for filthy habits. Feeling better now?"

Khouri nodded, but without any great conviction.

They moved through gulletlike tunnels whose walls glistened with damp secretions or beguilingly regular crystal patterns. Khouri brushed herself along with gloved hands. Now and then she recognised some old aspect of the ship—a conduit, bulkhead or inspection box—but typically it would be half-melted into its surroundings or surreally distorted. Hard surfaces had become fuzzily fractal, extending blurred grey boundaries into thin air. Varicoloured slimes and unguents threw back their torchlights in queasy diffraction patterns. Amoebalike blobs drifted through the air, following—or at times swimming against, it seemed—the prevailing shipboard air-currents.

Via grinding locks and wheels they transferred to the part of the ship that was still rotating. Khouri was grateful for the gravity, but with it came an unanticipated unpleasantness. Now there was somewhere for the fluids and secretions to run to. They dripped and dribbled from the walls in miniature cataracts, congealing on the floor before finding their way to a drainage aperture or hole. Certain secretions had formed stalagmites and stalactites, amber and snot-green prongs fingering between floor and ceiling. Khouri did her best not to brush against them, but it was not the easiest of tasks. She noticed that Volyova had no such inhibitions. Within minutes her jacket was smeared and swabbed with several varieties of shipboard effluent.

"Relax," Volyova said, noticing her discomfort. "It's perfectly safe. There's nothing on the ship that can harm either of us. You—um—have had those gunnery implants taken out, haven't you?"

"You should remember. You did it."

"Just checking."

"Ha. You're actually enjoying this, aren't you?"

"I've learned to take my pleasures where I can find them, Ana. Especially in times of deep existential crisis . . . " Ilya Volyova flicked a cigarette butt into the shadows and lit herself another.

They continued in silence. Eventually they reached one of the elevator shafts that threaded the ship lengthwise, like the main elevator shaft in a skyscraper. With the ship rotating rather than being under thrust it was much easier to move along its lateral axis. But it was still four kilometres from the tip of the ship to its tail, so it made sense to use the shafts wherever possible. To Khouri's surprise, a car was waiting for them in the shaft. She followed Volyova into it with moderate trepidation, but the car looked normal inside and accelerated smoothly enough.

"The elevators are still working?" Khouri asked.

"They're a key shipboard system," Volyova said. "Remember, I've got tools for containing the plague. They don't work perfectly, but I can at least steer the disease clear of anything I don't want to become too corrupted. And the Captain himself is occasionally willing to assist. The transformations aren't totally out of his control, it seems."

Volyova had finally raised the matter of the Captain. Until that moment Khouri had been clinging to the hope that it might all turn out to be a bad dream she had confused with reality. But there it was. The Captain was very much alive.

"What about the engines?"

"Still functionally intact, as far as I can tell. But only the Captain has control of them."

"Have you been talking with him?"

"I'm not sure talking is quite the word I'd use. Communicating, possibly . . . but even that might be stretching things."

The elevator veered, switching between shafts. The shaft tubes were mostly transparent, but the elevator spent much of its time whisking between densely packed decks or boring through furlongs of solid hull material. Now and then, through the window, Khouri saw dank chambers zoom by. Mostly they were too large for her to see the other side in the weakly reflected light of the elevator. There were five chambers which were the largest of all, huge enough to hold cathedrals. She thought of the one Volyova had shown her during her first tour of *Infinity,* the one that held the forty horrors. There were fewer than forty of them now, but that was surely still enough to make a difference. Even, perhaps, against an enemy like the Inhibitors. Provided that the Captain could be persuaded.

"Have you and him patched up your differences?" Khouri asked.

"I think the fact that he didn't kill us when he had the chance more or less answers that question."

"And he doesn't blame you for what you did to him?"

For the first time there was a sign of annoyance from Volyova. "Did to him? Ana, what I 'did to him' was an act of extreme mercy. I didn't punish him at all. I merely . . . stated the facts and then administered the cure."

"Which by some definitions was worse than the disease."

Now Volyova shrugged. "He was going to die. I gave him a new lease on life."

Khouri gasped as another chamber ghosted by, filled with fused metamorphic shapes. "If you call this living."

"Word of advice." Volyova leant closer, lowering her voice. "There's a very good chance he can hear this conversation. Just keep that in mind, will you? There's a good girl."

If anyone else had spoken to her like that they would have been nursing at least one interesting dislocation about two seconds later. But Khouri had long since learned to make allowances for Volyova.

"Where is he? Still on the same level as before?"

"Depends what you mean by 'him.' I suppose you could say his epicentre is still there, yes. But there's really very little point in distinguishing between him and the ship nowadays."

"Then he's everywhere? All around us?"

"All-seeing. All-knowing."

"I don't like this, Ilia."

"If it's any consolation, I very much doubt that he does either."

After many delays, reversals and diversions the elevator finally brought them to the bridge of *Nostalgia for Infinity*. To Khouri's considerable relief a consultation with the Captain did not seem to be imminent.

The bridge was much as she remembered it. The chamber was damaged and careworn, but most of the vandalism had been inflicted before the Captain changed. Khouri had even done some of it herself. Seeing the impact craters where her weapons discharges had fallen gave her a faint and mischievous sense of pride. She remembered the tense power-struggle that had taken place aboard the lighthugger when it was in orbit around the neutron star Hades, on the very edge of the present system.

It had been touch and go at times, but because they had survived she had dared to believe that a greater victory had been won. But the arrival of the Inhibitor machines suggested otherwise. The battle, in all likelihood, had already been lost before the first shots were fired. But they had at least bought themselves a little time. Now they had to do something with it.

Khouri settled into one of the seats facing the bridge's projection sphere. It had been repaired since the mutiny and now showed a real-time display of the Resurgam system. There were eleven major planets, but the display also showed their moons and the larger asteroids and comets—all were of potential importance. Their precise orbital positions were indicated, along with vectors showing the motion, prograde or retrograde, of the body in question. Pale cones radiating from the lighthugger showed the extent of the ship's instantaneous deep-sensor coverage, corrected for light-travel time. Volyova had strewn a handful of monitor drones on other orbits so that they could peer into blind spots and increase the interferometric baseline, but she used them cautiously.

"Ready for a recent-history lesson?" Volyova asked.

"You know I am, Ilia. I just hope this little jaunt turns out to be worth it, because I'm still going to have to answer some tricky questions when I get back to Cuvier."

"They may not seem so massively pressing when you've seen what I have to show you." She made the display zoom in, enlarging one of the moons spinning around the system's second-largest gas giant.

"This is where the Inhibitors have set up camp?" Khouri asked.

"Here and on two other worlds of comparable size. Their activities on each seem broadly the same."

Now dark shapes fluttered into view around the moon. They swarmed and scattered like agitated crows, their numbers and shapes in constant flux. In an instant they settled on to the surface of the moon, linking together in purposeful formations. The playback was evidently accelerated—hours compressed into seconds, perhaps—for transformations blistered across the moon's surface in a quick black inundation. Zoom-in showed a tendency for the structures to be formed of cubic subelements of widely differing sizes. Vast lasers pumped heat back into space as the transformations raged. Grotesque black machines the size of mountains clotted the landscape, ramping down the moon's albedo until only infra-red could tease out significant patterns.

"What are they doing?" Khouri asked.

"I couldn't tell at first."

One or two weeks had passed before what was taking place became clear. Dotted at regular intervals around the moon's equator were volcanic apertures, squat gape-mouthed machines that extended a hundredth of the moon's diameter into space. Without warning, they began to spew out rocky material in ballistic dust plumes. The matter was hot but not actually molten. It arced above the moon, falling into orbit. Another machine—Volyova had not noticed it until then—circled in the same orbit, processing the dust, shepherding, cooling and compactifying the plume. In its wake it left an organised ring system of processed and refined matter, gigatonnes of it in tidy lanes. Droves of smaller machines trailed behind like minnows, sucking in the pre-refined matter and subjecting it to even further purification.

"What's happening?"

"The machines seem to be dismantling the moon," Volyova said.

"That much I've figured out for myself. But it strikes me as a pretty cumbersome way of going about it. We've got crustbuster warheads that would do the same thing in a flash . . . "

"And in the process vaporise and disperse half of the moon's matter." Volyova nodded sagely. "I don't think that's quite what they wanted to do. I think they want all that matter, processed and refined as efficiently as possible. More, in fact, since they're ripping apart three moons. There's a lot of volatile material they won't be able to process into solids, not unless they're going to be doing some heavy-duty alchemy, but my guess is they'll still give themselves around a hundred billion billion tonnes of raw material."

"That's a lot of rubble."

"Yes. And it rather begs the question: what, precisely, do they need it for?"

"I suppose you've got a theory."

Ilia Volyova smiled. "Not much more than guesswork at this stage. The lunar dismantling's still in progress, but I think it's reasonably clear that they want to build something. And do you know what? I strongly suspect that whatever it is may not have our absolute best interests at heart."

"You think it's going to be a weapon, don't you?"

"Obviously I'm getting predictable in my old age. But yes, I rather fear a weapon is on the cards. What kind, I can't begin to guess. Clearly they could have already destroyed Resurgam if that was their immediate intention—and they wouldn't need to dismantle it neatly."

"Then they've got something else in mind."

"It would seem so."

"We've got to do something about it, Ilia. We've still got the cache. We could make some kind of difference, even now."

Volyova turned off the display sphere. "At the moment they seem not to be aware of our presence—we appear to fall beneath their detection threshold unless we're in the vicinity of Hades. Would you be willing to compromise that by using the cache weapons?"

"If I felt it was our last best hope, I might. So would you."

"I'm just saying there won't be any going back. We have to be completely clear about that." Volyova was silent for a moment. "There's something else as well . . . "

"Yes?"

She lowered her voice. "We can't control the cache, not without his help. The Captain will need to be persuaded."

Of course they did not call themselves the Inhibitors. They had never seen any reason to name themselves anything. They simply existed to perform a duty of astonishing importance, a duty vital to the future existence of intelligent life itself. They did not expect to be understood, or sympathised with, so any name—or any hint of justification—was entirely superfluous. Yet they were passingly aware that this was a name that they had been given, assigned to them after the glorious extinctions that had followed the Dawn War. Through a long, tenuous chain of recollection the name had been passed from species to species, even as those species were wiped from the face of the galaxy. The Inhibitors: those that Inhibit, those that suppress the emergence of intelligence.

The overseer recognised, ruefully, that the name was indeed an accurate description of its work.

It was difficult to say exactly where and when the work had begun. The Dawn War had been the first significant event in the history of the inhabited galaxy, a clashing of a million newly emergent cultures. These were the first starfaring species to arise, the players at the beginning of the game.

The Dawn War, ultimately, had been about a single precious resource.

It had been about metal.

She returned to Resurgam.

In Inquisition House there were questions to be answered.

She fielded them with as much insouciance as she could muster. She had been in the wilderness, she said, handling a highly sensitive field report from an agent who had stumbled on an exceptionally good lead. The trail to the Triumvir, she told her doubters, was hotter than it had been in years. To prove this she reactivated certain closed files and had old suspects invited back to Inquisition House for follow-up interviews. Inwardly, she felt sick at what had to be done to maintain the illusion of probity. Innocents had to be detained and made, for the sake of realism, to feel as if their lives, or at least their liberties, were in extreme jeopardy. It was a detestable business. Once she had sweetened it by making sure that she only terrorised people who were known to have evaded punishment for other crimes, revealed by judicious snooping of the files of rival government departments. It had worked for a time, but then even that had begun to seem morally questionable.

But now it was worse. She had doubters in the administration, and to silence their qualms she had to make her investigations unusually efficient and ruthless. There had to be plausible rumours circulating Cuvier of the degrees to which Inquisition House was prepared to go. People had to suffer for the sake of her cover.

She reassured herself that it was all, ultimately, in their best interests, that what she was doing was for the greater good of Resurgam; that a few terrified souls here and there were a small price to pay when set against the protection of an entire world.

She stood at the window of her office in Inquisition House, looking down towards the street, watching another guest being bundled into a blunt grey electric car. The man stumbled as the guards walked him to it. His head was covered and his hands were tied behind his back. The car would speed through the city until it reached a residential zone—it would be dusk by then—and the man would be dumped into the gutter a few blocks from his home.

His bonds would have been loosened, but the man would likely lie still on the ground for several minutes, breathing hard, gasping at the realisation that he had been released. Perhaps a gang of friends would find him as they made their way to a bar or back from the repair factories. They would not recognise him at first, for the beating he had taken would have swollen his face and made it difficult for him to talk. But when they did they would help the man back to his house, glancing warily over their shoulders in case the government agents who had dumped him were still abroad.

Or perhaps the man would find his own feet and, peering through the slits of bloodied, bruised eyelids, might somehow contrive to find his own way home. His wife would be waiting, perhaps more scared now than anyone in Cuvier. When her husband came home she would experience something of the same mingled relief and terror that he had experienced upon regaining consciousness. They would hold each other despite the pain that the man was in. Then she would examine his wounds and clean what could be cleaned. There would be no broken bones, but it would take a proper medical examination to be sure of that. The man would assume that he had been lucky, that the agents who had beaten him had been weary after a hard day in the interrogation cells.

Later, perhaps, he would hobble to the bar to meet his friends. Drinks would be bought and in some quiet corner he would show them the worst of the bruises. And word would spread that he had acquired them in Inquisition House. His friends would ask him how he could ever have fallen under suspicion of being involved with the Triumvir, and he would laugh and say that there was no stopping Inquisition House; not now. That anyone even remotely suspected of impeding the House's enquiries was fair game; that the pursuit of the criminal had been notched up to such an intensity that any misdemeanour against any government branch could be assumed to indicate tacit support for the Triumvir.

Khouri watched the car glide away and pick up speed. Now she could barely remember what the man had looked like. They all began to look the same after a while, the men and women blurring into one homogenous terrified whole. Tomorrow there would be more.

She looked above the buildings, into the bruise-coloured sky. She imagined the processes that she now knew were taking place beyond Resurgam's atmosphere. No more than one or two light-hours away, vast and implacable alien machinery was engaged in reducing three worlds to fine metallic dust. The machines seemed unhurried, unconcerned with doing things on a recognisably human timescale. They went about their business with the quiet calm of undertakers.

Khouri recalled what she had already learned of the Inhibitors, information vouchsafed to her after she had infiltrated Volyova's crew. There had been a war at the dawn of time, a war that had encompassed the entire galaxy and numerous cultures. In the desolate aftermath of that war, one species—or collective of species—had determined that intelligent life could no longer be tolerated. They had unleashed dark droves of machines whose only function was to watch and wait, vigilant for the signs of emergent starfaring cultures. They left traps dotted through space, glittery baubles designed to attract the unwise. The traps both alerted the Inhibitors to the presence of a new outbreak of intelligence and also served as psychological probing mechanisms, constructing a profile of the soon-to-be-culled fledglings.

The traps gauged the technological prowess of an emergent culture and suggested the manner in which they might attempt to counter the Inhibitor threat. For some reason that Khouri did not understand, and which had certainly never been explained to her, the response to the emergence of intelligence had to be proportionate; it was not enough simply to wipe out all life in the galaxy or even in a pocket of the galaxy. There was, she sensed, a deeper purpose to the Inhibitor culls that she did not yet grasp, and might not ever be capable of grasping.

And yet the machines were imperfect. They had begun to fail. It was nothing that could be detected over any timescale shorter than a few million years. Most species did not endure that long, so they saw only grim continuity. The only way that the decline could be observed was in the much longer term, evidenced not in the records of individual cultures but in the subtle differences between them. The ruthlessness quotient of the Inhibitors remained as high as ever, but their methods were becoming less efficient, their response times slower. Some profound and subtle flaw in the machines' design had worked its way to the surface. Now and then a culture slipped through the net, managing to spread into interstellar space before the Inhibitors could contain and cull it. The cull then became more difficult; less like surgery and more like butchery.

The Amarantin, the birdlike creatures who had lived on Resurgam a million years earlier, had been one such species. The effort to cleanse them had been protracted, allowing many of them to slip into various hidden sanctuaries. The last act of the culling machines had been to annihilate Resurgam's biosphere by triggering a catastrophic stellar flare. Delta Pavonis had since settled down to normal sunlike activity, but it was only now that Resurgam was beginning to support life again.

Their work done, the Inhibitors had vanished back into the stellar cold. Nine hundred and ninety thousand years passed.

Then humans came, drawn to the enigma of the vanished Amarantin culture. Their leader had been Sylveste, the ambitious scion of a wealthy Yellowstone family. By the time Khouri, Volyova and *Nostalgia for Infinity* arrived in the system, Sylveste had put in place his plans for exploring the neutron star on the system's edge, convinced that Hades had something to do with the Amarantin extinction. Sylveste had coerced the crew of the starship into helping him, using its cache of weapons to break through shells of defensive machinery and finally penetrating to the heart of a moon-sized artefact—they called it Cerberus—which orbited the neutron star.

Sylveste had been right all along about the Amarantin. But in verifying his theory he had also sprung a primed Inhibitor trap. At the heart of the Cerberus object, Sylveste had died in a massive matter-antimatter explosion.

And at the same time he had not died at all. Khouri knew; she had met and spoken to Sylveste after his "death." So far as she was capable of understanding it, Sylveste and his wife had been stored as simulations in the crust of the neutron star itself. Hades, it turned out, was one of the sanctuaries that the Amarantin had used when they were being harried by the Inhibitors. It was an element of something much older than either the Amarantin or the Inhibitors, a transcendent information storage and processing system, a vast archive. The Amarantin had found a way inside it, and so, much later, had Sylveste. That was as much as Khouri knew, and as much as she wanted to know.

She had met the stored Sylveste only once. In the more than sixty years that had passed since then—the time that Volyova had spent carefully infiltrating the very society that feared and loathed her—Khouri had allowed herself to forget that Sylveste was still out there, was still in some sense alive in the Hades computational matrix. On those rare occasions when she did think about him, she found herself wondering if he ever gave a moment's thought to the consequences of his actions all those years ago; if memories of the Inhibitors ever stirred him from vain dreams of his own brilliance. She doubted it, for Sylveste had not struck her as someone overly troubled by the results of his own deeds. And in any case, by Sylveste's accelerated reckoning, for time passed very rapidly in the Hades matrix, the events must have been centuries of subjective time in his past, as inconsequential as childhood misdeeds. Very little could touch him in there, so what was the point of worrying about him?

But that hardly helped those who were still outside the matrix. Khouri and Volyova had spent only twenty of those sixty-plus years out of reefersleep, for their infiltration scheme had been necessarily slow and episodic. But of those twenty years, Khouri doubted that a single day had passed when she had not thought of—and worried about—the prospect of the Inhibitors.

Now at least her worry had transmuted into certainty. They were here; the thing that she had dreaded had finally started.

And yet it was not to be a quick, brutal culling. Something titanic was being brought into existence, something that required the raw material of three entire worlds. For the time being the activities of the Inhibitors could not be detected from Resurgam, even with the tracking systems put in place to spot approaching lighthuggers. But Khouri doubted that this could continue to be the case. Sooner or later the activities of the alien machines would exceed some threshold and the citizenry would begin to glimpse strange apparitions in the sky.

Very likely, all hell would break loose.

But by then it might not even matter.

TEN

Xavier saw one ship detach itself from the bright flow of other vessels on the main approach corridor to Carousel New Copenhagen, tugged down his helmet's binoculars and swept space until he locked on to the ship itself. The image enlarged and stabilised, the spined pufferfish profile of *Storm Bird* rotating as the ship executed a slow turn. The Taurus IV salvage tug was still nosing against its hull, like a parasite looking for one last nibble.

Xavier blinked hard, requesting a higher magnification zoom. The image swelled, wobbled and then sharpened.

"Dear God," he whispered. "What the hell have you done to my ship?"

Something awful had happened to his beloved *Storm Bird* since the last time he had seen it. Whole parts were gone, ripped clean away. The hull looked as if it had seen its last service some time during the *Belle Époque,* not a couple of months ago. He wondered where Antoinette had taken it—straight into the heart of Lascaille's Shroud, perhaps? Either that or she had had a serious run-in with well-armed banshees.

"It's not your ship, Xavier. I just pay you to look after it now and then. If I want to trash it, that's entirely my business."

"Shit." He had forgotten that the suit-to-ship comm channel was still open. "I didn't mean . . . "

"It's a lot worse than it looks, Xave. Trust me on that."

The salvage tug detached at the last minute, executed a needlessly complex pirouette and then was gone, curving away to its home on the other side of Carousel New Copenhagen. Xavier had already calculated how much the salvage tug was going to cost in the end. It didn't matter who ultimately picked up that tab. It was going to be one hell of a sting, whether it was him or Antoinette, since their businesses were so intertwined. They were well into the red at the favour bank, and it was going to take about a year of retroactive favours before they groped their way back into the black . . .

But things could have been worse. Three days ago he had more or less given up hope of ever seeing Antoinette again. It was depressing how quickly the elation at finding her alive had degenerated into his usual nagging worries about insolvency. Dumping that hauler certainly hadn't helped . . .

Xavier grinned. But hell, it had been worth it.

When she had announced her approach Xavier had suited up, gone out on to the carousel's skin and hired a skeletal thruster trike. He gunned the trike across the fifteen kilometres to *Storm Bird,* then orbited it around the ship, satisfying himself that the damage looked every bit as bad up close as he had first thought it was. None of it would cripple the ship for good; it was all technically fixable—but it would cost money to put right.

He swung around, bringing the trike forwards so that he was ahead of *Storm Bird*. Against the dark hull he saw the two bright parallel slits of the cabin windows. Antoinette was a tiny silhouetted figure in the uppermost cabin, the small bridge that she only used during delicate docking/undocking procedures. She was reaching up to work controls above her head, a clipboard tucked under one arm. She looked so small and vulnerable that all his anger drained out of him in an instant. Instead of worrying about the damage, he should have been rejoicing that the ship had kept her alive all this time.

"You're right; it's superficial," he said. "We'll get it fixed easily enough. Do you have enough thruster control to do a hard docking?"

"Just point me to the bay, Xave."

He nodded and flipped the trike over, arcing away from *Storm Bird*. "Follow me in, then."

Carousel New Copenhagen loomed larger again. Xavier led *Storm Bird* around the rim, tapping the trike's thrusters until he had matched rotation with the carousel, sustaining the pseudo-orbit with a steady rumble of power from the trike's belly. They passed over a complex of smaller bays, repair wells lit up with golden or blue lights and the periodic flashes of welding tools. A rim train snaked past, overtaking them, and then he saw *Storm Bird*'s shadow blot out his own. He looked back and behind. The freighter was coming in nice and steadily, although it looked as large as an iceberg.

The huge shadow slid and dipped, flowing over the hemispherical gouge in the rim known locally as Lyle's Crater, the impact point where the rogue trader's chemical-drive scow had collided with the carousel while trying to evade the authorities. It was the only serious damage that the carousel had sustained during wartime, and while it could have been repaired easily enough, it now made far more money as a tourist attraction than it would ever have had it been reclaimed and returned to normal use. People came in shuttles from all around the Rust Belt to gape at the damage and hear stories of the deaths and heroics that had followed the incident. Even now, Xavier saw a party of ghouls being led out on to the skin by a tourist guide, all of them hanging by harnesses from a network of lines spidering across the underside of the rim. Since he knew several people who had died during the accident, Xavier felt only contempt for the ghouls.

His repair well was a little further around the rim. It was the second largest on the carousel and it still looked as if it would be an impossibly tight fit, even allowing for all the bits of *Storm Bird* that Antoinette had helpfully removed . . .

The iceberg-sized ship came to a halt relative to the carousel and then tipped up, nose down to the rim. Through the gouts of vapour coming from the carousel's industrial vents and the ship's own popping micro-gee verniers, Xavier saw a loom of red lasers embrace *Storm Bird,* marking her position and velocity with ångström precision. Still applying a half-gee of thrust from its main motors, *Storm Bird* began to push itself into its allocated slot in the rim. Xavier held station, wanting to close his eyes, for this was the part that he dreaded.

The ship nosed in at a speed of no more than four or five centimetres per second. Xavier waited until the nose had vanished into the carousel, still leaving three-quarters of the ship out in space, and then guided his trike alongside, slipping ahead of *Storm Bird*. He parked the trike on a ledge, disembarked and authorised the trike to return to the place where he had hired it. He watched the skeletal thing buzz away, streaking back out into open space.

He did close his eyes now, hating the final docking procedure, and only opened them again after he had felt the rapid thunder of the docking latches, transmitted through the fabric of the repair bay to his feet. Below *Storm Bird,* pressure doors began to close. If she was going to be stuck here for a while, and it looked as if she would, they might even consider pumping the chamber so that Xavier's repair monkeys could work without suits. But that was something to worry about later.

Xavier made sure that the pressurised connecting walkways were aligned with and clamped to *Storm Bird*'s main locks, guiding them manually. Then he made his way to an airlock, passing out of the repair bay. He was in a hurry, so did not bother removing more than his gloves and helmet. He could feel his heart in his chest, knocking like an air pump that needed a new armature.

Xavier walked down the connecting tube to the airlock closest to the flight deck. Lights were pulsing at the end of the tube, indicating that the lock was already being cycled.

Antoinette was coming through.

Xavier stooped and placed his helmet and gloves on the floor. He started running down the tube, slowly at first and then with increasing energy. The airlock door was irising open with glorious slowness, condensation heaving out of it in thick white clouds. The corridor dilated ahead of him, time crawling the way it did when two lovers were running towards each other in a bad holo-romance.

The door opened. Antoinette was standing there, suited-up but for her helmet, which she cradled beneath one arm. Her blunt-cut blonde hair was dishevelled and plastered across her forehead with grease and filth, her skin was sallow and there were dark bags under her eyes. Her eyes were tired, bloodshot slits. Even from where Xavier was standing, she smelt as if she hadn't been near a shower in weeks.

He didn't care. He thought she still looked pretty great. He pulled her towards him, the tabards of their suits clanging together. Somehow he managed to kiss her.

"I'm glad you're home," Xavier said.

"Glad to be home," Antoinette replied.

"Did you . . . ?"

"Yes," she said. "I managed it."

He said nothing for several moments, desperately wishing not to trivialise what she had done, fully aware of how important it had been to her and that nothing must spoil that triumph.

She had been through enough pain already; the last thing he wanted to do was add to it.

"I'm proud of you."

"Hey. *I'm* proud of me. You bloody well should be."

"Count on it. I take it there were a few difficulties, though?"

"Let's just say I had to get into Tangerine's atmosphere a bit faster than I'd planned."

"Zombies?"

"Zombies *and* spiders."

"Hey, two for the price of one. But I don't imagine that's quite how you saw it. And how the hell did you get back if there were spiders out there?"

She sighed. "It's a long story, Xave. Some strange shit happened around that gas giant and I'm still not quite sure what to make of it."

"So tell me."

"I will. After we've eaten."

"Eaten?"

"Yeah." Antoinette Bax grinned, revealing filthy teeth. "I'm hungry, Xave. And thirsty. Really thirsty. Have you ever had anyone drink you under a table?"

Xavier Liu considered her question. "I don't think so, no."

"Well, now's your big chance."

They undressed, made love, lay together for an hour, showered, dressed—Antoinette wearing her best plum-coloured jacket—went out, ate well and then got royally drunk. Antoinette enjoyed nearly every minute of it. She enjoyed every instant of the lovemaking; that wasn't the problem. It was good to be clean, too—really clean, rather than the kind of grudging clean that was the best she could manage on the ship—and it was good to be back in some kind of gravity, even if it was only half a gee and even if it was centrifugal. No, the problem was that wherever she looked, whatever was happening around her, she couldn't help thinking that none of it was going to last.

The spiders were going to win the war. They would take over the entire system, the Rust Belt included. They might not turn everyone into hive-mind conscripts—they had more or less promised that that was the last thing they intended—but you could guarantee things were going to be different. Yellowstone had not exactly been a barrel of laughs under the last brief spider occupation. It was difficult to see where the daughter of a space pilot, with a single damaged, creaking ship to her name, was going to be able to fit in.

But hell, she thought, cajoling herself into a state of forced *bonhomie,* it wasn't going to happen *tonight,* was it?

They travelled by rim train. She wanted to eat at the bar under Lyle's Crater where the beer was great, but Xavier told her it would be heaving at this time of day and they were much better off going somewhere else. She shrugged, accepting his judgement, and was mildly puzzled when they arrived at Xavier's choice—a bar halfway around the rim called Robotnik's—and found the place nearly empty. When Antoinette synchronised her watch with Yellowstone Local Time she understood why: it was two hours past thirteen, in the middle of the afternoon. It was the graveyard shift on Carousel New Copenhagen, which saw most of its serious partying during the hours of Chasm City "night."

"We wouldn't have had any trouble getting into Lyle's," she told him.

"I don't really like that place."

"Ah."

"Too many damned animals. When you work with monkeys all day . . . or *not,* as the case may be . . . being served by machines begins to seem like a bloody good idea."

She nodded at him over the top of her menu. "Fair enough."

The gimmick at Robotnik's was that the staff were all servitors. It was one of the few places in the carousel, barring the heavy-industrial repair shops, where you saw any kind of machines doing manual labour. Even then the machines were ancient and clapped-out, the kind of cheap, rugged servitors that had always been immune to the plague, and which could still be manufactured despite the system's much reduced industrial capability in the wake of the plague and the war. There was a certain antique charm to them, Antoinette supposed, but by the time she had watched one limping machine drop their beers four times between the bar and their table, the charm had begun to wear a little thin.

"You don't actually like this place, do you?" she asked later. "It's just that you like Lyle's even less."

"You ask me, there's something a tiny bit sick about that place, turning a major civic catastrophe into a bloody tourist attraction."

"Dad would probably have agreed with you."

Xavier grunted something unintelligible. "So what happened with the spiders, anyway?"

Antoinette began picking the label off her beer bottle, just the way she had all those years ago when her father had first mentioned his preferred mode of burial. "I don't really know."

Xavier wiped foam from his lip. "Have a wild stab in the dark."

"I got into trouble. It was all going nicely—I was making a slow, controlled approach to Tangerine Dream—and then *wham*." She picked up a beer mat and stabbed a finger at it by way of explanation. "I've got a zombie ship dead ahead of me, about to hit the atmosphere itself. I painted it with my radar by mistake and got a bunch of attitude from the zombie pilot."

"But she didn't chuck a missile at you by way of thanks?"

"No. She must have been all out, or she didn't want to make things worse by revealing her position with a tube launch. See, the reason she was doing the big dive—the same as me—was that she had a spider ship chasing *her*."

"That wasn't good," Xavier said.

"No, not good at all. That's why I had to get into the atmosphere so quickly. Fuck the safeguards, let's get down there. Beast obliged, but there was a lot of damage on the way in."

"If it was that or get captured by the spiders, I'd say you did the right thing. I take it you waited down there until the spiders had passed on?"

"Not exactly, no."

"Antoinette . . . " Xavier chided.

"Hey, listen. Once I'd buried my father, that was the last place I wanted to hang around. And Beast wasn't enjoying it one bit. The ship wanted out as much as I did. Problem is, we got tokamak failure on the up and out."

"You were dead meat."

"We should have been," Antoinette said, nodding. "Especially as the spiders were still nearby."

Xavier leant back in his chair and swigged an inch of beer. Now that he had her safe, now that he knew how things had turned out, he was obviously enjoying hearing the story. "So what happened—did you get the tokamak to reboot?"

"Later, yes, when we were back in empty space. It lasted

long enough to get me back to Yellowstone, but I needed the tugs for the slow-down."

"So you managed to reach escape velocity, or were you still able to insert into orbit?"

"Neither, Xave. We were falling back to the planet. So I did the only thing I could, which was ask for help." She finished her own beer, watching his reaction.

"Help?"

"From the spiders."

"No shit? You had the nerve—the balls—to do that?"

"I'm not sure about the balls, Xave. But yes, I guess I had the nerve." She grinned. "Hell, what else was I going to do? Sit there and die? From my point of view, with a fuck of a lot of cloud coming up real fast, being conscripted into a hive mind suddenly didn't seem like the worst thing in the world."

"I still can't believe . . . even after that dream you've been replaying?"

"I figured that had to be propaganda. The truth couldn't be *quite* that bad."

"But maybe nearly as bad."

"When you're about to die, Xave, you take what you can get."

He pointed the open neck of the beer bottle at her. "But . . . "

She read his mind. "I'm still here, yeah. I'm glad you noticed."

"What happened?"

"They saved me." She said it again, almost having to reassure herself that it had really happened. "The spiders saved me. Sent down some kind of drone missile, or tug, or whatever it was. The thing clamped on to the hull and gave me a shove—a big shove—all the way out of Tangerine Dream's gravity well. Next thing I knew I was falling back to Yellowstone. Had to get the tokamak up and running, but at least now I had more than a few minutes to do it in."

"And the spiders . . . they left?"

She nodded vigorously. "Their main guy, this old geezer, he spoke to me just before they sent the drone. Gave me one hell of a warning, I admit. Said if we ever crossed paths again—like, *ever*—he'd kill me. I think he meant it, too."

"I suppose you have to count yourself lucky. I mean, not

everyone gets let off with a warning where the spiders are concerned."

"I guess so, Xave."

"This old man—the spider—anyone we'd have heard of?"

She shook her head. "Said his name was Clavain, that's all. Didn't mean shit to me."

"Not *the* Clavain, obviously?"

She stopped fiddling with the beer mat and looked at him. "And who would *the* Clavain be, Xave?"

He looked at her as if she was faintly stupid, or at the very least worryingly forgetful. "History, Antoinette, that boring stuff about the past. You know—before the Melding Plague, all that jazz?"

"I wasn't born then, Xave. It's not even of academic interest to me." She held her bottle up to the light. "I need another one. What are the chances of getting it in the next hour, do you think?"

Xavier clicked a finger at the nearest servitor. The machine spun around, stiffened itself, took a step in their direction and fell over.

But when she was back at their place, Antoinette began to wonder. In the evening, when she had blasted away the worst effects of the beer, leaving her head clear but ringingly delicate, she squirrelled herself into Xavier's office, powered up the museum-piece terminal and set about querying the carousel's data hub for information on Clavain. She had to admit that she was curious now, but even if she had been curious during the journey home from the gas giant she would have had to wait until now to access any extensive systemwide archives. It would have been too risky to send a query from *Storm Bird,* and the ship's own memories were not the most compendious.

Antoinette had never known anything except a post-plague environment, so she had no expectations of actually finding any useful information, even if the data she was looking for might once have existed. The system's data networks had been rebuilt almost from scratch during the post-plague years, and much that had been archived before then had been corrupted or erased during the crisis.

But to her surprise there was rather a lot out there about Clavain, or at least about *a* Clavain. The famous Clavain, the one that Xavier had known about, had been born on Earth way back in the twenty-second century, in one of the last perfect summers before the glaciers rolled in and the place became a pristine snowball. He had gone to Mars and fought against the Conjoiners in their earliest incarnation. Antoinette read that again and frowned: *against* the Conjoiners? But she read on.

Clavain had gained notoriety during his Martian days. They called him the Butcher of Tharsis, the man who had turned the course of the Battle of the Bulge. He had authorised the use of red-mercury, nuclear and foam-phase weapons against spider forces, gouging glassy kilometre-wide craters across the face of Mars. In some accounts his deeds made him an automatic war criminal. Yet according to some of the less partisan reports, Clavain's actions could be interpreted as having saved many millions of lives, both spider and allied, that would otherwise have been lost in a protracted ground campaign. Equally, there were reports of his heroism: of Clavain saving the lives of trapped soldiers and civilians; of him sustaining many injuries, recovering and going straight back to the front line. He had been there when the spiders brought down the aerial docking tower at Chryse, and had been pinned in the rubble for eighteen days with no food or water except the supplies in his skinsuit. When they pulled him out they found him clutching a cat that had also been trapped in the ruins, its spine snapped by masonry and yet still alive, nourished by portions from Clavain's own rations. The cat died a week later. It took Clavain three months to recover.

But that hadn't been the end of his career. He had been captured by the spider queen, the woman called Galiana who had created the whole spider mess in the first place. For months Galiana had held him prisoner, finally releasing him when the cease-fire was negotiated. Thereafter, there had always been a weird bond between the two former adversaries. When the uneasy peace had begun to crumble, it had been Clavain who went down to try to iron things out with the spider queen. And it was on that mission that he was presumed to have "defected," throwing in his lot with the Conjoiners, accepting their remodelling machines into his skull and becoming one of the hive-mind spiders.

And that was when Clavain more or less dropped out of history. Antoinette skimmed the remaining records and found numerous anecdotal reports of him popping up here and there over the next four-hundred-odd years. It was possible; she could not deny that. Clavain had been getting on a bit before he defected, but with freezing and the time dilation that naturally accompanied any amount of star travel, he might not have lived through more than a few decades of those four centuries. And that was not even allowing for the kind of rejuvenation therapies that had been possible before the plague. No, it *could* have been Clavain—but it could equally well have been someone else with the same name. What were the chances of Antoinette Bax's life intersecting with that of a major historical figure? Things like that just didn't happen to her.

Something disturbed her. There was a commotion outside the office, the sound of things toppling and scraping, Xavier's voice raised in protest. Antoinette killed the terminal and went outside.

What she found made her gasp. Xavier was up against one wall, his feet an inch from the floor. He was pinned there—painfully, she judged—by one manipulator of a multi-armed gloss-black police proxy. The machine—again it made her think of a nightmarish collision of pairs of huge black scissors—had barged into the office, knocking over cabinets and potted plants.

She looked at the proxy. Although they all appeared to be more or less identical, she just knew this was the same one, being slaved by the same pilot, that had come to pay her visit aboard *Storm Bird.*

"Fuck," Antoinette said.

"Miss Bax." The machine lowered Xavier to the ground, none too gently. Xavier coughed, winded, rubbing a raw spot beneath his throat. He tried to speak, but all that came out was a series of hoarse hacking vowels.

"Mr. Liu was impeding me in the course of my inquiries," the proxy said.

Xavier coughed again. "I . . . just . . . didn't get out of the way fast enough."

"Are you all right, Xave?" Antoinette asked

"I'm all right," he said, regaining some of the colour he had lost a moment earlier. He turned to the machine, which was occupying most of the office, flicking things over and examining other things with its multitude of limbs. "What the fuck do you want?"

"Answers, Mr. Liu. Answers to exactly the questions that were troubling me upon my last visit."

Antoinette glared at the machine. "This fucker paid you a visit while I was away?"

The machine answered her. "I most certainly did, Miss Bax—seeing as you were so unforthcoming, I felt it necessary."

Xavier looked at Antoinette.

"He boarded *Storm Bird,*" she confirmed

"And?"

The proxy overturned a filing cabinet, rummaging with bored intent through the spilled paperwork. "Miss Bax showed me that she was carrying a passenger in a reefersleep casket. Her story, which was verified by Hospice Idlewild, was that there had been some kind of administrative confusion, and that the body was in the process of being returned to the Hospice."

Antoinette shrugged, knowing she was going to have to bluff this one out. "So?"

"The body was already dead. And you never arrived at the Hospice. You steered for interplanetary space shortly after I departed."

"Why would I have done that?"

"That, Miss Bax, is precisely what I would like to know." The proxy abandoned the paperwork, kicking the cabinet aside with a whining flick of one sharp-edged piston-driven limb. "I asked Mr. Liu, and he was no help at all. Were you, Mr. Liu?"

"I told you what I knew."

"Perhaps I should take a special interest in you too, Mr. Liu—what do you think? You have a very interesting past, judging by police records. You knew James Bax very well, didn't you?"

Xavier shrugged. "Who didn't?"

"You worked for him. That implies a more than passing knowledge of the man, wouldn't you say?"

"We had a business arrangement. I fixed his ship. I fix a lot of ships. It didn't mean we were married."

"But you were undoubtedly aware that James Bax was a figure of concern to us, Mr. Liu. A man not overly bothered about matters of right and wrong. A man not greatly troubled by anything so inconsequential as the law."

"How was he to know?" Xavier argued. "You fuckers make the law up as you go along."

The proxy moved with blinding speed, becoming a whirling black blur. Antoinette felt the breeze as it moved. The next thing she knew it had Xavier pinned to the wall again, higher this time, and with what looked like a good deal more force. He was choking, clawing at the machine's manipulators in a desperate effort to free himself.

"Did you know, Mr. Liu, that the Merrick case has never been satisfactorily closed?"

Xavier couldn't answer.

"The Merrick case?" Antoinette asked.

"Lyle Merrick," the proxy replied. "You know the fellow. A trader, like your father. On the wrong side of the law."

"Lyle Merrick died . . . "

Xavier was beginning to turn blue.

"But the case has never been closed, Miss Bax. There have always been a number of loose ends. What do you know of the Mandelstam Ruling?"

"Another one of your fucking new laws, by any chance?"

The machine let Xavier fall to the floor. He was unconscious. She hoped he was unconscious.

"Your father knew Lyle Merrick, Miss Bax. Xavier Liu knew your father. Mr. Liu almost certainly knew Lyle Merrick. What with that and your propensity for ferrying dead bodies into the war zone for no logical reason that we can think of, it's hardly any wonder that you two are of such interest to us, is it?"

"If you touch Xavier one more time . . . "

"What, Miss Bax?"

"I'll . . . "

"You'll do nothing. You're powerless here. There aren't even any security cameras or mites in this room. I know. I checked first."

"Fucker."

The machine edged closer to her. "Of course, you could be carrying some form of concealed device, I suppose."

Antoinette pressed herself back against one wall of the office. "What?"

The proxy extended a manipulator. She squeezed back even

further, sucking in her breath, but it was no good. The proxy stroked its manipulator down the side of her face gently enough, but she was horribly aware of the damage it could do should the machine wish it. Then the manipulator caressed her neck and moved down, lingering over her breasts.

"You . . . fucker."

"I think you might be carrying a weapon, or drugs." There was a blur of metal, the same vile breeze. She flinched, but it was over in an instant. The proxy had torn her jacket off; her favourite plum jacket was ripped to shreds. Underneath she wore a tight black sleeveless vest with equipment pockets. She wriggled and swore, but the machine still held her tightly. It drew shapes on the vest, tugging it away from her skin.

"I have to be sure, Miss Bax."

She thought of the pilot, surgically inserted into a steel canister somewhere in the belly of the police cutter that had to be parked nearby, little more than a central nervous system and a few tedious add-ons.

"You sick fuck."

"I am only being . . . *thorough,* Miss Bax."

There was a crash and a clatter behind the machine. The proxy froze. Antoinette held her breath, just as puzzled. She wondered if the pilot had notified more proxies of the fun that was to be had.

The machine edged back from her and spun around very slowly. It faced a wall of shocking orange-brown and rippling black. By Antoinette's estimate there were at least a dozen of them, six or seven orang-utans and about the same number of enhanced silverback gorillas. They had all been augmented for full bipedality and they were all carrying makeshift—in some cases not so makeshift—weapons.

The main silverback had a comically huge wrench in its hands. When it spoke its voice was almost pure subsonics, something Antoinette felt more in her stomach than heard. "Let her go."

The proxy weighed its chances. Very probably it could have taken out all of the hyperprimates. It had tasers and glue-guns and other nasties. But there would have been a great deal of mess and a great deal of explaining to be done, and no guarantee that the proxy would not sustain a certain amount of damage before it had all the primates either pacified or dead.

It was not worth the bother, especially not when there were such powerful unions and political lobbies behind most of the hyperprimate species. The Ferrisville Convention would find it a lot harder to explain the death of a gorilla or orang-utan than a human, especially in Carousel New Copenhagen.

The proxy retreated, tucking most of its limbs away. For a moment the wall of hyperprimates refused to allow it to leave and Antoinette feared that there was going to be bloodshed. But her rescuers only wanted to make their point.

The wall parted; the proxy scuttled out.

Antoinette let out a sigh. She wanted to thank the hyperprimates, but her first and most immediate concern was for Xavier. She knelt down by him and touched the side of his neck. She felt hot animal breath on hers.

"He all right?"

She looked into the magnificent face of the silverback; it was like something carved from coal. "I think so. How did you know?"

The superbly low voice rumbled, "Xavier push panic button. We come."

"Thank you."

The silverback stood up, towering over her. "We like Xavier. Xavier treat us good."

Later, she inspected the remains of her jacket. Her father had given it to her on her seventeenth birthday. It had always been a little small for her—when she wore it, it looked more like a matador's jacket—but despite that it had always been her favourite, and she always felt she had made it look right. Now it was ruined beyond any hope of repair.

When the primates had gone, and when Xavier was back on his feet, shaken but basically unharmed, they did what they could to tidy up the mess. It took several hours, most of which were spent putting the paperwork back into order. Xavier had always been meticulous about his book-keeping; even as the company slid towards bankruptcy, he said, he was damned if he was going to give the money-grabbing creditor bastards any more ammunition than they already had.

By midnight the place looked respectable again. But Antoinette knew it was not over. The proxy was going to come back, and next time it would make sure there would be no primate rescue party. Even if the proxy never did get to the bottom of what she had been doing in the war zone, there would be a thousand ways that the authorities could put her out of business. The proxy could have impounded *Storm Bird* already. All the proxy was doing, and she had to keep reminding herself that there was a human pilot behind it, was playing with her, making her life a misery of worry while giving itself, or himself, something amusing to do when it wasn't harassing someone else.

She thought of asking Xavier why it was taking such an interest in her father's associates, most specifically the Lyle Merrick case, but then she decided to put the whole thing out of her mind, at least until the morning.

Xavier went out and bought a couple more beers, and they finished them off while they were putting the last few items of furniture back into place.

"Things will work out, Antoinette," he said.

"You're certain of that?"

"You deserve it," he said. "You're a good person. All you ever wanted to do was honour your father's wishes."

"So why do I feel like such an idiot?"

"You shouldn't," he said, and kissed her.

They made love again—it felt like days since the last time—and then Antoinette fell asleep, sinking through layers of increasingly vague anxiety until she reached unconsciousness. And then the Demarchist propaganda dream began to take over: the one where she was on a liner that was raided by spiders; the one where she was taken to their cometary base and surgically prepared for induction into their hive mind.

But there was a difference this time. When the Conjoiners came to open her skull and sink their machines into it, the one who leant over her pulled down a white surgical mask to reveal the face she now recognised from the history texts, from the most recent anecdotal sightings. It was the face of a white-haired, bearded old patriarch, lined and characterful, sad and jolly at the same time, a face that might, under any other circumstances, have seemed kind and wise and grandfatherly.

It was the face of Nevil Clavain.

"I told you not to cross my path again," he said.

The Mother Nest was a light-minute behind him when Clavain instructed the corvette to flip over and commence its deceleration burn, following the navigational data that Skade had given him. The starscape wheeled like something geared by well-oiled clockwork, shadows and pale highlights oozing over Clavain and the recumbent forms of his two passengers. A corvette was the nimblest vessel in the Conjoiner in-system fleet, but cramming three occupants into the hull resembled a mathematical exercise in optimal packing. Clavain was webbed into the pilot's position, with tactile controls and visual read-outs within easy reach. The ship could be flown without blinking an eyelid, but it was also designed to withstand the kind of cybernetic assault that might impair routine neural commands. Clavain flew it via tactile control in any case, though he had barely moved a finger in hours. Tactical summaries jostled his visual field, competing for attention, but there had been no hint of enemy activity within six light-hours.

Immediately to his rear, with their knees parallel to his shoulders, lay Remontoire and Skade. They were slotted into human-shaped spaces between the inner surfaces of weapons pods or fuel blisters and, like Clavain, they wore lightweight spacesuits. The black armoured surfaces of the suits reduced them to abstract extensions of the corvette's interior. There was barely room for the suits, but there was even less room to put them on.

Skade?

[Yes, Clavain?]

I think it's safe to tell me where we're headed now, isn't it?

[Just follow the flight plan and we'll arrive there in good time. The Master of Works will be expecting us.]

Master of Works? Anyone I've met? He caught the sly curve of Skade's smile, reflected in the corvette's window.

[You'll soon have the pleasure, Clavain.]

He didn't need to be told that wherever they were going was still in the same part of the cometary halo that contained the Mother Nest. There was nothing out here but vacuum and comets, and even the comets were scarce. The Conjoiners had turned some comets into decoys to lure in the enemy, and had placed sensors, booby-traps and jamming systems on others, but he was not aware of any such activities taking place so close to home.

He tapped into systemwide newsfeeds as they flew. Only the most partisan enemy agencies pretended that there was any chance of a Demarchist victory now. Most of them were talking openly of defeat, though it was always worded in more ambiguous terms: *cessation of hostilities; concession to some enemy demands; reopening of negotiations with the Conjoiners* . . . the litany went on and on, but it was not difficult to read between the lines.

Attacks against Conjoiner assets had grown less and less frequent, with a commensurately dwindling success rate. Now the enemy was concentrating on protecting its own bases and strongholds, and even there they were failing. Most of the bases needed to be resupplied with provisions and armaments from the main production centres, which meant convoys of robot craft strung out on long, lonely trajectories across the system. The Conjoiners picked them off with ease; it was not even worth capturing their cargoes. The Demarchists had launched crash programmes to recover some of the expertise in nanofabrication they had enjoyed before the Melding Plague, but the rumours coming out of their war labs hinted at grisly failures; of whole research teams turned into grey slurry by runaway replicators. It was like the twenty-first century all over again.

And the more desperate they got, the worse the failures became.

Conjoiner occupation forces had successfully seized a number of outlying settlements and quickly established puppet regimes, enabling day-to-day life to continue much as it had before. They had not so far embarked on mass neural conversion programmes, but their critics said it would only be a matter of time before the populaces were subjugated by Conjoiner implants, enslaved into their crushingly uniform hive mind. Resistance groups had made several damaging strikes against Conjoiner power in those puppet states, with loose alliances of Skyjacks, pigs, banshees and other systemwide ne'er-do-wells banding together against the new authority. All they were doing, Clavain thought, was hastening the likelihood that some form of neural conscription would have to take place, if only for the public good.

But so far Yellowstone and its immediate environs—the Rust Belt, the high-orbit habitats and carousels and the starship parking swarms—had not been contested. The Ferrisville Convention, though it had its own problems, was still maintaining a façade of control. It had long suited both sides to have a neutral zone, a place where spies could exchange information and where covert agents from both sides could mingle with third parties and sweet-talk possible collaborators, sympathisers or defectors. Some said that even this was only a temporary state of affairs; that the Conjoiners would not stop at occupying most of the system; they had held Yellowstone for a few short decades and would not throw away a chance to claim her for good. Their earlier occupation had been a pragmatic intervention at the invitation of the Demarchists, but the second would be an exercise in totalitarian control like nothing history had seen for centuries.

So it was said. But what if even that was a hopelessly optimistic forecast?

Skade had told him that the signals from the lost weapons had been detected more than thirty years earlier. The memories he had been given and the data he now had access to confirmed her story. But there was no explanation for why the recovery of the weapons had suddenly become a matter of vital urgency to the Mother Nest. Skade had said that the war had made it difficult to stage an attempt any sooner than now, but that was surely only part of the truth. There had to be something else: a crisis, or the threat of a crisis, which made the recovery of the weapons vastly more important than it had been before. Something had scared the Inner Sanctum.

Clavain wondered if Skade—and by implication the Inner Sanctum—knew something about the wolves that he had yet to be told. Since Galiana's return, the wolves had been classified as a disturbing but distant threat, something to worry about only when humankind began to push deeper into interstellar space. But what if some new intelligence had been received? What if the wolves were closer?

He wanted to dismiss the idea, but found himself unable to do so. For the remainder of the trip his thoughts circled like vultures, examining the idea from every angle, mentally stripping it to the bone. It was only when Skade again pushed her thoughts into his head that he forced himself to bury his internal enquiries beneath conscious thought.

[We're nearly there, Clavain. You appreciate that none of what you see here can be shared with the rest of the Mother Nest?]

Of course. I hope you were discreet about whatever you were doing out here. If you'd drawn the enemy's attention you could have compromised everything.

[But we didn't, Clavain.]

That's not the point. There weren't supposed to be any operations within ten light-hours of—

[Listen, Clavain.] She leaned forwards from the tight confines of her seat, the restraint webbing taut against the black curves of her spacesuit. [There's something you need to grasp: the war isn't our main concern any more. We're going to win it.]

Don't underestimate the Demarchists.

[Oh, I won't. But we must keep them in perspective. The only serious issue now is the recovery of the hell-class weapons.]

Does it have to be recovery? Or would you settle for destruction? Clavain watched her reaction carefully. Even after his admittance to the Closed Council Skade's mind was closed to him.

[Destruction, Clavain? Why on Earth would we want to destroy them?]

You told me that your main objective was to stop them from falling into the wrong hands.

[That remains the case, yes.]

So you'd allow them to be destroyed? That would achieve the same end, wouldn't it? And I imagine it'd be very much easier from a logistical point of view.

[Recovery is our preferred outcome.]

Preferred?

[Very much preferred, Clavain.]

Presently, the corvette's motors burned harder. Barely visible, a dark cometary husk hoved out of the darkness. The ship's forward floods glanced across its surface, hunting and questing. The comet spun slowly, more rapidly than the Mother Nest but still within reasonable limits. Clavain judged the size of the filthy snowball to be perhaps seven or eight kilometers across—an order of magnitude smaller than home. It could easily have been hidden within the Mother Nest's hollowed-out core.

The corvette hovered close to the frothy black surface of the comet, arresting its drift with stuttering spikes of violet-flamed thrust before firing anchoring grapples. They slammed into the ground, piercing the nearly invisible epoxy skein that had been thrown around the comet for structural reinforcement.

You've been busy little beavers. How many people have you got here, Skade, doing whatever it is they do?

[No one. Only a handful of us have ever visited here, and no one ever stays permanently. All activities have been totally automated. Periodically a Closed Council operative arrives to check on things, but for the most part the servitors have worked unsupervised.]

Servitors aren't that clever.

[Ours are.]

Clavain, Remontoire and Skade donned helmets and left the corvette via its surface lock, jumping across several metres of space until they collided with the reinforcement membrane. It caught them like flies on glue paper, springing back and forth until their impact energy was damped away. When the membrane had ceased its oscillations Clavain gently ripped his arm away from the adhesive surface and then levered himself into a standing position. The adhesive was sophisticated enough to yield to normal motions, but it would remain sticky against any action sufficiently violent to send someone away from the comet at escape velocity. Similarly, the membrane was rigid under normal forces, but would deform elastically if something impacted it at more than a few metres per second. Walking was possible provided it was done reasonably slowly, but anything more vigorous would result in the subject becoming embroiled and immobilised until they relaxed.

Skade, whose crested helmet made her difficult to mistake, led the way, following what must have been a suit homing trace. After five minutes of progress they arrived at a modest depression in the comet's surface. Clavain discerned a black entrance hole at the depression's lowest point, almost lost against the sooty blackness of the comet's surface. There was a circular gap in the membrane, protected by a ring-shaped collar.

Skade knelt by the blackness, the adhesive gripping her knees via oozing capillary flow. She knocked the rim of the collar twice and then waited. After perhaps a minute a servitor bustled from the darkness, unfolding a plethora of jointed legs and appendages as it cleared the tight restriction of the collar. The machine resembled a belligerent iron grasshopper. Clavain recognised it as a general construction model—there were thousands like it back at the Mother Nest—but there was something unnervingly confident and cocky about the way it moved.

[Clavain, Remontoire . . . let me introduce you to the Master of Works.]

The servitor?

[The Master's more than just a servitor, I assure you.]

Skade shifted to spoken language. "Master . . . we wish to see the interior. Please let us through."

In reply Clavain heard the buzzing, wasplike voice of the Master. "I am not familiar with these two individuals."

"Clavain and Remontoire both have Closed Council clearance. Here, read my mind. You'll see I am not being coerced."

There was a pause while the machine stepped closer to Skade, easing the full mass of its body from the collar. It had many legs and limbs, some tipped with picklike feet, others ending in specialised grippers, tools or sensors. On either side of its wedge-shaped head were major sensor clusters, packed together like faceted compound eyes. Skade stood her ground while the servitor advanced, until it was towering over her. The machine lowered its head and swept it from side to side, and then jerked backwards.

"I will want to read their minds as well."

"Be my guest."

The servitor moved to Remontoire, angled its head and swept him. It took a little longer with him than it had spent on Skade. Then, seemingly satisified, it proceeded to Clavain. He felt it rummaging through his mind, its scrutiny fierce and systematic. As the machine trawled him, a torrent of remembered smells, sounds and visual images burst into his consciousness, and then each image vanished to be replaced by another. Now and then the machine would pause, back up and retrieve an earlier image, lingering over it suspiciously. Others it skipped over with desultory disinterest. The process was mercifully quick, but it still felt like he was being ransacked.

Then the scanning stopped, the torrent ceased and Clavain's mind was his own again.

"This one is conflicted. He appears to have had doubts. I have doubts about him. I cannot retrieve deep neural structures. Perhaps I should scan him at higher resolution. A modest surgical procedure would permit . . . "

Skade interrupted the servitor. "That's not necessary, Master. He's entitled to his doubts. Let us through, will you?"

"This is not in order. This is most irregular. A limited surgical intervention . . . " The machine still had its clusters of sensors locked on to Clavain.

"Master, this is a direct command. Let us pass."

The servitor pulled away. "Very well. I comply under duress. I will insist that the visit be brief."

"We won't detain you," Skade said.

"No, you will not. You will also remove your weapons. I will not permit high-energy-density devices within my comet."

Clavain glanced down at his suit's utility belt, unclipping the low-yield boser pistol he had barely been aware he was carrying. He moved to place the pistol on the ice, but even as he did so there was a whiplike blur of motion from the Master of Works, flicking the pistol from his hand. He saw it spin off into the darkness above him, flung away at greater than escape velocity. Skade and Remontoire did likewise, and the Master disposed of their weapons with the same casual flick. Then the servitor spun round, its legs a dancing blur of metal, and then thrust itself back into the hole.

[Come on. It doesn't really like visitors, and it'll start getting irritated if we stay too long.]

Remontoire pushed a thought into their heads. [You mean it's not irritated *yet*?]

What the hell is it, Skade?

[A servitor, of course, only somewhat brighter than the norm . . . does that disturb you?]

Clavain followed her through the collar and into the tunnel, drifting more than walking, guiding himself between the throat-like walls of compactified ice. He had barely been aware of the pistol he carried until it had been confiscated, but now he felt quite vulnerable without it. He fingered his utility belt, but there was nothing else on it that would serve as a weapon against the servitor, should it chose to turn against them. There were a few clamps and miniature grapples, a couple of thumb-sized signalling beacons and a standard-issue sealant spray. The only thing approaching an actual weapon—while the spray looked like a gun, it had a range of only two or three centimetres—was a short-bladed piezo-knife, sufficient to pierce spacesuit fabric but not much use against an armoured machine or even a well-trained adversary.

You know damned well it does. I've never had my mind invaded by a machine . . . not the way that one just did.

[It just needs to know it can trust us.]

While it trawled him he had tasted the sharp metallic tang of its intelligence. *How clever is it, exactly? Turing-compliant?*

[Higher. As smart as an alpha-level, at the very least. Oh, don't give me that aura of self-righteous disgust, Clavain. You once accepted machines that were almost as intelligent as yourself.]

I've had time to revise my opinion on the subject.

[Is it that you feel threatened by it, I wonder?]

By a machine? No. What I feel, Skade, is pity. Pity that you let that machine become intelligent while forcing it to remain your slave. I didn't think that was quite what we believed in.

He felt Remontoire's quiet presence. [I agree with Clavain. We've managed to do without intelligent machines until now, Skade. Not because we fear them but because we know that any intelligent entity must choose its own destiny. Yet that servitor doesn't have any free will, does it? Just intelligence. The one without the other is a travesty. We've gone to war over less.]

Somewhere ahead of them was a pale lilac glow that picked out the natural patterning of the tunnel walls. Clavain could see the servitor's dark spindly bulk against the light source. It must have been listening in to this conversation, he thought, hearing them debate what it represented.

[I regret that we had to do it. But we didn't have any choice. We needed clever servitors.]

[It's slavery,] Remontoire insisted.

[Desperate times call for desperate measures, Remontoire.]

Clavain peered into the pale purple gloom. *What's so desperate? I thought all we were doing was recovering some lost property.*

The Master of Works brought them to the interior of Skade's comet, calling them to a halt inside a small, airless blister set into the interior wall of the hollowed-out body. They stationed themselves by hooking limbs into restraint straps attached to the blister's stiff alloy frame. The blister was hermetically sealed from the comet's main chamber. The vacuum that had been achieved within was so high-grade that even the vapour leakage from Clavain's suit would have caused an unacceptable degradation.

Clavain stared into the chamber. Beyond the glass was a cavern of dizzying scale. It was bathed in rapturous blue light, filled with vast machines and an almost subliminal sense of scurrying activity. For a moment the scene was far too much to take in. Clavain felt as if he was staring into the depths of perspective in a fabulous detailed medieval painting, beguiled by the interlocking arches and towers of some radiant celestial city, glimpsing hosts of silver-leaf angels in the architecture, squadron upon squadron of them as far as the eye could see, receding into the cerulean blue of infinity. Then he grasped the scale of things and realised with a perceptual jolt that the angels were merely distant machines: droves of sterile construction servitors traversing the vacuum by the thousand as they went about their tasks. They communicated with each other using lasers, and it was the scatter and reflection of those beams that drenched the chamber in such shivering blue radiance. And it was indeed cold, Clavain knew. Dotted around the walls of the chamber he recognised the nubbed black cones of cryo-arithmetic engines, calculating overtime to suck away the heat of intense industrial activity that would otherwise have boiled the comet away.

Clavain's attention flicked to the reason for all that activity. He was not surprised to see the ships—not even surprised to see that they were starships—but the degree to which they had been completed astonished him. He had been expecting half-finished hulks, but he could not believe that these ships were far from flight-readiness. There were twelve of them packed side by side in clouds of geodesic support scaffolding. They were identical shapes, smooth and black as torpedos or beached whales, barbed near the rear with the outflung spars and nacelles of Conjoiner drives. Though there were no obvious visual comparisons, he was certain that each of the ships was at least three or four kilometres long, much larger than *Nightshade*.

Skade smiled, obviously noting his reaction. [Impressed?]

Who wouldn't be?

[Now you understand why the Master was so concerned about the risk of an unintentional weapons discharge, or even a powerplant overload. Of course, you're wondering why we've started building them again.]

It's a fair question. Would the wolves have anything to do with it, by any chance?

[Perhaps you should tell me why you think we ever stopped making them.]

I'm afraid no one ever had the decency to tell me.

[You're an intelligent man. You must have formed a few theories of your own.]

For a moment Clavain thought of telling her that the matter had never really concerned him; that the decision to stop making starships had happened when he was in deep space, a *fait accompli* by the time he returned, and—given the immediate need to help his side win the war—not the most pressing issue at hand.

But that would have been a lie. It had always troubled him.

Generally it's assumed that we stopped making them for selfish economic reasons, or because we were worried that the drives were falling into the wrong hands—Ultras and other undesirables. Or that we discovered a fatal flaw in the design that meant that the drives had a habit of exploding now and again.

[Yes, and there are at least half a dozen other theories in common currency, ranging from the faintly plausible to the ludicrously paranoid. What was your understanding of the reason?]

We'd only ever had a stable customer relationship with the Demarchists. The Ultras bought their drives off second- or third-hand sources, or stole them. But once our relationship with the Demarchists began to deteriorate, which happened when the Melding Plague crashed their economy, we lost our main client. They couldn't afford our technology, and we weren't willing to sell it to a faction that showed increasing signs of hostility.

[A very pragmatic answer, Clavain.]

I never saw any reason to look for any deeper explanation.

[There is, of course, quite a grain of truth in that. Economic and political factors did play a role. But there was something else. It can't have escaped your attention that our own internal shipbuilding programme has been much reduced.]

We've had a war to fight. We have enough ships for our needs as it is.

[True, but even those ships have not been active. Routine interstellar traffic has been greatly reduced. Travel between Conjoiner settlements in other systems has been cut back to a minimum.]

Again, effects of a war—

[Had remarkably little to do with it, other than providing a convenient cover story.]

Despite himself, Clavain almost laughed. *Cover story?*

[Had the real reason ever come out, there would have been widespread panic across the whole of human-settled space. The socio-economic turmoil would have been incomparably greater than anything caused by the present war.]

And I don't suppose you're going to tell me why?

[You were right, in a sense. It was to do with the wolves, Clavain.]

He shook his head. *It can't have been.*

[Why not?]

Because we didn't learn about the wolves until Galiana returned. And Galiana didn't encounter them until after we separated. There was no need to remind Skade that both of these events had happened long after the edict to stop shipbuilding.

Skade's helmet nodded a fraction. [That's true, in a sense. Certainly, it wasn't until Galiana's return that the Mother Nest obtained any detailed intelligence concerning the nature of the machines. But the fact that the wolves existed—the fact that they were out there—that was already known, many years before.]

It can't have been. Galiana was the first to encounter them.

[No. She was merely the first to make it back alive—or at least the first to make it back in any sense at all. Before that, there had only been distant reports, mysterious instances of ships vanishing, the odd distress signal. Over the years the Closed Council collated these reports and came to the conclusion that the wolves, or something like the wolves, was stalking interstellar space. That was bad enough, yet there was an even more disturbing conclusion, one that led to the edict. The pattern of losses pointed to the fact that the machines, whatever they were, homed in on a specific signature from our engines. We concluded that the wolves were drawn to us by the tau-neutrino emissions that are a characteristic of our drives.]

And Galiana?

[When she returned we knew we'd been right. And she gave

a name to our enemy, Clavain. We owe her that much, if nothing else.]

Then Skade reached into his head and planted an image. What she showed him was pitiless blackness studded by a smattering of faint, feeble stars. The stars did nothing to nullify the darkness, serving only to make it more absolute and cold. This was how Skade now perceived the cosmos, as ultimately inimical to life as an acid bath. But between the stars was something other than emptiness. The machines lurked in those spaces, preferring the darkness and the cold. Skade made him experience the cruel flavour of their intelligence. It made the thought processes of the Master of Works seem comforting and friendly. There was something bestial in the way the machines thought, a furious slavering hunger that would eclipse all other considerations.

A feral, ravenous bloodlust.

[They've always been out there, hiding in the darkness, watching and waiting. For four centuries we've been extremely lucky, stumbling through the night, making noise and light, broadcasting our presence into the galaxy. I think in some ways they must be blind, or that there are certain kinds of signals they filter from their perceptions. They never homed in on our radio or television transmissions, for instance, or else they would have scented us *en masse* centuries ago. That hasn't happened yet. Perhaps they are designed only to respond to the unmistakable signs of a starfaring culture, rather than a merely technological one. Speculation, of course, but what else can we do but speculate?]

Clavain looked at the twelve brand-new starships. *And now? Why start ship-building again?*

[Because now we can. *Nightshade* was a prototype for these twelve much larger ships. They have quiet drives. With certain refinements in drive topology we were able to reduce the tau-neutrino flux by two orders of magnitude. Far from perfect, but it should allow us to resume intersellar travel without immediate fear of bringing down the wolves. The technology will, of course, have to remain strictly within Conjoiner control.]

Of course.

[I'm glad you see it that way.]

He looked at the ships again. The twelve black shapes were

larger, fatter versions of *Nightshade,* their hulls swelling out to a width of perhaps two hundred and fifty metres at the widest point. They were as fat-bellied as the old ramliner colonisation ships, which had been designed to carry many tens of thousands of frozen sleepers.

But what about the rest of humanity? What about all the old ships that are still being used?

[We've done what we can. Closed Council agents have succeeded in regaining control of a number of outlaw vessels. These ships were destroyed, of course: we can't use them either, and existing drives can't be safely converted to the stealthed design.]

They can't?

Into Clavain's mind Skade tossed the image of a small planet, perhaps a moon, with a huge bowl-shaped chunk gouged out of one hemisphere, glowing cherry-red.

[No.]

And I don't suppose that at any point you thought that it might help to disclose this information?

Behind the visor of her crested helmet she smiled tolerantly. [Clavain . . . Clavain. Always so willing to believe in the greater good of humanity. I find your attitude heartening, I really do. But what good would disclosure serve? This information is already too sensitive to share even with the majority of the Conjoined. I daren't imagine what effect it would have on the rest of humanity.]

He wanted to argue but he knew she was correct. It was decades since any utterance from the Conjoiners had been taken at face value. Even a warning as bluntly urgent as that would be assumed to have duplicitous intent.

Even if his side capitulated, their surrender would be taken as a ruse.

Maybe you're right. Maybe. But I still don't understand why you've suddenly begun shipbuilding again.

[As a purely precautionary measure, should we need them.]

Clavain studied the ships again. Even if each ship only had the capacity to carry fifty or sixty thousand sleepers—and they looked capable of carrying far more than that—Skade's fleet would have sufficed to carry nearly half the population of the Mother Nest.

Purely precautionary—that's all?

[Well, there is the small matter of the hell-class weapons. Two of the ships plus the prototype will constitute a taskforce for the recovery operation. They will be armed with the most advanced weapons in our arsenal, and will contain recently developed technologies of a tactically advantageous nature.]

Like, I suppose, the systems you were testing?

[Certain further tests must still be performed, but yes . . .]

Skade unhitched herself. "Master of Works—we're done here for now. My guests have seen enough. What is your most recent estimate for when the ships will be flight ready?"

The servitor, which had folded and entwined its appendages into a tight bundle, swivelled its head to address her. "Sixty-one days, eight hours and thirteen minutes."

"Thank you. Be sure to do all you can to accelerate that schedule. Clavain won't want to be detained a moment, will you?"

Clavain said nothing.

"Please follow me," said the Master of Works, flicking a limb towards the exit. It was anxious to lead them back to the surface.

Clavain made sure he was the first behind it.

He did his best to keep his mind as blank and calm as possible, concentrating purely on the mechanics of the task in hand. The journey back towards the surface of the comet seemed to take much longer than the trip down had. The Master of Works bustled ahead of them, straddling the tunnel bore, picking its way along it with fastidious care. The servitor's mood was impossible to read, but Clavain had the impression that it was very glad to be done with the three of them. It had been programmed to tend the operations here with zealous protectivity, and Clavain could not help but admire the grudging way it had entertained them. He had dealt with many robots and servitors in his lifetime, and they had been programmed with many superficially convincing personalities. But this was the first one that had seemed genuinely resentful of human company.

Halfway along the throat, Clavain halted suddenly. *Wait a moment.*

[What's wrong?]

I don't know. My suit's registering a small pressure leak in my glove. Something in the wall may have ripped the fabric.

[That's not possible, Clavain. The wall is mildly compacted cometary ice. It would be like cutting yourself on smoke.]

Clavain nodded. *Then I cut myself on smoke. Or perhaps there was a sharp chip embedded in the wall.*

Clavain turned around and held his hand up for inspection. A target-shaped patch on the back of his left gauntlet was flashing pink, indicating the general region of a slow pressure loss.

[He's right, Skade,] Remontoire said.

[It's not serious. He can fix it when we're back on the corvette.]

My hand feels cold. I've lost this hand once already, Skade. I don't intend to lose it again.

He heard her hiss, an unfiltered sound of pure human impatience. [Then fix it.]

Clavain nodded and fumbled the spray from his utility belt. He dialled the nozzle to its narrowest setting and pressed the tip against his glove. The sealant emerged like a thin grey worm, instantly hardening and bonding to the fabric. He worked the nozzle sinuously up and down and from side to side, until he had doodled the worm across the gauntlet.

His hand was cold, but it also hurt because he had pushed the blade of the piezo-knife clean through the gauntlet. He had done it without removing the knife from the belt, in one fluid gesture as he moved one hand across the belt and angled the knife with the other. Given the difficulties, he had done well not to escape a more severe injury.

Clavain returned the spray to his belt. There was a regular warning tone in his helmet and his glove continued to pulse pink—he could see the pink glow around the edges of the sealant—but the sense of cold was diminishing. There was a small residual leak, but nothing that would cause him any difficulties.

[Well?]

I think that's taken care of it. I'll take a better look at it when we're in the corvette.

To Clavain's relief the incident appeared closed. The servitor bustled on and the three of them followed it. Eventually the tunnel breached the comet's surface. Clavain had the usual expected moment of vertigo as he stood outside again, for the comet's weak gravity was barely detectable and it was very easy via a simple flip of the perceptions to imagine himself glued by the soles of his feet to a coal-black ceiling, head down over infinite nothingness. But then the moment passed and he was confident again. The Master of Works packed itself back into the collar and then vanished down the tunnel.

They made quick progress to the waiting corvette, a wedge of pure black tethered against the starscape.

[Clavain . . . ?]

Yes, Skade?

[Do you mind if I ask you something? The Master of Works reported that you had doubts . . . was that an honest observation, or was the machine confused by the extreme antiquity of your memories?]

You tell me.

[Do you appreciate the need to recover the weapons, now? I mean on a visceral level?]

Nothing's ever been clearer to me. I understand perfectly that we need those weapons.

[I sense your honesty, Clavain. You do understand, don't you?]

Yes, I think so. The things you showed me made it all a lot clearer.

He was ahead of Skade and Remontoire by ten or twelve metres, moving as quickly as he dared. Suddenly—when he had reached the corvette's nearest grappling line—he stopped and spun around, grasping the line with one hand. The gesture was enough to make Skade and Remontoire stop in their tracks.

[Clavain . . .]

He ripped the piezo-knife from his belt and plunged it into the plastic membrane that wrapped the comet. He had the knife set to maximum sharpness and worked it lengthways, gouging a gash in the membrane. Clavain edged along like a crab, slicing first a metre then a two-metre rift, the knife whistling through the membrane with the barest hint of resistance. He had to keep a firm hold of the grapple, so he was only able to open up a four-metre-wide gash.

Until he had made the cut, he had no way of judging whether it would be sufficiently long. But a sliding sensation in his gut told him that it was enough. The entire patch of membrane under the corvette was being tugged back by the elasticity of the rest of the fabric. The gash was ripping wider and longer without his encouragement: four metres, then six, then ten . . . unzipping in either direction. Skade and Remontoire, caught on the far side, were tugged away by the same elastic pull.

The whole thing had taken one or two seconds. That, however, was more than enough time for Skade.

Almost as soon as he had plunged the knife in he had felt her claw at his mind, understanding that he was attempting to escape. In that moment he sensed brutal neural power that he had never suspected before. Skade was unleashing everything that she had against him, damning caution and secrecy. He felt search-and-destroy algorithms scuttle across the vacuum on radio waves, burrowing into his skull, working their way through the layered strata of his mind, questing and grasping for the basal routines that would allow her to paralyse him, or throw him into unconsciousness, or simply kill him. Had he been a normal Conjoiner she would have succeeded in microseconds, instructing his neural implants to self-destruct in an incendiary orgy of heat and pressure, and he would have been lost. Instead he felt a pain as if someone were driving an iron piton into his skull, one cruel tap at a time.

He still slipped into unconsciousness. The moment could only have lasted two or three seconds, but when he emerged he felt a yawing dislocation, unable to remember where he was or what he was doing. All that remained was a searing chemical imperative, written in the adrenaline that was still flooding his blood. He didn't quite know what had caused it, but the feeling was inescapable: an ancient mammalian fear. He was running away from something and his life was in great danger. He was suspended by one hand from a taut metal line. He glanced along the line—up—and saw a ship, a corvette, hovering above him, and knew, or hoped, that this was where he needed to be.

He started to tug himself up the line towards the waiting ship, half-remembering something that he had initiated and that he needed to continue. Then the pain notched itself higher and he fell back into unconsciousness.

Clavain came around as he drifted to a halt-"fell" was too strong a word for it—against the plastic membrane. Again he felt a basic urgency and struggled to make sense of the predicament he vaguely knew himself to be in. There above him was the ship—he remembered it from last time. He had been inching up the line, trying to reach it. Or had he been inching down it, trying to get away from something aboard it?

He looked laterally across the surface of wherever he was and saw two figures beckoning him.

[Clavain . . .]

The voice—the female presence in his head—was forceful but not entirely lacking in compassion. There was regret there, but it was the kind of regret a teacher might entertain for a promising pupil that had let her down. Was the voice disappointed because he was about to fail, or disappointed because he had nearly succeeded?

He didn't know. He sensed that if he could only think things through, if only he could have a quiet minute alone, he could put all the pieces back together. There had been something, hadn't there? A huge room full of dark, menacing shapes.

All he needed was peace and quiet.

But there was also a ringing tone in his head: a pressure-loss alarm. He glanced at his suit exterior, searching for the telltale pulse of pink that would highlight the wound. There it was: a smudge of rose across the back of his hand, the one that now held a knife. He returned the knife to the vacant position on his belt and reached instinctively for the sealant spray. Then he realised that he had already used the spray; that the smudge of pink was leaking around the sides of an intricately curved and curled scab of hardened sealant. The solidified grey worm appeared to form a complex runic inscription.

He looked at the glove from a different angle and saw a message scrawled in the tangled track of the worm: *SHIP*.

It was his handwriting.

The two figures had reached the ends of the wound-shaped gash in the ice and were now converging on his position as quickly as they were able. He judged that they would arrive at the base of the grapple in under a minute. It would take him almost as long to work his way along the line. He wondered about jumping for it, hoping that he could judge it correctly and not sail past the corvette, but at the back of his mind he knew that the adhesive membrane would not allow him to kick off. He would have to shin up the line hand-over-hand, despite the pain in his head and the constant feeling that he was on the verge of teetering back into unconsciousness.

He blacked out again, but more briefly this time, and when he saw his glove and the figures converging below him he guessed that he was right to head for the ship. He reached the lock at the same time as the first of the figures—the one with the ridged helmet, he saw now—arrived at the barbed grapple.

His perceptions now told him that the surface of the comet was a vertical black wall, with the tether lines emerging horizontally. The two others were flies glued to that wall, crouched and foreshortened and about to traverse the same bridge he had just crossed. Clavain fell back into the lock and palmed the emergency repressurisation control. The outer door snicked silently shut; air began to flood in. Instantly he felt the pain in his head lessen, and gasped in the sheer relief of the moment.

The override permitted the inner door to open almost before the outer door had sealed. Clavain hurled himself into the corvette's interior, kicked off from the far wall, knocked his skull against a bulkhead and then collided with the front of the flight deck. He did not bother getting into his seat or fastening restraints. He simply fired the corvette's thrusters—full emergency burn—and heard a dozen klaxons scream at him that this was not an auspicious thing to do.

Advise immediate engine shutdown. Advise immediate engine shutdown.

"Shut up!" Clavain shouted.

For a moment the corvette pulled away from the comet's surface. The ship made perhaps two and a half meters before the grapple lines extended to their maximum tension and held taut. The jolt threw him against a wall; he felt something break like a dry twig somewhere between his heart and his waist. The comet had moved too, of course, but only imperceptibly; he might as well have been tethered to an immovable rock at the centre of the universe.

"Clavain." The voice came over the corvette's radio. It was extraordinarily calm. His memories had begun to reassemble, fitfully, and with some hesitation he felt able to apply a name to his tormentor.

"Skade. Hello." He spoke through pain, certain that he had broken at least one rib and probably bruised one or two others.

"Clavain . . . what exactly are you doing?"

"I seem to be attempting to steal this ship."

He pulled himself into the seat now, wincing at multiple flares of pain. He groaned as he stretched restraint webbing across his chest. The thrusters were threatening to go into autonomous shutdown mode. He threw desperate commands at the corvette. Grapple retraction wouldn't help his situation: it would just reel in Skade and Remontoire—he remembered both of them now—and then the two of them would be on the outside of the hull, where they would have to stay. They would probably be safe if he abandoned them in space, drifting, but this was a Closed Council mission. Almost no one else would know they were out here.

"Full thrust . . . " Clavain said aloud, to himself. He knew a burst of full thrust would get him away from the comet. Either it would sever the grapple lines or it would rip chunks of the comet's surface away with him.

"Clavain," said a man's voice, "I think you need to think about this."

Neither of them could reach him neurally. The corvette would not allow those kinds of signals through its hull.

"Thanks, Rem . . . but as a matter of fact, I've already given it a fair bit of thought. She wants those weapons too badly. It's the wolves, isn't it, Skade? You need the weapons for when the wolves come."

"I as good as spelled it out to you, Clavain. Yes, we need the weapons to defend ourselves against the wolves. Is that so reprehensible? Is ensuring our own survival such a damning thing to do? What would you prefer—that we capitulate, offer ourselves up to them?"

"How do you know they're coming?"

"We don't. We merely consider their arrival to be likely, based on the information available to us . . . "

"There's more to it than that." His fingers skated over the main thrust controls. In a few seconds he would have to use full burn or stay behind.

"We just know, Clavain. That's all you have to know. Now let us back aboard the corvette. We'll forget all about this, I assure you."

"Not good enough, I'm afraid."

He fired the main engine, working the other thrusters to steer the blinding violet arc of the drive flame away from the comet's surface. He did not want to hurt either of them. Clavain disliked Skade but wished her no harm. Remontoire was his friend, and he had only left him on the comet because he did not see the point of implicating him in what he was about to do.

The corvette stretched against its guys. He could feel the vibration of the engine working its way through the hull, into his bones. Overload indicators were flicking into the red.

"Clavain, listen to me," Skade said. "You can't take that ship. What are you going to do with it—defect to the Demarchists?"

"It's a thought."

"It's also suicide. You'll never make it to Yellowstone. If we don't kill you, the Demarchists will."

Something snapped. The shuttle yawed and then slammed against the restraints of the remaining grapple lines. Through the cockpit window Clavain saw the severed line whiplash into the surface of the comet, slicing through the caul of stabilising membrane. It gashed a meter-wide wound in the surface. Black soot erupted out like octopus ink.

"Skade's right. You won't make it, Clavain—there's nowhere for you to go. Please, as a friend—I beg you not to do this."

"Don't you understand, Rem? She wants those weapons so she can take them with her. Those twelve ships? They're not all for the taskforce. They're part of something bigger. It's an evacuation fleet."

He felt the jolt as another line snapped, coiling into the comet with savage energy.

"So what if they are, Clavain?" Skade said.

"What about the rest of humanity? What are those poor fools meant to do when the wolves arrive? Take their own chances?"

"It's a Darwinian universe."

"Wrong answer, Skade."

The final line snapped at that moment. Suddenly he was accelerating away from the comet at full burn, squashed into his seat. He yelped at the pain from his damaged ribs. He watched the indicators normalise, the needles trembling back into green or white. The motor pitch died away to subsonic; the hull oscillations subsided. Skade's comet grew smaller.

By eye, Clavain orientated himself toward the sharp point of light that was Epsilon Eridani.

ELEVEN

Deep within *Nostalgia for Infinity,* Ilia Volyova stood at the epicentre of the thing that had once been her Captain, the thing that in another life had called itself John Armstrong Brannigan. She was not shivering, and that still struck her as wrong. Visits to the Captain had always been accompanied by extreme physical discomfort, lending the whole exercise the faintly penitential air of a pilgrimage. On the occasions when they were not visiting the Captain to measure the extent of his growth—which could be slowed, but not stopped—they had generally been seeking his wisdom on some matter or other. It seemed only right and proper that some burden of suffering should be part of the bargain, even if the Captain's advice had not always been absolutely sound, or even sane.

They had kept him cold to arrest the progress of the Melding Plague. For a time, the reefersleep casket in which he was kept could maintain the cold. But the Captain's relentless growth had finally encroached on the casket itself, subverting and incorporating its systems into his own burgeoning template. The casket had continued functioning, after a fashion, but it had proved necessary to plunge the entire area around it into cryogenic cold. Trips to the Captain required the donning of many layers of thermal clothing. It was not easy to breathe the chill air that infested his realm: each inhalation threatened to shatter the lungs into a million glassy shards. Volyova had chain-smoked during those visits, though they were easier for her than for the others. She had no internal implants, nothing that the plague could reach and corrupt. The others—all dead now—had considered her squeamish and weak for not having them. But she saw the envy in their eyes when they were forced to spend time in the vicinity of the Captain. Then, if only for a few minutes, they wanted to be her. Desperately.

Sajaki, Hegazi, Sudjic . . . she could barely remember their names, it seemed like such a long time ago.

Now the place was no cooler than any other part of the ship, and much warmer than some areas. The air was humid and still. Glistening films textured every surface. Condensation ran in rivulets down the walls, dribbling around knobbly accretions. Now and then, with a rude eructation, a mass of noxious shipboard effluent would burst from a cavity and ooze to the floor. The ship's biochemical recycling processes had long ago escaped human control. Instead of crashing, they had evolved madly, adding weird feedback loops and flourishes. It was a constant and wearying battle to prevent the ship from drowning in its own effluent. Volyova had installed bilge pumps at thousands of locations, redirecting the slime back to major processing vats where crude chemical agents could degrade it. The drone of the bilge pumps provided a background to every thought, like a single sustained organ note. The sound was always there. She had simply stopped noticing it.

If one knew where to look, and if one had the particular visual knack for extracting patterns from chaos, one could just about tell where the reefersleep casket had been. When she had allowed him to warm—she had fired a flèchette round into the casket's control system—he had begun to consume the surrounding ship at a vastly accelerated rate, ripping it apart atom by atom and merging it with himself. The heat had been like a furnace. She had not waited to see what the effects of the transformations would be, but it had seemed clear enough that the Captain would continue until he had assimilated much of the ship. As horrific as that prospect had been, it had been preferable to letting the ship remain in the control of *another* monster: Sun Stealer. She had hoped that the Captain would succeed in wresting some control from the parasitic intelligence that had invaded *Nostalgia for Infinity*.

She had, remarkably, been right. The Captain had eventually subsumed the whole ship, warping it to his own feverish whim. There was, Volyova knew, something unique about this particular case of plague infection. As far as anyone knew there was only one strain of Melding Plague, and the contamination that had reached the ship was the same kind that had done such damage in the Yellowstone system and elsewhere. Volyova had seen images of Chasm City after the plague, the twisted and grotesque architecture that the city had assumed, like a sick dream of itself. But while those transformations possessed at times what appeared to have been purpose, or even artistry, no real intelligence could be said to lie behind them. The shapes the buildings had taken on were in some sense pre-ordained by their underlying biodesign principles. But what had happened on *Infinity* was different. The plague had inhabited the Captain for long years before reshaping him. Was it possible that some symbiosis had been achieved, and that when the plague finally went wild, consuming and altering the ship, the transformations were in some sense expressions of the Captain's subconscious?

She suspected so, and at the same time hoped not. For no matter which way one looked at it, the ship had become something monstrous. When Khouri had come up from Resurgam, Volyova had done her best to be blasé about the transformations, but that act had been as much for her benefit as Khouri's. The ship unnerved her on many levels. Shortly before she had allowed him to warm, she had come to an understanding of the Captain's crimes, gaining a fleeting glimpse into the cloister of guilt and hate that was his mind. Now it was as if that mind had been vastly expanded, to the point where she could walk around inside it. The Captain had become the ship. The ship had inherited his crimes and become a monument to its own villainy.

She studied the contours that marked where the casket had been. During the latter stages of the Captain's illness, the reefersleep unit, pressed up against one wall, had begun to extend silvery fronds in all directions. They could be traced back through the casket's fractured casing into the Captain himself, fused deeply with his central nervous system. Now those sensory feelers encompassed the entire ship, worming, bifurcating and reconnecting like immense squid axons. There were several dozen locations where the silver feelers converged into what Volyova had come to think of as major ganglial processing centres, fantastically intricate tangles. There was no physical trace of the Captain's old body now, but his intelligence, distended, confused, spectral, undoubtedly still inhabited the ship. Volyova had not decided whether those nodes were distributed brains or simply small components of a much larger shipwide intellect. All that she was sure of was that John Brannigan was still present.

Once, when she had been shipwrecked around Hades and

had assumed Khouri to be dead, she had been waiting for *Infinity* to execute her. She was expecting it. She had warmed the Captain by then, told him of the crimes she had uncovered, given him every reason to punish her.

But he had spared her and then rescued her. He had allowed her back aboard the ship, which was still in the process of being consumed and transformed. He had ignored all her attempts at communication, but had made it possible for her to survive. There had been pockets where his transformations were less severe, and she had found that she could live in them. She had discovered that they even moved around, if she decided to inhabit a different portion of the ship. So Brannigan, or whatever was running the ship, knew she was aboard, and knew what she needed to stay alive. Later, when she had found Khouri, the ship had allowed her to come aboard as well.

It had been like inhabiting a haunted house occupied by a lonely but protective spirit. Whatever they needed, within reason, the ship provided. But it would not relinquish absolute control. It would not move, except to make short in-system flights. It would not give them access to any of its weapons, let alone the cache.

Volyova had continued her attempts at communication, but they had all been fruitless. When she spoke to the ship, nothing happened. When she scrawled visual messages, there was no response. And yet she remained convinced that the ship was paying attention. It had become catatonic, withdrawn into its own private abyss of remorse and recrimination.

The ship despised itself.

But then Khouri had left, returning to Resurgam to infiltrate Inquisition House and lead the whole damned planet on a wild goose chase, just so she and Volyova could get into any place they needed without question.

Those first few months of solitude had been trying, even for Ilia Volyova. They had forced her to the conclusion that she quite liked human companionship after all. Having nothing for company except a sullen, silent, hateful mind had almost pushed her to the edge.

But then the ship, in its own small way, had begun to talk back. At first, she had almost not noticed its efforts. There had been a hundred things that needed doing each day, and no time to stop and be quiet and wait for the ship to make its fumbling gestures of conciliation. Rat infestations . . . bilge pump failures . . . the continual process of redirecting the plague away from critical areas, fighting it with nano-agents, fire, refrigerants and chemical sprays.

Then one day the servitors had started behaving oddly. Like the rats that had turned rogue, they had once been part of the ship's repair and redesign infrastructure. The smartest of them had been consumed by the plague, but the oldest, stupidest machines had endured. They continued to toil away at their allotted tasks, only dimly aware that the ship had changed around them. For the most part they neither helped nor hindered Volyova, so she had let them be. Very occasionally they were useful, but it was such a rare occurrence that she had long since stopped counting on it.

But then the servitors began to help her. It started with a routine bilge pump failure. She had detected the pump breakdown and travelled downship to inspect the problem. When she arrived, to her astonishment she had found a servitor waiting there, carrying more or less exactly the right tools she needed to fix the unit.

Her first priority had been to get the pump chugging again. When the local flood had subsided she had sat down and taken stock. The ship still looked the way it had when she had woken up. The corridors still stretched away like mucus-coated windpipes. Vile substances continued to ooze and drip from every orifice in the ship's fabric. The air remained cloying, and at the back of every thought was the constant Gregorian chant of the other bilge pumps.

But something had definitely changed.

She had put the tools back on the rack that the servitor carried. When she was done the machine had whipped smartly around on its tracks and whirred off into the distance, vanishing around the ribbed curve of the corridor.

"You can hear me, I think," she had said aloud. "Hear me and see me. You also know that I'm not here to hurt you. You could have killed me already, John, especially if you control the servitors—and you do, don't you?"

She had not been the least bit surprised when no answer was forthcoming. But she had persisted.

"You remember who I am, of course. I'm the one who warmed you. The one who guessed what you'd done. Perhaps you think I was punishing you for your actions. You'd be wrong. It's not my style; sadism bores me. If I wanted to punish you, I'd have killed you—and there were a thousand ways I could have done it. But it wasn't what I had in mind. I just want you to know that my personal opinion on the matter is that you've suffered enough. You have suffered, haven't you?" She had paused, listening to the musical tone of the pump, satisfying herself that it was not going to immediately fail again.

"Well, you deserved it," she said. "You deserved to spend time in hell for what you did. Perhaps you have. Only you will ever know what it was like to live like that, for so long. Only you will ever know if the state you're in now is any kind of improvement."

There had been a distant tremor at that point; she had felt it through the flooring. She wondered if it was just a scheduled pumping operation going on somewhere else in the ship or whether the Captain had been commenting on her remark.

"It's better now, isn't it? It has to be better. You've escaped now, and become the spirit of the ship you once commanded. What more could any Captain desire?"

There had been no answer. She had waited several minutes, hoping for another seismic rumble or some equally cryptic signal. Nothing had come.

"About the servitor," she had said. "I'm grateful, thank you. It was a help."

But the ship had said nothing.

What she found from then on, however, was that the servitors were always there to help her when they could. If her intentions could be guessed, the machines would race ahead to bring the tools or equipment she needed. If it was a long job, a servitor would even bring her food and water, transported from one of the functioning dispensaries. If she asked the ship directly to bring her something, it never happened. But if she stated her needs aloud, as if talking to herself, then the ship seemed willing to oblige. It could not always help her, but she had the distinct impression that it was doing its best.

She wondered if she was wrong, whether perhaps it was not John Brannigan who was haunting her, but some markedly lower-level intelligence. Perhaps the reason that the ship was keen to serve her was that its mind was only as complex as a servitor's, infected with the same obedient routines. Perhaps when she addressed her thoughts directly to Brannigan, talking to him as if he listened, she was imagining more intelligence present than was really the case.

Then the cigarettes had turned up.

She had not asked for them, nor even suspected that there was another hoard of them to be found anywhere on the ship now that she had exhausted the last of her personal supply. She had examined them with curiosity and suspicion. They looked as if they had been manufactured by one of the trading colonies that the ship had dealt with decades ago. They did not appear to have been made by the ship itself, from local raw materials. They smelt too good for that. When she lit one of them up and smoked it to a stub, it tasted too good as well. She had smoked another one, and that had also tasted fine.

"Where did you find these?" she asked. "Where in the name of . . . " She inhaled again, filling her lungs for the first time in weeks with something other than the taste of shipboard air. "Never mind. I don't need to know. I'm grateful."

From then on there had been no doubt in her mind: Brannigan was with her. Only another member of the crew could have known about her cigarette habit. No machine would have thought to bring her an offering like that, no matter how deeply ingrained its instinct for servility. So the ship must have wanted to make peace.

Progress had been slow since then. Now and then something had happened which had forced the ship back into its shell, the servitors shutting down and refusing to help her for days on end. It sometimes happened after she had been talking to the Captain too freely, trying to coax him out of his silence with cod-psychology. She was not good at psychology, she reflected ruefully. This whole horrible mess had begun when her experiments with Gunnery Officer Nagorny had driven him insane. If that hadn't happened, there would have been no need to recruit Khouri, and everything might have been different . . .

Afterwards, when shipboard life returned to a kind of normality and the servitors again did her bidding, she would be very careful what she did and said. Weeks would go by without her making any overt attempts at communication. But she would always try again, building up slowly to another catatonic episode. She persisted because she had the impression that she was making small but measurable progress between each crash.

The last crash had not happened until six weeks after Khouri's visit. The catatonic state had persisted for an unprecedented eight weeks after that. Another ten weeks had passed since then, and only now was she ready to risk another crash.

"Captain . . . listen to me," she said. "I've tried to reach you many times, and I think once or twice I've succeeded and that you've been fully cognisant of what I'm saying. But you haven't been ready to answer. I understand; I truly do. But now there's something I *have* to explain to you. Something about the outside universe, something about what's happening elsewhere in this system." She was standing in the great sphere of the bridge, talking aloud with her voice raised slightly louder than would have been strictly necessary for conversation. In all likelihood, she could have said her piece anywhere in the ship and he would have heard her. But here, in what had once been the ship's focus of command, the soliloquy felt slightly less absurd. The acoustics of the place lent her voice a resonance that she found pleasing. She was also gesticulating theatrically with the stub of a cigarette.

"Perhaps," she continued, "you already know of it. I know you have synaptic pathways to the hull sensors and cameras. What I don't know is how well you can interpret those data streams. After all, you weren't born to do it. It must be strange, even for you, to see the universe through the eyes and ears of a four-kilometre-long machine. But you always were an adaptable bastard. My guess is you'll figure it out eventually."

The Captain did not respond. But the ship had not immediately plunged into the catatonic state. According to the monitor bracelet on her wrist, ship-wide servitor activity continued normally.

"But I'll assume you don't know about the machines yet, aside from what you may have picked up during Khouri's last visit. What kind of machines, you ask? Alien ones, that's what. We don't know where they've come from. All that we know is that they're here, now, in the Delta Pavonis system. We think Sylveste—you remember him?—must have inadvertently summoned them here when he went into the Hades artefact." Of course he remembered Sylveste, if he was capable of remembering anything at all from his previous existence. It was Sylveste they had brought aboard to heal the Captain. But

Sylveste had only been playing with their wishes, his eye on Hades all along.

"Of course," she continued, "that's guesswork, but it seems to fit the facts. Khouri knows a lot about these machines, more than me. But the way she learned about them means she can't easily articulate everything she *knows*. We're still in the dark in a lot of areas."

She told the Captain about what had happened so far, replaying observations on the bridge's display sphere. She explained how the swarms of Inhibitor machines had begun dismantling three smaller worlds, sucking out their cores and processing the eviscerated material into highly refined belts of orbital matter.

"It's impressive," she said. "But it's not so far beyond our own capabilities that I'm quivering in my boots. Not just yet. But what worries me is what they have in mind next."

The mining operations had come to an abrupt and precise halt two weeks earlier. The artificial volcanoes studding the equators of the three worlds had stopped belching matter, leaving a final curtailed arc of processed material climbing into orbit.

By then, by Volyova's estimate, at least half the mass of each world had been elevated into orbital storage. Only hollowed-out husks remained below. It was fascinating to watch them subside once the mining was over, crumpling down into compact orange balls of radioactive slag. Some machines detached themselves from the surface, but many appeared to have served their purpose and were not recycled. The apparent wastefulness of that gesture chilled Volyova. It suggested to her that the machines did not care about the effort they had already expended in earlier replication cycles, that in some sense it made no difference compared with the importance of the task ahead.

Yet millions of smaller machines remained. The debris rings themselves had appreciable self-gravity and needed constant shepherding. Various breeds of processor swam through the ore lanes, ingesting and excreting. Volyova detected the occasional flare of exotic radiation from the vicinity of the works. Awesome alchemical mechanisms had been unleashed. The raw dirt of the worlds was being coaxed into specialised and rare new forms, types of matter that simply did not exist in nature.

But before the volcanoes had ceased spewing dirt, a new

process had already started. A matter stream had peeled away from the space around each world, a filament of processed material that extended in a long tongue until it was light-seconds in length. The shepherding machines had obviously injected enough energy into each stream to kick them out of the gravitational wells of their progenitor worlds. The tongues of matter were now on an interplanetary trajectory, following a soft parabolic which hugged the ecliptic. They distended until they were light-hours from end to end. Volyova extrapolated the parabolas—there were three of them—and found that they would converge on the same point in space, at precisely the same time.

There was nothing there at the moment. But by the time they got there, something else would have arrived: the system's largest gas giant. That conjunction, Volyova was inclined to think, was very unlikely to be coincidence. "Here's my guess," she told the Captain. "What we've seen so far was just the gathering of raw material. Now it's being assembled in the place where the real work is about to begin. They've got designs on Roc. What, I don't know. But it's undoubtedly part of their plan."

What she knew of the gas giant sprung on to the projection sphere. A schematic showed Roc cored open like an apple, revealing layers of annotated strata: a plunge into perplexing depths of weird chemistry and nightmarish pressure. Gases at more or less imaginable pressures and temperatures overlaid an ocean of pure liquid hydrogen that began only a scratch beneath the apparent outer layer of the planet. Beneath that, the very thought of its existence giving Volyova a faint migraine, was an ocean of hydrogen in its metallic state. Volyova did not like planets at the best of times, and gas giants struck her as an unreasonable affront to human scale and frailty. In that respect, they were almost as bad as stars.

But there was nothing about Roc that marked it as out of the ordinary. It had the usual family of moons, most of them icy and tidally locked to the larger world. Ions were boiling off the surfaces of the hotter moons, forming great toroidal plasma belts which encircled the giant, held in check by the giant's own savage magnetosphere. There were no large rocky moons, which was presumably why the initial dismantling operations had taken place elsewhere. There was a ring system with some interesting resonant patterns—bicycle spokes and odd little knots—but again, it was nothing Volyova had not seen already.

What did the Inhibitors want? What would begin when their matter streams had arrived at Roc?

"You understand my misgivings, Captain. I'm sure you do. Whatever those machines are up to, it isn't going to be good for us. They're engines of extinction. Wiping out sentient life is what they do. The question is, can we do anything about it?"

Volyova paused and took stock. She had not yet triggered a catatonic withdrawal, and that was good. The Captain was at least prepared to let her discuss the outside events. On the other hand, she had yet to raise any of the subjects that usually triggered a shutdown.

Well, it was now or never.

"I think we can, Captain. Perhaps not stop the machines for good, but at least throw a fairly large spanner into their works." She eyed her bracelet, noting that nothing unusual was happening elsewhere in the ship. "Of course, I'm talking about a military strike. I don't think reasoned argument is going to work against a force that dismantles three of your planets without even saying 'please' first."

There was something then, she thought. A tremor reaching her from somewhere else in the ship. It had happened before, and it seemed to mean something, but exactly what she was not prepared to say. It was certainly a kind of communication from whatever intelligence ruled the ship, but not necessarily of the sort she might have wished for. It was more a sign of irritation, like the low growl of a dog that did not like being disturbed.

"Captain . . . I understand this is difficult. I swear I do. But we have to do something, and soon. A deployment of the cache weapons would seem to me to be our only option. We have thirty-three of them left; thirty-nine if we can salvage and rearm the six I deployed against Hades . . . but I think even thirty-three will be sufficient if we can use them well and use them soon."

The tremor intensified, subsided. She was really touching a nerve now, she thought. But the Captain was still listening. "The weapon we lost on the edge of the system may have been the most powerful we had," she went on, "but the six we discarded were, by my estimate at least, at the lower end of the destructive scale of the others. I think we can make do, Captain. Shall I tell you my plan? I propose that we target the three worlds where the matter streams are coming from. Ninety per cent of the extracted mass is still in orbit around each collapsed body, although more and more is being pumped towards Roc. Most of the Inhibitor machines are still around those moons. They might not survive a surprise attack, and even if they do, we can disperse and contaminate those matter reservoirs."

She began to talk faster, intoxicated with the way the plan was unfolding in her mind. "The machines might be able to regroup, but they'll need to find new worlds to dismantle. But we can beat them at that as well. We can use the other cache weapons to rip apart as many probable candidates as we can find. We can poison their wells; stop them from doing any more mining. That'll make it harder—perhaps even impossible—for them to finish what they have in mind for the gas giant. We have a chance, but there's a catch, Captain. You'll have to help us do it."

She looked at the bracelet again. Still nothing had happened, and she allowed herself to breathe a mental sigh of relief. She would not push him much more now. Merely discussing the need for his co-operation had gone further than she had imagined would be possible.

But it came, then: a distant, growing howl of angry air. She heard it shrieking towards her through kilometres of corridor.

"Captain . . . "

But it was too late. The gale stormed the command sphere, knocking her to the floor with its ferocity. The cigarette butt flew from her hand and executed several orbits of the chamber, caught in a whirlwind of ship air. Rats and sundry other items of loose ship debris precessed with it.

She found it hard to talk. "Captain . . . I didn't mean . . . " But then even breathing became difficult. The wind sent her skidding across the floor, arms windmilling. The noise was excruciating, like an amplification of all the years, all the decades of pain that John Brannigan had known.

Then the gale died down, and the chamber was still again. Somewhere else in the ship all he had needed to do was open a pressure lock into one of the chambers that was normally under hard vacuum. Very likely no air had actually reached space during his show of strength, but the effect had been as unnerving as any hull rupture.

Ilia Volyova got to her feet. Nothing seemed to be broken.

She dusted herself down and, shaking, lit herself another cigarette. She smoked it for at least two minutes, until her nerves were as steady as they were going to get.

Then she spoke again, calmly and quietly, like a parent talking to a baby that had just thrown a tantrum. "Very well, Captain. You've made your point very effectively. You don't want to talk about the cache weapons. Fine. That's your prerogative, and I can't say I'm terribly surprised. But understand this: we're not just talking about a small local matter here. Those Inhibitor machines haven't just arrived around Delta Pavonis. They've arrived *in human space*. This is just the beginning. They won't stop here, not even after they've wiped out all life on Resurgam for the second time in a million years. That'll just be the warm-up exercise. It'll be somewhere else after that. Maybe Sky's Edge. Maybe Shiva-Parvati. Maybe Grand Teton, Spindrift, Zastruga—maybe even Yellowstone. Maybe even the First System. It probably doesn't matter, because once one goes, the others won't be far behind. It'll be the end, Captain. It might take decades or it might take centuries. Doesn't matter. It'll still be the end of everything, the final repudiation of every human gesture—every human thought—since the dawn of time. We'll have been erased from existence. I guarantee you something: it'll be one hell of a shooting match, even if the outcome isn't really in doubt. But you know what? We won't be around to see one damned moment of it. And that pisses me off more than you can imagine."

She took another drag on the cigarette. The rats had scampered back into the darkness and slime and the ship felt almost normal again. He appeared to have forgiven her that one indiscretion.

She continued, "The machines haven't paid us much attention yet. But my guess is they'll get around to it eventually. And do you want my theory as to why we haven't been attacked so far? It might be that they just don't see us yet; that their senses are attuned to signs of life on a much larger scale than just a single ship. It could also be that there's no need to worry about us; that it would be a waste of effort to go to the trouble of wiping us out individually when what they're working on will do the job just as effectively. I suspect that's how they think, Captain. On a much larger, slower scale than we're used to. Why go to the trouble of squashing a single fly when you're about to exterminate the entire species? And if we're going to do something about them, we have to start thinking a little bit like them. We need the cache, Captain."

The room shuddered; the display illumination and the surrounding lights failed. Volyova looked at her bracelet, unsurprised to see that the ship was in the process of going catatonic again. Servitors were shutting down on all levels, abandoning whatever tasks they had been assigned. Even some of her bilge pumps were dying; she could hear the subtle change in the background note as units dropped out of the chorus. Warrens of shipboard corridor would be plunged into darkness. Elevators would not be guaranteed to arrive. Life was about to get harder again, and for a few days—perhaps a few weeks—merely surviving aboard the ship would require most of her energies.

"Captain . . . " she said softly, doubtful that anything was now listening. "Captain, you have to understand: I'm not going to go away. And nor are they."

Alone, standing in darkness, Volyova smoked what remained of her cigarette then, when she was done, she pulled out her torch, flicked it on and left the bridge.

The Triumvir was busy. She had much work to do.

Remontoire stood on the adhesive skin of Skade's comet, waving at an approaching spacecraft.

It came in hesitantly, nosing towards the dark surface with evident suspicion. It was a small ship, only slightly larger than the corvette that had brought them here in the first place. Globular turrets bulged from its hull, swivelling this way and that. Remontoire blinked against the red glare of a targeting laser, then the beam passed, doodling patterns on the ground, surveying it for booby-traps.

"You said there were two of you," said the commander of the ship, his voice buzzing in Remontoire's helmet. "I see only one."

"Skade was injured. She's inside the comet, being looked after by the Master of Works. Why are you speaking to me vocally?"

"You could be a trap."

"I'm Remontoire. Don't you recognise me?"

"Wait. Turn a little to the left so I can see your face through your visor."

A moment passed while the ship loitered, scrutinising him. Then it eased closer and fired its own set of grapples, ramming them hard into the ground where the three severed lines were still anchored. Remontoire felt the impacts drum through the membrane, the epoxy tightening its grip on his soles.

He tried to establish neural communication with the pilot. *Do you accept that I'm Remontoire, now?*

He watched an airlock open near the front of the ship. A Conjoiner emerged, clad in full battle armour. The figure glided to the comet's surface and landed feet first only two metres from where he stood. The figure carried a gun that he pointed unwaveringly at Remontoire. Other guns on the ship were also trained on him. He could feel their wide-muzzled scrutiny, and had the sense that it would only take a slight wrong move for the weapons to open fire.

The Conjoiner connected neurally with Remontoire. [What are you doing here? Who is the Master of Works?]

Closed Council business, I'm afraid. All I can tell you is that Skade and I were here on a matter of Conjoiner security. This comet is one of ours, as you'll have gathered.

[Your distress message said that three of you came here. Where is the ship that brought you?]

That's where it gets a tiny bit complicated. Remontoire tried to push into the man's head—it would make it so much easier if he could just dump his memories directly—but the other Conjoiner's neural blockades were secure.

[Just tell me.]

Clavain came with us. He stole the corvette.

[Why would he do something like that?]

I can't really tell you, not without revealing the nature of this comet.

[Let me guess. Closed Council business again.]

You know what it's like.

[Where was he headed with the corvette?]

Remontoire smiled; there was no point in playing further cat-and-mouse games. *Probably towards the inner system. Where else? He won't be going back to the Mother Nest.*

[How long ago was this, exactly?]

More than thirty hours.

[He'll need fewer than three hundred to reach Yellowstone. You didn't think to alert us sooner?]

I did my best. We had something of a medical crisis to deal with. And the Master of Works needed a lot of persuasion before it would allow me to send a signal back to the Mother Nest.

[Medical crisis?]

Remontoire gestured back across the scabbed and gashed surface of the comet, towards the dimpled entry hole where the Master of Works had first appeared. *As I said, Skade was hurt. I think we should get her back to the Mother Nest as quickly as possible.*

Remontoire began walking, picking his way gingerly step by step. The ship-mounted guns continued to track him, ready to turn him into a miniature crater if he so much as flinched.

[Is she alive?]

Remontoire shook his head. *Not at the moment, no.*

TWELVE

Clavain woke from a period of forced sleep, rising through dreams of collapsed buildings and sandstorms. There was a moment of bleary readjustment while he synched with his surroundings and the memories of recent events tumbled into place. He recalled the session within the Closed Council and the trip out to Skade's comet. He recalled meeting the Master of Works and learning about the buried fleet of what were obviously intended to be evacuation ships. He remembered how he had stolen the corvette and pointed it towards the inner system at maximum burn.

He was still inside the corvette, still in the forward pilot's position. His fingers brushed against the tactile controls, calling up the display screens. They bustled into place around him, opening and brightening like sunflowers. He did not quite trust the corvette to communicate with him neurally, for Skade might have managed to plant an incapacitating routine in the ship's control web. He thought it unlikely that she had—the ship had obeyed him unquestioningly so far—but there was no sense in taking unnecessary risks.

The flowerlike screens filled with status read-outs, schematics of the corvette's manifold subsystems strobing by at frantic speed. Clavain upped his consciousness rate until the cascade of images slowed to something he could assimilate. There were some technical issues, reports of damage that the corvette had sustained during the escape, but nothing that would threaten the mission. The other read-outs showed summaries of the tactical situation in increasingly large volumes of space, spreading out from the corvette in powers of ten. Clavain studied the icons and annotations, noting the proximity of both Conjoiner and Demarchist vessels, drones, rover-mines and larger assets. There was a major battle taking place three light-hours away, but there was nothing closer. Nor was there any sign of a response from the Mother Nest. It didn't mean that there had been no response, since Clavain was relying on the tactical data that the corvette was intercepting using passive sensors and by tapping into systemwide communication nets rather than risking the use of its own active sensors, which would betray its position to anyone looking in the right direction. But at least there was—so far—no obvious response.

Clavain smiled and shrugged, and was immediately reminded of the broken rib he had sustained during the escape. The pain was duller than it had been before, since he had remembered to strap on a medical tabard before going to sleep. The tabard had directed magnetic fields into his chest, coaxing the bone into re-knitting. But the discomfort was still there, proving that none of it had been in his imagination. There was a patch on his hand, too, where the piezoknife had cut to the bone. But the wound had been clean and there was very little pain from the self-inflicted injury.

So he had done it. There had been a moment during that state of hazy reacquaintance with reality when he had dared to imagine that the memories of recent events stemmed only from a series of troubling dreams: the kind that afflicted any soldier with anything resembling a conscience; anyone who had lived through enough wars—enough history—to know that what appeared to be the right action at the time might later turn out to be the direst of mistakes. But he had gone through with it, betraying his people. And it *was* a betrayal, no matter how pure the motive. They had trusted him with a shattering secret, and he had violated that trust.

There had not been time to evaluate the wisdom of defection in anything but the most cursory manner. From the moment he had seen the evacuation fleet and understood what it meant he knew that he had one opportunity to leave, and that it would mean stealing the corvette there and then. If he had waited any longer—until they got back to the Mother Nest, for instance—Skade would surely have seen his intentions. She had already had suspicions, but it would take her time to pick through the unfamiliar architecture of his mind, his antique implants and half-forgotten neural-interface protocols. He could not afford to give her that time.

So he had acted, knowing that he would probably not see Felka again, since he did not expect to remain a free man—or even a living one—after he had entered into the next and most difficult phase of his defection. It would have been far better if he had been able to see her one last time; there would have been no hope of persuading her to come with him, and no way of arranging her escape even if she had been willing, but he could have let her know his intentions, certain that his secret was safe with her. He also thought she would have understood—not necessarily agreed, but she would not have tried to argue him out of it. And if there had been a final farewell, he thought, then she might have answered the question he had never quite had the courage to ask her; the question that went back to the time of Galiana's nest and the war-weary days on Mars when they had met for the first time. He would have asked her if she was his daughter, and she might have answered.

Now he would have to live without ever knowing, and though he might never have summoned the courage—in all the years before he had never managed it, after all—the permanence of his exile and the impossibility of ever knowing the truth felt as bleak and cold as stone.

Clavain decided he had better learn to live with it.

He had defected before, throwing away one life, and he had survived both emotionally and physically. He was older now, but not so old and weary that he could not do it again. The trick, for now, was to focus only on immediates: fact one was that he was still alive and that his injuries were minor. He thought it likely that missiles were on their way to him, but they could not have been launched until long after he had taken the corvette or they would have already shown up on the passive sensors. Someone, very probably Remontoire, had managed to delay matters sufficiently to give him this edge. It was not much of an edge, but it was a lot better than being already dead, surfing his own expanding cloud of ionised debris. That at least was worth another rueful smile. They might yet kill him, but it would not be close to home.

He scratched his beard, muscles labouring against the continual pull of acceleration. The corvette's motors were still firing at maximum sustainable thrust: three gees that felt as rock-solid and smooth as the pull of a star. Each second, the ship was annihilating a bacterium-sized speck of anti-matter, but the anti-matter and metallic-hydrogen reaction-mass cores had barely been scratched. The corvette would take him anywhere he wanted in the system, and it would get him there in only tens of days. He could even accelerate harder if he wished, though it would stress the engines.

Fact two was that he had a plan.

The corvette's antimatter thrusters were advanced—far more so than anything in the enemy's fleet—but they did not employ the same technology as the Conjoiner starship drive. They could not have pushed a million-tonne starship to within a whisker of light-speed, but they did have one significant tactical advantage: they were silent across the entire neutrino-emission spectrum. Since Clavain had disabled all the usual transponders, he could be tracked only by his emission flame: the torch of relativistic particles slamming from the corvette's exhaust apertures. But the corvette's exhaust was already as tightly collimated as a rapier blade. There was negligible scattering away from the axis of thrust, so effectively he could only be seen by anything or anyone sitting in a very narrow cone immediately to his rear. The cone widened as it reached further behind him, but it also became steadily attenuated, like a torch beam growing weaker with distance. Only an observer near its centre would detect sufficient numbers of photons to obtain an accurate fix on his position, and if Clavain allowed the cone's angle to tilt by no more than a handful of degrees, the beam would become too dim to betray him.

But a change in beam vector implied a change in course. The Mother Nest would not expect him to do that, only for him to maintain a minimum-time trajectory towards Epsilon Eridani, and then to Yellowstone, which huddled in a tight, warm orbit around the same star. He would get there in twelve days. Where else could he go? The corvette could not reach another system—it barely had the range to reach the cometary halo—and almost any other world apart from Yellowstone was still in nominal Demarchist control. Their hold might be faltering, but in their present paranoid state they would still attack Clavain, even if he claimed to be defecting with tactically valuable secrets. But Clavain knew all that. Even before he plunged the piezo-knife into the membrane around Skade's comet, he had formulated a plan—maybe not the most detailed or elegant of his career, and it was far from the most likely to succeed, but he had only had minutes to assemble it and he did not think he had done too badly. Even after reconsideration, nothing better had presented itself.

And all it needed was a little trust.

I want to know what happened to me.

They looked at her, and then at each other. She could almost feel the intense buzz of their thoughts crackling through the air like the ionisation breakdown that presaged a thunderstorm.

The first of the surgeons projected calm and reassurance. [Skade . . .]

I said I want to know what happened to me.

[You are alive. You were injured, but you survived. You are still in need of . . .] The surgeon's gloss of calm faltered.

In need of what?

[You still need to be properly healed. But everything can be made good.]

For some reason she could not see into any of their heads. For most Conjoiners, waking to experience such isolation would have been a profoundly disturbing experience. But Skade was equipped for it. She endured it stoically, reminding herself that she had experienced degrees of isolation almost as extreme during her time in the Closed Council. Those had ended; this would end. It would only be a matter of time until . . .

What is wrong with my implants?

[Nothing's wrong with your implants.]

She knew that the surgeon was a man named Delmar. *So why am I isolated?*

But almost before she had phrased the question she knew what the answer would be. It was because they did not want her to be able to see what she looked like through their eyes. Because they did not want her to know the immediate truth of what had happened to her.

[Skade . . .]

Never mind . . . I know. Why did you bother waking me?

[There is someone to see you.]

She could not move her head, only her eyes. Through the blur of peripheral vision she saw Remontoire approach the bed, or table, or couch, where they had woken her. He wore an electric-white medical tunic against a background of pure white. His head was an oddly disconnected sphere bobbing towards her. Swan-necked medical servitors moved out of his way. The surgeon folded his arms across his chest and looked on with an expression of stern disapproval. His colleagues had made a discreet exit, leaving only the three of them in the room.

Skade peered "down" towards the foot of the bed but could see only an out-of-focus whiteness that might have been illusory. There was a quiet mechanical humming, but nothing that she would not have expected in a medical room.

Remontoire knelt down beside her. [How much do you remember?]

You tell me what happened and I'll tell you what I remember.

Remontoire glanced back at the surgeon. He allowed Skade to hear the thought he pushed into Delmar's head. [I'm afraid you'll have to leave us. Your machines as well, since I'm certain that they have recording devices.]

[We'll leave you alone for exactly five minutes, Remontoire. Will that be sufficient?]

[It'll have to do, won't it?] Remontoire nodded and smiled as the man ushered his machines from the room, their swan-necks lowering elegantly to pass through the doorway. [Sorry . . .]

[Five minutes, Remontoire.]

Skade tried moving her head again, but still without success. *Come closer, Remontoire. I can't see you very easily. They won't show me what happened.*

[Do you remember the comet? Clavain was with us. You were showing him the buried ships.]

I remember.

[Clavain stole the corvette before you or I could get aboard. It was still tethered to the surface of the comet.]

She remembered taking Clavain to the comet but not the rest of it. *And did he get away?*

[Yes, but we'll come to that. The problem is what happened during his escape. Clavain applied thrust until the tethers gave way under the strain. They whiplashed back towards the comet. I'm afraid one of them caught you.]

It was difficult to respond, though she had known from the moment of waking that something bad had happened to her. *Caught me?*

[You were injured, Skade. Badly. If you hadn't been Conjoiner, hadn't had the machines in your head to help your body cope with the shock, you would very probably not have survived, even with the assistance that your suit was able to give you.]

Show me, damn you.

[I would if there was a mirror in this room. But there isn't, and I can't bypass the neural blockades that Delmar has installed.]

Describe it, then. Describe it, Remontoire!

[This isn't why I came, Skade . . . Delmar will put you back into a recuperative coma very shortly, and when you next wake you'll be healed again. I came to ask you about Clavain.]

For a moment she pushed aside her own morbid curiosity. *I take it he's dead?*

[Actually, they haven't managed to stop him yet.]

As angry as she was, and despite her morbid curiosity, she had to admit that the matter of Clavain was at least as fascinating to her as her own predicament. And the two things were not unconnected, were they? She did not yet fully understand what had happened to her, but it was enough to know that it had been Clavain's doing. It did not matter that it might not have been intentional.

There were no *accidents* in treason.

Where is he?

[That's the funny thing. No one seems to know. They had a fix on his exhaust. He was heading towards Eridani—towards what we assumed would be Yellowstone or the Rust Belt.]

The Demarchists would crucify him.

Remontoire nodded. [Clavain especially. But now it doesn't

look as if he was going there at all—not directly, anyway. He turned away from the sunward vector. We don't know how far into his journey, since we lost his drive flame.]

We have optical monitors strewn through the halo. Surely he'll have fallen into the line of sight of another one by now.

[The problem is that Clavain knows the positions of those monitors. He can make sure his beam doesn't sweep across them. We have to keep reminding ourselves that he's one of ours, Skade.]

Were missiles launched?

[Yes, but they never got close enough to establish their own fixes. They didn't have enough fuel to make it back to the Nest, so we had to detonate them.]

She felt drool loosen itself and trail down her chin. *We have to stop him, Remontoire. Grasp that.*

[Even if we pick up Clavain's signal again, he'd be out of effective missile range. And no other ships can catch a corvette.]

She bit down on her fury. *We have the prototype.*

[Even *Nightshade* isn't that fast, not over solar-system-type distances.]

Skade said nothing for several seconds, calculating how much she could prudently reveal. This was Inner Sanctum business, after all, sensitive even by the clandestine standards of Closed Council. *It is, Remontoire.*

The door opened. One of the servitors ducked under and in, followed by Delmar. Remontoire stood and extended his hands, palms facing forwards.

[We just need another moment . . .]

Delmar stood by the door, arms folded. [I'm staying here, I'm afraid.]

Skade hissed at Remontoire. He moved closer, bending down so that their heads were only centimetres apart, permitting mind-to-mind contact without amplification by the room's systems. *It can be done. The prototype has a higher acceleration ceiling than you have assumed.*

[How much higher?]

A lot. You'll see. But all you need to know is that the prototype can get close enough to Clavain's approximate position to pick up his trail again, and then close within weapons range. I'll need you on the crew, of course. You're a soldier, Remontoire. You know the weapons better than I do.

[Shouldn't we be thinking of ways to bring him back alive?]

It's a little bit late for that, wouldn't you say?

Remontoire said nothing, but she knew she had made her point. And he would come around to her viewpoint soon enough. He was a Conjoiner to the core, and would therefore accept any course of action, no matter how ruthless, that benefited the Mother Nest. That was the difference between Remontoire and Clavain.

[Skade . . .]

Yes, Remontoire?

[If I should consent to your proposal . . .]

You'd have a demand of your own?

[Not a demand. A request. That Felka be allowed to join us.]

Skade narrowed her eyes. She was about to refuse when she realised that her grounds for doing so—that the operation had to be remain entirely within the purview of the Closed Council—made no difference where Felka was concerned.

What possible good would Felka's presence serve?

[That depends. If you intend to make this an execution squad she will be of no use to us at all. But if you have any intention of bringing Clavain back alive—and I think you must—then Felka's usefulness cannot be underestimated.]

Skade knew he was right, though it pained her to admit it. Clavain would have been an immensely valuable asset to the operation to recover the hell-class weapons, and his loss would make the operation very much more difficult. On one level, she could see the attraction of bringing him back into the fold, so that he could be pinned down and his hard-won expertise sucked out like so much bone marrow. But a live capture would be inordinately more difficult than a long-range kill, and until she succeeded there would remain the possibility of him reaching the other side. The Demarchists would be fascinated to hear about the new shipbuilding programme, the rumours of evacuation plans and savage new weapons.

Skade could not be certain, but she thought that the news might be enough to reinvigorate the enemy, gaining them allies who had thus far remained neutral. If the Demarchists rallied and managed to launch some kind of lastditch attack on the Mother Nest, with the support of the Ultras and any number of previously neutral factions, all could be lost.

No. She had to kill Clavain; that was simply not open to debate. Equally, she had to give every impression that she was ready to act reasonably, just as she would have done under any other state of war. Which meant that she had to accept Felka's presence.

This is blackmail, isn't it?

[Not blackmail, Skade. Just negotiation. If any one of us can talk Clavain out of this, it has to be Felka.]

He won't listen to her, even if . . .

[Even if he thinks she's his daughter? Is that what you were going to say?]

He's an old man, Remontoire. An old man with delusions. They're not my responsibility.

The servitors moved aside to allow him to leave. She watched the seemingly detached ovoid of his face bob out of the room like a balloon. There had been instants in their conversation when she had almost sensed cracks in the neural blockade, pathways that Delmar had—through understandable oversight—not completely disabled. The cracks had been like strobe flashes, opening up brief frozen windows into Remontoire's skull. Very probably he had not even been aware of her intrusions. Perhaps she had even imagined them.

But if she had imagined them, she had also imagined the horror that went with them. And the horror came from what Remontoire was seeing.

Delmar . . . I really would like to know the facts . . .

[Later, Skade, after you've been healed. Then you can know. Until then, I'd rather put you back into coma.]

Show me now, you bastard.

He came closer to her side. The first of the swan-necked servitors towered over him, the chrome segments of its neck gleaming. The machine angled its head back and forth, digesting what lay below it.

[All right. But don't say you weren't warned.]

The blockades came down like heavy metal shutters: clunk, clunk, clunk through her skull. A barrage of neural data crashed in. She saw herself through Delmar's eyes. The thing down on the medical couch was her, recognisably so—her head was bizarrely unharmed—but she was not remotely the right shape. She felt a twisting spasm of revulsion, as if she had just accessed a photograph from some bleak pre-industrial archive of medical nightmares. She wanted desperately to turn the page, to move on to the next pitiful atrocity.

She had been bisected.

The tether must have fallen across her from her left shoulder to her right hip, a precise diagonal severance. It had taken her legs and her left arm. Carapacial machinery hugged the wounds: gloss-white humming scabs of medical armour, like huge pus-filled blisters. Fluid lines erupted from the machinery and trailed into white modules squatting by her side. She looked as if she was bursting out of a white steel chrysalis. Or being consumed by it, transformed into something strange and phantasmagoric.

Delmar . . .

[I'm sorry, Skade, but I did warn . . .]

You don't understand. This . . . state . . . doesn't concern me at all. We're Conjoiners, aren't we? There isn't anything we can't repair, given time. I know you can fix me, eventually. She felt his relief.

[Eventually, yes . . .]

But eventually isn't good enough. In a few days, three at the most, I need to be on a ship.

THIRTEEN

They had to drag Thorn to the Inquisitor's office. The great doors creaked open and there she was, her back to him, standing by the window. He studied the woman through gummed-up eyes, never having seen her before. She looked smaller and younger than he had expected, almost like a girl wearing adult clothes. She wore highly polished boots and dark trousers under a side-buttoned leather tunic that appeared slightly too large for her, so that her gloved hands were almost lost in the sleeves. The tunic's hem almost reached her knees. Her black hair was combed back from her forehead in tight, glistening rows that curved down to tiny curls like inverted question marks above the nape of her neck. Her face was in near-profile, her skin a tone darker than his, her thin nose hooked above a small, straight mouth.

She turned around and spoke to the guard waiting by the door. "You can leave us now."

"Ma'am . . . "

"I *said* you can leave us now."

The guard left. Thorn stood by himself, only wavering slightly. The woman moved in and out of focus. For a long, long time she just looked at him. Then she spoke, with the same voice he had heard coming out of the speaker grille. "Are you going to be all right? I'm sorry that they hurt you."

"Not as sorry as I am."

"I only wanted to talk to you."

"Maybe you should keep an eye on what happens to your guests, in that case." He tasted blood in his mouth as he spoke.

"Will you come with me, please?" She gestured across the room to what looked like a private chamber. "There's something that we need to discuss."

"I'm fine here, thank you."

"It wasn't an invitation. I have no interest in whether you are fine or not, Thorn."

He wondered if she had read his reaction—the minute dilation of his pupils that betrayed his guilt. Or perhaps she had a laser trained on the back of his neck, sampling his skin's salinity. Either way, she might have a good idea of what he thought of her assertion. Perhaps she even had a trawl somewhere in this building. It was rumoured that Inquisition House had at least one, lovingly tended since the early days of the colony.

"I don't know who you think I am."

"Oh, but you do. So why play games? Come with me."

He followed her into the smaller room. It was windowless. He glanced around, looking for signs of a trap or any indication that the room might double as an interrogation chamber, but it looked innocent enough. The walls were lined with bulging paperwork-stuffed shelves, except for one that was largely occupied by a map of Resurgam studded with many pins and lights. She offered him a chair on one side of the large desk that took up much of the floor space. Another woman was already seated opposite him, with her elbows propped on the edge of the desk, looking faintly bored. She was older than the Inquisitor, but possessed something of the same wiry build. She wore a cap and a heavy drab-coloured coat with a fleeced collar and cuffs. Both women struck him as faintly avian, thin yet quick and strong-boned. The one behind the desk was smoking.

He settled down into the seat that the Inquisitor had indicated.

"Coffee?"

"No thanks."

The other woman pushed her pack of cigarettes towards him. "Have a smoke, then."

"I'll pass on those as well." But he picked up the packet and turned it over, studying the odd markings and sigils. It hadn't been manufactured in Cuvier. In fact, it didn't look as if it had been manufactured anywhere on Resurgam. He pushed it back towards the older woman. "Can I go now?"

"No. We haven't even started yet." The Inquisitor eased into her own seat, next to the other woman, and fixed herself a mug of coffee. "Introductions, I think. You know who you are, and we know who you are, but you probably don't know much about us. You have an idea about me, of course . . . but probably not a very accurate one. My name is Vuilleumier. This is my colleague . . . "

"Irina," she said.

"Irina . . . yes. And you, of course, are Thorn; the man who has done so much harm of late."

"I'm not Thorn. The government doesn't have a clue who Thorn is."

"How would you know?"

"I read the papers, like everyone else."

"You're right. Internal Threats doesn't have much of an idea who Thorn is. But only because I have been doing my best to keep that particular department off your trail. Have you any idea how much effort that's cost me? How much personal anguish?"

He shrugged, doing his best to look neither interested nor surprised. "That's your problem, not mine."

"Hardly the gratitude I was expecting, Thorn. But we'll let it pass. You don't know the big picture yet, so it's understandable."

"What big picture?"

"We'll come to that in good time. But let's talk about you for a moment." She patted a fat government folder resting at the edge of the desk and then pushed it over to him. "Go on, open it. Have a gander."

He looked at her for several seconds before moving. He opened the folder at random and then thumbed back and forth through the paperwork jammed within. It was like opening a box of snakes. His whole life was here, annotated and cross-referenced in excruciating detail. His real name—Renzo; his personal details. Every public move he had made in the last five years. Every significant antigovernment action he had played any significant part in—voice transcripts, photographs, forensic evidence, long-winded reports.

"Makes interesting reading, doesn't it?" said the other woman.

He flicked through the rest of it in horror, a plummeting sensation in his gut. There was enough to have him executed many times over, after ten separate show trials.

"I don't understand," he said feebly. He did not want to give up now—not after so long—but anything else suddenly seemed futile.

"What don't you understand, Thorn?" asked Vuilleumier.

"This department . . . it's External Threats, not Internal Threats. You're the person in charge of finding the Triumvir. I'm not the . . . Thorn isn't the one you're interested in."

"You are now." She knocked back some coffee.

The other woman puffed on a cigarette. "The fact is, Thorn, my colleague and I have been engaged in a concerted effort to sabotage the activities of Internal Threats. We've been doing our best to make sure they don't catch you. That's why we've needed to know at least as much about you as they do, if not more."

She had a funny accent, this one. He tried to place it and found that he couldn't. Except . . . had he heard it once before, when he was younger? He racked his memory but nothing came.

"Why sabotage them?" he asked.

"Because we want you alive, not dead." She smiled, quick and fast like a monkey.

"Well, that's reassuring."

"You'll want to know why next," said Vuilleumier, "so I'll tell you. And this is where we start drifting into the arena of the big picture, if you get my drift, so please *do* pay attention."

"I'm all ears."

"This office, the department of Inquisition House called External Threats, is not at all that it appears to be. The whole business of tracking down the war criminal Volyova has always been a front for a much more sensitive operation. Matter of fact, Volyova died years ago."

He had the impression she was lying, but still telling him something that was far closer to the truth than he had ever heard before. "So why keep up the pretence of searching for her?"

"Because it's not her we really want. It's her ship, or a means of reaching it. But by focusing on Volyova we were able to follow much the same lines of inquiry without bringing the ship into the discussion."

The other woman, the one he thought had called herself Irina, nodded. "Essentially this entire government department is engaged in recovering her ship, and *nothing else*. Everything else is a smokescreen. A hugely complex one, and one that has involved internecine warfare with half a dozen other departments, but a smokescreen all the same."

"Why does it have to be so secret?"

The two woman exchanged glances.

"I'll tell you," said Irina, just as the other one started to say something. "The operation to find the ship had to be kept maximally secret for the simple reason that there would have been intense civil disorder if it ever came to light."

"I don't follow."

"It's a matter of panic," she said, waving her cigarette for emphasis. "The government's official policy has always been pro-terraforming, right back to the old Inundationist days under Girardieau. That policy only deepened after the Sylveste crisis. Now they're fully wedded to it in ideological terms. Anyone who criticises the programme is guilty of incorrect thought. You of all people shouldn't need to be told this."

"So where the does the ship come in?"

"As an escape route. One branch of government has determined a singularly disturbing fact." She puffed on her cigarette. "There's an external threat to the colony, but not quite the kind they originally imagined. Studies of the threat have been ongoing for some time. The conclusion is inescapable: Resurgam must be evacuated, perhaps within no more than one or two years. Half a decade at the optimistic side—and that's probably being *very* optimistic."

She watched him, undoubtedly waiting to observe the effects her words would have. Perhaps she assumed that she would need to repeat herself, that he would be too slow to take it all in at first go.

He shook his head. "Sorry, but you're going to have to try better than that."

Irina, or whoever she was, looked pained. "You don't believe my story?"

"I wouldn't be the only one, either."

The Inquisitor said, "But you've always wanted to leave Resurgam. You've always said the colony was in danger."

"I wanted to leave. Who wouldn't?"

"Listen to me," Vuilleumier said sharply. "You're a hero to thousands of people. Most of them wouldn't trust the government to tie their shoelaces. A certain fraction of those people have long believed that you know the whereabouts of one or two shuttles, and that you are planning a mass exodus into space for your believers."

He shrugged. "And?"

"It's not true, of course—the shuttles never existed—but it's not beyond the bounds of possibility that they *might* have, given everything that's gone on. Now." She leant forwards again. "Consider the following hypothesis. A special covert branch of government determines that there is an imminent global threat to Resurgam. The same branch of government, after much work, determines the whereabouts of Volyova's ship. An inspection of the ship indicates that it is damaged but flightworthy. More importantly, it has a passenger-carrying capacity. A *vast* passenger-carrying capacity. Enough to evacuate the entire planet, if some sacrifices are made."

"Like an ark?" he said.

"Yes," she said, clearly pleased by his answer. "Exactly like an ark."

Vuilleumier's friend cradled her cigarette elegantly between two fingers. Her exceedingly thin hands reminded Thorn of the splayed-out bones in a bird's wing. "But having a ship we can use as an ark is only half of the solution," she said. "The question is, might the government's announcement of the existence of such a ship be viewed with a trace of scepticism? Of course it would." She stabbed the cigarette in his direction. "That's where you come in. The people'll trust you where they won't trust us."

Thorn leant back in his seat until it was balancing on only two legs. He laughed and shook his head, the two women watching him impassively. "Was that why I was beaten up downstairs? To soften me into accepting a piece of drivel like this?"

Vuilleumier's friend held up the packet of cigarettes again. "These came from her ship."

"Did they? That's nice. I thought you said you had no means of reaching orbit."

"We didn't. But now we do. We hacked into the ship from the ground, got it to send down a shuttle."

He pulled a face, but could not swear that such a thing was impossible. Difficult, yes—unlikely, very probably—but certainly not impossible.

"And you're going to evacuate an entire planet with one shuttle?"

"Two, actually." Vuilleumier coughed and retrieved another folder. "The most recent census put the population of Resurgam at just under two hundred thousand. The largest shuttle can move five hundred people into orbit, where they can transfer to an in-system craft with a capacity about four times that. That means we'll need to make four hundred surface-to-orbit flights. The in-system ship will need to make about one hundred round trips to Volyova's ship. That's the real bottleneck, though—each of those round trips will take *at least* thirty hours, and that's assuming almost zero time for loading and unloading at either end. Better assume forty hours to be on the safe side. That means we're looking at nearly six standard months. We can shave some time off that by pressing another surface-to-orbit ship into service, but we'll be doing very well if we get it much below five months. And that, of course, is assuming that we can have two thousand people ready and waiting to be moved off Resurgam every forty hours . . . " Vuilleumier smiled. He could not help but like her smile, for all that he felt he should be associating it with pain and fear. "You begin to see why we need you, I think."

"Assuming I refuse to offer my assistance . . . just how would the government go about this?"

"Mass coercion would seem to be the only other option available to us," Irina said, as if this was a perfectly reasonable statement. "Martial law . . . internment camps . . . you get the idea. It wouldn't be pretty. There'd be civil disobedience, riots. There's a good chance a lot of people would end up dead."

"A lot of people will end up dead anyway," Vuilleumier said. "There's no way anyone could organise a mass evacuation of a planet without some loss of life. But we'd like to keep a lid on it."

"With my help?" he asked her.

"Let me outline the plan." She stabbed her finger against the tabletop between sentences. "We release you forthwith. You'll be free to go as you please, and you have my guarantee that we will continue to do our utmost to keep Internal Threats off your back. I'll also make sure that those bastards who hurt you are punished . . . you have my word on that. In return, you disseminate information to the effect that you have indeed located the shuttles. More than that, you have discovered a threat to Resurgam and the means to get everyone out of harm's way. Your organisation begins spreading the word that the evacuation will start shortly, with hints as to where interested parties should congregate. The government, meanwhile, will issue counterstatements discrediting your movement's position, but they won't be completely convincing. The people will begin to suspect that you are on to something, something that the government would rather they didn't know about. With me so far?"

He returned her smile. "So far."

"This is where it gets interesting. Once the idea has sunk into the public consciousness, and after some people have begun to take you seriously, you will be arrested. Or at least you'll be seen to be arrested. After some procrastination the government will concede that there is a genuine threat, and that your movement has indeed obtained access to Volyova's ship. At that point the evacuation operation falls under government control—but you'll be seen to give it your reluctant blessing, and you'll remain in charge as a figurehead, by public demand. The government will have egg on its face, but the public won't be so certain they're walking into a trap. You'll be a hero." She made eye contact with him for a moment longer than she had before, and then glanced away. "Everyone's a winner. The planet gets evacuated without too much panic. In the aftermath, you'll be released and honoured—all charges dismissed. Sounds tempting, doesn't it?"

"It would," he admitted, "but there are just two small flaws in your argument."

"Which are?"

"The threat, and the ship. You haven't told me why we have to evacuate Resurgam. I'd need to know that, wouldn't I? I'd also need to believe it, too. Can't convince anyone else if I don't believe it myself, can I?"

"Fair point, I suppose. And concerning the ship?"

"You told me you have the means to visit it. Fine." He looked at the two women in turn, the younger one and the older one, sensing without really knowing why that the two of them could be very dangerous individually and quite exquisitely lethal when working as a team.

"Fine, what?" said Vuilleumier.

"Take me to see it."

They were one light-second out from the Mother Nest when the peculiar thing happened.

Felka had watched the comet fall behind *Nightshade*. It dwindled so slowly at first that the whole departure had a curious dreamlike quality, like casting off from a lonely moonlit island. She thought of her atelier in the green heart of the comet, of her filigreed wooden puzzles, each as intricately worked as scrimshaw. Then she thought of her wall of faces and the glowing mice in her maze, and could not quite assure herself that she would ever see any of them again. Even if she returned, she thought, it would be to profoundly changed circumstances, with Clavain either dead or a prisoner. Denied his help, she knew that she would curl inwards, back into the comforting hollow of her past, when the only thing that had mattered in the world had been her beloved Wall. And the horrible thing was that the idea did not revolt her in the slightest, but rather left her with a nagging glow of anticipation. It would have been different when Galiana was alive; different even when she was gone but when Felka still had Clavain's companionship to anchor her to the real world, with all its crushing simplicities.

The last thing she had done, after sealing her atelier and assigning a servitor to look after her mice, had been to go down to the vault and visit Galiana, to say goodbye to her frozen body one final time. But the door into the vault had refused to open for her. There had been no time to make enquiries; it was either go now or miss *Nightshade*'s departure. So she had left, never having made that final farewell, and she wondered now why it made her feel so guilty.

All they shared was some genetic material, after all.

Felka had retired to her quarters once the Mother Nest was too small and dim to see with the naked eye. An hour after departure the ship ramped the gravity to one gee, instantly defining "up" as being towards the sharp prow of the long conic hull. After another two hours, during which the Mother Nest fell a light-second behind *Nightshade,* a message came across the ship's intercom. It was politely aimed at Felka; she was the only Conjoiner on the ship who was not routinely tuned into the general grid of neural communications.

The message instructed her to move up the ship, ascending in the direction of flight towards the prow, which was now above her head. When she dallied, a Conjoiner, one of Skade's technicians, politely ushered her through corridors and shafts until she was many levels above her starting point. She refused to allow a map of the ship to be burned into her short-term memory—such instant familiarity would have denied her the boredom-alleviating pleasure of working out *Nightshade*'s layout for herself—but it was easy enough to tell that she was closer to the prow. The curvature of the outer walls was sharper, and the individual rooms were smaller. It did not take her long to conclude that there could be no more than a dozen people on *Nightshade,* including Remontoire and herself. Her companions were all Closed Council, though she did not even attempt to unwrap their minds.

The rooms were spartan, usually windowless chambers that the ship had defined according to the current needs of the crew. The room where she found Remontoire was on the outer edge of the hull, with a blister-shaped observation cupola set into one wall. Remontoire was sitting on an extruded ledge, his expression calm and his fingers steepled neatly above one knee. He was deep in conversation with a white mechanical crab that was perched just below the rim of the cupola.

"What's happening?" Felka asked. "Why did I have to leave my quarters?"

"I'm not quite sure," Remontoire replied.

Then she heard a volley of muted clunks as dozens of armoured irised bulkheads snicked shut up and down the ship.

"You'll be able to return to your quarters shortly," the crab said. "This is just a precaution."

She recognised the voice, even if the timbre was not entirely as she remembered it. "Skade? I thought you were . . . "

"They've allowed me to slave this proxy," the crab said, wiggling the tiny jointed manipulators between its foreclaws. It was stuck to the wall by circular pads on the ends of its legs. From under the crab's glossy white shell protruded various barbs, muzzles and lacerating and stabbing devices. It was very clearly an old assassination device that Skade had commandeered.

"It's good of you to see us off," Felka said, relieved that Skade would not be accompanying them.

"See you off?"

"When the light-lag exceeds a few seconds, won't it be impracticable to slave the proxy?"

"What light-lag? I'm on the ship, Felka. My quarters are only a deck or two below your own."

Felka remembered being told that Skade's injuries were so severe that it required a roomful of Doctor Delmar's equipment just to keep her alive. "I didn't think . . . "

The crab waved a manipulator, dismissing her protestations. "It doesn't matter. Come down later; we'll have a little chat."

"I'd like that," Felka said. "There's a great deal you and I need to talk about, Skade."

"Of course there is. Well, I must be going; urgent matters to attend to."

A hole puckered open in one wall; the crab scuttled through it, vanishing into the ship's hidden innards.

Felka looked at Remontoire. "Seeing as we're all Closed Council, I suppose I can talk freely. Did she say anything more about the Exordium experiments when you were with Clavain?"

Remontoire kept his voice very low. It was no more than a gesture; they had to assume that Skade would be able to hear everything that went on in the ship, and would also be able to read their minds at source. But Felka understood precisely why he felt the need to whisper. "Nothing. She even lied about where the edict to cease shipbuilding came from."

Felka glared at the wall, forcing it to provide her with somewhere to sit down. A ledge pushed out from the wall opposite Remontoire and she eased herself on to it. It was good to be off her feet; she had spent far too long of late in the weightless environment of her atelier, and the gee of shipboard thrust was wearying.

She stared out through the cupola and down, and saw the lobed shadow of one of *Nightshade*'s engines silhouetted against an aura of chill flame.

"What did she tell him?" Felka asked.

"Some story about the Closed Council piecing together the evidence of the wolf attacks from a variety of ship losses."

"Implausible."

"I don't think Clavain believed her. But she couldn't mention Exordium; she obviously wanted him to know the bare minimum for the job, and yet she couldn't avoid talking about the edict to some extent."

"Exordium's at the heart of all this," Felka said. "Skade must have known that if she gave Clavain a thread to pull on he'd have unravelled the whole thing, right back to the Inner Sanctum."

"That's as far as he'd have been able to take it."

"Knowing Clavain, I wouldn't be so sure. She wanted him as an ally because he isn't the kind to stop at a minor difficulty."

"But why couldn't she have just told him the truth? The idea that the Closed Council picked up messages from the future isn't so shocking, when you think about it. And from what I've gathered the content of those messages was sketchy at best, little more than vague premonitionary suggestions."

"Unless you were part of it, it's difficult to describe what happened. But I only participated once. I don't know what happened in the other experiments."

"Was Skade involved in the programme when you participated?"

"Yes," she told him. "But that was after our return from deep space. The edict was issued much earlier, long before Skade was recruited to the Conjoined. The Closed Council must have already been running Exordium experiments before Skade joined us."

Felka eyed the wall again. It was entirely reasonable to indulge in speculation about something like Exordium, Felka knew—Skade could hardly object to it, given the fact that it was so central to what was now happening—but she still felt as if they were on the brink of committing some unspeakably treasonous act.

But Remontoire continued speaking, his voice low yet assured. "So Skade joined us . . . and before very long she was in the Closed Council and actively involved in the Exordium experiments. At least one of the experiments coincided with the edict, so we can assume there was a direct warning about the tau-neutrino effect. But what about the other experiments? What warnings came through during those? Were there even warnings?" He looked at Felka intently.

She was about to answer, about to tell him something, when the seat beneath her forced itself upwards, the suddenness of it taking her breath away. She expected the pressure to abate, but it did not. By her own estimation her weight, which had been uncomfortable enough beforehand, had just doubled.

Remontoire looked out and downwards, as Felka had done a few minutes before.

"What just happened? We seem to be accelerating harder," she observed.

"We are," he said. "Definitely."

Felka followed his gaze, hoping to see something different in the view. But as accurately as she could judge, nothing had changed. Even the blue glow behind the engines seemed no brighter.

Gradually, the acceleration became tolerable, if not something she would actually describe as pleasant. With forethought and economy she could manage most of what she had been doing before. The ship's servitors did their best to assist, helping people get in and out of seats, always ready to spring into action. The other Conjoiners, all somewhat lighter and leaner than Felka, adapted with insulting ease. The interior surfaces of the ship hardened and softened themselves on cue, aiding movement and limiting injury.

But after an hour it increased again. Two and a half gees. Felka could stand it no longer. She asked to be allowed back to her quarters, but learned it was still not possible to go into that part of the ship. Nonetheless the ship partitioned a fresh room for her and extruded a couch she could lie on. Remontoire helped her on to it, making it perfectly clear that he had no better idea than she did of what was happening.

"I don't understand," Felka said, wheezing between words. "We're just accelerating. It's what we always knew we'd have to do if we stood a chance of reaching Clavain."

Remontoire nodded. "But there's more to it than that. Those engines were already operating near their peak efficiency when we boosted to one gee. *Nightshade* may be smaller and lighter than most lighthuggers, but the engines are smaller as well. They were designed to sustain a one-gee cruise up to lightspeed, no more than that. Over short distances, yes, greater speed is possible, but that isn't what's happening."

"Meaning?"

"Meaning we shouldn't have been able to accelerate so much harder. And definitely not three times as hard. I didn't see any auxiliary boosters attached to our hull, either. The only other way Skade could have done it would be by jettisoning two-thirds of the mass we had when we left the Mother Nest."

With some effort Felka shrugged. She had a profound lack of interest in the mechanics of spaceflight—ships were a means to an end as far as she was concerned—but she could work her way through an argument easily enough. "So the engines must be capable of working harder than you assumed."

"Yes. That's what I thought."

"And?"

"They can't be. We both looked out. You saw that blue glow? Scattered light from the exhaust beam. It would have had to get a lot brighter, Felka, bright enough that we'd have noticed. It didn't." Remontoire paused. "If anything, it got fainter, as if the engines had been throttled back a little. As if they weren't having to work as hard as before."

"That wouldn't make any sense, would it?"

"No," Remontoire said. "No sense at all. Unless Skade's secret machinery had something to do with it."

FOURTEEN

Triumvir Ilia Volyova gazed into the abyss of the cache chamber, wondering if she was about to make the kind of dreadful mistake she had always feared would end her days.

Khouri's voice buzzed in her helmet. "Ilia, I really think we should give this just a tiny bit more thought."

"Thank you." She checked the seals on her spacesuit again, and then flicked through her weapon status indicators.

"I mean it."

"I know you mean it. Unfortunately I've already given it more than enough thought. If I gave it any more thought I might decide not to do it. Which, given the wider circumstances, would be even more suicidally dangerous and stupid than doing it."

"I can't fault your logic, but I've a feeling the ship . . . I mean the Captain . . . really isn't going to like this."

"No?" Volyova considered that a far from remote possibility herself. "Then perhaps he'll decide to co-operate with us."

"Or kill us. Have you considered that?"

"Khouri?"

"Yes, Ilia?"

"Please shut up."

They were floating inside an airlock that allowed entry into the chamber. It was a large lock, but there was still only just enough room for the two of them. It was not simply that their suits had been augmented with the bulky frames of thruster-packs. They also carried equipment, supplemental armour and a number of semi-autonomous weapons, clamped to the frames at strategic points.

"All right; let's just get it over with," Khouri said. "I've never liked this place, not from the first time you showed it to me. Nothing that's happened since has made me like it any more."

They powered out into the chamber, propelling themselves with staccato puffs of micro-gee thrust.

It was one of five similarly sized spaces in *Nostalgia for Infinity*'s interior: huge inclusions large enough to stow a fleet of passenger shuttles or several megatonnes of cargo, ready to be dropped down to a needy colony world. So much time had passed since the days when the ship had carried colonists that only scant traces of its former function remained, overlaid by centuries of adaptation and corruption. For years the ship had rarely carried more than a dozen inhabitants, free to wander its echoing interior like looters in an evacuated city. But beneath the accretions of time much remained more or less intact, even allowing for the changes that had come about since the Captain's transformations.

The smooth sheer walls of the chamber reached away in all directions, vanishing into darkness and only fitfully illuminated by the roving spotlights of their suits. Volyova had not been able to restore the chamber's main lighting system: that was one of the circuits the Captain now controlled, and he clearly did not like them entering this territory.

Gradually the wall receded. They were immersed in darkness now, and it was only the head-up display in Volyova's helmet that gave her any indication of where to aim for or how fast she was moving.

"It feels as if we're in space," Khouri said. "It's hard to believe we're still inside the ship. Any sign of the weapons?"

"We should be coming up on weapon seventeen in about fifteen seconds."

On cue, the cache weapon loomed out of the darkness. It did not float free in the chamber, but was embraced by an elaborate arrangement of clamps and scaffolds, which were in turn connected to a complicated three-dimensional monorail system which plunged through the darkness, anchored to the chamber walls by enormous splayed pylons.

This was one of thirty-three weapons that remained from the original forty. Volyova and Khouri had destroyed one of them on the system's edge after it went rogue, possessed by a splinter of the same software parasite that Khouri herself had carried aboard the ship. The other six weapons had been abandoned in space after the Hades episode. They were probably recoverable, but there was no guarantee they would work again, and by Volyova's estimate they were considerably less potent than those that remained.

They fired their suit thrusters and came to a halt near the first weapon.

"Weapon seventeen," Volyova said. "Ugly son of a *svinoi,* don't you think? But I've had some success with this one—reached all the way down to its machine-language syntax layer."

"Meaning you can talk to it?"

"Yes. Isn't that just what I said?"

None of the cache weapons looked exactly alike, though they were all clearly the products of the same mentality. This one looked like a cross between a jet engine and a Victorian tunnelling machine: an axially symmetric sixty-metre-long cylinder faced with what could have been cutting teeth or turbine blades, but which were probably neither. The thing was sheathed in a dull, battered alloy that seemed either green or bronze, depending on the way their lights played across it. Cooling flanges and fins leant it a rakish art deco look.

"If you can talk to it," Khouri said, "can't we just tell it to leave the ship and then use it against the Inhibitors?"

"That would be nice, wouldn't it?" Volyova's sarcasm could have etched holes in metal. "The problem is that the Captain can control the weapons as well, and at the moment his commands will veto any I send, since his come in at root level."

"Mm. And whose bright idea was that?"

"Mine, now you come to mention it. Back when I wanted all the weapons to be controlled from the gunnery, it seemed quite a good idea."

"That's the problem with good ideas. They can turn out to be a real fucking pain in the arse."

"So I'm learning. Now then." Volyova's tone became hushed and businesslike. "I want you to follow me, and keep your eyes peeled. I'm going to check my control harness."

"Right behind you, Ilia."

They orbited the weapon, steering their suits through the interstices of the monorail system.

The harness was a frame that Volyova had welded around the weapon, equipped with thrusters and control interfaces. She had achieved only very limited success in communicating with the weapons, and those that she had been most confident of controlling had been among those now lost. Once, she had attempted to interface all the weapons via a single controlling node: an implant-augmented human plugged into a gunnery seat. Though the concept had been sound, the gunnery had caused her no end of troubles. Indirectly, the whole mess they were in now could be traced back to those experiments.

"Harness looks sound," Volyova said. "I think I'll try to run through a low-level systems check."

"Wake the weapon up, you mean?"

"No, no . . . just whisper a few sweet nothings to it, that's all." She tapped commands into the thick bracelet encircling her spacesuited forearm, watching the diagnostic traces as they scrolled over her faceplate. "I'm going to be preoccupied while I do this, so it's down to you to keep an eye out for any trouble. Understood?"

"Understood. Um, Ilia?"

"What."

"We have to make a decision on Thorn."

Volyova did not like to be distracted, most especially not during an operation as dangerous as this. "Thorn?"

"You heard what the man said. He wants to come aboard."

"And I said he can't. It's out of the question."

"Then I don't think we'll be able to count on his help, Ilia."

"He'll help us. We'll *make* the bastard help us."

She heard Khouri sigh. "Ilia, he isn't some piece of machinery we can poke or prod until we get a certain response. He doesn't have a *root level*. He's a thinking human being, fully capable of entertaining doubts and fears. He cares desperately about his cause and he won't risk jeopardising it if he thinks we're holding anything back from him. Now, if we were telling the truth, there'd be no good reason for refusing him the visit he asked for. He knows we have a means to reach the ship, after all. It's only reasonable that he'd want to see the Promised Land he's leading his people into, and the reason why Resurgam has to be evacuated."

Volyova was through the first layer of weapons protocols, burrowing through her own software shell into the machine's native operating system. So far nothing she had done had incurred any hostile response from either the weapon or the ship. She bit her tongue. It all got trickier from hereon in.

"I don't think it's in the least bit reasonable," Volyova replied.

"Then you don't understand human nature. Look, trust me on this. He has to see the ship or he won't work with us."

"If he saw this ship, Khouri, he'd do what any sane person would do under the same circumstances: run a mile."

"But if we kept him away from the worst parts, the areas which have undergone the most severe transformations, I think he might still help us."

Volyova sighed, while keeping her attention on the work at hand. She had the horrible, overfamiliar feeling that Khouri had already given this matter some consideration—enough to deflect her obvious objections.

"He'd still suspect something," she countered.

"Not if we played our cards right. We could disguise the transformations in a small area of the ship and then keep him to that. Just enough so that we can appear to give him a guided tour, without seeming to be holding anything back."

"And the Inhibitors?"

"He has to know about them eventually—everyone will. So what's the problem with Thorn finding out now rather than later?"

"He'll ask too many questions. Before long he'll put two and two together and figure out who he's working for."

"Ilia, you know we have to be more open with him . . . "

"Do we?" She was angry now, and it was not merely because the weapon had refused to parse her most recent command. "Or do we just want to have him around because we like him? Think very carefully before you answer, Khouri. Our friendship might depend on it."

"Thorn means nothing to me. He's just convenient."

Volyova tried a new syntax combination, holding her breath until the weapon responded. Previous experience had taught her that she could only make so many mistakes when talking to a weapon. Too many and the weapon would either clam up or start acting defensively. But now she was through. In the side of the weapon, what had appeared to be seamless alloy slid open to reveal a deep machine-lined inspection well, glowing with insipid green light.

"I'm going in. Watch my back."

Volyova steered her suit along the weapon's flanged length until she reached the hatch, braked and then inserted herself with a single cough of thrust. She arrested her movement with her feet, coming to a halt inside the well. It was large enough for her to rotate and translate without any part of her suit coming into contact with the machinery.

Not for the first time, she found herself wondering about the dark ancestry of these thirty-three horrors. The weapons were of human manufacture, certainly, but they were far in advance of the destructive potential of anything else that had ever been invented. Centuries ago, long before she had joined the ship, *Nostalgia for Infinity* had found the cache tucked away inside a fortified asteroid, a nameless lump of rock circling an equally nameless star. Perhaps a thorough forensic examination of the asteroid might have revealed some clue as to who had made the weapons, or who had owned them up to that point, but the crew had been in no position to linger. The weapons had been spirited aboard the ship, which had then left the scene of the crime with all haste before the asteroid's stunned defences woke up again.

Volyova, of course, had theories. Perhaps the most likely was that the weapons were of Conjoiner manufacture. The spiders had been around long enough. But if these weapons belonged to them, why had they ever allowed them to slip out of their hands? And why had they never made an effort to reclaim what was rightfully theirs?

It was immaterial. The cache had been aboard the ship for centuries. No one was going to come and ask for it back *now*.

She looked around, inspecting the well. Naked machinery surrounded her: control panels, read-outs, circuits, relays and devices of less obvious function. Already there was an apprehensive feeling in the back of her mind. The weapon was focusing a magnetic field on part of her brain, instilling a sense of phobic dread.

She had been here before. She was used to it.

She unhooked various modules stationed around her suit's thruster frame, attaching them to the interior of the well via epoxy-coated pads. From these modules, which were of her own design, she extended several dozen colourcoded cables that she connected or spliced into the exposed machinery.

"Ilia . . ." Khouri said. "How are you doing?"

"Fine. It doesn't like me being in here very much, but it can't kick me out—I've given it all the right authorisation codes."

"Has it started doing the fear thing?"

"Yes, as a matter of fact it has." She experienced a moment of absolute screaming terror, as if someone was poking her brain with an electrode, stirring her most primal fears and anxieties into daylight. "Do you mind if we have this conversation later, Khouri? I'd like to get this . . . over . . . as soon as possible."

"We're still going to have to decide about Thorn."

"Fine. Later, all right?"

"He has to come here."

"Khouri, do me a favour: shut up about Thorn and keep your eye on the job, understand?"

Volyova paused and forced herself to focus. So far, despite the fear, it had gone as well as she had hoped it would. She had only once before gone this deep into the weapon's control architecture, and that was when she had prioritised the commands coming in from the ship. Since she was at the same level now she could theoretically, by issuing the right command syntax, lock out the Captain for good. This was only one weapon; there were thirty-two others, and some of those were utterly unknown to her. But she would surely not need the whole cache to make a difference. If she could gain control of a dozen or so weapons, it would hopefully be enough to throw a spanner into the Inhibitor's plans . . .

And she would not succeed by prevarication.

"Khouri, listen to me. Minor change of plan."

"Uh-oh."

"I'm going to go ahead and see if I can get this weapon to submit entirely to my control."

"You call that a *minor* change of plan?"

"There's absolutely nothing to worry about."

Before she could stop herself, before the fear became overwhelming, she connected the remaining lines. Status lights winked and pulsed; displays rippled with alphanumeric hash. The fear sharpened. The weapon *really* did not want her to tamper with it on this level.

"Tough luck," she said. "Now let's see . . . " And with a few discreet taps on her bracelet she released webs of mind-numbingly complicated command syntax. The three-valued logic that the weapon's operating system ran on was characteristic of Conjoiner programming, but it was also devilishly hard to debug.

She sat still and waited.

Deep inside the weapon, the legality of her command would be thrashed out and scrutinised by dozens of parsing modules. Only when it had satisfied all criteria would it be executed. If that happened, and the command did what she thought it would, the weapon would immediately delete the Captain from the list of authenticated users. There would then only be one valid way to work the weapon, which was through her control harness, a piece of hardware disconnected from the ship's Captain-controlled infrastructure.

It was a very sound theory.

She had the first indication that the command syntax had been bad an instant before the hatch slid shut on her. Her bracelet flashed red; she started assembling a particularly poetic sequence of Russish swearwords and then the weapon had locked her in. Next, the lights went out, but the fear remained. The fear, in fact, had grown very much stronger—but perhaps that was partly her own response to the situation.

"Damn . . . " Volyova said. "Khouri . . . can you hear me?"

But there was no reply.

Without warning machinery shifted around her. The chamber had become larger, revealing dimly glowing vaults plunging deeper into the weapon. Enormous fluidly shaped mechanisms floated in blood-red light. Cold blue lights flickered on the shapes or traced the flow lines of writhing intestinal power lines. The entire interior of the weapon appeared to be reorganising itself.

And then she nearly died of fright. She sensed something else inside the weapon, a presence that was coming closer, creeping through the shifting components with phantom slowness.

Volyova hammered on the hatch above her. "Khouri . . . !"

But the presence had reached her. She had not seen it arrive but she sensed its sudden proximity. It was shapeless, crouched behind her. She thought she could almost see it in her peripheral vision, but even as she wrenched her head around the presence flowed into her blind spot.

Suddenly her head hurt, the blinding pain making her squeal aloud.

* * *

Remontoire squeezed his lean frame into one of *Nightshade*'s viewing blisters, establishing by visual means that the engines had actually shut off. He had issued the correct sequence of neural commands, instantly feeling the shift to weightlessness as the ship ceased accelerating, but still he felt the need for additional confirmation that his order had been followed. Given what had happened already, he would not have been entirely surprised to see that the blue glow of scattered light was still present.

But he saw only darkness. The engines really had shut down; the ship was drifting at constant velocity, still falling towards Epsilon Eridani but far too slowly ever to catch Clavain.

"What now?" Felka asked quietly. She floated next to him, one hand hooked into a soft hoop that the ship had obligingly provided.

"We wait," he said. "If I'm right, Skade won't be long."

"She won't be pleased."

He nodded. "And I'll reinstate thrust as soon as she tells me what's going on. But before that I'd like some answers."

The crab arrived a few moments later, easing through a fist-sized hole in the wall. "This is unacceptable. Why have you . . ."

"The engines are my responsibility," Remontoire said pleasantly, for he had rehearsed exactly what he would say. "They're a highly delicate and dangerous technology, all the more so given the experimental nature of the new designs. Any deviation from the expected performance might indicate a serious, possibly catastrophic, problem."

The crab waggled its manipulators. "You know perfectly well that there was nothing at all wrong with the engines. I demand that you restart them immediately. Every second we spend drifting is to Clavain's advantage."

"Really?" Felka said.

"Only in the very loosest sense. If we're delayed any further our only realistic option will be a remote kill, rather than a live capture."

"Not that that's ever been under serious consideration, has it?" Felka asked.

"You'll never know if Remontoire persists with this . . . insubordination." "Insubordination?" Felka hooted. "Now you almost sound like a Demarchist."

"Don't play games, either of you." The crab pivoted around on its suckered feet. "Reinstate the engines, Remontoire, or I'll find a way to do it without you."

It sounded like a bluff, but Remontoire was prepared to believe that overriding his commands was within the capabilities of an Inner Sanctum member. It might not be easy, certainly less easy than having him do what she wanted, but he did not doubt that Skade was capable of it.

"I will . . . once you show me what your machinery does."

"My machinery?"

Remontoire reached over and prised the crab from the wall, each suckered foot detaching with a soft, faintly comical slurp. He held the crab at eye-level, looking into its tight assemblage of sensors and variegated weapons, daring Skade to hurt him. The little legs thrashed pathetically.

"You know exactly what I mean," he said. "I want to know what it is, Skade. I want to know what you've learned to do."

They followed the proxy through *Nightshade,* navigating twisting grey corridors and vertical interdeck shafts, moving steadily away from the prow of the ship—"down" as far as Remontoire's inner ear was concerned. The acceleration was now one and three-quarter gees, Remontoire having agreed to reinstate the engines at a low level of thrust. His mental map of the other occupants showed that they were all still crammed into the volume of the ship immediately aft of the prow, and that Felka and he were the only people this far downship. He had yet to discover where Skade's actual body was; she still had not spoken to him through any other medium than the crab's voice box, and his usual omniscient knowledge of the ship's layout had been replaced by a mental map riddled with precisely edited gaps, like the blocked-out text in a classified document.

"This machinery . . . whatever it is . . . "

Skade cut him off. "You'd have found out about it sooner or later. As would all of the Mother Nest."

"Was it something you learned from Exordium?"

"Exordium showed us the direction to follow, that's all. Nothing was handed to us on a plate." The crab skittered ahead of them and reached a sealed bulkhead, one of the mechanical doors that had closed before the increase in acceleration. "We have to go through here, into the part of the ship I sealed off. I should warn you that things will feel a little different on the other side. Not immediately, but this barricade more or less marks the point at which the effects of the machinery rise above the threshold of human sensitivity. You may find it disturbing. Are you certain that you wish to continue?"

Remontoire looked at Felka; Felka looked back at him and nodded.

"Lead on, Skade," said Remontoire.

"Very well."

The barricade wheezed open, revealing an even darker and deader space beyond it. They stepped through and then descended several further levels via vertical shafts, riding piston-shaped discs.

Remontoire examined his feelings but nothing was out of the ordinary. He raised a quizzical eyebrow in Felka's direction, to which she responded with a short shake of her head. She felt nothing unusual either, and she was a good deal more attuned to such matters than he was.

They continued on through normal corridors, pausing now and then until they regained the energy to continue. Eventually they arrived at a plain stretch of walling devoid of any indicators—real, holographic or entoptic—to mark it as out of the ordinary. Yet the crab halted at a certain spot and after a moment a hole opened in the wall at chest height, enlarging to form an aperture shaped like a cat's pupil. Red light spilled through the inverted gash.

"This is where I live," the crab told them. "Please come in."

They followed the crab into a large warm space. Remontoire looked around, realising as he did so that nothing he saw matched his expectations. He was simply in an almost empty room. There were a few items of machinery in it, but only one thing, resembling a small, slightly macabre piece of sculpture, that he did not instantly recognise. The room was filled with the soft hum of equipment, but again the sound was not unfamiliar.

The largest item was the first thing he had noticed. It was a black egg-shaped pod resting on a heavy rust-red pedestal inset with quivering analogue dials. The pod had the antique look of much modern space technology, like a relic from the earliest days of near-Earth exploration. He recognised it as an escape pod of Demarchist design, simple and robust. Conjoiner ships never carried escape pods.

This unit was marked with warning instructions in all the common languages—Norte, Russish, Canasian—along with icons and diagrams in bright primary colours. There were bee-stripes and cruciform thrusters; the grey bulges of sensors and communication systems; collapsed solar-wings and parachutes. There were explosive bolts around a door and a tiny triangular window in the door itself.

There was something in the pod. Remontoire saw a curve of pale flesh through the window, indistinct because it was embedded in a matrix of amber cushioning gel or some cloying medical nutrient. The flesh moved, breathing slowly.

"Skade . . . ?" he said, thinking of the injuries he had seen when he had visited her before their departure.

"Go ahead," the crab said. "Have a look. I'm sure it will surprise you."

Remontoire and Felka eased closer to the pod. There was a figure packed inside it, pink and foetal. Remontoire saw lines and catheters, and watched the figure move almost imperceptibly no more than once a minute. It was breathing.

It wasn't Skade, or even what had remained of Skade. It definitely wasn't human.

"What is it?" Felka asked, her voice barely a whisper.

"Scorpio," Remontoire said. "The hyperpig, the one we found on the Demarchist ship."

Felka touched the metal wall of the pod. Remontoire did likewise, feeling the rhythmic churning of life-support systems.

"Why is he here?" Felka asked.

"He's on his way back to justice," Skade said. "Once we're near the inner system we'll eject the pod and let the Ferrisville Convention recover him."

"And then?"

"They'll try him and find him guilty of the many crimes he is supposed to have committed," Skade said. "And then, under the present legislation, they'll kill him. Irreversible neural death."

"You sound as if you approve."

"We have to co-operate with the Convention," Skade said. "They can make life difficult for us in our dealings around Yellowstone. The pig has to be handed back to them one way or another. It would have been very convenient for us if he had died in our custody, believe me. Unfortunately, this way he has a small chance of survival."

"What kind of crimes are we talking about?" Felka asked.

"War crimes," Skade said breezily.

"That doesn't tell me anything. How can he be a war criminal if he isn't affiliated to a recognised faction?"

"It's very simple," Skade said. "Under the terms of the Convention virtually any extralegal act committed in the war zone becomes a war crime, by definition. And there's no shortage in Scorpio's case. Murder. Assassination. Terrorism. Blackmail. Theft. Extortion. Eco-sabotage. Trafficking in unlicensed alpha-level intelligences. Frankly, he's been involved in every criminal activity you can think of from Chasm City to the Rust Belt. If it were peacetime, they'd be serious enough. But in a time of war, most of those crimes carry a mandatory penalty of irreversible death. He'd have earned it several times over even if the nature of the murders themselves wasn't taken into consideration."

The pig breathed in and out. Remontoire watched the protective gel tremble as he moved and wondered if he were dreaming, and if so what shape those dreams assumed. Did pigs dream? He was not sure. He did not remember if Run Seven had had anything to say on the matter. But then, Run Seven's mind had not exactly been put together like other pigs'. He had been a very early and imperfectly formed specimen, and his mental state had been a long way from anything Remontoire would have termed sane. Which was not to say that he had been stupid, or lacking in ingenuity. The tortures and methods of coercion that the pirate had used on Remontoire had been adequate testimony to his intelligence and originality. Even now, somewhere at the back of his mind (there were days when he did not notice it) there was a scream that had never ended; a thread of agony that connected him with the past.

"What exactly were these murders?" Felka repeated.

"He likes killing humans, Felka. He makes something of an art of it. I don't pretend there aren't others like him, criminal scum making the most of the present situation." Skade's crab hopped through the air and landed deftly on the side of the pod. "But he's different. He revels in it."

Remontoire spoke softly. "Clavain and I trawled him. The memories we dug out of his head were enough to have him executed there and then."

"So why didn't you?" asked Felka.

"Under more favourable circumstances, I think we might have."

"The pig needn't detain us," Skade said. "It's his good fortune that Clavain defected, forcing us to make this journey to the inner system, or we'd have had to return a corpse, packed into a high-burn missile warhead. That option was seriously considered. We'd have been perfectly within our rights."

Remontoire stepped away from the pod. "I thought it might be you in there."

"And were you relieved to find it wasn't me?"

The voice startled him, because it had not come from the crab. He looked around and for the first time paid proper attention to the unfamiliar object he had only glanced at before. It had reminded him of a sculpture: a cylindrical silver pedestal in the middle of the room, supporting a detached human head.

The head vanished into the pedestal somewhere near the middle of the neck, joined to it by a tight black seal. The pedestal was only slightly wider than the head, flaring towards a thick base inset with various gauges and sockets. Now and then it gurgled and clicked with inscrutable medical processes.

The head swivelled slightly to greet them and then spoke, pushing thoughts into his head. [Yes, it's me. I'm glad you were able to follow my proxy. We're inside the range of the device now. Do you feel any ill effects?]

Only a little queasiness, Remontoire replied.

Felka stepped closer to the pedestal. "Do you mind if I touch you?"

[Be my guest.]

Remontoire watched her press her fingers lightly across Skade's face, tracing its contours with horrified care. *It is you, isn't it?* he asked.

[You seem a little surprised. Why? Does my state disturb you? I've experienced far more unsettling conditions than this, I assure you. This is merely temporary.]

But behind her thoughts he sensed chasms of horror; self-disgust so extreme that it had become something close to awe. He wondered if Skade was letting him taste her feelings deliberately, or whether her control was simply not good enough to mask what she really felt.

Why did you let Delmar do this to you?

[It wasn't his idea. It would have taken too long to heal my entire body, and Delmar's equipment was too bulky to bring along. I suggested that he remove my head, which was perfectly intact.]

She glanced down, though she could not tilt her head. [This life-support apparatus is simple, reliable and compact enough for my needs. There are some problems with maintaining the precise blood chemistry that my brain would experience if it were connected to a fully functioning body—hormones, that sort of thing—but apart from some slight emotional lability, the effects are pretty minor.]

Felka stepped back. "What about your body?"

[Delmar will have a replacement ready, fully clone-cultured, when I get back to the Mother Nest. The reattachment procedure won't cause him any difficulties, especially since the decortication happened under controlled circumstances.]

"Well, that's fine then. But unless I'm missing something, you're still a prisoner."

[No. I have a certain degree of mobility, even now.] The head spun around through a disconcerting two hundred and seventy degrees. From out of the room's shadows stepped what Remontoire had until then taken to be a waiting general-utility servitor, the kind one might find in any well-appointed household. The bipedal androform machine had a dejected, slumped appearance. It was headless, with a circular aperture between its shoulders.

[Help me into it, please. The servitor can do it, but it always seems to take an eternity to do it properly.]

Help you into it? Remontoire queried.

[Grasp the support pillar immediately beneath my neck.]

Remontoire placed both hands around the silver pedestal and pulled. There was a soft click and the upper part, along with the head, came loose in his hands. He elevated it, finding it much heavier than he had imagined it would be. Hanging beneath the place where the pedestal had separated was a knot of slimy wriggling cables. They thrashed and groped like a fistful of eels.

[Now carry me—gently—to the servitor.]

Remontoire did as she asked. Perhaps the possibility of dropping the head flickered through his mind once or twice, though rationally he doubted that the fall would do Skade very much harm: the floor would most likely soften to absorb the impact. But he fought to keep such thoughts as well censored as he could.

[Now pop me down into the body of the servitor. The connections will establish themselves. Gently now . . . gently does it.]

He slid the silver core into the machine until he encountered resistance. *Is that it?*

[Yes.] Skade's eyes widened perceptibly, and her skin took on a blush it had lacked before. [Yes. Connection established. Now, let's see . . . motor control . . .]

The servitor's forearm jerked violently forwards, the fist clenching and unclenching spasmodically. Skade pulled it back and held the outspread hand before her eyes, studying the mechanical anatomy of gloss-black and chrome with rapt fascination. The servitor was of a quaint design that resembled medieval armour; it was both beautiful and brutal.

You seem to have the hang of it.

The servitor took a shuffling step forwards, both arms held slightly in front of it. [Yes . . . This is my quickest adjustment yet. It almost makes me think I should instruct Delmar not to bother.]

"Not to bother doing what?" asked Felka.

[Healing my old body. I think I prefer this one. That's a joke, incidentally.]

"Of course," Felka said uneasily.

[But you should be grateful that this has happened to me. It makes me more likely to try to bring Clavain back into our possession alive.]

"Why's that?"

"Because I would very much like him to see what he has done to me." Skade turned around with a creak of metal. "Now, there is something else you wanted to see, I think. Shall we continue?"

The suit of armour led them out of the room.

FIFTEEN

A word pressed itself into Volyova's skull, as hard and searing as a cattle brand.

[Ilia.]

She could not speak, could only shape her own thoughts in response. *Yes. How do you know my name?*

[I've come to know you. You've shown such interest in me—in us—that it was difficult not to know you in return.]

Again she moved to hammer on the door that had sealed her inside the cache weapon, but when she tried to lift her arm nothing happened. She was paralysed, though still able to breathe. The presence, whatever it was, continued to feel as if it was directly behind her, looking over her shoulder.

Who . . . She sensed a terrible mocking delight in her own ignorance.

[The controlling subpersona of this weapon, of course. You can call me Seventeen. Who else did you think I was?]

You speak Russish.

[I know your preferred natural language filters. Russish is easy enough. An old language. It hasn't changed much since the time we were made.]

Why . . . now?

[You have never reached this deeply into one of us before, Ilia.]

I . . . have. Nearly.

[Perhaps. But never under quite these circumstances. Never with so much fear before you even began. You are quite desperate to use us, aren't you? More than you've ever been before.]

She felt, despite still being paralysed, a tiny easing of her terror. So the presence was a computer program, no more than that. She had simply triggered a layer of the weapon's control mechanism that she had never knowingly invoked before. The presence felt almost preternaturally evil, but that—and the paralysis—was obviously just a refinement of the usual fear-generation mechanism.

Volyova wondered how the weapon was talking to her. She had no implants, and yet the weapon's voice was definitely speaking directly into her skull. It could only be that the chamber she was in was functioning as a kind of high-powered inverse trawl, stimulating brain function by the application of intense magnetic fields. If it could make her feel terror, Volyova supposed, and with such finesse, it would not have been a great deal more difficult for it to generate ghost signals along her auditory nerve or, more probably, in the hearing centre itself, and to pick up the anticipatory neural firing patterns that accompanied the intention to speak.

These are desperate times . . .

[So it would seem.]

Who made you?

There was no immediate answer from Seventeen. For a moment the fear was gone, the neural thrall interrupted by a blank instant of calm, like the drawing of breath between agonised screams.

[We don't know.]

No?

[No. They didn't want us to know.]

Volyova marshalled her thoughts with the care of someone placing heavy ornaments on a rickety shelf. *I think the Conjoiners made you. That's my working hypothesis, and nothing you've told me has led me to think it might need reconsidering.*

[It doesn't matter who made us, does it? Not now.]

Probably not. I'd like to know for curiosity's sake, but the most important thing is that you're still capable of serving me.

The weapon tickled the part of her mind that registered amusement. [Serving you, Ilia? Whatever gave you that impression?]

You did what I asked of you, in the past. Not you specifically, Seventeen—I never asked anything of you—but whenever I asked anything of the other weapons, they always obeyed me.

[We didn't *obey* you, Ilia.]

No?

[No. We humoured you. It amused us to do what you asked of us. Often that was indistinguishable from following your commands—but only from your point of view.]

You're just saying that.

[No. You see, Ilia, whoever made us gave us a degree of free will. There must have been a reason for that. Perhaps we were expected to act autonomously, or to piece together a course of action from incomplete or corrupted orders. We must have been created to be doomsday weapons, you see, weapons of final resort. Instruments of End Times.]

You still are.

[And are these End Times, Ilia?]

I don't know. I think they might be.

[You were frightened before you came here, I can tell. We all can. What exactly is it that you want of us, Ilia?]

There's a problem you might have to attend to.

[A local problem?]

In this system, yes. I'd need you to deploy beyond the ship . . . beyond this chamber . . . and help me.

[But what if we decide not to help you?]

You will. I've looked after you for so long, taking care of you, keeping you safe from harm. I know you'll help me.

The weapon held her suspended, stroking her mind playfully. Now she knew what a mouse felt like after the cat had caught it. She felt that she was only an instant away from having her spine broken in two.

But as abruptly as it had come, the paralysis eased. The weapon still imprisoned her, but she was regaining some voluntary muscle control.

[Perhaps, Ilia. But let's not pretend that there aren't complicating factors.]

Nothing we can't work around . . .

[It will be very difficult for us to do anything without the cooperation of the other one, Ilia. Even if we wanted to.]

The other one?

[The other . . . entity . . . that continues to exert a degree of control over us.]

Her mind dwelled on the possibilities before she realised what the weapon had to be talking about. *You mean the Captain.*

[Our autonomy is not so great that we can act without the

other entity's permission, Ilia. No matter how cleverly you attempt to persuade us.]

The Captain just needs persuading, that's all. I'm sure he'll come around, in the end.

[You have always been an optimist, haven't you, Ilia?]

No . . . not at all. But I have faith in the Captain.

[Then we hope your powers of persuasion are up to the task, Ilia.]

I do too.

She gasped suddenly, as if she had been stomach-punched. Her head was empty again and the horrid sense of something sitting immediately behind her had gone, as abruptly as a slamming door. There was not even a hint of the presence in her peripheral vision. She was floating alone, and although she was still imprisoned in the weapon, the feeling that it was haunted had vanished.

Volyova gathered her breath and her composure, marvelling at what had just happened. In all the years she had worked with the weapons she had never once suspected that any of them harboured a guardian subpersona, much less a machine intelligence of at least high gamma-level status—even possibly low-to-medium beta-level.

The weapon had scared the living daylights out of her. Which, she supposed, had undoubtedly been the intended affect.

There was a bustle of motion around her. The access panel—in a totally different part of the wall than she remembered—budged open an inch. Harsh blue light rammed through the gap. Through it, squinting, Volyova could just make out another spacesuited figure. "Khouri?"

"Thank God. You're still alive. What happened?"

"Let's just say my efforts to reprogram the weapon were not an unqualified success, shall we, and leave it at that?" She hated discussing failure almost as much as she hated the thing itself.

"What, you gave it the wrong command or something?"

"No, I gave it the right command but for a different interpreter shell than I was actually accessing."

"But that would still make it the wrong command, wouldn't it?"

Volyova turned herself around until her helmet was aligned

with the slit of light. "It's more technical than that. How did you get the panel open?"

"Good old brute force. Or is that not technical enough?"

Khouri had wedged a crowbar from her suit utility kit into what must have been a hair-fine joint in the weapon's skin, and then levered back on that until the panel slid open.

"And how long did you take to do that?"

"I've been trying to get it open since you went inside, but it only just gave way, right this minute."

Volyova nodded, fairly certain that absolutely nothing would have happened until the weapon decided it was time to let her go. "Very good work, Khouri. And how long do you think it will take to get it open all the way?"

Khouri adjusted her position, re-attaching herself to the weapon so that she could apply more leverage to the bar. "I'll have you out of there in a jiffy. But while I've got you there, so to speak, can we come to some agreement on the Thorn issue?"

"Listen to me, Khouri. He only barely trusts us now. Show him this ship, give him even a hint of a reason to begin to guess who I am, and you won't see him for daylight. We'll have lost him, and with him the only possible means of evacuating that planet in anything resembling a humane manner."

"But he's even less likely to trust us if we keep finding excuses for why he can't come aboard . . . "

"He'll just have to deal with them."

Volyova waited for a response, and waited, and then noticed that there no longer appeared to be anyone on the other side of the gap. The hard blue light that had been coming from Khouri's suit was gone, and no hand was on the tool.

"Khouri . . . ?" she said, beginning to lose her calm again.

"Ilia . . . " Khouri's voice came through weakly, as if she were fighting for breath. "I think I have a slight problem."

"Shit." Volyova reached for the end of the crowbar and tugged it through to her side of the hatch. She braced herself and then worked the gap wider, until it was just wide enough for her to push her helmet through. In intermittent flashes she saw Khouri falling into the darkness, her suit harness tumbling away from her. Crouched on the side of the weapon she also saw the belligerent lines of a heavy-construction servitor. The mantislike machine must have been under the Captain's direct control.

"You vicious bastard! It was me who broke into the weapon, not her . . . "

Khouri was very distant now, perhaps halfway to the far wall. How fast was she moving? Three or four metres per second, perhaps. It was not fast, but her suit's armour was not designed to protect her against impacts. If she hit badly . . .

Volyova worked harder, forcing the hatch open inch by painful inch. Dully, she realised that she was not going to make it in time. It was taking too long. Khouri would reach the wall long before Volyova freed herself.

"Captain . . . you've really done it now."

She pushed harder. The crowbar slipped from her fingers, whacked the side of her helmet and went spinning into the dark depths of the machine. Volyova hissed her anger, knowing that she did not have time to go searching for the lost tool. The hatch was wide enough to wriggle through now, but to do so she would have to abandon her harness and life-support pack. She could survive long enough to fend for herself, but there would be no way to save Khouri.

"Shit," she said. "Shit . . . shit . . . shit."

The hatch slid open.

Volyova climbed through the hole and kicked off from the side of the weapon, leaving the servitor behind. There was no time to reflect on what had just happened, except to acknowledge that only Seventeen or the Captain could have made the hatch open.

She had her helmet drop a radar overlay over her faceplate. Volyova rotated and then got an echo from Khouri. Her fall was taking her through the long axis of the chamber, through a gallery of menacing stacked weapons. Judging by her trajectory she must have already glanced against one of the monorail tracks that threaded the chamber.

"Khouri . . . are you still alive?"

"I'm still here, Ilia . . . " But she sounded as if she had been hurt. "I can't stop myself."

"You don't have to. I'm on my way."

Volyova jetted after her, zooming between weapons that were both familiar to her and yet still quietly mysterious. The radar echo assumed definition and shape, becoming a tumbling human figure. Behind it, looming closer and closer, was the far wall. Volyova checked her own speed relative to it: six metres per second. Khouri could not have been moving much slower than that.

Volyova squirted more thrust from her harness. Ten . . . twenty metres per second. She saw Khouri now, grey and doll-like, with one arm flopping limply into space. The figure swelled. Volyova applied reverse thrust in incremental stabs, feeling the frame creak at the unusual load it was being expected to distribute. Fifty metres from Khouri . . . forty. She looked in a bad way: a human arm was definitely not meant to articulate that way.

"Ilia . . . that wall's coming up awfully fast."

"So am I. Hold on. There may be a slight . . . " They thumped together. " . . . impact."

Mercifully, the collision had not thrown Khouri off on another trajectory. Volyova held on to her by her unharmed arm just long enough to unwind a line and fasten it to Khouri's belt and then let her go. The wall was visible now, no more than fifty metres away.

Volyova braked, her thumb hard down on the thruster toggle, ignoring the protestations from the suit's subpersona. The line tethering Khouri extended to maximum tautness, Khouri hanging between her and the wall. But they were slowing. The wall was not rushing towards them with quite the same sense of inevitability.

"Are you all right?" Volyova asked.

"I think I may have broken something. How did you get out of the weapon? When the machine flicked me off, the hatch was still nearly shut."

"I managed to get it open a little wider. But I had some help, I think."

"The Captain?"

"Possibly. But I don't know if it means he's fully on our side after all." She concentrated on flying for a moment, keeping the tether taut as she swung around. The pale green ghosts of the thirty-three cache weapons loomed on her radar; she plotted a course through them back to the airlock.

"I still don't know why he set the servitor on you," Volyova said. Maybe he wanted to warn us off rather than kill us. As you say, he could have killed us already. Just possibly he prefers to have us around.'

"You're reading a lot into one hatch."

"That's why I don't think we should count on the Captain's assistance, Khouri."

"No?"

"There's someone else we could ask for help," Volyova said. "We could ask Sylveste."

"Oh no."

"You met him once before, inside Hades."

"Ilia, I had to die to get inside that fucking thing. It's not something I'm going to do twice."

"Sylveste has access to the stored knowledge of the Amarantin. He might know of a suitable response to the Inhibitor threat, or at the very least have some idea of how long we have left to come up with one. His information could be vital, Ana, even if he can't help us in a material sense."

"No way, Ilia."

"You don't actually remember dying, do you? And you're fine now. There were no ill effects."

Khouri's voice was very weak, like someone mumbling on the edge of sleep. "You fucking do it, if it's that easy."

Presently—and not a moment too soon—Volyova saw the pale rectangle which marked the airlock. She approached it slowly, winding Khouri in and depositing her first into the lock. By then the injured woman was unconscious.

Volyova pulled herself in, closed the door behind them and waited for the lock to pressurise. When the air pressure had reached nine-tenths of a bar she wrenched her own helmet off, her ears popping, and flicked sweat-drenched hair from her eyes. The biomedical displays on Khouri's suit were all in the green: nothing to worry about. All she had to do now was drag her to somewhere where she could get medical attention.

The door into the rest of the ship irised open. She pushed herself towards it, hoping she had the strength to haul Khouri's dead weight along behind her.

"Wait."

The voice was calm and familiar, yet it was not one she had heard in a long time. It reminded her of unspeakable cold, of a place where the other crewmembers had feared to tread. It was coming from the wall of the chamber, hollowly resonant.

"Captain?" she said.

"Yes, Ilia. It's me. I'm ready to talk now."

* * *

Skade led Felka and Remontoire down into the bowels of *Nightshade,* deep into the realm of influence of her machinery. By turns, Remontoire started to feel light-headed and feverish. At first he thought it was his imagination, but then his pulse started racing and his heart thundered in his chest. The sensations worsened with every level that they descended, as if they were lowering themselves into an invisible fog of psychotropic gas.

Something's happening.

The head snapped around to look at him, while the ebony servitor continued striding forwards. [Yes. We're well into the field now. It wouldn't be safe for us to descend much further, not without medical support. The physiological effects become quite upsetting. Another ten vertical metres, then we'll call it a day.]

What's going on?

[It's a little difficult to say, Remontoire. We're within the influence of the machinery now, and the bulk properties of matter here—all matter, even the matter in your body—have been changed. The field that the machinery generates is suppressing inertia. What do you think you know about inertia, Remontoire?]

He answered judiciously. *As much as anyone, I suppose. It isn't something I've ever needed to think about. It's just something we live with.*

[It doesn't have to be. Not now.]

What have you done? Learned how to switch it off?

[Not quite—but we've certainly learned to take the sting out of it.] Skade's head twisted around again. She smiled indulgently; waves of opal and cerise flickered back and forth along her crest, signifying, Remontoire imagined, the effort that was required to translate the concepts she took for granted into terms a mere genius could grasp. [Inertia is more mysterious than you might think, Remontoire.]

I don't doubt it.

[It's deceptively easy to define. We feel it every moment of our lives, from the moment we're born. Push against a pebble and it moves. Push against a boulder and it doesn't, or at least not very much. By the same token, if a boulder's rushing towards you, you aren't going to be able to stop it very easily. Matter is lazy, Remontoire. It resists change. It wants to keep on doing whatever it's doing, whether that's sitting still or moving.

We call that laziness inertia, but that doesn't mean we understand it. For a thousand years we've labelled it, quantified it, caged it in equations, but we've still only scratched the surface of what it really is.]

And now?

[We have an opening. More than a glimpse. Recently the Mother Nest has achieved reliable control of inertia on the microscopic scale.]

"Exordium gave you all that?" Felka asked, speaking aloud.

Skade answered without speaking, refusing to indulge in Felka's preferred mode of communication. [I told you that the experiment gave us a signpost. It was almost enough to know that the technique was possible; that such a machine could exist. Even then it still took us years to build the prototype.]

Remontoire nodded; he had no reason to think she might be lying. *From scratch?*

[No . . . not entirely. We had a head start.]

What kind of head start? He watched mauve and turquoise striations pulse along Skade's crest.

[Another faction had explored something similar. The Mother Nest recovered key technologies relating to their work. From those beginnings—and the theoretical clues offered by the Exordium messages—we were able to progress to a functioning prototype.]

Remontoire recalled that Skade had once been involved in a high-security mission into Chasm City, an operation that had resulted in the deaths of many other operatives. The operation had clearly been sanctioned at Inner Sanctum level; even as a Closed Council member he knew little other than that it had happened.

You helped recover those technologies, Skade? I understand you were lucky to get out alive.

[The losses were extreme. We were fortunate that the mission was not a complete failure.]

And the prototype?

[For years we worked to make it into something useful. Microscopic control of inertia—no matter how conceptually profound—was never of any real value. But lately we've had one success after another. Now we can suppress inertia on classical scales, enough to make a difference to the performance of a ship.]

He looked at Felka, then back to Skade. *Ambitious, I'll give you that.*

[Lack of ambition is for baseline humans.]

This other faction . . . the one you recovered the items from—why didn't they make the same breakthrough? He had the impression that Skade was framing her thoughts with extreme care.

[All previous attempts to understand inertia were doomed to failure because they approached the problem from the wrong standpoint. Inertia isn't a property of matter as such, but a property of the quantum vacuum in which matter is embedded. Matter itself has no intrinsic inertia.]

The vacuum imposes inertia?

[It isn't really a vacuum, not at the quantum level. It's a seething foam of rich interactions: a broiling sea of fluctuations, with particles and messenger-particles in constant existential flux, like glints of sunlight on ocean waves. It's the choppiness of that sea which creates inertial mass, not matter itself. The trick is to find a way to modify the properties of the quantum vacuum—to reduce or increase the energy density of the electromagnetic zero-point flux. To calm the sea, if only in a locally defined volume.]

Remontoire sat down. *I'll stop here, if you don't mind.*

"I don't feel well either," Felka said, squatting down next to him. "I feel sick and light-headed."

The servitor turned around stiffly, animated like a haunted suit of armour. [You're experiencing the physiological effects of the field. Our inertial mass has dropped to about half its normal value. Your inner ear will be confused by the drop in inertia of the fluid in your semi-circular canal. Your heart will beat faster: it evolved to pump a volume of blood with an inertial mass of five per cent of your body; now it has only half that amount to overcome, and its own cardiac muscle reacts more swiftly to the electrical impulses from your nerves. If we were to go much deeper, your heart would start fibrillating. You would die without mechanical intervention.]

Remontoire grinned at the armoured servitor. *Fine for you, then.*

[It wouldn't be comfortable for me, either, I assure you.]

So what does the machine do? Does all the matter within the bubble have zero inertia?

[No, not in the present operating mode. The radial effectiveness of the damping depends on the mode in which we're running the device. At the moment we're in an inverse square field, which means that the inertial damping becomes four times more efficient every time we halve our distance to the machine; it becomes near infinite in the immediate proximity of the machine, but the inertial mass never drops to absolute zero. Not in this mode.]

But there are other modes?

[Yes: other states, we call them, but they're all very much less stable than the present one.] She paused, eyeing Remontoire. [You look ill. Shall we return upship?]

I'll be fine for now. Tell me more about your magic box.

Skade smiled, as stiffly as usual, but with what looked to Remontoire like pride. [Our first breakthrough was in the opposite direction—creating a region of enhanced quantum vacuum fluctuation, thereby increasing the energy-momentum flux. We call that state one. The effect was a zone of hyper-inertia: a bubble in which all motion ceased. It was unstable, and we never managed to magnify the field to macroscopic scales, but there were fruitful avenues for future research. If we could freeze motion by ramping inertia up by many orders of magnitude we'd have a stasis field, or perhaps an impenetrable defensive barrier. But cooling—state two—turned out to be technically simpler. The pieces almost fell into place.]

I'll bet they did.

"Is there a third state?" Felka asked.

[State three is a singularity in our calculations that we don't expect to be physically realisable. All inertial mass vanishes. All matter in a state-three bubble would become photonic: pure light. We don't expect that to happen; at the very least it would imply a massive local violation of the law of conservation of quantum spin.]

"And beyond that—on the other side of the singularity? Is there a state four?"

[Now we're getting ahead of ourselves, I think. We've explored the properties of the device in a well-understood parameter space, but there's no point in indulging in wild speculation.]

How much testing, exactly?

[*Nightshade* was chosen to be the prototype: the first ship to be equipped with inertia-suppression machinery. I ran some tests during the earlier flight, dropping the inertia by a measurable amount—enough to alter our fuel consumption and verify the effectiveness of the field, but not enough to draw attention.]

And now?

[The field is much stronger. The ship's effective mass is now only twenty per cent of what it was when we left the Mother Nest—there's a relatively small part of the ship projecting ahead of the field, but we can do better than that simply by increasing the field strength.] Skade clapped her hands together with a creak of armour. [Think of it, Remontoire—we could squeeze our mass down to one per cent, or less—accelerate at a hundred gees. If our bodies were inside the bubble of suppressed inertia we'd be able to withstand it, too. We'd reach near-light cruise speed in a couple of days. Subjective travel between the closest stars in under a week of shiptime. There'd be no need for us to be frozen. Can you imagine the possibilities? The galaxy would suddenly be a much smaller place.]

But that's not why you developed it. Remontoire climbed to his feet. Still light-headed, he steadied himself against the wall. It was the closest he had come to intoxication in a great while. This excursion had been interesting enough, but he was now more than ready to return upship, where the blood in his body would behave as nature had intended.

[I'm not sure I understand, Remontoire.]

It was for when the wolves arrive—the same reason you've built that evacuation fleet.

[*Sorry?*]

Even if we can't fight them, you've at least given us a means of running away very, very quickly.

Clavain opened his eyes from another bout of forced sleep. Cool dreams of walking through Scottish forests in the rain seduced him for a few dangerous moments. It was so tempting to return to unconsciousness, but then old soldierly instincts forced him to snap into grudging alertness. There had to be a problem. He had instructed the corvette not to wake him until it had something useful or ominous to report, and a quick appraisal of the situation revealed that this was most emphatically the latter.

Something was following him. Details were available on request.

Clavain yawned and scratched at the now generous growth of beard that he sported. He caught a glimpse of himself in the cabin window and registered mild alarm at what he saw. He looked wild-eyed and maniacal, as if he had just stumbled from the depths of a cave. He ordered the corvette to stop accelerating for a few minutes, then gathered some water into his hands from the faucet, cupping the amoeba-like droplets between his palms, and then endeavoured to splash them over his face and hair, slicking and taming hair and beard. He glanced at his reflection again. The result was not a great improvement, but at least he no longer looked feral.

Clavain unharnessed himself and set about preparing coffee and something to eat. It was his experience that crises in space fell into two categories: those that killed you immediately, usually without much warning, and those that gave you plenty of time to ruminate on the problem, even if no solution was very likely. This, on the basis of the evidence, looked like the kind which could be contemplated after first sating his appetite.

He filled the cabin with music: one of Quirrenbach's unfinished symphonies. He sipped the coffee, leafing through the corvette's status log entries while he did so. He was pleased but not surprised to see that the ship had operated flawlessly ever since his departure from Skade's comet. There was still adequate fuel to carry him all the way to circum-Yellowstone space, including the appropriate orbital insertion procedures once he arrived. The corvette was not the problem.

Transmissions had been received from the Mother Nest as soon as his departure had become evident. They had been tightbeamed on to him, maximally encrypted. The corvette had unpacked the messages and stored them in time-sequence.

Clavain bit into a slice of toast. "Play 'em. Oldest first. Then erase immediately."

He could have guessed what the first few messages would be like: frantic requests from the Mother Nest for him to turn around and come home. The first few gave him the benefit of the doubt, assuming—or pretending to assume—that he had some excellent justification for what looked like a defection attempt. But they had been half-hearted. Then the messages gave up on that tack and simply started threatening him.

Missiles had been launched from the Mother Nest. He had turned off his course and lost them. He had assumed that would be the end of it. A corvette was fast. There was nothing else that could catch him, unless he turned to interstellar space.

But the next set of messages did not emanate from the Mother Nest at all. They came from a tiny but measurable angle away from its position, a few arc-seconds, and they were steadily blue-shifted, as if originating from a moving source.

He calculated the rate of acceleration: one point five gees. He ran the numbers through his tactical simulator. It was as he'd expected: no ship with that rate of acceleration could catch him in local space. For a few minutes he allowed himself to feel relief while still pondering the point of the pursuer. Was it merely a psychological gesture? It seemed unlikely. Conjoiners were not greatly enamoured of gestures.

"Open the messages," he said.

The format was audio-visual. Skade's head popped into the cabin, surrounded by an oval of blurred background. The communication was verbal; she knew that he would never allow her to insert anything into his head again.

"Hello, Clavain," she said. "Please listen and pay attention. As you may have gathered, we are pursuing you with *Nightshade*. You will assume that we cannot catch you, or come within missile or beam-weapon range. These assumptions are incorrect. We are accelerating and will continue to increase our acceleration at regular intervals. Study the Doppler shift of these transmissions carefully if you doubt me."

The disembodied head froze; vanished.

He scanned the next message originating from the same source. Its header indicated that it had been transmitted ninety minutes after the first. The implied acceleration was now two point five gees.

"Clavain. Surrender now and I guarantee you a fair hearing. You cannot win."

The transmission quality was poor: the acoustics of her voice were strange and mechanical, and whatever compression algorithm she had used had made her head seem fixed and immobile, only her mouth and eyes moving.

Next message: three gees.

"We have redetected your exhaust signature, Clavain. The temperature and blue shift of your flame indicates that you are accelerating at your operational limit. I want you to appreciate that we are nowhere near ours. This is not the ship you knew, Clavain, but something faster and more deadly. It is fully capable of intercepting you."

The masklike face contorted into a stiff ghoulish smile. "But there is still time for negotiation. I'll let you pick a place of rendezvous, Clavain. Just say the word and we'll meet on your terms. A minor planet, a comet, open space—it doesn't bother me in the slightest."

He killed the message. He was certain that Skade was bluffing about having detected his flame. The last part of the message, the invitation to reply, was just her attempt to get him to betray his position by transmitting.

"Sly, Skade," he said. "But unfortunately I'm a hell of a lot more sly."

But it still worried him. She was accelerating too hard, and although the blue shift could have been faked, applied to the message before it was transmitted, he sensed that in that respect at least there had been no bluff.

She was coming after him with a much faster ship than he had assumed available, and she was gaining ground by the second.

Clavain bit into his toast and listened to the Quirrenbach a bit longer.

"Play the rest," he said.

"You have no more messages," the corvette told him.

Clavain was studying newsfeeds when the corvette announced receipt of a new batch of messages. He examined the accompanying information, noting that there was nothing from Skade this time.

"Play them," he said cautiously.

The first message was from Remontoire. His head appeared, bald and cherubic. He was more animated than Skade, and there was a good deal more emotion in his voice. He leant towards the lens, his eyes beseeching.

"Clavain. I'm hoping you'll hear this and give it some thought. If you've listened to Skade then you'll know that we can catch you up. This isn't a trick. She'll kill me for what I'm about to say, but if I know you at all you'll have arranged for these messages to be wiped as soon as you play them, so there's no real danger of this information reaching enemy hands. So here it is. There's experimental machinery on *Nightshade*. You knew Skade was testing something, but not what. Well, I'll tell you. It's a machine for suppressing inertial mass. I don't pretend to understand how it works, but I've seen the evidence that it does with my own eyes. Felt it, even. We've ramped up to four gees now, though you'll be able to confirm that independently. Before very long you'll have parallactic confirmation from the origin of these signals, if you weren't already convinced. All I'm saying is it's real, and according to Skade it can keep suppressing more and more of our mass." He looked hard into the camera, paused and then continued, "We can read your drive flame. We're homing in on it. You can't escape, Clavain, so stop running. As a friend, I beg you to stop running. I want to see you again, to talk and laugh with you."

"Skip to next message," he said, interrupting.

The corvette obliged; Felka's image replaced Remontoire's. Clavain experienced a jolt of surprise. The matter of who would pursue him had never been entirely settled in his mind, but he could have counted on Skade: she would make sure she was there when the killing missile was launched, and she would do all in her power to be the one to give the order. Remontoire would come along out of a sense of duty to the Mother Nest, emboldened by the conviction that he was executing a solemn task and that only he was truly qualified to hunt Clavain.

But Felka? He had not expected to see Felka at all.

"Clavain," she said, her voice revealing the strain of talking under four gees. "Clavain . . . *please*. They're going to kill you. Skade won't go to any great trouble to arrange a live capture, no matter what she says. She wants to confront you, to rub your nose in what you've done . . . "

"What I've done?" he said to her recording.

" . . . and while she'll capture you if she can, I don't think she'll keep you alive for long. But if you turn around and surrender, and let the Mother Nest know what you're doing, I think there might be a hope. Are you listening, Clavain?" She reached out and traced shapes across the lens between them, exactly as if she were mapping his face, relearning its shape for the thousandth time. "I want you to come home safe and sound, that's all. I don't even disagree with what you've done. I have my doubts about a lot of things, Clavain, and I can't say I wouldn't have . . . "

She lost whatever thread she was following, staring into infinity before refocusing. "Clavain . . . there's something I have to tell you, something that I think might make a difference. I've never spoken of this to you before, but now I think the time is right. Am I being cynical? Yes, avowedly. I'm doing this because I think it might persuade you to turn back; no other reason than that. I hope you can forgive me."

Clavain clicked a finger at the corvette's wall, making it drop the volume of the music. For a heartbreaking moment there was near silence, Felka's face hovering before him. Then she spoke again.

"It was on Mars, Clavain, when you were Galiana's prisoner for the first time. She kept you there for months and then released you. You must remember what it was like back then."

He nodded. Of course he remembered. What difference did four hundred years make?

"Galiana's nest was hemmed in from all sides. But she wouldn't give up. She had plans for the future, big plans, the kind that involved expanding the numbers of her disciples. But the nest lacked genetic diversity. Whenever new DNA came her way, she seized it. You and Galiana never made love on Mars, Clavain, but it was easy enough for her to obtain a cell scraping without your knowledge."

"And?" he whispered.

Felka's message continued seamlessly. "After you'd gone back to your side, she combined your DNA with her own, splicing the two samples together. Then she created me from the same genetic information. I was born in an artificial womb, Clavain, but I am still Galiana's daughter. And still your daughter, too."

"Skip to next message," he said, before she could say another word. It was too much; too intense. He could not process the information in one go, even though she was only telling him what he had always suspected—prayed—was the case.

But there were no other messages.

Fearfully, Clavain asked the corvette to spool back and replay Felka's transmission. But he had been much too thorough: the ship had dutifully erased the message, and now all that remained was what he carried in his memory.

He sat in silence. He was far from home, far from his friends, embarked on something that even he was not sure he believed in. It was entirely likely that he would die soon, uncommemorated except as a traitor. Even the enemy would not do him the dignity of remembering him with any more affection than that. And now this: a message that had reached across space to claw at his feelings. When he had said goodbye to Felka he had managed a singular piece of self-deception, convincing himself that he no longer thought of her as his daughter. He had believed it, too, for the time it took to leave the Nest.

But now she was telling him that he had been right all along. And that if he did not turn around he would never see her again.

But he could not turn around.

Clavain wept. There was nothing else to do.

SIXTEEN

Thorn took his first tentative steps aboard *Nostalgia for Infinity*. He looked around with frantic, wide-eyed intent, desperate not to miss a single detail or nuance of detail that might betray deception or even the tiniest hint that things were not completely as claimed. He was afraid to blink. What if some vital slip that would have exposed the whole thing as a façade happened when he had his eyes closed? What if the two of them were *waiting* for him to blink, like conjurors playing with an audience's attention?

Yet there appeared to be no deception here. Even if the trip in the shuttle had not convinced him of that fact—and it was difficult to imagine how that could have been faked—the supreme evidence was here.

He had travelled through space. He was no longer on Resurgam, but inside a colossal spacecraft: the Triumvir's long-lost lighthugger. Even the gravity felt different.

"You couldn't have made this . . . " he said, as he walked alongside his two companions. "Not in a hundred years. Not unless you were Ultras to begin with. And then why would you need to fake it anyway?"

"So you're prepared to believe our story?" the Inquisitor asked him.

"You've got your hands on a starship. I can hardly deny that. But even a ship this size, and from what I've seen it's at least as big as *Lorean* ever was, even a ship this size can't accommodate two hundred thousand sleepers. Can it?"

"It won't need to," the other woman told him. "Remember, this is an evacuation operation, not a pleasure cruise. Our objective is only to get people away from Resurgam. We'll put the most vulnerable into reefersleep. But the majority will have to stay awake and suffer rather cramped conditions. They won't enjoy it, but it's a hell of an improvement on being dead."

There was no arguing with that. None of his own plans had ever guaranteed a luxurious ride off the planet.

"How long do you think people will have to spend here, before they can return to Resurgam?" he asked.

The women exchanged glances. "Returning to Resurgam may never be an option," the older one said.

Thorn shrugged. "It was a sterile rock when we arrived. We can start from scratch if we have to."

"Not if the planet doesn't exist. It *could* be that bad, Thorn." She knuckled the wall of the ship as they walked on. "But we can keep people here as long as we need to—years, decades even."

"We could reach another star system, then," he countered. "This is a starship, after all."

Neither of them said anything.

"I still want to see what it is we're so frightened of," he said. "Whatever it is that's posing such a threat."

The older one, Irina, said, "Do you sleep well at night, Thorn?"

"As well as anyone."

"I'm afraid all that's about to end. Follow me, will you?"

* * *

Antoinette was aboard *Storm Bird,* running systems checks, when the message came in. The freighter was still berthed in the rim repair bay in Carousel New Copenhagen, but most of the serious damage had been rectified or patched over. Xavier's monkeys had worked around the clock, since neither he nor Antoinette could afford to occupy this bay for an hour longer than necessary. The monkeys had agreed to work even though most of the other hyperprimate workers in the carousel were on strike or sick with an extremely rare prosimian virus that had mysteriously crossed a dozen species barriers overnight. Xavier detected, so he claimed, a degree of sympathy from the workers. None of them were great fans of the Ferrisville Convention, and the fact that Antoinette and Xavier were being persecuted by the police only made the primates more willing to break the usual labour rules. Nothing came without costs, of course, and Xavier would end up owing the workers rather more than he might have wished, but there were certain trade-offs that one simply had to accept. That was a rule Antoinette's father had quoted often enough, and she had grown up with the same resolutely pragmatic approach.

Antoinette was tapping through tokamak field configuration settings, a compad tucked under one arm and a pen between her teeth, when the console chimed. Her first thought was that something she had done had triggered an error somewhere else in the ship's control web.

She spoke with the pen still in place, knowing that Beast would be able to make sense of her gruntings. "Beast . . . fix that, will you?"

"Little Miss, the signal in question is a notification of the arrival of a message."

"Xavier?"

"Not Mr. Liu, Little Miss. The message, in so far as one can deduce from the header information, originated well outside the carousel."

"Then it's the cops. Funny. They don't usually call; they just show up, like a turd on the doorstep."

"It doesn't appear to be the authorities either, Little Miss. Might one suggest that the most prudent course of action would be to view the message in question?"

"Clever clogs." She pulled the pen from her mouth and

tucked it behind her ear. "Pipe it through to my 'pad, Beast."

"Very well, Little Miss."

The screen of tokamak data shuffled aside. In its place a face resolved, speckled with coarse-resolution pixels. Whoever was sending was trying to get away with taking up as little bandwidth as possible. Nonetheless, she recognised the face very well.

"Antoinette . . . it's me again. I hope you made it back safely." Nevil Clavain paused, scratching at his beard. "I'm bouncing this transmission through about fifteen relays. Some of them are pre-plague, some of them may even go back to the Amerikano era, so the quality may not be of the best. I'm afraid there's no possibility of you being able to reply, and no possibility of my being able to send another message; this is emphatically my one and only shot. I need your help, Antoinette. I need your help very badly." He smiled awkwardly. "I know what you're thinking: that I said I'd kill you if our paths ever crossed again. I meant it, too, but I said it because I hoped you'd take me seriously and stay out of trouble. I really hope you believe that, Antoinette, or else there isn't much chance that you're likely to agree to my next request."

"Your next request?" she mouthed, staring in disbelief at the compad.

"What I need, Antoinette, is for you to come and rescue me. I'm in rather a lot of trouble, you see."

She listened to what he had to say, but there was not a great deal more to the message. Clavain's request was simple enough, and it was, she admitted, within her capabilities to do what he wanted. Even the co-ordinates he had given her were precise enough that she would not have to do any real searching. There was a tight time window, very tight, actually, and there was a not inconsiderable degree of physical risk, quite aside from any associated with Clavain himself. But it was all very feasible. She could tell that Clavain had worked through the details himself before calling her, anticipating almost all the likely problems and objections she might have. In that respect, she could not help but admire his dedication.

But it still didn't make a shred of difference. The message was from Clavain, the Butcher of Tharsis; the same Clavain who had lately started inhabiting her dreams, personifying what had previously been the merely faceless terror of the spider induction wards. It was Clavain who presided over the glistening machines as they lowered themselves into her brainpan.

It didn't matter that he had once saved her life.

"You have got to be fucking kidding," Antoinette said.

Clavain floated alone in space. Through his spacesuit visor he watched the corvette curve away on automatic pilot, dwindling slowly but surely until its sleek flintlike shape was difficult to distinguish from a faint star. Then the corvette's main drive flicked on, a hard and bright violet-blue spike, carefully angled away from his best guess for the position of *Nightshade*. The acceleration would certainly have crushed him had he remained aboard. He watched until even that spike of light had become the slightest pale scratch against the stars, until the point where he blinked and lost it altogether.

He was alone, about as truly alone as it was possible to be.

As rapid as the corvette's acceleration now was, it was nothing that the ship could not sustain. In a few hours the burn would take it to a point in space and give it a velocity consistent with its last recorded position as determined by *Nightshade*. The drive would ramp down then, back to a thrust level consistent with carrying a human passenger. Skade would redetect the corvette's flame, but she would also see that the flame was flickering with some irregularity, indicating an unstable fusion burn. That, at least, was what Clavain hoped she would think.

For the last fifteen hours of his flight he had pushed the corvette's motors as hard as he could, deliberately circumventing the safety overrides. With all the excess mass aboard the corvette—weapons, fuel, life-support mechanisms—the corvette's effective acceleration ceiling had not been far above his own physiological tolerance limit. It had been prudent to accelerate as hard as he could stand, of course, but Clavain had also wanted Skade to think that he was pushing things just slightly too hard.

He had known that she must be watching his flame, studying it for any hint of a mistake on his part. So, by tapping into the engine-management system he had introduced evidence of an imminent failure mode. He had forced the engine to operate erratically, cycling its temperature, allowing unfused impurities to clot the exhaust, showing every sign that it was about to blow.

After fifteen hours he had simulated an abrupt stuttering

drive failure. Skade would recognise the failure mode; it was almost textbook stuff. She would doubtless think that Clavain had been unlucky not to die in an instant painless blast. Now she would be able to catch up with him, and his death would be rather more protracted. If Skade recognised the type of failure mode he had hoped to simulate, she would conclude that it would require about ten hours for the ship's own auto-repair mechanisms to fix the fault. Even then, for that particular failure mode only a partial repair would be possible. Clavain might be able to get the antimatter-catalysed fusion torch re-lit, but the drive would never function at full capacity. At the very best, Clavain might manage to squeeze six gees out of the corvette, and he would not be able to sustain that acceleration for long.

As soon as she saw the corvette's flame, as soon as she recognised the telltale flicker, Skade would know that success was hers. She would never know that he had used the ten hours of grace not to repair a defective engine, but to deposit himself somewhere else entirely. At least, he hoped she would never guess that.

His last act had been to send a message to Antoinette Bax, making sure that the signal could not possibly be interdicted by Skade or any other hostile forces. He had told Antoinette where he would be floating, and he had told her exactly how long he could reasonably survive in a single low-endurance spacesuit with no sophisticated recycling systems. By his own estimation she could reach him in time and then ferry him out of the war zone before Skade had a chance to realise what was happening. All Antoinette would need to do was approach the rough volume of space he had defined and then sweep it with her radar; sooner or later she would pick out his figure.

But she only had one window of opportunity. He only had one chance to convince her, and she had to act immediately. If she decided to call his bluff or to wait a couple of days, agonising about what to do, he was dead.

He was in her hands. Totally.

Clavain did what he could to extend the suit's durability. He brought up certain rarely used neural routines that allowed him to slow his own metabolism, so that he would use as little air and power as possible. There was no real point in staying conscious; it gained him nothing except the opportunity to endlessly reflect on whether he was going to live or die.

Drifting alone in space, Clavain prepared to sink into unconsciousness. He thought of Felka, who he did not believe he would ever see again, and wondered about her message. He did not know if he wanted it to be true or not. He hoped also that she would find a way to come to terms with his defection, that she would not hate him for it and that she would not resent the fact that he had continued with it despite her plea.

He had originally defected to the side of the Conjoiners because he had believed it was the right thing to do under the circumstances. There had been almost no time to plan his defection or evaluate the correctness of it. The moment had arisen when he had to make his choice, there and then. He had known that there was no going back.

It was the same now. The moment had presented itself . . . and he had seized it, mindful of the consequences, knowing that he might turn out to be wrong, that his fears might turn out to be groundless or the paranoid delusions of an old, old man, but knowing that it must be done.

That, he suspected, was the way it would always be for him.

He remembered a time when he lay under fallen rubble, in a pocket of air beneath a collapsed structure on Mars. It had been about four standard months after the Tharsis Bulge campaign. He remembered the broken-spined cat that he had kept alive, how he had shared his rations with the injured animal even when the thirst had felt like acid etching away his mouth and throat; even when the hunger had been far, far worse than the pain of his own injuries. He remembered that the cat had died shortly after the two of them had been pulled from the rubble, and wondered whether the kindest thing would have been for it to have died earlier, rather than have its own painful existence prolonged for a few more days. And yet he knew that if the same thing were to happen again he would keep the cat alive, no matter how pointless the gesture. It was not just that keeping the cat alive had given him something to focus on other than his own discomfort and fear. There had been something more. What, he couldn't easily say. But he had a feeling that it was the same impulse that was driving him towards Yellowstone, the same impulse that had made him seek Antoinette Bax's help.

Alone and fearful, far from any world, Nevil Clavain fell into unconsciousness.

SEVENTEEN

The two women brought Thorn to a room within *Nostalgia for Infinity*. The centrepiece of the room was an enormous spherical display apparatus, poised in the middle of the chamber like a single grotesque eyeball. Thorn had an unshakeable feeling of intense scrutiny, as if not just the eye but also the entire fabric of the ship was studying him with great owl-like interest and not a little malice. Then he began to take in the particulars of what confronted him. There was evidence of damage everywhere. Even the display apparatus itself appeared to have been subjected to recent and crude repairs.

"What happened here?" Thorn asked. "It looks as if there was a gunfight or something."

"We'll never know for sure," Inquisitor Vuilleumier said. "Clearly the crew wasn't as united as we thought during the Sylveste crisis. It looks from the internal evidence as if there was some sort of factional dispute aboard the ship."

"We always suspected this was the case," the other woman, Irina, added. "Evidently there was trouble brewing just below the surface. Seems that whatever happened around Cerberus/Hades was enough to spark off a mutiny. The crew must have killed each other, leaving the ship to take care of itself."

"Handy for us," Thorn said.

The women exchanged glances. "Perhaps we should move on to the item of interest," Vuilleumier said.

They played a movie for him. It was holographic, running in the big eye. Thorn assumed that it was a computer synthesis assembled from data that the ship had gathered from a multitude of sensor bands and viewpoints. What it presented was a God's-eye view, the view of a being able to apprehend entire planets and their orbits.

"I must ask you to accept something," Irina said. "It is difficult to accept, but it must be done."

"Tell me," Thorn said.

"The entire human species is poised on the brink of sudden and catastrophic extinction."

"That's quite a claim. I hope you can justify it."

"I can, and I will. The important thing to grasp is that the extinction, if it is to happen, will begin here, now, around Delta Pavonis. But this is merely the start of something that will become greater and bloodier."

Thorn could not help but smile. "Then Sylveste was right, is that it?"

"Sylveste knew nothing about the details, or the risks he was taking. But he was correct in one assumption: he believed that the Amarantin had been wiped out by external intervention, and that it had something to do with their sudden emergence as a spacefaring culture."

"And the same thing's going to happen to us?"

Irina nodded. "The mechanism will be different this time, it seems. But the agents are the same."

"And they are?"

"Machines," Irina told him. "Starfaring machines of immense age. For millions of years they've hidden between the stars, waiting for another culture to disturb the great galactic silence. All they exist to do is detect the emergence of intelligence and then suppress it. We call them the Inhibitors."

"And now they're here?"

"The evidence would suggest so."

They showed him what had happened so far, how a squadron of Inhibitor machines had arrived in the system and set about the dismantling of three worlds. Irina shared with Thorn her suspicion that Sylveste's activities had probably drawn them, and that there might even be further waves converging on the Resurgam system from further out, alerted by the expanding wavefront of whatever signal had activated the first machines.

He watched the three worlds die. One was a metallic planet; the other two were rocky moons. The machines swarmed and multiplied on the surfaces of the moons, covering them in a plaque of specialised industrial forms. From the equators, plumes of mined matter belched into space. The moons were being cored out like apples. The matter plumes were directed into the maws of three colossal processing engines orbiting the dying bodies. Streams of refined matter, segregated into distinct ores and isotopes and granularities, were then flung into interplanetary space, arcing out along lazy parabolas.

"That was just the start," Vuilleumier said.

They showed him how the mass streams from the three dismantled moons converged on a single point in space. It was a point in the orbit of the system's largest gas giant, and the giant planet would arrive at that point at exactly the same time as the three mass streams.

"That was when our attention switched to the giant," Irena said.

The Inhibitor machines were fearfully difficult to detect. It was only with the greatest of effort that she had managed to discern the presence of another smaller swarm of machines around the giant. For a long time they had done nothing but wait, poised for the arrival of the matter streams, the hundred billion billion tonnes of raw material.

"I don't understand," Thorn said. "There are plenty of moons around the gas giant itself. Why did they go to the trouble of dismantling moons elsewhere if they were going to be needed here?"

"Those aren't the right sort of moon," Irina said. "Most of the moons around the giant aren't much more than ice balls, small rocky cores surrounded by frozen or liquid-state volatiles. They needed to rip apart metallic worlds, and that meant looking further afield."

"And now what are they going to do?"

"Make something else, it seems," Irina said. "Something bigger still. Something that needs one hundred billion billion tonnes of raw material."

Thorn returned his attention to the eye. "When did this start? When did the matter streams reach Roc?"

"Three weeks ago. The thing—whatever it is—is beginning to take shape." Irena tapped at a bracelet around her wrist, causing the eye to zoom in on the giant's immediate neighbourhood.

Most of the planet remained in shadow. Above the one limb that was illuminated—an off-white crescent shot through with pale bars of ochre and fawn—*something* was suspended: a filamentary arc that must have been many thousands of kilometres from end to end. Irina zoomed in further, towards the middle of the arc.

"It's a solid object, so far as we can tell," Vuilleumier said. "An arc of a circle one hundred thousand kilometres in radius. It's in an equatorial orbit around the planet, and the ends are growing."

Irina zoomed in again, focusing on the precise midpoint of the growing arc. There was a swelling, little more than a lozenge-shaped smudge at the current resolution. She tapped more controls on the bracelet and the smudge bloomed into clarity, expanding to fill the entire display volume.

"It was a moon in its own right," Irina said, "a ball of ice a few hundred kilometres from side to side. They circularised its orbit above the equator in a few days, without the moon breaking apart under the dynamic stresses. Then the machines built structures inside it, what we must assume to be additional processing equipment. One of the matter streams falls into the moon *here,* via this maw-shaped structure. We can't speculate about what goes on inside, I'm afraid. All we know is that two tubular structures are emerging from either end of the moon, fore and aft of its orbital motion. On this scale they appear to be whiskers, but the tubes are actually fully fifteen kilometres in thickness. They currently extend seventy thousand kilometres either side of the moon, and are growing in length by a rate of around two hundred and eighty kilometres every hour."

Irina nodded, noting Thorn's evident incredulity. "Yes, that's quite correct. What you see here has been achieved in the last ten standard days. We are dealing with an industrial capacity beyond anything in our experience, Thorn. Our machines can turn a small metal-rich asteroid into a starship in a few days, but even that would seem astonishingly slow by comparison with the Inhibitor processes."

"Ten days to form that arc." The hairs on the back of Thorn's neck were standing up, to his embarrassment. "Do you think they'll keep growing it until the ends meet?"

"It seems likely. If the ends are to form a ring, they'll meet in a little under ninety days."

"Three months! You're right. We couldn't do that. We never could; not even during the *Belle Époque*. Why, though? Why throw a ring around the gas giant?"

"We don't know. Yet. There's more, though." Irina nodded at the eye. "Shall we continue?"

"Show me," Thorn said. "I want to see it all."

"You won't like it."

She showed him the rest, explaining how the three individual mass streams had followed near-ballistic trajectories from their points of origin, like chains of pebbles tossed in precise formation. But near the gas giant they were tightly orchestrated, steered and braked by machines too small to see. They were forced to curve sharply, aimed towards whichever constructional focus was their destination. One stream rained down into the maw of the moon that was extruding out the whiskers. The other two streams plunged into similar mawlike structures on two other moons, both of which had been lowered into orbits just above the cloud layer, well within the radius at which they should have been shattered by tidal forces.

"What are the other two moons doing?" Thorn asked.

"Something else, it seems," Irina said. "Here, take a look. See if you can make more sense of it than we've been able to."

It was difficult to surmise exactly what was going on. There was a whisker of material emerging from each of the two lower moons, ejected aft, against the direction of orbital motion. The whiskers appeared to be about the same size as the arc that was being built by the higher moon, but they each followed a sinuous snakelike curve that took them from a tangent to the orbital motion into the atmosphere itself, like great telegraph cables being reeled into the sea by a ship. Immediately behind the impact point of each tube was an eyelike wake of roiling and disturbed atmosphere many thousands of kilometres long.

"They don't come out again, as far as we can see," Vuilleumier said.

"How fast are they being laid?"

"We can't tell. There aren't any reference points on the tubes themselves, so we can't calculate how fast they're emerging from the moons. There's no way we can get a Doppler measurement, not without revealing our interest. But we know that the flux of matter falling into each of the three moons is about the same, and the tubes are all about the same width."

"Then they're probably being spooled into the atmosphere at the same speed as the arc is being formed, is that it? Two hundred and eighty kilometres per hour, or thereabouts." Thorn looked at the two women, searching their faces for clues. "Any ideas, then?"

"We can't begin to guess," Irina said.

"But you don't think this is good news, do you?"

"No, Thorn, I don't. My guess, frankly, is that whatever is taking place down there is part of something even larger."

"And that something means we have to evacuate Resurgam?"

She nodded. "We still have time, Thorn. The outer arc won't be finished for eighty days, but it seems very unlikely that anything catastrophic will happen immediately after that. More likely, another process will start, something that might take as long again to complete as the building of the arcs. We may have many months beyond that."

"Months, though, not years."

"We only need six months to evacuate Resurgam."

Thorn remembered the calculations they had explained to him, the dry arithmetic of shuttle flights and passenger capacities. It could be done in six months, yes, but only if human behaviour was factored out of the sums. People did not behave like bulk cargo. Especially not people who had been cowed and intimidated by an oppressive regime for the last five decades.

"What you told me before—that we might have a few years to get this done?"

Vuilleumier smiled. "We told a few white lies, that's all."

Later, following what seemed to him to be an unnecessarily tortuous route through the ship, they took Thorn to view a cavernous hangar bay where many smaller spacecraft waited. They hung in their parking racks, transatmospheric and ship-to-ship shuttles like sleek-skinned sharks or bloated, spined angelfish. Most of the ships were too small to be of any use in the proposed evacuation plan, but he could not deny that the view was impressive.

They even helped him into a spacesuit with a thruster pack so that he could be taken on a tour through the chamber itself, inspecting the ships that would lift the people off Resurgam and ferry them across space to *Nostalgia for Infinity* itself. If he had harboured any suspicions that any of this was being faked, he discarded them now. The sheer vastness of the chamber and the overwhelming fact of the ships' existence rammed aside any lingering misgivings, at least with respect to the reality of *Infinity*.

And yet . . . and yet. He had seen the ship with his own eyes, had walked on it and felt the subtle difference of its spin-generated artificial gravity compared with the pull of Resurgam that he had known all his adult life. The ship could not be faked, and it would have taken extreme measures to fake the fact that the bay was full of smaller craft. But the threat itself? That was where it all broke down. They had shown him much, but not nearly enough. Everything concerning the threat to Resurgam had been shown to him second-hand. He had seen none of it with his own eyes.

Thorn was a man who needed to see things for himself. He could ask either of the two women to show him more evidence, but that would solve nothing. Even if they took him outside the ship and let him look through a telescope pointed at the gas giant, there would be no way for him to be sure that the view was not being doctored in some way. Even if they let him look with his own eyes towards the giant, and told him that the dot of light he was seeing was in some way different because of the machines' activities, he would still be taking it on trust.

He was not a man to take things on trust.

"Well, Thorn?" Vuilleumier said, helping him out of the suit. "I take it you've seen enough now to know we aren't lying? The sooner we get you back to Resurgam, the sooner we can move ahead with the exodus. Time's precious, as we said."

He nodded at the small dangerous-looking woman with the smoke-coloured eyes. "You're right. You've shown me a lot, I admit. Enough for me to be sure you aren't lying about all of it."

"Well, then."

"But that's not good enough."

"No?"

"You're asking me to risk too much to take any of it on trust, Inquisitor."

There was steel in her voice when she answered. "You saw your dossier, Thorn. There's enough there to send you to the Amarantin."

"I don't doubt it. I'll give you more, if you want. It doesn't change a thing. I'm not going to lead the people into anything that looks like a government trap."

"You still think this is a conspiracy?" Irina asked, ending her remark with an odd clucking noise.

"I can't discount it, and that's all that matters."

"But we showed you what the Inhibitors are doing."

"No," he said. "What you showed me was some data in a projection device. I still have no objective evidence that the machines are real."

Vuilleumier looked at him imploringly. "Dear God, Thorn. How much more have we got to show you?"

"Enough," he said. "Enough that I can believe it completely. How you do that is entirely your problem."

"There isn't time for this, Thorn."

He wondered, then. She said it with such urgency that it almost cut through his doubts. He could hear the fear in her voice.

Whatever else was going on, she was truly scared about something . . .

Thorn looked back towards the hangar bay. "Could one of those ships get us closer to the giant?"

The Dawn War had been about metal.

Almost all the heavy elements in the observable universe had been brewed in the cores of stars. The Big Bang itself had made little except hydrogen, helium and lithium, but each successive generation of stars had enriched the palette of elements available to the cosmos. Massive suns assembled the elements lighter than iron in delicately balanced fusion reactions, block by block, cascading through increasingly desperate reactions as lighter elements were depleted. But once stars started burning silicon, the end was in sight. The end-stage of silicon fusion was a shell of iron imprisoning the star's core, but iron itself could not be fused. Barely a day after the onset of silicon fusion, the star would become catastrophically and suddenly unstable, collapsing under its own gravity. Rebounding shockwaves from the collapse would lift the star's carcass into space, outshining all other stars in the galaxy. The supernova itself would create new elements, pumping cobalt, nickel, iron and a stew of radioactive decay products back into the tenuous clouds of gas that lay between all stars. It was this interstellar medium that would provide the raw material for the next generation of stars and worlds. Nearby, a clump of gas that had until then been stable against collapse would ripple with the shockwave of the super-

nova, forming knots and whorls of enhanced density. The clump, which had already been metal-enriched by earlier supernovae, would begin to collapse under its own ghostly gravity. It would form hot, dense stellar nurseries, birthing places of eager young stars. Some were cool dwarves that would consume their star fuel so slowly that they would outlast the galaxy itself. But others were faster burners, supermassive suns that lived and died in a galactic eyeblink. In their death throes they strewed more metals into the vacuum and triggered yet more cycles of stellar birth.

The process continued, until the dawn of life itself. Hot blasts of dying stars peppered the galaxy, and with each blast the raw materials for world-building—and life itself—became more abundant. But the steady enrichment of metals did not happen uniformly across the disc of the galaxy. In the outlying regions of the galaxy, the cycles of stardeath and starbirth happened on a much slower timescale than in the frantic core zones.

So it was that the first stars to host rocky worlds formed closer to the core, where the metals reached the critical level first. It was from the core zones, within a thousand kiloparsecs of the galactic centre itself, that the first starfaring cultures emerged. They looked out into the galactic wilderness, flung envoys across thousands of light-years and imagined themselves alone and unique and somehow privileged. It was a time both of sadness and chilling cosmic potential. They imagined themselves to be lords of creation.

But nothing in the galaxy was that straightforward. Not only were there other cultures emerging at more or less the same galactic epoch, in the same band of habitable stars, but there were also pockets of higher metallicity out in the cold zone: statistical fluctuations which allowed machine-building life to emerge where it ought not to have been possible. There were to be no all-encompassing galactic dominions, for none of these nascent cultures managed to spread across the galaxy before encountering the expansion wave of another rival. It had all happened with blinding speed once the initial conditions were correct.

And yet the initial conditions were themselves changing. The great stellar furnaces had not fallen quiet. Several times a century, heavy stars died as supernovae, outshining all others.

Usually they did so behind sooty veils of dust, and their deaths went unrecorded save for a chirp of neutrinos or a seismic tremor of gravitational waves. But the metals that they made still found their way into the interstellar medium. New suns and worlds were still coalescing out of the clouds that had been enriched by each previous stellar cycle. This ceaseless cosmic industry rumbled on, oblivious to the intelligence that it had allowed to flourish.

But near the core the metallicity was becoming higher than optimum. The new worlds that were forming around new suns were very heavy indeed, their cores laden with heavy elements. Their gravitational fields were stronger and their chemistries more volatile than those of existing worlds. Plate tectonics no longer functioned, since their mantles could no longer support the burden of rigid floating crusts. Without tectonics, topography—and hence changes in elevation—became less pronounced. Comets were tugged into collisions with these worlds, drenching them with water. Vast world-engulfing oceans slumbered beneath oppressive skies. Complex life rarely evolved on these worlds, since there were few suitable niches and little climatic variation. And those cultures that had already achieved starflight found these new core worlds lacking in usefulness or variety. When a pocket of the right metallicity threatened to condense down into a solar system with the prospect of being desirable, the elder cultures often squabbled over property rights. The ensuing catfights were the most awesome displays of energy that the galaxy had seen beyond its own blind processes of stellar evolution. But they were nothing compared with what was to come.

So, avoiding conflict where they could, the elder cultures turned outwards. But even then they were thwarted. In half a billion years the zone of optimum habitability had crept a little further from the galactic core. The lifewave was a single ripple, spreading out from the centre to the galaxy's edge. Sites of stellar formation that had previously been too metal-poor to form viable solar systems were now sufficiently enriched. Again, squabbles broke out. Some of them lasted ten million years, leaving scars on the galaxy that took another fifty million to heal over.

And still these were nothing compared with the coming Dawn War.

For the galaxy, as much as it was a machine for making metals, and thereby complex chemistry, and thereby life, could also be seen as a machine for making wars. There were no stable niches in the galactic disc. On the kind of timescale that mattered to galactic supercultures, the environment was constantly changing. The wheel of galactic history forced them into eternal conflict with other cultures, new and old.

And so the war to end wars had come, the war that ended the first phase of galactic history, and the one that would yet come to be known as the Dawn War, because it had happened so far in the past.

The Inhibitors remembered little of the war itself. Their own history had been chaotic, muddled and almost certainly subject to crude retroactive tampering. They could not be sure what was documented fact and what was a fiction some earlier incarnation of themselves had manufactured for the purposes of cross-species propaganda. It was probable that they had once been organic, spined, warm-blooded land-dwellers with bicameral minds. The faint shadow of that possible past could be discerned in their cybernetic architectures.

For a long time they had clung to the organic. But at some point their machine selves had become dominant, sloughing their old forms. As machine intelligences, they roamed the galaxy. The memory of planetary dwelling became dim, and then was erased entirely, no more relevant than the memory of tree dwelling.

All that mattered was the great work.

In her quarters, after she had made certain that Remontoire and Felka were aware that the mission's objective had been achieved, Skade had the armour return her head to the pedestal. She found that her thoughts took on a different texture when she was sessile. It was something to do with the slight differences between the blood recirculation systems, the subtle flavouring of neuro-chemicals. On the pedestal she felt calm and inwardly focused, open to the presence that she always carried with her.

[Skade?] The Night Council's voice was tiny, almost child-like, but utterly unignorable. She had come to know it well.

Yes.

[You feel that you have been successful, Skade?]

Yes.

[Tell us, Skade.]

Clavain is dead. Our missiles reached him. The kill still has to be confirmed . . . but I'm certain of it.

[Did he die well, in the Roman sense?]

He didn't surrender. He kept running all the while, even though he must have known he'd never get far enough away with his engines damaged.

[We didn't think he would ever surrender, Skade. Still, it was quick for him. You've done well, Skade. We are satisfied. More than satisfied.]

Skade wanted to nod, but the pedestal prevented it. *Thank you.*

The Night Council allowed her time to gather her thoughts. It was always mindful of her, always patient with her. On more than one occasion the voice had told Skade that it valued her as highly as it valued any of the elite few, perhaps more so. The relationship, in so far as Skade appreciated it, was like that between a teacher and a gifted, keenly inquisitive pupil.

Skade did not often ask herself where the voice came from or what precisely it represented. The Night Council had warned her not to dwell on such matters, for fear that her thoughts might be intercepted by others.

Skade found herself recalling the occasion on which the Night Council had first made itself known to her and revealed something of its nature.

[We are a select core of Conjoiners,] it had told her, [a Closed Council so secret, so hyper-secure, that our existence is not known, or even suspected, by the most senior orthodox Council members. We are deeper than the Inner Sanctum, though the Sanctum is at times our unwitting client, our puppet in wider Conjoiner affairs. But we do not lie within it. Our relationship to these other bodies can only be expressed in the mathematical language of intersecting sets. The details need not concern you, Skade.]

The voice had gone on to tell her that she had been singled out. She had performed excellently in the most dangerous of recent Conjoiner operations, a covert mission deep into Chasm City to recover key elements vital to the inertia-suppression technology programme. No one else had made it out alive except Skade.

[You did well. Our collective eye had been on you for some

time, Skade, but that was your chance to shine. It did not escape our attention. That is why we have made ourselves known to you now: because you are the kind of Conjoiner capable of the difficult work that lies ahead. This is not flattery, Skade, but a cold statement of the facts.]

It was true that she had been the only survivor of the Chasm City operation. The precise details of that job had necessarily been scrubbed from her memory, but she knew that it had been an exquisitely dangerous high-risk venture that had not played out according to Closed Council plans.

There was a paradox in Conjoiner operations. Those troops who could be deployed along battle lines, within Contested Volumes, could never be allowed to hold sensitive information in their heads. But deep insertions, covert forays into enemy space, were a different matter. They were highly delicate operations that drew on expert Conjoiners. More than that, they required the use of agents who had been psychologically primed to tolerate isolation from their fellows. Those individuals who could work alone, far behind enemy lines, were rare indeed, and regarded with ambivalence by the others. Clavain was one.

Skade was another.

When she had returned to the Mother Nest, the voice had entered her skull for the first time. It had told her that she must speak of the matter to no one.

[We value our secrecy, Skade. We will protect it at all costs. Serve us, and you will be serving the greater good of the Mother Nest. But betray us, even involuntarily, and we will be forced to silence you. It will not amuse us, but it will be done.]

Am I the first?

[No, Skade. There are others like you. But you will never know who they are. That is our will.]

What do you want of me?

[Nothing, Skade. For now. But you will hear from us when we have need of you.]

And so it had been. Over the months, and then years, that followed she had come to assume that the voice had been illusory, no matter how real it had seemed at the time. But the Night Council had returned, in a quiet moment, and its guidance had begun. The voice did not ask much of her at first: action by omission, mostly. Skade's promotion into the Closed Council appeared to have been won through her own efforts, not the intervention of the voice. Later, the same could be said of her admission into the Inner Sanctum.

She often wondered who exactly made up the Night Council. Amongst the faces she saw in Closed Council sessions, and in the wider Mother Nest, it was certain that some belonged to the officially nonexistent Council which the voice represented. But there was never a hint, not even a glance that appeared out of place. In the wash of their thoughts there was never a suspicious note; never a sense that the voice was speaking to her through other channels. And she did her best not to think about the voice when she was not in its presence. At other times she merely did its bidding, refusing to examine the source of her compulsion. It felt good to serve something higher than herself.

By turns, Skade's influence reached further and further. The Exordium programme had already been re-opened by the time Skade became one of the Conjoined, but she was instructed to manoeuvre herself into a position where she could dominate the programme, make maximum use of its discoveries and determine its future direction. As she ascended through layers of secrecy, Skade became aware of just how vital had been the technological items she had harvested from Chasm City. The Inner Sanctum had already made faltering attempts to construct inertia-suppressing machinery, but with the items from Chasm City—and still Skade did not remember exactly what had happened during that mission—the pieces fell into place with beguiling ease. Perhaps it was the case that there were other individuals serving the voice, as the voice itself had suggested, or perhaps it was simply that Skade was herself a skilled and ruthless organiser. The Closed Council was her shadow theatre. Its players moved to her will with contemptible eagerness.

And still the voice had urged her on. It drew her attention to the signal from the Resurgam system, to the diagnostic pulse that indicated that the remaining hell-class weapons had been re-armed.

[The Mother Nest needs those weapons, Skade. You must expedite their recovery.]

Why?

The voice had crafted images in her skull: a swarm of implacable black machines, dark and heavy and busy like a flutter of ravens' wings. [There are enemies between the stars, Skade, worse than anything we have imagined. They are coming closer. We must protect ourselves.]

How do you know?

[We know, Skade. Trust us.]

She had felt something in that childlike voice that she had not sensed until then. It was pain, or torment, or both.

[Trust us. We know what they can do. We know what it is like to be harried by them.]

And then the voice had fallen silent again, as if it had said too much.

Now the voice pushed a new, nagging thought into her head, pulling her out of her reverie. [When can we be *certain* that he is dead, Skade?]

Ten, eleven hours. We'll sweep through the kill zone and sift the interplanetary medium for an enhancement in trace elements, the kind we'd expect to find in this situation. And even if the evidence is not conclusive, we can be confident . . .

The response was brusque, petulant. [No, Skade. Clavain cannot be allowed to reach Chasm City.]

I've killed him, I swear.

[You are clever, Skade, and determined. But so is Clavain. He tricked you once. He can always trick you again.]

It doesn't matter.

[No?]

If Clavain reaches Yellowstone, the information he has still won't be of any ultimate benefit to the enemy or the Convention. They can attempt to recover the hell-class weapons for themselves, if they wish. But we have Exordium and the inertia-suppression machinery. They give us an edge. Clavain, and whatever bunch of allies he manages to surround himself with, won't succeed.

The voice hovered in her head. For a moment she wondered if it had gone, leaving her alone.

She was wrong.

[So you think he might still be alive?]

She fumbled for an answer. *I . . .*

[He had better not be, Skade. Or we will be bitterly disappointed with you.]

He was cradling an injured cat, its spine severed somewhere near the lower vertebrae so that its rear legs hung limply. He was trying to persuade it to sip water from the plastic teat of his skinsuit rations pack. His own legs were pinned under tonnes of collapsed masonry. The cat was blind, burned, incontinent and in obvious pain. But he would not give it the easy way out.

He mumbled a sentence, more for his own benefit than the cat's. "You are going to live, my friend. Whether you want to or not."

The words came out sounding like one sheet of sandpaper being scraped against another. He needed water badly. But there was only a tiny amount left in the rations pack, and it was the cat's turn.

"Drink, you little fucker. You've come this far . . ."

"Let me . . . die," the cat told him.

"Sorry, puss. Not the way it's going to happen."

He felt a breeze. It was the first time he had felt any stirring at all of the air bubble in which the cat and he lay trapped. From somewhere distant he heard the thunderous rumble of collapsing concrete and metal. He hoped to God that the sudden airflow was only caused by a shifting of the air bubble; that perhaps an obstruction had collapsed, linking one bubble to another. He hoped it was not part of the external wall giving way, or else the cat would shortly get its wish. The air bubble would depressurise and they would be left trying to breathe Martian atmosphere. He had heard that dying that way was not at all pleasant, despite what they tried to make you think in the Coalition's morale-boosting holo-dramas.

"Clavain . . . save yourself."

"Why, puss?"

"I die anyway."

The first time the cat had spoken to him he had assumed that he had begun to hallucinate, imagining a loquacious companion where none actually existed. Then, belatedly, he had realised that the cat really was talking, that the animal was a rich tourist's bioengineered affectation. A civilian dirigible had been parked on the top of the aerial docking tower when the spiders had hit it with their foam-phase artillery shells. The pet must have escaped from the dirigible gondola long before the attack itself, making its way down to the basement levels of the tower. Clavain thought that bioengineered talking animals were an affront against God, and he was reasonably certain that the cat was not a legally recognised sentient entity. The Coalition for Neural

Purity would have had fits if it had known he had dared share his water rations with the forbidden creature. It hated genetic augmentation as much as it hated Galiana's neural tinkering.

Clavain forced the teat into the cat's mouth. Some reflex made it gulp down the last few drops of water.

"We all get it one day, puss."

"Not so . . . soon."

"Drink up and stop moaning."

The cat lapped up the last few drops. "Thank . . . you."

That was when he felt the breeze again. It was stronger this time, and with it came a more insistent rumble of shifting masonry. In the dim illumination that was afforded by the biochemical thermal/light-stick he had cracked open an hour earlier, he saw dust and debris scud across the ground. The cat's golden fur rippled like a field of barley. The injured animal tried to raise its head in the direction of the wind. Clavain touched the animal's head with his hand, doing his best to comfort it. Its eyes were bloody sockets.

The end was coming. He knew it. This was no relocation of air within the ruin; it was a major collapse on the perimeter of the fallen structure. The cell of air was leaking out into the Martian cold.

When he laughed it was like scraping his own throat with razor wire.

"Something . . . funny?"

"No," he said. "No. Not at all."

Light speared through the darkness. A wave of pure cold air hit his face and rammed into his lungs.

He stroked the cat's head again. If this was dying, then it was nowhere near as bad as he had feared.

"Clavain."

His name was being spoken calmly and insistently.

"Clavain. Wake up."

He opened his eyes, an effort that immediately sapped half the strength he felt he had left. He was somewhere so bright that he wanted to squint, resealing the eyelids that had nearly gummed shut. He wanted to retreat back into his own past, no matter how painful and claustrophobic the dream might be.

"Clavain. I'm warning you . . . if you don't wake up I'm going to . . . "

He forced his eyes as wide as he could, realising that just before him was a shape that had yet to shift into focus. It was leaning over him. It was the shape that was talking to him.

"Fuck . . . " he heard the woman's voice say. "I think he's lost his mind or something."

Another voice, sonorous, deferential, but just the tiniest bit patronising, said, "Begging your pardon, Little Miss, but it would be unwise to assume anything. Especially if the gentleman in question is a Conjoiner."

"Hey, as if I needed reminding."

"One merely means to point out that his medical condition may be both complex and deliberate."

"Space him now," said another male voice.

"Shut up, Xave."

Clavain's vision sharpened. He was bent over double in a small white-walled chamber. There were pumps and gauges set into the walls, along with decals and printed warnings that had been worn nearly away. It was an airlock. He was still wearing his suit, the one he had been wearing, he remembered now, when he had sent the corvette away, and the figure leaning over him was wearing a suit as well. She—for it was the woman—had been the one who had opened his visor and glare shield, allowing light and air to reach him.

He groped in the ruins of his memory for a name. "Antoinette?"

"Got it in one, Clavain." She had her visor up as well. All that he could see of her face was a blunt blonde fringe, wide eyes and a freckled nose. She was attached to the wall of the lock by a metal line, and she had one hand on a heavy red lever.

"You're younger than I thought," he said.

"Are you all right, Clavain?"

"I've felt better," he said. "But I'll be all right in a few moments. I put myself into deep sleep, almost a coma, to conserve my suit's resources. Just in case you were a little late."

"What if I hadn't arrived at all?"

"I assumed you would, Antoinette."

"You were wrong. I very nearly didn't come. Isn't that right, Xave?"

One of the other voices—the third—he had heard earlier answered, "You don't realise how lucky you are, man."

"No," Clavain said. "I probably don't."

"I still say we should space him," the third voice repeated.

Antoinette looked over her shoulder, through the window of the inner airlock door. "After we came all this way?"

"It's not too late. Teach him a lesson about taking things for granted."

Clavain made to move. "I didn't . . . "

"Whoah!" Antoinette had extended a hand, clearly indicating that it would be very unwise of him to move another muscle. She nodded towards the lever she held in her other hand. "Check this out, Clavain. You do one thing that I don't like—like so much as bat an eyelid—and I pull this lever. Then it's back into space again, just like Xave said."

He mulled over his predicament for several seconds. "If you weren't prepared to trust me, at least slightly, you wouldn't have come out to rescue me."

"Maybe I was curious."

"Maybe you were. But maybe you also felt I might have been sincere. I saved your life, didn't I?"

With her free hand she worked the other airlock controls. The inner door slid aside, offering Clavain a brief glimpse into the rest of her ship. He saw another spacesuited figure waiting on the far side, but no sign of anyone else.

"I'm going now," Antoinette said.

In one deft movement she unclipped her restraint line, slipped through the open doorway and then made the inner airlock door close again. Clavain stayed still, waiting until her face appeared in the window. She had removed her helmet and was running her fingers through the unruly mop of her hair.

"Are you going to leave me here?" he asked.

"Yes. For now. It makes sense, doesn't it? I can still space you if you do anything I don't like."

Clavain reached up and removed his own helmet, twisting it free. He let it drift away, tumbling across the lock like a small metal moon. "I'm not planning on doing anything that might annoy any of you."

"That's good."

"But listen to me carefully. You're in danger just being out here. We need to get out of the war zone as quickly as possible."

"Relax, guy," the man said. "We've got time to service some systems. There aren't any zombies for light-minutes in any direction."

"It's not the Demarchists you need to worry about. I was running from my own people, from the Conjoiners. They have a stealthed ship out here. Not nearby, I grant you, but it can move quickly, it has long-range missiles and I guarantee that it is looking for me."

Antoinette said, "I thought you said you'd faked your death."

He nodded. "I'm assuming Skade will have taken out my corvette with those same long-range missiles. She'll have assumed I'm aboard it. But she won't stop there. If she's as thorough as I think she is, she'll sweep the area with *Nightshade* just to make sure, searching for trace atoms."

"Trace atoms? You're joking. By the time they get to where the blast happened . . . " Antoinette shook her head.

Clavain shook his in return. "There'll still be a slightly enhanced density—one or two atoms per cubic metre—of the kind of elements you don't normally find in interplanetary space. Hull isotopes, that kind of thing. *Nightshade*'s hull will sample and analyse the medium. The hull is covered with epoxy-coated patches that will snare anything larger than a molecule, and then there are mass spectrometers that will sniff the atomic constituency of the vacuum itself. Algorithms will process the forensic data, comparing the curves and histograms of abundance and isotope ratios against plausible scenarios for the destruction of a vessel of the corvette's composition. The results won't be unambiguous, for the statistical errors will be almost as large as the effects Skade's attempting to measure. But I've seen it done before. The pull of the data will be in favour of there having been very little organic matter aboard the corvette." Clavain reached up and touched the side of his head, slowly enough that it could not be seen as threatening. "And then there are the isotopes in my implants. They'll be harder to detect, a lot harder, but Skade will expect to find them if she looks hard enough. And when she doesn't . . . "

"She'll figure out what you did," Antoinette said.

Again Clavain nodded. "But I took all that into consideration. It will take time for Skade to make a thorough search. You can still make it back into neutral territory, but only if you start home immediately."

"You're really that keen to get to the Rust Belt, Clavain?" asked Antoinette. "They'll eat you alive, whether it's the Convention or the zombies."

"No one said defecting was a risk-free activity."

"You defected once already, right?" Antoinette asked.

Clavain caught his drifting helmet and secured it to his belt by the helmet's chin loop. "Once. It was a long time ago. Probably a bit before your time."

"Like four hundred years before my time?"

He scratched his beard. "Warm."

"Then it *is* you. You are him."

"Him?"

"*That* Clavain. The historical one. The one everyone says has to be dead by now. The Butcher of Tharsis."

Clavain smiled. "For my sins."

EIGHTEEN

Thorn hovered above a world that was being prepared for death. They had made the trip from *Nostalgia for Infinity* in one of the smaller, nimbler ships that the two women had shown him in the hangar bay. The craft was a two-seat surface-to-orbit shuttle with the shape of a cobra's head: a hoodlike wing curving smoothly into fuselage, with the cabin viewing windows positioned either side of the hull like snake eyes. The undercurve was scabbed and warted by sensors, latching pods and what he took to be various sorts of weapon. Two particle-beam muzzles jutted from the front like hinged venom fangs, and the ship's entire skin was mosaiced with irregular scales of ceramic armour, shimmering green and black.

"This will get us there and back?" Thorn had asked.

"It will," Vuilleumier had assured him. "It's the fastest ship here, and probably the one with the smallest sensor footprint. Light armour, though, and the weapons are more for show than anything else. You want something better armoured, we'll take it—just don't complain if it's slow and easily tracked."

"I'll let you be the judge."

"This is very foolish, Thorn. There's still time to chicken out."

"It isn't a question of foolishness or otherwise, Inquisitor." He could not snap out of the habit of calling her that. "I simply won't co-operate until I know that this threat is real. Until I can verify that for myself—with my own eyes, and not through a screen—I won't be able to trust you."

"Why would we lie to you?"

"I don't know, but you are, I think." He had studied her carefully, their eyes meeting, he holding her gaze for a moment longer than was comfortable. "About something. I'm not sure what, but neither of you are being totally honest with me. Yet some of the time you are, and that's the part I don't fully understand."

"All we want to do is save the people of Resurgam."

"I know. I believe that part, I really do."

They had taken the snake-headed ship, leaving Irina back aboard the larger vessel. The departure had been rapid, and though he had done his best, Thorn had not been able to sneak a look backwards. He had still not seen *Nostalgia for Infinity* from the outside, not even on the approach from Resurgam. Why, he wondered, would the two of them go to such lengths to hide the outside of their ship? Perhaps he was just imagining it, and he would get that view on the way back.

"You can take the ship yourself," Irina had told him. "It doesn't need flying. We can program a trajectory into it and let the autonomics handle any contingency. Just tell us how close you want to get to the Inhibitors."

"It doesn't have to be close. A few tens of thousands of kilometres should be good enough. I'll be able to see that arc, if it's bright enough, and probably the tubes that are being dropped into the atmosphere. But I'm not going out there on my own. If you want me badly enough, one of you can come with me. That way I'll know it really isn't a trap, won't I?"

"I'll go with him," Vuilleumier had offered.

Irina had shrugged. "It's been nice knowing you."

The trip out had been uneventful. As on the journey from Resurgam, they had spent the boring part of it asleep—not in reefersleep, but in a dreamless drug-induced coma.

Vuilleumier did not wake them until they were within half a

light-second of the giant. Thorn awoke with a vague sense of irritation, a bad taste in his mouth and various aches and pains where there had been none before.

"Well, the good news is that we're still alive, Thorn. The Inhibitors either don't know we're here, or they just don't care."

"Why wouldn't they care?"

"They must know from experience that we can't offer them any real trouble. In a little while we'll all be dead, so why worry about one or two of us now?"

He frowned. "Experience?"

"It's in their collective memory, Thorn. We're not the first species they've done this to. The success rate must be pretty high, or else they'd revise the strategy."

They were in free-fall. Thorn unhitched from his seat, tugging aside the acceleration webbing, and kicked over to one of the slitlike windows. He felt a little better now. He could see the gas giant very clearly, and it did not look like a well planet.

The first things that he noticed were the three great matter streams curving in from elsewhere in the system. They twinkled palely in the light from Delta Pavonis, thin ribbons of translucent grey like great ghostly brushstrokes daubed across the sky, flat to the ecliptic and sweeping away to infinity. The flow of matter along the streams was just tangible, as one boulder or another caught the sun for an instant; it was a fine-grained creep that reminded Thorn of the sluggish currents in a river on the point of freezing. The matter was travelling at hundreds of kilometres per second, but the sheer immensity of the scene rendered even that speed glacial. The streams themselves were many, many kilometres wide. They were, he supposed, like planetary rings that had been unwound.

His gaze followed the streams to their conclusions. Near the gas giant, the smooth mathematical curves—arcs describing orbital trajectories—were curtailed by abrupt hairpins or doglegs as the streams were routed to particular moons. It was as if the artist painting the elegant swathes had been jolted at the last instant. The orientation of the moons with respect to the arriving streams was changing by the hour, of course, so the stream geometries were themselves subject to constant revision. Now and then a stream would have to be dammed back, the flow stopped while another intersected it. Or perhaps it was done with astonishingly tight timing, so that the streams passed through each other without any of the constituent masses actually colliding.

"We don't know how they steer them like that," Vuilleumier told him, her voice low and confidential. "There's a lot of momentum in those streams, mass fluxes of billions of tonnes a second. Yet they change direction easily. Maybe they've got tiny little black holes positioned up there, so they can slingshot the streams around them. That's what Irina thinks, anyway. Scares the hell out of me, I can tell you. Although she thinks they might also be able to turn off inertia when they need to, so they can make the streams swerve like that."

"That doesn't sound much more encouraging."

"No, it doesn't. But even if they *can* do that to inertia, or make black holes to order, they obviously can't do it on a huge scale or we'd be dead already. They have their limitations. We *have* to believe that."

The moons, a few dozen kilometres wide, were visible as tight knots of light, barbs on the ends of the infalling streams. The matter plunged into each moon through a mouthlike aperture, perpendicular to the plane of orbital motion. By rights, the unbalanced mass flux should have been forcing each moon into a new orbit. Nothing like that was happening, which suggested that, again, the normal laws of momentum conservation were being suppressed, or ignored, or put on hold until some later reckoning.

The outermost moon was laying the arc that would eventually enclose the gas giant. When Thorn had seen it from *Nostalgia for Infinity* it had been possible to believe that it was never destined for closure. No such assurance was possible now. The ends had continued moving outwards from the moon, the tube being extruded at a rate of a thousand kilometres every four hours. It was emerging as quickly as an express train, an avalanche of super-organised matter.

It was not magic, just industry. Thorn reminded himself of that, difficult as it was to believe it. Within the moon, mechanisms hidden beneath its icy crust were processing the incoming matter stream at demonic speed, forging the unguessable components that formed the thirteen-kilometre-wide tube. The two women had not speculated in his presence about whether the tube was solid or hollow or crammed with twinkling alien clockwork.

But it was not magic. Physical laws as Thorn understood them might be melting like toffee in the vicinity of the Inhibitor engines, but that was only because they were not the ultimate laws they appeared to be, rather mere statutes or regulations to be adhered to most of the time but broken under duress. Yet even the Inhibitors were constrained to some degree. They could work wonders, but not the impossible. They needed matter, for instance. They could work it with astonishing speed, but they could not, on the evidence gleaned so far, conjure it from nothing. It had been necessary to shatter three worlds to fuel this inferno of creativity.

And whatever they were doing, vast though it was, was necessarily slow. The arc had to be grown around the planet at a *mere* two hundred and eighty metres a second; it could not be created instantly. The machines were mighty, but not Godlike.

That was, Thorn decided, about all the consolation they were going to get.

He turned his attention to the two lower moons. The Inhibitors had moved them into perfectly circular orbits just above the cloud layer. Their orbits intersected periodically, but the slow, diligent cable-laying continued unabated.

This part of the process was much clearer now. Thorn could see the elegant curves of the extruded tubes emerging whip-straight from the trailing face of each moon, before flexing down towards the cloud deck. Several thousand kilometres aft of each moon, the tubes plunged into the atmosphere like syringes. The tubes were moving with orbital speed when they touched air—many kilometres per second—and they gouged livid claw marks into the atmosphere. There was a thin band of agitated rust-red immediately beneath the track of each moon which reached two or three times around the planet, each pass offset from the previous one because of the gas giant's rotation. The two moons were etching a complex geometric pattern into the shifting clouds, a pattern that resembled an extravagant calligraphic flourish. On some level Thorn appreciated that it was beautiful, but it was also quietly sickening. Something atrocious and final was surely going to happen to the planet. The calligraphic marks were elaborate funerary rites for a dying world.

"I take it you believe us now," Vuilleumier said.

"I'm inclined to," Thorn said. He rapped the window. "I suppose this might not be glass, as it appears, but some three-dimensional screen . . . but I don't think I'll presume that much ingenuity on your behalf. Even if I went outside in a suit, to look at it for myself, I wouldn't be certain that the faceplate was glass either."

"You're a suspicious man."

"I've learned that it helps one get by." Thorn returned to his seat, having seen enough for the moment. "All right. Next question. What's going on down there? What are they up to?"

"It's not necessary to know, Thorn. The fact that something bad is going to happen is information enough."

"Not for me."

"Those machines . . . " Vuilleumier gestured at the window. "We know what they do, but not how they do it. They wipe out cultures, slowly and painstakingly. Sylveste brought them here—unwittingly, perhaps, although I wouldn't take anything as read where that bastard's concerned—and now they've come to do the job. That's all you or any of us need to know. We just have to get everyone away from here as quickly as possible."

"If these machines are as efficient as you say, that won't do us a great deal of good, will it?"

"It'll buy us time," she said. "And there's something else. The machines are efficient, but they're not *quite* as efficient as they used to be."

"You told me they were self-replicating machines. Why would they become less efficient? If anything they should keep getting cleverer and faster as they learn more and more."

"Whoever made them didn't want them to get too clever. The Inhibitors created the machines to wipe out emergent intelligence. It wouldn't have made much sense if the machines filled the niche they were supposed to be keeping empty."

"I suppose not . . . " Thorn was not going to let it lie that easily. "There's more you have to tell me, I think. But in the meantime I want to get closer."

"How much closer?" she asked guardedly.

"This ship's streamlined. It can take atmosphere, I think."

"That wasn't in the agreement."

"So sue me." He grinned. "I'm naturally inquisitive, just like you."

Scorpio came to cold, clammy consciousness, shivering uncontrollably. He pawed at himself, peeling a glistening layer of fatty gel from his naked skin. It came away in revolting semi-translucent scabs, slurping as it detached from the underlying flesh. He was careful with the area around the burn scar on his right shoulder, fingering its perimeter with tentative fascination. There was no inch of the burn that he did not know intimately, but in touching it, tracing the wrinkled topology of its shoreline where smooth pig flesh changed to something with the leathery texture of cured meat, he was reminded of the duty that was his and his alone, the duty that he had set himself since escaping from Quail. He must never forget Quail, and nor must he forget that—as altered as the man had been—Quail was fully human in the genetic sense, and that it was humans who had to bear the brunt of Scorpio's retribution.

There was no pain now, not even from the burn, but there *was* discomfort and disorientation. His ears roared continually, as if he had his head shoved up a ventilation duct. His vision was blurred, revealing little more than vague amorphic shapes. Scorpio reached up and peeled more of the transparent gel from his face. He blinked. Things were clearer now, but the roaring remained. He looked around, still shivering and cold, but alert enough to take note of where he was and what was happening to him.

He had awakened inside one half of what appeared to be a cracked metal egg, curled in an unnatural foetal position with his lower half still immersed in the revolting mucous gel. Plastic pipes and connectors lay around him. His throat and nasal passages were sore, as if the pipes had recently been shoved into him. They did not appear to have been removed with the utmost care. The other half of the metal egg lay just to one side, as if the two halves had only recently been disunited. Beyond it, and all around, was the instantly identifiable interior of a spacecraft: all polished blue metal and curved, perforated struts that reminded him of ribs. The roar in his ears was the sound of thrust. The ship was travelling somewhere, and the fact that he could hear the motors told him that the ship was probably a small one, not large enough for force-cradled engines. A shuttle, then, or something similar. Definitely in-system.

Scorpio flinched. A door had opened in the far end of the ribbed cabin revealing a little chamber with a ladder in it that led upwards. A man was just stepping off the last rung. He stooped through the opening and walked calmly towards Scorpio, evidently unsurprised to see Scorpio awake.

"How do you feel?" the man asked.

Scorpio forced his unwilling eyes to snap into focus. The man was known to him, though he had changed since their last meeting. His clothes were as neutral and dark as before, but now they were not of recognisably Conjoiner origin. His skull was covered with a very fine layer of black hair, where it had been shaven before. He looked a degree less cadaverous.

"Remontoire," Scorpio said, spitting vile gobbets of gel from his mouth.

"Yes, that's me. Are you all right? The monitor told me you hadn't suffered any ill effects."

"Where are we?"

"In a ship, near the Rust Belt."

"Come to torture me again, have you?"

Remontoire did not look him quite in the eye. "It wasn't torture, Scorpio . . . just re-education."

"When do you hand me over to the Convention?"

"That's no longer on the agenda. At least, it doesn't have to be."

Scorpio judged that the ship was small, probably a shuttle. It was entirely possible that he and Remontoire were the only two occupants. Likely, even. He wondered how he would fare trying to fly a Conjoiner-designed ship. Not well, perhaps, but he was willing to give it a try. Even if he crashed and burned, it had to be a lot better than a death sentence.

He lunged for Remontoire, springing out of the bowl in an explosion of gel. Pipes and tubing went flying. In an instant his ill-made hands were seeking the pressure points that would drop anyone, even a Conjoiner, into unconsciousness and then death.

Scorpio came around. He was in another part of the ship, strapped into a seat. Remontoire was sitting opposite him, hands folded neatly in his lap. Behind him was the impressive curve of a control panel, its surface covered with numerous read-outs, command systems and hemispherical navigation displays. It was lit up like a casino. Scorpio knew a thing or two about ship design. A Conjoiner control interface would have been minimalist to the point of invisibility, like something designed by New Quakers.

"I wouldn't try that again," Remontoire said.

Scorpio glared at him. "Try what?"

"You had a go at strangling me. It didn't work, and I'm afraid it never will. We put an implant in your skull, Scorpio—a very small one, around your carotid artery. Its only function is to constrict the artery in response to a signal from another implant in my head. I can send that signal voluntarily if you threaten me, but I don't have to. The implant will emit a distress code if I suffer sudden unconsciousness or death. You will die shortly afterwards."

"I'm not dead now."

"That's because I was nice enough to let you off with a warning."

Scorpio was clothed and dry. He felt better than when he had come around in the egg. "Why should I care, Remontoire? Haven't you just given me the perfect means to kill myself, instead of letting the Convention do it for me?"

"I'm not taking you to the Convention."

"A little private justice, is that it?"

"Not that either." Remontoire swung his seat around so that he faced the lavish control panel. He played it like a pianist, hands outstretched, not needing to watch where his fingers were going. Above the panel and on either side of the cabin, windows puckered into what had been blue steel. The cabin illumination dropped softly. Scorpio heard the roar of the thrust change pitch and felt his stomach register a change in the axis of gravity. A vast ochre crescent hoved into view beyond. It was Yellowstone: most of the planet was in night. Remontoire's ship was nearly in the same plane as the Rust Belt. The string of habitats was hardly visible against dayside—just a dark sprinkling, like a fine line of cinnamon—but beyond the terminator they formed a jewelled thread, spangling and twinkling as habitats precessed or trimmed their immense mirrors and floodlights. It was impressive, but Scorpio knew that it was only a shadow of what it had been. There had been ten thousand habitats before the plague; now only a few hundred were fully utilised. But against night the derelicts vanished, leaving only the fairy-dust trail of illuminated cities, and it was almost as if the wheel of history had never turned.

Beyond the Belt, Yellowstone looked hurtingly close. He could almost hear the urban hum of Chasm City droning up through the clouds like a seductive siren song. He thought of the warrens and strongholds that the pigs and their allies maintained in the deepest parts of the city's Mulch, a festering outlaw empire composed of many interlocked criminal fiefdoms. After his escape from Quail, Scorpio had entered that empire at the very lowest level, a scarred immigrant with barely a single intact memory in his head, other than how to stay alive from hour to hour in a dangerous foreign environment, and—equally importantly—how to turn the apparatus of that environment to his advantage. That at least was something he owed Quail, if nothing else. But it did not mean that he was grateful.

Scorpio remembered very little of his life before meeting Quail. He was aware that much of what he did recall was second-hand memory, for although he had pieced together only the major details of his former existence—his life aboard the yacht—his subconscious had wasted no time in filling in the aching gaps that remained with all the enthusiasm of gas rushing into a vacuum. And as he remembered those memories, not quite real in themselves, he could not help but impress even more sensory details upon them. The memories might accord precisely with what had really happened, but Scorpio had no way of knowing for sure. And yet it made no difference as far as he was concerned. No one else was going to contradict him now. Those who might have been able to do so were dead, butchered at the hands of Quail and his friends.

Scorpio's first clear memory of Quail was amongst the most frightening. He had come to consciousness after a long period of sleep, or something deeper than sleep, standing in a cold armoured room with eleven other pigs, disorientated and shivering, much as he had been upon waking aboard Remontoire's ship. They wore crudely fashioned clothes, sewn together from stiff squares of dark, stained fabric. Quail had been there with them: a tall asymmetrically augmented human whom Scorpio identified as being either an Ultra or from one of the other occasionally chimeric factions, such as the Skyjacks or the Atmosphere Dredgers. There were other augmented humans, too, half a dozen of them crowding behind Quail. They all carried weapons, ranging from knives to wide-muzzled low-velocity slug-guns, and they all viewed the assembled pigs with undisguised anticipation. Quail, whose language Scorpio understood without effort, explained that the twelve pigs had been brought aboard his ship—for the room was inside a much larger vessel—to provide amusement for his crew after a run of unprofitable deals.

And in a sense, though perhaps not in quite the sense that Quail had intended, that was precisely what they had done. The crew had anticipated a hunt, and for a little while that was what they got. The rules were simple enough: the pigs were allowed free run of Quail's ship, to hide anywhere they desired and to improvise tools and weapons from whatever was at hand. After five days an amnesty would be declared on any surviving pigs, or at least that was what Quail promised. It was up to the pigs to choose whether they hid *en masse* or split into smaller teams. They had six hours' lead on the humans.

That turned out to make precious little difference. Half the pigs were dead by the end of the first day's hunt. They had accepted the terms unquestioningly; even Scorpio had felt a strangely eager obligation to do whatever was asked of him, a sense that it was his duty to do whatever Quail—or any other human—required. Though he was afraid, and had an immediate desire to safeguard his own survival, it was to be nearly three days before he would think about striking back, and even then the thought only pushed its way into his head against great resistance, as if violating some sacrosanct personal paradigm.

At first Scorpio had sought shelter with two other pigs, one of them mute, the other only able to form broken sentences, but they had functioned well enough as a team, anticipating each other's actions with uncanny ease. Scorpio knew, even then, that the twelve pigs had worked together before, though he could not yet assemble a single clear memory of his life before waking in Quail's chamber. But even though the team had functioned well, Scorpio had chosen to go off on his own after the first eighteen hours. The other two wanted to remain hiding in the cubbyhole they had found, but Scorpio was sure that the only hope of survival lay in continuous ascent, moving ever upwards along the ship's axis of thrust.

It was then that he had made the first of three discoveries. Crawling through a duct, he had ripped away part of his clothing, revealing the edge of a shining green shape that covered much of his right shoulder. He ripped away more of the clothing, but it was only when he found a reflective panel that he was able to examine the entire shape properly and see that it was a highly stylised green scorpion. As he touched the emerald tattoo, tracing the curved line of its tail, almost feeling the sting of its barb, he felt as if it was imbued with power, a personal force that he alone was able to channel and direct. He sensed that his identity was bound up with the scorpion; that everything that mattered about him was locked within the tattoo. The moment was a startling instant of self-revelation, for at last he realised that he had a name, or could at least *give* himself a name that had some significant connection with his past.

Perhaps half a day later he made the second discovery: glimpsed through a window was another ship, much smaller. On closer inspection, Scorpio recognised the lean, efficient lines of an in-system yacht. The hull gleamed with pale green alloy, a lusciously streamlined manta shape with cowled air-intakes like the mouths of basking sharks. As he looked at the yacht, Scorpio could almost see its blueprint glowing beneath the skin. He knew that he could crawl aboard that yacht and make it fly almost without thinking, and that he could repair or remedy any technical fault or imperfection; he felt an almost overwhelming urge to do just that, sensing perhaps that only in the belly of the yacht, surrounded by machines and tools, would he be truly happy.

Tentatively, he formed his hypothesis: the twelve pigs must have been the crew of that yacht when Quail had captured their ship. The yacht had been taken as bounty, the crew put into deep freeze until they were required to spice up the humdrum existence on board Quail's ship. That accounted for the amnesia, at least. He felt delight in discovering a link with his own past. It was still with him when he made the third discovery.

He had found the two pigs he had left behind in the cubbyhole. They had been caught and killed, just as he had feared. Quail's hunters had suspended them by chains from the perforated spars bridging a corridor. They had been eviscerated and skinned, and at some point in the process Scorpio was certain that they had still been alive. He was also certain that the clothes they had been wearing—the clothes he continued to wear—were themselves made from the skins of other pigs. The twelve were not the first victims, but merely the latest in a game that had been playing for much longer than he had at first suspected; he began to feel a fury beyond anything he had known before. Something snapped; suddenly he was able to consider, at least as a theoretical possibility, what had previously been the unthinkable: he could imagine how it would feel to hurt a human, and to hurt a human very badly indeed. And he could even think of ways that he might go about it.

Scorpio, who turned out to be both resourceful and technically minded, began to infiltrate the machinery of Quail's ship. He turned bulkhead doors into vicious scissoring traps. He turned elevators and transit pods into deadfalls or crushing pistons. He sucked air from certain parts of the ship and replaced it with poisonous gases or vacuum, and then fooled the sensors that would have alerted Quail and his company to the ruse. One by one he executed the pigs' hunters, often with considerable artistry, until only Quail remained alive, alone and fearful, finally grasping the terrible error of judgement he had made. But by then the other eleven pigs were also dead, so Scorpio's victory was mingled with a sour sense of abject personal failure. He had felt an obligation to protect the other pigs, most of who had lacked the language skills he took for granted. It was not simply that some of them were unable to talk, lacking the vocal mechanisms necessary for producing speech sounds, but they did not even comprehend spoken language with the same fluency that he did. A few words and phrases, perhaps, but nothing more than that. Their minds were wired differently from his, lacking the brain functions that coded and decoded language. For him it was second nature. There was no escaping it, but he was a lot closer to human than they were. And he had let them down, even though none of them had elected him as their protector.

Scorpio kept Quail alive until they were near circum-Yellowstone space, at which point he arranged for his own passage into Chasm City. He had taken the yacht. By the time he reached the Mulch Quail was dead, or was at least experiencing the final death agonies of the execution device Scorpio had made for him, crafted with loving care from the robotic surgery systems he had removed from the yacht's medical bay.

He was almost home and dry, but there was one final discovery that had to be made: the yacht had never belonged to himself, or to any of the other pigs. The craft—*Zodiacal Light*—had been run by humans, with the twelve pigs serving as indentured slaves, crammed belowdecks, each with their own area of specialisation. Replaying the yacht's video log, Scorpio saw the human crew being murdered by Quail's boarders. It was a quick, clean series of murders, almost humane compared with the slow hunting of the pigs. And, via the same logs, Scorpio saw that the twelve pigs had all been tattooed with a different zodiacal sign. The symbol on his shoulder was a mark of identity, just as he had suspected, but it was also a mark of ownership and obedience.

Scorpio found a welding laser, adjusted the yield to its minimum setting and scorched it deep into tissue, watching with horrified fascination as it burned away the flesh, effacing the green scorpion in crackling stutters of pulsed light. The pain was indescribable, yet he chose not to smother it with anaesthetic from the medical kit. Nor did he do anything to assist the healing of the damaged skin. As much as he needed the pain as a symbolic bridge to be crossed, he needed that mark to show what he had done. Through the pain he reclaimed himself, snatched back his own identity. Perhaps he had never truly had one before, but in the agony he forged one for himself. The scarring would serve to remind him of what he had done, and if ever his hatred of humans began to lapse—if ever he was tempted to *forgive*—it would be there to guide him. Yet, and this was the thing he could never quite understand, he elected to keep the name. In calling himself Scorpio he would become an engine of hate directed at humanity. The name would become a synonym for fear, something that human parents would tell their children about at night to keep them from misbehaving.

In Chasm City his work had begun, and it was in Chasm City that it would continue, if he could escape from Remontoire. Even then he knew that it would be difficult to move freely, but once he made contact with Lasher his difficulties would be greatly diminished. Lasher had been one of his first real allies: a moderately well-connected pig with influence reaching to Loreanville and the Rust Belt. He had remained loyal to Scorpio. And even if he did end up being held prisoner by someone, which seemed at least likely given the circumstances, his captors would have to keep a very close watch on him indeed. The army of pigs, the loose alliance of gangs and factions which Scorpio and Lasher had webbed into something resembling a cohesive force, had struck against the authorities several times before, and while they had suffered dreadful losses, they had never been fully defeated. True, the conflicts had not cost the powers greatly—mostly it had been a matter of retaining pig-held manors of the Mulch—but Lasher and his associates were not afraid of widening the terms of reference. The pigs had allies in the banshees, which meant they had the means to expand their criminal activities far beyond the Mulch. Having been out of circulation for so long, Scorpio was curious to learn how that alliance now fared.

He nodded towards the line of habitats. "It still looks as if we're headed for the Belt."

"We are," Remontoire told him. "But we're not headed towards the Convention. There's been a slight change of plan, which is why we put that nasty little implant into your head."

"You were right to."

"Because you'd have killed me otherwise? Perhaps. But you wouldn't have got very far." Remontoire caressed the control panel and smiled apologetically. "You can't operate this ship, I'm afraid. Beneath the surface the systems are entirely Conjoiner. But we have to pass muster as a civilian vessel."

"Tell me what's going on."

Remontoire swung the seat around again. He parked his hands in his lap and leaned towards Scorpio; dangerously close, were it not for the implant. Scorpio was prepared to believe he would die if he tried anything again, so he let Remontoire speak, while imagining how good it would feel to murder him.

"You met Clavain, I believe."

Scorpio sniffed hard.

Remontoire continued, "He was one of us. A good friend of mine, in fact. Better than that: he was a good Conjoiner. He'd been one of us for four hundred years, and we wouldn't be here now if it wasn't for his deeds. He was the Butcher of Tharsis once, you know. But that's ancient history now; I don't imagine you've even heard of Tharsis. All that matters is that Clavain defected, or is in the process of defecting, and he must be stopped. Because he was—is—a friend, I would sooner that we stopped him alive rather than dead, but I accept that it might not be possible. We tried killing him once, when it was the only option we had. I'm almost glad that we failed. Clavain tricked us; he used his corvette to drop himself off in empty space. When we destroyed the corvette, he wasn't aboard it."

"Clever guy. I like him better already."

"Good. I'm glad to hear it. Because you're going to help me find him."

He was good, Scorpio thought. The way Remontoire said it, it was almost as if he believed it might happen. "Help you?"

"We think he was rescued by a freighter. We can't be certain, but it looks as if it was the same one we encountered earlier, around the Contested Volume—just before we captured *you,* as a matter of fact. Clavain helped the pilot of the freighter then, and he must have hoped she'd pay back the favour. That ship just made an unscheduled, illegal detour into the war zone. It's just possible that it rendezvoused with Clavain, picked him up from empty space."

"Then shoot the fucking thing down. I don't see what your problem is."

"Too late, I'm afraid. By the time we pieced this together, the freighter had already returned to Ferrisville Convention air-space." Remontoire gestured over his shoulder to the line of habitats slashed across the darkening face of Yellow-stone. "By now, Clavain will have gone to ground in the Rust Belt, which happens to be more your territory than mine. Judging by your record, you know it almost as intimately as you know Chasm City. And I'm sure you'll be very eager to be my guide." Remontoire smiled and tapped a finger gently against his own temple. "Won't you?"

"I could still kill you. There are always ways."

"You'd die, though, and what good would that do? We have a bargaining position, you see. Assist us—assist the Conjoined—and we will ensure that you never reach Convention custody. We'll supply the Convention with a body, an identical replica cloned from your own. We'll tell them that you died in our care. That way you not only get your freedom, but you'll also no longer have an army of Convention investigators after you. We can supply you with finances and credible false documentation. Scorpio will be dead, but there's no reason why you can't continue."

"Why haven't you done that already? If you can fake my body, you could have given them a corpse by now."

"There'll be repercussions, Scorpio, severe ones. It is not a path we would ordinarily choose. But at this point we need Clavain back rather more than we need the Convention's good will."

"Clavain must mean a lot to you."

Remontoire turned back to the control panel and played it again, his fingers arpeggiating like a maestro. "He does mean a lot to us, yes. But what he carries in his head means even more."

Scorpio considered his position, his survival instincts clicking in with their usual ruthless efficiency, just as they always did in times of personal crisis. Once it was Quail, now it was a frail-looking Conjoiner with the power to kill him by thought alone. He had every reason to believe that Remontoire was sincere in his threat, and that he would be handed over to the Convention if he did not co-operate. With no opportunity to alert Lasher to his return, he was as good as dead if that happened. But if he assisted Remontoire he would at least be prolonging his arrest. Perhaps Remontoire was telling the truth when he said that he would be allowed to go free. But even if the Conjoiner was lying about that—and he did not think that he was—then there would be still more opportunities to contact Lasher and make his ultimate escape. It sounded like the sort of offer one would be very foolish to refuse. Even if it meant, for the time being at least, working with someone he still considered human. "You must be desperate," he said.

"Perhaps I am," said Remontoire. "At the same time, I really don't think it's much of your business. So, are you going to do what I asked?"

"If I say no . . ."

Remontoire smiled. "Then there won't be any need for that cloned corpse."

About once every eight hours Antoinette opened the airlock door long enough to pass him food and water. Clavain took what she had to offer gratefully, remembering to thank her and to show not the least sign of resentment that he was still a prisoner. It was enough that she had rescued him and that she was taking him back to the authorities. He imagined that in her shoes he would have been even less trusting, especially since he knew what a Conjoiner was capable of doing. He was much less her prisoner than she believed.

His confinement continued for a day. He felt the floor pitch and shift under him as the ship changed its thrust pattern, and when Antoinette appeared at the door she confirmed, before passing another bulb of water and a nutrition bar through to him, that they were *en route* back to the Rust Belt.

"Those thrust changes," he said, peeling back the foil covering the bar. "What were they for? Were we in danger of running into military activity?"

"Not exactly, no."

"What, then?"

"Banshees, Clavain." She must have seen his look of incomprehension. "They're pirates, bandits, brigands, rogues, whatever you want to call them. Real badass sons of bitches."

"I haven't heard of them."

"You wouldn't have unless you were a trader trying to make an honest living."

He chewed on the bar. "You almost said that with a straight face."

"Hey, listen. I bend the rules now and then, that's all. But what these fuckers do—it makes the most illegal thing I've ever done look like, I don't know, a minor docking violation."

"And these banshees . . . they used to be traders too, I take it?"

She nodded. "Until they figured out it was easier to steal cargo from the likes of me rather than haul it themselves."

"But you've never been directly involved with them before?"

"A few run-ins. Everyone who hauls anything in or near the Rust Belt has been shadowed by banshees at least once. Normally they leave us alone. *Storm Bird*'s pretty fast, so it doesn't make an easy target for a forced docking. And, well, we have a few other deterrents."

Clavain nodded wisely, thinking that he knew exactly what she meant. "And now?"

"We've been shadowed. A couple of banshees latched on to us for an hour, holding off at one-tenth of a light-second. Thirty-thou klicks. That's pissing-distance out here. But we shook 'em off."

Clavain took a sip from the drinking bulb. "Will they be back?"

"Dunno. It's not normal to meet them this far from the Rust Belt. I'd almost say . . . "

Clavain raised an eyebrow. "What—that I might have something to do with it?"

"It's just a thought."

"Here's another. You were doing something unusual and dangerous:traversing hostile space. From the banshees' point of view it might have meant you had valuable cargo, something worthy of their interest."

"I suppose so."

"I swear I had nothing to do with it."

"I didn't think you did, Clavain—I mean, not intentionally. But there's a lot of weird shit going down these days."

He took another sip from the bulb. "Tell me about it."

They let him out of the airlock eight hours later. That was when Clavain had his first decent look at the man Antoinette had called Xavier. Xavier was a rangy individual with a pleasing, cheerful face and a bowl-shaped mop of shiny black hair that gleamed blue under *Storm Bird*'s interior lighting. In Clavain's estimation he was perhaps ten or fifteen years older than Antoinette, but he was prepared to believe that his guess might be seriously wrong and that she might be the older one of the partnership. That said, he was certain that neither of them had been born more than a few decades ago.

When the lock opened he saw that Xavier and Antoinette were still wearing their suits, with their helmets hitched to their belts. Xavier stood between the posts of the lock's doorframe and pointed at Clavain.

"Take your suit off. Then you can come into the rest of the ship."

Clavain nodded and did as he was told. Removing the suit was awkward in the confined space of the lock—it was awkward enough anywhere—but he managed it within five minutes, stripping down to the skintight thermal layer.

"I take it I can stop now?"

"Yes."

Xavier stood aside and let him move into the main body of the ship. They were under thrust, so he was able to walk. His socked feet padded against the cleated metal flooring.

"Thank you," Clavain said.

"Don't thank me. Thank her."

Antoinette said, "Xavier thinks you should stay in the lock until we get to the Rust Belt."

"I don't blame him for that."

"But if you try anything . . . " Xavier started.

"I understand. You'll depressurise the entire ship. I'll die, since I'm not suited-up. That makes a lot of sense, Xavier. It's exactly what I would have done in your situation. But can I show you something?"

They looked at each other.

"Show us what?" Antoinette asked.

"Put me back in the airlock, then close the door."

They did as he asked. Clavain waited until their faces appeared in the window, then sidled closer to the door itself, until his head was only a few inches from the locking mechanism and its associated control panel. He narrowed his eyes and concentrated, dredging up neural routines that he had not used in many years. His implants detected the electrical field generated by the lock circuitry, superimposing a neon maze of flowing pathways on to his view of the panel. He understood the lock's logic and saw what needed to be done. His implants began to generate a stronger field of their own, suppressing certain current flows and enhancing others. He was talking to the lock, interfacing with its control system.

He was a little out of practice, but even so it was almost childishly simple to achieve what he wanted. The lock clicked. The door slid open, revealing Antoinette and Xavier. They stood there wearing horrified expressions.

"Space him," Xavier said. "Space him now."

"Wait," Clavain said, holding up his hands. "I did that for one reason only: to show you how easy it would have been for me to do it before. I could have escaped at any time. But I didn't. That means you can trust me."

"It means we should kill you now, before you try something worse," Xavier said.

"If you kill me you'll be making a terrible mistake, I assure you. This is about more than just me."

"And that's the best defence you can offer?" Xavier asked.

"If you really feel you can't trust me, weld me into a box," Clavain said reasonably. "Give me a means to breathe and some water and I'll survive until we reach the Rust Belt. But please don't kill me."

"He sounds like he means it, Xave," Antoinette said.

Xavier was breathing heavily. Clavain realised that the man was still desperately afraid of what he might do.

"You can't mess with our heads, you know. Neither of us has any implants."

"It's not something I had in mind."

"Or the ship," Antoinette added. "You were lucky with that airlock, but a lot of the mission-critical systems are opto-electronic."

"You're right," he said, offering his palms. "I can't touch those."

"I think we have to trust him," Antoinette said.

"Yes, but if he so much . . . " Xavier halted and looked at Antoinette. He had heard something.

Clavain had heard it too: a chime from somewhere else in the ship, harsh and repetitious.

"Proximity alert," Antoinette breathed.

"Banshees," Xavier said.

Clavain followed them through the clattering metal innards of the ship until they reached a flight deck. The two suited figures slipped ahead of him, buckling into massive antique-looking acceleration couches. While he searched for somewhere to anchor himself, Clavain appraised the flight deck, or bridge, or whatever Antoinette called it. Though it was about as far from a corvette or *Nightshade* as a space vessel could be in terms of capability, function and technological elegance, he had no difficulty orientating himself. It was easy when you had lived through so many centuries of ship design, seen so many cycles of technological boom-and-bust. It was simply a question of dusting off the right set of memories.

"There," Antoinette said, jabbing a finger at a radar sphere. "Two of the fuckers, just like before." Her voice was low, evidently intended for Xavier's ears alone.

"Twenty-eight thousand klicks," he replied, in the same near-whisper, looking over her shoulder at the tumbling digits of the distance indicator. "Closing at . . . fifteen klicks a second, on a near-perfect intercept trajectory. They'll start slowing soon, ready for final approach and forced hard docking."

"So they'll be here in . . . what?" Clavain ran some numbers through his head. "Thirty, forty minutes?"

Xavier stared back at him with a strange look on his face. "Who asked you?"

"I thought you might value my thoughts on the matter."

"Have you dealt with banshees before, Clavain?" Xavier asked.

"Until a few hours ago I don't think I'd ever heard of them."

"Then I don't think you're going to be a fuck of a lot of use, are you?"

Antoinette spoke softly again. "Xave . . . how long do *you* think we've got before they're on us?"

"Assuming the usual approach pattern and deceleration tolerances . . . thirty . . . thirty-five minutes."

"So Clavain wasn't far off."

"A lucky guess," Xavier said.

"Actually, it wasn't a lucky guess at all," Clavain said, folding down a flap from the wall and strapping himself to it. "I may not have dealt with banshees before, but I've certainly dealt with hostile approach-and-boarding scenarios." He decided they could stand not knowing that he had often been the one doing the hostile boarding.

"Beast," Antoinette said, raising her voice, "you ready with those evasion patterns we ran through before?"

"The relevant routines are uploaded and ready for immediate execution, Little Miss. There is, however, a not inconsiderable problem."

Antoinette sighed. "Lay it on me, Beast."

"Our fuel-consumption margins are already slender, Little Miss. Evasive patterns eat heavily into our reserve supplies."

"Do we have enough left to throw another pattern and still make it back to the Belt before hell freezes over?"

"Yes, Little Miss, but with very little . . . "

"Yeah, yeah." Antoinette's gauntleted hands were already on the controls, ready to execute the ferocious manoeuvres that would convince the banshees not to bother with this particular freighter.

"Don't do it," Clavain said.

Xavier looked at him with an expression of pure contempt. "What?"

"I said don't do it. You can assume these are same banshees as before. They've already seen your evasive patterns, so they know exactly what you're capable of doing. It may have given them pause for thought once, but you can be certain they've already decided that the risk is worth it."

"Don't listen . . . " Xavier said.

"All you'll do is burn fuel you might need later. It won't make a blind bit of difference. Trust me. I've been here a thousand times, in about as many wars."

Antoinette looked at him questioningly. "So what the fuck do you want me to do, Clavain? Just sit here and lap it up?"

He shook his head. "You mentioned additional deterrents earlier on. I had a feeling I knew what you meant."

"Oh no."

"You must have weapons, Antoinette. In these times you'd be foolish not to."

NINETEEN

Clavain did not know whether to laugh or cry when he saw the weapons and realised how antiquated and ineffective they were compared with the oldest, lowest-lethality weapons of a Conjoiner corvette or Demarchist raider. They had obviously been cobbled together from several centuries' worth of black market jumble sales, more on the basis of how sleek and nasty they looked than on how much damage they could really do. Apart from the handful of firearms stored inside the ship to be used to repel boarders, the bulk of the weapons were stowed in concealed hull hatches or packed into dorsal or ventral pods that Clavain had earlier assumed held communications equipment or sensor arrays. Not all of the weapons were even functional. About a third of them had either never worked or had broken down, or had run out of whatever ammunition or fuel-source they needed to work.

To access the weapons, Antoinette had pulled back a hidden panel in the floor. A thick metal column had risen slowly from the well, unfolding control arms and display devices as it ascended. A schematic of *Storm Bird* rotated in one sphere, with the active weapons pulsing red. They were linked back into the main avionics web by snaking red data pathways. Other spheres and readouts on the main panel showed the immediate volume of space around the ship at various magnifications. At the lowest magnification, the banshee ships were visible as indistinct radar-echo smudges creeping closer to the freighter.

"Fifteen thousand klicks," Antoinette said.

"I still say we should pull the evasive pattern," Xavier murmured.

"Burn that fuel when you need it," Clavain said. "Not until then. Antoinette, are all those weapons deployed?"

"Everything we've got."

"Good. Do you mind if I ask why you were unwilling to deploy them earlier?"

She tapped controls, finessing the weapons' deployment, reallocating data flows through less congested parts of the web.

"Two reasons, Clavain. One: it's a hanging offence to even think of installing weps on a civilian ship. Two: all those juicy guns might just be the final incentive the banshees need to come in and rob us."

"It won't come to that. Not if you trust me."

"Trust you, Clavain?"

"Let me sit there and operate those weapons."

She looked at Xavier. "Not a hope in hell."

Clavain leaned back and folded his arms. "You know where I am if you need me, in that case."

"Pull the evasive . . . " Xavier began.

"No." Antoinette tapped something.

Clavain felt the entire ship rumble. "What was that?"

"A warning shot," she said.

"Good. I'd have done the same."

The warning shot had probably been a slug, a cylinder of foam-phase hydrogen accelerated up to a few dozen klicks per second in a stubby railgun barrel. Clavain knew all about foam-phase hydrogen; it was one of the main weapons left in the Demarchist arsenal now that they could no longer manipulate antimatter in militarily useful quantities.

The Demarchists mined hydrogen from the oceanic hearts of gas giants. Under conditions of shocking pressure, hydrogen underwent a transition to a metallic state a little like mercury but thousands of times denser. Usually that metallic state was unstable: release the confining pressure and it would revert to a low-density gas. The foam phase, by contrast, was only quasi-unstable; with the right manipulation it could remain in the metallic state even when the external pressure dropped by many orders of magnitude. Packed into shells and slugs, foam-phase munitions were engineered to retain their stability until the moment of impact. Then they would explode catastrophically. Foam-phase weapons were either used as destructive devices in their own right, or as initiators for fission/fusion bombs.

Antoinette was right, Clavain thought. The foam-phase slug cannon might have been an antique in military terms, but just thinking of owning such a weapon was enough to send one to an irreversible neural death.

He saw the firefly smudge of the slug crawl across the distance to the closing pirate ships, missing them by mere tens of kilometres.

"They're not stopping," Xavier said, several minutes later.

"How many more slugs do you have?" Clavain asked.

"One," Antoinette said.

"Save it. You're too far out now. They can get a radar lock on the slug and dodge it before it reaches them."

He unstrapped himself from the folding flap, clambering down the length of the bridge until he was immediately behind Antoinette and Xavier. Now that he had the chance he took a better look at the weapons plinth, mentally assaying its functionality.

"What else have you got?"

"Two gigawatt excimers," Antoinette said. "One Breitenbach three-millimetre boser with a proton-electron precursor. Couple of solid-state close-action slug guns, megahertz firing rate. A cascade-pulse single-use graser, not sure of the yield."

"Probably mid-gigawatt. What's that?" Clavain pointed at the only active weapon she had not described.

"That? That's a bad joke. Gatling gun."

Clavain nodded. "No, that's good. Don't knock Gatling guns; they have their uses."

Xavier spoke. "Picking up reverse thrust plumes. Doppler says they're slowing."

"Did we scare them off?" Clavain asked.

"Sorry, no; this looks exactly like a standard banshee approach," Xavier replied.

"Fuck," Antoinette said.

"Don't do anything until they're closer," Clavain said. "Much closer. They won't attack you; they won't want to risk damaging your cargo."

"I'll remind you of that when we're having our throats slit," Antoinette said.

Clavain raised an eyebrow. "Is that what they do?"

"Actually, that's at the nice humane end of the spectrum."

The next twelve minutes were amongst the most tense Clavain could remember. He understood how his hosts felt, sympathising with their instinct to shoot at the enemy. But it would have been suicidal. The beam weapons were too low-powered to guarantee a kill, and the projectile weapons were too slow to have any effectiveness except at very short range. At the very best they might succeed in taking out one banshee, but not two at once. At the same time Clavain wondered why the banshees had not taken the earlier warning. Antoinette had given them plenty of hints that stealing her imagined cargo would not be easy. Clavain would have thought that they would have decided to cut their losses and move on to a less nimble, less well-armed target. But according to Antoinette it was already unusual for banshees to foray this far into the zone.

When they were just under a hundred klicks out, the two ships slowed and split up, one of them arrowing around to the other hemisphere before resuming its approach. Clavain studied the magnified visual grab of the closest ship. The image was fuzzy—*Storm Bird*'s optics were not military quality—but it was enough to disperse any doubts they might have had about the ship's identity. The view showed a wasp-waisted civilian vessel a little smaller than *Storm Bird*. But it was night-black and studded with grapples and welded-on weapons. Jagged neon markings on the hull suggested skulls and sharks' teeth.

"Where do they come from?" Clavain asked.

"No one knows," Xavier said. "Somewhere in the Rust Belt/Yellowstone environment, but beyond that . . . no one has a fucking clue."

"And the authorities just tolerate them?"

"The authorities can't do dick. Not the Demarchists, not the Ferrisville Convention. That's why everyone's so shit-scared of the banshees." Xavier winked at Clavain. "I tell you, even if you guys do take over it isn't going to be a picnic, not while the banshees are still around."

"Luckily it isn't likely to be my problem," Clavain said.

The two ships crept closer, pinning *Storm Bird* from either side. The optical views sharpened, allowing Clavain to pick out points of weakness and strength, and to make a guess at the capability of the enemy ships' weapons. Scenarios tumbled through his head by the dozen. At sixty kilometres he nodded and spoke quietly and calmly. "All right, listen carefully. At this range you have a chance of doing some damage, but only if you listen to me and do precisely what I say."

"I think we should ignore him," Xavier said.

Clavain licked his lips. "You can, but you'll die. Antoinette: I want you to set up the following firing pattern in preprogrammed mode, without actually moving any of your weapons until I say. You can bet the banshees have us in their sights, and they'll be watching to see what happens."

She looked at him and nodded, her fingers poised over the controls of the weapons plinth. "Say it, Clavain."

"Hit the starboard ship with a two-second excimer pulse as close to amidships as you can get it. There's a sensor cluster there; we want to take it out. At the same time use the rapid-fire slug gun to put a spread over the port ship, say a megahertz salvo with a hundred millisecond sustain. That won't kill them, but it'll sure as hell damage that rack launcher and probably buckle those grapple arms. In any case it'll provoke a response, and that's good."

"It is?" She was already programming his firing pattern into the plinth.

"Yes. See how she's keeping her hull at that angle? At the moment she's in a defensive posture. That's because her main weapons are delicate; now that they're deployed she won't want to bring them into our field of fire until she can guarantee a kill. And she'll think we've hit with our heaviest toys first."

Antoinette brightened. "Which we won't have."

"No. That's when we hit them—both ships—with the Breitenbach."

"And the single-use graser?"

"Hold it back. It's our medium-range trump card, and we don't want to play it until we're in a lot more danger than this."

"And the Gatling gun?"

"We'll keep that back for dessert."

"I hope you're not bullshitting us, Clavain," Antoinette warned.

He grinned. "I sincerely hope I'm not bullshitting you, too."

The two ships continued their approach. Now they were visible through the cabin windows: black dots that occasionally pulsed out white or violet spikes of steering thrust. The dots enlarged, becoming slivers. The slivers took on hard mechanical form, until Clavain could quite clearly see the neon patterning of the pirate ships. The markings had only been turned on during their final approach; at that point, needing to trim speed with thruster bursts, there was no further prospect of remaining camouflaged against the darkness of space. The markings were there to inspire fear and panic, like the Jolly Roger of the old sailing ships.

"Clavain . . . "

"In about forty-five seconds, Antoinette. But not a moment before. Got that?"

"I'm worried, Clavain."

"It's natural. It doesn't mean you're going to die."

That was when he felt the ship shudder again. It was almost the same movement he had felt earlier, when the foam-phase slug had been fired as a warning shot. But this was more sustained.

"What just happened?" Clavain asked.

Antoinette frowned. "I didn't . . . "

"Xavier?" Clavain snapped.

"Not me, guy. Must have been the . . . "

"Beast!" Antoinette shouted.

"Begging your pardon, Little Miss, but one . . . "

Clavain realised that the ship had taken it upon itself to fire the megahertz slug gun. It had been directed towards the port banshee, as he had specified, but much too soon.

Storm Bird shook again. The flight deck console lit up with blocks of flashing red. A klaxon began to shriek. Clavain felt a tug of air, and then immediately heard the rapid sequential slamming of bulkheads.

"We've just taken a hit," Antoinette said. "Amidships."

"You're in deep trouble," Clavain said.

"Thanks. I gathered that."

"Hit the starboard banshee with the ex—"

Storm Bird shuddered again, and this time half the lights on the console blacked out. Clavain guessed that one of the pirates had just hit them with a penetrating slug equipped with an EMP warhead. So much for Antoinette's boast that all the critical systems were routed through opto-electronic pathways . . .

"Clavain . . . " she looked back at him with wild, frightened eyes. "I can't get the excimers to work . . . "

"Try a different routing."

Her fingers worked the plinth controls, and Clavain watched the spider's web of data connections shift as she assigned data to scurry along different paths. The ship shook again. Clavain leaned over and looked through the port window. The banshee was looming large now, arresting its approach with a continuous blast of reverse thrust. He could see grapples and claws unfolding, articulating away from the hull like the barbed and hooked limbs of some complicated black insect just emerging from a cocoon.

"Hurry up," Xavier said, looking at what Antoinette was doing.

"Antoinette." Clavain spoke as calmly as he could. "Let me take over. Please."

"What fucking good . . . "

"Just let me take over."

She breathed in and out for five or six seconds, just looking at him, and then unbuckled herself and eased out of the seat. Clavain nodded and squeezed past her, settling by the weapons plinth.

He had already familiarised himself with it. By the time his hands touched the controls, his implants had begun to accelerate his subjective consciousness rate. Things around him moved glacially, whether it was the expressions on the faces of his hosts or the pulsing of the warning messages on the control panel. Even his hands moved as if through treacle, and the delay between sending a nerve signal and watching his hands respond was quite noticeable. He was used to that, though. He had done this before, too many times, and he naturally made allowances for the sluggish response of his own body.

As his consciousness rate reached fifteen times faster than normal, so that every actual second felt like fifteen seconds to him, Clavain willed himself on to a plateau of detached calm. A second was a long time in war. Fifteen seconds was even longer. There was a lot you could do, a lot you could think, in fifteen seconds.

Now then. He began to set the optimum control pathways for the remaining weapons. The spider's web shifted and reconfigured. Clavain explored a number of possible solutions, forcing himself not to accept second best. It might take two actual seconds to find the perfect arrangement of data flows, but that would be time well spent. He glanced at the short-range radar sphere, amused to see that its update cycle now looked like the slow beating of some immense heart.

There. He had regained control of the excimer cannons. All he needed now was a revised strategy to deal with the changed situation. That would take a few seconds—a few actual seconds—for his mind to process.

It would be tight.

But he thought he would make it.

Clavain's efforts destroyed one banshee and left the other crippled. The damaged ship scuttled back into darkness, its neon patterning flickering spastically like a short-circuiting firefly. After fifty seconds they saw the glint of its fusion torch and watched it fall ahead of them, back towards the Rust Belt.

"How to win friends and influence people," Antoinette said as she watched the ruined one tumble away. Half its hull was gone, revealing a skeletal confusion of innards belching grey spirals of vapour. "Good work, Clavain."

"Thanks," he said. "Unless I'm very much mistaken, that's two reasons for you to trust me. And now, if you don't mind, I'm going to have to faint."

He fainted.

The rest of the journey passed without incident. Clavain was unconscious for eight or nine hours after the battle against the banshees, while his mind recovered from the ordeal of such a protracted spell of rapid consciousness. Unlike Skade, his brain was not built to support that kind of thing for more than one or two actual seconds, and he had suffered the equivalent of a massive and sudden heatstroke.

But there had been no lasting ill effects and he had earned their trust. It was a price he was more than willing to pay. For the remainder of the trip he was free to move around the ship as he pleased, while the other two gradually divested themselves of their outer spacesuit layers. The banshees never came back, and *Storm Bird* never ran into any military activity. Clavain still felt the need to make himself useful, however, and with Antoinette's consent he helped Xavier with a number of minor in-flight repairs or upgrades. The two of them spent hours tucked away in tight cable-infested crawlspaces, or rummaging through layers of archaic source code.

"I can't really blame you for not trusting me before," Clavain said, when he and Xavier were alone.

"I care about her."

"It's obvious. And she took a hell of a risk coming out here to rescue me. If I'd been in your shoes I'd have tried to talk her out of it as well."

"Don't take it personally."

Clavain dragged a stylus across the compad he had balanced on his knees, rerouting a number of logic pathways between the control web and the dorsal communications cluster. "I won't."

"What about you, Clavain? What's going to happen when we get to the Rust Belt?"

Clavain shrugged. "Up to you. You can drop me wherever it suits you. Carousel New Copenhagen's as good as anywhere else."

"And then what?"

"I'll hand myself over to the authorities."

"The Demarchists?"

He nodded. "Although it'd be much too dangerous for me to approach them directly, out here in open space. I'll need to go through a neutral party, such as the Convention."

Xavier nodded. "I hope you get what you're hoping for. You took a risk as well."

"Not the first, I assure you." Clavain paused and lowered his voice. It was unnecessary—they were many dozens of metres away from Antoinette—but he felt the need all the same. "Xavier . . . while we're alone . . . there's something I've been meaning to ask you."

Xavier peered at him through scuffed grey data-visualisation goggles. "Go ahead."

"I gather you knew her father, and that you handled the repair of this ship when he was running it."

"True enough."

"Then I suppose you know all about it. Perhaps more than Antoinette?"

"She's a damned good pilot, Clavain."

Clavain smiled. "Which is a polite way of saying she's not very interested in the technical aspects of this ship?"

"Nor was her father," Xavier said, with a touch of defensiveness. "Running a commercial operation like this is enough trouble without worrying about every subroutine."

"I understand. I'm no expert myself. But I couldn't help noticing back there, when the subpersona intervened . . . " He left the remark hanging.

"You thought that was odd."

"It nearly got us killed," Clavain said. "It fired too soon, against my direct orders."

"They weren't orders, Clavain, they were recommendations."

"My mistake. But the point is, it shouldn't have happened. Even if the subpersona had some control over the weapons—and in a civilian ship I'd regard that as unusual, to say the least—it still shouldn't have acted without a direct command. And it definitely shouldn't have panicked."

Xavier's laugh was hard and nervous. "Panicked?"

"That's what it felt like to me." Clavain couldn't see Xavier's eyes behind the data goggles.

"Machines don't panic, Clavain."

"I know. Especially not gamma-level subpersonae, which is what Beast would have to be."

Xavier nodded. "Then it can't have been panic, can it?"

"I suppose not." Clavain frowned and returned to his compad, dragging the stylus through the bright ganglia of logic pathways like someone stirring a plate of spaghetti.

They docked in Carousel New Copenhagen. Clavain was prepared to go on his way there and then, but Antoinette and Xavier were having none of it. They insisted that he join them for a farewell meal elsewhere in the carousel. After giving the matter a few moments' thought, Clavain happily assented; it would only take a couple of hours and it would give him a valuable chance to acclimatise before he commenced what he imagined would be a perilous solo journey. And he still felt he owed them thanks, especially after Xavier allowed him to take whatever he wanted from his wardrobe.

Clavain was taller and thinner than Xavier, so it took some creativity to both dress himself and not feel that he was taking anything particularly valuable. He retained the skintight spacesuit inner layer, slipping on a bulging high-collared vest that looked faintly like the kind of inflatable jacket pilots wore when they ditched in water. He found a pair of loose black trousers that came down to his shins, which looked terrible, even with the skintight, until he found a pair of rugged black boots that reached nearly to his knees. When he inspected himself in a mirror he concluded that he looked odd rather than bizarre, which he supposed was a step in the right direction. Finally he trimmed his beard and moustache and neatened his hair by combing it back from his brow in snowy waves.

Antoinette and Xavier were waiting for him, already freshened up. They took an intra-rim train from one part of Carousel New Copenhagen to another. Antoinette told him that the line had been put in after the spokes were destroyed; until then the quickest way to get about had been to go up to the hub and down again, and by the time the intra-rim line was installed it could not take the most direct route. It zigzagged its way along the rim, swerving and veering and occasionally taking detours out on to the skin of the habitat, just to avoid a piece of precious interior real estate. As the train's direction of travel shifted relative to the carousel's spin vector, Clavain felt his stomach knot and unknot in a variety of queasy ways. It reminded him of dropship insertions into the atmosphere of Mars.

He snapped back to the present as the train arrived in a vast interior plaza. They disembarked on to a glass-floored and glass-walled platform that was suspended many tens of metres above an astonishing sight.

Beneath their feet, thrusting through the inner wall of the carousel's rim, was the front of an enormous spacecraft. It was a blunt-nosed, rounded design, scratched, gouged and scorched, with all its appendages—pods, spines and antennae—ripped clean away. The spacecraft's cabin windows, which ran around the pole of the nose in a semicircle, were shattered black apertures, like eye-sockets. Around the collar of the ship where it met the fabric of the carousel was a congealed grey foam of solidified emergency sealant that had the porous texture of pumice.

"What happened here?" Clavain asked.

"A fucking idiot called Lyle Merrick," Antoinette said.

Xavier took over the story. "That's Merrick's ship, or what's left of it. Thing was a chemical-rocket scow, about the most primitive ship still making a living in the Rust Belt. Merrick stayed in business because he had the right clients—people the authorities would never, ever suspect of trusting their cargo to such a shit-heap. But Merrick got into trouble one day."

"It was about sixteen, seventeen years ago," Antoinette said. "The authorities were chasing him, trying to force him to let them board and inspect his cargo. Merrick was trying to get under cover—there was a repair well on the far side of the carousel that could just accommodate his ship. But he didn't make it. Fluffed his approach, or lost control, or just bottled out. Stupid twat rammed straight into the rim."

"You're only looking at a small part of his ship," Xavier said. "The rest of it, trailing behind, was mostly fuel tank. Even with foam-phase catalysis you need a lot of fuel for a chemical rocket. When the front hit, she went clean through the carousel's rim, deforming it with the force of the impact. Lyle made it, but the fuel tanks blew up. There's one hell of a crater out there, even now."

"Casualties?" Clavain asked.

"A few," Xavier said.

"More than a few," said Antoinette. "A few hundred."

They told him that suited hyperprimates had sealed the rim, with only a few deaths amongst the emergency team. The animals had done such a good job of sealing the gap between the shuttle and the rim wall that it had been decided that the safest thing to do was to leave the remains of the ship exactly where they were. Expensive designers had been called in to give the rest of the plaza a sympathetic face-lift.

"They call it 'echoing the ship's brutalist intrusion,'" Antoinette said.

"Yeah," said Xavier. "Or else, 'commenting on the accident in a series of ironic architectural gestures, while retaining the urgent spatial primacy of the transformative act itself.'"

"Bunch of overpaid wankers is what I call them," Antoinette said.

"It was your idea to come here in the first place," Xavier responded.

There was a bar built into the nose cone of the ruined ship. Clavain tactfully suggested that they situate themselves as unobtrusively as possible. They found a table in one corner, next to a cavernous tank of bubbling water. Squid floated in the water, their conic bodies flickering with commercials.

A gibbon brought beers. They attacked them with enthusiasm, even Clavain, who had no particular taste for alcohol. But the drink was cold and refreshing and he would have gladly drunk anything in the current spirit of celebration. He just hoped he would not spoil things by revealing how gloomy he really felt.

"So, Clavain . . . " Antoinette said. "Are you going to tell us what this is all about, or are you just going to leave us wondering?"

"You know who I am," he said.

"Yes." She glanced at Xavier. "We think so. You didn't deny it before."

"You know that I defected once already, in that case."

"A way back," Antoinette said.

Clavain noticed that she was peeling the label from her beer bottle with great care. "Sometimes it seems like only yesterday. But it *was* four hundred years ago, give or take the odd decade. For most of that time I have been more than willing to serve my people. Defecting certainly isn't something I take lightly."

"So why the big change of heart?" she asked.

"Something very bad is going to happen. I can't say what exactly—I don't know the full story—but I know enough to say that there's a threat, an external threat, which is going to pose a great danger to all of us. Not just Conjoiners, not just Demarchists, but all of us. Ultras. Skyjacks. Even you."

Xavier glared into his beer. "And on that cheering note . . . "

"I didn't mean to spoil things. That's just the way it is. There's a threat, and we're all in trouble, and I wish it were otherwise."

"What kind of threat?" Antoinette asked.

"If what I learned was correct, then it's alien. For some time now, we—the Conjoiners, rather—have known that there are hostile entities out there. I mean *actively* hostile, not just occasionally dangerous and unpredictable, like the Pattern Jugglers or Shrouders. And I mean extant, in the sense that they've posed a real threat to some of our expeditions. We call them the wolves. We think that they're machines, and that somehow we've only now begun to trigger a response from them." Clavain paused, certain now that he had the attention of his young hosts. He was not overly concerned about revealing what were technically Conjoiner secrets; in a very short while he hoped to be saying exactly the same things to the Demarchist authorities. The quicker the news was spread, the better.

"And these machines . . . ?" Antoinette said. "How long have you known about them?"

"Long enough. For decades we were aware of the wolves, but it seemed they wouldn't cause us any local difficulties provided that we took certain precautions. That's why we stopped building starships. They were luring the wolves to us, like beacons. Only now we've found a way to make our ships quieter. There's a faction in the Mother Nest, led—or influenced, at the very least—by Skade."

"You've mentioned that name already," Xavier said.

"Skade's chasing me down. She doesn't want me to reach the authorities because she knows how dangerous the information I hold is."

"And this faction, what have they been doing?"

"Building an exodus fleet," Clavain told Antoinette. "I've seen it. It's easily large enough to carry all the Conjoiners in this system. They're planning on evacuating, basically. They've determined that a full-scale wolf attack is imminent—that's my guess, anyway—and they've decided that the best thing they can do is run away."

"What's so abhorrent about that?" Xavier asked. "We'd do the same thing if it meant saving our skins."

"Perhaps," Clavain said, feeling a weird admiration for the young man's cynicism. "But there's an added complication. Some time ago the Conjoiners manufactured a stockpile of doomsday weapons. And I mean doomsday weapons—nothing like them has ever been made again. They were lost, but now they've been found again. The Conjoiners are trying to get their hands on them, hoping that they'll be an additional safeguard against the wolves."

"Where are they?" Antoinette asked.

"Near Resurgam, in the Delta Pavonis system. About twenty years' flight time from here. Someone—whoever now owns the weapons—has re-armed them, causing them to emit diagnostic signals that we picked up. That's worrying in itself. The Mother Nest was putting together a recovery squad which they, not unnaturally, wanted me to lead."

"Wait a sec," Xavier said. "You'd go all the way there just to pick up a bunch of lost weapons? Why not make new ones?"

"The Conjoiners can't," Clavain said. "It's as simple as that. These weapons were made a long time ago according to principles which were deliberately forgotten after their construction."

"Sounds a bit fishy to me."

"I never said I had all the answers," Clavain replied.

"All right. Assuming these weapons exist . . . what next?"

Clavain leaned closer, cradling his beer. "My old side will still do their best to recover them, even without me. My purpose in defecting is to persuade the Demarchists or whoever will listen that they need to get there first."

Xavier glanced at Antoinette. "So you need someone with a ship, and maybe some weapons. Why didn't you just go straight to the Ultras?"

Clavain smiled wearily. "It's Ultras we'll be trying to take the weapons from, Xavier. I don't want to make things more difficult than they already are."

"Good luck," Xavier said.

"Yes?"

"You're going to need it."

Clavain nodded and held his bottle aloft. "To me, in that case."

Antoinette and Xavier raised their own bottles in toast. "To you, Clavain."

Clavain said goodbye to them outside the bar, asking only that they give him directions as to which rim train to take. There had been no customs checks coming into Carousel New Copenhagen, but according to Antoinette he would have to pass through a security check if he wanted to travel elsewhere in the Rust Belt. That suited him very well; he could think of no better way to introduce himself to the authorities. He would be examined, trawled, his Conjoiner identity established. A few more tests would prove beyond reasonable doubt that he was indeed who he claimed to be, since his largely unmodified DNA would mark him as a man born on Earth in the twenty-second century. From that point he had no real idea what would happen. He hoped that the response would not be his immediate execution, but it was not something he could rule out. He just hoped he would be able to convey the gist of his message before it was too late.

Antoinette and Xavier showed him which rim train to take and made sure he had enough money to cover the fare. He waved goodbye as the train slid out of the station, the battered ruin of Lyle Merrick's ship vanishing around the gentle curve of the carousel.

Clavain closed his eyes, willing his consciousness rate into a three-to-one ratio, snatching a few moments of calm before he arrived at his destination.

TWENTY

Thorn had been ready to argue with Vuilleumier, but she had agreed to his wishes with surprising ease. It was not that she viewed the prospect of diving into the heart of the Inhibitor activity around Roc with anything less than deep concern, she told him, but that she wanted him to believe that she was totally sincere about the threat. If the only way to convince him of that was to let him see things in close-up, then she would have to go along with his wishes.

"But make no mistake, Thorn. This is dangerous. We're in uncharted territory now."

"I'd say we were never exactly safe, Inquisitor. We could have been attacked at any moment. We've certainly been within range of *human* weapons for the last few hours, haven't we?"

The snake-headed ship plunged towards the top of the gas giant's atmosphere. The trajectory would take them close to the impact point of one of the extruded tubes, only a thousand kilometres from the roiling chaos of tortured air around the eyelike collision zone. Their sensors could not glimpse anything beneath that confusion, only the vaguest suggestion that the tube continued to plunge deeper into Roc, unharmed by the impact.

"We're dealing with alien machinery, Thorn. Alien machine psychology, if you want. It's true that they haven't attacked us yet, or shown the slightest interest in any of our activities. They haven't even bothered wiping life off the surface of Resurgam. But that doesn't mean there isn't a threshold we might inadvertently cross if we're not very careful."

"And you think this might constitute being not very careful?"

"It worries me, but if this is what it takes . . . "

"It's about more than just convincing me, Inquisitor."

"Do you have to keep calling me that?"

"I'm sorry?"

She made an adjustment to the controls. Thorn heard an orchestrated creaking as the ship's hull reshaped itself for optimum transatmospheric insertion. The gas giant Roc was about all they could see outside now. "You don't have to call me that all the time."

"Vuilleumier, then?"

"My first name is Ana. I'm a lot more comfortable with that, Thorn. Perhaps I shouldn't call you Thorn, either."

"Thorn will do. It's a name I've grown into. It seems to fit me rather well. And I wouldn't want to help Inquisition House in its investigations too much, would I?"

"We know exactly who you are. You've seen the dossier."

"Yes. But I have the distinct impression you'd be less than eager to use it against me, wouldn't you?"

"You're useful to us."

"That's not quite what I meant."

They continued their descent into Roc without speaking for several minutes. Only the occasional chirp or spoken warning from the console interrupted the silence. The ship was not at all enthusiastic about what was being asked of it, and kept offering suggestions as to what it would rather be doing.

"I think we're like insects to them," Vuilleumier said eventually. "They've come here to wipe us out, like pest-control specialists. They're not going to bother killing one or two of us—they know it won't make enough of a difference to matter. Even if we sting them, I'm not sure we'd provoke the response we were expecting. They'll just keep on doing their work, slowly and methodically, knowing that it will be more than sufficient in the long run."

"Then we're safe now, is that it?"

"It's just a theory, Thorn—it isn't something I particularly want to bet my life on. But it's clear that we don't understand all that they're doing. There has to be a higher purpose to their activity. There has to be a reason for it; it can't simply be the annihilation of life for its own sake. Even if it was, even if they were nothing more than mindless killing machines, there'd be more efficient ways of doing it."

"So what are you saying?"

"Only that we shouldn't count on our understanding of events to be correct, any more than an insect understands about pest-control programmes." With that, she clenched her jaw and palmed a control. "All right. Hold on. This is where it gets a little bumpy."

A pair of armoured eyelids snicked down over the windows, blocking the view. Almost immediately Thorn felt the ship rumble, the way a car did when it left a smooth road and hit dirt. He had weight, too—it was the tiniest pressure squeezing him back into his seat, but it would keep growing and growing.

"Who are you exactly, Ana?"

"You know who I am. We've been over that."

"Not to my entire satisfaction, we haven't. There's something funny about that ship, isn't there? I couldn't put my finger on what it was exactly, but the whole time I was aboard it, I had the feeling you and the other woman, Irina, were holding your breath. It was as if you couldn't wait to get me off it."

"You have urgent work to do on Resurgam. Irina didn't agree with you coming aboard in the first place. She'd much rather you stayed on the planet, putting in the groundwork for the evacuation operation."

"A few days won't make much difference. No, that definitely wasn't it. There was something else. You two were hiding something, or hoping I wouldn't notice something. I just can't work out exactly what it was."

"You have to trust us, Thorn."

"You make it difficult, Ana."

"What else could we do? We showed you the ship, didn't we? You saw that it was real. It has enough capacity to evacuate the planet. We even showed you the shuttle hangar."

"Yes," he said. "But it's everything that you didn't show me that makes me wonder."

The rumbling had increased. The ship felt as if it was tobogganing down an ice-slope, hitting the occasional buried rock. The hull creaked and reshaped itself again and again, struggling to smooth out the transition. Thorn found himself excited and terrified at the same time. He had entered a planet's atmosphere only once before in his life, when his parents had brought him as a child to Resurgam. He had been frozen and unconscious at the time, and had no more recollection of it than he did of his birth in Chasm City.

"We didn't show you everything because we don't know that the whole of the ship is safe," Vuilleumier said. "We don't know what sorts of traps Volyova's crew left behind."

"You didn't even let me see it from outside, Ana."

"It wasn't convenient. Our approach—"

"Had nothing to do with it. There's something about that ship that you can't let me see, isn't there?"

"Why are you asking me this now, Thorn?"

He smiled. "I thought the gravity of the situation would focus your attention."

She said nothing.

Presently, the ride became smoother. The airframe creaked and reshaped one last time. Vuilleumier waited another few minutes and then raised the armoured eyelids. Thorn blinked against the sudden intrusion of daylight. They were inside the atmosphere of Roc.

"How do you feel?" she asked. "Your weight has doubled since we were aboard the ship."

"I'll manage." He was fine provided he did not have to move around. "How deep did you take us?"

"Not far. Pressure's about half an atmosphere. Wait . . . " At that moment she frowned at something on one of her displays, tapping controls below it so that the image shifted through pastel-coloured bands. Thorn saw a simplified silhouette of the ship they were in, surrounded by pulsing, concentric circles. He suspected it was some form of radar, and saw a small smudge of light wink in and out of existence on the limit of the display. She tapped another control and the concentric circles tightened, bringing the smudge closer. Now it was there, now it was gone, now it was there again.

"What's that?" Thorn asked.

"I don't know. Passive radar says there's something following us, about thirty thousand klicks astern. I didn't see anything on our approach. It's small and it doesn't seem to be getting any closer, but I don't like it."

"Could it be a mistake, an error that the ship's making?"

"I'm not sure. I suppose the radar might be confused, picking up a false return from our wake vortex. I could switch to a focused active sweep, but I really don't want to provoke anything I don't have to. I suggest we get away from here while we still can. I'm a firm believer in listening to warnings."

Thorn tapped the console. "And how do I know that you didn't arrange for that bogey to appear?"

She laughed the sudden, nervous laugh of a person caught completely unawares. "I didn't, believe me."

Thorn nodded, sensing that she was telling the truth—or at least lying very well indeed. "Perhaps not. But I still want you to steer us towards the impact site, Ana. I'm not leaving until I see what's happening here."

"You're serious, aren't you?" She waited for him to answer, but Thorn said nothing, looking at her unflinchingly. "All right," Vuilleumier said finally. "We'll get close enough that you can see things for yourself. But no closer than that. And if that other thing shows any signs of coming nearer, we're out of here. Got that?"

"Of course," he said mildly. "What do you think I am, suicidal?"

Vuilleumier plotted an approach. The impact point was moving at thirty kilometres per second relative to Roc's atmosphere, its pace determined by the orbital motion of the moon that was extruding the tube. They came in from the rear, shadowing the impact point, increasing their speed. The hull contorted itself again, dealing with the increasing Mach numbers; all the while the smudge on the passive radar lingered behind them, shifting in and out of clarity, sometimes vanishing entirely, but never moving relative to their own position.

"I feel lighter," Thorn said.

"You will. We're nearly orbiting again. If we went much faster I'd have to apply thrust to hold us down."

In the wake of the impact the atmosphere was curdled and turbulent, rare chemistries staining cloud layers with sooty reds and vermilions. Lightning flickered from horizon to horizon, arcing across the sky in stuttering silver bridges as transient charge differentials were smoothed out. Furious eddies whirled like dervishes. The ship's manifold passive sensors probed ahead, groping for a trajectory between the worst of the storms.

"I don't see the tube yet," Thorn said.

"You won't, not until we're much closer. It's only thirteen kilometres across, and I doubt that we could see more than a hundred kilometres in any direction even without the storm."

"Do you have any idea what they're doing?"

"I wish I did."

"Planetary engineering, obviously. They ripped apart three worlds for this, Ana. They must mean business."

They continued their approach, the ride becoming rougher. Vuilleumier dipped them up and down by tens of kilometres, until she decided not to risk any further use of the Doppler radar. Thereafter she held a steady altitude, the ship bucking and shaking as it slammed through vortices and shear walls. Alarms went off every other minute, and now and again Vuilleumier would swear and tap a rapid sequence of commands into the control panel. The air around them was growing pitch-dark. Mighty black clouds billowed and surged, contorted into looming visceral shapes. Thunderheads larger than cities whipped past in an instant. Ahead, the air pulsed and blazed with constant electrical discharges: blinding forked white branches and twisting sheets of baby blue. They were flying into a small pocket of hell.

"Doesn't seem like quite such a good idea now, does it?" Vuilleumier commented.

"Never mind," Thorn said. "Just keep us on this heading. The bogey hasn't come any closer, has it? Maybe it was just a reflection from our wake." As he spoke, something else snared Vuilleumier's attention on the console. An alarm started whooping, a chorus of multilingual voices shouting incomprehensible warning messages.

"Mass sensor says there's something up ahead, seventy-odd kilometres distant," she said. "Elongated, I think—the field geometry's cylindrical, with an inverse 'r' attenuation. That's got to be our baby."

"How long until we see it?"

"We'll be there in five minutes. I'm slowing our rate of approach. Hold on."

Thorn pitched forwards in his seat restraints as Vuilleumier killed the speed. He counted out five minutes, then another five. The smudge on the passive radar display held its relative position, slowing as they did. Strangely, the ride became even smoother. The clouds began to thin out; the savage electrical activity became little more than a constant distant strobing on either side of them. There was a horrible sense of unreality about it.

"Air pressure's dropping," Vuilleumier said. "I think there must be a low-pressure wake behind the tube. It's slicing through the atmosphere supersonically, so that the air can't immediately rush around and close the gap. We're inside the Mach cone of the tube, as if we were flying right behind a supersonic aircraft."

"You sound like you know what you're talking about—for an Inquisitor, anyway."

"I've had to learn, Thorn. And I've had a good teacher."

"Irina?" he asked, amusedly.

"We make a pretty good team. But it wasn't always the case." Then she looked ahead and pointed. "Look. I can see something, I think. Let's try some magnification and then get the hell back out into space." On the main console display appeared an image of the tube. It plunged down into the atmosphere from above them, angled to the horizontal by forty or forty-five degrees. Against the slate background of the atmosphere it was a line of shining silver, like the funnel of a twister. They could see perhaps eighty kilometres of its length; above and below it vanished into haze or roiling clouds. There was no sense of motion along the tube, even though it was flowing into the depths at a rate of a kilometre every four seconds. It appeared to be suspended, even unmoving.

"No sign of anything else," Thorn said. "I don't know quite what I was expecting, but I thought there'd be something else. Deeper, maybe. Can you take us forwards?"

"We'll have to pass through the transonic boundary. It'll be a lot rougher than anything we've gone through so far."

"Can we handle it?"

"We can try." Vuilleumier grimaced and worked the controls again. The air in front of the tube was perfectly steady and calm, utterly unaware of the shock wave that was racing towards it. Even the last passage of the tube on the previous swing-round of the moon had been thousands of kilometres to one side of its present trajectory. Air immediately in front of the tube was compressed into a fluid layer only centimetres thick, forming a v-shaped shock wave at each point along the tube's length. There was no way to get ahead of the tube without passing through that wing of savagely compressed and heated air;

not unless Vuilleumier accepted a detour of many thousands of kilometres.

They passed to one side of the tube. It shone cherry-red along the leading edge, evidence of the frictional energies dissipated in its passage. But there was no sign of any harm being done to the alien machinery.

"It's being fed downwards," Thorn said. "But there isn't anything down there. Just a lot of gas."

"Not all the way down," said Vuilleumier. "The gas turns into liquid hydrogen a few hundred kilometres down. Below that, there's pure metallic hydrogen. And somewhere below that there's a rocky core."

"Ana, if they wanted to take apart a planet like this to get at that rocky matter, have you any idea how they might go about it?"

"I don't know. Maybe we're about to find out."

They hit the transonic boundary. For a moment Thorn thought the ship would break up; that they had finally asked too much of it. The hull had creaked before; now—for an instant—he heard it actively scream. The console flared red and flickered out. For a horrible moment all was silent. Then they were through, ghosting in still air. The console stuttered back into life and a chorus of warning voices began to shriek out of the walls.

"We're through," Vuilleumier said. "In one piece, I think. But let's not push our luck, Thorn . . ."

"I agree. But now that we've come all this way . . . well, it would be silly not to look a little deeper, wouldn't it?"

"No."

"If you want me to help you, I want to know what I'm getting myself into."

"The ship can't take it."

Thorn smiled. "It just took more crap than you said it would ever be able to take. Stop being such a pessimist."

The Demarchist representative entered the white holding room and looked at him. Behind her stood three Ferrisville police, the ones he had surrendered to in the departure terminal, and four Demarchist soldiers. The latter had surrendered their firearms but still managed to look foreboding in their fiery red power-armour. Clavain felt old and fragile, knowing that he was completely at the mercy of his new hosts.

"I am Sandra Voi," the woman said. "You must be Nevil Clavain. Why did you have me come here, Clavain?"

"I'm in the process of defecting."

"That's not what I mean. I mean why me in particular? According to the Convention officials you specifically asked for me."

"I thought you'd give me a fair hearing, Sandra. I used to know one of your relatives, you see. Who would she have been, your great-grandmother? I can never get the hang of generations these days."

The woman pulled up the other white chair and stationed herself in it, opposite Clavain. Demarchists pretended that their political system made rank an outmoded concept. Instead of captains they had shipmasters; instead of generals they had strategic planning specialists. Naturally, such specialisations required visual signifiers, but Voi would have frowned at any suggestion that the many bars and bands of colour across the breast of her tunic indicated anything as outmoded as military status.

"There hasn't been another Sandra Voi for four hundred years," she said.

"I know. The last one died on Mars, during an attempt to negotiate peace with the Conjoiners."

"You're talking ancient history now."

"Which doesn't mean it isn't true. Voi and I were part of the same peace-keeping mission. I defected to the Conjoiners shortly after she died, and I've been on their side ever since."

The eyes of the younger Sandra Voi momentarily glazed over. Clavain's implants sensed the scurry of data traffic in and out of her skull. He was impressed. Since the plague few Demarchists carried very much in the way of neural augmentation.

"Our records don't agree."

Clavain raised an eyebrow. "They don't."

"No. Our intelligence indicates that Clavain did not live for more than a century and a half after his defection. You can't possibly be him."

"I left human space on an interstellar expedition and only returned recently. That's why there hasn't been much record of me lately. Does it matter, though? The Convention's already verified that I'm a Conjoiner."

"You could be a trap. Why would you wish to defect?"

Again, she had surprised him. "Why shouldn't I?"

"Maybe you've been reading too many of our newspapers. If you have, I've got some real news for you: your side is about to win this war. A single spider defection won't make any difference now."

"I never thought it would," Clavain said.

"And?"

"That's not why I'd like to defect."

Down, down they went, always remaining ahead of the transonic shock wave of the Inhibitor machinery. The smudge on the passive radar display—the thing that shadowed them at a distance of thirty thousand kilometres—remained present, fading in and out of clarity but never leaving them completely. The daylight grew steadily darker, until the sky overhead was only fractionally lighter than the unmoving black depths below. Ana Khouri turned off the spacecraft's cabin illumination, hoping that it would make the exterior brighter, but the improvement was marginal. The only real source of light was the cherry-red slash of the tube's leading edge, and even that was duller than it had been before. The tube moved at only twenty-five kilometres per second now, relative to the atmosphere: it had steepened its descent, too, plunging nearly vertically towards the transition zones where the atmosphere thickened to liquid hydrogen.

She winced as another pressure warning sounded. "We can't go much deeper. I'm serious now. We'll crush. It's already fifty atmospheres outside, and that thing is still sitting on our tail."

"Just a little closer, Ana. Can we reach the transition zone?"

"No," she said emphatically. "Not in this ship. She's an air-breather. She'll stall in liquid hydrogen, and then we'll fall and be crushed by hull implosion. It's *not* a nice way to go, Thorn."

"The tube doesn't seem bothered by the pressure, does it? I think it probably goes a lot deeper. How much do you think they've laid already? One kilometre every four seconds, isn't it? That's not far off a thousand kilometres in an hour. By now there must be enough to loop around the planet quite a few times."

"We don't know that that's what's happening."

"No, but we can make an educated guess. Do you know what I keep thinking of, Ana?"

"I'm sure you're going to tell me."

"Windings. Like in an electric motor. I could be wrong, of course." Thorn smiled at her.

He moved suddenly. She was not expecting it and for a moment—for all her soldier training—she was frozen in surprise. He was out of his seat, pushing himself towards her across the cabin. He had some weight, since they were moving at much less than orbital speed, but he still swung across with ease, his movements fluid and pre-planned. Gently, he pulled her out of the pilot's position. She fought back, but Thorn was much stronger and knew enough to parry her defensive moves. It was not that she had forgotten her soldiering, but there was only so much advantage that technique could give, especially against an equally skilled opponent.

"Easy, Ana, easy. I'm not going to hurt you."

Before she knew what was happening, Thorn had her in the passenger seat. He forced her to sit on her hands, then tugged the crash webbing tight across her chest. He asked her if she could breathe, then tugged it tighter. She wriggled, but the webbing contracted snugly, holding her in place.

"Thorn . . . " she said.

Thorn eased himself into the pilot's seat. "Now. How shall we play this? Are you going to tell me everything I want to know, or do I have to supply some additional persuasion?"

He worked the controls. The ship lurched; alarms sounded.

"Thorn . . . "

"Sorry. It looked easy enough when I watched you do it. Maybe there's a bit more to it than meets the eye, eh?"

"You can't fly this thing."

"I'm having a damned good go, aren't I? Now . . . what does this do? Let's see . . . " There was another violent reaction from the ship. More alarms sounded. But, sluggishly, the ship had begun to answer his commands. Khouri saw the artificial horizon indicator tilt. They were banking. Thorn was executing a hard turn to starboard.

"Eighty degrees . . . " he read off. "Ninety . . . one hundred . . . "

"Thorn, no. You're taking us straight back towards the shock wave."

"That's pretty much the idea. Do you think the hull will cope? You seemed to think it was already a little on the stressed side. Well, I suppose we're about to find out, aren't we?"

"Thorn, whatever you're planning—"

"I'm not planning anything, Ana. I'm just trying to put us in a position of real and imminent danger. Isn't that abundantly clear?"

She had another go at wriggling free, but it was futile. Thorn had been very clever. No wonder the bastard had eluded the government for so long. She had to admire him for that, even if her admiration was grudging. "We won't make it," she said.

"No, perhaps we won't. And my flying won't help matters, I think. Which makes it all the easier, then. Answers, that's what I want."

"I've told you everything . . . "

"You've told me precisely nothing. I want to know who you are. Do you know when I started having suspicions?"

"No," she said, realising that he would do nothing until she answered.

"It was Irina's voice. I was certain I'd heard it before, you know. Well, finally I remembered. It was Ilia Volyova's address to Resurgam, shortly before she started blasting colonies off the surface. It was a long time ago, but old wounds take a long time to heal. More than a family resemblance there, I'd say."

"You've got it all wrong, Thorn."

"Have I? Then are you going to enlighten me?"

More alarms sounded. Thorn had pulled their speed down, but they were still moving at several kilometres per second towards the shock wave. She hoped it was her imagination, but she thought she could see that slash of cherry-red coming at them through the blackness.

"Ana . . . ?" he asked again, his voice all sweetness and light.

"Damn you, Thorn."

"Ah. Sounds like progress to me."

"Pull up. Turn us around."

"In a moment. Just as soon as I hear the magic words from you. A confession, that's all I'm looking for."

She breathed in deeply. Here it was, then. The ruination of all their slow and measured plans. They had bet on Thorn and Thorn had been cleverer than them. They should have seen it coming, really they should. And Volyova, damn her too, had been right. It had been a mistake ever allowing him anywhere near *Nostalgia for Infinity*. They should have found another way to convince him. Volyova should have ignored Khouri's protests . . .

"Say the words, Ana."

"All right. *All right,* God damn it. She is the Triumvir. We told you a pack of fucking lies from word one. Happy now?"

Thorn did not answer immediately. To her gratitude, he took the time to swing the ship around. Acceleration pressed her even further into the couch as he applied thrust to outrun the shock wave. And from the blackness it came hurtling towards them, a livid line of red, like the bloody edge of an executioner's sword. She watched it swell until the rear view was a wall of scarlet as bright as molten metal. The collision alarms whooped and the multilingual warning voices merged into a single agitated chorus. Then a background of sky started to close in on either side of the red line, like two iron-grey curtains. The thread began to diminish in width, falling behind them.

"I think we made it," Thorn said.

"Actually, I think we didn't."

"What?"

She nodded at the radar display. There was now no sign of the smudge that had been behind them ever since they had entered Roc's atmosphere, but a host of radar signatures were crowding in on all sides. There were at least a dozen new objects, and they lacked the transient quality of the earlier echo. They were closing at kilometres per second, clearly converging on Khouri's ship.

"I think we just provoked a response," she said, her own voice sounding much calmer than she had expected. "Looks like there is a threshold after all, and we just crossed it."

"I'll get us up and out as quickly as possible."

"You think it'll make any damned difference? They're going to be here in about ten seconds. Guess you got the proof you wanted, Thorn. Either that or you're about to get it. Enjoy the moment, because it might not last very long."

He looked at her with what she thought was quiet admiration. "You've been here before, haven't you?"

"Here, Thorn?"

"On the point of death. It doesn't mean much to you."

"I'd rather be somewhere else, don't get me wrong."

The converging forms had transgressed the final concentric circle on the display. They were now within a few kilometres of the ship, slowing as they neared it. Khouri knew there was no longer any harm in directing the active sensors at the approaching things. Their position was already betrayed, and they would lose nothing by taking a closer look at the converging objects. They were approaching from all sides, and although there were still large gaps between them, it would have been utterly futile to attempt to run away. A minute ago the things had not been there at all; clearly, they were able to slip through the atmosphere as if it hardly existed. Thorn had put them into a steep climb, and while she would have done exactly the same thing, she knew it was not going to make any difference. They had come too close to the heart of things, and now they were going to pay for their curiosity, just as Sylveste had all those years ago.

The active radar returns were confused by the shifting forms of the approaching machines. Mass sensors registered phantom signals at the edge of their sensitivity, barely separable from the background of Roc's own field. But the visual evidence was unequivocal. Discrete dark shapes were swimming towards the ship through the atmosphere. Swimming was the right word, Khouri realised, because that was exactly how it appeared: a squirming, flowing, undulating complexity of motion, the way an octopus moved through water. The machines were as large as her ship and formed of many millions of smaller elements, a slithering, restless dance of black cubes on many scales. Almost no detail was visible beyond the absolute shifting black of the silhouettes, but every now and then blue or mauve light flickered within the blocky masses, throwing this or that appendage into relief. Clouds of smaller black shapes attended each major assemblage, and as the assemblages neared each other they threw out extensions between each other, umbilical lines of flowing black daughter machines. Waves of mass pulsed between the main cores, and now and then one of the primaries fissioned or merged with its neighbour. The purple lightning continued to flicker between the inky shapes, occasionally forming a geometric shell around Khouri's ship, before collapsing back to something which appeared much more random. Despite herself, despite the certain feeling that she was going to die, the approach was fascinating. It was also sickening: simply looking at the Inhibitor machines inspired a feeling of dreadful nausea, for she was apprehending something that had clearly never been shaped by human intelligence. It was breathtakingly strange, the way the machines moved, and in her heart she knew that Volyova and she had—if such a thing were possible—terribly underestimated their enemy. They had seen nothing yet.

The machines were now only a hundred metres from her ship. They formed a closing black shell, oozing tighter around their prey. The sky was being locked out, visible only between the tentacular filaments of the exchanging machines. Limned in violet arcs and sprays of lightning—quivering sheets and dancing baubles of contained plasma energy—Khouri saw thick trunks of shifting machinery probing inwards, obscenely and hungrily. The ship's exhaust was still thrusting behind them, but the machines were quite oblivious to it, and it seemed to pass right through the shell.

"Thorn?"

"I'm sorry," he said, with what sounded like genuine regret. "It's just that I had to know. I've always been one to push things."

"I don't really blame you. I might have done the same thing, if the tables were turned."

"That means we'd have both been stupid, Ana. It isn't any excuse."

The hull clanged, then clanged again. The whooping alarm changed its tone: no longer reporting imminent pressure collapse or a stall warning, but indicating that the hull was being damaged, prodded from outside. There was a vile metallic scraping sound, like nails dragged down tin, and the wide grasping end of a trunk of Inhibitor machinery splayed itself across the cockpit windows. The circular end of the trunk squirmed with a moving mosaic of tiny thumb-sized black cubes, the swirling motion possessing a weird hypnotic quality. Khouri tried to reach the controls that would shutter the windows, imagining it might make one or two seconds' difference.

The hull creaked. More black tentacles attached themselves. One by one the sensor displays began to blank out or haze with static.

"They could have killed us by now . . . " Thorn said.

"They could, but I think they want to know what we're like."

There was another sound, one she had been dreading. It was the squeal of metal being torn aside. Her ears popped as pressure fell within the ship, and she assumed that she would be dead a second or two later. To die by depressurisation was not the most desirable of deaths, but she imagined that it was preferable to being smothered by Inhibitor machinery. What would the grasping black shapes do when they reached her—dismantle her the same way they were pulling the ship apart? But just as she had formulated that consolatory thought, the sensation of pressure drop ceased and she realised that if there had been a hull rupture it had been brief.

"Ana," Thorn said. "Look."

The bulkhead door that led into the flight deck was a wall of rippling ink, like a suspended tidal wave of pure darkness. Khouri felt the breeze of that constant bustling motion, as if a thousand silent fans were being flicked back and forth. Only now and then did a pulse of pink or purple light strobe within the blackness, hinting at dreadful machine-filled depths. She sensed hesitation. The machines had reached this far into her ship, and they must have been aware that they had arrived at its delicate organic core.

Something began to emerge from the wall. It began as a domelike blister as wide across as Khouri's thigh, and then it extended, taking on the form of a tree trunk as it probed further into the cabin. Its tip was a blunt nub like one extremity of a slime mould, but it waggled to and fro as if sniffing the air. A blurred haze of tiny black machines made the edge difficult to focus on. The process took place in silence, save for the occasional distant snap or crackle. The nub grew out from the wall until it was a metre long, and as many metres again from Khouri and Thorn. For a moment it ceased extending and swung to one side and then the other. Khouri saw a black thing the size of a bluebottle flit past her brow and then settle back into the main mass of the trunk. Then, with dire inevitability, the trunk bifurcated and resumed its extrusion. The split ends forked, one aiming for Khouri, the other for Thorn. It grew via oozing waves of cubes pulsing along the length of it, the cubes swelling or contracting before locking into their final positions.

"Thorn," Khouri said. "Listen to me. We can destroy the ship."

He nodded once. "What do I do?"

"Free me and I'll do it. It won't accept the destruct order from you."

He made to move, but had shifted barely an inch before the black tentacle had whipped out another appendage to pin him down. It was done with care—the machinery was clearly still unwilling to harm them inadvertently—but Thorn was now immobilised.

"Nice try," Khouri said. The tips were only an inch from her. They had bifurcated and re-bifurcated on their final approach, so that now a many-fingered black hand was poised before her face, fingers—or appendages—ready to be plunged into eyes, mouth, nose, ears, even through skin and bone. The fingers were themselves split into tinier and tinier black spikes, vanishing into a grey-black bronchial haze.

The trunk pulled back an inch. Khouri closed her eyes, thinking the machinery was preparing itself to strike. Then she felt a sharp prick of coldness beneath her eyelids, a sting so quick and localised that it was hardly pain at all. A moment later she felt the same thing somewhere within her auditory canal, and an instant after that—though she had no real idea of how rapidly time was actually passing now—the Inhibitor machinery reached her brain. There was a torrent of sensation, confused feelings and images cascading by in rapid, random succession, followed by a sense that she was being unravelled and inspected like a long magnetic tape. She wanted to scream or make some recognisable human response, but she was pinned hard. Even her thoughts had become gelid, impeded by the invasive presence of the black machines. The tarlike mass had crept into every part of her, until there was almost no space left for the entity that had once thought of itself as Khouri. And yet enough remained to sense that even as the machine pushed itself into her there was a two-way flow of data. As it established communicational feeds into her skull, she became dimly cognisant of its smothering black vastness, extending beyond her head, back along the trunk, back through the ship and into the clump of machines that had surrounded the ship.

She even sensed Thorn, linked into the same information-gathering network. His own thoughts, such as they were, echoed hers precisely. He was paralysed and compressed, unable to scream or even imagine the release that would come from screaming. She tried to reach out to him, to at least let him know that she was still present and that somone else in the universe was aware of what he was going through. And at the same time she felt Thorn do likewise, so that they linked fingers through neural space, like two lovers drowning in ink. The process of being analysed continued, the blackness seeping into the oldest parts of her mind. It was the worst thing she had ever experienced, worse than any torture or simulation of torture that she had ever known on Sky's Edge. It was worse than anything the Mademoiselle had done to her, and the only respite lay in the fact that she was only dwindlingly aware of her own identity. When that was gone she would be free.

And then something changed. At the limit of what she was feeling through the data-gathering channels, there was a disturbance on the periphery of the cloud that had englobed her ship. Thorn sensed it as well: she felt a pathetic flicker of hope reach her through the bifurcation. But there was nothing to be hopeful about. They were just feeling the machines regroup, ready for the next phase of the smothering process.

She was wrong.

She felt a third mind enter her thoughts, quite separate from Thorn's. This mind was bell-clear and calm, and its thoughts remained unclotted by the oppressive black choke of the machinery. She sensed curiosity and not a little hesitation, and while she also sensed fear, she did not detect the outright terror that Thorn was radiating. The fear was only an extreme kind of caution. And at the same time she gained back a little of herself, as if the black crush had relented.

The third mind skirted closer to her own, and she realised, with as much shock as she was capable of registering, that it was a mind she knew. She had never encountered it on this level before, but the force of its personality was so pervasive that it was like a trumpet blast sounding a familiar refrain. It was the mind of a man and it was the mind of a man who had never had much time for doubt, or humility, or much in the way of compassion for the affairs of others. At the same time she detected the tiniest gleam of remorse and something that might even have been concern. But even as she came to that conclusion the mind snapped back, shrouding itself again, and she felt the powerful wake of its withdrawal.

She screamed, properly, for she was able to move her body again. In the same moment the trunk shattered, breaking apart with a high-pitched tinkle. When she opened her eyes she was surrounded by a cloud of jostling black cubes, tumbling in disarray. The black wall across the bulkhead was breaking up. She watched the cubes attempt to merge with each other, occasionally forming larger black aggregates that lasted only a second or so before they too broke apart. Thorn was no longer pinned to his seat. He moved, shoving aside black cubes, until he was able to release Khouri from the webbing.

"Have you any idea what the hell just happened?" he asked, slurring his words as he spoke.

"I do," she said. "But I'm not sure if I believe it."

"Talk to me, Ana."

"Look, Thorn. Look outside."

He followed her gaze. Beyond the ship, the surrounding black mass was experiencing the same inability to cohere as the cubes within the ship. Windows were opening back into empty sky, closing and then re-opening elsewhere. And there was, she realised, something else out there as well. It was within the rough black shell that encompassed the ship but not of it, and as it moved—for it appeared to be orbiting the ship, looping around it in lazy open curves—the coagulated black masses moved nimbly out of its way. The shape of the object was difficult to focus on, but the impression Khouri retained later was of a whirling iron-grey gyroscope, a roughly spherical thing made out of many spinning layers. At its core, or buried somewhere within it, was a flickering source of dark red light, like a carnelian. The object—it also made her think of a spinning marble—was perhaps a metre across, but because its periphery swelled and retracted as it spun, it was difficult to be certain. All Khouri knew, all she could be sure of, was that the object had not been there before, and that the Inhibitor machinery appeared strangely apprehensive of it.

"It's opening a window for us," Thorn said, wonderingly. "Look. It's given us a way to escape."

Khouri eased him from the pilot's position. "Then let's use it," she said. They nosed out of the swarm of Inhibitor machines and arced towards space. On the radar Khouri watched the shell fall behind, fearful that it would smother the flickering red marble and come after them again. But they were allowed to leave. It was only later that something came up hard and fast from behind, with the same tentative radar signature that they had seen before. But the object only zipped past them at frightening acceleration, heading out into interplanetary space. Khouri watched it fall out of range, heading in the general direction of Hades, the neutron star on the system's edge.

But she had expected that.

* * *

Where did the great work come from? What had instigated it? The Inhibitors did not have access to that data. All that was clear was that the work was theirs to perform and theirs alone, and that the work was the single most important activity that had ever been instigated by an intelligent agency in the history of the galaxy, perhaps even in the history of the universe itself.

The nature of the work was simplicity itself. Intelligent life could not be allowed to spread across the galaxy. It could be tolerated, even encouraged, when it confined itself to solitary worlds or even solitary solar systems.

But it must not infect the galaxy.

Yet it was not acceptable to simply extinguish life wholesale. That would have been technologically feasible for any mature galactic culture, especially one that had the galaxy largely to itself. Artificial hypernovae could be kindled in stellar nurseries, sterilising blasts a million times more effective than supernovae. Stars could be steered and tossed into the event horizon of the sleeping supermassive black hole at the galaxy's core, so that their disruption would fuel a cleansing burst of gamma rays. Binary neutron stars could be encouraged to collide by delicate manipulation of the local gravitational constant. Droves of self-replicating machines could be unleashed to rip worlds to rubble, in every single planetary system in the galaxy. In a million years, every old rocky world in the galaxy could have been pulverised. Prophylactic intervention in the protoplanetary discs out of which worlds coalesced could have prevented any more viable planets from forming. The galaxy would have choked in the dust of its own dead souls, glowing red across the megaparsecs.

All this could have been done.

But the point was not to extinguish life, rather to hold it in check. Life itself, despite its apparent profligacy, was held sacrosanct by the Inhibitors. Its ultimate preservation, most especially that of thinking life, was what they existed for.

But it could not be allowed to spread.

Their methodology, honed over millions of years, was simple. There were too many viable suns to watch all the time; too many worlds where simple life might suddenly bootstrap itself towards intelligence. So they established networks of triggers, puzzling artefacts dotted across the face of the galaxy. Their placement was such that an emergent culture was likely to stumble on one sooner rather than later. Equally, they were not intended to lure cultures into space inadvertently. They had to be tantalising, but not too tantalising.

The Inhibitors waited between the stars, listening for the signs that one of their glittering contraptions had attracted a new species.

And then, quickly and mindlessly, they converged on the site of the new outbreak.

The military shuttle Voi had arrived in was docked outside, clamped to the underside of Carousel New Copenhagen via magnetic grapples. Clavain was marched aboard and told where to sit. A black helmet was lowered over his head, with only a tiny glass viewing window in the front. It was intended to block neural signals, preventing him from interfering with ambient machinery. Their caution did not surprise him in the slightest. He was potentially valuable to them—in spite of Voi's earlier comments to the contrary, any kind of defector might make some difference, even this late in the war—but as a spider he could also cause them considerable harm.

The military ship undocked and fell away from Carousel New Copenhagen. The windows in the armoured hull were quaintly fixed. Through the scratched and scuffed fifteen-centimetre-thick glass Clavain saw a trio of slim police craft shadowing them like pilot fish.

He nodded at the ships. "They're taking this seriously."

"They'll escort us out of Convention airspace," Voi said. "It's normal procedure. We have very good relations with the Convention, Clavain."

"Where are you taking me? Straight to Demarchist HQ?"

"Don't be silly. We'll take you somewhere nice and secure and remote to begin with. There's a small Demarchist camp on the far side of Marco's Eye . . . of course, you know all about our operations."

Clavain nodded. "But not your precise debriefing procedures. Have you had to do many of these?"

The other person in the room was a male Demarchist, also of high status, whom Voi had introduced as Giles Perotet. He had a habit of constantly stretching the fingers of his gloves, one after the other, from hand to hand.

"Two or three a decade," he said. "Certainly you are the first in a while. Do not expect the red-carpet treatment, Clavain. Our expectations may have been coloured by the fact that eight of the eleven previous defectors turned out to be spider agents. We killed them all, but not before valuable secrets had been lost to them."

"I'm not here to do that. There wouldn't be much point, would there? The war is ours anyway."

"So you came to gloat, is that it?" Voi asked.

"No. I came to tell you something that will put the war into an entirely different perspective."

Amusement ghosted across her face. "That'd be some trick."

"Does the Demarchy still own a lighthugger?"

Perotet and Voi exchanged puzzled glances before the man replied, "What do you think, Clavain?"

Clavain didn't answer him for several minutes. Through the window he saw Carousel New Copenhagen diminishing, the vast grey arc of the rim revealing itself to be merely one part of a spokeless wheel. The wheel itself grew smaller until it was nearly lost against the background of the other habitats and carousels that formed the Rust Belt.

"Our intelligence says you don't," Clavain said, "but our intelligence could be wrong, or incomplete. If the Demarchy had to get its hands on a lighthugger at very short notice, do you think it could?"

"What is this about, Clavain?" Voi asked.

"Just answer my question."

Her face flared red at his insolence, but she held her temper well. Her voice remained calm, almost businesslike. "You know there are always ways and means. It just depends on the degree of desperation."

"I think you should start making plans. You will need a starship, more than one, if you can manage it. And troops and weapons."

"We're not exactly in a position to spare resources, Clavain," Perotet said, removing one glove completely. His hands were milky white and very fine-boned.

"Why? Because you will lose the war? You're going to lose it anyway. It'll just have to happen a little sooner than you were expecting."

Perotet replaced the glove. "Why, Clavain?"

"Winning this war is no longer the Mother Nest's primary concern. Something else has taken precedent. They're going through the motions of winning now because they don't want you or anyone else to suspect the truth."

Voi asked, "Which is?"

"I don't know all the details. I had to make a choice between staying to learn more and defecting while I had a chance to do so. It wasn't an easy decision, and I didn't have a lot of time for second thoughts."

"Just tell us what you do know," Perotet said. "We'll decide if the information merits further investigation. We'll find out what you know eventually, you realise. We have trawls, just like your own side. Maybe not as fast, maybe not as *safe* . . . but they work for us. You'll lose nothing by telling us something now."

"I'll tell you all that I know. But it's valueless unless you act on it." Clavain felt the military ship adjust its course. They were headed for Yellowstone's only large moon, Marco's Eye, which orbited just beyond the Ferrisville Convention's jurisdictional limit.

"Go ahead," Perotet said.

"The Mother Nest has identified an external threat, one that concerns all of us. There are aliens out there, machinelike entities that suppress the emergence of technological intelligences. It's why the galaxy is such an empty place. They've wiped it clean. I'm afraid we're next on the list."

"Sounds like supposition to me," Voi said.

"It isn't. Some of our own deep-space missions have already encountered them. They are as real as you or I, and you have my word that they're coming closer."

"We've managed fine until now," Perotet said.

"Something we've done has alerted them. We may never know precisely what it was. All that matters is that the threat is real and the Conjoiners are fully aware of it. They do not think they can defeat it." He went on to tell them much the same story that he had already told Xavier and Antoinette about the Mother Nest's evacuation fleet and the quest to recover the lost weapons.

"These imaginary weapons," Voi asked. "Are we supposed to think that they'd make any practical difference against hostile aliens?"

"I suppose if they were not considered to be of value, my people would not be so eager to recover them."

"And where do we come in?"

"I'd like you to recover the weapons first. That's why you'll need a starship. You could leave a few weapons behind for Skade's exodus fleet, but beyond that . . . " Clavain shrugged. "I think they'd be better off in the control of orthodox humanity."

"You're quite a turncoat," Voi said admiringly.

"I've tried not to make a career out of it."

The ship lurched. There had been no warning until that moment, but Clavain had flown in enough ships to know the difference between a scheduled and unscheduled manoeuvre.

Something was wrong. He could see it instantly in Voi and Perotet: all composure dropped from their faces. Voi's expression became a mask, her throat trembling as she went into subvocal communication with the shuttle's shipmaster. Perotet moved to one window, making sure he had at least one limb attached to a grappling point.

The vessel lurched again. A hard blue flash lit the cabin. Perotet looked away, his eyes squinting against the glare.

"What's happening?" Clavain asked.

"We're being attacked." He sounded fascinated and appalled at the same time. "Someone just took out one of the Ferrisville escort craft."

"This shuttle looks lightly armoured," Clavain said. "If someone was attacking us, wouldn't we be dead by now?"

Another flash. The shuttle lurched and yawed, the hull vibrating as the engine load intensified. The shipmaster was applying an evasive pattern.

"That's two down," Voi said from the other side of the cabin.

"Would you mind releasing me from this chair?" Clavain asked.

"I see something approaching us," Perotet called. "Looks like another ship—maybe two. Unmarked. Looks civilian, but can't be. Unless . . . "

"Banshees?" suggested Clavain.

They appeared not to hear him.

"There's something on this side too," Voi said. "Shipmaster doesn't know what's happening either." Her attention flicked to Clavain. "Could your side have got this close to Yellowstone?"

"They want me back pretty badly," Clavain said. "I suppose anything's possible. But this is against every rule of war."

"Those could still be spiders," Voi said. "If Clavain's right, then the rules of war don't apply any more."

"Can you retaliate?" Clavain asked.

"Not here. Our weapons are electronically pacified inside Convention airspace." Perotet unhooked from one restraint and scudded to another on the far wall. "The other escort's damaged—she must have taken a partial hit. She's outgassing and losing navigational control. She's falling behind us. Voi, how long until we're back in the war zone?"

Her eyes glazed again. It was as if she had been stunned momentarily. "Four minutes to the frontier, then weps will depacify."

"You haven't got four minutes," Clavain said. "Is there a spacesuit aboard this thing, by any chance?"

Voi looked at him oddly. "Of course. Why?"

"Because it's pretty obvious that it's me they want. No sense in us all dying, is there?"

They showed him to the spacesuit locker. The suits were of Demarchist design, all ribbed silvery-red metal, and while they were neither more nor less technologically advanced than Conjoiner suits, everything worked differently on them. Clavain could not have put the suit on without the assistance of Voi and Perotet. Once the helmet had latched shut, the faceplate border lit up with a dozen unfamiliar status read-outs, worming traces and shifting histograms labelled with acronyms that meant nothing to Clavain. Periodically a small, polite feminine voice would whisper something in his ear. Most of the traces were green rather than red, which he took to be a good sign.

"I keep thinking this must be a trap," Voi said. "Something you'd always planned. That you meant to come aboard our ship and then be rescued. Perhaps you've done something to us, or planted something . . . "

"Everything I told you was true," Clavain said. "I don't know who those people outside are, and I don't know what they want with me. They could be Conjoiners, but if they are, their arrival's nothing I've planned."

"I wish I could believe you."

"I admired Sandra Voi. I hoped that my knowing her might

help my cause with you. I was perfectly sincere about that."

"If they are Conjoiners . . . will they kill you?"

"I don't know. I think they might have done that already, if that was what they wanted. I don't think Skade would have spared you, but perhaps I'm misjudging her. If indeed it is Skade . . . " Clavain shuffled into the airlock. "I'd best be going. I hope they leave you alone once they see I'm outside."

"You're scared, aren't you?"

Clavain smiled. "Is it that obvious?"

"It makes me think you might not be lying. The information you gave us . . . "

"You really should act on it."

He stepped into the lock. Voi did the rest. The traces on the faceplate registered the shift to vacuum. Clavain heard his suit creak and click in unfamiliar ways as it adjusted to space. The outer door heaved open on heavy pistons. He could see nothing but a rectangle of darkness. No stars; no worlds; no Rust Belt. Not even the marauding ships.

It always took courage to step out of any spacecraft, most especially in the absence of any means of returning. Clavain judged that single footstep and push-off to be amongst the two or three hardest things he had ever done in his life.

But it had to be done.

He was outside. He turned slowly, the claw-shaped Demarchist shuttle coming into view and then passing by him. It was unharmed, save for one or two scorch marks on the hull where it had been struck by scalding fragments from the escort ships. On the sixth or seventh turn the engines pulsed and the shuttle began to put increasing distance between itself and him. Good. There was no sense sacrificing himself if Voi did not take advantage of it.

He waited. Perhaps four minutes passed before he became aware of the other ships. Evidently they had moved away after the attack. There were three of them, as Perotet and Voi had thought.

Their hulls were black, stencilled with neon skulls, eyes and sharks' teeth. Now and then a thruster aperture would bark a pulse of steering gas, and the flash would pick out more details, limning the sleek curves of transatmospheric surfaces and the cowled muzzles of retractable weapons or hinged grappling gear. The weapons could be packed away and the ships would look innocent enough: sleek rich kids' toys, but nothing you would bet on against armed Convention escorts.

One of the three banshees broke from the pack and loomed large. A yellow-lit airlock irised open in the belly of her hull. Two figures bustled out, black as space themselves. They jetted towards Clavain and braked expertly when they were on the point of colliding with him. Their spacesuits were like their ships: civilian in origin but augmented with armour and weapons. They made no effort to speak to him on the suit channel; all he heard as he was snared and taken aboard the black ship was the repetitious soft voice of the suit subpersona.

There was just room for the three of them in the belly airlock. Clavain looked for markings on the suits of the other two, but even up close they were perfectly black. The faceplate visors were heavily tinted, so that all he caught was the occasional flash of an eye.

His status indicators shifted again, registering the return of air pressure. The inner door irised open and he was pushed forwards into the main body of the black ship. The spacesuited pair followed him. Once they were inside, their helmets detached themselves automatically and flew away to storage points. Two men had brought him aboard the ship. They could easily have been twins, even down to the nearly identical broken nose on each face. One of the men had a gold ring through one eyebrow, the other through the lobe of one ear. Both were bald except for an exceptionally narrow line of dyed-green hair that bisected their skulls from temple to nape. They wore wraparound tortoiseshell goggles and neither man had any trace of a mouth.

The one with the ring through his eyebrow motioned to Clavain that he should remove his own helmet. Clavain shook his head, unwilling to do that until he was certain that he was in breathable air. The man shrugged and reached for something racked on the wall. It was a bright-yellow axe.

Clavain raised a hand and began to fiddle with the connecting latch of the Demarchist suit. He could not find the release mechanism. After a moment the man with the pierced ear shook his head and brushed Clavain's hand aside. He worked the latch and the soft voice in Clavain's ear became shriller, more insistent. The status displays flicked mostly into red.

The helmet came off with a gasp of air. Clavain's ears popped.

The pressure on the black ship was not quite Demarchist standard. He breathed cold air, his lungs working hard.

"Who . . . who are you?" he asked, when he had the energy for words.

The man with the pierced eyebrow replaced the yellow axe on the wall. He drew a finger across his own throat.

Then another voice, one that Clavain did not recognise, said, "Hello."

Clavain looked around. The third person also wore a spacesuit, though it was much less cumbersome than the suits worn by her fellows. Despite its bulk she still managed to appear thin and spare. She hovered within the frame of a bulkhead door, resting calmly with her head cocked slightly to one side. Perhaps it was the play of light on her face, but Clavain thought he saw ghostly blades of faded black against the perfect white of her skin.

"I hope the Talkative Twins treated you well, Mr. Clavain."

"Who are you?" Clavain said again.

"I am Zebra. That's not my real name, of course. You won't ever need to know my real name."

"Who are you, Zebra? Why have you done this?"

"Because I was told to. What did you expect?"

"I didn't expect anything. I was trying . . . " He paused and waited until his breath had returned. "I was trying to defect."

"We know."

"We?"

"You'll find out soon enough. Come with me, Mr. Clavain. Twins, secure and prepare for high-burn. The Convention will be swarming like flies by the time we get back to Yellowstone. It's going to be an interesting trip home."

"I'm not worth killing innocent people for."

"No one died, Mr. Clavain. The two Convention escorts we destroyed were remotes, slaved to the third. We wounded the third, but its pilot won't have been harmed. And we conspicuously avoided harming the zombies' shuttle. Did they make you step outside, I wonder?"

He followed her forwards, through the bulkhead into a flight deck area. There was only one other person aboard as far as Clavain could tell: a wizened-looking man strapped into the pilot's position. He was not wearing a suit. His ancient age-spotted hands gripped the controls like prehensile twigs.

"What do you think?" Clavain asked.

"It's possible they might have, but I think it more likely that you chose to leave."

"It doesn't matter now, does it? You've got me."

The ancient man glanced at Clavain with only a flicker of interest. "Normal insertion, Zebra, or do we take the long way home?"

"Follow the normal corridor, Manoukhian, but be ready to deviate. I don't want to engage the Convention again."

Manoukhian, if that was indeed his name, nodded and applied pressure to the ivory-handled control sticks. "Get the guest strapped down, Zebra. You too."

The striped woman nodded. "Twins? Help me secure Mr. Clavain."

The two men shifted Clavain's suited form into a contoured acceleration couch. He let them do whatever they wanted; he was too weak to offer more than token resistance. His mind probed the immediate cybernetic environment of the spacecraft, and while his implants sensed something of the data traffic through the control networks, there was nothing he could influence. The people were also beyond his reach. He did not even think any of them had implants.

"Are you the banshees?" Clavain asked.

"Sort of, but not exactly. The banshees are a bunch of thuggish pirates. We do things with a little more finesse. But their existence gives us the cover we need for our own activities. And you?" The stripes on her face bunched as she smiled. "Are you really Nevil Clavain, the Butcher of Tharsis?"

"You didn't hear that from me."

"That's what you told the Demarchists. And those kids in Copenhagen. We have spies everywhere, you see. There's not a lot that escapes us."

"I can't prove I'm Clavain. But then why should I bother?"

"I think you are," Zebra said. "I *hope* you are, anyway. It would be such a letdown if you turned out to be an impostor. My boss wouldn't be at all happy."

"Your boss?"

"The man we're on our way to meet," Zebra said.

TWENTY-ONE

When they were safely clear of the atmosphere and the carnelian-red marble had vanished from the extreme range of her ship's radar, Khouri found the courage to take hold of one of the black cubes that had been left behind when the main mass of Inhibitor machinery had fragmented. The cube was shockingly cold to the touch, and when she let go of it she left behind two thin films of detached flesh on opposite faces of the cube, like pink fingerprints. Her fingertips were now red-raw and smooth. For a moment she thought the removed skin would stay adhered to the smooth black sides, but after a few seconds the two sheets of flesh peeled away of their own accord, forming delicate translucent flakes like insects' discarded wings. The cube's cold black sides were as pitilessly dark and unmarred as before. But she noticed that the cube was shrinking, the contraction so odd and unexpected that her mind interpreted it as the cube receding into an impossible distance. All around her, the other cubes were echoing the contraction, their size diminishing by a half with every second that passed.

Within a minute there was nothing left in the cabin but films of grey-black ash. She even felt ash accumulate at the corners of her eyes, like a sudden attack of sleepy dust, and was reminded that the cubes had reached into her head before the marble had arrived.

"Well, you got your demonstration," she said to Thorn. "Was it worth it, just to make a point?"

"I had to know. But I couldn't know *what* was going to happen."

Khouri rubbed circulation back into her hands where they had grown numb. It was good to be out of the restraint webbing that Thorn had put her in. He apologised for that, without very much in the way of conviction. She had to admit that she would never have confessed to the truth without such extreme coercion.

"What did happen, by the way?" Thorn added.

"I don't know. Not all of it anyway. We provoked a response, and I'm pretty sure we were about to die, or at least to be swallowed up by that machinery."

"I know. I had that feeling as well."

They looked at each other, conscious that the period of union in the Inhibitor data-gathering network had permitted them a level of intimacy neither had expected. They had shared very little other than fear, but Thorn at least had been shown that her fear was every bit as intense as his own, and that the Inhibitor attack had not been something she had arranged for his benefit. But there had been something more than fear, hadn't there? There had been concern for each other's welfare. And when the third mind had arrived, there had also been something very close to remorse.

"Thorn . . . did you feel the other mind?" Khouri asked.

"I felt something. Something other than you, and something other than the machinery."

"I know who it was," she said, knowing that it was far too late for lies and evasion now, and that Thorn needed to be told as much of the truth as she understood. "At least, I think I recognised him. The mind was Sylveste's."

"Dan Sylveste?" he asked cautiously.

"I knew him, Thorn. Not well, and not for long, but enough to recognise him again. And I know what happened to him."

"Start at the beginning, Ana."

She rubbed the grit from the edge of her eye, hoping that the machinery was truly inert and not simply sleeping. Thorn was right. Her admission had been the first crack in an otherwise perfect façade. But the crack could not be unmade. It would spread, extending fracturing fingers. All she could offer now was damage limitation.

"Everything you think you know about the Triumvir is wrong. She isn't the maniacal tyrant that the populace thinks. The government built up her image. It needed a demon, a hate figure. If the people hadn't had the Triumvir to hate, they would have directed their anger, their sense of frustration, at the government itself. That couldn't be allowed to happen."

"She murdered a whole settlement."

"No . . ." She was suddenly weary. "No. It didn't happen like that. She just made it seem that way, don't you understand? Nobody actually died."

"And you can be sure of that, can you?"

"I was there."

The hull creaked and reconfigured itself again. Shortly they would be outside the electromagnetic influence of the gas giant. The Inhibitor processes continued unabated: the slow laying of the sub-atmospheric tubes, the building of the great orbital arc. What had just happened within Roc had made no difference to that grander scheme.

"Tell me about it, Ana. Is that really your name, or is it another layer of untruth that I need to peel back?"

"It is my name," she said. "But Vuilleumier isn't. That was a cover. It was a colonist name. We created a history for me, the necessary past that enabled me to infiltrate the government. My true name is Khouri. And yes, I was part of the Triumvir's crew. I came here aboard *Nostalgia for Infinity*. We came to find Sylveste."

Thorn folded his arms. "Well, now we're finally getting somewhere."

"The crew wanted Sylveste, that's all. They had no grudge against the colony. They used misinformation to make you think that they were more willing to use force than was really the case. But Sylveste double-crossed us. He needed a way to explore the neutron star and the thing in orbit around it, the Cerberus/Hades pair. He persuaded the Ultras to help him with their ship."

"And afterwards? What happened then? Why did the two of you come back to Resurgam if you had a starship to yourselves?"

"There was trouble on the ship, as you guessed. Serious fucking trouble."

"A mutiny?"

Khouri bit her lip and nodded. "Three of us, I suppose, turned against the rest. Ilia and myself, and Sylveste's wife, Pascale. We didn't want Sylveste to explore the Hades pair."

"Pascale? As in Pascale Girardieau, you mean?"

Khouri remembered that Sylveste's wife had been the

daughter of one of the most powerful colonial politicians; the man whose regime had taken power after Sylveste was deposed for his beliefs.

"I didn't know her that well. She's dead now. Well, sort of."

"Sort of?"

"This isn't going to be easy, Thorn. You'll just have to accept what I say, understand? No matter how insane or unlikely it sounds. Although given what's just happened, I have a feeling you'll be more receptive than before."

He touched a finger to his lip. "Try me."

"Sylveste and his wife entered Hades."

"You mean the other object, surely? Cerberus?"

"No," she said emphatically. "I mean Hades. They entered the neutron star, although it turned out that it's a lot more than just a neutron star. It's not really a neutron star at all, actually; more a kind of giant computer, left behind by aliens."

He shrugged. "Like you say, it's not as if I haven't seen some strange things today. And? What happened next?"

"Sylveste and his wife are inside the computer, running like programs. Like alpha-levels, I guess." She raised a finger, anticipating his point. "I know this, Thorn, because I took a stroll inside it myself. I encountered Sylveste, after he'd been mapped into Hades. Pascale too. As a matter of fact, there's probably a copy of me in there as well. But I—this me—didn't stay. I came back out here into the real universe, and I haven't been back since. Matter of fact, I'm not planning on ever going back. There's no easy way into Hades, not unless you count dying by being ripped apart by gravitational tidal stresses."

"But you think the mind we met was Sylveste's?"

"I don't know," she said, sighing. "Sylveste's been inside Hades for subjective centuries, Thorn—subjective aeons, probably. What happened to us all sixty years ago must just be a dim, distant memory from the dawn of time for him. He's had time to evolve beyond anything our imaginations can deal with. And he's immortal, since nothing within Hades has to die. I can't guess how he'd act now, whether we'd even recognise his mind. But it sure as hell felt like Sylveste to me. Maybe he was able to recreate himself the way he used to be, just so I'd know what it was that saved us."

"He'd take an interest in us?"

"He's never shown any sign of it before. But then again,

nothing very much has happened in the outside world since he was mapped into Hades. But now, all of a sudden, the Inhibitors have arrived and they've started ripping the place up. Information must still be reaching him inside Hades, even if it's only on an emergency basis. But think about it, Thorn. There is some serious shit going down here. It might even affect Sylveste. We can't know that, but we can't say for sure it isn't true either."

"So what was that thing?"

"An envoy, I suppose. A chunk of Hades, sent out to gather information. And Sylveste sent a copy of himself along with it. The envoy learned what it could, buzzed around the machinery, shadowed us, and then headed back to Hades. Presumably when it gets there it'll merge back into the matrix. Maybe it was never totally disconnected—there could have been a filament of nuclear matter a single quark wide stretching all the way from the marble back to the edge of the system, and we'd never have known it."

"Go back a bit. What happened after you left Hades? Did Ilia come with you?"

"No. She was never mapped into the matrix. But she survived and we met up again in orbit around Hades, inside *Nostalgia for Infinity*. The logical thing to have done would have been to get away from this system, a long way away, but it wasn't happening. The ship was, well, not exactly damaged, but changed. It had suffered a kind of psychotic episode. It didn't want to have any further dealings with the external universe. It was all we could do to get it back to the inner system, within an AU of Resurgam."

"Hm." Thorn had his chin propped on his knuckle. "This gets better, it really does. The odd thing is, I actually think you might be telling the truth. If you were going to lie, you'd at least come up with something that made sense."

"It does make sense, you'll see."

She told him the rest of it, Thorn listening quietly and patiently, nodding occasionally and asking her to clarify certain aspects of her story. She told him that everything they had already told him about the Inhibitors was the truth in so far as they knew it, and that the threat was as real as they had claimed.

"That much I think you've convinced me of," Thorn said.

"Sylveste brought them down, unless they were already on

their way here. That's why he might still feel some obligation to protect us, or at least take a passing interest in the external universe. The thing around Hades was a kind of trigger, we think. Sylveste knew there was risk in what he did, but he didn't care."

Khouri scowled, feeling a surge of anger. "Fucking arrogant scientist. I was supposed to kill him, you know. That's why I was on that ship in the first place."

"Another delicious complication." He nodded approvingly. "Who sent you?"

"A woman from Chasm City. Called herself the Mademoiselle. She and Sylveste went years back. She knew what he was up to, and that he had to be stopped. That was my job. Trouble was, I fucked up."

"You don't look like the sort to commit cold-blooded murder."

"You don't know me, Thorn. Not at all."

"Not yet, perhaps." He looked at her long and hard until, with some reluctance, she turned away from his gaze. He was a man she felt attracted to and she knew that he was a man who believed in something. He was strong and brave—she had seen that for herself, in Inquisition House. And it was true, even if she did not necessarily want to admit it, that she had engineered this situation with some inkling of how it might play out, from the moment she had insisted that they bring Thorn aboard. But there was no escaping the single painful truth that continued to define her life, even after so much had happened. She was a married woman.

Thorn added, "But there's always time, as they say."

"Thorn . . . "

"Keep talking, Ana. Keep talking." Thorn's voice was very soft. "I want to hear it all."

Later, when they had put a light-minute between themselves and the gas giant, the console signalled an incoming tight-beam transmission relayed from *Nostalgia for Infinity*. Ilia must have tracked Khouri's ship with deep-look sensors, waiting until there was sufficient angular separation between it and the Inhibitor machines. Even with the relay drones she was deeply anxious not to compromise her position.

"I see you are on your way home," she said, intense displeasure etched into every word. "I see also that you went much closer to the heart of their activity than we agreed. That is not good. Not good at all."

"She doesn't sound happy," Thorn whispered.

"What you did was exceptionally dangerous. I just hope you learned something for your efforts. I demand that you make all haste back to the starship. We mustn't detain Thorn from his urgent work on Resurgam . . . nor the Inquisitor from her duties in Cuvier. I will have more to say on this matter when you return." She paused before adding, "Irina out."

"She still doesn't know that I know," Thorn said.

"I'd better tell her."

"That doesn't sound terribly wise to me, Ana."

She looked at him. "No?"

"Not just yet. We don't know how she'd take it. Probably better that we act as if I still think . . . et cetera." He made a spiralling gesture with his forefinger. "Don't you agree?"

"I kept something from Ilia once before. It was a serious mistake."

"This time you'll have me on your side. We can break it to her gently once we're safe and sound aboard the ship."

"I hope you're right."

Thorn narrowed his eyes playfully. "It will work out in the end, I promise you that. All you have to do is trust me. That isn't so hard, is it? After all, it's no more than you asked of me."

"The trouble was we were lying."

He touched her arm, a contact that might have seemed accidental had he not prolonged it for several artful seconds. "We'll just have to put that behind us, won't we?"

She reached over and delicately removed his hand, which closed gently around her own, and for a moment they were frozen like that. Khouri was conscious of her own breathing. She looked at Thorn, knowing full well what she wanted and knowing that he wanted it too.

"I can't do this, Thorn."

"Why not?" He spoke as if there were no valid objection she could possibly raise.

"Because . . . " She slipped her hand from his. "Because of what I still am. Because of a promise I made to someone."

"Who?" Thorn asked.

"My husband."

"I'm sorry. I never thought for a moment that you might be

married." He sat back in his seat, putting a sudden distance between them. "I don't mean that in an insulting way. It's just one minute you're the Inquisitor, the next you're an Ultra. Neither exactly fitted my preconceptions of a married woman."

She raised a hand. "It's all right."

"Who is he, if you don't mind my asking?"

"It isn't that simple, Thorn. I honestly wish it was."

"Tell me. Please. I *do* want to know." He paused, perhaps reading something in her expression. "Is your husband dead, Ana?"

"It isn't *that* simple, either. My husband was a soldier. I used to be one as well. We were both soldiers on Sky's Edge, in the Peninsula wars. I'm sure you've heard of our quaint little civil dispute." She did not wait for his answer. "We were fighting together. We were wounded and shipped into orbit unconscious. But something went wrong. I was misidentified, mis-tagged, put on the wrong hospital ship. I still don't know all the details. I ended up being loaded aboard a bigger ship heading outsystem. A lighthugger. By the time the error was discovered I was around Epsilon Eridani, Yellowstone."

"And your husband?"

"I still don't know. At the time I was led to think that he'd been left behind around Sky's Edge. Thirty, forty years, Thorn—that's how long he'd have had to wait, even if I'd managed to get on a ship making the immediate return trip."

"What kind of longevity therapies did you have on Sky's Edge?"

"None at all."

"So there would have been a good chance of your husband being dead by the time you got back?"

"He was a soldier. Life expectancy in a freeze/thaw battalion was already pretty damned short. And anyway, there *wasn't* any ship headed straight back." She rubbed her eyes and sighed. "That was what I was told had happened to him. But I still don't know for sure. He might have come with me on the same ship; everything *else* might have been a lie."

Thorn nodded. "So your husband might still be alive, but in the Yellowstone system?"

"Yes—supposing he ever got there, and supposing he didn't ship back on the next outbound ship. But even then he'd be old. I spent a long time frozen in Chasm City before I came here.

And I've spent even more time frozen since then, while Ilia and I waited for the wolves."

Thorn was silent for a minute. "So you're married to a man you still love, but who you probably won't ever see again?"

"Now you understand why it isn't easy for me," she said.

"I do," Thorn said quietly, with something close to reverence in his voice. "I do, and I'm sorry." Then he touched her hand again. "But maybe it's still time to let go of the past, Ana. We all have to one day."

It took much less time to reach Yellowstone than Clavain had expected. He wondered if Zebra had drugged him, or whether the thin cold air in the cabin had caused him to slip into unconsciousness . . . but there appeared to be no gap in the sequence of his thoughts. The time had simply passed very rapidly. Three or four times Manoukhian and Zebra had spoken quietly and urgently between themselves, and shortly thereafter Clavain had felt the ship change its vector, presumably to avoid another tangle with the Convention. But there had never been any tangible sense of panic.

He had the impression that Zebra and Manoukhian regarded another conflict as something to be avoided out of a sense of decorum or neatness, rather than a pragmatic matter of survival. Whatever else they were, they were professionals.

The ship looped above the Rust Belt, avoiding it by many thousands of kilometres, and then made a spiralling approach towards Yellowstone's cloud layers. The planet swelled, filling every window within Clavain's field of view. A skin of neon-pink ionisation gases surrounded the ship as she cleaved into atmosphere. Clavain felt his gravity return after hours of weightlessness. It was, he reminded himself, the first *actual* gravity that he had felt in years.

"Have you visited Chasm City before, Mr. Clavain?" Zebra asked him, when the black ship had completed its atmospheric insertion.

"Once or twice," he said. "Not lately. I take it that's where we're going?"

"Yes, but I can't say where exactly. You'll have to find out for yourself. Manoukhian, can you hold her steady for the next minute or so?"

"Take your time, Zeb."

She unbuckled from her acceleration couch and stood over Clavain. It appeared that the stripes were zones of distinct pigmentation rather than tattoos or skin paint. Zebra flipped open a locker and slid out a metallic-blue box the size of a medical kit. She opened it and dithered her finger over the contents, like someone puzzling over a box of chocolates. She pulled out a hypodermic device.

"I'm going to put you under, Mr. Clavain. While you're unconscious I'll run some neurological tests, just to verify that you really are a Conjoiner. I won't wake you until we've arrived at our destination."

"There's no need to do that."

"Ah, but there is. My boss is very protective of his secrets. He'll want to decide for himself what you get to know." Zebra leaned over him. "I can get this into your neck, I think, without getting you out of that suit."

Clavain saw that there was no point in arguing. He closed his eyes and felt the cold tip of the hypodermic prick his skin. Zebra was good, no doubt about that. He felt a second flush of cold as the drug hit his bloodstream.

"What does your boss want with me?" he asked.

"I don't think he really knows yet," Zebra said. "He's just curious. You can't blame him for that, can you?"

Clavain had already willed his implants to neutralise whatever agent Zebra had injected into him. There might be a slight loss of clarity as the medichines filtered his blood—he might even lapse into brief unconsciousness—but it would not last. Conjoiner medichines were good against any . . .

He was sitting upright in an elegant chair fashioned from scrolls of rough black iron. The chair was anchored to something tremendously solid and ancient. He was on planetary ground, no longer in Zebra's ship. The blue-grey marble beneath the chair was fabulously veined, streaked and whorled like the gas flows in some impossibly gaudy interstellar nebula.

"Good afternoon, Mr. Clavain. How are you feeling now?"

It was not Zebra's voice this time. Footsteps padded across the marble without haste. Clavain looked up, taking in more of his surroundings.

He had been brought to what appeared to be an immense conservatory or greenhouse. Between pillars of veined black marble were finely mullioned windows that reached tens of metres high before curving over to intersect above him. Trellised sheets climbed nearly to the apex of the structure, tangled with vivid green vines. Between the trellises were many large pots or banks of earth that held too many kinds of plant for Clavain to identify, beyond a few orange trees and what he thought was some kind of eucalyptus. Something like a willow loomed over his seat, its dangling vegetation forming a fine green curtain that effectively blocked his vision in a number of directions. Ladders and spiral staircases provided access to aerial walkways spanning and encircling the conservatory. Somewhere, out of Clavain's field of view, water trickled constantly, as if from a miniature fountain. The air was cool and fresh rather than cold and thin.

The man who had spoken stepped softly before him. He was Clavain's height and dressed in similarly dark clothes—Clavain had been divested of his spacesuit—though there the resemblance ended. The man's apparent physiological age was two or three decades younger than Clavain's, his slick backcombed black hair merely feathered by grey. He was muscular, but not to the point where it looked ridiculous. He wore narrow black trousers and a knee-length black gown cinched above his waist. His feet and chest were bare, and he stood before Clavain with his arms folded, looking down on him with an expression somewhere between amusement and mild disappointment.

"I asked . . . " the man began again.

"You have obviously examined me," Clavain said. "What more can I tell you that you don't already know?"

"You seem displeased." The man spoke Canasian, but with a trace of stiffness.

"I don't know who you are or what you want, but you have no idea of the damage you have done."

"Damage?" the man asked.

"I was in the process of defecting to the Demarchists. But of course you know all that, don't you?"

"I'm not sure how much Zebra told you," the man said. "It's true we know something about you, but not as much as we'd like to know. That's why you're here now, as our guest."

"Guest?" Clavain snorted.

"Well, that may be stretching the usual definition of the term, I admit. But I do not want you to consider yourself our prisoner. You are not. Nor are you our hostage. It is entirely possible that we will decide to release you very shortly. What harm will have been done then?"

"Tell me who you are," Clavain said.

"I will in a moment. But first, why don't you come with me? I think you will find the view most rewarding. Zebra told me this wasn't your first visit to Chasm City, but I am not sure you'll have ever seen it from quite this perspective." The man leaned down and offered Clavain his hand. "Come, please. I assure you I will answer all of your questions."

"All of them?"

"Most of them."

Clavain pushed himself from the iron seat with the man's assistance. He realised that he was still a little weak, now that he had to stand on his own, but he was able to walk without difficulty, his own bare feet cold against the marble. He remembered that he had removed his shoes before getting into the Demarchist spacesuit.

The man led him to one of the spiral staircases. "Can you manage this, Mr. Clavain? It's worth it. The windows are a little dusty below."

Clavain followed the man up the rickety spiral staircase until they reached one of the aerial walkways. It wound its way through panes of trelliswork until Clavain lost all sense of direction. From the vantage point of his seat he had been aware only of indistinct shapes beyond the windows and a pale ochre light that suffused everything with its own melancholic glow, but now he saw the view more clearly. The man ushered him to a balustrade.

"Behold, Mr. Clavain: Chasm City. A place I have to come to know and, while not actually love, perhaps not to detest with quite the same missionary zeal as when I first arrived."

"You're not from here?" Clavain asked.

"No. Like you I have travelled far and wide."

The city crawled away in all directions, festering into a distant urban haze. There were not more than two dozen buildings taller than the one they were in, although some of those were very much taller, plunging into overlying cloud so that their tops were invisible. Clavain saw the dark, distant line of the encircling rim wall looming over the haze many tens of kilometres away. Chasm City was built inside a caldera which itself contained a gaping hole in Yellowstone's crust. The city surrounded the great belching chasm, teetering on the edge, thrusting clawlike taplines down into the depths. Structures leaned shoulder to shoulder, intertwined and fused into deliriously strange shapes. The air was infested with aerial traffic, a constant shifting mass that made the eye struggle to stay in focus. It seemed quite impossible that there could be that many journeys to be made at any one time, that many vital errands and deputations. But Chasm City was vast. The aerial traffic represented a microscopic portion of the real human activity taking place beneath the spires and towers, even in wartime.

It had been different, once. The city had seen three approximate phases. The longest had been the *Belle Époque,* when the Demarchists and their presiding families had held absolute power. Back then the city had sweltered under the eighteen merged domes of the Mosquito Net. All the power and chemistry that the city needed had been drawn from the chasm itself. Within the domes, the Demarchists had pushed their mastery of matter and information to its logical conclusion. Their longevity experiments had given them biological immortality, while the regular downloading of neural patterns into computers had made even violent death no more than a nuisance. Their expertise with what some of them still quaintly termed "nanotechnology" had enabled them to reshape their environments and bodies almost at will. They had become protean, a people for whom stasis of any kind was abhorrent.

The city's second phase had come only a century ago, with the emergence of the Melding Plague. The plague had been very democratic, attacking people as eagerly as it attacked buildings. Belatedly, the Demarchists had realised that their Eden had always held a particularly vicious serpent. Until then the changes had been harnessed, but the plague ripped them from human control. Within a few months the city had been utterly transformed. Only a few hermetic enclaves existed where people could still walk around with machines in their bodies. The buildings contorted into mocking shapes, reminding the Demarchists of what they had lost. Technology had crashed back to an almost pre-industrial state. Predatory factions stalked the city's lawless depths.

Chasm City's dark age lasted nearly forty years.

It was a matter of debate whether the city's third state had already ended or was still continuing under different stewardship. In the immediate aftermath of the plague, the Demarchists had lost most of their former sources of wealth. Ultras took their trade elsewhere. A few high families struggled on, and there were always pockets of financial stability in the Rust Belt, but Chasm City itself was ripe for economic takeover. The Conjoiners, confined until then to a few remote niches throughout the system, had seen their moment.

It was not an invasion in the usual sense. They were too few in number, too militarily weak, and they had no wish to convert the populace to their mode of thinking. Instead they had bought out the city a chunk at a time, rebuilding it into something glittering and new. They tore down the eighteen merged domes. In the chasm they installed a vast item of bioengineered machinery called the Lilly, which vastly increased the efficiency of chemical conversion of the chasm's native gases. Now the city lived in a pocket of warm breathable air, sustained by the Lilly's slow exhalations. The Conjoiners had torn down many of the warped structures, replacing them with elegant bladelike towers that reached far above the breathable pocket, turning like yacht's sails to minimise their wind profile. More resilient forms of nanotechnology were cautiously introduced back into the environment. Conjoiner medicines allowed longevity therapies to be pursued again. Sniffing prosperity, Ultras again made Yellowstone a key stopover on their trade intineraries. Around Yellowstone, resettlement of the Rust Belt proceeded apace.

It should have been a new Golden Age.

But the Demarchists, the city's former masters, never adjusted to the role of historical has-beens. They chafed at their reduced status. For centuries they had been the Conjoiners' only allies, but all that was about to end. They would go to war to win back what they had lost.

"Can you see the chasm, Mr. Clavain?" His host pointed towards a dark elliptical smear almost lost beyond a profusion of spires and towers. "They say the Lilly is dying now. The Conjoiners aren't here to keep it alive, since they were evicted. The air quality is not what it was. There is even speculation that the city will have to be re-domed. But perhaps the Conjoiners will soon be able to reoccupy what was once theirs, eh?"

"It would be difficult to draw another conclusion," Clavain said.

"I do not care who wins, I must admit. I was able to make a living before the Conjoiners came, and I have continued to do so in their absence. I did not know the city under the Demarchists, but I don't doubt that I would have found a way to survive."

"Who are you?"

"Where are we might be a better question. Look down, Mr. Clavain."

Clavain looked down. The building he was in was high, that much was obvious from the elevated view, but he had not quite grasped how very high it really was. It was as if he stood near the summit of an immensely tall and steep mountain, looking down at subsidiary peaks and shoulders many thousands of metres below, secondary summits which themselves towered over the majority of the surrounding buildings. The highest air-traffic corridor was far below; indeed, he saw that some of the traffic flowed through the building itself, diving through immense arches and portals. Below lay other traffic layers, then a gridlike haze of elevated roadways, and below that yet more space, and then a blurred suggestion of tiered parks and lakes, so far below that they resembled faded two-dimensional markings on a map.

The building was black and monumental in its architecture. He could not guess its true shape, but he had the impression that had he viewed it from some other part of Chasm City it would have resembled something black and dead and faintly foreboding, like a solitary tree that had been struck by lightning.

"All right," Clavain said. "It's a very nice view. Where are we?"

"Château des Corbeaux, Mr. Clavain. The House of Ravens. I trust you remember the name?"

Clavain nodded. "Skade came here."

The man nodded. "So I gather."

"Then you had something to do with what happened to her, is that it?"

"No, Mr. Clavain, I did not. But my predecessor, the person who last inhabited this building, most certainly did." The man turned around and offered Clavain his right hand. "My name is H, Mr. Clavain. At least, that is the name under which I currently choose to do business. Shall *we* do business?"

Before Clavain could respond, H had taken his hand and

squeezed it. Clavain withdrew his hand, taken aback. He noticed that there was a tiny spot of red on his palm, like blood.

H took Clavain downstairs, back to the marbled floor. They walked past the fountain Clavain had heard earlier—it consisted of an eyeless golden snake belching a constant stream of water—and then took another long flight of marbled steps down to the floor immediately below.

"What do you know about Skade?" Clavain asked. He did not trust H, but saw no harm in asking a few questions.

"Not as much as I would like," H said. "But I will tell you what I have learned, within certain limits. Skade was sent to Chasm City on an espionage operation for the Conjoiners, one that concerned this building. That's correct, isn't it?"

"You tell me."

"Come now, Mr. Clavain. As you will discover, we have very much more in common than you might imagine. There's no need to be defensive."

Clavain wanted to laugh. "I doubt that you and I have much in common at all, H."

"No?"

"I am a four-hundred-year-old man who has probably seen more wars than you've seen sunsets."

H's eyes wrinkled in amusement. "Really?"

"My perspective on things is bound to be just a tiny bit different from yours."

"I don't doubt it. Would you follow me, Mr. Clavain? I'd like to show you the former tenant."

H led him along high-ceilinged black corridors lit only by the narrowest of windows. Clavain observed that H walked with the tiniest of limps, caused by a slight imbalance in length between one leg and the other that he managed to overcome most of the time. He seemed to have the whole immense building to himself, or at least this mansion-sized district of it, but perhaps that was an illusion fostered by the building's sheer immensity. Clavain had already sensed that H controlled an organisation of some influence.

"Start at the beginning," Clavain said. "How did you get mixed up in Skade's business?"

"Through a mutual interest, I suppose you'd say. I've been here on Yellowstone for a century, Mr. Clavain. In that time I have cultivated certain interests—obsessions, you might almost call them."

"Such as?"

"Redemption is one of them. I have what you might charitably refer to as a chequered past. I have done some very bad things in my time. But then again, who hasn't?" They halted at an arched doorway set into black marble. H made the door open and ushered Clavain into a windowless room that had the still, spectral atmosphere of a crypt.

"Why would you be interested in redemption?"

"To absolve myself, of course. To make some recompense. In the current era, even allowing for the present difficulties, one can live an inordinately long life. In past times a heinous crime marked one for life, or at least for the biblical three score years and ten. But we may live for centuries now. Should such a long life be sullied by a single unmeritorious act?"

"You said you'd done more than one bad thing."

"As indeed I have. I have signed my name to many nefarious deeds." H walked over to a roughly welded upright metal box in the middle of the room. "But the point is this: I do not see why my present self should be locked into patterns of behaviour merely because of something my much younger self did. I doubt that there is a single atom of my body shared by both of us, after all, and very few memories."

"A criminal past doesn't give you a unique moral perspective."

"No, it doesn't. But there is such a thing as free will. There is no need for us to be puppets of our past." H paused and touched the box. It had, Clavain realised, the general dimensions and proportions of a palanquin, the kind of travelling machine that the hermetics still used.

H drew in a deep breath before speaking again. "A century ago I came to terms with what I had done, Mr. Clavain. But there was a price to be paid for that reconciliation. I vowed to put right certain wrongs, many of which directly concerned Chasm City. They were difficult vows, and I am not one to take such things lightly. Unfortunately, I failed in the most important one of all."

"Which was?"

"In a moment, Mr. Clavain. First I want you to see what has become of her."

Her?'

"The Mademoiselle. She was the woman who lived here before I did, the woman who occupied this building at the time of Skade's mission." H slid aside a black panel at head-height, revealing a tiny dark window set into the side of the box.

"What was her real name?" Clavain asked.

"I don't actually know," H told him. "Manoukhian may know a little more about her, I think—he used to be in her service, before he swapped allegiances. But I've never extracted the truth from him, and he's much too useful, not to say fragile, to risk under a trawl."

"What *do* you know about her, then?"

"Only that she was a very powerful influence in Chasm City for many years, without anyone realising it. She was the perfect dictator. Her control was so pervasive that no one noticed they were in her thrall. Her wealth, as estimated by the usual indices, was practically zero. She did not 'own' anything in the usual sense. Yet she had webs of coercion that enabled her to achieve whatever she wanted silently, invisibly. When people acted out of what they imagined was pure self-interest, they were often following the Mademoiselle's hidden script."

"You make her sound like a witch."

"Oh, I don't think there was anything supernatural about her influence. It was just that she saw information flows with a clarity most people lack. She could see the precise point where pressure needed to be applied, the point where the butterfly had to flap its wings to cause a storm half a world away. That was her genius, Mr. Clavain. An instinctive grasp of chaotic systems as applied to human psychosocial dynamics. Here, take a look."

Clavain stepped up to the tiny window set into the box.

There was a woman inside. She appeared to have been embalmed, and was sitting in an upright position within the box. Her hands were folded neatly in her lap, holding an outspread paper fan of translucent delicacy. She wore a high-necked brocaded gown that Clavain judged to be a century out of date. Her forehead was high and smooth, dark hair raked back from it in severe furrows. From Clavain's vantage point it was impossible to tell whether her eyes were truly closed or whether she was just looking down at the fan. She rippled, as if she were a mirage.

"What happened to her?" Clavain asked.

"She is dead, in so far as I understand the term. She has been dead for more than thirty years. But she has not changed at all since the moment of her death. There has been no decay, no evidence of the usual morbid processes. And yet there cannot be a vacuum in there, or she could not have breathed."

"I don't understand. Did she die in this thing?"

"It was her palanquin, Mr. Clavain. She was in it when I killed her."

"You killed her?"

H slid the little plate closed, obscuring the window. "I used a type of weapon designed by Canopy assassins for the specific purpose of murdering hermetics. They call it a crabber. It attaches a device to the side of the palanquin that bores through the armour while at the same time maintaining perfect hermetic integrity. There can be unpleasant things *inside* palanquins, you see, especially when the occupants suspect they may be the targets of assassination attempts. Subject-specific nerve gas, that sort of thing."

"Go on," Clavain said.

"When the crabber reaches the interior it injects a slug which detonates with sufficient force to kill any organism inside, but not enough to shatter the window or any other weak point. We employed something similar against tank crews on Sky's Edge, so I had some familiarity with the principles involved."

"If the crabber worked," he said, "there shouldn't be a body inside."

"Quite right, Mr. Clavain, there shouldn't. Believe me, I know—I've seen what it looks like when these things do work."

"But you did kill her."

"I did *something* to her; what, I'm not quite sure. I could not examine the palanquin until several hours after the crabber had done its work, since we had the Mademoiselle's allies to deal with as well. When I did look through the window I expected to see nothing except the usual dripping red smear on the other side of the glass. But her body was nearly intact. There were wounds, quite evident wounds which would normally have been fatal in their own right, but over the next few hours I watched them heal. The clothes as well—the damage undid itself. She has been like this ever since. More than thirty years, Mr. Clavain."

"It isn't possible."

"Did you notice the way you seemed to be viewing her body

as if through a layer of shifting water? The way she shimmered and warped? It was no optical illusion. There is something in there with her. I wonder how much of what we can see was ever human."

"You're talking as if she was some kind of alien."

"I think there was something alien about her. Beyond that, I would not care to speculate."

H led him out of the room. Clavain risked one rearward glance at the palanquin, a glance that chilled him. H obviously kept it here because there was nothing else to be done with it. The corpse could not be destroyed, might even be dangerous in other hands. So she remained entombed here, in the building she had once inhabited.

"I have to ask . . ." Clavain began.

"Yes?"

"Why did you kill her?"

His host closed the door behind them. There was a palpable feeling of relief. Clavain had the distinct impression that even H did not greatly relish visits to the Mademoiselle.

"I killed her, Mr. Clavain, for the very simple and obvious reason that she had something I wanted."

"Which was?"

"I'm not entirely sure. But I think it was the same thing Skade was after."

TWENTY-TWO

Xavier was working on *Storm Bird*'s hull when the two peculiar visitors arrived at the repair shop. He checked on the monkeys, satisfying himself that they could be trusted to get on with things by themselves for a few minutes. He wondered who Antoinette had pissed off now. Like her father, she was pretty good at not pissing off the right people. That was how Jim Bax had stayed in business.

"Mr. Gregor Consodine?" asked a man, standing up from a seat in the waiting area.

"I'm not Gregor Consodine."

"I'm sorry. I thought this was . . . "

"It is. I'm just minding things while he's off in Vancouver for a couple of days. Xavier Liu." He beamed helpfully. "How may I be of assistance?"

"We are looking for Antoinette Bax," the man said.

"Are you?"

"It's a matter of some urgency. I gather that's her ship parked in your service well."

The back of Xavier's neck bristled. "And you'd be . . . ?"

"I am called Mr. Clock."

Mr. Clock's face was an exercise in anatomy. Xavier could see the bones beneath the skin. Mr. Clock looked like a man very close to death, and yet he moved with the light step of a ballet dancer or mime artiste.

But it was the other one that really bothered him. Xavier's first careless glance at the visitors had revealed two men, one tall and thin like a storybook undertaker, the other short and wide, built like a professional wrestler. The more squat man had his head down and was thumbing through a brochure on the coffee table. Between his feet was a featureless black box the size of a toolkit.

Xavier looked at his own hands.

"My colleague is Mr. Pink."

Mr. Pink looked up. Xavier did his best to conceal a moment of surprise. The other man was a pig, not a baseline human at all. He had a smooth rounded brow beneath which little dark eyes studied Xavier. His nose was small and upturned. Xavier had seen humans with stranger faces, but that was not the point. Mr. Pink never had *been* human.

"Hello," the pig said, and then turned his attention back to his reading matter.

"You haven't answered my question," Clock said.

"Your question?"

"Concerning the ship. It does belong to Antoinette Bax, doesn't it?"

"I was just told to do some hull work on it. That's all I know."

Clock smiled and nodded. He stepped back to the office door and closed it. Mr. Pink turned over a page and chuckled at something in the brochure. "That's not quite the truth, is it, Mr. Liu?"

"I'm sorry?"

"Have a seat, Mr. Liu." Clock gestured at one of the chairs. "Please, take the weight off your feet. We need to have a little talk, you and me."

"I really need to get back to my monkeys."

"I'm sure they won't get up to any mischief in your absence. Now." Clock gestured again and the pig looked up and fixed his gaze on Xavier. Xavier sunk down into the seat, weighing his options. "Concerning Miss Bax. Traffic records, freely available traffic records, indicate that her vessel is the one currently parked in the service bay, the one you are working on. You are aware of this, aren't you?"

"I might be."

"Please, Mr. Liu, there's really no point in being evasive. The data we have amassed points to a very close working relationship between yourself and Miss Bax. You are perfectly aware that *Storm Bird* belongs to her. As a matter of fact, you know *Storm Bird* very well indeed, isn't that true?"

"What is this about?"

"We'd like to have a little word with Miss Bax herself, if that isn't too much trouble."

"I can't help you there."

Clock raised one fine, barely present eyebrow. "No?"

"If you want to speak to her, you'll have to find her yourselves."

"Very well. I hoped it wouldn't come to this, but . . . " Clock looked at the pig. The pig put down the brochure and stood up. He had the bulky presence of a gorilla. When he walked it seemed as if he was engaged in a balancing act that was always on the point of collapsing. The pig pushed past him, carrying the black box.

"Where's he going?" Xavier asked.

"To her ship. He's very good mechanically, Mr. Liu. Very good at fixing things, but also, it must be said, very good at breaking things as well."

H took him down another flight of steps, his broad-backed form descending one or two paces ahead of Clavain. Clavain looked down on the brilliant blue-black grooves of his greased hair. H appeared quite unconcerned that Clavain might attack him or attempt to make his escape from the monstrous black Château. And Clavain felt a strange willingness to co-operate with his new host. It was, he supposed, mostly curiosity. H knew things about Skade that Clavain did not, even if H himself did not pretend to know all the facts. Clavain, in turn, was clearly of interest to H. The two of them could indeed learn much from each other.

But this situation could not continue, Clavain knew. As urbane and interesting as his host might have been, Clavain had still been kidnapped. And he had business that needed to be attended to.

"Tell me more about Skade," Clavain said. "What did she want from the Mademoiselle?"

"It gets a little complicated. I shall do my best, but you must forgive me if I seem not to understand all the details. The truth of the matter is that I doubt that I ever will."

"Start at the beginning."

They arrived at a hallway. H strolled along it, passing many irregular sculptures resembling the sloughed scabs and scales of some immense metallic dragon, each of which rested on a single annotated plinth.

"Skade was interested in technology, Mr. Clavain."

"What kind?"

"An advanced technology concerning the manipulation of the quantum vacuum. I am not a scientist, Mr. Clavain, so I cannot pretend to have more than the shakiest grasp of the relevant principles. But it is my understanding that certain bulk properties of matter—inertia, for instance—stem directly from the properties of the vacuum in which they are embedded. Pure speculation, of course, but wouldn't a means to control inertia be of use to the Conjoiners?"

Clavain thought of the way *Nightshade* had been able to pursue him across the solar system at such great speed. A technique for suppressing inertia would have allowed that, and might also explain what Skade had been doing aboard the ship during the previous mission. She must have been fine-tuning her technology, testing it in the field. So the technology probably existed, albeit in prototype form. But H would have to learn that for himself.

"I've no knowledge of a programme to develop that kind of ability," Clavain told him, choosing his words so as to avoid an outright lie.

"Doubtless it would be secret, even amongst the Conjoiners. Very experimental and no doubt dangerous."

"Where did the technology come from in the first place?"

"That's the interesting part. Skade—and by extension the Conjoiners—seem to have had a well-developed idea of what they were looking for before they came here, as if what they sought here was merely the final part of a puzzle. As you know, Skade's operation was viewed as a failure. She was the only survivor and she did not escape back to your Mother Nest with more than a handful of stolen items. Whether they were sufficient or not, I couldn't guess . . . " H glanced back over his shoulder with a knowing smile.

They reached the end of the corridor. They had arrived on a low-walled ledge that circumnavigated an enormous slope-floored room many storeys deep. Clavain peered over the edge, noting what appeared to be pipes and drainage vents set into the sheer black walls.

"I'll ask again," Clavain said. "Where did the technology come from in the first place?"

"A donor," H answered. "Around a century ago I learned an astonishing truth. I gained knowledge of the whereabouts of an individual, an alien individual, who had been waiting undisturbed on this planet for many millions of years, shipwrecked and yet essentially unharmed." He paused, evidently watching Clavain's reaction.

"Continue," Clavain said, determined not to be fazed.

"Unfortunately, I was not the first to learn of this hapless creature. Other people had discovered that he could give them something of considerable value provided that they held him prisoner and administered regular jolts of pain. This would have been abhorrent under any circumstances, but the creature in question was a highly social animal. Intelligent, too—his was a starfaring culture of great extent and antiquity. In fact, the wreck of his ship still contained functioning technologies. Do you see where this is heading?"

They had walked along one length of the vaultlike chamber. Clavain had still not deduced its function.

"Those technologies," Clavain asked, "did they include the inertia-modifying process?"

"So it would appear. I must confess that I had something of a head start in this matter. Some considerable amount of time ago I met another of these creatures, so I already knew a little of what to expect from this one."

"A less open-minded man than myself might find all this a tiny bit difficult to accept," Clavain said.

H paused at the corner, placing both hands on the top of the low marble walling. "Then I will tell you more, and perhaps you will begin to believe me. It cannot have escaped your attention that the universe is a hazardous place. I'm certain that the Conjoiners have learned this for themselves. What is the current toll—thirteen known extinct intelligent cultures, or is it fourteen now? And one or two possibly extant alien intelligences that unfortunately are so alien that they don't do anything that might enable us to say for certain how intelligent they really are. The point being that the universe seems to have a way of stamping out intelligence before it gets too big for its boots."

"That's one theory." Clavain did not reveal how well it chimed with what he already knew; how it was perfectly consistent with Galiana's message about a cosmos stalked by wolves that slavered and howled at the scent of sapience.

"More than a theory. The grubs—that's the race-name of the species of which the unfortunate individual was a member—had been harried to the point of extinction themselves. They lived only between the stars, shying away from warmth and light. Even there they were nervous. They knew how little it would take to bring the killers down upon them again. In the end they evolved a rather desperate protective strategy. They were not naturally hostile, but they learned that other noisier species sometimes had to be silenced to protect themselves." H resumed his stroll, brushing one hand along the wall. It was his right hand, Clavain noticed, and it left behind a thin red smear.

"How did you learn about the alien?"

"It's a long story, Mr. Clavain, and one I don't intend to detain you with. Suffice it only to say the following. I vowed to save the creature from his tormentors—part of my plan for personal atonement, you might say. But I could not do it immediately. It took planning, a vast amount of forethought. I amassed a team of trusted helpers and made elaborate preparations. Years passed but the moment was never right. Then a decade went by. Two decades. Every night I dreamed of that thing suffering, and every night I renewed my vow to help him."

"And?"

"It's possible that someone betrayed me. Or else her intelligence was better than my own. The Mademoiselle reached the creature before I did. She brought him here, to this room. How, I don't know; that alone must have taken enormous planning."

Clavain looked down again, struggling to comprehend what kind of animal had needed a room this large as a prison. "She kept the creature here, in the Château?"

H nodded. "For many years. It was no simple matter to keep him alive, but the people who had imprisoned him before her had worked out exactly what needed to be done. The Mademoiselle had no particular interest in torturing him, I think; she was not cruel in that sense. But every instant of the creature's continued existence was a kind of torture, even when his nervous system was not being poked and prodded with high-voltage electrodes. But she refused to let him die. Not until she had learned all that she could from him."

H went on to tell Clavain that the Mademoiselle had found a way to communicate with the creature. As clever as the Mademoiselle had been, it was the creature that had expended the greater effort.

"I gather there was an accident," H said. "A man fell into the creature's pen, from all the way up here. He died instantly, but before they could get him out the creature, which was unrestrained, ate what remained of him. They had been feeding him morsels, you see, and until that moment he did not have very much idea of what his captors actually looked like."

H's voice grew quietly enthusiastic. "Anyway, a strange thing happened. A day later a wound appeared in the creature's skin. The wound enlarged, forming a hole. There was no bleeding, and the wound looked very symmetrical and well formed. Structures lurked behind it, moving muscles. The wound was becoming a mouth. Later, it began to make humanlike vowel sounds. Another day or so passed and the creature was attempting recognisable words. Another day, and he was stringing those words together into simple sentences. The chilling part, from what I have gathered, was that the creature had inherited more than just the means to make language from the man he had eaten. He had absorbed his memories and personality, fusing them with his own."

"Horrible," Clavain said.

"Perhaps." H appeared unconvinced. "Certainly, it might be a useful strategy for an interstellar trading species that expected to encounter many other cultures. Instead of puzzling over translation algorithms, why not simply decode language at the level of biochemical representation? Eat your trading partner and become more like him. It would require some co-operation from the other party, but perhaps this was an accepted form of business millions of years ago."

"How did you learn all this?"

"Ways and means, Mr. Clavain. Even before the Mademoiselle beat me to the alien, I had become dimly aware of her existence. I had my own webs of influence in Chasm City, and she had hers. For the most part we were discrete, but now and then our activities would brush against each other. I was curious, so I tried to learn more. But she resisted my attempts to infiltrate the Château for many years. It was only when she had the creature that I think she became distracted by him, consumed by his alien puzzle. Then I was able to get agents into the building. You've met Zebra? She was one of them. Zebra learned what she could and put in place the conditions I needed for the takeover. But that was long after Skade had come here."

Clavain thought things through. "So Skade must have known something about the alien?"

"Evidently. You're the Conjoiner, Mr. Clavain—shouldn't you know?"

"I've learned too much already. That's why I chose to defect."

They walked on, exiting the prison. Clavain was as relieved to be out of it as when he had left the room holding the palanquin. Perhaps it was his imagination, but he felt as if some of the creature's isolated torment had imprinted itself on the room's atmosphere. There was a feeling of intense dread and confinement that only abated once he had left the room.

"Where are you taking me now?"

"To the basement first, because I think there is something there that will interest you, and then I will take you to some people I would very much like you to meet."

Clavain said, "Do these people have something to do with Skade?"

"I think everything's to do with Skade, don't you? I think something may have happened to her when she visited the Château."

H showed him to an elevator. The car was a skeletal affair fashioned from iron spirals and filigrees. The floor was a cold iron grillework with many gaps in it. H slid shut a creaking door formed from scissoring iron chevrons, latching it just as the elevator began its descent. At first the progress was ponderous, Clavain guessing that it would take the better part of an hour to reach the building's lower levels. But the elevator, in its creaking fashion, accelerated faster and faster, until a substantial wind was ramming through the perforated flooring.

"Skade's mission was deemed a failure," Clavain said over the rumble and screech of the elevator's descent.

"Yes, but not necessarily from the Mademoiselle's point of view. Consider: she had extended her web of influence into every facet of Chasm City life. Within limits, she could make anything happen that she wished. Her reach included the Rust Belt, all the major foci of Demarchist power. She even had, I think, some hold over the Ultras, or at least the means to make them work for her. But she had nothing on the Conjoiners."

"And Skade may have been her point of entry?"

"I think it must be considered likely, Mr. Clavain. It may not be accidental that Skade was allowed to survive when the rest of her team were killed."

"But Skade is one of us," Clavain said feebly. "She would never betray the Mother Nest."

"What happened to Skade afterwards, Mr. Clavain? Did she by any chance widen her influence within the Conjoined?"

Clavain recalled that Skade had joined the Closed Council in the aftermath of the mission. "To some extent."

"Then I think the case is closed. That would always have been the Mademoiselle's strategy, you see. Infiltrate and orchestrate. Skade might not even think she is betraying your people; the Mademoiselle was always clever enough to play on loyalty. And although Skade's mission was judged a failure, she did recover some of the items of interest, did she not? Enough to benefit the Mother Nest?"

"I've already told you that I don't know about any secret project concerning the quantum vacuum."

"Mm. And I didn't find your denial wholly convincing the first time, either."

Clock, the one with the bald egg-shaped skull, told Xavier to call Antoinette.

"I'll call her," Xavier said. "But I can't make her come here, even if Mr. Pink starts damaging the ship."

"Find a way," Clock said, stroking the waxy olive leaf of one of the repair shop's potted plants. "Tell her you found something you can't fix, something that needs her expertise. I'm sure you can improvise, Mr. Liu."

"We'll be listening in," Mr. Pink added. To Xavier's relief, the pig had returned from inside *Storm Bird* without inflicting any obvious damage to the ship, although he had the impression that Mr. Pink had merely been scoping out possibilities for inflicting harm later on.

He called Antoinette. She was halfway around Carousel New Copenhagen, engaged in a frantic round of business meetings. Ever since Clavain had left things had gone from bad to worse.

"Just get here as quickly as you can," Xavier told her, one eye on his two visitors.

"Why the big rush, Xave?"

"You know how much it's costing us to keep *Storm Bird* parked here, Antoinette. Every hour makes a difference. Just this phone call is killing us."

"Holy shit, Xave. Cheer me up, why don't you?"

"Just get here." He hung up on her. "Thanks for making me do that, you bastards."

Clock said, "Your understanding is appreciated, Mr. Liu. I assure you no harm will come to either of you, most especially not to Antoinette."

"You'd better not hurt her." He looked at both of them, unsure which one he trusted the least. "All right. She'll be here in about twenty minutes. You can speak to her here, and then she can be on her way."

"We'll talk to her in the ship, Mr. Liu. That way there's no chance of either of you running away, is there?"

"Whatever," Xavier said, shrugging. "Just give me a minute to sort out the monkeys."

The elevator slowed and came to a halt, shaking and creaking even though it was stationary. Far above Clavain, metallic echoes chased each other up and down the lift-shaft like hysterical laughter.

"Where are we?" he asked.

"The deep basement of the building. We're well below the old Mulch now, Mr. Clavain, into Yellowstone bedrock." H ushered Clavain onwards. "This is where it happened, you see."

"Where what happened?"

"The disturbing event."

H led him along corridors—tunnels, more accurately—that had been bored through solid rock and then only lightly faced. Blue lanterns threw the ridges and bulges of the underlying geology into deep relief. The air was damp and cold, the hard stone floor uncomfortable beneath Clavain's feet. They passed a room containing many upright silver canisters arrayed across the floor like milk churns, and then descended via a ramp that took them even deeper.

H said, "The Mademoiselle protected her secrets well. When we stormed the Château she destroyed many of the items she had recovered from the grub's spacecraft. Others, Skade had taken with her. But enough remained for us to make a start. Recently, progress has been gratifyingly swift. Did you notice how easily my ships outran the Convention, how easily they slipped unnoticed through tightly policed airspace?"

Clavain nodded, remembering how quick the journey to Yellowstone had appeared. "You've learned how to do it too."

"In a very modest fashion, I admit. But yes, we've installed inertia-suppressing technology on some of our ships. Simply reducing the mass of a ship by four-fifths is enough to give us an edge over a Convention cutter. I imagine the Conjoiners have done rather better than that."

Grudgingly, Clavain admitted, "Perhaps."

"Then they'll know that the technology is extraordinarily dangerous. The quantum vacuum is normally in a very stable minimum, Mr. Clavain, a nice deep valley in the landscape of possible states. But as soon as you start tampering with the vacuum—cooling it, to damp the fluctuations that give rise to inertia—you change the entire topology of that landscape. What were stable minima become precarious peaks and ridges. There are adjacent valleys that are associated with very different properties of immersed matter. Small fluctuations can lead to violent state transitions. Shall I tell you a horror story?"

"I think you're going to."

"I recruited the very best, Mr. Clavain, the top theorists from the Rust Belt. Anyone who had shown the slightest interest in the nature of the quantum vacuum was brought here and made to understand that their wider interests would be best served by helping me."

"Blackmail?" Clavain asked.

"Good grief, no. Merely gentle coercion." H glanced back at Clavain and grinned, revealing sharply pointed incisors. "For the most part it wasn't even necessary. I had resources that the Demarchists lacked. Their own intelligence network was crumbling, so they knew nothing of the grub. The Conjoiners had their own programme, but to join them would have meant becoming Conjoined as well—no small price for scientific curiosity. The workers I approached were usually more than willing to come to the Château, given the alternatives." H paused, and his voice took on an elegiac tone it had lacked before. "One amongst their number was a brilliant defector from the Demarchists, a woman named Pauline Sukhoi."

"Is she dead?" Clavain asked. "Or something worse than dead?"

"No, not at all. But she has left my employment. After what happened—the disturbing event—she couldn't bring herself to continue. I understood perfectly and made sure that Sukhoi found alternative employment back in the Rust Belt."

"Whatever happened, it must have been truly disturbing," Clavain said.

"Oh, it was. For all of us, but especially for Sukhoi. Many experiments were in progress," said H. "Down here, in the basement levels of the Château, there were a dozen little teams working on different aspects of the grub technology. Sukhoi had been on the project for a year, and had shown herself to an excellent if fearless researcher. It was Sukhoi who explored some of the less stable state transitions."

H led him past several doors that opened into large dark chambers, until they arrived at one in particular. He did not enter the room. "Something terrible happened here. No one associated with the work would ever go into this room afterwards. They say damp records the past. Do you feel it also, Mr. Clavain? A sense of foreboding, an animal instinct that you *should not enter*?"

"Now that you've planted the suggestion that there's something odd about the room, I can't honestly say what I feel."

"Step inside," H said.

Clavain entered the room, stepping down to the smooth flat floor. The room was cold, but then again, the entire basement level had been cold. He waited for his eyes to adjust to the gloom, picking out the generous dimensions of the chamber. Here and there the floor and walls and ceiling were interrupted by metal struts or sockets, but no apparatus or analysis equipment remained. The room was completely empty and very clean.

He walked around the perimeter. He could not say that he enjoyed being in the room, but everything he felt—a mild sense of panic, a mild sense of presence—could have been psychosomatic. "What happened?" he asked.

H spoke from the door. "There was an accident in this room, involving only Sukhoi's project. Sukhoi was injured, but not critically, and she soon made a good recovery."

"And none of the other people in Sukhoi's team were injured?"

"That was the odd thing. There *were* no other people—Sukhoi had always worked alone. We had no other victims to worry about. The technology was slightly damaged, but soon showed itself to be capable of limited self-repair. Sukhoi was conscious and coherent, so we assumed that when she was on her feet again she would go back down to the basement."

"And?"

"She asked a strange question. One that, if you will pardon the expression, made the hairs on the back of my neck stand on end."

Clavain rejoined H near the door. "Which was?"

"She asked what had happened to the other experimenter."

"Then there was some neurological damage. False memories." Clavain shrugged. "Hardly surprising, is it?"

"She was quite specific about the other worker, Mr. Clavain. Even down to his name and history. She said that the man had been called Yves, Yves Mercier, and that he had been recruited from the Rust Belt at the same time that she had."

"But there was no Yves Mercier?"

"No one of that name, or any name like it, had ever worked in the Château. As I said, Sukhoi had always tended to work alone."

"Perhaps she felt the need to attach the blame for the accident to another person. Her subconscious manufactured a scapegoat."

H nodded. "Yes, we thought that something like that might have happened. But why transfer blame for a minor incident? No one had been killed, and no equipment had been badly damaged. As a matter of fact, we had learned much more from the accident that we had with weeks of painstaking progress. Sukhoi was blameless, and she knew it."

"So she made up the name for another reason. The subconscious is an odd thing. There doesn't have to be a perfectly obvious rationale for anything she said."

That's precisely what we thought, but Sukhoi was adamant. As she recovered, her memories of working with Mercier only sharpened. She recalled the minutest details about him—what he had looked like, what he had liked to eat and drink, his sense of humour, even his background; what he had done before he came to the Château. The more we tried to convince her that Mercier had not been real, the more hysterical she became.'

"She was deranged, then."

"Every other test said she wasn't, Mr. Clavain. If she had a delusional system, it was focused solely on the prior existence of Mercier. And so I began to wonder."

Clavain looked at H and nodded for him to continue.

"I did some research," H added. "It was easy enough to dig into Rust Belt records—those that had survived the plague, anyway. And I found that certain aspects of Sukhoi's story checked out with alarming accuracy."

"Such as?"

"There had been someone named Yves Mercier, born in the same carousel that Sukhoi claimed."

"It can't be that unusual a name amongst Demarchists."

"No, probably not. But in fact there was only one. And his date of birth accorded precisely with Sukhoi's recollections. The only difference was that this Mercier—the real one—had died many years earlier. He had been killed shortly after the Melding Plague destroyed the Glitter Band."

Clavain forced a shrug, but with less conviction that he would have wished. "A coincidence, then."

"Perhaps. But you see, this particular Yves Mercier was already a student at the time. He was well advanced on studies into exactly the same quantum-vacuum phenomena that would, according to Sukhoi, eventually bring him into my orbit."

Clavain no longer wanted to be in the room. He stepped up, back into the blue-lanterned corridor. "You're saying her Mercier really existed?"

"Yes, I am. At which point I found myself faced with two possibilities. Either Sukhoi was somehow aware of the dead Mercier's life story, and for one reason or another chose to believe that he had not in fact died, or that she was actually telling the truth."

"But that isn't possible."

"I rather think it may be, Mr. Clavain. I think everything Pauline Sukhoi told me may have been the literal truth; that in some way we can't quite comprehend, Yves Mercier *never died* for her. That she worked with him, here in the room you have just left, and that Mercier was present when the accident happened."

"But Mercier did die. You've seen the records for yourself."

"But suppose he didn't. Suppose that he survived the Melding Plague, went on to work on general quantum-vacuum theory, and eventually attracted my attention. Suppose also that he ended up working with Sukhoi, together on the same experiment, exploring the less stable state transitions. And suppose then that there was an accident, one that involved a shift to a very dangerous state indeed. According to Sukhoi, Mercier was much closer to the field generator than she was when it happened."

"It killed him."

"More than that, Mr. Clavain. It made him cease to have existed." H watched Clavain and nodded with tutorly patience. "It was as if his entire life story, his entire world-line, had been unstitched from our reality, right back to the point when he was killed during the Melding Plague. That, I suppose, was the most logical point at which he could have died in our mutual world-line, the one you and I share."

"But not for Sukhoi," Clavain said.

"No, not for her. She remembered how things had been before. I suppose she was close enough to the focus that her memories were entangled, knotted-up with the prior version of events. When Mercier was erased, she nonetheless retained her memories of him. So she was not mad at all, not remotely delusional. She was merely the witness to an event so horrific that it transcends all understanding. Does it chill you, Mr. Clavain, to think that an experiment could have this outcome?"

"You already told me it was dangerous."

"More than we ever realised at the time. I wonder how many world-lines were wrenched out of existence before there was ever a witness close enough to feel the change?"

Clavain said, "What exactly was it that these experiments were related to, if you don't mind my asking?"

"That's the interesting part. State transitions, as I have said—exploring the more exotic quantum-vacuum manifolds. We can suck some of the inertia out of matter, and depending on the field state we can *keep* sucking it out until the matter's inertial mass becomes asymptotic with zero. According to Einstein, matter with no mass has no choice but to travel at the speed of light. It will have become photonic, light-like."

"Is that what happened to Mercier?"

"No—not quite. In so far as I understood Sukhoi's work, it appeared that the zero-mass state would be very difficult to realise physically. As it neared the zero-mass state, the vacuum would be inclined to flip to the other side. Sukhoi called it a tunnelling phenomenon."

Clavain raised an eyebrow. "The other side?"

"The quantum-vacuum state in which matter has imaginary inertial mass. By imaginary I mean in the purely mathematical sense, in the sense that the square root of minus one is an imaginary number. Of course, you immediately see what that would imply."

"You're talking about tachyonic matter," Clavain said. "Matter travelling faster than light."

"Yes." Clavain's host seemed pleased. "It appears that Mercier and Sukhoi's final experiment concerned the transition between tardyonic—the matter we are familiar with—and tachyonic matter states. They were exploring the vacuum states that would allow the construction of a faster-than-light propulsion system."

"That's simply not possible," Clavain said.

H put a hand on his shoulder. "Actually, I don't think that is quite the right way to think about it. The grubs knew, of course. This technology had been theirs, and yet they chose to crawl between the stars. That should have told us all we needed to know. It is not that it is impossible, merely that it is very, very inadvisable."

For a long time they stood in silence, on the threshold of the bleak room where Mercier had been unthreaded from existence.

"Has anyone attempted those experiments again?" Clavain asked.

"No, not after what happened to Mercier. Quite frankly, no one was very keen to do any further work on the grub machinery. We'd learned enough as it was. The basement was evacuated. Almost no one ever comes down here these days. Those who do sometimes say they see ghosts; perhaps they're the residual shadows of all those who suffered the same fate as Mercier. I've never seen the ghosts myself, I have to say, and people's minds do play tricks on them." He forced false cheer into his voice, an effort that had the opposite effect to that intended. "One mustn't credit such things. You don't believe in ghosts, do you, Mr. Clavain?"

"I never used to," he said, wishing devoutly to be somewhere other than in the basement of the Château.

"These are strange times," H said, with no little sympathy. "I sense that we live at the end of history, that great scores are soon to be settled. Difficult choices must soon be made. Now, shall we go and see the people I mentioned earlier on?"

Clavain nodded. "I can't wait."

Antoinette left the rim train at the closest station to the rented repair shop. Something about Xavier's attitude had struck her as unusual, but it was nothing she could quite put her finger on. With some trepidation she checked out the repair shop's waiting area and business desk. Nothing doing there, just a "closed for business" sign on the door. She double-checked that the repair bay was pressurised and then pushed through to the interior of the bay itself. She took the nearest connecting catwalk, never looking down. The air in the bay was heady with aerosols. She was sneezing by the time she reached the ship's own airlock, and her eyes were itching.

"Xavier . . ." she called.

But if he was deep inside *Storm Bird* he would never hear her. She would either have to find him or wait until he came out. She had told him she would arrive in twenty minutes.

She went through into the main flight deck. Everything looked normal. Xavier had called up some of the less commonly used diagnostic read-outs, some of which were sufficiently obscure that even Antoinette viewed them with mild incomprehension. But that was exactly what she would have expected when Xavier had half the ship's guts out on the table.

"I'm really, really sorry."

She looked around, seeing Xavier standing behind her with an expression on his face that meant he was begging forgiveness for something. Behind him were two people she did not recognise. The taller of the two strangers indicated that she should follow them back into the lounge area aft of the main bridge.

"Please do as I tell you, Antoinette," the man said. "This shouldn't take long."

Xavier said, "I think you'd better do it. I'm sorry I made you come here, but they said they'd start trashing the ship if I didn't."

Antoinette nodded, stooping back along the connecting corridor. "You did right, Xave. Don't eat yourself up over it. Well, who are these clowns? Have they introduced themselves?"

"The tall one's Mr. Clock. The other one, the pig, he's Mr. Pink."

The two of them nodded in turn as Xavier spoke their names.

"But who are they?"

"They haven't said, but here's a wild stab in the dark. They're interested in Clavain. I think they might possibly be spiders, or working for the spiders."

"Are you?" Antoinette asked.

"Hardly," Remontoire said. "And as for my friend here . . ."

Mr. Pink shook his gargoylelike head. "Not me."

"I'd let you examine us if the circumstances were more amenable," Remontoire continued. "I assure you there are no Conjoiner implants in either of us."

"Which doesn't mean you aren't spider stooges," Antoinette said. "Now, what do I need to do in order for you to get the fuck off my ship?"

"As Mr. Liu correctly judged, we're interested in Nevil Clavain. Have a seat . . ." The one called Clock said it with steely emphasis this time. "Please, let's be civil."

Antoinette folded out a chair from the wall and parked herself in it. "I've never heard of anyone called Clavain," she said.

"But your partner has."

"Yeah. Nice one, Xave." She gave him a look. Why couldn't he have just pleaded ignorance?

"It's no good, Antoinette," Clock said. "We know that you brought him here. We are not in any way angry with you for doing that—it was the human thing to do, after all."

She folded her arms. "And?"

"All you have to do is tell us what happened next. Where Clavain went once you brought him to Carousel New Copenhagen."

"I don't know."

"So he just magically disappeared, is that it? Without a word of thanks, or any indication of what he was going to do next?"

"Clavain told me the less I knew the better."

Clock looked at the pig for a moment. Antoinette decided that she had scored a point. Clavain *had* wanted her to know as little as possible. It was only through her own efforts that she had found out a little more, but Clock did not have to know that.

She added, "Of course, I kept asking him. I was curious about what he was doing here. I knew he was a spider, too. But he wouldn't tell me. Said it was for my own good. I argued, but he stuck to his guns. I'm glad he did now. There's nothing you can force me to tell you because I simply don't know."

"So just tell us exactly what happened," Clock said soothingly. "That's all you have to do. We'll work out what Clavain had in mind, and then we'll be on our way. You'll never hear from us again."

"I told you, he just left. No word of where he was going, nothing. Goodbye and thanks. That was all he said."

"He wouldn't have had documentation or money," Clock said, as if to himself, "so he couldn't have got far without a little help from you. If he didn't ask for money, he's probably still on Carousel New Copenhagen." The thin, deathly pale man leaned toward her. "So tell me. Did he ask for anything?"

"No," she said, with just the tiniest hesitation.

"She's lying," the pig said.

Clock nodded gravely. "I think you're right, Mr. Pink. I hoped it wouldn't come to this, but there you have it. Needs must, as they say. Do you have the item, Mr. Pink?"

"The item, Mr. Clock? You mean . . . "

Between the pig's feet was a perfectly black box, like an oblong of shadow. He pushed it forwards, leaned down and touched some hidden mechanism. The box shuffled open to reveal many more compartments than appeared feasible from its size. Each held a piece of polished silver machinery nesting in precisely shaped cushioning foam. Mr. Pink took out one of the pieces and held it up for scrutiny. Then he took out another piece and connected the two together. Despite the clumsiness of his hands he worked with great care, his eyes focused sharply on the work in progress.

"He'll have it ready in a jiffy," Clock said. "It's a field trawl, Antoinette. Of spider manufacture, I'm obliged to add. Do you know a great deal about trawls?"

"Fuck off."

"Well, I'll tell you anyway. It's perfectly safe, isn't it, Mr. Pink?"

"Perfectly safe, Mr. Clock."

"Or at least, there's no reason why it shouldn't be. But field trawls are a different matter, aren't they? They're not nearly as proven as the larger models. They have a much higher probability of leaving the subject with neural damage. Even death isn't entirely unheard of, is it, Mr. Pink?"

The pig looked up from his activities. "One hears things, Mr. Clock. One hears things."

"Well, I'm sure the detrimental effects are exaggerated . . . but nonetheless, it's not at all advisable to use a field trawl when there are alternative procedures available." Clock made eye contact with Antoinette again. His eyes were sunk deep inside their sockets and his appearance made her want to look away. "Are you quite sure Clavain didn't say where he was going?"

"I told you, he didn't . . . "

"Continue, Mr. Pink."

"Wait," Xavier said.

They all looked at him, even the pig. Xavier started to say something else. And then the ship began to shake, quite without warning, yawing and twisting against its docking constraints. Its chemical thrusters were firing, loosing pulses of gas in opposing directions, the din of it like a cannonade.

The airlock behind Antoinette closed. She grabbed at a railing for support, and then tugged a belt across her waist.

Something was happening. She had no idea what, but it was definitely something. Through the nearest window she saw the repair bay choking in dense orange propellant fumes. Something broke free with a screech of severed metal. The ship lurched even more violently.

"Xavier . . ." she mouthed.

But Xavier had already got himself into a seat.

And they were falling.

She watched the pig and Clock scramble for support. They folded down their own seats and webbed themselves in. Antoinette seriously doubted that they had much more of an idea than she did about what was going on. Equally, they were smart enough not to want to be untethered aboard a ship that gave every indication that it was about to do something violent.

They hit something. The collision compressed every bone in her spine. The repair bay door, she thought—Xavier had pressurised the well so he and his monkeys could work without suits. The ship had just rammed into the door.

The ship rose again. She felt the lightness in her belly.

And then it dropped.

This time there was only a muffled bump as they hit the door. Through the window Antoinette saw the orange smoke vanish in an instant. The repair bay had just lost all its air. The walls slid past as the ship pushed its way into space.

"Make this stop," Clock said.

"It's out of my hands, buddy," Xavier told him.

"This is a trick," the spider said. "You wanted us aboard the ship all along."

"So sue me," Xavier said.

"Xavier . . . " Antoinette did not have to shout. It was perfectly silent aboard *Storm Bird,* even as she scraped through what remained of the bay door. "Xavier . . . please tell me what's happening."

"I rigged an emergency program," Xavier said. "Figured it'd come in handy one day, if we ever got into just this situation."

"Just this situation?"

"I guess it was worth it," he said.

"Is that why there were no monkeys working?"

"Hey." He feigned insult. "Credit me with some foresight, will you?"

They were weightless. *Storm Bird* fell away from Carousel New Copenhagen, surrounded by a small constellation of debris. Fascinated despite herself, Antoinette inspected the damage they had left behind. They had punched a ship-shaped hole through the door.

"Holy shit, Xave. Have you any idea what that'll cost us?"

"So we'll be a little bit longer in the red. I figured it was an acceptable trade-off."

"It won't help you," Clock said. "We're still here, and there's nothing you can do to us that won't hurt yourselves at the same time. So forget about depressurisation, or executing high-gee-load thrust patterns. They won't work. The problem you had to deal with five minutes ago hasn't gone away."

"The only difference," Mr. Pink said, "is that you just burned a lot of goodwill."

"You were about to rip her head open to get at her memories," Xavier said. "If that's your idea of goodwill, you can stick it where the sun doesn't shine."

Mr. Pink's half-assembled trawl was floating through the cabin. He had let go of it during the escape.

"You wouldn't have learned anything anyway," Antoinette said, "because I don't know what Clavain was going to do. Maybe I'm not putting that in sufficiently simple terms for you."

"Get the trawl, Mr. Pink," Remontoire said. The pig glared at him until Clock added, with distinct overemphasis, "*Please,* Mr. Pink."

"*Yes,* Mr. Clock," the pig said, with the same snide undertone.

The pig fumbled at his webbing. He was almost out of it when the ship surged forward. The trawl was the only thing not tied down. It smashed against one of *Storm Bird*'s unyielding walls, breaking into half a dozen glittering pieces.

Xavier couldn't have programmed that in, could he? Antoinette wondered.

"Clever," Clock said. "But not clever enough. Now we'll have to get it out of you via some other means, won't we?"

The ship was under constant steady thrust now. Still Antoinette heard nothing, and that started her worrying. Chemical rockets were noisy: they transmitted their sound right through the framework of the hull even though the ship was in vacuum. Ion thrust was silent, but it couldn't sustain this kind of acceleration. But the tokamak fusion motor was totally silent, suspended in a loom of magnetic fields.

They were on fusion thrust.

Holy shit . . .

There was a mandatory death sentence for using fusion motors within the Rust Belt. Even using nuclear rockets this close to a carousel would have brought heinous penalties; almost certainly she would never have flown in space again. But fusion thrust was an instrument of potential lethality. A misdirected fusion flame could sever a carousel in seconds . . .

"Xavier, if you can do anything about this, get us back on to chems immediately."

"Sorry, Antoinette, but I figured this was for the best."

"You did, did you?"

"Yes, and I'll take the rap for it if it comes to that. But listen, we're being held hostage here. That changes the rules. Right now we want the police to pay us a visit. All I'm doing is waving a flag."

"That sounds great in theory, Xave, but . . ."

"No buts. It'll work. They'll see that I deliberately kept the flame away from habitations. Matter of fact, there's even an SOS modulation buried in the pulse pattern, though it's much too rapid for us to feel."

"You think the cops'll notice that?"

"No, but they'll sure as hell be able to verify it afterwards, which is all that matters. They'll see that this was a clear attempt at signalling for help."

"I admire your optimism," Clock said. "But it won't come to a court of law. They'll simply shoot you out of the sky for violating protocol. You'll never have a chance to explain yourself."

"He's right," Mr. Pink said. "You want to live, you'd better turn this ship around and scuttle back to Carousel New Copenhagen."

"Back to square one? You've got to be joking."

"It's that or die, Mr. Liu."

Xavier undid his seat restraints. "You two," he said, pointing at the two visitors, "had better stay put. It's for your own good."

"What about me?" Antoinette said.

"Stay where you are—it's safer. I'll be back in a minute."

She had no choice but to trust him. Only Xavier knew the details of the program he had loaded into Beast, and if she started moving around as well she might come to harm if the ship made another violent thrust change. There would be arguments later, she knew—she was not happy that he had installed this set of tricks without even telling her—but for now she had to admit that Xavier had the upper hand. Even if all it might gain them was a few minutes of breathing time.

Xavier was gone, off towards the flight deck.

She glared at Clock. "I liked Clavain a lot better than you, you know."

Xavier entered *Storm Bird*'s flight deck, making sure the door was sealed behind him, and settled into the pilot's seat. The console displays were still in deep-diagnostic mode, not at all what one would expect of a ship in mid-flight. Xavier spent his first thirty seconds restoring the normal avionics readouts, bringing the ship into something resembling routine flight status. Immediately a synthetic voice started screeching at him that he needed to shut down fusion thrust, because according to at least eight local transponder beacons he was still within the Rust Belt, and thereby obliged to use nothing more energetic than chemical rockets . . .

"Beast?" Xavier whispered. "Better do it. They'll have seen us by now, I'm pretty sure."

Beast said nothing.

"It's safe," Xavier said, still whispering. "Antoinette's staying downship with the two creeps. She's not going anywhere soon."

When the ship spoke to him, its voice was much lower and softer than it ever was when it addressed Antoinette. "I hope we did the right thing, Xavier."

The ship rumbled as fusion thrust was smoothly supplanted by nuclear rockets. Xavier was pretty sure they were still within fifty kilometres of Carousel New Copenhagen, which meant even using nuclear rockets was in contravention of a list of rules as long as his arm, but he still wanted to attract some attention.

"I do too, Beast. Guess we'll know soon enough."

"I can depressurise, I think. Can you get Antoinette into a suit without the other two causing any trouble?"

"Not going to be easy. I'm already worried about leaving them alone down there. I don't know how long it will be before they decide to risk moving around. I suppose if I could get them into one compartment, and her into another . . . "

"I might be able to selectively depressurise, yes. Never tried it before, though, so I don't know if it'll work first time."

"Maybe it won't come to that, if the Convention's goons get to us first."

"Whatever happens, there's going to be trouble."

Xavier read Beast's tone of voice well enough. "Antoinette, you mean?"

"She might have some difficult questions for you to answer, Xavier."

Xavier nodded grimly. It was the last thing he needed to be reminded about now, but the point was inarguable. "Clavain had his doubts about you, but had the good sense not to ask Antoinette what was going on."

"Sooner or later she's going to have to know. Jim never meant for this to be a secret her whole life."

"But not today," Xavier said. "Not here, not now. We've got enough to deal with for the moment."

That was when something on the console caught his eye. It was on the three-dimensional radar plot: three icons daggering in from the direction of the carousel. They were moving quickly, on vectors that would bring them around *Storm Bird* in a pincer movement.

"Well, you wanted a response, Xavier," Beast said. "Looks like you've got one."

These days, the Convention's cutters were never very far from Carousel New Copenhagen. If they were not harassing Antoinette—and usually they were—then it was someone else. Very likely the authorites had been alerted that something unusual was happening as soon as *Storm Bird* had left the repair bay. Xavier just hoped it was not the particular Convention officer who had taken such an interest in Antoinette's affairs.

"Do you think it's true, that they'd kill us without even asking why we were on fusion thrust?"

"I don't know, Xavier. At the time I wasn't exactly spoilt for other options."

"No . . . you did fine. It's what I would have done. What Antoinette would have done, probably. And definitely what Jim Bax would have done."

"The ships will be within boarding range in three minutes."

"Make it easy for them. I'll go back and see how the others are doing."

"Good luck, Xavier."

He worked his way back to where Antoinette was waiting. To his relief, Clock and the pig were still in their seats. He felt his weight diminishing as Beast cut power to the nuclear rockets.

"Well?" Antoinette asked.

"We're OK," Xavier said, with more confidence than he felt. "The police will be here any moment."

He was in his seat by the time they were weightless. A few seconds later he felt a series of bumps as the police craft grappled on to the hull. So far, so good, he thought: they were at least going to get a boarding, which was better than being shot out of the sky. He would be able to argue his case, and even if the bastards insisted that someone still had to die, he thought he could keep Antoinette out of too much trouble.

He felt a breeze. His ears popped. It felt like decompression, but it was over before he had started to feel real fear. The air was still again. Distantly, he heard clunks and squeals of buckling and shearing metal.

"What just happened?" asked Mr. Pink.

"Police must have cut their way through our airlock," Xavier said. "Slight pressure differential between their air and ours. There was nothing to stop them coming in normally, but I guess they weren't prepared to wait for the lock to cycle."

Now he heard approaching mechanical sounds.

"They've sent a proxy," Antoinette said. "I hate proxies."

It arrived less than a minute later. Antoinette flinched as the machine unfolded itself into the room, enlarging like a vile black origami puzzle. It swept rapier-edged limbs through the room in lethal arcs. Xavier flinched as one bladed arm passed inches from his eyes, parting air with a tiny whipcrack. Even the pig looked as if there were places he would rather be.

"This wasn't clever," Mr. Pink said.

"We weren't going to hurt you," Clock added. "We just wanted information. Now you're in a great deal more trouble."

"You had a trawl," Xavier said.

"It wasn't a trawl," Mr. Pink said. "It was just an eidetic playback device. It wouldn't have harmed you."

The proxy said, "The registered owner of this vessel is Antoinette Bax." The machine moved to crouch over her, close enough that she could hear the constant low humming that it gave out and smell the tingle of ozone from the sparking taser. "You have contravened Ferrisville Convention regulations relating to the use of fusion propulsion within the Rust Belt, formerly known as the Glitter Band. This is a category-three civil offence that carries the penalty of irreversible neural death. Please submit for genetic identification."

"What?" said Antoinette.

"Open your mouth, Miss Bax. Do not move."

"It's you, isn't it?"

"Me, Miss Bax?" The machine whipped out a pair of rubber-tipped manipulators and braced her head. It hurt, and continued to hurt, as if her skull were being slowly compressed in a vice. Another manipulator whisked out of a previously concealed part of the machine. It ended in a tiny curved blade, like a scythe.

"Open your mouth."

"No . . . " She felt tears coming.

"Open your mouth."

The evil little blade—which was still large enough to nip off a finger—hovered an inch from her nose. She felt the pressure increase. The machine's humming intensified, becoming a low orgasmic throb.

"Open your mouth. This is your last warning."

She opened her mouth, but it was as much to groan in pain as to give the proxy what it wanted. Metal blurred, much to quick for her to see. There was a moment of coldness in her mouth, and the feeling of metal brushing her tongue for an instant.

Then the machine withdrew the blade. The limb articulated, tucking the blade into a separate aperture in the proxy's compact central chassis. Something hummed and clicked within: a rapid sequencer, no doubt, tallying her DNA against the Convention's records. She heard the rising whine of a centrifuge. The proxy still had her head in a vicelike grip.

"Let her go," Xavier said. "You've got what you want. Now let her go."

The proxy released Antoinette. She gasped for breath, wiping tears from her face. Then the machine turned towards Xavier.

"Interfering in the activities of an official or officially designated mechanism of the Ferrisville Convention is a category-one . . ."

It did not bother to complete the sentence. Contemptuously, it flicked the taser arm across Xavier so that the sparking electrodes skimmed his chest. Xavier made a barking noise and convulsed. Then he was very still, his eyes open and his mouth agape.

"Xavier . . . " Antoinette gasped.

"It's killed him," Clock said. He started unfastening his restraint webbing. "We must do something."

Antoinette snapped, "What the fuck do you care? You brought this about."

"Difficult as it may be to believe, I do care." Then he was up from his seat, grappling for the nearest anchorage point. The machine gyred to face him. Clock stood his ground, the only one of them who had not flinched when the proxy had arrived. "Let me through. I want to examine him."

The machine lurched towards Clock. Perhaps it expected him to feint out of the way at the last moment, or huddle protectively. But Clock did not move at all. He did not even blink. The proxy halted, humming and clicking furiously. Evidently it did not know quite what to make of him.

"Get back," it ordered.

"Let me through, or you will have committed murder. I know there is a human brain driving you, and that you understand the concept of execution as well as I do."

The machine brought the taser up again.

"It won't do any good," Clock said.

It pressed the taser against him, just below his collarbone. The sparking bar of current dancing between the poles like a trapped eel ate into the fabric of his clothes. But Clock remained unparalysed. There was no trace of pain on his face.

"It won't work on me," he said. "I am a Conjoiner. My nervous system is not fully human."

The taser was beginning to chew into his skin. Antoinette smelt what she knew without ever having smelt it before to be burning flesh.

Clock was trembling, his skin even more pale and waxy than it had been before. "It won't . . . " His voice sounded strained. The machine pulled back the taser, revealing a scorched-black trench half an inch deep. Clock was still trying to complete the sentence he had started.

The machine knocked him sideways with the blunt circular muzzle of its Gatling gun. Bone cracked; Clock crashed against the wall and was immediately still. He looked dead, but then again there had never been a time when he had looked particularly alive. The stink of his burned skin still filled the cabin. It was not something Antoinette was going to forget in a hurry.

She looked at Xavier again. Clock had been on his way to do something for him. He had been "dead" for perhaps half a minute already. Unlike Clock, unlike any spider, Xavier did not have an ensemble of fancy machines in his head to arrest the processes of brain damage that accompanied loss of circulation. He did not have much more than another minute . . .

"Mr. Pink . . . " she pleaded.

The pig said, "Sorry, but it isn't my problem. I'm dead anyway."

Her head still hurt. The bones were bruised, she was sure of it. The proxy had nearly shattered her skull. Well, they were dead anyway. Mr. Pink was right. So what did it matter if she got hurt some more? She couldn't let Xavier stay like that, without doing something.

She was out of her seat.

"Stop," the proxy said. "You are interfering with a crime scene. Interference with a designated crime scene is a category . . . "

She carried on moving anyway, springing from handhold to handhold until she was next to Xavier. The machine advanced on her—she heard the crackle of the taser intensify. Xavier had been dead for a minute. He was not breathing. She felt his wrist, trying to locate a pulse. Was that the right way to do it, she wondered frantically? Or was it the side of the neck . . .

The proxy heaved her aside as easily as if she were a bundle of sticks. She went at it again, angrier than she had ever been in her life, angry and terrified at the same time. Xavier was going to die—was, in fact, *already dead.* She, it seemed, would soon be following him. Holy shit . . . half an hour ago all she had been worried about had been *bankruptcy.*

"Beast!" she cried out. "Beast, if you can do something . . . now might not be a bad time."

"Begging your pardon, Little Miss, but one is unable to do anything that would not inconvenience you more than it would inconvenience the proxy." Beast paused and added, "I am really, really sorry."

Antoinette glanced at the walls, and a moment of perfect stillness enclosed her, an eye in the storm. Beast had never sounded like that before. It was as if the subpersona had spontaneously clicked into a different identity program. When had it ever called itself "I" before?

"Beast . . . " she said calmly. "Beast . . . ?"

But then the proxy was on her, the diamond-hard, scimitar-sharp alloy of its limbs scissoring around her, Antoinette thrashing and screaming as the machine pried her away from Xavier. She could not help cutting herself against the proxy's limbs. Her blood welled out from each wound in long beadlike processions, tracing ruby-red arcs through the air. She began to feel faint, consciousness lapping away.

The pig moved. Mr. Pink was on the machine. The pig was small but immensely strong for his size and the proxy's servitors whined and hummed in protest as the pig fought the bladed limbs. The whips and whorls of his own shed blood mingled with Antoinette's. The air hazed scarlet as the beads broke down into smaller and smaller droplets. She watched the machine inflict savage gashes in Mr. Pink. He bled curtains of blood, rippling out of him like aurorae. Mr. Pink roared in pain and anger, and yet he kept fighting. The taser arced a stuttering blue curve through the air. The muzzle of the Gatling gun began to rotate even more rapidly, as if the proxy were preparing to spray the cabin.

Antoinette crawled her way back to Xavier. Her palms were crisscrossed with cuts. She touched Xavier's forehead. She could have saved him a few minutes ago, she thought, but it was pointless trying now. Mr. Pink was fighting a brave battle, but he was, inexorably, losing. The machine would win, and it would pick her off Xavier again; and then, perhaps, it would kill her too.

It was over. And all she should have done, she thought, was follow her father's advice. He had told her never to get involved with spiders, and although he could not have guessed the circumstances that would entangle her with them, time had proved him right.

Sorry, Dad, Antoinette thought. *You were right, and I thought I knew better. Next time I promise I'll be a good girl . . .*

The proxy stopped moving, its servo motors falling instantly silent. The Gatling gun spun down to a low rumble and then stopped. The taser buzzed, sparked and then died. The centrifuge wound down until Antoinette could no longer hear it. Even the humming had ended. The machine was simply frozen there, immobile, a vile blood-lathered black spider spanning the cabin from wall to wall.

She found some strength. "Mr. Pink . . . what did you do?"

"I didn't do anything," Mr. Pink said. And then the pig nodded at Xavier. "I'd concentrate on him, if I were you."

"Help me. Please. I'm not strong enough to do this myself."

"Help yourself."

Mr. Pink, she saw, was quite seriously injured himself. But though he was losing blood, he appeared not to have suffered anything beyond cuts and gashes; he did not seem to have lost any digits or received any broken bones.

"I'm begging you. Help me massage his chest."

"I said I'd never help a human, Antoinette."

She began to work Xavier's chest anyway, but each depression sapped more strength from her, strength that she did not have to spare.

"Please, Mr. Pink . . . "

"I'm sorry, Antoinette. It's nothing personal, but . . . "

She stopped what she was doing. Her own anger was supreme now. "But what?"

"I'm afraid humans just aren't my favourite species."

"Well, Mr. Pink, here's a message from the human species. Fuck you and your attitude."

She went back to Xavier, mustering the strength for one last attempt.

TWENTY-THREE

Clavain and H rode the rattling iron elevator back up from the Château's basement levels. On the way up, Clavain ruminated on what his host had shown and told him. Under any other circumstances, the story about Sukhoi and Mercier would have strained his credulity. But H's apparent sincerity and the dread atmosphere of the empty room had made the whole thing difficult to dismiss. It was much more comforting to think that H had simply told him the story to play with his mind, and for that reason Clavain chose, provisionally, to opt for the less comforting possibility, just as H had done when he had investigated Sukhoi's claims.

In Clavain's experience, it was the less comforting possibility that generally turned out to be the case. It was the way the universe worked.

Little was said on the ascent. Clavain was still convinced that he had to escape from H and continue his defection. Equally, however, what H had revealed to him so far had forced him to accept that his own understanding of the whole affair was far from complete.

Skade was not just working for her own ends, or even for the ends of a cabal of faceless Conjoiners. She was in all likelihood working for the Mademoiselle, who had always desired influence within the Mother Nest. And the Mademoiselle herself was an unknown, a figure entirely outside Clavain's experience. And yet, like H, she had evidently had some profound interest in the alien grub and his technology, enough that she had brought the creature to the Château and learned how to communicate with him. She was dead, it was true, but perhaps Skade had become such a willing agent of hers that one might as well think of Skade and the Mademoiselle as inseparable now.

Whatever Clavain had imagined he was dealing with, it was

bigger—and it went back further—than he had ever imagined.

But it changes nothing, he thought. The crucial matter was still the acquisition of the hell-class weapons. Whoever was running Skade wanted those weapons more than anything.

And so I have to get them instead.

The elevator rattled to a halt. H opened the trelliswork door and led Clavain through another series of marbled corridors until they reached what appeared to be an absurdly spacious hotel room. A low, ornately plaster-moulded ceiling receded into middle distance, and various items of furniture and ornamentation were stationed here and there, much like items in a sculptural installation: the tilted black wedge of a grand piano; a grandfather clock in the middle of the room, as if caught in the act of gliding from wall to wall; a number of black pillars supporting obscure alabaster busts; a pair of lion-footed settees in dark scarlet velvet; and three golden armchairs as large as thrones.

Two of the three armchairs were occupied. In one sat a pig dressed like H in a simple black gown and trousers. Clavain frowned, realising—though he could not be absolutely certain—that the pig was Scorpio, the prisoner he had last seen in the Mother Nest. In the other sat Xavier, the young mechanic Clavain had met in Carousel New Copenhagen. The odd juxtaposition made Clavain's head ache as he tried to construct some plausible scenario for how the two came to be together, here.

"Are introductions necessary?" H asked. "I don't think so, but just to be on the safe side—Mr. Clavain, meet Scorpio and Xavier Liu." He nodded first at Xavier. "How are you feeling now?"

"I'm all right," Xavier said.

"Mr. Liu suffered heart failure. He was attacked with a taser weapon aboard Antoinette Bax's spacecraft *Storm Bird*. The voltage setting would have dropped a hamadryad, let alone a human."

"Attacked?" Clavain said, feeling it was polite to say something.

"By an agent of the Ferrisville Convention. Oh, don't worry, the individual involved won't be doing that again. Or much else, as it happens."

"Have you killed him?" Xavier asked.

"Not as such, no." H turned to Clavain. "Xavier's lucky to be alive, but he'll be fine."

"And Antoinette?" Clavain asked.

"She'll be fine, too. A few cuts and bruises, nothing too serious. She'll be along shortly."

Clavain sat down in the vacant yellow chair, opposite Scorpio. "I don't pretend to understand why Xavier and Antoinette are here. But you . . . "

"It's a long story," Scorpio said.

"I'm not going anywhere. Why not start at the beginning? Shouldn't you be in custody?"

H said, "Matters have become complicated, Mr. Clavain. I gather the Conjoiners brought Scorpio to the inner system with the intention of handing him over to the authorities."

Xavier looked at the pig, doing a double take. "I thought H was joking when he called you Scorpio before. But he wasn't, was he? Holy fuck. You *are* him, the one they've been trying to catch all this time. *Holy fuck!*"

"Your reputation precedes you," H said to the pig.

"What the fuck were you doing in Carousel New Copenhagen?" Xavier asked, easing back into his seat. He appeared disturbed to be in the same building as Scorpio, let alone the same room.

"I was coming after him," Scorpio said, nodding at Clavain.

Now it was Clavain's turn to blink. "Me?"

"They gave me a deal, the spiders. Said they'd let me go, wouldn't turn me over, if I helped them track you down after you gave them the slip. I wasn't going to say no, was I?"

H said, "They provided Scorpio with credible documentation, enough that he would not be arrested on sight. I believe they were sincere in their promise that he would be allowed to go free if he assisted in bringing you back into the fold."

"But I still don't . . . "

"Scorpio and his associate—another Conjoiner—followed your trail, Mr. Clavain. Naturally it took them to Antoinette Bax. That was how Xavier became involved in the whole unfortunate business. There was a struggle, and some damage was done to the carousel. The Convention already had an eye on Antoinette, so it did not take them long to reach her ship. The injuries that were sustained, including Scorpio's, all took place when the Convention proxy entered *Storm Bird*."

Clavain frowned. "But that doesn't explain how they come to be . . . oh, wait. You were shadowing them, weren't you?"

H nodded with what Clavain thought was a trace of pride. "I expected the Conjoiners to send someone after you. For my own curiosity I was determined to bring them here, too, so that I might determine what part they played in this whole curious affair. My ships were waiting around Copenhagen, looking for anything untoward—and especially anything untoward concerning Antoinette Bax. I am only sorry that we did not intervene sooner, or a little less blood might have been shed."

Clavain turned around at the sound of metronomic ticking, coming nearer. It was a woman wearing stiletto heels. An enormous black cloak fanned behind her, as if she walked in her own private gale. He recognised her.

"Ah, Zebra," H said, smiling.

Zebra strode up to him and then wrapped her arms around him. They kissed, more like lovers than friends.

"Are you certain that you don't need some rest?" H asked. "Two busy jobs in one day . . . "

"I'm fine, and so are the Talkative Twins."

"Did you—um—make arrangements concerning the Convention employee?"

"We dealt with him, yes. Do you want to see him?"

"I imagine it might amuse my guests. Why not?" H shrugged, as if all that was being debated was whether to have afternoon tea now rather than later.

"I'll fetch him," Zebra said. She turned around and clicked into the distance.

Another pair of footsteps approached. Clavain corrected himself. It was really two pairs of footsteps, but which fell in near-perfect synchrony. It was the two huge mouthless men wheeling a chair between the settees. Antoinette was sitting in the chair, looking tired but alive. She had many bandages on her hands and forearms.

"Clavain . . . " she started to say.

"I'm fine," he said. "And pleased to hear that you're well. I'm sorry to learn that there was trouble on my account. I sincerely hoped that when I left, that would be the last of it for you."

"Life's just never that simple, is it?" Antoinette said.

"I suppose not. But I'm sorry all the same. If I can make amends, I will."

Antoinette looked at Xavier. "You're OK? She said you were, but I didn't know if I should believe her."

"I'm fine," Xavier told her. "Right as rain."

But neither of them had the energy to get out of their chairs, it seemed.

"I didn't think I'd manage it," Antoinette said. "I was trying to get your heart started, but I didn't have the strength. I could feel myself slipping into unconsciousness, so I gave it one last try. I guess it worked."

"Actually, it didn't," H said. "You passed out. You'd done your best, but you'd lost a lot of blood yourself."

"Then who . . . ?"

H nodded at Scorpio. "Our friend the pig saved Xavier. Didn't you?"

The pig grunted. "It wasn't anything."

Antoinette said, "Maybe not to you, Mr. Pink. But it made a hell of a difference to Xavier. I suppose I should say thank you."

"Don't cut yourself up over it. I'll live without your gratitude."

"I'll still say it. Thanks."

Scorpio looked at her and then grunted something unintelligible before looking away.

"What about the ship?" Clavain said, breaking the awkward silence that followed. "Is the ship OK?"

Antoinette looked at H. "I guess it isn't, right?"

"Actually, she's fine. As soon as Xavier was conscious, Zebra asked him to instruct *Storm Bird* to fly on automatic pilot to some coordinates we provided. We have secure holding facilities in the Rust Belt, vital for some of our other operations. The ship is intact and out of harm's way. You have my word on that, Antoinette."

"When can I see it again?"

"Soon," H said. "But exactly how soon I am not willing to say."

"Am I a prisoner, then?" Antoinette asked.

"Not exactly. You are all my guests. I would just rather you did not leave until we have all had a chance to talk. Mr. Clavain may have his own opinion on the matter, perhaps justifiably, but I think it is fair to say that some of you owe me for saving your lives." He held up a hand, cutting off any objections before anyone had a chance to speak. "I do not mean that I hold any of you in debt to me. I merely ask that you indulge me with a little of your time. Like it or not," and he glanced at all of them in turn, "we are all players in something larger than any of us can readily grasp. Unwilling players, perhaps, but then it has always been thus. By defecting, Mr. Clavain has precipitated something momentous. I believe we have no option but to follow events to their outcome. To play, if you like, our predetermined roles. That includes all of us—even Scorpio."

There was a squeaking sound, accompanied by more of the metronomic clicking. Zebra had returned. Ahead of her she propelled an upright metal cylinder the size of a large tea urn. It was burnished to a high gleam and sprouted all manner of pipes and accoutrements. It sat propped on the cushion of a wheelchair, the same kind that Antoinette had arrived in.

The cylinder was, Clavain noticed, rocking slightly from side to side, as if something inside was struggling to escape.

"Bring it here," H said, gesturing Zebra forwards.

She wheeled the cylinder between them. It was still wobbling. H leaned over and rapped it softly with his knuckles. "Hello there," he said, raising his voice. "Nice that you could make it. Do you know where you are, I wonder, or what has happened to you?"

The cylinder wobbled with increasing agitation.

"Let me explain," H said to his guests. "What we have here is the life-support system of a Convention cutter. The pilot of a cutter never leaves his spacecraft for his entire term of service, which can be many years. To reduce mass, most of his body is surgically detached and held in cold storage back at Convention headquarters. He doesn't need limbs when he can drive a proxy via a neural interface. He doesn't need a lot of other things, either. They are all removed, labelled and stored."

The cylinder lurched back and forth.

Zebra reached down and held it steady. "Whoah," she said.

"Inside this cylinder," H said, "is the pilot of the cutter responsible for the recent unpleasantness aboard Miss Bax's spacecraft. Nasty little fellow, aren't you? What fun it must be, terrifying innocent crews who have done nothing worse than violate a few silly old laws. What larks."

"It isn't the first time we've done business," Antoinette said.

"Well, I'm afraid our guest has gone just a little bit too far this time," H said. "Haven't you, old fellow? It was a simple matter to detach your life-support core from the rest of the ship. I hope it didn't cause you too much discomfort, although I imagine there must have been no little pain as you were disconnected from your ship's nervous system. I'll apologise for that now, because torture really isn't my business."

The cylinder was suddenly very still, as if listening.

"But I can't very well let you go unpunished, can I? I am a very moral man, you see. My own crimes have sharpened my sense of ethics to a quite unprecedented degree." He leaned close to the cylinder, until his lips were almost kissing the metal. "Listen carefully, because I don't want there to be any doubt in your mind as to what is to happen to you."

The cylinder rocked softly.

"I know what I need to do to keep you alive. Power here, nutrients there—it's not rocket science. I imagine that you can exist in this can for decades, provided I keep you fed and watered. And that is precisely what I am going to do, until the moment you die." He glanced at Zebra and nodded. "I think that'll be all, don't you?"

"Shall I put him in the same room as the others, H?"

"I think that will do very nicely." He beamed at his guests and then watched with obvious fondness as Zebra wheeled the prisoner away.

When she was out of earshot Clavain said, "You're a cruel man, H."

"I am not cruel," he said. "Not in the sense you mean. But cruelty is a useful tool if one can only recognise the precise moment when it must be used."

"That fucker had it coming," Antoinette said. "Sorry, Clavain, but I'm not going to lose any sleep over that bastard. He'd have killed us all if it wasn't for H."

Clavain still felt cold, as if one of the ghosts they had recently discussed had just walked through him. "What about the other victim?" he asked with sudden urgency. "The other Conjoiner. Was it Skade?"

"No, it wasn't Skade. A man this time. He was injured, but there's no reason why he won't make a full recovery."

"Might I see him?"

"Shortly, Mr. Clavain. I am not done with him yet. I wish to make absolutely certain that he can't do me any harm before I bring him to consciousness."

"He lied, then," Antoinette said. "Bastard told us he didn't have any implants left in his head."

Clavain turned to her. "He'll have kept them while they were still useful, only flushing them out of his body when he was about to pass through some kind of security check. It doesn't take long for the implants to dismantle themselves—a few minutes, and then all you're left with are trace elements in the blood and urine."

Scorpio said, "Be careful. Be very fucking careful."

"Any particular reason why I should be?" H asked.

The pig pushed himself forwards in his seat. "Yeah. The spiders put something in my head, tuned to his implants. Like a little valve or something, around one vein or artery. He dies, I die—it's simple."

"Mm." H had one finger on his lip. "And you're totally certain of this?"

"I already passed out once, when I tried strangling him."

"Friendly relationship you two had, was it?"

"Marriage of convenience, pal. And he knew it. That was why he had to have a hold on me."

"Well, there may have been something there once," H said. "But we examined all of you. You have no implants, Scorpio. If there was anything in your head, he flushed it out before you reached us."

Scorpio's mouth dropped open in a perfectly human expression of astonishment and intense self-disgust. "No . . . the fucker couldn't have . . ."

"Very probably, Scorpio, you could have walked away at any time and there wouldn't have been a thing in the world he could have done to stop you."

"It's like my father told me," Antoinette said. "You can't trust the spiders, Scorpio. Ever."

"Like I need to be told that?"

"You were the one they tricked, Scorpio, not me."

He sneered at her, but remained silent. Perhaps, Clavain thought, he knew there was nothing he could say that would not make his position worse.

"Scorpio," H said, with renewed seriousness, "I meant it when I said you were not my prisoner. I have no particular admiration for the things you did. But I have done terrible things myself, and I know that there are sometimes reasons that others don't see. You saved Antoinette, and for that you have my gratitude—and, I suspect, the gratitude of my other guests."

"Get to the point," Scorpio grunted.

"I will honour the agreement that the Conjoiners made with you. I will let you leave, freely, so that you can rejoin your associates in the city. You have my word on that."

Scorpio pushed himself from the seat, with noticeable effort. "Then I'm out of here."

"Wait." H had not raised his voice, but something in his tone immobilised the pig. It was as if all that had come before was mere pleasantry, and that H had finally revealed his true nature: that he was not a man to be trifled with when he moved on to matters of gravity.

Scorpio eased back into his seat. Softly he asked, "What?"

"Listen to me and listen well." He looked around, his expression judicial in its solemnity. "All of you. I won't say this more than once."

There was silence. Even the Talkative Twins seemed to have fallen into a deeper state of speechlessness.

H moved to the grand piano and played six bleak notes before slamming the cover down. "I said that we live in momentous times. End times, perhaps. Certainly a great chapter in human affairs appears to be drawing to a close. Our own petty squabbles—our delicate worlds, our childlike factions, our comical little wars—are about to be eclipsed. We are children stumbling into a galaxy of adults, adults of vast age and vaster power. The woman who lived in this building was, I believe, a conduit for one or other of those alien forces. I do not know how or why. But I believe that through her these forces have extended their reach into the Conjoiners. I can only surmise that this has happened because a desperate time draws near."

Clavain wanted to object. He wanted to argue. But everything he had discovered for himself, and everything that H had shown him, made that denial harder. H was correct in his assumption, and all Clavain could do was nod quietly and wish that it were otherwise.

H was still speaking. "And yet—and this is what terrifies me—even the Conjoiners seem frightened. Mr. Clavain is an honourable man." H nodded, as if his statement needed affirmation. "Yes. I know all about you, Mr. Clavain. I have studied your career and sometimes wished that I could have walked the line you have chosen for yourself. It has been no easy path, has it? It has taken you between ideologies, between worlds, almost between species. All along, you have never followed anything as fickle as your heart, anything as meaningless as a flag. Merely your cold assessment of what, at any given moment, it is *right* to do."

"I've been a traitor and a spy," Clavain said. "I've killed innocents for military ends. I've made orphans. If that's honour, you can keep it."

"There have been worse tyrants than you, Mr. Clavain, trust me on that. But the point I make is merely this. These times have driven you to do the unthinkable. You have turned against the Conjoiners after *four hundred years*. Not because you believe the Demarchists are right, but because you sensed how your own side had become poisoned. And you realised, without perhaps seeing it clearly yourself, that what lies at stake is bigger than any faction, bigger than any ideology. It is the continued existence of the human species."

"How would you know?" Clavain asked.

"Because of what you have already told your friends, Mr. Clavain. You were voluble enough in Carousel New Copenhagen, when you imagined no one else could be listening. But I have ears everywhere. And I can trawl memories, like your own people. You have all passed through my infirmary. Do you imagine I wouldn't stoop to a little neural eavesdropping when so much is at stake? Of course I would."

He turned to Scorpio again, the force of his attention making the pig edge even further back into his seat. "Here is what is going to happen. I am going to do what I can to help Mr. Clavain complete his assignment."

"To defect?" Scorpio asked.

"No," H said, shaking his head. "What would be the good of that? The Demarchists don't even have a single remaining starship, not in this system. Mr. Clavain's gesture would be wasted. Worse than that, once he's back in Demarchist hands I doubt even my influence would be able to free him again. No. We need to think beyond that to the issue itself, to why Mr. Clavain was defecting in the first place." He nodded at Clavain, like a prompter. "Go on, tell us. It'll be good to hear it from your lips, after all that I've said."

"You know, don't you?"

"About the weapons? Yes."

Clavain nodded. He did not know whether to feel defeated or

victorious. There was nothing to do but talk. "I wanted to persuade the Demarchists to put together an operation to recover the hell-class weapons before Skade can get her hands on them. But H is right: they don't even have a starship. It was a folly, a futile gesture to make me feel that I was doing something." He felt long-postponed weariness slide over him, casting a dark shadow of dejection. "That's all it ever was. One old man's stupid final gesture." He looked around at the other guests, feeling as if he owed them some kind of apology. "I'm sorry. I've dragged you all into this, and it was for nothing."

H moved behind the chair and placed two hands on Clavain's shoulders. "Don't be so sorry, Mr. Clavain."

"It's true, isn't it? There's nothing we can do."

"You spoke to the Demarchists," H said. "What did they say when you broached the topic of a ship?"

Clavain recalled his conversation with Perotet and Voi. "They told me they didn't have one."

"And?"

Clavain laughed humourlessly. "That they could get their hands on one if they really needed to."

"And they probably could," H said. "But what would it gain you? They're weak and exhausted, corrupt and battle-weary. Let them find a ship—I won't stop them. After all, it doesn't matter who recovers those weapons, so long as it isn't the Conjoiners. I just think someone else might stand a slightly better chance of actually succeeding. Especially someone who has access to some of the same technology that your side now possesses."

"And who would that be?" Antoinette asked, but she must have already had an inkling.

Clavain looked at his host. "But you don't have a ship either."

"No," H said, "I don't. But like the Demarchists I might know where to find one. There are enough Ultra ships in this system that it would not be impossible to steal one, if we had the necessary will. As a matter of fact, I have already drawn up contingency plans for the taking of a lighthugger, should the need ever arise."

"You'd need a small army to take one of their ships," Clavain said.

"Yes," H said, as if this was the first time it had occurred to him. "Yes, I probably would." Then he turned to the pig. "Wouldn't I, Scorpio?"

* * *

Scorpio listened carefully to what H had to say concerning the delicate matter of stealing a lighthugger. The audacity of the act he was proposing was astounding, but, as H pointed out, the army of pigs had performed audacious crimes before, if not on quite so great a scale. They had taken control of entire zones of the Mulch, usurping power from what was still laughingly called the authorities. They had made a mockery of the Ferrisville Convention's attempts to extend martial law into the darkest niches of the city, and by way of reply the pigs and their allies had established lawless enclaves throughout the Rust Belt. These bubbles of controlled criminality had simply been edited off the map, treated as if they had never been reclaimed after the Melding Plague. But that did not make them any less real or negate the fact that they were often more harmonious environments than the habitats under full and legal Ferrisvillle administration.

H mentioned also the activities that the pigs and the banshees had extended across the system, using them to illustrate his thesis that the pigs already had all the necessary expertise and resources to steal a lighthugger. What remained was simply a question of organisation and timing. A ship would have to be selected some considerable period in advance, and it would have to be the ideal target. There could be no prospect of failure, even a failure that cost the pigs little in terms of lives or resources. The instant the Ultras suspected that there was an attempt being made to possess one of their precious ships, they would tighten their security by an order of magnitude, or leave the system *en masse*. No: the attack would have to take place quickly and it would have to succeed first time.

H told Scorpio that he had already run a number of simulations of theft strategies, and he had concluded that the best time was when a lighthugger was already in its departure phase. His studies had shown that this was when the Ultras were at their most vulnerable, and when they were most likely to neglect their usual security measures. It would be even better to select a ship that had not done well in the usual trade exchanges, as these were the ships that were likely to have sold some of their defence systems or armour as collateral. That was the kind of deal that the Ultras kept to themselves, but H had already placed spies in the parking swarm network routers that intercepted and filtered Ultra trade dialogues. He showed Scorpio the latest transcripts, skimming through reams of commercial argot, highlighting the lucrative deals. In the process he drew Scorpio's attention to one ship already in Yellowstone space that was doing badly in the latest rounds.

"Nothing wrong with the ship itself," H said, lowering his voice confidentially. "Technically sound, or at least nothing that couldn't be fixed on the way to Delta Pavonis. I think she might be our one, Scorpio." He paused. "I've even had a quiet word with Lasher . . . your deputy? He's aware of my intentions, and I've asked him to put together an assault squad for the operation—a few hundred of the best. They don't have to be pigs, although I suspect many of them will be."

"Wait. Wait." Scorpio raised his clumsy stub of a hand. "You said Lasher. How the fuck do you know Lasher?"

H was amused rather than irritated. "This is my city, Scorpio. I know everyone and everything in it."

"But Lasher . . . "

"Remains fiercely loyal to you, yes. I'm aware of that, and I made no attempt to turn his loyalty. He used to be a fan of yours before he became your deputy, didn't he?"

"You know shit about Lasher."

"I know enough that he would kill himself if you gave the word. And as I said, I made no effort to turn him. I . . . anticipated your consent, Scorpio. That's all. Anticipated that you would accept my request and do what I ask. I told Lasher that you had already ordered him to assemble the army, and that I was merely relaying the order. So I took a liberty, I admit. As I intimated earlier, these are not times for hesitant men. We aren't hesitant men, are we?"

"No . . . "

"That's the spirit." He slapped him on the shoulder in a gesture of boisterous camaraderie. "The ship's *Eldritch Child,* out of Macro Hektor Industria's trade halo. Do you think you and Lasher can take her, Scorpio? Or have I come to the wrong pigs?"

"Fuck you, H."

The man beamed. "I'll take that as 'yes.' "

"I'm not done. I pick my team. Not just Lasher, but whoever

else I say. No matter where they are in the Mulch, no matter the shit they're in or the shit they've done, you get them to me. Understand?"

"I will do what I can. I have my limits."

"Fine. And when I'm done, when I've set Clavain up with a ship . . ."

"You will ride that same ship. There isn't any other way, you see. Did you seriously imagine you could melt back into Stoner society? You can walk out of here now, with my blessing, but I won't give you my protection. And as loyal as Lasher may be, the Convention has scented blood. There is no reason for you to stay behind, any more than there's a reason for Antoinette and Xavier to stay here. Like them, you'll go with Clavain if you're wise."

"You're talking about leaving Chasm City."

"We all have to make choices in life, Scorpio. They aren't always easy. Not the ones that count, anyway." H waved his hand dismissively. "It doesn't have to be for ever. You weren't born here, any more than I was. The city will still be around in a hundred or two hundred years. It may not look the way it does now, but what does that matter? It may be better or worse. It would be up to you to find your place in it. Of course, you may not wish to return by then."

Scorpio looked back to the scrolling lines of trade argot. "And that ship . . . the one you've fingered . . . ?"

"Yes?"

"If I took her—gave her to Clavain—and then chose to stay aboard her . . . there's something I'd insist on."

H shrugged. "One or two demands on your side would not be unreasonable. What is it you want?"

"To name it. She becomes *Zodiacal Light*. And that isn't open to negotiation."

H looked at him with a cool, distant interest. "I'm sure Clavain would have no objections. But why that name? Does it mean something to you?"

Scorpio left the question unanswered.

Later, much later, when he knew that the ship was on its way—successfully captured, its crew ousted, and now ramming out of the system towards the star Delta Pavonis, around which orbited a world he had barely heard of called Resurgam—H walked out on to one of the middle-level balconies of the Château des Corbeaux. A warm breeze flicked the hem of his gown against his trousers. He took a deep breath of that air, savouring its scents of unguents and spices. Here the building was still inside the bubble of breathable atmosphere being belched out of the chasm by the ailing Lilly, that vast item of bioengineering that the Conjoiners had installed during their brief halcyon tenancy. It was night, and by some rare alignment of personal mood and exterior optical conditions he found that Chasm City looked extraordinarily beautiful, as all human cities are obliged to at some point in their lives. He had seen it through so many changes. But they were nothing compared with the changes he had lived through himself.

It's done, he thought.

Now that the ship was on its way, now that he had assisted Clavain in his mission, he had finally done the one incontrovertibly good act of his life. It was not, he supposed, adequate atonement for all that he had done in the past, all the cruelties he had inflicted, all the kindnesses he had omitted. It was not even enough to expiate his failure to rescue the tormented grub before the Mademoiselle had beaten him to it. But it was better than nothing.

Anything was better than nothing.

The balcony extended from one black side of the building, bordered by only the lowest of walls. He walked to the very edge, the warm breeze—it was not unlike a constant animal exhalation—gaining in strength until it was not really a breeze at all. Down below, dizzying kilometres below, the city splayed out in tangled jetstreams of light, like the sky over his home town after one of the dogfights he remembered from his youth.

He had sworn that when he finally achieved atonement, when he finally found an act that could offset some of his sins, he would end his life. Better to end with the score not fully settled than risk committing some even worse deed in the future. The power to do bad was still in him, he knew; it lay buried deep, and it had not surfaced for many years, but it was still there, tight and coiled and waiting, like a hamadryad. The risk was too great.

He looked down, imagining how it would feel. In a moment it would be over save for the slow, elegant playing out of gravity and mass. He would have become no more than an exercise in ballistics. No more capacity for pain; no more hunger for redemption.

A woman's voice cut across the night. "No, H!"

He did not look around, but remained poised on the edge. The mesmeric city still pulled him towards itself.

She crossed the balcony, her heels clicking. He felt her arm slip around his waist. Gently, lovingly, she pulled him back from the edge.

"No," she whispered. "This is not how it ends. Not here, not now."

TWENTY-FOUR

"There's the getaway car," said the swarthy little man, nodding at the solitary vehicle parked on the street.

Thorn observed the slumped shadow behind the car's window. "The driver looks asleep."

"He's not." But to be on the safe side, Thorn's driver pulled up next to the other car. The two vehicles were identical in shape, conforming to the standard government-sponsored design. But the getaway car was older and drabber, the rain matt against irregular patches of repaired bodywork. His driver got out and trudged through puddles to the other car, rapping smartly on the window. The other driver wound down his window and the two of them spoke for a minute or so, Thorn's driver reinforcing his points with many hand gestures and facial expressions. Then he came back and got in with Thorn, muttering under his breath. He released the handbrake and their own car eased away with a hiss of tyres.

"There aren't any other vehicles parked on this street," Thorn said. "It looks conspicuous, waiting there like that."

"Would you rather there was no car, on a piss-poor night like this?"

"No. But just make sure the lazy sod has a good story in case

Vuilleumier's goons decide to have a nice little chat with him."

"He's got an explanation, don't worry about that. Thinks his missis is cheating on him. See that residential apartment over there? He's watching it in case she shows up when she's supposed to be working nights."

"Maybe he should wake up a bit, then."

"I told him to look lively." They sped around a corner. "Relax, Thorn. You've done this a hundred times, and we've run a dozen local area meetings in this part of Cuvier. The reason you have me work for you is so you don't have to worry about details."

"You're right," Thorn said. "I suppose it's just the usual nerves."

The man laughed at this. "You, nervous?"

"There's a lot at stake. I don't want to let them down. Not after we've come so far."

"You won't let them down, Thorn. They won't let you. Don't you realise it yet? They love you." The man flicked a switch on the dashboard, making the windscreen wipers pump with renewed vigour. "Fucking terraformers, eh? Like we haven't had enough rain lately. Still, it's good for the planet, or so they say. Do you think the government is lying, by the way?"

"About what?" Thorn said.

"That weird thing in the sky."

Thorn followed the organiser into the designated building. He was led through a brief series of unlit corridors until he reached a large windowless room. It was full of people, all of whom were seated facing a makeshift stage and podium. Thorn walked amongst them, stepping nimbly on to the stage. There was quiet applause, respectful without being ecstatic. He looked down at the people and established that there were about forty of them, as he had been promised.

"Good evening," Thorn said. He planted both hands on the podium and leaned forward. "Thank you for coming here tonight. I appreciate the risks that you have all taken. I promise you that it will be worth it."

His followers were from all walks of Resurgam life except the very core of government. It was not that government workers did not sometimes attempt to join the movement, nor that they weren't occasionally sincere. But it was too much of a security risk to allow them in. They were screened out long before they ever got near Thorn. Instead there were technicians, cooks and truck drivers, farmers, plumbers and teachers. Some of them were very old, and had adult memories of life in Chasm City before the *Lorean* had brought them to Resurgam. Others had been born since the Girardieau regime, and to them *that* period—barely less squalid than the present—was the "good old days," as difficult as that was to believe. There were few like Thorn who had only childhood memories of the old world.

"Is it true, then?" a woman asked from the front row. "Tell us, Thorn, now. We've all heard the rumours. Put us out of our misery."

He smiled, patient despite the woman's lack of respect for his script. "What rumour would that be, exactly?"

She stood up, looking around before speaking. "That you've found them—the ships. The ones that are going to get us off this planet. And that you've found the starship too, and it's going to take us back to Yellowstone."

Thorn didn't answer her directly. He looked over the heads of the audience and spoke to someone at the back. "Could I have the first picture, please?" Thorn stepped aside so that he did not block the projection thrown on to the chipped and stained rear wall of the room.

"This is a photograph taken exactly twenty days ago," he said. "I won't say where it was taken from just yet. But you can see for yourselves that this is Resurgam and that the picture must be quite recent—see how blue the sky is, how much vegetation there is in the foreground? You can tell that it's low ground, where the terraforming programme's been the most successful."

The flat-format picture showed a view down into a narrow canyon or defile. Two sleek metallic objects were parked in the shadows between the rock walls, nose to nose.

"They're shuttles," Thorn said. "Large surface-to-orbit types, each with a capacity of around five hundred passengers. You can't judge size very well from this view, but that small dark aperture *there* is a door. Next, please."

The picture changed. Now Thorn himself stood beneath the hull of one of the shuttles, peering up at the formerly tiny-looking door.

"I climbed down the slope. I didn't believe they were real

myself until I got close. But there they are. So far as we can tell they are perfectly functional, as good as the day they came down."

"Where are they from?" another man asked.

"The *Lorean*," Thorn said.

"They've been down here all that time? I don't believe it."

Thorn shrugged. "They're built to keep themselves in working order. Old tech, self-regenerating. Not like the new stuff we've all grown used to. These shuttles are relics from a time when things didn't break down or wear out or become obsolescent. We have to remember that."

"Have you been inside? The rumours say you've been inside, even got the shuttles to come alive."

"Next."

The picture showed Thorn, another man and a woman on the flight deck of the shuttle, all of them smiling into the camera, the instrumentation lit up behind them.

"It took a long time—many days—but we finally got the shuttle to talk to us. It wasn't that it didn't want to deal with us, simply that we'd forgotten all the protocols that its builders had assumed we'd know. But as you can see, the ship is at least nominally functional."

"Can they fly?"

Thorn looked serious. "We don't know for sure. We have no reason to assume that they can't, but so far we've only scratched the surface of those diagnostic layers. We have people there now who are learning more by the day, but all we can say at the moment is that the shuttles *should* fly, given everything that we know about *Belle Époque* machinery."

"How did you find them?" asked another woman.

Thorn lowered his eyes, marshalling his thoughts. "I have been looking for a way off this planet my entire life," he said.

"That isn't what I asked. What if those shuttles are a government trap? What if they planted the clues that led you to them? What if they're designed to kill you and your followers, once and for all?"

"The government knows nothing about any way to leave this planet," Thorn told her. "Trust me on that."

"How can you be so sure?"

"Next."

Thorn now showed them a picture of the thing in the sky,

waiting while the projector lurched in and out of focus. He studied the reaction of his audience. Some of them had seen this image before; some had seen pictures that showed the same thing but with much less resolution; some had seen it with their own eyes, as a faint ochre smudge in the sky chasing the setting sun like a malformed comet. He told them that the picture was the latest and best image available to the government, according to his sources.

"But it isn't a comet," Thorn said. "That's the government line, but it isn't true. It isn't a supernova either, or any of the other rumours they've put about. They've been able to get away with those lies because not many people down here know enough about astronomy to realise what that thing is. And those that do have been too intimidated to speak out, since they know that the government is lying for a reason."

"So what is it?" someone asked.

"While it doesn't have anything like the right morphology to be a comet, it isn't something outside our solar system either. It moves against the stars, a little each night, and it's sitting in the ecliptic along with the other planets. There's an explanation for that, quite an obvious one, really." He looked them all up and down, certain that he had their attention. "It *is* a planet, or rather what used to be one. The smudge is where there used to be a gas giant, the one we call Roc. What we're seeing is Roc's disembowelled corpse. The planet is being pulled apart, literally dismantled." Thorn smiled. "That's what the government doesn't want you to know, because there's nothing they can do about it."

He nodded towards the back. "Next."

He showed them how it had begun, over a year earlier.

"Three medium-sized rocky worlds were dismantled first, ripped apart by self-replicating machines. Their rubble was collected, processed and boosted across the system to the gas giant. Other machines were already waiting there. They turned three of Roc's moons into colossal factories, eating megatonnes of rubble by the second and spewing out highly organised mechanical components. They spun an arc of matter around the gas giant, a vast metallic ring, unbelievably dense and strong. You can see it here, very faintly, but you'll have to take my word that it's more than a dozen kilometres thick. At the same time they were threading tubes of similar material down into the atmosphere itself."

"Who?" another man asked. "Who is doing this, Thorn?"

"Not who," he said. "What. The machines aren't of human origin. The government's pretty certain about that. They have a theory, too. It was something Sylveste did. He set off some kind of trigger that brought them here."

"Just like the Amarantin must have done?"

"Perhaps," Thorn said. "There's certainly speculation along those lines. But there's no sign that any major planets have ever been dismantled in this system before, no resonance gaps in orbits where a Jovian would have belonged. But then again, it was a million years ago. Maybe the Inhibitors tidied up after they'd done their dirty work."

"Inhibitors?" asked a bearded man whom Thorn recognised as an unemployed palaeobotanist.

"That's what the government calls the alien machines. I don't know why, but it seems as good a name as any."

"What will they do to us?" asked a woman who had exceptionally bad teeth.

"I don't know." Thorn tightened his fingers around the edge of the podium. He had felt the mood of the room change within the last minute. It always happened this way, when they saw what was happening. Those who knew of the thing in the sky had viewed it with alarm from the moment the rumours began. For most of the year it had not been visible at all from Cuvier's latitude, where most of the citizenry still lived. But no one had been of the opinion that it was likely to be a good omen. Now it had hoved into the evening sky, unignorable.

The government's experts had their own ideas about what was going on around the giant. They had correctly deduced that the activities could only be the result of intelligent forces, rather than some outlandish astronomical cataclysm, although that had, for a while, been considered. A minority considered it likely that the agency behind the destruction was human: the Conjoiners, perhaps, or a new and belligerent group of Ultras. A smaller and less credible minority thought that the Triumvir herself, Ilia Volyova, had to have something to do with it. But the majority had correctly deduced that alien intervention was the most likely explanation, and that it was in some way a response to Sylveste's investigations.

But the government's experts had access only to the sketchiest of data. They had not glimpsed the alien machinery in close-up, as Thorn had.

Volyova and Khouri had their own theories.

As soon as the arc was finished, as soon as the giant had been girdled, there had been a dramatic change in the properties of the planet's magnetosphere. An intense quadrupole field had been set up, orders of magnitude more intense than the planet's natural field. Loops of magnetic flux curled between lines of latitude from equator to pole, ramming far out of the atmosphere. The field was clearly artificial, and it could only have been produced by current flow along conductors laid along those lines of latitude, great metallic loops wound around the planet like motor windings.

That was the process Thorn and Khouri had observed with their own eyes. They had watched the loops being laid, spooled deep into the atmosphere. But they had no idea how deep they had gone. The windings must have sunk far into the metallic hydrogen ocean, deep enough to achieve some kind of torque coupling with the planet's shrivelled yet immensely metal-rich rocky kernel. An exterior acceleration force transmitted to the windings would be transferred to the planet itself.

Meanwhile, around the planet, the orbital arc generated a pole-to-pole current flow, passing through the giant and returning to the arc via the magzetospheric plasma. The charge elements in the ring reacted against the field in which they were embedded, forcing a tiny change in angular momentum in the motor windings.

Imperceptibly at first, the gas giant began to rotate faster.

The process had continued for most of a year. The effect had been catastrophic: as the planet had spun faster and faster, so it had been pushed closer and closer towards the critical break-up velocity when its own gravity could no longer stop it from flying apart. Within six months, half the mass of the planet's atmosphere had been flung into space, ejected into the half-beautiful, half-repulsive new circum-planetary nebula that was visible from Resurgam as a thumb-sized smudge in the evening sky. Now most of the atmosphere was gone. Relieved of the compressive weight of the overlying layers, the liquid-hydrogen ocean had returned to the gaseous state, liberating squalls of energy that had been pumped smoothly back into the spin-up machinery. The metallic-hydrogen ocean had undergone a similar but even more convulsive state change. That too had been part of the plan, for the great process of dismantling had not faltered once.

Now all that remained was a husk of tectonically unstable core matter spinning close to its own fragmentation speed. The machines were surrounding it even as Thorn spoke, processing and refining. In the nebula, revealed as shadowy knots of coherent shape and density, other structures were taking shape, larger than worlds in their own right.

Thorn said again, "I don't know what's happening. I don't think anyone does. But I do have an idea. What they've done so far has been very hierarchical. The machines are awesome, but they have limitations. Matter has to come from somewhere, and they couldn't immediately start smashing apart the gas giant. They had to make the tools to do that, and that meant smashing three smaller worlds first. They need raw material, you see. Energy doesn't seem to be a problem—maybe they can draw it directly from the vacuum—but they obviously can't condense it back down into matter with any precision or efficiency. So they have to work in stages, one step at a time. Now they've ripped apart a gas giant, liberating perhaps one-tenth of one per cent of the entire useful mass in this system. Based on what we've seen so far, that liberated mass will be used to make something else. What, I don't know. But I'm willing to hazard a guess. There's only one place to go now, only one hierarchy above a gas giant. It has to be the sun. I think they're going to take it apart."

"You're not serious," someone said.

"I wish I wasn't. But there has to be a reason why they haven't smashed Resurgam yet. I think it's obvious: they don't have to. In a while, perhaps much sooner than we'd like, there won't be any need for them to worry about it. It'll be gone. They'll have ripped this solar system apart."

"No . . . " someone exclaimed.

Thorn started to answer, ready to work on their understandable doubts. He had been through this before, and he knew the truth took a while to sink in. That was why he told them about the shuttles first, so that there would be something they could pin their hopes on. It was the end of the world, he would say, but that didn't mean they all had to die. There was an escape route.

All anyone needed was the courage to trust him, the courage to follow him.

But then Thorn realised that the person had said "no" for an entirely different reason. It had nothing to do with his presentation.

It was the police. They were coming through the door.

Act as you would if you thought your life was in danger, Khouri had told him. It has to look totally credible. If this is going to work—and it has to work, for all our sakes—they have to believe that you've been arrested without any foreknowledge of what was going on. You had better struggle, Thorn, and be prepared to get hurt.

He jumped from the podium. The police were masked, unrecognisable. They came in with sprays and pacifiers at the ready, moving through the stunned and frightened audience with quick jerky movements and no audible communication. Thorn hit the ground and dashed towards the escape route, the one that would lead to the getaway car two blocks away. Make it look real. Make it look bloody real. He heard chairs scraping as people stood or tried to stand. The crack of fear-gas grenades and the buzz-snap of stun guns filled the room. He heard someone cry out, followed by the sound of armour on bone. There had been a moment of near calm; now it was over. The room erupted into a panicked frenzy as everyone tried to get out.

His exit was blocked. The police were coming in that way as well.

Thorn spun around. Same story the other way. He started coughing, feeling panic rise in him unexpectedly, like a sudden urge to sneeze. The effect of the fear-gas was so absolute that it made him want to crawl into a corner and cower rather than stand his ground. But Thorn fought through it. He grabbed one of the chairs and raised it aloft as a shield as the police stormed towards him.

The next thing he knew he was on his knees, and then his hands, and the police were hitting him with sticks, expertly aimed so that he would have bruises but no major broken bones or internal injuries.

Out of the corner of his eye, Thorn saw another group of police laying into the woman with the bad teeth. She disappeared under them, like something mobbed by rooks.

* * *

While it waited for the singer to finish building itself, the overseer dug playfully through the stratalike memories of its earlier incarnations.

The overseer did not exist in any single Inhibitor machine. That would have been too vulnerable a concentration of expertise. But when a swarm was drawn to the site where a local cleansing would be required—typically a volume of space no more than a few light-hours wide—a distributed intelligence would be generated from many less than sentient subminds. Light-speed communications bound together the dumb elements, weaving slow, secure thoughts. More rapid processing was assigned to individual units. The overseer's larger thought processes were necessarily sluggish, but this was a limitation that had never handicapped the Inhibitors. Nor had they ever attempted to weave together an overseer's subelements with superluminal communication channels. There were too many warnings in the archive concerning the hazards of such experiments, entire species that had been edited out of galactic history because of a single foolish episode of causality violation.

The overseer was not only slow and distributed. It was also temporary, permitted to achieve only fleeting consciousness. Even as its sense of self had come into being it had known with grim fatality that it would die once its duties were accomplished. But it felt no sense of bitterness at the inevitability of this fate, even after it had sifted through archived memories of its previous apparitions, memories laid down during other cleansings. It was simply the way things had to be. Intelligence, even machine intelligence, was something that could not be allowed to infect the galaxy until the coming crisis had been averted. Intelligence was, quite literally, its own worst enemy.

It found itself remembering some of the earlier cleansings. Of course, it had not really been the same overseer that had masterminded those extinction episodes. When Inhibitor swarms met, which was rarely, they traded knowledge of recent kills and outbreaks, methods and anecdotes. Lately, those meetings had become more rare, which was why there had been only one significant addition to the library of starcide techniques in the last five hundred million years. Swarms, isolated from each other for so long, reacted cautiously when they met. There were even rumours of different Inhibitor factions clashing over extinction rights.

Something had certainly gone wrong since the old days, when the kills had happened cleanly and methodically, and no major outbreaks slipped through the net. The overseer could not avoid drawing conclusions. The great galaxy-encompassing machine for holding back intelligence—the machine of which the overseer was one dutiful part—was failing. Intelligence was starting to slip through the cracks, threatening infestation. The situation had certainly worsened in the last few million years, and yet this was nothing compared with the thirteen Galactic Turns—the three billion years—that lay ahead, before the time of crisis arrived. The overseer had grave doubts that intelligence could be held in check until then. It was almost enough to make it give up now, and let this particular species go uncleansed. They were quadrupedal vertebrate oxygenbreathers, after all. Mammals. It felt a distant echo of kinship, something that had never troubled it when it was extinguishing ammonia-breathing gasbags or spiny insectoids.

The overseer forced itself out of this mood. Very probably it was just this sort of thinking that was decreasing the success rate of cleansings.

No, the mammals would die. That was the way, and that was how it would be.

The overseer looked on the extent of its works around Delta Pavonis. It knew of the previous cleansing, the wiping out of the avians who had last inhabited this local sector of space. The mammals had probably not even evolved locally, meaning that this would only be phase one of a more protracted cleansing. The last lot had really botched things up, it thought. Of course, there was always a desire to perform a cleansing with the minimum amount of environmental damage. Worlds and suns were not to be converted into weapons unless a class-three breakout was imminent, and even then it was to be avoided wherever possible. The overseer did not like inflicting unnecessary devastation. It had a keen sense of the irony of ripping apart stars now, when the whole point of its work was to avoid greater destruction three billion years down the line. But what was done was done. A certain amount of additional damage had now to be tolerated.

Messy. But that, as the overseer reflected, was "life."

* * *

The Inquisitor looked out across rain-soaked Cuvier. Her own reflection hovered beyond the window, a spectral figure stalking the city.

"Will you be all right with this one, ma'am?" the guard who had brought him asked.

"I'll cope," she said, not yet turning around. "If I can't, you're only a room away. Undo his cuffs and then leave us alone."

"Are you certain, ma'am?"

"Undo his cuffs."

The guard wrenched the plastic restraints apart. Thorn stretched his arms and touched his face nervously, like an artist checking paint that might not have dried.

"You can go now," the Inquisitor said.

"Ma'am," the guard replied, closing the door after him.

There was a seat waiting for Thorn. He collapsed into it. Khouri continued to look out of the window, her hands clasped behind her back. The rain drooled in great curtains from the overhang above the window. The night sky was a featureless haze somewhere between red and black. There were no stars tonight, no troubling omens in the sky.

"Did they hurt you?" she asked.

He remembered to keep in character. "What do you think, Vuilleumier? That I did this to myself because I like the sight of blood?"

"I know who you are."

"So do I—I'm Renzo. Congratulations."

"You're Thorn. The one they've been looking for." Her voice was raised a little bit louder than normal. "You're very lucky, you know."

"I am?"

"If Counter-Terrorism had found you, you'd be in a morgue by now. Maybe several morgues. Luckily the police who arrested you had no idea who they were dealing with. I doubt they'd have believed me if I'd told them, quite frankly. Thorn's like the Triumvir to them, a figure of myth and revulsion. I think they were expecting a giant among men, someone who could pull them apart with his bare hands. But you're just a normal-looking man who could walk unnoticed down any street in Cuvier."

Thorn rummaged around in his mouth with the tip of one finger. "I'd apologise for being such a disappointment if I was Thorn."

She turned around and walked towards him. Her bearing, her expression, even the aura she radiated, was not of Khouri. Thorn experienced a dreadful moment of doubt, the thought flashing through his mind that perhaps everything that had happened since his last meeting here had been a fantasy, that there was no Khouri at all.

But Ana Khouri was real. She had told him her secrets, not just concerning her identity and the identity of the Triumvir, but the hurting secrets that went deeper, those that concerned her husband and the way they had been cruelly separated. He never doubted for one instant that she was still terribly in love with the man. At the same time he desperately wanted to break her away from her own past, to make her see that she had to accept what had happened and move on. He felt bad about it because he knew that there was a streak of self-justification in what he wanted to do, that it was not all about—or even mainly about—helping Khouri. He also wanted to make love to her. He despised himself for it, but the urge was still there.

"Can you stand?" she asked.

"I walked in here."

"Come with me, then. Do not attempt anything, Thorn. It will be very bad for you if you do."

"What do you want with me?"

"There's a matter we need to discuss in private."

"Here's fine by me," he said.

"Would you like me to turn you over to Counter-Terrorism, Thorn? It's very easily arranged. I'm sure they'd be delighted to see you."

She took him into the room he remembered from his first visit, with the walls covered in shelves loaded with bulging paperwork. Khouri shut the door behind her-it sealed tightly and hermetically—and then removed a slim silver cylinder the size of a cigar from a desk drawer. She held it aloft and slowly turned around in the centre of the room, while tiny lights buried in the cigar flicked from red to green.

"We're safe," she said, after the lights had remained green

for three or four minutes. "I've had to take extra precautions lately. They got a bug in here when I was up on the starship."

Thorn said, "Did they learn much?"

"No. It was a crude device and by the time I got back it was already faulty. But they've made another attempt since, a bit more sophisticated. I can't take any chances, Thorn."

"Who is it? Another branch of government?"

"Perhaps. Could be this one, even. I promised them the Triumvir's head on a plate and I haven't delivered. Someone's getting suspicious."

"You've got me."

"Yes, so I suppose there are some consolations. Oh, shit." It was as if she had only noticed him properly then. "Look at what they did to you, Thorn. I'm so sorry you had to go through this." From another drawer she produced a small medical kit. Khouri tipped disinfectant into a wad of cotton wool and jammed it against Thorn's split eyebrow.

"That hurts," Thorn said.

Her face was very close to his. He could see every pore, and because she was so close he could look into her eyes without feeling that he was staring.

"It will. Did they really rough you up badly?"

"Nothing your friends downstairs haven't done to me before. I'll live, I think." He winced. "They were pretty ruthless."

"They weren't given any special orders, only the usual tip-off. I'm sorry, but that's the way it had to be. If there's a single detail about your arrest that looks stage-managed we're finished."

"Do you mind if I sit down?"

She helped him to a seat. "I'm sorry other people had to get hurt, too."

Thorn remembered the police piling into the woman with bad teeth. "Can you make sure they all get out all right?"

"No one will be detained. That's part of the plan."

"I mean it. Those people don't deserve to suffer just because there had to be witnesses, Ana."

She applied more disinfectant. "They'll suffer a hell of a lot more if this doesn't work, Thorn. No one will set foot on those shuttles unless they trust you to lead them. A little pain now is worth it if it means not dying later." As if to emphasise her point she pressed the wad against his brow, Thorn groaning at the needlelike discomfort.

"That's a cold way of looking at things," he said. "Makes me think you spent more time with those Ultras than you told me."

"I'm not an Ultra, Thorn. I used them. They used me. That doesn't make us the same." She closed up the medical kit and slammed it back into the desk. "Try to keep that in mind, will you?"

"I'm sorry. It's just that this whole business is so God-damned brutal. We're treating the people of this planet like sheep, herding them to where we know is best for them. Not trusting them to make their own minds up."

"They haven't got time to make their minds up, that's the problem. I'd love to do this democratically, I really would. I'd like nothing better than a clean conscience. But it ain't going to happen that way. If the people know what's going to happen to them—that what they've got in store, other than remaining on this doomed fuckhole of a planet, is a trip to a starship which just happens to have been consumed and transformed by the plague-infected body of its former captain, who incidentally happens to be a totally deranged murderer—do you think there's going to be a stampede for those shuttles? Throw in the fact that rolling out the red carpet when they get there will be Triumvir Ilia Volyova, Resurgam's number-one hate figure, and I think a lot of people will say 'thanks, but no thanks,' don't you?"

Thorn said, "At least they'd have made their own minds up."

"Yeah. A lot of consolation that'll be when we watch them getting incinerated. Sorry, Thorn, but I'll take the bitch option now and worry about ethics later, when we've saved a few lives."

"You won't save everyone even if your plan works."

"I know. We could, but we won't. It's inevitable. There are two hundred thousand people out there. If we started now, we could get all of them off this planet in six months, although a year is more likely given all the variables. But even that might not be enough time. I think I'll have to consider this operation a success if we save only half of them. Maybe fewer than that. I don't know." She rubbed her face, suddenly looking very much older and wearier than she had before. "I'm trying not to think how badly this might all go."

The black telephone on her desk rang. Khouri let it ring for a few seconds, one eye on the silver cylinder. The lights stayed green. She motioned to Thorn to stay quiet and then picked up the heavy black handset, holding it against the side of her head.

"Vuilleumier. I hope this is important. I'm interviewing a suspect in the Thorn inquiry."

The voice on the other end of the phone spoke back to her. Khouri let out a sigh and then closed her eyes. The voice continued talking. Thorn could hear none of the actual words, but enough of the voice's tone reached him for a certain rising desperation to become apparent. Someone sounded as if they were trying to explain something that had gone awfully wrong. The voice reached a crescendo and then fell silent.

"I want the names of those involved," Khouri said, and then placed the handset back on to its cradle.

She looked at Thorn. "I'm sorry."

"What for?"

"They killed someone, when the police broke up the meeting. She died a few minutes ago. A woman . . . "

He stopped her. "I know which one you mean."

Khouri said nothing. The silence filled the room, amplified and trapped by the masses of paperwork surrounding them; lives annotated and documented in numbing precision, all for the purposes of suppression.

"Did you know her name?" Khouri asked.

"No. She was just a follower. Just someone who wanted a way to leave Resurgam."

"I'm sorry." Khouri reached across the desk and took his hand. "I'm sorry. I mean it, Thorn. I didn't want it to begin this way."

Despite himself he laughed hollowly. "Well, she got it, didn't she? What she wanted. A way off this planet. She was the first."

TWENTY-FIVE

Armoured in black, Skade strode through the ship that was now fully hers. For the time being they were safe, having slipped undetected through the last shell of Demarchist perimeter defences. Now there was nothing between *Nightshade* and its destination except empty light-years.

Skade brushed her steel fingers against the corridor plating, loving the sleek conjunction of artificial things. For a time the ship had carried Clavain's stench of ownership, and even after he had defected there had been Remontoire to contend with, Clavain's sympathiser and ally, but now they were both gone, and she could rightfully consider *Nightshade* her own. She could, if she were minded, change the name to one of her own choosing, or perhaps discard the very idea of naming the ship at all, so resolutely against the grain of Conjoiner thinking. But Skade decided that there was a perverse pleasure to be had in keeping the old name. There would be enjoyment in turning Clavain's prized weapon against himself, and that enjoyment would be all the sweeter if the weapon still carried the name he had bestowed upon it. It would be a final humiliation, rich reward for all that he had done to her.

Yet, for all that she despised what he had done, she could not deny that she was adjusting to her new state of body in a way that might have alarmed her weeks earlier. Her armour was becoming her. She admired her form in the gleam of bulkheads and portals. The initial clumsiness was gone now, and in the privacy of her quarters she spent long hours amusing herself with astonishing tricks of strength, dexterity and prestidigitation. The armour was learning to anticipate her movements, freeing itself from any need to wait for signals to crawl up and down her spine. Skade played lightning-fast one-handed fugues on a holoclavier, her gauntleted fingers becoming a blur of metal as quick and lethal as threshing machinery. *Toccata in D,* by someone called Bach, collapsed under her mastery. It became a rapid blast of sound like Gatling-gun fire, requiring neural post-processing to separate it into anything resembling "music."

It was all a distraction, of course. Skade might have slipped through the Demarchists' final line of defences, but in the last three days she had become aware that her difficulties were not entirely at an end. There was something following her, coming out of the Yellowstone system on a very similar trajectory.

It was time, Skade decided, to share this news with Felka.

Nightshade was silent. Skade's footsteps were all she heard as she made her way down to the sleep bay. They rang hard and regular as hammers in a foundry. The ship was accelerating at two gees, the inertia-suppressing machinery running smooth and quiet, but walking for Skade was effortless.

Skade had frozen Felka shortly after news reached Skade of her most recent failure. At that point it had become clear, following scrutiny of news items around Yellowstone, that Clavain had eluded her again; that Remontoire and the pig had not succeeded in capturing him but had themselves fallen victim to local bandits. It would have been attractive at that point to assume that Clavain himself was dead, but she had made that mistake before and was not about to fall into the same error again. That was precisely why she had kept Felka back, as leverage to be used in any future negotiations with Clavain. She knew what he thought about Felka.

It wasn't true, but that didn't matter.

Skade had intended to return to the Mother Nest on completion of the mission, but the failure to kill Clavain forced her to reconsider. *Nightshade* was capable of continuing into interstellar space, and any minor technical issues could be dealt with on the way to Delta Pavonis. The Master of Works did not need her direct supervision to finish building the evacuation fleet either. Once the fleet was flight-ready and equipped with inertia-suppressing machinery, part of it would follow Skade towards the Resurgam system, while the rest would set off in a different direction, loaded with sleeping evacuees. A single crustbuster warhead would finish off the Mother Nest.

Skade would attempt to recover the weapons. If she failed on her first attempt, she would have only to wait for her backup fleet to arrive. Those were much larger starships and they could carry larger armaments than *Nightshade,* up to heavy relativistic railguns. Once she had obtained possession of the lost weapons, she would rendezvous with the rest of the evac fleet in a different system, in the opposite half of the sky from Delta Pavonis, as far away from the Inhibitor encroachment as they could get.

Then they would set off into even deeper space, many dozens, perhaps even hundreds of light-years into the galactic plane. It was time to say goodbye to local solar space. None of them were very likely to see it again.

The constellations will shift, Skade thought; not just by a few small degrees, but enough to wrench them out of shape. For the first time in history they would live under truly alien skies, uncomforted by the mythic shapes of their childhood, those chance alignments of stars which human consciousness had imprinted with meaning. And at the same time they would know those skies to be cruel, as infested with monsters as any enchanted forest.

She felt her weight shift, as if she had been on a sea vessel in a sudden squall. Skade steadied herself against the wall and established a link to Jastrusiak and Molenka, her two inertia-suppression systems experts.

Something up?

Molenka, the female of the two, responded to Skade's query. [Nothing, Skade. Just a small bubble instability. Nothing unexpected.]

I want to know if anything untoward happens, Molenka. We may need much more out of this equipment, and I want to have absolute confidence in it.

Now it was Jastrusiak's turn. [We have everything under control, Skade. The machinery is in a perfectly stable state-two condition. Small instabilities are damped back to the mean.]

Good. But try to keep those instabilities in check, will you?

Skade was about to add that they terrified her, but thought better of it. She must not reveal her fears to the others, not when so much depended on them accepting her leadership. It was difficult enough to make members of a hive mind submit to her will, and the one thing that would have undermined her control would have been the faintest hint of doubt in her own abilities.

There were no more irregularities in the field. Satisfied, Skade continued her journey to the sleeper bay.

Only two of the reefersleep caskets were occupied. Skade

had instigated Felka's wake-up cycle six hours earlier. Now the nearer of the two caskets was easing open, exposing Felka's unconscious form. Skade softened her approach to the casket, crouching down on her metal haunches until she was level with Felka. The casket's diagnostic aura told her that Felka was merely sleeping now, in a mild REM state. Skade observed the tremble of her eyelids and placed a steel hand on to Felka's forearm. She squeezed gently, and Felka moaned and shifted.

Felka. Felka. Wake up now.

Felka came around slowly. Skade waited patiently, doting on Felka with something close to affection.

Felka. Understand me. You are coming out of reefersleep. You have been frozen for six weeks. You will feel discomfort and disorientation, but it will fade. You have nothing to fear.

Felka opened her eyes to a pained squint, affronted even by the dim blue lighting of the sleep bay. She moaned again and tried to get out of the casket, but the effort was too much for her, especially under two gees.

Easy.

Felka mumbled and slurred a series of sounds, over and over, until they formed recognisable words. "Where am I?"

Aboard Nightshade. *You remember, don't you? We went after Clavain, into the inner system.*

"Clavain . . . " She said nothing more for ten or fifteen seconds, before adding, "Dead?"

I don't think so, no.

Felka succeeded in opening her eyes a little wider. "Tell me . . . what happened."

Clavain fooled us with the corvette. He made it to the Rust Belt. You remember that much, I think. Remontoire and Scorpio went in after him. No one else could go—they were the only ones who stood a chance of moving covertly through Yellowstone space. I wouldn't let you go, for obvious reasons. Clavain cares about you, Felka, and that makes you valuable to me.

"Hostage?"

No, of course not. Merely one of us. Clavain is the lamb that has left the fold, not you. Clavain is the one we want back, Felka. Clavain is the prodigal son.

They went to *Nightshade*'s flight deck. Felka sipped a chocolate-flavoured broth laced with restorative medichines.

"Where are we?" she asked.

Skade showed Felka a display of the rear starfield, with one dim yellow-red star outlined in green. That was Epsilon Eridani, two hundred times fainter than it had been even from the remote vantage point of the Mother Nest. It was now ten million times fainter than the sun that burned in Yellowstone's sky. They were truly in interstellar space now, for the first time in Skade's life.

Six weeks out from Yellowstone, over thirteen hundred AU. We've been maintaining two gees for most of that time, which means that we've already reached one-quarter light-speed. A conventional ship would be struggling to reach an eighth of the speed of light by now, Felka. But we can do better than this if we have to.

Which was true, Skade knew, but there would be little practical advantage in accelerating harder. Relativity ensured that. Arbitrarily high acceleration would compress the subjective duration of their journey to Resurgam, but it would make almost no difference to the *objective* time that the journey consumed. And it was that objective time which was the only relevant factor in the wider picture: it would still take the same amount of time to reach Resurgam as measured by external observers, and more decades still to rendezvous with the other elements of the exodus fleet.

Still, there were other reasons to consider an increase in acceleration. And at the back of Skade's mind was a dangerous and alluring possibility that would change the rules entirely.

"And the other ship?" Felka asked. "Where is that?"

Skade had already told her about the vessel behind them. Now a second circle bisected by two cross hairs appeared on the display almost exactly centred above the one that demarked Epsilon Eridani.

That's it. It's very faint, but there's a clear tau-neutrino source there, and it's moving on the same course as us.

"But a long way behind," Felka said.

Yes. Three or four weeks behind us, easily.

"It could be a commercial ship, Ultras or something, on a similar heading."

Skade nodded. *I've considered that possibility, but I don't find it likely. Resurgam isn't a very popular destination for Ultras, and if that ship were headed for another colony in the same part of the sky, we'd have seen lateral motion by now. We haven't—she's dead on our tail, Felka.*

"A stern chase."

Yes, deliberately following us. They have a modest tactical advantage, you see. Our flame points towards them; theirs points away from us. I can track them because we have military-grade neutrino detectors, but it is still difficult. But they need no finesse to spot us. I have separated our thrust beams into four components and given them a small angular offset, but they need only detect a tiny amount of leaked radiation to fix our position. We are neutrino-quiet, however, and that will give us a definitive advantage after turnover, when we have to point our flame towards Resurgam. But it won't come to that. That ship can't ever catch us, no matter how hard it tries.

"The ship should be falling behind already," Felka said. "Is ti?"

No. So far she has maintained two gees all the way out from the Rust Belt.

"I didn't think normal ships could accelerate that hard."

They can't, not usually. But there are methods, Felka. Do you know the story of Irravel Veda?

"Of course," Felka said.

When she was pursuing Run Seven she modified her own ship to manage two gees. But she did it the crude way—not by improving the efficacy of her Conjoiner drives, but by stripping her ship down to a skeleton. She left all her passengers behind on a comet to save mass.

"And you think that other ship must be doing something similar?"

There's no other explanation. But it won't help them. Even at two gees they cannot close the gap between us, and the gap will widen if we increase our inertia-suppression effect. They cannot match three gees, Felka; there is only so much mass you can strip out of a ship before you haven't got a ship at all. They must be very near the limit already.

"It must be Clavain," she said.

You seem very certain.

"I never thought he'd give up, Skade. It just isn't his style. He wants those weapons very badly, and he isn't going to let you get your cold steel hands on them without a fight."

Skade wanted to shrug, but her armour would not allow it.

Then it confirms what I have always suspected, Felka. Clavain is not a rationalist. He is a man fond of gestures, no matter how futile or stupid they might be. This is merely his grandest and most hopeless gesture to date.

Clavain ran into the first of Skade's traps eight hundred AU from Yellowstone, one hundred light-hours into the crossing. Clavain had been expecting her to try something; he would, in fact, have been disappointed and a little alarmed had she not. But Skade had not let him down.

Nightshade had sown mines behind it. Over a period of weeks, Skade had dropped them from her ship's stern: small, automated, highly autonomous drones stealthed for maximum invisibility against Clavain's forward-looking sensors. The drones were small enough that Skade could afford to manufacture and deploy them by the hundreds, littering Clavain's forward path with hidden obstacles.

The drones did not have to be very clever or have great range. Skade could be quite certain of the trajectory that Clavain would be obliged to follow, just as he could be quite certain of hers. Even a small deviation away from the direct line between Epsilon Eridani and Delta Pavonis would cost Clavain precious weeks, further delaying his arrival. He was already lagging behind, and would not wish to incur any further hold-ups if he could help it. So Skade would have known that Clavain would remain on the same heading except for short-term deviations.

That still meant she had a lot of space to cover. Explosions were not an efficient means of inflicting harm on space vessels at anything other than extreme close range, since vacuum did not propagate shock waves. Skade would know that the odds of one of her mines coming within a thousand kilometres of Clavain's ship were so small as to be negligible, so there would be no point putting crustbuster-class warheads in them. Clavain expected, instead, that the mines would be designed to identify and fire at his ship across a typical range of light-seconds. They would be single-use launchers, particle beams, very probably. It was exactly what he would have done if he were being chased by a similar ship.

But Skade had used crustbusters. She had inserted them, so far as Clavain could judge, into every twentieth mine, with a statistical bias towards the edge of her swarm. The warheads were primed to detonate as soon as he came within one light-hour of them, as near as he could tell. There would be a distant prick of hard blue light, shading into violet, red-shifted from Clavain's rest frame by a few hundred kilometres per second. And then, hours or tens of hours later, another would detonate, sometimes two or three in close succession, stammering out of the night like a cascade of fireworks. Some were closer than others, but they were all much too distant to do any harm to Clavain's ship. Clavain ran a regression analysis on the spread pattern and concluded that Skade's bombs had only a one in one thousand chance of damaging his ship. The chances of a destructive strike were a factor of one hundred less favourable. Clearly, they were not meant for that purpose.

Skade, he realised, was using the crustbusters purely to increase the targeting accuracy of her other weapons, flooding Clavain's ship with strobelike flashes which nailed its instantaneous position and velocity. Her other mines would be sniffing space for the backscatter of reflected photons from his own hull. It was a way of compensating for the fact that Skade's mines were too small to carry neutrino detectors, and were therefore reliant on outdated positional estimates transmitted back from *Nightshade,* many light-hours further into interstellar space. The crustbusters smoked Clavain's ship out of darkness, allowing Skade's directed-energy weapons to latch on to it. Clavain did not see the beams of those weapons, only the flash of their triggering explosions. The yields were about one hundredth of a crustbuster burst, which was sufficient to power a particle beam or graser with a five-light-second extreme kill range. If the beam missed him, he never saw it at all. In interstellar space there were so few ambient dust grains that even a beam passing within kilometres of Clavain's ship would suffer insufficient scattering to reveal itself. Clavain was a blind and deaf man stumbling across no man's land, oblivious to the bullets zipping past him, not even feeling the wind of their passage.

The irony was, he probably wouldn't even know it if a beam hit.

Clavain evolved a strategy that he hoped might work. If Skade's weapons were firing across typical distances of five light-seconds, they were dependent on positional estimates that were *at least* ten seconds out of date, and probably more like thirty seconds. The targeting algorithms would be extrapolating his course, bracketing his likely future position with a spread of less likely estimates. But thirty seconds gave Clavain enough of an edge to make that strategy enormously inefficient for Skade. In thirty seconds, under a steady two gees of thrust, a ship changed its relative position by nine kilometres, more than twice its hull length. Yet if Clavain stuttered the thrust randomly, Skade would not know for sure where in that nine-kilometre box to direct her weapons. She would have to assign more resources to obtain the same probability of a kill. It was a numbers game, not a guaranteed method of avoiding being killed, but Clavain had been a soldier long enough to know that this was, ultimately, what most combat situations boiled down to.

It appeared to work. A week passed, and then another, and then the smaller bursts of the particle beams ceased. There remained only the occasional, much more distant flash of a crust-buster. She was keeping her eye on him, but for now she had abandoned the idea of taking him out with anything as simple as a particle beam.

Clavain remained watchful and nervous. He knew Skade.

She wouldn't give up that easily.

He was right. Two months later a fifth of the army were dead, with many more injured and likely to die in the weeks ahead. The first hint of trouble had been innocuous indeed: a tiny change in the pattern of light that they were detecting from *Nightshade*. It seemed impossible that such a trifling change could have any impact on their own ship, but Clavain knew that Skade would do nothing without excellent reason. So once the change had been verified and shown to be deliberate, he assembled his senior crew on the bridge of the stolen lighthugger.

The ship—Scorpio had named her *Zodiacal Light,* for obscure reasons of his own—was a typical trade lighthugger, manufactured more than two hundred years earlier. The ship had been through several cycles of repair and redesign in the intervening time, but the core of the vessel remained mostly unchanged. At four kilometres long the lighthugger was much larger than *Nightshade,* her hull voided by cavernous cargo bays large enough to swallow a flotilla of medium-sized spacecraft. The hull itself was approximately conic, tapering to a needle-sharp prow in the direction of flight, with a blunter tail to stern. Two interstellar drives were attached to the hull via flanged spars flung out from the cone's widest point. The drives were barnacled with two centuries' worth of later accretions, but the basic shape of Conjoiner technology was evident beneath the growth layers. The rest of the hull had the dark smoothness of wet marble, except for the prow, which was cased in a matrix of ablative ice sewn through with hyperdiamond filaments. As H had said, the ship itself was essentially sound; it was the former crew's business methods that had made them insolvent. The army of pigs, trained not to harm anything irreplaceable, had succeeded in minimising damage during the capture itself.

The bridge was a third of the way back from the prow, one point three five kilometres of vertical distance when the ship was accelerating. Most of the technology in it—indeed, most of the technology aboard the ship—was ancient, both in feel and function. Nothing about that surprised Clavain: Ultras were notoriously conservative, and it was precisely because they hadn't adopted nano-technologies to any great degree that they continued to play a role in these post-plague days. There were general-purpose manufactories in the belly of the ship, now running full-time on weapons production, with no capacity to be spared to upgrade the fabric and infrastructure of *Zodiacal Light*. It had not taken Clavain very long to settle into the museumlike ambience of the huge old ship; he knew such robustness would serve them well in any battle against Triumvir Volyova.

The bridge itself was a spherical chamber within a gimballed arrangement that permitted it to swivel according to whether the ship was under thrust or rotating. The walls were quilted with projection systems, showing exterior views of the ship captured by drones, tactical representations of the immediate volume of space and simulations of various approach strategies for the arrival in the Resurgam system. Other parts of the walls were filled with scrolling text in old-fashioned Norte script, a steady litany of shipboard faults and the automatic systems that were triggered to fix them.

A railinged, circular dais made of grilled red metal held seats, display and control systems. The dais could accommodate about twenty people before it became uncomfortable; Clavain judged that it was somewhere near its maximum capacity right now. Scorpio was there, of course, with Lasher, Shadow, Blood and Cruz: three of his pig deputies and a one-eyed human woman from the same criminal underworld. Antoinette Bax and Xavier Liu, filthy from hastily abandoned repairwork, sat near the back, and the rest of the dais was taken up by a broad mixture of pigs and baseline humans, many of who had come directly from the Château's employment. They were experts in the technology H had pieced together and, like Scorpio and his associates, had been convinced that they were better off joining Clavain's expedition than staying behind in Chasm City or the Rust Belt. Even Pauline Sukhoi was there, ready to return to the work that had wrenched askew her personal reality. To Clavain she looked like a woman who had just stumbled out of a haunted house.

"There's been a development," Clavain said when he had their attention. "I don't quite know what to make of it."

A cylindrical display tank, an antique imaging system, sat in the middle of the dais. The interior of the tank contained a single transparent blade of helical profile that could be rotated at great speed. Coloured lasers buried in the base of the tank pulsed beams of light upwards, where they were intercepted by the moving surface of the blade.

A perfectly flat square of light appeared in the tank, rotating slowly to bring itself into view of all those on the bridge. "This is a two-dimensional image of the sky ahead of us," Clavain said. "Already there are strong relativistic effects: the stars shifted out of their usual positions, and their spectra shifted into the blue. Hot stars appear dimmer, since they were already emitting most of their flux in the UV. Dwarf stars pop out of nowhere, since we're suddenly seeing IR flux that used to be invisible. But it isn't the stars I'm interested in today." He pointed to the middle of the square, to one dim, starlike object. "This thing here, which looks like a star as well, is the exhaust signature from Skade's lighthugger. She's done her best to make her drive invisible, but we're still seeing enough stray photons from *Nightshade* to maintain a fix."

"Can you estimate her thrust output?" Sukhoi asked.

Clavain nodded. "Yes. The temperature of her flame says she's running her drive at nominal thrust—that would give her a gee of acceleration, for a typical million-tonne ship. *Nightshade*'s engines are smaller, but she's also a small ship by lighthugger standards. It shouldn't make that much difference, yet she's managing two gees, and she's occasionally pushed it to three. Like us, she has inertia-suppressing machinery. But I know she can push it much harder than this."

"We can't," Sukhoi said, turning paler than ever. "Quantum reality is a nest of snakes, Clavain, and we are already poking it with a very sharp stick."

Clavain smiled patiently. "Point taken, Pauline. But whatever Skade manages, we must find a way to do as well. That isn't what's troubling me, though. It's this." The wheeling images changed almost imperceptibly. Skade's signature became slightly brighter.

"She's thrusting harder, or she's changed her beam geometry," Antoinette said.

"No, that's what I thought, but the additional light is different. It's coherent, peaked sharply in the optical in Skade's rest frame."

"Laser light?" Lasher asked.

Clavain looked at the pig, Scorpio's most trusted ally. "So it would seem. High-power optical lasers, probably a battery of them, shining back along her line of flight. We're probably not seeing all the flux, either, just a fraction of it."

"What good will that do her?" Lasher said. He had a black scar on his face, slashed like a pencil line from brow to cheek. "She's much too far ahead of us for that to make any sense as a weapon."

"I know," Clavain said. "And that's what worries me. Because Skade won't do anything unless there's a good reason for it."

"This is an attempt to kill us?" the pig asked.

"We just have to figure out how she hopes to succeed," Clavain replied. "And then hope to hell that we can do something about it."

Nobody said anything. They stared at the slowly wheeling square of light, with the malign little star of *Nightshade* burning at its heart.

The government spokesman was a small, neat man with fastidiously well-maintained fingernails. He despised dirt or contamination of any sort, and when the prepared statement was handed to him—a folded piece of synthetic grey government vellum—

he took it between his thumb and forefinger only, achieving the minimum possible contact between skin and paper. Only when he was seated at his desk in Broadcasting House, one of the squat buildings adjoining Inquisition House, did he contemplate opening the statement, and then only when he had satisfied himself that there were no crumbs or grease spots on the table itself. He placed the paper on the desk, geometrically aligned with the table's edges, and then levered it open along its fold, slowly and evenly, in the manner of someone opening a box that might possibly contain a bomb. He employed his sleeve to encourage the paper to lie flat on the surface, stroking it across the text diagonally. Only when this process was complete did he lower his eyes and begin scanning the text for meaning, and then only so that he would be certain of making no mistakes when delivering it.

On the other side of the desk, the operator aimed the camera at him. The camera was a cantilevered boom with an old float-cam attached to the end of it. The float-cam's optical system still worked perfectly, but its levitation motors were long expired. Like many things in Cuvier, it was a taunting reminder of how much better things had been in the past. But the spokesman put such thoughts from his mind. It was not his duty to reflect on the present standard of living, and—if truth be told—he lived a comfortable enough existence by comparison with the majority. He had a surplus of food rations and he and his wife lived in a larger than average domicile in one of the better quarters of Cuvier.

"Ready, sir?" asked the camera operator.

He did not answer immediately, but scanned once more through the prepared text, his lips moving softly as he familiarised himself with the wording. He had no idea where the piece had originated, who had drafted and refined it or puzzled over the precise language. It was not his business to worry about such matters. He knew only that the machinery of government had functioned, as it always did, and that great, solid, well-oiled apparatus had delivered the text into his hands, for him to deliver to the people. He read the piece once more, and then looked up at the operator.

"Yes," he said. "I believe we are ready now."

"We can run through it again if you're not happy with the first reading. This isn't going out live."

"I believe one take should suffice."

"Right you are, then . . . "

The spokesman cleared his throat, feeling a spasm of inner revulsion at the thought of the phlegm being dislodged and resettled by that particular bodily action. He began to read.

"The Democratic Government of Cuvier wishes to make the following statement. One week ago the fugitive known as Thorn was successfully apprehended following a combined operation involving Inquisition House and the Bureau of Counter-Terrorism. Thorn is now in custody and no longer poses a threat to the law-abiding citizens of Cuvier or its satellite communities. Once again, the Democratic Government of Cuvier refutes in the strongest possible terms those irresponsible rumours that have been circulated by misguided sympathisers of the fugitive Thorn. There is no evidence that the colony itself is in imminent danger of destruction. There is no evidence for the existence of a pair of intact shuttles with surface-to-orbit capability. There is no evidence that covert evacuation camps have already been established, nor is there evidence that there have already been mass migrations from any of the major population centres towards these fictitious camps. There is, furthermore, absolutely no evidence that the Triumvir's starship has been located, and no evidence that it is capable of evacuating the entire populace of Resurgam."

The spokesman paused, re-establishing eye contact with the camera. "Only twenty-six hours ago, Thorn himself publicly criticised his own complicity in the spreading of these rumours. He has denounced those who have assisted in the spreading of these malicious untruths, and has sought the government's forgiveness for any inconvenience that may have been caused by his participation in these acts."

The spokesman's face betrayed not a hint of inner dissonance as he read these words. It was true that on his first scan through the text he had racked his own memory at that part and failed to come up with any recollection of Thorn making any kind of public statement, let alone a public criticism of his own activities. But such things were not unknown, and it was entirely possible that he had missed the appearance in question.

He soldiered on, changing his tone. "On a related matter . . . recent studies released by the Mantell Scientific Institute have led to a reassessment of the likely nature of the object visible in the evening sky. It is now thought less likely that the object in question is cometary in nature. A more probable explanation is that the object is related to the system's largest gas giant. The Democratic Government of Cuvier, however, strongly refutes any suggestion that the planet itself has been, or is in the process of being, destroyed. Any rumours to this effect are malicious in origin and are to be condemned in the strongest possible terms."

He paused again and allowed the tiniest trace of a smile to ghost his lips. "And that concludes this statement from the Democratic Government of Cuvier."

Aboard *Nostalgia for Infinity,* with no great enjoyment, Ilia Volyova smoked to a stub one of the cigarettes the ship had furnished her with. She was thinking, and thinking furiously, her mind humming like an overworked turbine room. Her booted feet squelched through secreted ship slime that had the precise consistency of mucus. She had a mild headache, which was not in any way alleviated by the constant drone of the bilge pumps. And yet she was in one sense elated, for she could finally see a clear course of action before her.

"It's so good that you've decided to talk to me, Captain," she said. "You can't believe what it means after all this time."

His voice emerged from all around her, simultaneously near and distant, immense and ageless as a God's. "I'm sorry it took so long."

She felt the entire fabric of the ship tremble with each syllable. "Do you mind if I ask why it took quite as long as it did, Captain?"

His answers, when they came, were seldom immediate. Volyova had the impression that the marshalling of his thoughts took time; that with immense size had come immense slowness, so that his dealings with her did not really represent the true rate of his thought processes.

"There were things I had to come to terms with, Ilia."

"What things, Captain?"

Another almighty pause. This was not the first conversation they had enjoyed since the Captain had resumed communications. During the first few hesitant exchanges, Volyova had feared that the silences signalled the Captain's withdrawal into another protracted state of catatonia. The withdrawals had appeared less severe than before—normal shipboard functions had continued—but she had still feared the tremendous setback that those silences could mean. Months, perhaps, before he could be coaxed back into communication. But it had never been that bad. The silences merely indicated periods of reflection, the time it took for signals to rattle back and forth through the enormous synaptic fabric of the transformed ship and then assembled into thoughts. The Captain appeared infinitely more willing to discuss those subjects that had previously been out of bounds.

"The things I did, Ilia. The crimes I committed."

"We've all committed crimes, Captain."

"Mine were exceptional."

Yes, she thought: there was no denying that. With the unwitting collusion of alien co-conspirators, the Pattern Jugglers, the Captain had committed a grievous act against another member of his crew. He had employed the Jugglers to imprint his own consciousness into another man's head, invading his skull: a personality transfer infinitely more effective than anything that could be achieved by technological means. And so for many years of shiptime he had existed as two men, one of whom was slowly succumbing to the infection of the Melding Plague.

Because his crime was so vile he had been forced to hide it from the other members of the crew. It had only come to light during the climactic events around the neutron star, the very events that had led to the Captain being allowed to engulf and transform his own ship. Volyova had forced that fate upon him as a kind of punishment, though it would have been equally easy for her to kill him. She had also done it because she hoped it might increase her own chances of survival. The ship had already been under the control of one hostile agent—the plague—and having the Captain take over instead had struck her as the marginally lesser of two evils. It was not, she would readily admit, a decision she had subjected to a great deal of analysis at the time.

"I know what you did," she said. "And you know that I abhor it. But you have suffered for it, Captain; no one would deny that. It's time to put it behind us and move on, I think."

"I feel tremendous guilt for what I did."

"And I feel tremendous guilt for what I did to the gunnery

officer. I'm as much to blame for any of this as you, Captain. If I hadn't driven him mad, I doubt that any of this would have happened."

"I'd still have my crime to live with."

"It was a long time ago. You were frightened. What you did was terrible, but it was not the work of a rational man. That doesn't make it excusable, but it does make it a little easier to understand. Were I in your situation, Captain—barely human, and perhaps infected with something I *knew* was going to kill me, or worse—I can't say for sure that I wouldn't consider something just as extreme."

"You would never murder, Ilia. You are better than that."

"They think of me as a war criminal on Resurgam, Captain. Sometimes I wonder if they are right, you know. What if we *did* destroy Phoenix after all?"

"You didn't."

"I hope not."

There was another long pause. She walked on through the slime, noting how the texture and colour of the secreted matter was never quite the same from district to district of the ship. Left to its own devices, the ship would be engulfed by the slime in a few short months. She wondered if that would help or hinder the Captain, and hoped that it was an experiment she would never see performed.

"What exactly do you want, Ilia?"

"The weapons, Captain. Ultimately, you control them. I've attempted to work them myself, but it wasn't a roaring success. They're too thoroughly integrated into the old gunnery weapons network."

"I don't like the weapons, Ilia."

"I don't either, but now I think we need them. You have sensors, Captain. You've seen what we've seen. I showed you when the rocky worlds were dismantled. That was only the start."

After another worrying silence, he said, "I've seen what they've done to the gas giant."

"Then you'll also have seen that something new is taking shape, assembling in the cloud of liberated matter from the giant. It's sketchy at the moment, no more fully formed than a foetus. But it is clearly deliberate. It is something vast, Captain, vaster than anything in our experience. Thousands of kilometres across, even now, and it may become larger still as it grows."

"I have seen it."

"I don't know what it is, or what it will do. But I can guess. The Inhibitors are going to do something to the sun, to Delta Pavonis. Something terminal. We're not just talking about triggering a major flare now. This is going to be much bigger than any mass ejection we've ever heard of."

"What kind of weapon can kill a sun?"

"I don't know, Captain. I don't know." She drew hard on the butt of the cigarette, but it was well and truly dead. "That isn't, however, my primary concern at the moment. I'm more interested in another question. What kind of weapon can kill a weapon like that?"

"You think the cache may suffice?"

"One of those thirty-three horrors ought to do the trick, don't you think?"

"You want my assistance," the Captain said.

Volyova nodded. She had reached the critical point in the conversation now. If she got through this bit without triggering a catatonic shutdown, she would have made significant progress in her dealings with Captain John Brannigan.

"Something like that," she said. "You control the cache, after all. I've done my best, but I can't make it do much without your co-operation."

"It would be very dangerous, Ilia. We're safe now. We haven't done anything to provoke the Inhibitors. Using the cache . . . even a single weapon from the cache . . . " The Captain trailed off. There was absolutely no need to labour the point.

"It's a bit on the risky side, I know."

"A bit on the risky side?" The Captain's chuckle of amusement was like a small earthquake. "You were always one for understatement, Ilia."

"Well. Are you going to help me or not, Captain?"

After a glacial intermission he said, "I'll give it quite some thought, Ilia. I'll give it quite some thought."

That, she supposed, had to count as progress.

TWENTY-SIX

There was almost no warning of Skade's strike. For weeks Clavain had expected something, but there had been no guessing the exact nature of the attack. His own knowledge of *Nightshade* was useless: with the manufactories aboard a military lighthugger, Skade could weave new weapons almost as quickly as she could imagine them, tailoring each to the flexing demands of battle. Like a crazed toymaker, she could spin the darkest of fabulations into existence in mere hours, and then unleash them against her enemy.

Zodiacal Light had reached half the speed of light. Relativistic effects were now impossible to ignore. For every hundred minutes that passed on Yellowstone, eighty-six passed aboard Clavain's ship. That time-dilation effect would become steadily more acute as they nosed closer and closer to light-speed. It would compress the fifteen actual years of the journey into only four years of shiptime; still fewer if a higher rate of acceleration was used.

Yet half the speed of light was still not radically relativistic, especially when they were dealing with an enemy moving in almost the same accelerated frame. At their fastest, the mines that Skade had dropped behind her had slammed past *Zodiacal Light* with relative velocities of only a few thousand kilometres per second. It was fast only by the standards of solar war. Although the mines were difficult to detect until *Zodiacal Light* was within their "volume of denial," there was no danger of actually colliding with them. A direct collision would be a very effective way of taking out a starship, but Clavain's simulations argued that it was beyond Skade's capability to mount such an attack. His analyses showed that for any conceivable spread of obstacles that Skade dropped in her wake—even if she dismantled most of *Nightshade* to convert into mines—he could always detect the obstacles sufficiently far ahead to steer a path through them.

And yet there was a terrible flaw in Clavain's thinking, and in the thinking of all his advisors.

The obstacle, when *Zodiacal Light*'s forward sensors detected it, was moving much faster towards him than Clavain had expected. Relativity distorted classical expectations in a way that Clavain still did not find entirely intuitive. Slam two objects towards each other, each with individual velocities just below light-speed, and the classical result for their closing velocity would be the sum of their individual speeds: just under twice the speed of light. Yet the true result, confirmed with numbing precision, was that the objects saw each other approach with a combined speed that was *still* just below the speed of light. Similarly, the relativistic closing velocity for two objects moving towards each other with individual speeds of one-half of light-speed was not light-speed itself, but eight-tenths of it. It was the way the universe was put together, and yet it was not something the human mind had evolved to accept.

The Doppler echo from the approaching obstacle indicated a closing speed of just above 0.8 c, which meant that Skade's obstacle was itself moving back towards Yellowstone at half the speed of light. And it was also astonishingly large: a circular structure one thousand kilometres from side to side. The mass sensor could not see it at all.

Had the object been on a direct collision course, nothing could have been done to avoid it. But the projected impact point was only a dozen kilometres from one edge of the oncoming obstacle. *Zodiacal Light*'s systems instigated an emergency collision-avoidance procedure.

That was what killed them, not the obstacle itself.

Zodiacal Light was forced to execute a five-gee swerve, with only seconds of warning. Those who were near seats were able to get into them and allow cushioning webs to engulf their bodies. Those who were near servitors were offered some protection by them. In certain parts of the ship, its structural fabric was able to deform to minimise injuries as bodies slammed into walls. But not all were that lucky. Those who were training in the larger bays were killed by the impact. Machinery that had not been adequately secured killed others, including Shadow and two of his senior platoon leaders. Most of the pigs who had been working outside on the hull, preparing attachment points for future armaments, were swept into interstellar space; none were recovered.

The damage to the ship was equally grave. It had never been designed for such a violent course correction, and the hull suffered many fractures and fatigue points, particularly along the attachment spars that held the Conjoiner motors. By Clavain's estimate there was at least a year's worth of repairs to be done merely to get back to where they had been before the attack. Interior damage had been just as bad. Even *Storm Bird* had been harmed as it strained against its scaffolding, all of Xavier's work undone in a moment.

But, Clavain reminded himself, it could have been so much worse. They had not actually hit Skade's obstacle. If they had, the dissipation of relativistically boosted kinetic energy would almost certainly have ripped his ship apart in an eyeblink.

They had almost hit a light-sail, possibly one of many hundreds that Skade had dropped behind her. The sails were probably close to being monolayers: films of matter stretched to a thickness of one atom, but with artificially boosted inter-atomic rigidity. The sails must have been unfurled when they were some distance behind *Nightshade,* so that its exhaust would not incinerate them. Probably they had been spun up for additional rigidity.

Then she had trained her lasers on them. That was why they had seen coherent light emanating from *Nightshade*. The photon pressure from the lasers had rammed against the sails, pushing them back, decelerating them at hundreds of gees until they were moving only slowly in the local stellar rest frame. But the tightly focused lasers had kept pushing, accelerating and kicking the sails back towards Clavain. Skade's positional fix was sufficiently good that the sails could be aimed directly at *Zodiacal Light*.

It was, as ever, a numbers game. God only knew how many sails they had nearly collided with, until one appeared directly in front of them. Perhaps Skade's gambit had never had a high probability of success, but knowing her the odds would not have been too bad.

There were, Clavain was certain, many other sails out there.

Even when the worst of the damage was being repaired, Clavain and his cohort of experts were devising a counter-strategy. Simulations showed that it should be possible to blast their way through an incoming sail, opening an aperture large enough to fly through, but only if the sails were detected further out than was currently possible. They would also need something to blast with, but the program to install hull weapons had been one of those hampered by Skade's attack. The short-term solution was for a shuttle to fly one hundred thousand kilometres ahead of *Zodiacal Light,* serving as a buffer against any further sail strikes. The shuttle was uncrewed, stripped down to little more than an unpressurised shell. Periodically it had to be refuelled with antimatter from the other craft parked in the lighthugger's spacecraft hold, which necessitated an energy-costly round-trip with another ship, including a hazardous fuel transfer operation. *Zodiacal Light* needed no antimatter herself, but it was essential to conserve some for operations around Delta Pavonis. Clavain was only prepared to use half of his reserve supplying the buffer shuttle, which gave them one hundred days to find a longer-term solution.

In the end the answer was obvious: a single sail could kill a starship, but it would only take another sail to kill a sail. *Zodiacal Light*'s own manufactories could be programed to make light-sails—the process did not require complex nanotechnology—and they did not need to be anywhere near as large as Skade's, nor manufactured in any great number. The ship's anti-collision lasers, never sufficiently effective as weapons, could be easily tuned to provide the necessary photon pressure. Skade's sails had to be pushed at hundreds of gees; Clavain's only had to be pushed at two.

They called it the shield sail. It was ready in ninety-five days, with a reserve of sails ready to be pushed out and deployed should the first be destroyed. In any case, the sails had a fixed lifetime due to the steady ablation caused by interstellar dust grains. This only became worse as *Zodiacal Light* climbed closer and closer to light-speed. But they could keep replacing the sails all the way to Resurgam and they would only have expended one per cent of the ship's total mass.

When the shield sail was in place, Clavain allowed himself to breathe again. He had the feeling that Skade and he were making up the rules of interstellar combat as they went on. Skade had won one round by killing a fifth of his crew, but he had responded with a counter-strategy that rendered her current strategy obsolete. She was undoubtedly watching him, puzzling over a smudge of photons far to her stern. Very probably Skade would figure out what he had done from that sparse data alone, even if she had not sewn high-resolution imaging drones along her flight path, designed to capture images of his ship. And then, Clavain knew, Skade would try something else, something different and currently unguessable.

He would just have to be ready for her, and hope that he still had some luck on his side.

Skade, Molenka and Jastrusiak, the two inertia-suppression systems experts, were deep in *Nightshade*'s bowels, well into the bubble of suppressed inertia. Skade's armour coped well with the physiological changes, but even she had to admit that she did not feel entirely normal. Her thoughts shifted and coalesced with frightening speed, like clouds in a speeded-up film. She flickered between moods she had never known before, terror and elation revealed as opposed facets of the same hidden emotion. It was not just the effect of the armour's blood chemistry, although that was considerable, but the field itself, playing subtle games with the normal ebb and flow of neurochemicals and synaptic signals.

Molenka's concern was obvious. [Three gees? Are you certain?]

I wouldn't have ordered it otherwise.

The curved black walls of the machinery folded around them, as if they were crouched inside a cavern carved into smooth and surreal shapes by patient aeons of subterranean water. She sensed the tech's disquiet. The machinery was in a stable regime now, and she saw no reason to tamper with it.

[Why?] Molenka persisted. [Clavain can't reach you. He might have squeezed two gees out of his own ship, but that must have been at enormous expense, shedding every gram of nonessential mass. He's far behind, Skade. He can't catch you up.]

Then increase to three gees. I want to observe his reaction to see if he attempts to match our new rate of acceleration.

[He won't be able to.]

Skade reached up with one steel hand and caressed Molenka under the chin with her forefinger. She could crush her now, shattering bone into fine grey dust, if she dared.

Just do it. Then I'll know for certain, won't I?

* * *

Molenka and Jastrusiak were not happy, of course, but she had expected nothing less. Their protestations were a form of ritual that had to be endured. Later, Skade felt the acceleration load increase to three gees and knew that they had acquiesced. Her eyeballs sagged in their sockets, her jaw feeling like solid iron. It was no more of an effort to walk since the armour took care of that, but she was aware now of how unnatural it was.

She walked to Felka's quarters, heels pounding the floor with jackhammer precision. Skade did not hate Felka, nor even blame her for hating her back. Felka could hardly be expected to endure Skade's attempts to kill Clavain. Equally, however, Felka had to see the necessity of Skade's actions. No other faction could be allowed to obtain the lost weapons. It was a matter of Conjoiner survival, a matter of loyalty to the Mother Nest. Skade could not tell Felka about the governing voices that told her what to do, but even without that information she must see that the mission was vital.

The door to Felka's quarters was shut, but Skade had the authority to enter any part of the ship. She knocked politely nonetheless, and waited five or six seconds before entering.

Felka. What are you doing?

Felka was on the floor, sitting down cross-legged. She appeared calm, nothing in her composure betraying the increased effort of performing virtually any activity under three gees. She wore thin black pyjamas that made her look very pale and childlike to Skade.

She had surrounded herself with small white rectangles, many dozens of them, each of which was marked with a particular set of symbols. Skade saw reds and blacks and yellows. The rectangles were something she had encountered before, but she could not remember where. They were arrayed in excessively neat arcs and spokes, radiating out from Felka. Felka was moving them from place to place, as if exploring the permutations of some immense abstract structure.

Skade bent down, picking up one of the rectangles. It was a piece of glossy white card or plastic, printed on one side only. The other side was perfectly blank.

I recognise these. It's a game they play in Chasm City. There are fifty-two cards in a set, thirteen cards for each symbol, just as there are thirteen hours on a Yellowstone clock face.

Skade put the card back where she had found it. Felka continued rearranging the cards for some minutes. Skade waited, listening to the slick sound that the cards made as they passed across each other.

"Its origins are a bit older than that," Felka said.

But I'm right, aren't I? They do play this there.

"There are many games, Skade. This is just one of them."

Where did you find the cards?

"I had the ship make them. I remembered the numbers."

And the patterns? Skade selected another card, this one marked with a bearded figure. *This man looks like Clavain.*

"It's just a King," Felka said dismissively. "I remembered the patterns as well."

Skade examined another: a long-necked, regal-looking woman dressed in something that resembled ceremonial armour. *She could almost be me.*

"She's the Queen."

Why, Felka? What precisely is the point of this? Skade stood again and gestured at the configuration of cards. *The number of permutations must be finite. Your only opponent is blind chance. I don't see the attraction.*

"You probably wouldn't."

Again Skade heard the slick rasp of card on card. *What is the objective, Felka?*

"To maintain order."

Skade barked out a short laugh. *Then there is no end-state?*

"This isn't a problem in computation, Skade. The means *is* the end. The game has no halting state other than failure." Felka bit her tongue, like a child working on some particularly tortuous piece of colouring-in. In a flurry of movement she moved six cards, dramatically altering the larger pattern in a way Skade would have sworn was not possible a moment earlier.

Skade nodded, understanding. *This is the Great Wall of Mars, isn't it?*

Felka looked up, but said nothing before resuming her work.

Skade knew that she was right: that the game she saw Felka playing here, if indeed it could be called a game, was only a surrogate for the Wall itself. The Wall had been destroyed four hundred years earlier, and yet it had played such a vital part in Felka's childhood that she regressed towards her memories of it at the slightest sign of external stress.

Skade felt anger. She knelt down again and destroyed the pattern of cards. Felka froze, her hand hovering above the space where a card had been. She looked at Skade, incomprehension on her face.

As was sometimes the case with Felka, she framed her question as a flat, uninflected statement. "Why."

Listen to me, Felka. You must not do this. You are one of us now. You cannot retreat back into your childhood just because Clavain isn't here any more.

Pathetically, Felka tried to regather the cards. But Skade reached out and grabbed her hand.

No. Stop this, Felka. You cannot regress. I won't allow it. Skade tilted Felka's head towards her own. *This is about more than just Clavain, Felka. I know that he means something to you. But the Mother Nest means more. Clavain was always an outsider. But you are one of us, to the marrow. We need you, Felka. As you are now, not as you were.*

But when she released her hold, Felka only looked down. Skade stood up and backed away from the cross-legged figure. She had committed a cruel act, she knew. But it was no less than Clavain would have done, had he caught Felka retreating back into her childhood. The Wall was a mindless God to worship, and it sucked her soul into itself, even in memory.

Felka began to lay the cards back down again.

She pushed Galiana's casket through the empty warrens of *Nightshade*. Her armour moved in measured, funereal steps, one cautious pace at a time. With each clangorous footfall, Skade heard the whining of gyroscopes struggling to maintain balance under the new acceleration. The weight of her own skull was a cruel compressive force squeezing down on the upper vertebrae of her truncated spine. Her tongue was an unresponsive mass of sluggish muscle. Her face looked different, the skin tugged down from her cheekbones as if by invisible guylines. Slight distortion of the visual field revealed the effect of the gravity on her eyeballs.

Only one-quarter of the ship's mass remained now. The rest was being suppressed by the field, the bubble of which had now swallowed up half the ship's length from the stern towards the midpoint.

They were sustaining four gees.

Skade seldom went into the bubble itself now: the physiological effects, even though buffered by the mechanisms of her armour, were simply too uncomfortable. The bubble lacked a sharply defined edge, but the effects of the field fell off so sharply that they were almost immeasurably small beyond the nominal boundary. The field geometry was not spherically symmetrical, either: there were occlusions and hairpins within it, ventricles and fissures where the effect dropped or rose in interplay with other variables. The strange topology of the machinery itself imposed its own structure on the field, too. When the machinery moved, as it was obliged to, the field changed as well. At other times it seemed to be the field that was making the machinery move. Her technicians only pretended that they understood all that was happening. What they had was a set of rules that told them what would happen under certain conditions. But those rules were valid only in a narrow range of states. They had been happy suppressing half of the ship's mass, but were much less so now. Occasionally, the delicate quantum-field instrumentation that the techs had positioned elsewhere in the ship registered excursions of the bubble as it momentarily swelled and contracted, engulfing the entire ship. Skade convinced herself that she felt those instants, even though they lasted much less than a microsecond. At two gees of suppression, the excursions had been rare. Now they happened three or four times a day.

Skade wheeled the casket into an elevator and rode downship, towards the bubble boundary. She could see the undercurve of Galiana's jaw through the casket's viewing window. Her expression was one of infinite calm and composure. Skade was very glad that she had had the presence of mind to bring Galiana with her, even when the mission's sole scope had been stopping Clavain. At the back of her mind even then she must have suspected that they might have to turn into interstellar space, and that at some point it would be necessary to seek Galiana's dangerous advice. It had cost her nothing to bring the woman's frozen corpse aboard; now all she needed was the nerve to consult it.

She propelled the casket into a clean white room. Behind her, the door sealed invisibly. The room was full of eggshell-pale machinery that was only truly visible when it moved. The machinery was ancient, lovingly and fearfully tended since the days of Galiana's earliest experiments on Mars. It had also cost Skade nothing to bring it with her aboard *Nightshade*.

Skade opened Galiana's casket. She elevated the corpse's core temperature by fifty millikelvin and then ushered the pale machinery into position. It swung and fluttered around Galiana, never quite touching her skin. Skade stepped back with a stiff whirr of servos. The pale machinery made her uneasy; it always had. There was something deeply unsettling about it, so much so that it had almost never been used. Even on those rare occasions when it had been used, it had done dreadful things to those who dared to open their minds to it.

Skade was not about to use the machinery to its fullest capability. Not yet. For now she wished merely to speak to the Wolf, and that required only a subset of the machinery's functionality, exploiting its extreme isolation and sensitivity, its ability to pluck and amplify the faintest of signals from a churning sea of neural chaos. She would not be attempting coherence coupling unless she had very good reason, and so there was no rational reason for the sense of disquiet Skade felt.

But Skade knew what the machinery could do, and that was enough.

Skade readied herself. The external indicators showed that Galiana had been warmed enough to wake the Wolf. The machinery was already picking up the familiar constellations of electrical and chemical activity that showed she was beginning to think again.

Skade closed her eyes. There was a moment of transition, a perceptual jolt followed by a disorientating sense of rotation. And then she was standing on a flat hard rock just large enough to accommodate her feet. The rock was one of many; they reached into mist all around her, positioned like stepping-stones in shallow grey water, linked by sharp, barnacled ridges. It was impossible to see more than fifteen or twenty metres in any direction. The air was cold and damp, scented with brine and the stench of something like rotting seaweed. Skade shivered and pulled her black gown tighter. Beneath it she was naked, her bare toes curling over the edge of the rock. Wet dark hair flicked against her eyes. She reached up and pushed it back from her brow. There was no crest on her scalp, and the absence of it made her inhale in sharp surprise. She was fully human again; the Wolf had restored her body. She heard, distantly, the crowdlike roar of ocean waves. The sky above her was a pale grey-green inseparable from the mist that reached to the ground. It made her feel nauseous.

The first fumbling attempts at communication between Skade and the Wolf had been through Galiana's mouth, which proved to be hopelessly one-dimensional and slow compared with mind-to-mind linkage. Since then, Skade had agreed to meet the Wolf in a rendered environment, a three-dimensional simulation in which she was fully participatory.

The Wolf chose it, not her. It wove a space that Skade was obliged to enter under the Wolf's strict terms. Skade could have overlaid this reality with something of her own choosing, but she feared that there might have been some nuance or detail that she was missing.

It was better to play the game according to the Wolf's rules, even if she felt in less than complete control of the situation. It was, Skade knew, a dangerously double-edged sword. She would have trusted nothing that the Wolf told her, but Galiana was in there as well, somewhere. And Galiana had learned much that might still be useful to the Mother Nest. The trick was to distinguish the Wolf from its host, which was why Skade had to be so attuned to the nuances of the environment. She never knew when Galiana might break through, if only for an instant.

I'm here. Where are you?

The tidal roar increased. The wind dragged a curtain of hair across her face. She felt precarious, surrounded by so many sharp-edged ridges. But without warning the mist opened up a little before her, and a mist-grey figure hovered into existence at the edge of vision. The figure was really no more than a suggestion of the human form; there were no details at all, and the mist continually thickened and thinned around it. It could just as easily have been a stump of weatherworn wood. But Skade felt its presence, and the presence was familiar. There was a frightening cold intelligence beaming out from the figure like a narrow searchlight. It was intelligence without consciousness; thought without emotion or any sense of self. Skade sensed only analysis and inference.

The distant roar of the tide shaped words. "What is it that you want of me now, Skade?"

The same thing . . .

"Use your voice."

She obeyed without question. "The same thing that I always want: advice."

The tide said, "Where are we, Skade?"

"I thought you decided that."

"That isn't what I meant. I mean, where exactly is her body?"

"Aboard a ship," Skade said. "In interstellar space, midway between Epsilon Eridani and Delta Pavonis." She wondered how the Wolf had been able to tell that they were no longer in the Mother Nest. Perhaps it had been a lucky guess, she told herself, with no real sense of conviction.

"Why?"

"You know why. The weapons are around Resurgam. We must recover them before the machines arrive."

The figure became momentarily clearer. For an instant there was a hint of snout, dark canine eyes and a lupine glint from steely incisors.

"You must appreciate that I have mixed feelings about such a mission."

Skade tugged her gown even tighter. "Why?"

"You already know why. Because that of which I am a part would be inconvenienced by the use of those weapons."

"I don't want a debate," Skade said, "just assistance. You have two choices, Wolf. Let the weapons fall into someone else's hands—someone you have no influence over—or help *me* to recover them. You see the logic, don't you? If any human faction has to obtain them, surely it had better be one you know, one you have already infiltrated."

Above, the sky became less opaque. A silver sun scoured through the pale green canopy. Light sparkled on the ridges linking the rockpools and stones, tracing a pattern that reminded Skade of the synaptic pathways revealed by a slice through brain tissue. Then the mist closed in again and she was colder than before, colder and more vulnerable.

"So what is the problem?"

"There's a ship behind me. It's been on my tail ever since we left Yellowstone space. We have inertia-suppression machinery, Wolf. Our inertial mass is twenty-five per cent at the moment. Yet the other ship is still playing catchup, as if it has the same technology aboard it."

"Who is operating this other ship?"

"Clavain," she said, watching the Wolf's reaction with great interest. "At least, I'm reasonably certain it must be him. I was trying to bring him back to the Mother Nest after he defected. He gave me the slip around Yellowstone. He got his hands on another ship, stealing it from the Ultras. But I don't know where he got the technology from."

The Wolf appeared troubled. It shifted in and out of the mist, its form contorting with each moment of clarity. "Have you tried killing him?"

"Yes, but I haven't managed it—he's very tenacious, Wolf. And he hasn't been deterred, which was my next hope."

"That's Clavain for you." Skade wondered whether that was the Wolf or Galiana speaking, or some incomprehensible fusion of the two. "Well, what did your precious Night Council suggest, Skade?"

"That I push the machinery harder."

The Wolf faded, returned. "And if Clavain continues to match you step for step . . . ? Have you considered what you might do then?"

"Don't be absurd."

"Fears must be faced, Skade. The unthinkable must be contemplated. There is a way to slip ahead of him, if only you have the nerve to do it."

"I won't do it. I don't know *how* to do it." Skade felt dizzy, on the point of toppling from the smooth platform of rock. The ridges looked sharp enough to cut her skin. "We know nothing about how the machinery operates in that regime."

"You can learn," the Wolf told her teasingly. "Exordium would show you what you needed to do, wouldn't it?"

"The more exotic the technology, the more difficult it is to interpret the messages describing it, Wolf."

"But I could help you."

Skade narrowed her eyes. "Help me?"

"In Exordium. Our minds are linked now, Skade. There's no reason why we couldn't continue to the next phase of the experiment. My mind could filter and process the Exordium information. With the clues we will receive, I could show you exactly what you need to do to make the state-four transition."

"It's that easy? You'd help me, just to make sure I get the weapons?"

"Of course." For a moment the Wolf's voice was playful. There was that flash of incisor again. "But of course, it wouldn't just be you and me."

"I'm sorry?"

"Bring Felka."

"No, Wolf . . . "

"Bring Felka, or I won't help you."

She started to argue, knowing how futile it would be; knowing that ultimately she had no choice but to do what the Wolf wished. The mist had closed in again. The analytic scrutiny of the Wolf's mind suddenly ceased, like a torch beam being switched off. Skade was quite alone. She shivered against the cold, hearing the long slow groan of the distant tide.

"No . . . "

The mist closed in further. The rockpool swallowed the stone beneath her feet, and then with the same perceptual twist she was back in the metal prison of her armour aboard *Nightshade*. The gravity was an oppressive crush. She traced a steel finger down the alloy curve of her thigh, remembering how flesh had felt, remembering the sense of cold and the porous texture of the rock beneath her feet. Skade felt the stirrings of unwanted emotions: loss, regret, horror, the aching memory of wholeness. But there were things that needed to be done that transcended such concerns. She crushed the emotions out of existence, preserving only the thinnest residue of anger.

That would help her, in the days that lay ahead.

TWENTY-SEVEN

On the rare occasions when he made any kind of ship-board journey at all, Clavain moved around *Zodiacal Light* in an exoskeletal support, constantly bruised and chafed by the pressure points of the framework. They were at five gees now, accelerating in close lock-step with *Nightshade,* which was now only three light-days ahead. Each time Skade had ramped up her acceleration, Clavain had persuaded Sukhoi to increase theirs to an even higher rate, and this, with no little reluctance, she had done. Little more than a week of shiptime later, Skade would be seen to respond with an increase of her own. The pattern was obvious: even Skade was unwilling to push the machinery any harder than was absolutely necessary.

Pauline Sukhoi did not use an exoskeletal rig herself. When she met with Clavain she did so in a form-fitting travelling couch in which she lay almost horizontally, on her back, labouring for breath between each utterance. Like much else on the ship the couch had a crudely welded makeshift look. The manufactories were running around the clock to make weapons, combat equipment, reefersleep caskets and spare parts; anything else had to be knocked together in less sophisticated workshops.

"Well?" Sukhoi asked, the force of the acceleration heightening her haunted appearance by pulling her skin deep into her eye sockets.

"I need seven gees," Clavain said. "Six and a half at the very least. Can you give it to me?"

"I've given you everything I can, Clavain."

"That's not quite the answer I wanted."

She threw a schematic against one wall, hard red lines against corroded brown metalwork. It was a cross section of the ship with a circle superimposed over the thickened midship and stern where the hull was widest and where the motors were attached.

"See this, Clavain?" Sukhoi made the circle flare brighter. "The bubble of suppressed inertia swallows most of our length now, which is enough to drop our effective mass to a fifth of what it should be. But we still feel the full force of that five gees *here,* in the front of the ship." She indicated the small cone of the hull, jutting forwards of the bubble's edge.

Clavain nodded. "The field's so weak here that you need fancy detectors to measure it at all."

"Correct. Our bodies, and the fabric of the ship around us, still have nearly their full quota of inertial mass. The floor of the ship pushes against us at five gees, so we feel five gees of force. But that's only because we're outside the bubble."

"What are you getting at?"

"This." Sukhoi altered the picture, making the circle expand until it enclosed the entire volume of the starship. "The field geometry is complex, Clavain, and it depends complicatedly on the degree of inertial suppression. At five gees, we can exclude the entire inhabited portion of the ship from the major effects of the machinery. But at six . . . it doesn't work. We fall within the bubble."

"But we're already effectively inside it," Clavain said.

"Yes, but not so much that we feel anything. At six gees, however, the field effects would rise above the threshold of physiological detectability. Sharply, too: it isn't a linear effect. We'd go from experiencing five gees to experiencing only one."

Clavain adjusted his position, trying to find a posture that would relieve one or more pressure points. "That doesn't sound too bad."

"But we'd also feel our inertial mass to be a fifth of what it should be. Every part of your body, every muscle, every organ, every bone, every fluid, has evolved under normal conditions of inertia. Everything changes, Clavain, even the viscosity of blood." Sukhoi steered her couch around him, collecting her breath. "I have seen what happens to people who fall into fields of extreme inertial suppression. Very often they die. Their hearts stop beating properly. There are other things that can happen to them, too, especially if the field isn't stable . . . " With effort, she looked him in the eye. "Which it won't be, I assure you."

Clavain said, "I still want it. Will routine machinery still work normally? Reefersleep caskets, that kind of thing?"

"I won't make any promises, but . . . "

He smiled. "Then this is what we do. We freeze Scorpio's army, or as many of them as we can manage, in the new caskets. Anybody who we can't freeze, or who we might need to consult, we can rig-up to a life-support system, enough to keep them breathing and pumping blood at the right rate. That will work, won't it?"

"Again, no promises."

"Six gees, Sukhoi. That's all I'm asking of you. You can do it, can't you?"

"I can. And I will, if you insist upon it. But understand this: the quantum vacuum is a nest of snakes . . . "

"And we're poking it with a very sharp stick, yes."

Sukhoi waited until he was done. "No. That was before. At

six gees we are down in the pit with the snakes, Clavain."

He let her have her moment, then patted the iron husk of the travel couch. "Just do it, Pauline. I'll worry about the analogies."

She spun the couch around and wheeled off towards the elevator that would ferry her downship. Clavain watched her go, then winced as another pressure sore announced itself.

The transmission came in a little while later. Clavain scrubbed it for buried informational attack, but it was clean.

It was from Skade, in person. He took it in his quarters, enjoying a brief respite from the high acceleration. Sukhoi's experts had to crawl over their inertial machinery and they did not like doing that while the systems were functional. Clavain sipped on tea while the recording played itself out.

Skade's head and shoulders appeared in an oval projection volume, blurred at the edges. Clavain remembered the last time he had seen her like this, when she had transmitted a message to him when he was still on his way to Yellowstone. He had assumed at the time that Skade's stiff posture was a function of the message format, but now that he saw it again he began to have doubts. Her head was immobile while she spoke, as if clamped in the kind of frame surgeons used when making precise operations on the brain. Her neck vanished into absurd gloss-black armour, like something from the Middle Ages. And there was something else strange about Skade, although he could not quite put his finger on it . . .

"Clavain," she said. "Please do me the courtesy of viewing this transmission in its entirety and giving careful consideration to what I am about to propose. I do not make this offer lightly, and I will not make it twice."

He waited for her to continue.

"You have proven difficult to kill," Skade said. "All my attempts have failed so far, and there is no assurance that anything I try in the future will work either. That doesn't mean I expect you to live, however. Have you looked behind you recently? Rhetorical question: I'm sure that you have. You must be aware, even with your limited detection capabilities, that there are more ships out there. Remember the task force you were supposed to lead, Clavain? The Master of Works has finished those ships. Three of them are approaching you from behind. They are better armed than *Nightshade*: heavy relativistic railguns, ship-to-ship boser and graser batteries, not to mention long-range stingers. And they have a bright target to aim at."

Clavain knew about the other ships, even though they only showed up at the extreme limit of his detectors. He had started turning Skade's light-sails to his own side, training his own optical lasers on to them as they passed in the night and steering them into the paths of the chasing ships. The chances of a collision remained small, and the pursuers could always deploy similar anti-sail defences of the sort Clavain had invented, but it had been enough to force Skade to abandon sail production.

"I know," he whispered.

Skade continued, "But I'm willing to make a deal, Clavain. You don't want to die, and I don't really want to kill you. Frankly, there are other problems I would sooner expend energy on."

"Charming." He sipped at his tea.

"So I will let you live, Clavain. And, more importantly, I will let you have Felka back."

Clavain put his cup aside.

"She is very ill, Clavain, retreating back into dreams of the Wall. All she does now is make circular structures around herself, intricate games that demand her total attention every hour of the day. They are surrogates for the Wall. She has abandoned sleep, like a true Conjoiner. I'm worried for her, I really am. You and Galiana worked so hard to make her more fully human . . . and yet I can see that work crumbling away by the day, just as the Great Wall crumbled away on Mars." Skade's face formed a stiff sad smile. "She doesn't recognise people at all, now. She shows no interest in anything outside her increasingly narrow set of obsessions. She doesn't even ask about you, Clavain."

"If you hurt her . . . " he found himself saying.

But Skade was still talking. "But there may still be time to make a difference, to repair some of the harm, if not all of it. It's up to you, Clavain. Our velocity differential is small enough now that a transfer operation is possible. If you turn away from my course and show no sign of returning to it, I will send Felka to you aboard a corvette—fired into deep space, of course."

"Skade . . . "

"I will expect your response immediately. A personal transmission would be nice, but, failing that, I will expect to see a change in your thrust vector." She sighed, and it was in that moment that Clavain realised what had been troubling him about Skade since the start of the transmission. It was the way she never drew breath, never once stopped to take in air.

"One final thing. I'll give you a generous margin of error before I decide that you have rejected my offer. But when that margin has ended, I will still put Felka aboard a corvette. The difference is, I won't make it easy for you to find her. Think of that, Clavain, will you? Felka, all alone between the stars, so far from companionship. She might not understand. Then again, she very well might." Skade hesitated, then added, "You'd know, I suppose, better than anyone. She's your daughter, after all. The question is, how much does she really mean to you?"

Skade's transmission ended.

Remontoire was conscious. He smiled with quiet amusement as Clavain entered the room that served as both his quarters and his prison. He could not be said to look sparklingly well—that would never be the case—but neither did he look like a man who had only recently been frozen, and before that, technically, deceased.

"I wondered when you'd pay me a visit," he said, with what struck Clavain as disarming cheerfulness. He lay on his back, his head on a pillow, his hands steepled across his chest, but in every sense appearing relaxed and calm.

Clavain's exoskeleton eased him into a sitting position, shifting pressure from one set of sores to another.

"I'm afraid things have been a tiny bit difficult," Clavain said. "But I'm glad to see that you're in one piece. It wasn't propitious to have you thawed until now."

"I understand," Remontoire said, with a dismissive wave of one hand. "It can't . . . "

"Wait." Clavain looked at his old friend, taking in the slight changes in his facial appearance that had been necessary for Remontoire to function as an agent in Yellowstone society. Clavain had become used to him being totally hairless, like an unfinished mannequin.

"Wait what, Clavain?"

"There are some ground rules you need to be aware of, Rem. You can't leave this room, so please don't embarrass me by making an attempt to do so."

Remontoire shrugged, as if this was no great matter. "I wouldn't dream of it. What else?"

"You can't communicate with any system beyond this room, not while you're in here. So, again, please don't try."

"How would you know if I did try?"

"I would."

"Fair enough. Anything else?"

"I don't know if I can trust you yet. Hence the precautions, and my general reluctance to wake you before now."

"Perfectly understandable."

"I'm not finished. I dearly want to trust you, Rem, but I'm not certain that I can. And I can't afford to risk the success of this mission." Remontoire started to speak, but Clavain raised a finger and continued talking. "That's why I won't be taking any chances. None at all. If you do anything, no matter how apparently trivial, that I think might be in any way to the detriment of the mission, I'll kill you. No ifs, no buts. Absolutely no trial. We're a long way from the Ferrisville Convention now, a long way from the Mother Nest."

"I gathered we were on a ship," Remontoire said. "And we're accelerating very, very hard. I wanted to find something I could drop to the floor, so that I might have an idea of exactly how hard. But you've done a very good job of leaving me with nothing. Still, I can guess. What is it now—four and a half gees?"

"Five," Clavain said. "And we'll soon be pushing to six and higher."

"This room doesn't remind me of any part of *Nightshade*. Have you captured another lighthugger, Clavain? That can't have been easy."

"I had some help."

"And the high rate of acceleration? How did you manage that without Skade's magic box of tricks?"

"Skade didn't create that technology from scratch. She stole it, or enough pieces to figure out the rest. She wasn't the only one with access to it, however. I met a man who had tapped the same motherlode."

"And this man is aboard the ship?"

"No, he left us to our own devices. It's my ship, Rem." Clavain whipped out an arm encased in the support rig and patted the rough metal wall of Remontoire's cell. "She's called *Zodiacal Light*. She's carrying a small army. Skade's ahead of us, but I'm not going to let her get her hands on those weapons without a struggle."

"Ah. Skade." Remontoire nodded, smiling.

"Something amusing you?"

"Has she been in touch?"

"In a manner of speaking, yes. That's why I woke you. What are you getting at?"

"Did she make it clear what had . . . " Remontoire trailed off, leaving Clavain aware that he was being observed closely. "Evidently not."

"What?"

"She nearly died, Clavain. When you escaped from the comet, the one where we met the Master of Works."

"Clearly she got better."

"Well, that very much depends . . . " Again, Remontoire trailed off. "This isn't about Skade, is it? I can see that concerned paternal look in your eye." In one easy movement he swung himself off the bed, sitting quite normally on the edge, as if the five gees of acceleration did not apply to him at all. Only a tiny twitching vein in the side of his head betrayed the tension he was under. "Let me guess. She still has Felka, doesn't she."

Clavain said nothing, waiting for Remontoire to continue.

"I tried to have Felka come with me and the pig," he said, "but Skade wasn't having it. Said Felka was more useful to her as a bargaining chip. I couldn't talk her out of it. If I'd have argued too strenuously, she wouldn't have let me come after you at all."

"You came to kill me."

"I came to stop you. My intention was to persuade you to come back with me to the Mother Nest. Of course, I'd have killed you if it came to it, but then you'd have done precisely the same to me if it was something you believed in sufficiently." Remontoire paused. "I believed I could talk you out of it. No one else would have given you a chance."

"We'll talk about that later. It's Felka who matters now."

There was a long silence between the two men. Clavain adjusted his position, determined that Remontoire should not see how uncomfortable he was.

"What's happened?" Remontoire asked.

"Skade's offered to turn Felka over provided I abandon the

chase. She'll drop her behind *Nightshade,* in a shuttle. At maximum burn it can shift to a rest frame we can reach with one of our shuttles."

Remontoire nodded. Clavain sensed his friend thinking deeply, chewing over permutations and possibilities.

"And if you refuse?"

"She'll still ditch Felka, but she won't make it easy for us to catch her. At best, I'll have to forfeit the chase to ensure a safe recovery. At worst, I'll never find her. We're in interstellar space, Rem. There's a hell of a lot of nothing out there. With Skade's flame ahead of us and ours behind, there are huge deadspots in our sensor coverage."

There was another long silence while Remontoire thought again. He eased back on to the bed, assisting the flow of blood to his brain.

"You can't trust Skade, Clavain. She has absolutely no need to convince you of her sincerity, since she doesn't think you'll ever have anything she needs or anything that can hurt her. This is not a two-prisoner game, like they taught you back on Deimos."

"I must have scared her," Clavain said. "She wasn't expecting us to catch up so easily."

"Even so . . . " Remontoire hovered on the edge of saying something for several minutes.

"You realise why I woke you now."

"Yes, I think I do. Run Seven was in a similar position to Skade when he had Irravel Veda on his tail, trying to get back her passengers."

"Seven made you serve him. You were forced to give him advice, tactics he could use against Irravel."

"It's an entirely different situation, Clavain."

"There are enough similarities for me." Clavain made his frame elevate him to a standing position. "Here's the picture, Rem. Skade will expect a response from me in a matter of days. You're going to help me choose that response. Ideally, I want Felka back without losing sight of the objective."

"You thawed me out in desperation, then? Better the devil you know, as they say?"

"You're my oldest and closest friend, Rem. I just don't know if I can trust you any more."

"And should the advice I give you be good . . . ?"

"That might put me in a more trusting frame of mind, I suppose." Clavain forced a smile. "Of course, I'd also have Felka's advice on that as well."

"And if we fail?"

Clavain said nothing. He just turned and left.

Four small shuttles arced away from *Zodiacal Light,* each falling into its own half-hemisphere of the relativistically distorted starscape. The exhaust streams of the ships glittered in the backwash from *Zodiacal Light*'s main flames. The trajectories were achingly beautiful, flung out from the mother ship like the curved arms of a chandelier.

If only this wasn't an action in a war, Clavain thought, *then it might almost be something to be proud of . . .*

He watched their departure from an observation cupola near the prow of his ship, feeling an obligation to wait until he could no longer make them out. Each shuttle carried a valued crewmember, plus a quota of fuel that he would rather not have had to spend before reaching Resurgam. If all went well, Clavain would get back the four shuttles and their crew. But he would never see most of the fuel again. There was only a tiny margin of error, enough that one ship could bring back a human-mass payload in addition to its pilot.

He hoped he was playing this one correctly.

It was said that the taking of hard decisions was something that became easier with repetition, like any difficult activity. There was, perhaps, some truth in that assertion. But if so, Clavain found that it most certainly did not apply in his own case. He had taken several extraordinarily difficult decisions lately, and each had been, in its own unique way, harder than the last. So it was with the matter of Felka.

It was not that he did not want Felka back, if there was a way that could be achieved. But Skade knew how much he wanted the weapons as well. She also knew that it was not a selfish issue with Clavain. He could not be bargained with in the usual sense, since he did not want the weapons for his own personal gain. But with Felka she had the perfect instrument of negotiation. She knew that the two of them had a special bond, one that went back to Mars. Was Felka really his daughter? He didn't know, even now. He had convinced himself that she might be, and she had told him she was . . . but that had been under possible duress, when she had been trying to persuade him not to defect. If anything, that admission had only served to slowly undermine his own certainties. He would not know for sure until he was again in her presence, and he could ask her properly.

And should it really matter? Her value as a human being had nothing to do with any hypothetical genetic connection with himself. Even if she was his daughter, he hadn't known that, or even suspected it, until long after he had rescued her from Mars. And yet something had made him go back into Galiana's nest, at great risk to himself, because he had felt a need to save her. Galiana had told him it was pointless, that she wasn't a thinking human being in any sense that he recognised it, just a mindless information-processing vegetable.

And he had proven her wrong. It was probably the only time in his life when he had ever done that to Galiana.

And yet still it didn't matter. This was all about humanity, Clavain thought, not about blood ties or loyalty. If he forgot that, then he might as well let Skade take the weapons with her. And he might as well defect back to the spiders and leave the rest of the human race to its fate. And yet if he failed to recover the weapons, what use was a single human gesture, no matter how well intentioned?

The four ships were gone. Clavain hoped and prayed that he had made the right decision.

A beetle-backed government car hissed through the streets of Cuvier. It had been raining again, but recently the clouds had cleared. The dismantled planet was now clearly visible during many hours of each evening. The cloud of liberated matter was a lacy many-armed thing. It gleamed red and ochre and pale green and occasionally flickered with slow electrical storms, pulsing like the courtship display of some uncatalogued deep-sea animal. Hard shadows and bright symmetric foci marked the sites within the cloud where Inhibitor machinery was coming into existence, aggregating and solidifying. There had been a time when it was possible to think that what had happened to the planet was some rare but natural event. Now no such comfort existed.

Thorn had seen the way people in Cuvier dealt with the phenomenon. For the most part they ignored it. When the thing was in the sky they walked down the streets without looking up.

Even when the fact of its existence could not be ignored, they seldom looked at the thing directly, or even referred to it in anything but the most oblique terms. It was as if a massive act of collective denial might make it go away, an omen that the people had decided to reject.

Thorn sat in one of the car's two rear seats, behind the driver's partition. There was a small flickering television screen sunk into the back of the driver's seat. Blue light played across Thorn's face as he watched footage taken from far outside the city. The clip was fuzzy and hand-held shaky, but it showed all that it needed to. The first of the two shuttles was still on the ground—the camera panned over it, lingering on the surreal juxtaposition of sleek machine and jumbled rockscape—but the second was in the air, coming back down from orbit. The shuttle had already made several trips to just above Resurgam's atmosphere where the much larger in-system craft was in orbit. Now the camera view jogged upwards, catching the descending ship as it lowered itself towards the landing site, settling down on a tripod of flames.

"It could be faked," Thorn said quietly. "I know it isn't, but that's what people will think."

Khouri was sitting next to him, dressed as Vuilleumier. She said, "You can fake anything if you try hard enough. But it isn't as easy as it used to be, not now that everything's stored using analogue media. I'm not sure even a whole government department could produce something convincing enough."

"The people will still be suspicious."

The camera panned across the sparse, nervous-looking crowd that was still on the ground. There was a small encampment three hundred metres from the parked shuttle, the dusty tents difficult to distinguish from fallen boulders. The people looked like refugees from any world, any century. They had come thousands of kilometres, converging on this point from a variety of settlements. It had cost them greatly: roughly a tenth of their number had not completed the journey. They had brought enough possessions to make the overland crossing, while knowing—if the underground intelligence network was efficient in its dissemination of information—that they would be allowed to bring nothing aboard the ship but the clothes they stood in. Near the encampment was a small hole in the ground where belongings were tossed before each party boarded the shuttle. These were possessions that had been treasured until the last possible moment, even though the logical thing would have been to leave them behind at home, before making the difficult journey across Resurgam. There were photographs and children's toys, and all of them would be buried, human relics to add to the million-year-old store of Amarantin artefacts that the planet still held.

"We've taken care of that," Khouri said. "Some of the witnesses who made it this far have returned to the major population centres. They needed persuading, of course, to turn around when they'd got that far, but . . . "

"How did you manage it?"

The car negotiated a bend with a swish of tyres. The cubiform buildings of the Inquisition House district loomed into view, grey and slab-sided as granite cliffs. Thorn eyed them apprehensively.

"They were told they'd be allowed to take a small quota of personal effects on to the ship with them when they came back."

"Bribery, in other words." Thorn shook his head, wondering if any great good deed could be entirely untainted by corruption, no matter how useful a purpose that corruption served. "But I suppose you had to get the word back somehow. How many, now?"

Khouri had the numbers ready. "Fifteen hundred in orbit, at the last count. A few hundred still on the ground. When we've got five hundred we'll make the next trip up from the surface, and then the transfer ship will be full, ready to shuttle them to *Nostalgia*."

"They're brave," Thorn said. "Or very, very foolish. I'm not sure which."

"Brave, Thorn, there's no doubt about that. And scared, too. But you can't blame them for that."

They were brave, it was true. They had made the journey to the shuttles based only on the scantiest of evidence that the machines even existed. After Thorn's arrest, rumours had run rife amongst the exodus movement. The government had continued to issue carefully engineered denials, each of which was designed to nurture in the populace's mind the idea that Thorn's shuttles might in fact be real. Those people who had made it to the shuttles so far had done so expressly against government advice, risking imprisonment and death as they trespassed into prohibited territory.

Thorn admired them. He doubted that he would have had the courage to follow those rumours to their logical conclusion had he not been the man who had initiated the whole movement. But he could take no pride in their achievement. They were still being deceived about their ultimate fate, a deception in which he was entirely complicit.

The car arrived at the rear of Inquisition House. Thorn and Khouri walked into the building, past the usual security checks. Thorn's identity was still a closely guarded secret, and he had been issued with a full set of papers allowing free movement in and around Cuvier. The guards assumed he was merely another official from the House, on government business.

"Do you still think this will work?" he asked, hurrying to keep up with Khouri as she strode up the stairs ahead of him.

"If it doesn't, we're fucked," she replied, in the same hushed voice.

The Triumvir was waiting in the Inquisitor's larger room, sitting in the seat usually reserved for Thorn. She was smoking, flicking ash on to the highly polished floor. Thorn felt a spasm of irritation at this act of studied carelessness. But doubtless the Triumvir's argument would have been that the whole planet was going to be ash before very long, so what difference did a little more make?

"Irina," he said, remembering to use the name she had adopted for her Cuvier persona.

"Thorn." She stood up, grinding out her cigarette on the chair's arm. "You look well. Government custody obviously isn't as bad as they say."

"If that's a joke, it isn't in very good taste."

"Of course." She shrugged, as if an apology would be superfluous. "Have you seen what they've done lately?"

"They?"

Triumvir Ilia Volyova was looking through the window, towards the sky. "Have a guess."

"Of course. You can't miss it now. Do you know what's taking shape in that cloud?"

"A mechanism, Thorn. Something to destroy our sun, I'd say."

"Let's talk in the office," Khouri said.

"Oh, let's not," said Volyova. "There are no windows, Ana, and the view does so focus the mind, don't you think? In a matter of minutes the fact of Thorn's collusion will be public knowledge." She looked at him sharply. "Won't it?"

"If you want to call it collusion."

Thorn had already taped his "statement"—the one where he spoke for the government, revealing that the shuttles were real, that the planet was indeed in imminent danger and that the government had, reluctantly, asked him to become the figurehead of the official exodus operation. It would be transmitted on all Resurgam television channels within the hour, to be repeated at intervals throughout the next day.

"It won't be viewed as collusion," Khouri said, eyeing the other woman coldly. "Thorn will be seen to be acting out of concern for the people, not his own self-interest. It will be convincing because it happens to be the truth." Her attention flicked to him. "Doesn't it?"

"I'm only voicing what will be common doubts," said Volyova. "Never mind, anyway. We'll know soon enough what the reaction is. Is it true there have already been acts of civil disturbance in some of the outlying settlements, Ana?"

"They were crushed pretty efficiently."

"There'll be worse, for certain. Don't be surprised if there's an attempt to overthrow this regime."

"That won't happen," Khouri said. "Not when the people realise what's at stake. They'll see that the apparatus of government has to remain in place so that the exodus can be organised smoothly."

The Triumvir smirked in Thorn's direction. "See how hopelessly optimistic she still is, Thorn?"

"Irina's right, unfortunately," Thorn said. "We can expect a lot worse. But you never imagined you'd get everyone off this planet in one piece."

"But we have the capacity . . . " Khouri said.

"People aren't payloads. They can't be shipped around like neat little units. Even if the majority buy into the idea that the government is somehow sincere about the evacuation—and that will be a small miracle in its own right—it'll only take a minority of dissenters to cause major trouble."

"You made a career out of being one of them," Khouri said.

"I did, yes." Thorn smiled sadly. "Unfortunately, I'm not the only one out there. Still, Irina's right. We'll know soon enough what the general reaction will be. How are the internal complications, anyway? Aren't the other branches of government getting a little suspicious about all these machinations?"

"Let's just say that one or two discreet assassinations may still have to be performed," Khouri said. "But that should take care of our worst enemies. The rest we only have to hold off until the exodus is finished."

Thorn turned to the Triumvir. "You've studied that thing in the sky more closely than any of us, Irina. Do you know how long we've got?"

"No," she said curtly. "Of course I can't say how long we've got, not without knowing what it is that they're building up there. All I can do is make an extremely educated guess."

"So indulge us."

She sniffed and then walked stiffly along the entire length of the window. Thorn eyed Khouri, wondering what she made of this performance. He had noticed a tension between the two women that he did not recall from his previous meetings with them. Perhaps it had always been there and he had simply missed it before, but he rather doubted it.

"I'll say this," the Triumvir stated, her heels squeaking as she turned to face the two of them. "Whatever it is, it's big. Much bigger than any structure we could imagine building, even if we had the raw materials and the time. Even the smallest structures that we can single out in the cloud ought to have collapsed under their own self-gravity by now, becoming molten spheres of metal. But they haven't. That tells me something."

"Go on," Thorn said.

"Either they can persuade matter to become many orders of magnitude more rigid than ought to be possible, or they have some local control of gravity. Perhaps some combination of the two, even. Accelerated streams of matter can serve the same structural functions as rigid spars if they can be controlled with sufficient finesse . . . " She was evidently thinking aloud, and for a moment she trailed off, before remembering her audience. "I suspect that they can manipulate inertia when it becomes necessary. We saw how they redirected those matter flows, bending them through right angles. That implies a profound knowledge of metric engineering, tampering with the basic substrate of space-time. If they have that ability, they can probably control gravity as well. We haven't seen that before, I think, so it might be something they can only do on a large scale: a broad brush, so to speak. Everything we've seen so far—the disassembly of the rocky worlds, the Dyson motor around the gas giant—all that was watchmaker stuff. Now we're seeing the first hints of Inhibitor heavy engineering."

"Now you're scaring me," Thorn said.

"Entirely my intention." She smiled quickly. It was the first time he had seen her smile that evening.

"So what is it going to be?" Khouri asked. "A machine to make the sun go supernova?"

"No," the Triumvir replied. "We can rule that out, I think. They may have a technology that can do it, but it would only work on heavy stars, the kind that are already predestined to blow up. That would be a formidable weapon, I admit. You could sterilise a volume of space dozens of light-years wide if you could trigger a premature supernova. I don't know how you would do it—maybe by tuning the nuclear cross sections to prohibit fusion for elements lighter than iron, thereby shifting the peak in the curve of binding energy. The star would suddenly have nothing to fuse, no means to support its outer envelope against collapse. They may have done it once, you know. Earth's sun is in the middle of a bubble in the interstellar medium, blown open by a recent supernova. It intersects other structures right out to the Aquila Rift. They may have been natural events, or we might be seeing the scars left behind by Inhibitor sterilisation events millions of years before the Amarantin xenocide. Or the bubbles might have been blown open by the weapons of fleeing species. We'll probably never know, no matter how hard we look. But that won't happen here. There are no supergiant stars in this part of the galaxy now, nothing capable of undergoing a supernova. They must have evolved different weapons for dealing with lower-mass stars like Delta Pavonis. Less spectacular—no use for sterilising more than a solar system—but perfectly effective on that level."

"How would you kill a star like Pavonis?" Thorn asked.

"There are several ways one might go about it," the Triumvir said thoughtfully. "It would depend on the resources available, and the time. The Inhibitors could assemble a ring around the star, just like they did with the gas giant. Something larger this time, of course, and perhaps functioning differently. There's no solid surface to a star, not even a solid core. But they might encircle the star with a ring of particle accelerators, perhaps. If they established a particle-beam flux through the ring, they could create a vast magnetic force by tightening and loosening the ring in waves. The field from the ring would strangle the star like a constricting snake, pumping chromospheric material away from the star's equator towards the poles. That's the only place it could go, and the only place it could escape. Hot plasma would ram away from the star's north and south poles. You might even be able to use those plasma jets as weapons in their own right, turning the whole star into a flame-thrower—all you'd need is more machinery above and below the poles to direct and focus the jets where you wanted them. You could incinerate every world in a solar system with a weapon like that, stripping atmosphere and ocean. You wouldn't even need to dismantle the entire star. Once you'd removed enough of its outer envelope, its core would adjust its fusion rate and the whole star would become cooler and much longer-lived. That might suit their longer-term plans, I suppose."

"That sounds as if it would take a long time," Khouri said. "And if all you're going to do is incinerate the worlds, why waste half a star doing it?"

"They could dismantle the whole thing, if they wished. I'm merely pointing out the possibilities. There's another method they might consider, too. They dismantled the gas giant by spinning it until it flew apart. They could do that to a sun, too: wrap accelerators around it again, this time in pole-to-pole loops, and start rotating them. They'd couple with the star's magnetosphere and start dragging the whole thing along with them, until it was spinning faster than its own centrifugal break-up speed. Matter would lift off the star's surface. It would come apart like an onion."

"Sounds slow, too."

Volyova nodded. "Perhaps. And there's another thing we need to consider. The machinery that's being assembled out there isn't ringlike, and there's no sign of any preparatory activity around the sun itself. The Inhibitors are going to use a different method again, I think."

"How else do you destroy a star, if pumping or spinning it won't work?" Khouri asked.

"I don't know. Let's assume they can manipulate gravity to some extent. If that's the case, they might be able to make a planet-mass black hole from the matter they've already accumulated. Say ten Earth masses, perhaps." She held her hands slightly apart, as if weaving an invisible cat's cradle. "This big, that's all. At most, they might have the resources to make a black hole ten or twenty times larger—a few hundred Earth masses."

"And if they dropped it into the star?"

"It would begin eating its way through it, yes. They would need to take great care to place it where it would do the maximum harm, though. It would be very difficult to insert it exactly in the star's nuclear-burning heart. The black hole would be inclined to oscillate, following an orbital trajectory through the star. It would have an effect, I am sure—the mass density near the black hole's Schwarzschild radius would reach the nuclear-burning threshold, I think, so the star would suddenly have two sites of nucleation, one orbiting the other. But it would only eat the star slowly, since its surface area is so small. Even when it had swallowed half the star, it would still only be three kilometres wide." She shrugged. "But it might work. It would depend acutely on the way in which matter fell into the hole. If it became too hot, its own radiation pressure would blast back the next layer of infalling material, slowing the whole process. I'll have to do some sums, I think."

"What else?" Thorn asked. "Assuming it isn't a black hole?"

"We could speculate endlessly. The nuclear-burning processes in the heart of any star are a delicate balance between pressure and gravity. Anything that tipped that balance might have a catastrophic effect on the overall properties of the star. But stars are resilient. They will always try to find a new balance point, even if that means switching to the fusion of heavier elements." The Triumvir turned to look out of the window again, tapping her fingers against the glass. "The exact mechanism that the Inhibitors will use may not even be comprehensible to us. It doesn't matter, because they will never get that far."

Khouri said, "I'm sorry?"

"I do not intend to wait this out, Ana. For the first time the Inhibitors have concentrated their activity at one focus point. I believe they are now at their most vulnerable. And for the first time, the Captain is willing to do business."

Khouri flashed a glance in Thorn's direction. "The cache?"

"He's given me his assurance that he will allow its use." She continued tapping the glass, still not turning to face them. "Of course, there's a risk. We don't know exactly what the cache is capable of. But damage is damage. I am certain we can put back their plans."

"No," Thorn said. "This isn't right. Not now."

The Triumvir turned from the window. "Why ever not?"

"Because the exodus operation is *working*. We've begun to lift people from the surface of Resurgam."

Volyova scoffed. "A few thousand. Hardly a dent, is it?"

"Things will change when the exodus operation becomes official. That's what we always counted on."

"Things could get very much worse, too. Are you willing to take that chance?"

"We had a plan," Khouri said. "The weapons were always there, to be used when we needed them. But it's senseless to provoke a reaction from the Inhibitors now, after all that we've achieved."

"She's right," Thorn said. "You have to wait, Irina. At least until we've evacuated a hundred thousand. Then use your precious weapons if you have to."

"By then it will be too late," she said, turning back to the window.

"We don't know that," Thorn said.

"Look." Volyova spoke quietly. "Can you see it?"

"See what?"

"In the distance, between those two buildings. There, beyond Broadcasting House. You can't miss it now."

Thorn walked to the window, Khouri next to him. "I don't see anything."

"Has your statement been broadcast yet?" Volyova asked.

Thorn checked the time. "Yes . . . yes. It should just have gone out, at least in Cuvier."

"There's your first reaction, then: a fire. Not much of one yet, but I don't doubt that we'll see more before the evening's out. The people are terrified. They've been terrified for months, with that thing in the sky. And now they know the government has been systematically lying to them. Under the circumstances I'd be a little angry. Wouldn't you?"

"It won't last," Thorn said. "Trust me, I know the people. When they understand that there's an escape route, that all they have to do is act rationally and do what I say, they'll calm down."

Volyova smiled. "Either you are a man of unusual ability, Thorn, or a man with a rather inadequate grasp of human nature. I just hope it's the former."

"You deal with your machines, Irina, and I'll deal with the people."

"Let's go upstairs," Khouri said. "On to the balcony. We'll be able to see things more clearly."

There were vehicles moving around now, more than normal for a rainy night. Below, police vans were assembling outside the building. Thorn watched riot officers troop into the vans, jostling each other with their armour, shields and electrically tipped prods. One by one the vans whisked away, dispersing the police to trouble spots. Other vans were being driven into a cordon around the building, the spaces between them spanned by metal barricades that had been perforated with narrow slits.

On the balcony it was much clearer. City sounds reached them through the rain. There were bangs and crashes, sirens and shouting. It almost sounded like a carnival, except there was no music. Thorn realised that it had been a long time since he had heard music of any kind.

Presently, despite the best efforts of the police, there was a crowd massing outside Inquisition House. There were simply too many people to hold back, and all the police could do was prevent them from entering the building itself. A number of people were already lying on the ground at the front of the crowd, stunned by grenades or prods. Their friends were doing their best to get them to safety. One man was thrashing in an epileptic frenzy. Another man looked dead, or at least deeply unconscious. The police could have murdered most of the people in the crowd in a few seconds, Thorn knew, but they were holding back. He studied the faces of the police as well as he was able. They appeared just as frightened and confused as the crowd they were supposed to be pacifying. Special orders had obviously decreed that their response should be measured rather than brutal.

The balcony was surrounded by a low fretted wall. Thorn

walked to the edge and looked over, peering down towards street level. Khouri followed him, Triumvir Volyova remaining out of sight.

"It's time," Thorn said. "I need to speak to the people in person. That way they'll know the statement wasn't faked up."

He knew that all he needed to do was shout and someone would hear him, even if it were only one person in the crowd. Before very long everyone would be looking upwards, and they would know, even before he spoke, who he was.

"Make it good," Volyova said, barely raising her voice above a whisper. "Make it very good, Thorn. A lot will depend on this little performance."

He looked back at her. "Then you'll reconsider?"

"I didn't say that."

"Irina . . . " Khouri said. "Please think about this. At least give us a chance here, before you use the weapons."

"You'll have a chance," Volyova said. "Before I use the weapons, I'll move them across the system. That way, even if there is a response from the Inhibitors, *Infinity* won't be the obvious target."

"That will take some time, won't it?" Khouri asked.

"You have a month, no more than that. Of course, I'm not expecting you to have the entire planet evacuated by then. But if you've kept to the agreed schedule—and perhaps improved on it a little—I may consider delaying the use of the weapons a while longer. That's reasonable, isn't it? I can be flexible, you see."

"You're asking too much of us," Khouri said. "No matter how efficient our operation on the surface is, we can't move more than two thousand people at a time between low orbit and the starship. That's an unavoidable bottleneck, Ilia." She seemed unaware that she had spoken the Triumvir's real name.

"Bottlenecks can always be worked around, if it matters enough," she said. "And I've given you every incentive, haven't I?"

"It's Thorn, isn't it?" Khouri said.

Thorn glanced back at her. "What about me?"

"She doesn't like the way you've come between us," Khouri told him.

The Triumvir made the same derisive snort he had heard before.

"No. It's true," Khouri said. "Isn't it, Ilia? You and I had a perfect working relationship until I brought Thorn into the arrangement. You'll never forgive either me or him for destroying that beautiful little partnership."

"Don't be absurd," Volyova said.

"I'm not being absurd, I'm just . . ."

But the Triumvir whipped past her.

"Where are you going?" Khouri asked.

She stopped long enough to answer her. "Where do you think, Ana? Back to my ship. I have work to do."

"*Your* ship, suddenly? I thought it was *our* ship."

But Volyova had said all she was going to say. Thorn heard her footsteps recede back into the building.

"Is that true?" he asked Khouri. "Do you really think she's resentful of me?"

But she said nothing either. Thorn, after a long moment, turned back to the city. He leaned out into the night, formulating the crucial speech he was about to deliver. Volyova was right: a lot depended on it.

Khouri's hand closed around his own.

The air reeked of fear-gas. Thorn felt it worming into his brain, brewing anxiety.

TWENTY-EIGHT

Skade stalked around her ship. Nothing felt right aboard *Nightshade* now. The pressure on her spine had eased and her eyeballs had returned to more or less the right shape, but those were the only real compensations. Every living thing inside the ship was now within the field's detectable sphere of influence, embedded in a bubble of artificially modified quantum vacuum. Nine-tenths of the inertial mass of every particle in the field no longer existed.

The ship was hurling itself towards Resurgam at ten gees.

Even though Skade had her armour, and was therefore insulated from the more physiologically upsetting effects of the field, she still moved around as little as possible. Walking was not in itself difficult since the acceleration that the armour felt was only a gee, a tenth of the actual value. The armour no longer laboured under the extra load, and Skade had lost the feeling that a fall would automatically dash her brains out. But everything else was worse. When she willed the armour to move a limb, it accommodated her wishes too quickly. When she moved what should have been a heavy piece of equipment, it shifted too easily. It was as if the apparently substantial furniture of the ship had been replaced by a series of superficially convincing paper-thin façades. Even changing the direction of her gaze took care. Her eyeballs, no longer distorted by gravity, were now too responsive and tended to overshoot and then overcompensate for the overshooting. She knew this was because the muscles that steered them, which were anchored to her skull, had evolved to move a sphere of tissue with a certain inertial mass; now they were confused. But knowing all this did not make dealing with it any easier. She had turned off her *Area Postrema* permanently, since her inner ear was profoundly disturbed by the modified inertial field.

Skade reached Felka's quarters. She entered and found Felka where she had left her last time, sitting cross-legged on a part of the floor that she had instructed to become soft. Her clothes had a stale, crumpled look. Her flesh was pasty and her hair was a nestlike tangle of greasy knots. Here and there Skade saw patches of raw pink scalp, where Felka had tugged out locks of her own hair. She sat perfectly still, one hand on either knee. Her chin was raised slightly and her eyes were closed. There was a faint glistening trail of mucus leading from one nostril to the top of her lip.

Skade audited the neural connections between Felka and the rest of the ship. To her surprise, she detected no significant traffic. Skade had assumed that Felka must have been roaming through a cybernetic environment, as had been the case on her last two visits. Skade had explored them for herself and found vast puzzlelike edifices of Felka's own making. They were clearly surrogates for the Wall. But this was not the case on this occasion. After abandoning the real, Felka had taken the next logical step, back to the place where it had all begun.

She had gone back into her skull.

Skade lowered herself to Felka's level, then reached out and touched her brow. She expected Felka to flinch against the cold metal contact, but she might as well have been touching a wax dummy.

Felka . . . can you hear me? I know you're in there somewhere. This is Skade. There is something you need to know.

She waited for a response; none came. *Felka. It concerns Clavain. I've done what I can to make him turn away, but he hasn't responded to any of my attempts at persuasion. My last effort was the one I thought most likely to persuade him. Shall I tell you what it was?*

Felka breathed in and out, slowly and regularly.

I used you. I promised Clavain that if he turned back, I'd give you back to him. Alive, of course. I thought that was fair. But he wasn't interested. He made no response to my overture. Do you see, Felka? You can't mean as much to him as his beloved mission.

She stood up and then strolled around the seated meditative figure. *I hoped you would, you know. It would have been the best solution for both of us. But it was Clavain's call, and he showed where his priorities lay. They weren't with you, Felka. After all those years, all those centuries, you didn't mean as much to him as forty mindless machines. I'll admit, I was surprised.*

Still Felka said nothing. Skade felt an urge to dive into her skull and find the warm and comforting place into which she had retreated. Had Felka been a normal Conjoiner, it would have been within Skade's capabilities to invade her most private mental spaces. But Felka's mind was put together differently. Skade could skim its surface, occasionally glimpse its depths, but no more than that.

Skade sighed. She had not really wanted to torment Felka, but she had hoped to prise her out of her withdrawal by turning her against Clavain.

It had not worked.

Skade stood behind Felka. She closed her eyes and issued a stream of commands to the spinal medical device she had attached to Felka. The effect was immediate and gratifying. Felka collapsed, sagging in on herself. Her mouth lolled open, oozing saliva.

Delicately, Skade picked her up and carried her out of the room.

The silver sun burned overhead, a blank coin shining through a caul of grey sea fog. Skade settled into a flesh-and-blood body, as she had before. She was standing on a flat-topped rock; the air was cold to the bone and prickled with ozone and the briny stench of rotting seaweed. In the distance, a billion pebbles sighed orgasmically under the assault of another sea wave.

It was the same place again. She wondered if the Wolf was becoming just the tiniest bit predictable.

Skade peered into the fog around her. There, no more than a dozen paces from her, was another human figure. But it was neither Galiana nor the Wolf this time. It was a small child, crouched on a rock about the same size as the one Skade stood on. Cautiously, Skade hopped and skipped her way from rock to rock, dancing across the pools and the razor-edged ridges that linked them. Being fully human again was both disturbing and exhilarating. She felt more fragile than she had ever done before Clavain had hurt her, conscious that beneath her skin was only soft muscle and brittle bone. It was good to be invincible. But at the same time it was good to feel the universe chemically invading her through every pore of her skin, to feel the wind stroking every hair on the back of her hand, to feel every ridge and crack of the seaworn rock beneath her feet.

She reached the child. It was Felka—no surprise there—but as she must have been on Mars, when Clavain rescued her.

Felka sat cross-legged, much as she had been in the cabin. She wore a damp, filthy, seaweed-stained torn dress that left her legs and arms bare. Her hair, like Skade's, was long and dark, falling in lank strands across her face. The sea fog lent the scene a bleached, monochrome aspect.

Felka glanced up at her, made eye contact for a second and then returned to the activity she had been engaged in before. Around her, forming a ragged ring, were many tiny parts of hard-shelled sea-creatures: legs and pincers, claws and tail pieces, whiplike antennae, broken scabs of carapacial shell, aligned and orientated with maniacal precision. The conjunctions of the many pale parts resembled a kind of anatomical algebra. Felka stared at the arrangement silently, occasionally pivoting around on her haunches to examine a different part of it. Only now and then would she pick up one of the pieces—a hinged, barbed limb, perhaps—and reposition it elsewhere. Her expression was blank, not at all like a child at play. It was more as if she was engaged in some task that demanded her solemn and total attention, an activity too intense to be pleasurable.

Felka . . .

She looked up again, questioningly, only to return to her game.

The distant waves crashed again. Beyond Felka the grey wall of mist lost some of its opacity for a moment. Skade could still not make out the sea, but she could see much farther than had been possible before. The pattern of rockpools stretched into the distance, a mind-wrenching tessellation. But there was something else out there, at the limit of vision. It was only slightly darker than the grey itself, and it shifted in and out of existence, but she was certain that there was something there. It was a grey spire, a vast towerlike thing ramming into the greyness of the sky. It appeared to lie a great distance away, perhaps beyond the sea itself, or thrusting out of the sea some distance from land.

Felka noticed it too. She looked at the object, her expression unchanging, and only when she had seen enough of it did she return to her animal parts. Skade was just wondering what it could be when the fog closed in again and she became aware of a third presence.

The Wolf had arrived. It—or she—stood only a few paces beyond Felka. The form remained indistinct, but whenever the fog abated or the form became more solid, Skade thought she saw a woman rather than an animal.

The roar of the waves, which had always been there, shifted into language again. "You brought Felka, Skade. I'm pleased."

"This representation of her," Skade asked, remembering to speak aloud as the Wolf had demanded of her before. She nodded towards the girl. "Is that how she sees herself now—as a child again—or how *you* wish *me* to see her?"

"A little of both, perhaps," said the Wolf.

"I asked for your help," Skade said. "You said that you would be more cooperative if I brought Felka with me. Well, I have. And Clavain is still behind me. He hasn't shown any sign of giving up."

"What have you tried?"

"Using her as a bargaining chip. But Clavain didn't bite."

"Did you imagine he ever would?"

"I thought he cared about Felka enough to have second thoughts."

"You misunderstand Clavain," the Wolf said. "He won't have given up on her."

"Only Galiana would know that, wouldn't she?"

The Wolf did not answer Skade directly. "What was your response, when Clavain failed to retreat?"

"I did what I said I would. Launched a shuttle, which he will now have great difficulty in intercepting."

"But an interception is still possible?"

Skade nodded. "That was the idea. He won't be able to reach it with one of his own shuttles, but his main ship will still be able to achieve a rendezvous."

There was amusement in the Wolf's voice. "Are you certain that one of his shuttles can't reach yours?"

"It isn't energetically feasible. He would have had to launch long before I made my move, and guess the direction I was going to send my shuttle in."

"Or cover every possibility," the Wolf said.

"He couldn't do that," Skade said, with a great deal less certainty than she thought she should feel. "He'd need to launch a flotilla of shuttles, wasting all that fuel on the off-chance that one . . . " She trailed off.

"If Clavain deemed the effort worth it, he would do exactly that, even if it cost him precious fuel. What did he expect to find in the shuttle, incidentally?"

"I told him I'd return Felka."

The Wolf shifted. Now its form lingered near Felka, though it was no more distinct that it had been an instant earlier. "She's still here."

"I put a weapon in the shuttle. A crustbuster warhead, set for a teratonne detonation."

She saw the Wolf nod appreciatively. "You hoped he would have to steer his ship to the rendezvous point. Doubtless you arranged some form of proximity fuse. Very clever, Skade. I'm actually quite impressed by your ruthlessness."

"But you don't think he'll fall for it."

"You'll know soon enough, won't you?"

Skade nodded, certain now that she had failed. Distantly, the sea mist parted again, and she was afforded another glimpse of the pale tower. In all likelihood it was actually very dark when seen up close. It rose high and sheer, like a sea-stack. But it looked less like a natural formation than a giant taper-sided building.

"What is that?" Skade asked.

"What is what?"

"That . . . " But when Skade looked back towards the tower, it was no longer visible. Either the mist had closed in to conceal it, or it had ceased to exist.

"There's nothing there," the Wolf said.

Skade chose her words carefully. "Wolf, listen to me. If Clavain survives this, I am prepared to do what we discussed before."

"The unthinkable, Skade? A state-four transition?"

Even Felka halted her game, looking up at the two adults. The moment was pregnant, stretching eternally.

"I understand the dangers. But we need to do it to finally slip ahead of him. We need to make a jump through the zero-mass boundary into state four. Into the tachyonic-mass phase."

Again that horrible lupine glint of a smile. "Very few organisms have ever travelled faster than light, Skade."

"I'm prepared to become one of them. What do I need to do?"

"You know full well. The machinery you have made is almost capable of it, but it will require a few modifications. Nothing that your manufactories can't handle. But to make the changes you will need to take advice from Exordium."

Skade nodded. "That's why I'm here. That's why I brought Felka."

"Then let us begin."

Felka went back to her game, ignoring the two of them. Skade issued the coded sequence of neural commands that would make the Exordium machinery initiate coherence coupling.

"It's starting, Wolf."

"I know. I can feel it, too."

Felka looked up from her game.

Skade sensed herself become plural. From out of the sea fog, from a direction she could neither describe nor point to, came a feeling of something receding into vast, chill distance, like a white corridor reaching to the bleak edge of eternity. The hairs on the back of Skade's neck prickled. She knew that there was something profoundly wrong about what she was doing. The premonitionary sense of evil was quite tangible. But she had to stand her ground and do what had to be done.

Like the Wolf said, fears had to be faced.

Skade listened intently. She thought she heard voices whispering down the corridor.

"Beast?"

"Yes, Little Miss?"

"Have you been completely honest with me?"

"Why would one have been anything other than honest, Little Miss?"

"That's exactly what I'm wondering, Beast."

Antoinette was alone on the lower flight deck of *Storm Bird*. Her freighter was locked in a loom of heavy repair scaffolding in one of *Zodiacal Light*'s shuttle bays, braced to withstand even the increased acceleration rate of the light-hunger. The freighter had been here ever since they had taken the lighthugger, the damage it had sustained painstakingly being put right under Xavier's expert direction. Xavier had relied on hyperpigs and shipboard servitors to help him do the work, and at first the repairs had gone more slowly than they would have with a fully trained monkey workforce. But although they had some dexterity problems, the pigs were ultimately cleverer than hyperprimates, and once the initial difficulties had been overcome and the servitors programmed properly, the work had gone very well. Xavier hadn't just repaired the hull; he had completely rearmoured it. The engines, from docking thrusters right up to the main tokamak fusion powerplant, had been overhauled and tweaked for improved performance. The deterrents, the many weapons buried in camouflaged hideaways around the ship, had been upgraded and linked into an integrated weapons command net. There was no point pussyfooting now, Xavier had said. They had no reason to pretend that *Storm Bird* was just a freighter any more. Where they were headed, there would be no nosey authorities to hide anything from.

But once the acceleration rate had increased and they all had to either stay still or submit to the use of awkward, bulky exoskeletons, Antoinette had made fewer visits to her ship. It was not just that the work was nearly done, and there was nothing for her to supervise; there was something else that kept her away.

She supposed that on some level she had always had her suspicions. There had been times when she felt that she was not alone on *Storm Bird*; that Beast's vigilance extended to more than just the mindless watchful scrutiny of a gamma-level persona. That there had been something more to him.

But that would have meant that Xavier—and her father—had lied to her. And that was something she was not prepared to deal with.

Until now.

During a brief lull when the acceleration was throttled back for technical checks, Antoinette had boarded *Storm Bird*. Out of sheer curiosity, expecting the information to have been erased from the ship's archives, she had looked for herself to see whether they had anything to say on the matter of the Mandelstam Ruling.

They had, too.

But even if they hadn't, she thought she would have guessed.

The doubts had begun to surface properly after the whole business with Clavain had started. There had been the time when Beast jumped the gun during the banshee attack, exactly as if her ship had "panicked," except that for a gamma-level intelligence that was simply not possible.

Then there had been time when the police proxy, the one that was now counting out the rest of its life in a dank cellar in the Château, had quizzed her on her father's relationship with Lyle Merrick. The proxy had mentioned the Mandelstam Ruling.

It had meant nothing to her at the time.

But now she knew.

Then there had been the time when Beast had inadvertently referred to itself as "I," as if a scrupulously maintained façade had just, for the tiniest of moments, slipped aside. As if she had glimpsed the true face of something.

"Little Miss . . . ?"

"I know."

"Know what, Little Miss?"

"What you are. Who you are."

"Begging your pardon, Little Miss, but . . . "

"Shut the fuck up."

"Little Miss . . . if one might . . . "

"I said shut the fuck up." Antoinette hit the panel of the flight deck console with the heel of her hand. It was the closest thing she could find to hitting Beast, and for a moment she felt a warm glow of retribution. "I know all about what happened. I found out about the Mandelstam Ruling."

"The Mandelstam Ruling, Little Miss?"

"Don't sound so fucking innocent. I know you know all about it. It's the law they passed just before you died. The one about irreversible neural death sentences."

"Irreversible neural death, Little . . . "

"The one that says that the authorities—the Ferrisville Convention—have the right to impound and erase any beta- or alpha-level copies of someone sentenced to permanent death. It says that no matter how many backups of yourself you make, no matter whether they're simulacra or genuine neural scans, the authorities get to round them up and wipe them out."

"That sounds rather extreme, Little Miss."

"It does, doesn't it? And they take it seriously, too. Anyone caught harbouring a copy of a sentenced felon is in just as much trouble themselves. Of course, there are loopholes—a simulation can be hidden almost anywhere, or beamed to somewhere beyond Ferrisville jurisdiction. But there are still risks. I checked, Beast. The authorities have caught people who sheltered copies, against the Mandelstam Ruling. They all got the death sentence, too."

"It would seem a rather cavalier thing to do."

She smiled. "Wouldn't it just? But what if you didn't even know you were sheltering one? How would that change the equation?"

"One hesitates to speculate."

"I doubt it would change the equation one fucking inch. Not where the cops are concerned. Which would make it all the more irresponsible, don't you think, for someone to trick *someone else* into harbouring an illegal simulation?"

"Trick, Little Miss?"

She nodded. She was there now. No more pussyfooting here either. "The police proxy knew, didn't it? Just couldn't get the evidence together, I guess—or maybe it was just letting me stew, waiting to see how much I knew."

The mask slipped again. "I'm not entire . . . "

"I guess Xavier had to be in on it. He knows this ship like the back of his hand, every subsystem, every Goddamned wire. He certainly would have known how to hide Lyle Merrick aboard it."

"Lyle Merrick, Little Miss?"

"You know. You remember. Not *the* Lyle Merrick, of course, just a copy of him. Beta- or alpha-level, I don't know. Don't very much care either. Wouldn't have made a fuck of a lot of difference in a court of law, would it?"

"Now . . . "

"It's you, Beast. You're him. Lyle Merrick died when the authorities executed him for the collision. But that wasn't the end, was it? You kept on going. Xavier hid a copy of Lyle aboard my father's fucking ship. You're it."

Beast said nothing for several seconds. Antoinette watched the slow, hypnotic play of colours and numerics on the console. She felt as if a part of her had been violated, as if everything in the universe she had ever felt she could trust had just been wadded up and thrown away.

When Beast answered, the tone of his voice was mockingly unchanged. "Little Miss . . . I mean Antoinette . . . You're wrong."

"Of course I'm not wrong. You've as good as admitted it."

"No. You don't understand."

"What part don't I understand?"

"It wasn't Xavier who did this to me. Xavier helped—Xavier knew all about it—but it wasn't his idea."

"No?"

"It was your father, Antoinette. He helped me."

She hit the console again, harder this time. And then walked out of her ship, intending never to set foot in it again.

Lasher the pig slept for most of the trip out from *Zodiacal Light*. There was nothing for him to do, Scorpio had said, except at the very end of the operation, and even then there was only a one-in-four chance that he would be required to do anything other than turn his ship around. But at the back of his mind he had always known it would be him who had to do the dirty work. He registered no surprise at all when the tight-beam message from *Zodiacal Light* told him that his shuttle was the one in the right quadrant of the sky to intercept the vessel Skade had dropped behind her larger ship.

"Lucky old Lasher," he said to himself. "You always wanted the glory. Now's your big chance."

He did not take the duty lightly, nor underestimate the risks to himself. The recovery operation was fraught with danger. The amount of fuel his shuttle carried was precisely rationed, just enough so that he could get back home again with a human-mass payload. But there was no room for error. Clavain had made it clear that there were to be no pointless heroics. If the trajectory of Skade's shuttle took it even a kilometre outside the safe volume in which a rendezvous was possible, Lasher—or whoever the lucky one was—was to turn back, ignoring it. The only concession to be made was that each of Clavain's shuttles carried a single modified missile, the warhead stripped out and replaced with a transponder. If they got within range of Skade's shuttle they could attach the beacon to its hull. The beacon would keep emitting its signal for a century of subjective time, five hundred years of worldtime. It would not be easy, but there would remain a faint chance of homing in on it again, before it fell beyond the well-mapped sphere of human space. It was enough to know that they would not have abandoned Felka entirely.

Lasher saw it now. His shuttle had homed in on Skade's, following updated coordinates from *Zodiacal Light*. Skade's shuttle was now in free-fall, having burned its last microgram of antimatter. It was visible in his forward window: a gunmetal barb illuminated by his forward floods.

He opened the channel back to the lighthugger. "This is Lasher. I see it now. It's definitely a shuttle. Can't tell you what type, but it doesn't look like one of ours."

He slowed his approach. It would have been nice to wait for Scorpio's response, but that was a luxury he did not have. There was already a twenty-minute timelag back to *Zodiacal Light,* and the distance was stretching continually as the larger ship maintained its ten-gee acceleration. He was permitted exactly thirty minutes here, and then he had to begin his return journey. If he stayed a minute longer he would never catch up with the lighthugger.

It would be just enough time to establish airlock connections between two unfamiliar ships, just enough time for him to get aboard and find Clavain's daughter, or whoever she was.

He didn't care who he was rescuing, only that Scorpio had told him to do it. So what if Scorpio was only doing what Clavain had told him to do? It didn't matter, did not reduce in any way the burning soldierly admiration Lasher felt for his leader. He had followed Scorpio's career almost from the moment Scorpio had arrived in Chasm City.

It was impossible to underestimate the effect of Scorpio's coming. Before, the pigs had been a squabbling rabble, content to snuffle around in the shittiest layers of the fallen city. Scorpio had galvanised them. He had become a criminal messiah, a figure so mythic that many pigs doubted that he even existed. Lasher had collected Scorpio's crimes, committing them to memory with the avidity of a religious acolyte. He had studied them, marvelling at their brutal ingenuity, their haiku-like simplicity. How must it feel, he had wondered, to have been the author of such jewel-like atrocities? Later, he had moved into Scorpio's realm of influence, and then ascended through the shadowy hierarchies of the criminal underworld. He remembered his first meeting with Scorpio, the sense of mild disappointment when he turned out to be just another pig like himself. Gradually, however, that realisation had only sharpened his admiration. Scorpio was flesh and blood, and that made his achievements all the more remarkable. Lasher, nervously at first, became one of Scorpio's main operatives, and then one of his deputies.

And then Scorpio had vanished. It was said that he had gone into space, off to engage in sensitive negotiations with some other criminal group elsewhere in the system—the Skyjacks, perhaps.

It was unsafe for Scorpio to move at any time, but most especially during war. Lasher had forced himself to deal with the likely but unpalatable truth: Scorpio was probably dead.

Months had passed. Then Lasher had heard the news: Scorpio was in custody, or a kind of custody. The spiders had captured him, it turned out, maybe after the zombies had already picked him up. And now the spiders were being pressured into turning Scorpio over to the Ferrisville Convention.

That was it, then. Scorpio's bright, inglorious reign had come to an end. The Convention could make any charge stick, and in wartime there was almost no crime that didn't carry the death penalty. They had Scorpio, the prize they had sought for so long. There would be a show trial and then an execution, and Scorpio's passage into legend would be complete.

But it hadn't happened that way. There had been the usual contradictory rumours, but some of them had spoken of the same thing—that Scorpio was alive and well, and no longer in anyone's custody; that Scorpio had made it back to Chasm City and was now holed up in the darkly threatening structure some of the pigs knew as the Château des Corbeaux, the one they said had the haunted cellar. And that he was the guest of the Château's mysterious tenant, and was now putting together the fabled thing that had often been spoken of but which had never quite come into existence before.

The army of pigs.

Lasher had rejoined his old master and learned that the rumours were true. Scorpio was working for, or in some strange collaboration with, the old man they called Clavain. And the two of them were plotting the theft of a ship belonging to the Ultras, something that the orthodox criminal rulebook said could not even be contemplated, let alone attempted. Lasher had been intrigued and terrified, even more so when he learned that the theft was just the prelude to something even more audacious.

How could he resist?

And so here, light-years from Chasm City, light-years from anything he could call familiar, he was. He had served Scorpio and served him well, not just treading in his footsteps but anticipating them; even, sometimes, dancing ahead of his master, earning Scorpio's quiet praise.

He was near the shuttle now. It had the smooth worn-pebble look of Conjoiner machinery. It was completely dark. He tracked the floods across it, searching for the point where Clavain had told him he would find an airlock: an almost invisibly fine seam in the hull that would only reveal itself when he was close by. Distance to the hull was now fifteen metres, with a closing speed of one metre per second. The shuttle was small enough that he would have no difficulty finding the hostage aboard it, provided Skade had kept her word.

It happened when he was ten metres from the hull. It grew from the heart of the Conjoiner spacecraft: a mote of light, like the first spark of the rising sun.

Lasher did not have time to blink.

* * *

Skade saw the fairy-light glint of the crustbuster proximity device. It was not difficult to recognise. There were no stars aft of *Nightshade* now, only an inky spreading pool of total blackness. Relativity was squeezing the visible universe into a belt that encircled the ship. But Clavain's ship was in nearly the same velocity frame as *Nightshade,* so it still appeared to lie directly behind her. The pinprick flare of the weapon studded that darkness like a single misplaced star.

Skade examined the light, corrected it for modest differential red shift and determined that the multiple-teratonne blast yield was consistent only with the device itself detonating, plus a small residual mass of antimatter. A shuttle-sized spacecraft had been destroyed by her weapon, but not a starship. The explosion of a lighthugger, a machine which had already sunk claws deep into the infinite energy well of the quantum vacuum, would have outshone the crustbuster by three orders of magnitude.

So Clavain had been cleverer than her again. No, she corrected herself: not cleverer, but precisely *as clever*. Skade had made no mistakes yet, and though Clavain had parried all her attacks, he had yet to strike at her. The advantage was still hers, and she was certain that she had inconvenienced him with at least one of her attacks. At the very least she had forced him to burn fuel he would sooner have conserved. More probably she had made him divert his efforts into countering her attacks rather than preparing for the battle that lay ahead around Resurgam. In every military sense she had lost nothing except the ability ever to bluff convincingly again.

But she had never been counting on that anyway.

It was time to do what had to be done.

"You lying fuck."

Xavier looked up as Antoinette stormed into their quarters. He was lying on his back on the bunk, a compad balanced between his knees. Antoinette had a momentary glimpse of lines of source code scrolling down the 'pad, the symbols and sinuous indentations of the programming language resembling the intricately formalised stanzas of some alien poetry. Xavier had a stylus gripped between his teeth. It dropped from his mouth as he opened it in shock. The compad tumbled to the floor.

"Antoinette?"

"I know."

"You know what?"

"About the Mandelstam Ruling. About Lyle Merrick. About *Storm Bird*. About Beast. About you."

Xavier slid around on the bunk, his feet touching the floor. He pushed a few fingers through the black mop of his hair, bashfully.

"About what?"

"Don't lie to me, you fuck!"

Then she was on him in a blind, pummelling rage. There was no real violence behind her punches; under any other circumstances they would have been playful. But Xavier hid his face, absorbing her anger against his forearms. He was trying to say something to her. She was blanking him out in her fury, refusing to listen to his snivelling little justifications.

Finally the rage turned to tears. Xavier stopped her from hitting him, taking her wrists gently.

"Antoinette," he said.

She hit him one last time, then started weeping in earnest. She hated him and loved him at the same time.

"It's not my fault," Xavier said. "I swear it's not my fault."

"Why didn't you tell me?"

He looked at her, she returning his gaze through the blur of her tears. "Why didn't I tell you?"

"That's what I asked."

"Because your father made me promise not to."

When Antoinette had calmed down, when she was ready to listen, Xavier told her something of what had happened.

Jim Bax had been a friend of Lyle Merrick's for many years. The two of them had been freighter pilots, both working within and around the Rust Belt. Normally two pilots operating in the same trading sphere would have found it difficult to sustain a genuine friendship through the ups and downs of a systemwide economy; there would have been too many occasions where their interests overlapped. But because Jim and Lyle operated in radically different niches with very different client lists, rivalry had never threatened their relationship. Jim Bax hauled heavy loads on rapid high-burn trajectories, usually at short notice and usually, though not always, more or less within the bounds of legality. Certainly Jim did not court criminal clients, although it was not exactly true to say that he turned them away, either. Lyle, by contrast, worked almost exclusively with criminals. They recognised that his slow, frail, unreliable chemical-drive scow was about the least likely ship to attract the attention of the Convention's customs and excise cutters. Lyle could not guarantee that his loads would arrive at their destinations quickly, or sometimes at all, but he could almost always guarantee that they would arrive uninspected, and that there would be no inconvenient lines of questioning extending back to his clients. So, in a more than modest fashion, Lyle Merrick prospered. He went to a great deal of trouble to hide his earnings from the authorities, maintaining a fastidious illusion of being constantly on the edge of insolvency. But behind the scenes, and by the standards of the day, he was a moderately wealthy man, far wealthier, in fact, than Jim Bax would ever be. Wealthy enough, indeed, to afford to have himself backed-up once a year at one of the alpha-level scanning facilities in Chasm City's high canopy.

And for many years his act worked. Until the day a bored police cutter decided to pick on Lyle for no other reason than that he had never troubled them before, and so therefore had to be up to something. The cutter had no difficulty matching trajectories with Lyle's scow. It requested that he initiate main-engine cut-off and prepare for boarding. But Lyle knew he could not possibly comply with the enforced main-engine cut-off. His entire reputation hinged on the fact that his hauls were never inspected. Had he allowed the proxy aboard, he would have been signing his own bankruptcy notice.

He had no choice but to run.

Fortunately—or not, as the case proved—he was already on final approach for Carousel New Copenhagen. He knew that there was a repair well on the rim just large enough to hold his ship. It would be tight, but if he could get inside the bay, he would at least be able to destroy the cargo before the proxies forced their way aboard. He would still be in a lot of trouble, but at least he would not have broken client confidentiality, and that, for Lyle, mattered a lot more than his own wellbeing.

Lyle, of course, never made it. He screwed up his last approach burn, harried by the cutters—there were now four of them swooping in to escort him, and they had already fired retarder grapples on to his hull—and collided with the outer face of the rim itself. Surprisingly, and no one was more surprised than Lyle, he survived the impact. The blunt life-support and habitat module of his freighter had pushed itself through the skin of the carousel like a baby bird's beak ripping through eggshell. His velocity at impact had only been a few tens of metres per second, and although he had been bruised and battered, he suffered no serious injuries. His luck continued even when the main propulsion section—the swollen lungs of the chemical fuel tanks—went up. The blast rammed the nose module further into the carousel, but again Lyle survived.

But even as he realised his good fortune, he knew that he was in grave trouble. The impact had not occurred in the most densely inhabited portion of the carousel's ring, but there were still many casualties. A vault of the rim interior had decompressed as his ship plunged through the rim, the air gushing through the wound in the carousel's fabric. The chamber had been a recreational zone, a miniature glade and forest lit by suspended lamps.

On any other night, there might have been no more than a few dozen people and animals enjoying the synthetic scenery by moonlight. But on the night Lyle crashed there had been a midnight recital of one of Quirrenbach's more populist efforts, and several hundred people had been there. Thankfully most had survived, though many had been seriously injured. But there had still been fatalities: forty-three dead at the final count, excluding Lyle himself. It was certainly possible that more had been killed.

Lyle made no attempt to escape. He knew that his fate was sealed. He would have been lucky to avoid the death penalty just for refusing to comply with the boarding order, but even if he had wriggled out of that—and there were ways and means—there was nothing that could be done for him now. Since the Melding Plague, when the once glorious Glitter Band had been reduced to the Rust Belt, acts of vandalism against habitats were considered the most heinous of crimes. The forty-three dead were almost a detail.

Lyle Merrick was arrested, tried and sentenced. He was found guilty on all counts relating to the collision. His sentence was irreversible neural death. Since he was known to have been scanned, the Mandelstam Ruling was to apply.

Designated Ferrisville officials, nicknamed eraserheads, were assigned to track down and nullify all extant alpha- or beta-level simulations of Lyle Merrick. The eraserheads had the full legal machinery of the Convention behind them, together with an arsenal of plague-tolerant hunter-seeker software tools. They could comb any known database or archive and ferret out the buried patterns of an illegal simulation. They could erase any public database even suspected of holding a forbidden copy. They were very good at their work.

But Jim Bax wasn't going to let down his friend. Before the net closed, and with the help of Lyle's other friends, some of who were extremely frightening individuals, the most recent alpha-level backup was spirited out of the hands of the law. Deft alteration of the records at the scanning clinic made it appear as if Lyle had missed his last appointment. The eraserheads lingered over the evidence, puzzling over the anomalies for many days. But in the end they decided that the missing alpha had never existed. They had done their work in any case, rounding up all other known simulations.

So, in a sense, Lyle Merrick escaped justice.

But there was a catch, and it was one that Jim Bax insisted upon. He would shelter Lyle's alpha-level persona, he said, and he would shelter it in a place the authorities were very unlikely ever to think of looking. Lyle would replace the subpersona of his ship, the alpha-level scan of a real human mind supplanting the collection of algorithms and subroutines that was a gamma-level persona. A real mind, albeit a simulation of the neural patterns of a real mind, would replace a purely fictitious persona.

A real ghost would haunt the machine.

"Why?" Antoinette asked. "Why did Dad want it to happen this way?"

"Why do you think? Because he cared about his friend and his daughter. It was his way of protecting both of you."

"I don't understand, Xave."

"Lyle Merrick was dead meat if he didn't agree. Your father wasn't going to risk his neck by sheltering the simulation any other way. At least this way Jim got something out of deal, other than the satisfaction of saving part of his friend."

"Which was?"

"He got Lyle to promise to look after you when Jim wasn't around."

"No," Antoinette said flatly.

"You were going to be told. That was always the plan. But the years slipped by, and when Jim died . . . " Xavier shook his head. "This isn't easy for me, you know. How do you think I've felt, knowing this secret all these years? Sixteen Goddamned years, Antoinette. I was about as young and green as they come when your father first took me under his employment, helping him with *Storm Bird*. Of course I had to know about Lyle."

"I don't follow. What do you mean, look after me?"

"Jim knew he wasn't going to be around for ever, and he loved you more than, well . . . " Xavier trailed off.

"I know he loved me," Antoinette said. "It's not like we had one of those dysfunctional father-daughter relationships like they always have on the holo-shows, you know. All that 'you never told me you loved me' crap. We actually got along pretty damned well."

"I know. That was the point. Jim cared about what'd happen to you afterwards, when he was gone. He knew you'd want to inherit the ship. Wasn't anything he could do about that, or even *wanted* to do about it. Hell, he was proud. Really proud. He thought you'd make a better pilot than he ever did, and he was damned sure you had more business sense."

Antoinette suppressed half a smile. She had heard that sort of thing from her father often enough, but it was still pleasing to hear it from someone else; evidence—if she needed it—that Jim Bax had *really* meant it.

"And?"

Xavier shrugged. "Guy still wanted to look out for his daughter. Not such a crime, is it?"

"I don't know. What was the arrangement?"

"Lyle got to inhabit *Storm Bird*. Jim told him he had to play along with being the old gamma-level; that you were never to suspect that you had a, well, guardian angel looking over you. Lyle was supposed to look after you, make sure you never got into too much trouble. It made sense, you know. Lyle had a strong instinct for self-preservation."

She remembered the times that Beast had tried to talk her out of doing something. There had been many, and she had always put them down to an over-protective quirk of the subpersona. Well, she had been right. Dead right. Just not in quite the way she had assumed.

"And Lyle just went along with it?" she asked.

Xavier nodded. "You've got to understand: Lyle was on a serious guilt and recrimination trip. He really felt bad for all the people he had killed. For a while he wouldn't even run himself—kept going into hibernation, or trying to persuade his friends to destroy him. The guy wanted to die."

"But he didn't."

"Because Jim gave him a reason to live. A way to make a difference, looking after you."

"And all that 'Little Miss' shit?"

"Part of the act. Got to hand it to the dude, he kept it up pretty good, didn't he? Until the shit came down. But then you can't blame him for panicking."

Antoinette stood up. "I suppose not."

Xavier looked at her expectantly. "Then . . . you're OK about it?"

She turned around and looked him hard in the eyes. "No, Xave, I'm not OK about it. I understand it. I even understand why you lied to me all those years. But that doesn't make it OK."

"I'm sorry," he said, looking down into his lap. "But all I ever did was make a promise to your father, Antoinette."

"It's not your fault," she said.

Later, they made love. It was as good as any time she could remember with him; all the more so, perhaps, given the emotional fireworks that were still going off in her belly. And it was true what she had said to Xavier. Now that she had heard his side of the story, she understood that he could never have told her the truth, or at least not until she had figured out most of it for herself. She did not even particularly blame her father for what he had done. He had always looked after his friends, and he had always thought the world of his daughter. Jim Bax had done nothing out of character.

But that did not make the truth of it any easier to take. When she thought of all the time she had spent alone on *Storm Bird* now knowing that Lyle Merrick had been there, haunting her—perhaps even *watching* her—she felt a wrenching sense of betrayal and stupidity.

She did not think it was something she was capable of getting over.

A day later, Antoinette walked out to visit her ship, thinking that by entering it again she might find some forgiveness for the lie that had been visited on her by the one person in the universe she had thought she could trust. It hardly mattered that the lie had been a kind one, intended to protect her.

But when she reached the base of the scaffolding that embraced *Storm Bird,* she could go no farther. She gazed up at the vessel, but the ship looked threatening and unfamiliar. It no longer looked like her ship, or anything that she wanted to be part of.

Crying because something had been stolen from her that could never be returned, Antoinette turned around and walked away.

Things moved with startling swiftness once the decision had been made. Skade throttled her ship down to one gee and then had the techs make the bubble contract to sub-bacterial size, maintained by only a trickle of power. This allowed much of the machinery to be disconnected. Then she gave the command that would cause a drastic reshaping of the ship, in accordance with the information that she had gleaned from Exordium.

Buried in the rear of *Nightshade* were many plague-hardened nanomachine repositories, dark tubers crammed with clades of low-level replicators. Upon Skade's command the machines were released, programmed to multiply and diversify until they had formed a scalding slime of microscopic matter-transforming engines. The slime swarmed and infiltrated every niche of the rear part of the ship, dissolving and regurgitating the very fabric of the lighthugger. Much of the machinery of the device succumbed to the same transforming blight. In their wake, the replicators left glistening obsidian structures, filamental arcs and helices threading back into space behind the ship like so many trailing tentacles and stingers. They were studded with the nodes of subsidiary devices, bulging like black suckers and venom sacs. In operation, the machinery would move with respect to itself, executing a hypnotic thresherlike motion, whisking and slicing the vacuum. In the midst of that scything motion, a quark-sized pocket of state-four quantum vacuum would be conjured into existence. It would be a pocket of vacuum in which inertial mass was, in the strict mathematical sense, imaginary.

The quark-sized bubble would quiver, fluctuate and then—in much *less* than an instant of Planck time—it would engulf the entire spacecraft, undergoing an inflationary type phase transition to macroscopic dimensions. The machinery that would continue to hold it in check was engineered to astonishingly fine tolerances, down to the very threshold of Heisenberg fuzziness. How much of this was necessary, no one could guess. Skade was not prepared to second-guess what the whispering voices of Exordium had told her. All she could do was hope that any deviations would not affect the functioning of the machine, or at least affect it so profoundly that it did not work at all. The thought of it working, but working wrongly, was entirely too terrifying to contemplate.

But nothing happened the first time. The machinery had powered up and the quantum-vacuum sensors had picked up strange, subtle fluctuations . . . but equally precise measurements established that *Nightshade* had not moved an ångström further than it would have under ordinary inertia-suppressing propulsion. Angry as much with herself as anyone else, Skade made her way through the interstices of the curved black machinery. Soon, she found the person she was looking for: Molenka, the Exordium systems technician. Molenka looked drained of blood.

What went wrong?

Molenka fumbled out an explanation, dumping reams of technical data into the public part of Skade's mind. Skade absorbed the data critically, skimming it for the essentials. The configuration of the field-containment systems had not been perfect; the bubble of state-two vacuum had evaporated back into state zero before it could be pushed over the potential barrier into the magical tachyonic state four. Skade appraised the machinery. It appeared undamaged.

Then you've learned what went wrong, I take it? You can make the appropriate corrective changes and attempt the transition again?

[Skade . . .]

What?

[Something did happen. I can't find Jastrusiak anywhere. He was much closer to the equipment than I was when we attempted the experiment. But he isn't there now. I can't find him anywhere, or even any evidence of him.]

Skade listened to this without registering any expression beyond tolerant interest. Only when the woman had finished speaking and there had been several seconds of silence did she reply. *Jastrusiak?*

[Yes . . . Jastrusiak.]

The woman seemed relieved. [My partner in this. The other Exordium expert.]

There was never anyone called Jastrusiak on this ship, Molenka.

Molenka turned—so it appeared to Skade—a shade paler. Her reply was little more than an exhalation. [No . . .]

I assure you, there was no one called Jastrusiak. This is a small crew, and I know everyone on it.

[That isn't possible. I was with him not twenty minutes ago. We were in the machinery, readying it for the transition. Jastrusiak stayed there to make last-minute adjustments. I swear this!]

Perhaps you do. Skade was tempted, very tempted, to reach into Molenka's head and install a mnemonic blockade, wiping out Molenka's memory of what had just happened. But that would not bury the evident conflict between what she thought to be true and what was objective reality.

Molenka, I know this will be difficult for you, but you have to continue working with the equipment. I'm sorry about Jastrusiak—I forget his name for a moment. We'll find him, I promise you. There are many places where he could have ended up.

[I don't . . .]

Skade cut her off, one of her fingers suddenly appearing beneath Molenka's chin. *No. No words, Molenka. No words, no thoughts. Just go back into the machinery and make the necessary adjustments. Do that for me, will you? Do it for me, and for the Mother Nest?*

Molenka trembled. She was, Skade judged, quite exquisitely terrified. It was the resigned, hopeless terror of a small mammal caught in something's claws. [Yes, Skade.]

The name Jastrusiak stuck in Skade's mind, tantalisingly familiar. She could not dislodge it. When the opportunity presented itself, she tapped into the Conjoiner collective memory and retrieved all references connected to the name, or anything close to it. She was determined to understand what had made Molenka's subconscious malfunction in such a singularly creative fashion, weaving a non-existent individual out of nothing in a moment of terror.

To her moderate surprise, Skade learned that Jastrusiak was a name known to the Mother Nest. There had been a Jastrusiak amongst the Conjoined. He had been recruited during the Chasm City occupation. He had quickly gained Inner Sanctum clearance, where he worked on advanced concepts such as breakthrough propulsion theory. He had been one of a team of Conjoiner theorists who had established their own research base on an asteroid. They had been working on methods to convert existing Conjoiner drives to the stealthed design.

It was tricky work, it turned out. Jastrusiak's team had been amongst the first to learn exactly how tricky. Their entire base, along with a sizeable chunk of that hemisphere of the asteroid, had been wiped out in an accident.

So Jastrusiak was dead—had, in fact, been dead for many years.

But had he lived, Skade thought, he would have been exactly the kind of expert she would have recruited for her own team aboard *Nightshade*. Very probably he would have been of similar calibre to Molenka, and would have ended up working alongside her.

What did it mean? It was, she supposed, no more than uncomfortable coincidence.

Molenka called her back. [We're ready, Skade. We can try the experiment again.]

Skade hesitated, almost about to tell her that she had discovered the truth about Jastrusiak. But then she thought better of it. *Make it so,* Skade told her.

She watched the machinery move, the curved black arms whisking back and forth and, it appeared, through each other, knitting and threshing time and space like some infernal weaving machine, coaxing and cradling the bacterium-sized speck of altered metric into the tachyonic phase. Within seconds the machinery had become a knitting blur behind *Nightshade*. The gravity wave and exotic particle sensors registered squalls of deep spatial stress as the quantum vacuum on the boundary of the bubble was curdled and sheared on microscopic scales. The pattern of those squalls, filtered and processed by computers, told Molenka how the bubble's geometry was behaving. She transmitted this data to Skade, permitting her to visualise the bubble as a glowing globule of light, pulsing and quivering like a drop of mercury suspended in a magnetic cradle. Colours, not all of them within the normal human spectrum, shifted in prismatic waves across the skin of the bubble, signifying arcane nuances of quantum-vacuum interaction. None of that concerned Skade; all that mattered to her were the accompanying indices that told her that the bubble was behaving normally, or as normally as could be expected of something that had no real right to exist in this universe. There was a soft blue glow from the bubble as particles of Hawking radiation were snatched into the tachyonic state and whisked away from *Nightshade* at superluminal speed.

Molenka signalled that they were ready to expand the bubble, so that *Nightshade* itself would be trapped inside its own sphere of tachyonic-phase spacetime. The process would happen in a flash, and the field, according to Molenka, would collapse back to its microscopic scale in subjective picoseconds, but that instant of stability would be sufficient to translate Skade's ship across a light-nanosecond of space, about one-third of a metre. Disposable probes had already been deployed beyond the expected radius of the bubble, ready to capture the instant when the ship made its tachyonic shift. One-third of a metre was not enough to make a difference against Clavain, of course, but in principle the jump procedure could be extended in duration and repeated almost immediately. By far the hardest thing would be to do it once; thereafter it was only a question of refinements.

Skade gave Molenka permission to expand the bubble. At the same time Skade willed her implants into their maximum state of accelerated consciousness. The normal activity of the ship became a barely changing background; even the whisking black arms slowed so that she was able to appreciate their hypnotic dance more clearly. Skade examined her state of mind and found nervous anticipation, mingled with the visceral fear that she was about to commit a grave mistake. She recalled that the Wolf had told her that very few organic entities had ever moved faster than light. Under other circumstances, she might have chosen to heed the Wolf's unspoken warning, but at the same time the Wolf had been goading her on, urging her to this point. Its technical assistance had been vital in decoding the Exordium instructions, and she assumed that it had some interest in preserving its own existence. But perhaps it simply enjoyed seeing her conflicted, caring nothing for its own survival.

Never mind. It was done now. The whisking arms were already altering the field conditions around the bubble, stroking the boundary with delicate quantum caresses, encouraging it to expand. The wobbling bubble enlarged, swelling in a series of lopsided expansions. The scale changed in a series of logarithmic jumps, but not nearly fast enough. Skade knew immediately that something was wrong. The expansion should have happened too rapidly to be sensed, even in accelerated consciousness. The bubble should have engulfed the ship by now, but instead it had only inflated to the size of a swollen grapefruit. It hovered within the grasp of the whisking arms, horribly, tauntingly wrong. Skade prayed for the bubble to shrink back down to bacterium size, but she knew from what Molenka had said that it was much more likely to expand in an uncontrolled fashion. Horrified and enraptured, she watched as the grapefruit-sized bubble flexed and undulated, becoming peanut-shaped one instant and then squirming into a torus, a topological transformation that Molenka had sworn was impossible. Then it was a bubble again, and then, as random bulges and dents pulsed in an out of the membrane's surface, Skade swore she saw a gargoyle face leer at her. She knew that it was the fault of her subconscious, imprinting a pattern where none existed, but the impression of inchoate evil was inescapable.

Then the bubble expanded again, swelling up to the size of a small spacecraft. Some of the whisking arms did not swing out of the way in time, and their sharp extremities punched through the undulating membrane. The sensors flipped into overload, unable to process the howling torrent of gravitational and particle flux. Inexorably, matters were shifting out of control. Vital control systems in the rear of *Nightshade* were shutting down. The arms began to move spasmodically, lashing against each other like the limbs of ill-orchestrated dancers. Nodules and flanges sheered off. Scarves of glowing plasma ripped between the boundary and its encasing machinery. The boundary bloated again; its membrane swallowed cubic hectares of support machinery. The failing machinery could no longer hold it stable. Dim explosions pulsed within the bubble. A major control arm severed itself and swung back into the side of *Nightshade*'s hull. Skade sensed a chain of explosions surging along the side of her ship, pink blossoms cascading towards the bridge. Her beautiful machinery was ripping itself to pieces. The bubble squirmed larger, oozing through the failing constraints of the sheered and buckled arms. Emergency alarms sounded, internal barricades clanging down throughout the ship. Whiteness glared from the heart of the bubble as matter within it underwent a partial transition to the pure photonic state. A catastrophic reversion to the state-three quantum vacuum, in which all matter was massless . . .

The photo-leptonic flash surged through the membrane. The few arms that were still functioning were snapped backwards like broken fingers. There was a brief, furious sizzle of plasma discharge and then the bubble swept larger, engulfing *Nightshade* and dissipating at the same time. Skade felt it slam through her, like a sudden cold front on a warm day. At the same time a shock wave shook the ship, throwing Skade against a wall. Ordinarily the wall would have deformed to absorb the energy of the collision, but this time the impact was hard and metallic.

Yet the ship remained around her. She was able to think. She could still hear klaxons and emergency messages, and the barricades were still closing. But the excursion event had passed. The bubble had shattered, but while it had damaged her ship—perhaps profoundly, perhaps beyond the point of repair—it had not destroyed it.

Skade willed her consciousness rate back down to her normal processing speed. Her crest throbbed with the excess blood heat it had to dissipate—she felt light-headed—but that would soon pass. She appeared to have suffered no injuries, even in the violent crash against the wall. Her armour moved at her will, undamaged by the impact. She took hold of a wall restraint and tugged herself into the middle of the corridor. She had no weight, for *Nightshade* was drifting and had never been equipped for spin-generated gravity.

Molenka?

There was no response. The entire shipboard network was down, preventing neural communication unless the subjects were extremely close to each other. But she knew where Molenka had been before the bubble had swelled out of control. She called aloud, but there was still no answer, and then set off in the direction of the machinery. The critical volume was still pressurised, though she had to persuade the internal doors to let her through.

The glossy, curved surfaces of the alien machinery, like black glass, had shifted since she was last within this part of the ship. She wondered how much of the change had happened during the failed attempt to expand the bubble. The air prickled with ozone and a dozen less familiar smells, and against the continuous background of klaxons and spoken alarms she heard sparking and shearing sounds.

"Molenka?" she called again.

[Skade.] The neural response was incredibly weak, but it was recognisably Molenka. She was close now, certainly.

Skade pushed forwards, hand over hand, the movements of her armour stiff. The machinery surrounded her on all sides, smooth black ledges and protrusions, like the water-carved rock in some ancient underground cavern. It widened out, admitting her to an occlusion five or six metres from side to side. The scalloped walls were studded with data-input sockets. A window set into the far side of the chamber offered a view of the smashed and buckled containment machinery jutting from the rear of her ship. Even now some of the arms were still moving, ticking lazily back and forth like the last twitching limbs of a dying creature. Seen with her eyes, the damage appeared much worse than she had been led to believe. Her ship had been gutted, its viscera ripped out for inspection.

But that was not what drew Skade's attention. In the approximate centre of the occlusion floated an undulating sac, its skin a milky translucence behind which something shifted in and out of visibility. The sac was five-pointed, throwing out blunt pseudopodia that corresponded in proportion and arrangement to the head and limbs of a human. Indeed, Skade saw, the thing within it was human, a shape she glimpsed in shattered parts rather than any unified whole. There was a ripple of dark clothing and a ripple of paler flesh.

Molenka?

Though she was only metres away, the reply felt astonishingly distant.

[Yes. It's me. I'm trapped, Skade. Trapped inside part of the bubble.]

Skade shivered, impressed by the woman's calm. She was

clearly going to die, and yet her reporting of her predicament had an admirable detachment. It was the attitude of a true Conjoiner, convinced that her essence would live on in the wider consciousness of the Mother Nest, and that physical death amounted only to the removal of an inessential peripheral element from a much more significant whole. But, Skade reminded herself, they were a long way from the Mother Nest now. *The bubble, Molenka?*

[It fragmented as it passed through the ship. It glued itself to me, almost deliberately. Almost as if it was looking for someone to surround, someone to embed within itself.] The five-pointed thing wobbled revoltingly, hinting at some awful instability that was on the point of collapsing.

What state are you in, Molenka?

[It must be state one, Skade . . . I don't feel any different. Just trapped . . . and *distant.* I feel very, very distant.] The bubble fragment began to contract, exactly as Molenka had said it was likely to do. The body-shaped membrane shrunk down until its surface conformed closely with Molenka's body. For a dreadful moment she looked quite normal, except that she was covered in a shifting glaze of pearly light. Skade dared to hope that the bubble would choose that instant to collapse, freeing Molenka. But at the same time she knew it was not about to happen.

The bubble quivered again, hiccoughed and twitched. Molenka's expression—it was quite visible—became obviously frightened. Even through the faint neural channel that connected them, Skade felt the woman's fear and apprehension. It was as if the glaze was tightening around her.

[Help me, Skade. I can't breathe.]

I can't. I don't know what to do.

Molenka's skin was tight against the membrane. She was starting to suffocate. Normal speech would have been impossible by now, but the automatic routines in her head would have already started shutting down non-essential parts of her brain, conserving vital resources to squeeze three or four extra minutes of consciousness from her last breath. [Help me. Please . . .]

The membrane tightened further. Skade watched, unable to turn away, as it squeezed Molenka. Her pain gushed across the neural link. It was all that Skade recognised: there was no further room for rational thought. She reached out, desperate to do something even if the gesture was hopeless. Her fingers skimmed the surface of the membrane. It shrank further, hastened by the contact. The neural link began to break up. The collapsing membrane was crushing Molenka alive, the pressure destroying the delicate loom of Conjoiner implants that floated in her skull.

The membrane halted, quivered, and then shrank down with shocking speed. When Molenka was three-quarters of her normal size, the figure within the membrane turned abruptly scarlet. Skade felt the screaming howl of abrupt neural severance before her own implants curtailed the link. Molenka was dead. But the human-shaped form lingered even as it collapsed further. Now it was a mannequin, now a horrid marionette, now a doll, now a thumb-sized figurine, losing shape and definition as the material within liquefied. Then the contraction stopped, the milky envelope stabilising.

Skade reached out and grasped the marble-sized thing that had been Molenka, knowing that she must dispose of it into vacuum before the field contracted even further. The matter within the membrane—that matter that had once been Molenka—was already under savage compression, and she did not want to think about what would happen should it spontaneously expand.

She tugged at the marble, but the thing barely moved, as if it were locked rigid at that precise point in space and time. She increased her suit's strength and finally the marble began to shift. It had all of Molenka's inertial mass within it, perhaps more, and it would be just as difficult to stop or steer.

Skade began to make her laborious way to the nearest dorsal airlock.

The projection helix spun up to speed. Clavain stood with his hands on the railing that surrounded it, peering at the indistinct shape that appeared within the cylinder. It resembled a squashed bug, a fan of soft ropelike entrails spilling from one end of a hard, dark carapace.

"She isn't going anywhere in a hurry," Scorpio said.

"Dead in the water," Antoinette Bax concurred. She whistled. "She's drifting, just falling through space. Holy shit. What do you think happened to her?"

"Something bad, but not something catastrophic," Clavain said quietly, "or else we wouldn't see her at all. Scorp, can you zoom in and enhance the rear section? It looks like something happened there."

Scorpio was controlling the hull cameras, slaved to pan over the drifting starship as they slammed past it with a velocity differential of more than a thousand kilometres per second. They would be within effective weapons range for only an hour. *Zodiacal Light* was not even accelerating at the moment; the inertia-suppressing systems were switched off and the engines were quiet. Great flywheels had spun the lighthugger's habitation core up to one gee of centrifugal gravity. Clavain enjoyed not having to struggle around under higher gravity or wear an exoskeletal rig. It was even more pleasant not having to suffer the disturbing physiological effects of the inertia-suppression field.

"There," Scorpio said when he had finished adjusting the settings. "That's as clear as it's going to get, Clavain."

"Thanks."

Remontoire, the only one amongst them still wearing an exoskeletal rig, stepped closer to the cylinder, brushing past Pauline Sukhoi with a whirr of servos.

"I don't recognise those structures, Clavain, but they look intentional."

Clavain nodded. That was his opinion as well. The basic shape of the lighthugger was still as it should have been, but from her rear erupted a complicated splay of twisted filaments and arcs, like the mainsprings and ratchets of some clockwork mechanism caught in the act of exploding.

"Would you care to speculate?" Clavain asked Remontoire.

"She was desperate to escape us, desperate to pull ahead. She might have considered something extreme."

"Extreme?" Xavier asked. He had one hand around Antoinette's waist. The two of them were filthy with machine oil.

"She already had inertia suppression," Remontoire said. "But I think this was something else—a modification of the same equipment to push it into a different state."

"Such as?" Xavier asked.

Clavain looked at Remontoire, too.

Remontoire said, "The technology will suppress inertial mass—that's what Skade called a state-two field—but it doesn't remove it entirely. In a state-three field, however, all inertial mass drops to zero. Matter becomes photonic, unable to travel at anything other than the speed of light. Time dilation becomes infinite, so the ship would remain frozen in the photonic state until the end of time."

Clavain nodded at his friend. Remtontoire appeared perfectly willing to wear the exoskeleton even though it was functioning as a form of restraint, capable of immobilising him should Clavain decide that he could not be trusted.

"What about state four?" Clavain asked.

"That might be more useful," Remontoire said. "If she could tunnel through state three, skipping it entirely, she might be able to achieve a smooth transition to a state-four field. Inside that field, the ship would flip into a tachyonic mass state, unable to do anything but travel faster than light."

"Skade tried that?" Xavier asked reverently.

"It's as good an explanation as any I can think of," Remontoire said.

"What do you think happened?" Antoinette asked.

"Some sort of field instability," Pauline Sukhoi said, the pale reflection of her haunted face hanging in the display tank. She spoke slowly and solemnly. "Managing a bubble of altered space-time makes fusion containment look like the kind of game children play on their birthdays. My suspicion is that Skade first created a microscopic bubble, probably sub-atomic, certainly no larger than a bacterium. At that scale, it's deceptively easy to manipulate. See those sickles and arms?" She nodded at the image, which had rotated slightly since it had first appeared. "Those would have been her field generators and containment systems. They would have been supposed to allow the field to expand in a stable fashion until it encased the ship. A bubble expanding at light-speed would take less than half a millisecond to swallow a ship the size of *Nightshade,* but altered vacuum expands superluminally, like inflationary space-time. A state-four bubble has a characteristic doubling time in the order of ten to the minus forty-three seconds. That doesn't give much time to react if things start going wrong."

"And if the bubble kept growing . . . ?" Antoinette asked.

"It won't," Sukhoi said. "At least, you wouldn't ever know about it if it does. No one would."

"Skade's lucky she has a ship left," Xavier said.

Sukhoi nodded. "It must have been a small accident, probably during the transition between states. She may have hit state three, converting a small chunk of her ship to pure white light. A small photo-leptonic explosion."

"It looks survivable," Scorpio said.

"Are there life-signs?" Antoinette asked.

Clavain shook his head. "None. But there wouldn't be, not with *Nightshade*. The prototype's designed for maximum stealth. Our usual scanning methods won't work."

Scorpio adjusted some settings, causing the colours of the image to shift to spectral greens and blues. "Thermal," he said. "She still has power, Clavain. If there'd been a major systems blow-out, her hull would be five degrees cooler by now."

"I don't doubt that there are survivors," Clavain said.

Scorpio nodded. "Some, maybe. They'll lie low until we're ahead of them, out of sensor range. Then they'll kick into repair mode. Before you know it they'll be on our tail, just as much a problem as they ever were."

"I've thought about that, Scorp," said Clavain.

The pig nodded. "And?"

"I'm not going to attack them."

Scorpio's wild dark eyes flared. "Clavain . . . "

"Felka is still alive."

There was an awkward silence. Clavain felt it press around him. They were all looking at him, even Sukhoi, each of them thanking their stars that they did not have to take this decision.

"You don't know that," Scorpio said. Clavain saw the lines of tension etched into his jaw. "Skade lied before and killed Lasher. She hasn't given us any evidence that she really has Felka. That's because she doesn't have her, or because Felka is dead now."

Calmly, Clavain said, "What evidence could she give? There isn't anything she couldn't fake."

"She could have learned something from Felka, something only she would know."

"You never met Felka, Scorp. She's strong—much stronger than Skade assumes. She wouldn't give Skade anything Skade could use to control me."

"Then perhaps she does have her, Clavain. But that doesn't mean she's awake. She's probably in reefersleep, so she doesn't cause any trouble."

"What difference would that make?" Clavain asked.

"She wouldn't feel anything," Scorpio said. "We have enough weapons now, Clavain. *Nightshade* is a sitting duck. We can take her out instantly, painlessly. Felka won't know a thing."

Clavain reached for his anger, forcing it to lie low. "Would you say that if she hadn't murdered Lasher?"

The pig thumped the railing. "She did, Clavain. That's all that matters."

"No . . . " Antoinette said. "It isn't all that matters. Clavain's right. We can't start acting like a single human life doesn't matter. We become as bad as the wolves if we do that."

Xavier, next to her, beamed proudly. "I agree," he said. "Sorry, Scorpio. I know she killed Lasher, and I know how much that pissed you off."

"You have no idea," Scorpio said. He did not sound angry so much as regretful. "And don't tell me a single human life suddenly matters. It's just because you know her. Skade is human, too. What about her, and her allies aboard that ship?"

Cruz, who had been silent until then, spoke softly. "Listen to Clavain. He's right. We'll get another chance to kill Skade. This just doesn't feel right."

"Might I make a suggestion?" Remontoire said.

Clavain looked at Remontoire uneasily. "What, Rem?"

"We are just—just—within shuttle range. It would cost us more antimatter, a fifth of our remaining stocks, but we may never get another chance like this."

"Another chance to do what?" Clavain asked.

Remontoire blinked, surprised, as if this was entirely too obvious to state. "To rescue Felka, of course."

TWENTY-NINE

Remontoire's calculation had been unerringly accurate; so much so that Clavain suspected he had already costed the energy expenditure of the shuttle flight before the rescue operation had been more than a glint in Clavain's eye.

Three of them went out: Scorpio, Remontoire and Clavain.

There was mercifully little time to make the shuttle ready. Merciful because had Clavain been granted hours or days, he would have spent the entire time convulsed in doubt, endlessly balancing one additional weapon or piece of armour against the fuel that would be saved by leaving it behind. As it was they had to make do with one of the stripped-down shuttles that had been used to resupply the defence shuttle before they had brought the laser-powered shield sail into use. The shuttle was just a skeleton, a wispy geodesic sketch of black spars, struts and naked silvery subsystems. It looked, to Clavain's eyes, faintly obscene. He was used to machines that kept their innards decently covered. But it would do the job well enough, he supposed. If Skade mounted any serious defence, armour wouldn't help them anyway.

The flight deck was the only part of the ship that was shielded from space, and even then it was not pressurised. They would have to wear suits for the entire operation and take an additional suit with them for Felka to wear on the return leg. There was also room to stow a reefersleep casket if it turned out she was frozen. But in that case, Felka's return mass would have to be offset by leaving behind weapons and fuel tanks at the halfway point.

Clavain took the middle seat, with the flight controls plugged into his suit. Scorpio sat on his left, Remontoire on his right; both could assume control of the avionics should Clavain need a rest.

"Are you sure you trust me enough to have me along for the operation?" Remontoire had asked with a playful smile when they were deciding who would go on the mission.

"I guess I'll find out, won't I?" Clavain had said.

"I won't be much use to you in an exoskeleton. You can't put a standard suit over one, and we don't have powered armour ready."

Clavain had nodded at Blood, Scorpio's deputy. "Get him out of the exoskeleton. If he tries anything, you know what to do."

"I won't, Clavain," Remontoire had assured him.

"I almost believe you. But I'm not sure I'd take the risk if there was someone else who knew *Nightshade* as well as you do. Or Skade, for that matter."

"I'm coming too," Scorpio had insisted.

"We're going to get Felka," Clavain had said. "Not to avenge Lasher."

"Perhaps." In so far as Clavain could read his expression, Scorpio had not looked fully convinced. "But let's be honest. Once you've got Felka, you're not going to walk out of there without doing some damage, are you?"

"I'll accept Skade's surrender gratefully," Clavain had said.

"We'll take pinhead munitions," Scorpio had said. "You won't miss a little hot dust, Clavain, and it'll sure put a hole in *Nightshade*."

"I'm grateful for your help, Scorpio. And I understand your feelings towards Skade after what she did. But we need you here, to supervise the weapons programme."

"And we don't need you?"

"This is about me and Felka," Clavain had said.

Scorpio had put a hand on his arm. "So take help when it's offered. I'm not in the habit of co-operating with people, Clavain, so make the most of this rare display of magnanimity and shut the fuck up."

Clavain had shrugged. He had not felt optimistic about the mission, but Scorpio's enthusiasm for a fight was oddly infectious.

He had turned to Remontoire. "Looks as if he's along for the ride, Rem. Certain you want to be on the team now?"

Remontoire had looked at the pig, then back at Clavain. "We'll manage," he had said.

Now that the mission had begun the two of them were silent, letting Clavain concentrate on the business of flying. He gunned the shuttle away from *Zodiacal Light,* homing in on the drifting *Nightshade,* trying not to think of how fast they were actually moving. The two major ships were falling through space at only two per cent below the speed of light, but there was still no strong visual cue that they were moving so rapidly. The stars had been shifted in both position and colour by relativistic effects, but they still appeared perfectly fixed and stationary, even at this high tau factor. Had their trajectory taken them close to a luminous body like a star, they might have seen it swing by in the night, squashed away from sphericity by Lorentz-Fitzgerald contraction. But even then it would not have slammed past unless they were nearly skimming its atmosphere. The exhaust flare of another ship, heading back to Yellowstone, would have been visible, but they had the corridor to themselves. And though the hulls of both ships glowed in the near infra-red, heated by the slow, constant abrasion of interstellar hydrogen and microscopic dust grains, this was nothing Clavain's mind could process into any visceral sense of speed. He was aware that the same collisions were a problem for the shuttle, too, though its much smaller cross section made them less likely. But cosmic rays, relativistically boosted by their motion, were eating into him every second. That was why there was armour around the flight deck.

The trip to *Nightshade* passed quickly, perhaps because Clavain was fearful of what he would find upon his arrival. The trio spent most of the journey unconscious, conserving suit power, knowing that there was realistically nothing they could do should Skade launch an attack.

Clavain and his companions came around when they were in visual range of the crippled lighthugger.

She was dark, of course—they were in true interstellar space here—but Clavain could see her because *Zodiacal Light* was shining one of its optical lasers on to her hull. He could not make out all the details he wanted to, but he could see enough to feel decidedly ill at ease. The effect was that of moonlight on a foreboding gothic edifice. The shuttle threw a tracery of moving shadows across the larger ship, making it appear to squirm and move.

The weird augmentations looked even stranger up close.

Their complexity had not really been apparent before, nor the extent to which they had been twisted and sheared by the accident. But Skade had been remarkably fortunate, since the damage was largely confined to the tapering rear part of her ship. The two Conjoiner drives, thrust out from either side of the thoraxlike hull, had suffered only superficial harm. Clavain steered the shuttle closer, convincing himself that any attack would already have happened. Delicately, he nosed the skeletal craft between the stingerlike curves and arcs of the ruined faster-than-light drive.

"She was desperate," he said to his companions. "She must have known there was no way we were going to get to Resurgam ahead of her, but that wasn't good enough for Skade. She wanted to get there years ahead of us."

Scorpio said, "She had the means, Clavain. Why are you surprised that she used them?"

"He's right to be surprised," Remontoire cut in before Clavain could answer. "Skade was perfectly aware of the risks of toying with the state-four transition. She denied any interest in it when I asked her about it, but I had the impression she was lying. Her own experiments must already have revealed the risks."

"Once thing's for sure," Scorpio said. "She wanted those guns badly, Clavain. They must mean a fuck of a lot to her."

Clavain nodded. "But we're not really dealing with Skade, I think. We're dealing with whatever it was that got to her in the Château. The Mademoiselle wanted the weapons, and she just planted the idea in Skade's mind."

"This Mademoiselle interests me greatly," Remontoire said. He had been told some of what had happened in Chasm City. "I'd have liked to have met her."

"Too late," Scorpio said. "H had her corpse in a box—didn't Clavain tell you?"

"He had *something* in a box," Remontoire said testily. "But evidently not the part of her that mattered. That part reached Skade. *Is* Skade now, for all we know."

Clavain slid the shuttle through the last pair of scissorlike blades and back into open space. This side of *Nightshade* was pitch black, save where the shuttle's own floods picked out details. Clavain crept along the hull, observing that the antiship weapons were all stowed behind their invisibly seamed hatches.

It meant very little: it would only require an eyeblink to deploy them, but it was undeniably reassuring that they were not already pointed at the shuttle.

"You two know your way around this thing?" Scorpio said.

"Of course," Remontoire said. "It used to be our ship. You should recognise it as well. It's the same one that pulled you out of Maruska Chung's cruiser."

"The only thing I remember about that is you trying to put the fear of the devil into me, Remontoire."

With some relief, Clavain realised that they had reached the airlock he had been looking for. There was still no sign of a reaction from the crippled ship: no lights or indications of proximity sensors coming alive. Clavain guyed them to the hull with epoxy-tipped grapples, holding his breath as the suckerlike grapple feet adhered to the ablative hull armour. But nothing happened.

"This is the difficult part," Clavain said. "Rem, I want you to remain here on the shuttle. Scorpio's coming inside with me."

"Might I ask why?"

"Yes, although I was hoping you wouldn't. Scorp has more experience of hand-to-hand combat than you do, almost more than me. But the main reason is I don't trust you enough to have you inside."

"You trusted me to come this far."

"And I'm prepared to trust you to sit tight on the shuttle until we get out." Clavain checked the time. "In thirty-five minutes we're out of return range. Wait half an hour and then leave. Not a minute more, even if Scorp and I are already coming back out of the airlock."

"You're serious, aren't you?"

"We've budgeted enough fuel to return the three of us plus Felka. If you return alone you'll have fuel to spare—fuel that we'll badly need later. That's what I trust you with, Rem: that responsibility."

"But not to come aboard," Remontoire said.

"No. Not with Skade on that ship. I can't run the risk of you defecting back to her side."

"You're wrong, Clavain."

"Am I?"

"I didn't defect. Neither did you. It was Skade and the rest of them that changed sides, not us."

"C'mon," Scorpio said, tugging at Clavain's arm. "We've got twenty-nine minutes now."

The two of them crossed over to *Nightshade*. Clavain fumbled around the rim of the airlock until he found the nearly invisible recess that concealed the external controls. It was just wide enough to take his gloved hand. He felt the familiar trinity of manual switches—standard Conjoiner design—and tugged them to the open position. Even if there had been a general shipwide power failure, cells within the lock would have retained power to open the door for about a century. Even if that failed, there was a manual mechanism on the other side of the rim.

The door slid aside. Blood-red lighting glared back from the interior chamber. His eyes had become highly dark-adapted. He waited for them to adjust to the brightness and then ushered Scorpio into the generously proportioned space. He followed the pig, their bulky suits knocking together, and then sealed and pressurised the chamber. It took an eternity.

The inner door opened. The interior of the ship was bathed in the same blood-red emergency lighting. But at least there was power. That meant there might be survivors, too.

Clavain studied the ambient data read-out in his faceplate field of view, then turned off his suit air and slid up the faceplate. These clumsy old suits, the best that *Zodiacal Light* had been able to provide, had limited air and power, and he saw no sense in wasting resources. He motioned for Scorpio to do likewise.

The pig whispered, "Where are we?"

"Amidships," Clavain told him in a normal speaking voice. "But everything looks different in this light, and without gravity. The ship doesn't feel as familiar as I had expected. I wish I knew how many crew we could expect to find."

"Skade never gave any indication?" he hissed back.

"No. You could run a ship like this with a few experts, and no more. There's no need to whisper either, Scorp. If there's anyone around to know we're here, they know we're here."

"Remind me why we didn't come with guns?"

"No point, Scorp. They'd have heavier and better armaments here. Either we take Felka painlessly or we negotiate our way out." Clavain tapped his utility belt. "Of course, we do have a negotiating aid."

They had brought pinheads aboard Skade's ship. The microscopic fragments of antimatter suspended in a pin-sized containment system, which was in turn shielded within a thumb-sized armoured grenade, would blow *Nightshade* cleanly out of the sky.

They moved down the red-lit corridor hand over hand. Every now and then, randomly, one of them would unclip a pinhead device, smear it with epoxy and push it into place in a corner or shadow. Clavain was confident that a well-organised search would be able to locate all the pinheads in a few tens of minutes. But a well-organised search looked like exactly the kind of thing the ship was not going to be capable of mounting for quite some time.

They had been working their way along for eight minutes when Scorpio broke the silence. They had reached a trifurcation in the corridor. "Recognise anything yet?"

"Yes. We're near the bridge." Clavain pointed one way. "But the reefersleep chamber is down here. If she has Felka frozen, that's where she might be. We'll check it first."

"We've got twenty minutes, then we have to be out."

Clavain knew that the time limit was, in a sense, artificially imposed. *Zodiacal Light* could backtrack and recover the shuttle even if they delayed their departure, but only at a wasteful expenditure of time, one that would instil a lethal seed of complacency into the rest of the crew. He had considered the risks and concluded that it would be better for all three of them to die—or at least be marooned here—rather than let that happen. Their deputies and sub-deputies could continue the operation even if Remontoire did not make it back alive, and they had to believe that every second really counted. As indeed it did. It was tough. But that was war, and it was a long way from the toughest decision Clavain had ever had to make.

They worked their way down to the reefersleep chamber.

"Something ahead," Scorpio said, after they had crawled and clambered wordlessly for several minutes.

Clavain slowed his progress, peering into the same red gloom, envious of Scorpio's augmented eyesight. "Looks like a body," he said.

They approached it carefully, pulling themselves along from one padded wall-staple to another. Clavain was mindful of every minute that elapsed; every half-minute of each minute; every cruel second.

They reached the body.

"Do you recognise it?" Scorpio asked, fascinated.

"I'm not sure whether anyone would be able to recognise it for certain," Clavain said, "but it isn't Felka. I don't think it could have been Skade, either."

Something dreadful had happened to the body. It had been sliced down the middle, exactly and neatly, in the fastidious fashion of an anatomical model. The interior organs were packed into tightly coiled or serpentine formations, glistening like glazed sweetmeats. Scorpio reached out a gloved trotter and pushed the half-figure; it drifted slackly away from the slick walling where it had come to rest.

"Where do you think the rest of it is?" he asked.

"Somewhere else," Clavain replied. "This half must have drifted here."

"What did that to it? I've seen what beam-weapons can do and it isn't nice, but there isn't any sign of scorching on this body."

"It was a causal gradient," said a third voice.

"Skade . . . " Clavain breathed.

She was behind them. She had approached with inhuman silence, not even breathing. Her armoured bulk filled the corridor, black as night save for the pale oval of her face.

"Hello, Clavain. And hello, Scorpio, too, I suppose." She looked at him with mild interest. "So you didn't die then, pig?"

"Actually, Clavain was just pointing out how lucky I am to have met the Conjoiners."

"Sensible Clavain."

Clavain looked at her, horrified and awestruck at the same time. Remontoire had forewarned him about Skade's accident, but that warning had been insufficient to prepare him for this meeting. Her mechanical armour was androform, even—in an exaggerated, faintly medieval way—feminine, swelling at the hips and with the suggestion of breasts moulded into the chest plate. But Clavain knew now that it was not armour at all but a life-support prosthesis; that the only organic part of her was her head. Skade's crested skull was plugged stiffly into the neck-piece of the armour. The brutal conjunction of flesh and machinery screamed wrongness, a wrongness that became even more acute when Skade smiled.

"You did this to me," she said, obviously speaking aloud for Scorpio's benefit. "Aren't you proud?"

"I didn't do it to you, Skade. I know exactly what happened. I hurt you, and I'm sorry it happened that way. But it wasn't intentional and you know it."

"So your defection was involuntary? If only it were that easy."

"I didn't cut your head off, Skade," Clavain said. "By now Delmar could have healed the injuries I gave you. You'd be whole again. But that didn't fit with your plans."

"You dictated my plans, Clavain. You and my loyalty to the Mother Nest."

"I don't question your loyalty, Skade. I just wonder exactly what it is you're loyal to."

Scorpio whispered, "Thirteen minutes, Clavain. Then we have to be out of here."

Skade's attention snapped on to the pig. "In a hurry, are you?"

"Aren't we all?" Scorpio said.

"You've come for something. I don't doubt that your weapons could already have destroyed *Nightshade* were that your intention."

"Give me Felka," Clavain said. "Give me Felka, then we'll leave you alone."

"Does she mean that much to you, Clavain, that you'd have held back from destroying me when you had the chance?"

"She means a great deal to me, yes."

Skade's crest rippled with turquoise and orange. "I'll give you Felka, if it makes you leave. But first I want to show you something."

She reached up with the gauntleted arms of her suit, placing one hand on either side of her neck as if about to strangle herself. But her metal hands were evidently capable of great gentleness. Clavain heard a click somewhere within Skade's chest, and then the metal pillar of her neck began to rise from between her shoulders. She was removing her own head. Clavain watched, entranced and repelled, as the lower part of the pillar emerged. It ended in thrashing, segmented appendages. They dribbled pink baubles of coloured fluid—blood, perhaps, or something entirely artificial.

"Skade . . . " he said. "This isn't necessary."

"Oh, it is very necessary, Clavain. I want you to apprehend fully what it is you've done to me. I want you to feel the horror of it."

"I think he's getting the picture," Scorpio said.

"Just give me Felka, then I'll leave you."

She hefted her own head, cradling it in one hand. It continued to speak. "Do you hate me, Clavain?"

"None of this is personal, Skade. I just think you're misguided."

"Misguided because I care about the survival of our people?"

"Something got to you, Skade," Clavain said. "You were a good Conjoiner once, one of the best. You truly served the Mother Nest, just as I did. But then you were sent on the Château operation."

He had pricked her interest. He saw the involuntary widening of her eyes. "The Chateau des Corbeaux? What does that have to do with anything?"

"A lot more than you'd like to think," Clavain said. "You were the only survivor, Skade, but you didn't come back alone. You probably don't remember very much of what actually happened down there, but that doesn't matter. Something got to you, I'm certain of that. It's responsible for everything that's happened lately." He tried to smile. "That's why I don't hate you, or even much blame you. You're either not the Skade I knew, or you think you're serving something higher than yourself."

"Ridiculous."

"But possibly true. I should know, Skade, I went there myself. How do you think we stayed on your tail all this time? The Château was the source for the technology you and I both used. Alien technology, for manipulating inertia. Except you used it for much more than that, didn't you?"

"I used it to serve an end, that's all."

"You tried to move faster than light, just the way Galiana did." He saw another flicker of interest at the mention of Galiana's name. "Why, Skade? What was so important that you had to do this? They're just weapons."

"You want them badly, too."

Clavain nodded. "But only because I've seen how badly you want them. You showed me that fleet, too, and that made me think you were planning on getting away from this part of space. What is it, Skade? What have you seen in your crystal ball?"

"Shall I show you, Clavain?"

"Show me?" he asked.

"Allow me access to your mind and I'll implant exactly what I was shown. Then you will know. And perhaps see things my way."

"Don't . . . " Scorpio said.

Clavain lowered his mental defences. Skade's presence was sudden and intrusive, so much so that he flinched. But she did not attempt to do more than paint images in his mind, as she had promised.

Clavain saw the end of everything. He saw chains of human habitats spangling with bright pinpricks of annihilating fire. Nuclear garlands dappled the surfaces of worlds too unimportant to dismantle. He saw comets and asteroids being steered into colonies, wave upon wave of them, far too many to be neutralised by the existing defences. Flares were lifted from the surfaces of stars, focused and daubed across the faces of worlds, sterilising all in their path. He saw rocky worlds being pulverised, smashed into hot clouds of interplanetary rubble. He saw gas giants being spun apart, ruined like the toys of petulant children. He saw stars themselves dying, poisoned so that they shone too hot or too cold, or ripped apart in a dozen different ways. He saw ships detonating in interstellar space, when they imagined they were safe from harm. He heard a panicked chorus of human radio and laser transmissions that was at first a multitude, but which thinned out to a handful of desperate lone voices, which were themselves silenced one by one. Then he heard only the mindless warbling of machine transmissions, and even those began to fall silent as humanity's last defences crumbled.

The cleansing was spread across a volume many dozens of light-years wide. It took many decades to complete, but it was over in a flash compared with the slow grind of galactic history.

And all around, orchestrating this cleansing, he sensed dim, ruthless sentience. It was an ensemble of machine minds, most of which hovered just beneath the threshold of consciousness.

They were old, older than the youngest stars, and they were expert only in the art of extinction. Nothing else concerned them.

"How far in the future is this?" he asked Skade.

"It's already begun. We just don't know it yet. But within half a century the wolves reach the core colonies, those closest to the First System. Within a century, the human race consists of a few huddling groups too afraid to travel or attempt any communication with each other."

"And the Conjoiners?"

"We're amongst them but just as vulnerable, just as predated. No Mother Nest remains. Conjoiner nests in some systems have been wiped out completely. That's when they send the message back in time."

He absorbed what she had said and nodded guardedly, prepared to accept it for the time being. "How did they do it?"

"Galiana's Exordium experiments," Skade's decorporated head answered. "She explored the linkage of human minds with coherent quantum states. But matter in a state of quantum superposition is entangled, in a ghostly sense, with every particle that has ever existed, or ever *will* exist. Her experiments were only intended to explore new modes of parallel consciousness, but she opened a window to the future, too. The conduit was imperfect, so that only faint echoes reached back to Mars. And every message sent through the channel increased the background noise. The conduit had a finite information capacity, you see. Exordium was a precious resource that could only be used at times of extreme crisis."

Clavain felt a dizzying sense of vertigo. "Our history's already been changed, hasn't it?"

"Galiana learned enough to make the first starship drive. It was a question of energy, Clavain, and the manipulation of quantum wormholes. At the heart of a Conjoiner drive is one end of a microscopic wormhole. The other end is anchored fifteen billion years in the past, sucking energy out of the quarkgluon plasma of the primordial fireball. Of course, the same technology can be applied to the manufacturing of doomsday weapons."

"The hell-class weapons," he said.

"In our original history we had neither of these advantages. We did not achieve starflight until a century later than the *Sandra Voi*'s first flight. Our ships were slow, heavy, fragile, incapable of reaching more than a fifth of light-speed. The human expansion was necessarily retarded. In four hundred years only a handful of systems were successfully settled. Yet still we attracted the wolves, even in that timeline. The cleansing was brutally efficient. This version of history—the one you have known—was an attempt at an improvement. The pace of human expansion was quickened and we were given better weapons to deal with the threat once it arose."

"I see now," Clavain said, "why the hell-class weapons couldn't be made again. Once Galiana had been shown how to make them, she destroyed the knowledge."

"They were a gift from the future," she said pridefully. "A gift from our future selves."

"And now?"

"Even in this timeline decimation happened. Again the wolves were alerted to our emergence. And it turned out that the drives were easy for them to track, across light-years of space."

"So our future selves tried another tweak."

"Yes. This time they reached back only into the recent past, intervening much later in Conjoiner history. The first message was an edict warning us to stop using Conjoiner drives. That was why we stopped shipbuilding a century ago. Later, we were given clues that enabled us to build stealthed drives of the kind *Nightshade* carries. The Demarchists thought we had built her to gain a tactical advantage over them in the war. In fact, she was designed to be our first weapon against the wolves. Later, we were given information regarding the construction of inertia-suppressing machinery. Although I didn't know it at the time, I was sent to the Château to obtain the fragments of alien technology which would enable us to assemble the prototype inertia-suppressing machine."

"And now?"

She answered him with a smile. "We've been given another chance. This time, flight is the only viable solution. The Conjoiners must leave this volume of space before the wolves arrive *en masse*."

"Run away, you mean?"

"Not really your style, is it, Clavain? But sometimes it's the only response that makes any sense. Later, we can consider a return—even a confrontation with the wolves. Other species have failed, but we are different, I think. We have already had the nerve to alter our past."

"What makes you think the other poor suckers didn't try it as well?"

"Clavain . . . " It was Scorpio. "We really need to be out of here, now."

"Skade . . . you've shown me enough," Clavain said. "I accept that you believe you are acting justly."

"And yet you still think I am the puppet of some mysterious agency?"

"I don't know, Skade. I certainly haven't ruled it out."

"I serve only the Mother Nest."

"Fine." He nodded, sensing that no matter what the truth was Skade believed that she was acting correctly. "Now give me Felka and I'll leave."

"Will you destroy me once you have left?"

He doubted that she knew of the pinhead charges he and Scorpio had deployed. He said, "What will happen to you, Skade, if I leave you here, drifting? Can you repair your ship?"

"I don't need to. The other craft are not far behind me. They are your real enemy, Clavain. Vastly better armed than *Nightshade,* and yet just as nimble and difficult to detect."

"That still doesn't mean I'd be better off not killing you."

Skade turned around and raised her voice. "Bring Felka here."

Half a minute later, two other Conjoiners appeared behind Skade, burdened with a spacesuited figure. Skade allowed them to pass it forwards. The visor was open so that Clavain could tell that the figure was Felka. She appeared unconscious, but he was certain that she was still alive.

"Here. Take her."

"What's wrong with her?"

"Nothing fundamental," Skade said. "I told you she was becoming withdrawn, didn't I? She misses her Wall very much. Perhaps she will improve in your care. But there is something you need to know, Clavain."

He looked at her. "What?"

"She isn't your daughter. She never was. Everything she told you was a lie, to make you more likely to return. A plausible lie, and perhaps one she almost wanted to believe was true, but a lie nonetheless. Do you still want her now?"

He knew she was telling the truth. Skade would lie to hurt him, but only if it served her wider ambitions. She was not doing that now, although he dearly wished that she were.

His voice caught in his throat. "Why should I want her less?"

"Be honest, Clavain. It might have made a difference."

"I came here to save someone I care for, that's all." He fought to keep his voice from breaking. "Whether she's my blood or not . . . it doesn't matter."

"No?"

"Not at all."

"Good. Then I believe our business here is done. Felka has served us both well, Clavain. She protected me from you, and she was able to bring out the co-operative side of the Wolf, something I could never have done on my own."

"The Wolf?"

"Oh, sorry, didn't I mention the Wolf?"

"Let's leave," Scorpio said.

"No. Not just yet. I want to know what she meant."

"I meant exactly what I said, Clavain." With loving care, Skade replaced her own head, blinking at the moment when it clicked home. "I brought the Wolf with me because I imagined it might prove valuable. Well, I was right."

"You mean you brought Galiana's body?"

"I brought Galiana," Skade corrected. "She isn't dead, Clavain. Not in the way you always thought she was. I reached her shortly after she returned from deep space. Her personality and memories were still there, perfectly intact. We had conversations, she and I. She asked about you—and of Felka—and I told her a small white lie; it was better for all of us that she think you dead. She was already losing the battle, you see. The Wolf was trying to take her over, and in the end she wasn't strong enough to fight it. But it didn't kill her, even then. It kept her mind intact because it found her memories useful. It also knew that Galiana was precious to us, and so we would do nothing against it that would harm her."

Clavain looked at her, hoping against hope that she was lying to him as she had lied before, but knowing that this was now the truth. And although he knew the answer she would give, he had to ask the question all the same.

"Will you give her to me?"

"No." Skade raised a black metal finger. "You leave with Felka only, or you leave with nothing. It's your choice. But Galiana stays here." Almost as an afterthought she added, "Oh, and in case you were wondering, I do know about the pinhead munitions you and the pig left behind you."

"You won't find them all in time," Scorpio said.

"I won't have to find them," Skade said. "Will I, Clavain? Because having Galiana protects me as fully as when I had Felka. No. I won't show her to you. It isn't necessary. Felka will tell you that she is here. She met the Wolf, too—didn't you?"

But Felka did not stir.

"C'mon," Scorpio said. "Let's leave before she changes her mind."

Clavain was with Felka when she came around. He was sitting in a seat next to her bed, scratching at his beard, a grasshopper-like *scritch, scritch, scritch* that burrowed remorselessly into her subconscious and tugged her towards wakefulness. She had been dreaming of Mars, dreaming of her Wall, dreaming of being lost in the endless, consuming task of maintaining the Wall's inviolability.

"Felka." His voice was sharp, almost stern. "Felka. Wake up. This is Clavain. You're amongst friends now."

"Where is Skade?" she asked.

"I left Skade behind. She isn't your concern now." Clavain's hand rested on hers. "I'm just relieved that you're all right. It's good to see you again, Felka. There were times when I never thought this would happen."

She had come around in a room that did not look like any of those she had seen on *Nightshade*. It had a slightly rustic feel. She was clearly aboard a ship, but it was not a sleekly engineered thing like the last vessel.

"You never said goodbye to me before you defected," she said.

"I know." Clavain poked a finger into the folds of one eye. He looked weary, older than she remembered him from their last meeting. "I know, and I apologise. But it was deliberate. You'd have talked me out of it." His tone became accusatory. "Wouldn't you?"

"I only wanted you to take care of yourself. That was why I convinced you to join the Closed Council."

"On balance, that was probably a mistake, wasn't it?" His tone had softened. He was, she was reasonably certain, smiling.

"If you call this taking care of yourself, then yes, I'd have to admit it wasn't quite what I had in mind."

"Did Skade take care of you?"

"She wanted me to help her. I didn't. I became . . . withdrawn. I didn't want to hear that she had killed you. She tried very hard, Clavain."

"I know."

"She has Galiana."

"I know that as well," he said. "Remontoire, Scorpio and I placed demolition charges across her ship. Even now we could destroy it, if I was prepared to delay our arrival at Resurgam."

Felka forced herself into a sitting position. "Listen to me carefully, Clavain."

"I'm listening."

"You must kill Skade. It doesn't matter that she has Galiana. It's what Galiana would want you to do."

"I know," Clavain said. "But that doesn't make it any easier to do."

"No." Felka raised her voice, not afraid to sound angry with the man who had just saved her. "No. You don't understand. I mean it is exactly what Galiana would want you to do. I *know*, Clavain. I touched her mind again, when we met the Wolf."

"There's no part of Galiana still there, Felka."

"There is. The Wolf did its best to hide her, but . . . I could sense her." She looked into his face, studying its ancient, latent mysteries. Of all the faces she knew, this was the one she had the least trouble recognising, but what exactly did that mean? Were they united by anything more than contingency, circumstance and shared history? She remembered how she had lied to Clavain about being his daughter. Nothing in his mood suggested that he had learned of that lie.

"Felka . . . "

"Listen to me, Clavain." She clasped his hand, squeezing it to demand his attention. "Listen to me. I never told you this before because it disturbed me too much. But in the Exordium experiments, I became aware of a mind reaching towards mine, from the future. I sensed unspeakable evil. But I also sensed something that I recognised. It was Galiana."

"No . . . " Clavain said.

She squeezed his hand harder. "It's the truth. But it wasn't her fault. I see it now. It was her mind, after the Wolf had taken her over. Skade allowed the Wolf to participate in the experiments. She needed its advice about the machinery."

Clavain shook his head. "The Wolf would never have collaborated with Skade."

"But it did. She convinced it that it needed to help her. That way she would recover the weapons, not you."

"How would that benefit the Wolf?"

"It wouldn't. But it was better that the weapons be seized by an agency that the Wolf had some influence over, rather than a third party like yourself. So it agreed to help her, knowing that it could always find a way to destroy the weapons once they were close at hand. I was there, Clavain, in its domain."

"The Wolf allowed that?"

"It demanded it. Or rather, the part of it that was still Galiana did." Felka paused. She knew how difficult this must be for Clavain. It was agonising for her, and yet Galiana had meant even more to Clavain.

"Then there would have to be a part of Galiana that still remembers us, is that what you mean? A part that still remembers what it was like before?"

"She still remembers," Clavain. She still remembers, and she still feels.' Again Felka paused, knowing that this was going to be the hardest part of all. "That's why you have to do it."

"Do what?"

"What you always planned to do before Skade told you that she had Galiana. You have to destroy the Wolf." Again she looked into his face, marvelling at its age, feeling sorrow for what she was doing to him. "You have to destroy the ship."

"But if I do that," Clavain said suddenly and excitedly, as if he had spotted a fatal flaw in Felka's argument, "I'll kill Galiana."

"I know," Felka said. "I know. But you still have to do it."

"You can't know that."

"I can, and I do. I felt her, Clavain. I felt her willing you to do this."

He watched it alone and in silence, from the vantage point of the observation cupola near *Zodiacal Light*'s prow. He had given instructions that he was to remain undisturbed until he made himself available again, even though that might mean many hours of solitude.

After forty-five minutes his eyes had become highly dark-adapted. He stared into the sea of endless night behind his ship, waiting for the sign that the work was done. The occasional cosmic ray scratched a false trail across his vision, but he knew that the signature of the event would be different and impossible to mistake. Against that darkness, too, it would be unmissable.

It grew from the heart of blackness: a blue-white glint that flared to its maximum brightness over the course of three or four seconds, and then declined slowly, ramping down through spectral shades of red and rust-brown. It burned a vivid hole into his vision, a searing violet dot that remained even when he closed his eyes.

He had destroyed *Nightshade*.

Skade, despite her best efforts, had not located all the demolition charges that they had glued to her ship. And because they were pinheads, it had only taken one to do the necessary work. The demolition charge had merely been the initiator for the much larger cascade of detonations: first the antimatter-fuelled and -tipped warheads, and then the Conjoiner drives themselves. It would have been instantaneous, and there would have been no warning.

He thought of Galiana, too. Skade had assumed that he would never attack the ship once he knew or even suspected that she was aboard.

And perhaps Skade had been right, too.

But Felka had convinced him that it had to be done. She alone had touched Galiana's mind and felt the agony of the Wolf's presence. She alone had been able to convey that single, simple message back to Clavain.

Kill me.

And so he had.

He started weeping as the full realisation of what he had done hit home. There had always been the tiniest possibility that she could be made well again. He had, he supposed, never fully come to terms with her absence because that tiny hope had always made it possible to deny the fact of her death.

But no such succour was possible now.

He had killed the thing he most loved in the universe.

Clavain began to weep, silently and alone.

I'm sorry, I'm sorry, I'm sorry . . .

* * *

He felt her approaching the monstrosity that he had become. Through senses that had no precise human analogue, the Captain became aware of the blunt metallic presence of Volyova's shuttle sidling close to him. She did not think that his omniscience was this total, he knew. In the many conversations that they had enjoyed he had learned that she still viewed him as a prisoner of *Nostalgia for Infinity,* albeit a prisoner who had in some sense merged with the fabric of his prison. And yet Ilia had assiduously mapped and catalogued the nerve bundles of his new, vastly enlarged anatomy, tracing the way they interfaced with and infiltrated the ship's old cybernetic network. She must be fully aware, on an analytical level, that there was no point in distinguishing between the prison and the prisoner any more. Yet she appeared unable to make that last mental leap, unable to cease viewing him as something *inside* the ship. It was, perhaps, just too violent a readjustment of their old relationship. He could not blame her for that final failure of imagination. He would have had grave difficulties with it himself had the tables been reversed.

The Captain felt the shuttle intrude into him. It was an indescribable sensation, really: as if a stone had been pushed through his skin, painlessly, into a neat hole in his abdomen. A few moments later he felt a series of visceral tremors as the shuttle latched itself home.

She was back.

He turned his attention inwards, becoming acutely and overwhelming aware of what was going on inside him. His awareness of the external universe—everything beyond his hull—stepped down a level of precedence. He descended through scale, focusing first on a district of himself, then on the arterial tangle of corridors and service tubes that wormed through that district. Ilia Volyova was a single corpuscular presence moving down one corridor. There were other living things inside him, as there were inside any living thing. Even cells contained organisms that had once been independent. He had the rats: scurrying little presences. But they were only dimly sentient, and ultimately they moved to his will, incapable of surprising or amusing him. The machines were even duller. Volyova, by contrast, was an invading presence, a foreign cell that he could kill but never control.

Now she was speaking to him. He heard her sounds, picking

them up from the vibrations she caused in the corridor material.

"Captain?" Ilia Volyova asked. "It's me. I'm back from Resurgam."

He answered her through the fabric of the ship, his voice barely a whisper to himself. "I'm glad to see you again, Ilia. I've been a little lonely. How was it down on the planet?"

"Worrying," she said.

"Worrying, Ilia?"

"Things are moving to a head. Khouri thinks she can hold it together long enough to get most of them off the surface, but I'm not convinced."

"And Thorn?" the Captain asked delicately. He was very glad that Volyova appeared more concerned about what was going on down on Resurgam than the other matter. Perhaps she had not noticed the incoming laser signal at all yet.

"Thorn wants to be the saviour of the people; the man who leads them to the Promised Land."

"You seem to think more direct action is appropriate."

"Have you studied the object lately, Captain?"

Of course he had. He still had morbid curiosity, if nothing else. He had watched the Inhibitors dismantle the gas giant with ridiculous ease, spinning it apart like a child's toy. He had seen the dense shadows of new machines coming into existence in the nebula of liberated matter, components as vast as worlds themselves. Embedded in the glowing skein of the nebula, they resembled tentative, half-formed embryos. Clearly the machines would soon assemble into something even larger. It was, perhaps, possible to guess what it would look like. The largest component was a trumpet-shaped maw, two thousand kilometres wide and six thousand kilometres deep. The other shapes, the Captain judged, would plug into the back of this gigantic blunderbuss.

It was a single machine, nothing like the extended ring-shaped structures that the Inhibitors had thrown around the gas giant. A single machine that could maim a star, or so Volyova believed. Captain John Brannigan almost thought it would be worth staying alive to see what the machine would do.

"I've studied it," he told Volyova.

"It's nearly finished, I think. A matter of months, perhaps, maybe less, and it will be ready. That's why we can't take any chances."

"You mean the cache?"

He sensed her trepidation. "You told me you would consider letting me use it, Captain. Is that still the case?"

He let her sweat before answering. She really did not appear to know about the laser signal. He was certain it would have been the first thing on her mind had she noticed it.

He asked, "Isn't there some risk in using the cache, Ilia, when we have come so far without being attacked?"

"There's even more risk in leaving it too late."

"I imagine Khouri and Thorn were less than enthusiastic about hitting back now if the exodus is proceeding according to plan."

"They've moved barely two thousand people off the surface, Captain—one per cent of the total. It's no more than a gesture. Yes, things will move more quickly once the government is handling the operation. But there will be a great deal more civil unrest, too. That's why we have to consider a pre-emptive strike against the Inhibitors."

"We would surely draw their fire," he pointed out. "Their weapons would destroy me."

"We have the cache."

"It has no defensive value, Ilia."

"Well, I've thought about that," she said testily. "We'll deploy the weapons at a distance of several light-hours from this ship. They can move themselves into position before we activate them, just like they did against the Hades artefact."

There was no need to remind her that the attack against the Hades artefact had gone less than swimmingly. But, in fairness to Volyova, it was not the weapons themselves that had let her down.

He groped for another token objection. He must not appear too willing, or she would begin to have suspicions. "What if they were traced back to us . . . to me?"

"By then we'll have inflicted a decisive blow. If there is a response, we'll worry about it then."

"And the weapons that you had in mind . . . ?"

"Details, Captain, details. You can leave that part to me. All you have to do is assign control of them to me."

"All thirty-three weapons?"

"No . . . that won't be necessary. Just the ones I've earmarked for use. I don't plan to throw everything against the Inhibitors. As you kindly reminded me, we may need some weapons later, to deal with any reprisal."

"You've thought all this through, haven't you?"

"Let's just say there have always been contingency plans," she told him. Then her tone of voice changed expectantly. "Captain, one final thing."

He hesitated before replying. Here, perhaps, it came. She was going to ask him about the laser signal spraying repeatedly against his hull, the signal that he had been very unwilling to bring to her attention.

"Go on, Ilia," he said, heavy-hearted.

"I don't suppose you've got any more of those cigarettes, have you?"

THIRTY

She toured the cache chamber, riding through it like a queen inspecting her troops. Thirty-three weapons were present, no two of them alike. She had spent much of her adult life studying them, together with the seven others that were now lost or destroyed. And yet in all that time she had come to no more than a passing familiarity with most of the weapons. She had tested very few of them in any meaningful sense. Indeed, those she had known most about were the ones that were now lost. Some of the remaining weapons, she was certain, could not even *be* tested without wasting the one opportunity that existed to use them. But they were not all like that. The tricky part was distinguishing amongst the subclasses of cache weapon, cataloguing them according to their range, destructive capability and the number of times they could be used. Though she had always concealed her ignorance from her colleagues, Volyova had no more than the sketchiest idea about what at least half of her weapons were capable of doing. But she had worked scrupulously hard to gain even that inadequate understanding.

Based on what she had learned in her years of study, she had come to a decision as to which weapons would be deployed against the Inhibitor machinery. She would release eight of the weapons, retaining twenty-five aboard *Nostalgia for Infinity*. They were low-mass weapons, so they could be deployed across the system quickly and discreetly. Her studies had also suggested that the eight were weapons with sufficient range to strike the Inhibitor site, but there was a lot of guesswork involved in her calculations. Volyova hated guesswork. She was even less sure that they would be able to do enough damage to make a difference to the Inhibitors' work. But she was certain of one thing: they *would* get noticed. If the human activity in the system had so far been on the buzzing-fly level—irritating without being actively dangerous—she was about to notch it up to a full-scale mosquito attack.

Swat this, you bastards, she thought.

She passed each weapon amongst the eight, slowing down her propulsion pack long enough to make sure nothing had changed since her last inspection. Nothing had. The weapons hung in their armoured cradles precisely as she had left them. They looked just as foreboding and sinister, but they had not done anything unexpected.

"These are the eight I'll need, Captain," she said.

"Just the eight?"

"They'll do for now. Mustn't put all our chicks in one egg, or whatever the metaphor is."

"I'm sure there's something suitable."

"When I say the word, I'll need you to deploy each weapon one at a time. You can do that, can't you?"

"When you say 'deploy,' Ilia . . . ?"

"Just move them outside the ship. Outside you, I mean," she corrected herself, having noticed that the Captain now tended to refer to himself and the ship as the same entity. She did not want to do anything, no matter how slight, that might interfere with his sudden spirit of co-operation. "Just to the outside," she continued. "Then, when all eight weapons are outside, we'll run another systems check. We'll keep you between them and the Inhibitors, just to be on the safe side. I don't have the feeling that we're being monitored, but it makes sense to play safe."

"I couldn't agree more, Ilia."

"Right then. We'll start with good old weapon seventeen, shall we?"

"Weapon seventeen it is, Ilia."

The motion was sudden and startling. It was such a long time since any of the cache weapons had moved in any way that she had forgotten what it was like. The cradle that held the weapon began to glide along its support rail so that the whole obelisk-sized mass of the weapon slid smoothly and silently aside. Everything in the cache chamber took place in silence, of course, but nonetheless it seemed to Volyova that there was a more profound silence here, a silence that was judicial, like the silence of a place of execution.

The network of rails allowed the cache weapons to reach the much smaller chamber immediately below the main one. The smaller chamber was just large enough to accommodate the largest weapon, and had been rebuilt extensively for just this purpose.

She watched weapon seventeen vanish into the chamber, remembering her encounter with the weapon's controlling subpersona "Seventeen," the one that had shown worrying signs of free will and a marked lack of respect for her authority. She did not doubt that something like Seventeen existed in all the weapons. There was no sense worrying about it now; all she could do was hope that the Captain and the weapons continued to do what she asked of them.

No sense worrying about it, no. But she did have a dreadful sense of foreboding all the same.

The connecting door closed. Volyova switched her suit's monitor feed to tap into the external cameras and sensors so that she could observe the weapon as it emerged beyond the hull. It would take a few minutes to get there, but she was in no immediate hurry.

And yet something very unexpected was happening. Her suit, via the monitors on the hull, was telling her that the ship was being bombarded by optical laser light.

Volyova's first reaction was a crushing sense of failure. Finally, for whatever reason, she had alerted the Inhibitors and drawn their attention. It was as if just intending to deploy the weapons had been sufficient. The wash of laser light must be from their long-range sensor sweeps. They were noticing the ship, sniffing it out of the darkness.

But then she realised that the emissions were not coming from the right part of the sky.

They were coming from interstellar space.

"Ilia . . . ?" the Captain asked. "Is something wrong? Shall I abort the deployment?"

"You knew about this, didn't you?" she said.

"Knew about what?"

"That someone was firing laser light at us. Communications frequency."

"I'm sorry, Ilia, but I just . . . "

"You didn't want me to know about it. And I didn't until I tapped into those hull sensors to watch the weapon emerging."

"What emissions . . . ah, wait." His great deific voice hesitated. "Wait. I see what you mean now. I didn't notice them—there was too much else going on. You're more attuned to such concerns than me, Ilia . . . I am very self-focused these days. If you wait, I will backtrack and determine when the emissions began . . . I have the sensor data, you know . . . "

She didn't believe him, but knew there was no way to prove otherwise. He controlled everything, and it was only through a slip of his concentration that she had learned about the laser light at all.

"Well. How long?"

"No more than a day, Ilia. A day or so . . . "

"What does 'or so' mean, you lying bastard?"

"I mean . . . a matter of days. No more than a week . . . at a conservative estimate."

"*Svinoi*. Lying pig bastard. Why didn't you tell me sooner?"

"I assumed you were already aware of the signal, Ilia. Didn't you pick it up as your shuttle approached me?"

Ah, she thought. So it was a *signal* now, not just a meaningless blast of laser light. What else did he know?

"Of course I didn't. I was asleep until the very last moment, and the shuttle wasn't programmed to watch for anything other than in-system transmissions. Interstellar communications are blue-shifted out of the usual frequency bands. What was the blue shift, Captain?"

"Modest, Ilia . . . ten per cent of light. Just enough to shift it out of the expected frequency band."

She did the sums. Ten per cent of light . . . a lighthugger couldn't slow down from that kind of speed in much less than thirty days. Even if a starship was breaking into the system, she still had half a month before it would arrive. It wasn't much of a breathing space, but it was a lot better than finding out they were mere days away.

"Captain? The signal must be an automated transmission locked on repeat, or they wouldn't have kept up it up for so long. Patch it through to my suit. Immediately."

"Yes, Ilia. And the cache weapons? Shall I abandon the deployment?"

"Yes . . . " she started saying, before correcting herself. "No. No! Nothing changes. Keep deploying the fucking things—it'll still take hours to get all eight of them outside. You heard what I said before, didn't you? I want your mass screening them from the Inhibitors."

"What about the source of the signal, Ilia?"

Had the option been available to her, she would have kicked part of him then. But she was floating far from anything kickable. "Just play the fucking thing."

Her faceplate opaqued, blanking out the view of the cache chamber. For a moment she stared into a dimensionless sea of white. Then a scene formed, a slow dissolve into an interior. She appeared to be standing at one end of a long austerely furnished room, with a black table between her and the three people at the table's far end. The table was a wedge of pure darkness.

"Hello," said the only human male among the three. "My name is Nevil Clavain, and I believe you have something I want."

At first glance he appeared to be an extension of the table. His clothes were the same unreflective black, so that only his hands and head loomed out of the shadows. His fingers were laced neatly in front of him. Ropelike veins curled across the backs of his hands. His beard and hair were white, his face notched here and there by crevasses of extreme shadow.

"He means the devices inside your ship," said the person sitting next to Clavain. She was a very young-looking woman who wore a similarly black quasi-uniform. Volyova struggled with her accent, thinking it sounded like one of the local Yellowstone dialects. "We know you have thirty-three of them. We have a permanent fix on their diagnostic signatures, so don't even think of bluffing."

"It won't work," said the third speaker, who was a pig. "We are very determined, you see. We captured this ship, when they said it couldn't be done. We've even given the Conjoiners a bloody nose. We've come a long way to get what we want and we won't be going home empty-handed." As he spoke he reinforced his points with downward swipes of one trotterlike hand.

Clavain, the first speaker, leaned forward. "Scorpio's right. We have the technical means to repossess the weapons. The question is, do you have the good sense to hand them over without a fight?"

Volyova felt as if Clavain was waiting for her to answer. The urge to say something even though she knew this was not a real-time message was almost overwhelming. She began to speak, knowing that the suit could capture whatever she was saying and uplink it back to the intruding ship. There would be a hell of a turnaround on the signal, though: three days out, at the very least, which meant she could not expect a reply for a week.

But Clavain was speaking again. "Let's not be too dogmatic, however. I appreciate you have local difficulties. We've seen the activity in your system, and we understand how it might give cause for concern. But that doesn't change our immediate objective. We want those weapons ready to be handed over as soon as we break into circumstellar space. No tricks, no delays. That isn't negotiable. But we *can* discuss the details, and the benefits of mutual co-operation."

"Not when you're half a month out, you can't," Volyova whispered.

"We will arrive shortly," Clavain said. "Perhaps sooner than you expect. But for now we're outside efficient communications range. We will continue transmitting this message until we arrive. In the meantime, to facilitate negotiations I have prepared a beta-level copy of myself. I am sure you are familiar with the necessary simulation protocols. If not, we can also supply technical documentation. Otherwise, you can proceed to a full and immediate installation. By the time this message has cycled one thousand times, you will have all the data you need to implement my beta-level." Clavain smiled reasonably, spreading his hands in a gesture of openness. "Please, will you consider it? We will of course make any reciprocal arrangements for your own beta-level, should you wish to uplink a negotiating proxy.

We await your reaction with interest. This is Nevil Clavain, for *Zodiacal Light,* signing off."

Ilia Volyova swore to herself. "Of course we're familiar with the fucking protocols, you patronising git."

The message had cycled more than a thousand times, which meant that the necessary data to implement the beta-level had already been recorded.

"Did you get that, Captain?" she asked.

"Yes, Ilia."

"Scrub the beta-level, will you? Check it for any nasties. Then find a way to implement it."

"Even if it contained some kind of military virus, Ilia, I doubt very much that it would harm me in my present state. It would be a little like a man with advanced leprosy worrying about a mild skin complaint, or the captain of a sinking ship concerning himself with a minor incident of woodworm, or . . ."

"Yes, I get the point, thank you. But do it anyway. I want to talk to Clavain. Face to face."

She reached up and de-opaqued her faceplate just in time to see the next cache weapon commence its crawl towards space. She was furious beyond words. It was not simply the fact that the newcomers had arrived so unexpectedly, or made such awkward and specific demands. It was the way the Captain appeared to have gone out of his way to conceal the whole business from her.

She did not know what he was playing at, but she did not like it at all.

Volyova took a step back from the servitor.

"Start," she said, not without a little wariness.

The beta-level had conformed to the usual protocols, backwardly compatible with all major simulation systems since the mid *Belle Époque*. It also revealed itself to be free of any contaminating viruses, either deliberate or accidental. Volyova still did not trust it, so she spent another half-day verifying the fact that the simulation had not, in some exceedingly devious way, managed to infiltrate and modify her virus filters. It appeared that it had not, but she still did her best to make sure it was isolated from as much of the ship's control network as possible.

The Captain, of course, was entirely correct: he was, in all major respects, now the ship. What attacked the ship attacked him. And since he had become the ship thanks to his own takeover by a super-adapted alien plague, it appeared highly unlikely that anything of merely human origin would be able to piggyback its way into him. He had already been stormed and corrupted by an expert invader.

Abruptly, the servitor moved. It took a step back from her, almost toppling before it righted itself. Dual camera-eyes looked in different directions and then snapped into binocular mode, locking on to her. Mechanical irises snicked open and shut. The machine took another step, towards her this time.

She raised a hand. "Halt."

She had installed the beta-level into one of the ship's few fully androform machines. The servitor was a skeletal assemblage of parts, all spindly openwork. She felt no sense of threat in its vicinity, or at least no rational sense of threat, since she was physically stronger and more robust than the machine.

"Talk to me," she said. "Are you properly installed?"

The machine's voice box buzzed like a trapped fly. "I am a beta-level simulation of Nevil Clavain."

"Good. Who am I?"

"I don't know. You haven't introduced yourself."

"I am Triumvir Ilia Volyova," she said. "This is my ship, *Nostalgia for Infinity*. I've installed you in one of our general-mech servitors. It's a frail machine, deliberately so, so don't think of trying any monkey business. You're wired for self-destruct, but even if that wasn't the case I could rip you apart with my fingers."

"Monkey business is the last thing on my mind, Triumvir. Or Ilia. What shall I call you?"

"Sir. This is my turf now."

It appeared not to have heard her. "Did you arrange for your own beta-level to be transmitted to *Zodiacal Light,* Ilia?"

"What's it to you if I did?"

"I'm curious, that's all. There'd be a pleasing symmetry if we were both represented by our respective beta-levels, wouldn't there?"

"I don't trust beta-levels. And I don't see the point, either."

Clavain's servitor looked around, its dual eyes clicking and whirring. She had activated it in a relatively normal part of the ship—the Captain's transformations were very mild here—but she supposed she had become accustomed to surroundings that were still quite odd by the usual criteria. Arcs of hardened, glistening plague-matter spanned the chamber like whale ribs. They were slick with chemical secretions. Her booted feet sloshed through inches of foul black effluent.

"You were saying?" she prompted.

The machine snapped its attention back on to her. "Using beta-levels makes perfect sense, Ilia. Our two ships are out of effective communication range now, but they're getting closer. The beta-levels can speed up the whole negotiation process, establishing the ground rules, if you like. When the ships are closer the betas can download their experiences. Our flesh progenitors can review what has been discussed and take appropriate decisions much more rapidly than would otherwise be possible."

"You sound plausible, but all I'm talking to is a set of algorithmic responses; a predictive model for how the real Clavain would respond in a similar situation."

The servitor made itself shrug. "And your point is?"

"I've no guarantee that this is exactly how Clavain really would respond, were he standing here."

"All, *that* old fallacy. You sound like Galiana. The fact is, the real Clavain might respond differently in any number of instances where he was presented with the same stimuli. So you lose nothing by dealing with a beta-level." The machine lifted up one of its skeletal arms, peering at her through the hollow spaces between the arm's struts and wires. "You realise this won't help matters, though?"

"I'm sorry?"

"Putting me in a body like this, something so obviously mechanical. And this voice . . . it's not me, not me at all. You saw the transmission. This just doesn't do me justice, does it? I actually have a slight lisp. Even play it up sometimes. I suppose you could say it's part of my character."

"I told you already . . . "

"Here's what I suggest, Ilia. Allow the machine to access your implants, will you, so that it can map a perceptual ghost into your visual/auditory field."

She felt oddly defensive. "I have no implants, Clavain."

The buzzing voice sounded astonished. "But you're an Ultra."

"Yes, but I'm also *brezgatnik*. I've never had implants, not even before the plague."

"I thought I understood Ultras," Clavain's beta-level said thoughtfully. "You surprise me, I admit. But you must have some way of viewing projected information, surely, when a hologram won't work?"

"I have goggles," she admitted.

"Fetch them. It will make life a lot easier, I assure you."

She did not like being told what to do by the beta-level, but she was prepared to admit that its suggestion made sense. She had another servitor bring her the goggles and an earpiece. She slipped the ensemble on, and then allowed the beta-level to modify the view she saw through the goggles. The spindly robot was edited out of her visual field and replaced by an image of Clavain, much as she had seen him during the transmission. The illusion was not perfect, which was a useful reminder that she was not dealing with a flesh-and-blood human. But on the whole it was a great improvement on the servitor.

"There," Clavain's real voice said in her ear. "Now we can do business. I've asked already, but will you consider uplinking a beta-level of yourself to *Zodiacal Light*?"

He had her in a spot. She did not want to admit that she had no provision for such a thing; that would really have made her look odd.

"I'll consider it. In the meantime, Clavain, let's get this little chat over with, shall we?" Volyova smiled. "You caught me in the middle of something."

Clavain's image smiled back. "Nothing too serious, I hope."

Even while she busied herself with the servitor, she continued the operation to deploy the cache weapons. She had told the Captain that she did not want him to make his presence known while the servitor was on, so his only means of speaking to her was through the same earpiece. He, in turn, was able to read her subvocal communications.

"I don't want Clavain learning any more than he has to," she had told the Captain. "Especially about you, and what's happened to this ship."

"Why should Clavain learn anything? If the beta-level discovers something we don't want it to know, we'll just kill it."

"Clavain will ask questions later."

"If there *is* a later," the Captain had said.

"Meaning what?"

"Meaning . . . we aren't intending to negotiate, are we?"

She escorted the servitor through the ship to the bridge, doing her best to pick a route that took her through the least strange parts of the interior. She observed the beta-level taking in its surroundings, obviously aware that something peculiar had happened to the ship. Yet it did not ask her any questions directly related to the plague transformations. It was, frankly, a lost battle in any case. The approaching ship would soon have the necessary resolution to glimpse *Infinity* for itself, and then it would learn of the baroque external transformations.

"Ilia," Clavain's voice said. "Let's not beat about the bush. We want the thirty-three items now in your possession, and we want them very badly. Do you admit knowledge of the items in question?"

"It would be a tiny bit implausible to deny it, I think."

"Good." Clavain's image nodded emphatically. "That's progress. At least we're clear that the items exist."

Volyova shrugged. "So if we're not going to beat about the bush, why don't we call them what they are? They're weapons, Clavain. You know it. I know it. *They* know it, in all likelihood."

She slipped her goggles off for a moment. Clavain's servitor strode around the room, its movements almost but not quite fluidly human. She replaced the goggles, and the overlaid image moved with the same puppetlike strides.

"I like you better already, Ilia. Yes, they're weapons. Very old weapons, of rather obscure origin."

"Don't bullshit me, Clavain. If you know about the weapons, you probably have just as much idea as me about who made them, maybe more. Well, here's my guess: I think the Conjoiners made them. What do you say to that?"

"You're warm, I'll give you that."

"Warm?"

"Hot. Very hot, as it happens."

"Start telling me what the hell this is all about, Clavain. If they're Conjoiner weapons, how have you only just found out about them?"

"They emit tracer signals, Ilia. We homed in on them."

"But you're not Conjoiners."

"No . . . " Clavain conceded this point with a sweep of one arm, neatly synchronised with the servitor. "But I'll be honest with you, if only because it might help swing the negotiations in my favour. The Conjoiners do want those weapons back. And they're on their way here as well. As a matter of fact, there's a whole fleet of heavily armed Conjoiner vessels immediately behind *Zodiacal Light*."

She remembered what the pig, Scorpio, had said about Clavain's crew bloodying the noses of the spiders. "Why tell me this?" Volyova said.

"It alarms you, I see. I don't blame you for that. I'd be alarmed, too." The image scratched its beard. "That's why you should consider negotiating with me first. Let me take the weapons off your hands. I'll deal with the Conjoiners."

"Why do you think you'd have any more luck than me, Clavain?"

"Couple of reasons, Ilia. One, I've already outsmarted them on a few occasions. Two, and perhaps more pertinent, until very recently I was one."

The Captain whispered in her ear. "I've done a check, Ilia. There was a Nevil Clavain with Conjoiner connections."

Volyova addressed Clavain. "And you think that would make a difference, Clavain?"

He nodded. "The Conjoiners aren't vindictive. They'll leave you alone if you have nothing to offer them. If you still have the weapons, however, they'll take you apart."

"There's a small flaw in your thinking," Volyova said. "If I had the weapons, wouldn't I be the one doing the taking apart?"

Clavain winked at her. "Know how to use them that well, do you?"

"I have some experience."

"No, you don't. You've barely switched the bloody things on, Ilia. If you had, we'd have detected them centuries ago. Don't overestimate your familiarity with technologies you barely understand. It could be your undoing."

"I'll be the judge of that, won't I?"

Clavain—she had to stop thinking of *it* as Clavain—scratched his beard again. "I didn't mean to offend. But the weapons are dangerous. I'm quite sincere in my suggestion that you hand them over now and let me worry about them."

"And if I say no?"

"We'll do just what we promised: take them by force."

"Look up, Clavain, will you? I want to show you something.

You alluded to some knowledge of it before, but I want you to be completely certain of the facts."

She had programmed the display sphere to come alive at that moment, filled with an enlargement of the dismantled world. The cloud of matter was curdled and torn, flecked by dense nodes of aggregating matter. But the trumpetlike object growing at its heart was ten times larger than any other structure, and now appeared almost fully formed. Although it was difficult for her sensors to see with any clarity through the megatonnes of matter that still lay along the line of sight, there was a suggestion of immense complexity, a bewildering accretion of lacy detail, from a scale of many hundreds of kilometres across to the limit of her scanning resolution. The machinery had a muscular, organic look, knotted and swollen with gristle, sinews and glandular nodes. It did not look like anything a human imagination would have produced by design. And even now layers of matter were being added to the titanic machine: she could see the density streams where mass flows were still taking place. But the thing looked worrying close to being finished.

"Have you seen much of that before now, Clavain?" she asked.

"A little. Not as clearly as this."

"What did you make of it?"

"Why don't you tell me what you've made of it first, Ilia?"

She narrowed her eyes. "I came to the obvious conclusion, Clavain. I watched three small worlds get ripped apart by machines, before they moved on to this one. They're alien. They were drawn here by something Dan Sylveste did."

"Yes. We assumed he had something to do with it. We know about these machines, too—at least, we've had our suspicions that they exist."

"Who is 'we,' exactly?" she asked.

"The Conjoiners, I mean. I only defected recently." He paused before continuing. "A few centuries ago, we launched expeditions into deep interstellar space, much further out than anything achieved by any other human faction. Those expeditions encountered the machines. We codenamed them wolves, but I think we can assume we're seeing essentially the same entities here."

"They have no name for themselves," Volyova said. "But we

call them the Inhibitors. It's the name they gained during their heyday."

"You learned all that from observation?"

"No," Volyova said. "Not as such."

She was telling him too much, she thought. But Clavain was so persuasive that she could almost not help herself. Before very long, if she were not careful, she would have told him everything about what had happened around Hades: how Khouri had been given a glimpse into the galaxy's dark prehuman history, endless chapters of extinction and war stretching back to the dawn of sentient life itself . . .

There were things she was prepared to discuss with Clavain, and there were things she would rather keep to herself, for now.

"You're a woman of mystery, Ilia Volyova."

"I'm also a woman with a lot of work to do, Clavain." She made the sphere zoom in on the burgeoning machine. "The Inhibitors are building a weapon. I have strong suspicions that it will be used to trigger some kind of cataclysmic stellar event. They triggered a flare to wipe out the Amarantin, but I think this will be different—much larger and probably more terminal. And I simply cannot allow it to happen. There are two hundred thousand people on Resurgam, and they will all die if that weapon is used."

"I sympathise, believe me."

"Then you'll understand that I won't be handing over any weapons, now or at any point in the future."

For the first time Clavain appeared exasperated. He rubbed a hand through his shock of hair, bristling it into a mess of jagged white spikes. "Give me the weapons and I'll see that they're used against the wolves. What's wrong with that?"

"Nothing," she said cheerfully. "Except that I don't believe you. And if these weapons are as potent as you say, I'm not sure I'm willing to hand them over to any other party. We've looked after them for centuries, after all. No harm was done. I'd say that puts us in rather a good light, wouldn't you? We've been responsible custodians. It would be quite cavalier of us to let any old bunch of rogues get their hands on them now, wouldn't it?" She smiled. "Especially as you admit that you're not the rightful owners, Clavain."

"You'll regret dealing with the Conjoiners, Ilia."

"Mm. But at least I'll be dealing with a legitimate faction."

Clavain pushed the fingers of his right hand against his brow, like someone fighting a migraine. "No, you won't be. Not in the sense you think. They only want the weapons so they can scuttle off into deep space with them."

"And I suppose you have some vastly more magnanimous use in mind?"

Clavain nodded. "I do, as a matter of fact. I want to put them back into the hands of the human race. Demarchists . . . Ultras . . . Scorpio's army . . . I don't care who takes them over, so long as they convince me that they'll do the right thing with them."

"Which is?"

"Fight the wolves. They're coming closer. The Conjoiners knew it, and what's happening here proves it. The next few centuries are going to be very interesting, Ilia."

"Interesting?" she repeated.

"Yes. But not in quite the way we'd wish."

She switched the beta-level off for the time being. The image of Clavain shattered into speckles and then faded away, leaving only the skeletal shape of the servitor where he had been standing. The transition was quite jarring: she had felt a palpable sense of being in his presence.

"Ilia?" It was the Captain. "We're ready now. The last cache weapon is outside the hull."

She tugged the earpiece out and spoke normally. "Good. Anything to report?"

"Nothing major. Five weapons deployed without incident. Of the remaining three, I noted a transient anomaly with the propulsion harness of weapon six, and an intermittent fault with the guidance subsystems of weapons fourteen and twenty-three. Neither has recurred since deployment."

She lit a cigarette and smoked a quarter of it before answering. "That doesn't sound like nothing major to me."

"I'm sure the faults won't happen again," boomed the Captain's voice. "The electromagnetic environment of the cache chamber is quite different from that beyond the hull. The transition probably caused some confusion, that's all. The weapons will settle down now that they're outside."

"Make a shuttle ready, please."

"I'm sorry?"

"You heard me. I'm going outside to check on the weapons." She stamped her feet, waiting for his answer.

"There's no need for that, Ilia. I can monitor the well-being of the weapons perfectly well."

"You may be able to control them, Captain, but you don't know them as well as I do."

"Ilia . . ."

"I won't need a large shuttle. I'd even consider taking a suit, but I can't smoke in one of those things."

The Captain's sigh was like the collapse of a distant building. "Very well, Ilia. I'll have a shuttle ready for you. You'll take care, won't you? You can keep to the side of the ship that the Inhibitors can't see, if you're careful."

"They're a long way from taking any notice of us. That isn't about to change in the next five minutes."

"But you appreciate my concern."

Did the Captain really care for her? She was not certain that she really believed it. Granted, he might be a little lonely out here, and she was his only chance of human companionship. But she was also the woman who had exposed his crime and punished him with this transformation. His feelings towards her were bound to be a little on the complex side.

She had finished enough of the cigarette. On a whim she inserted the butt-end into the wirework head assembly of the servitor, jamming it between two thin metal spars. The tip burned dull orange.

"Filthy habit," Ilia Volyova said.

She took the two-seater snake-headed shuttle that Khouri and Thorn had used to explore the Inhibitor workings around the former gas giant. The Captain had already warmed the craft and presented it to an air lock. The craft had sustained some minor damage during the encounter with the Inhibitor machinery inside Roc's atmosphere, but most of it had been easy to repair from existing component stocks. The defects that remained certainly did not prevent the shuttle being used for short-range work like this.

She settled into the command seat and assayed the avionics

display. The Captain had done a very good job: even the fuel tanks were brimming, although she would not be taking the ship more than a few hundred metres out.

Something nagged at the back of her mind, a feeling she could not quite put her finger on.

She took the shuttle outside, transiting through the armoured doors until she reached naked space. She exited near the much larger aperture where the cache weapons had emerged. The weapons themselves had vanished around the mountainous curve of the great ship's hull, out of the Inhibitors' line of sight. Volyova followed the same path, watching the nebulous mass of the shredded planet fall beneath the sharp horizon of the hull.

The eight cache weapons came into view, lurking like monsters. They were all different, but had clearly been shaped by the same governing intellects. She had always suspected that the builders were the Conjoiners, but it was unsettling to have this confirmed by Clavain. She saw no reason for him to have lied. Why, though, had the Conjoiners brought into existence such atrocious tools? It could only have been because they had some intention, at some point, of using them. Volyova wondered whether the intended target had been humanity.

Around each weapon was a harness of girders to which were attached steering rockets and aiming subsystems, as well as a small number of defensive armaments, purely to protect the weapons themselves. The harnesses were able to move the weapons around, and in principle they could have positioned them anywhere within the system, but they were too slow for her requirements. Instead, she had lately fastened sixty-four tug rockets on to the harnesses, eight apiece, positioned at opposing corners of each weapon's frame. It would take fewer than thirty days to move the eight weapons to the other side of the system.

She nosed the shuttle towards the group of weapons. The weapons, sensing her approach, shifted their positions. She slid through them, then banked, circled and slowed, examining the specific weapons that the Captain had reported difficulties with. Diagnostic summaries, terse but efficient, scrolled on to her wrist bracelet. She called up each weapon, paying meticulous attention to what she saw.

Something was wrong.

Or rather, something was not wrong. There appeared to be nothing the matter with any of the eight weapons.

She felt again that prickly sense of wrongness, the sense that she had been steered into doing something which only felt as if it had been her choice. The weapons were perfectly healthy; indeed, there was no evidence that there had been any faults at all, transient or otherwise. But that could only mean that the Captain had lied to her: that he had reported problems where none existed.

She composed herself. If only she had not taken him at his word, but had checked for herself before leaving the ship . . .

"Captain . . . " she said hesitantly.

"Yes, Ilia?"

"Captain, I'm getting some funny readings here. The weapons all appear to be healthy, no problems at all."

"I'm quite sure there were transient errors, Ilia."

"Are you?"

"Yes." But he did not sound so convinced of himself. "Yes, Ilia, quite sure. Why would I have reported them otherwise?"

"I don't know. Perhaps because you wanted to get me outside the ship for some reason?"

"Why would I have wanted to do that, Ilia?" He sounded affronted, but not quite as affronted as she would have liked.

"I don't know. But I have a horrible feeling I'm about to find out."

She watched one of the cache weapons—it was weapon thirty-one, the quintessence-force weapon—detach from the group. It slid sideways spouting bright sparks from its steering jets, the smooth movement belying the enormous mass of machinery that was being shunted so effortlessly. She examined her bracelet. Gyroscopes spun up, shifting the harness about its centre of gravity. Ponderously, like a great iron finger moving to point at the accused, the enormous weapon was selecting its target.

It was swinging back towards *Nostalgia for Infinity*.

Belatedly, stupidly, cursing herself, Ilia Volyova understood precisely what was happening.

The Captain was trying to kill himself.

She should have seen it coming. His emergence from the catatonic state had only ever been a ploy. He must have had it in mind all along to end himself, to finally terminate whatever extreme state of misery he found himself in. And she had given him the ideal means. She had begged him to let her use the cache weapons, and he had—too easily, she now saw—obliged.

"Captain . . . "

"I'm sorry, Ilia, but I have to do this."

"No. You don't. Nothing *has* to be done."

"You don't understand. I know you want to, and I know you think you do, but you can't know what it is like."

"Captain . . . listen to me. We can talk about it. Whatever it is that you feel you can't deal with, we can discuss it."

The weapon was slowing its rotation, its flowerlike muzzle nearly pointed at the lighthugger's shadowed hull.

"It's long past the time for discussion, Ilia."

"We'll find a way," she said desperately, not even believing herself. "We'll find a way to make you as you were: human again."

"Don't be silly, Ilia. You can't unmake what I've become."

"Then we'll find a way to make it tolerable . . . to end whatever pain or discomfort you're in. We'll find a way to make it better than that. We can do it, Captain. There isn't anything you and I couldn't achieve, if we set our minds to it."

"I said you didn't understand. I was right. Don't you realise, Ilia? This isn't about what I've become, or what I was. This is about what I did. It's about the thing I can't live with any more."

The weapon halted. It was now pointed directly at the hull.

"You killed a man," Volyova said. "You murdered a man and took over his body. I know. It was a crime, Captain, a terrible crime. Sajaki didn't deserve what you did to him. But don't you understand? The crime has already been paid for. Sajaki died twice: once with his mind in his body and once with yours. That was the punishment, and God knows he suffered for it. There isn't any need for further atonement, Captain. It's been done. You've suffered enough, as well. What happened to you would be considered justice enough by anyone. You've paid for that deed a thousand times over."

"I still remember what I did to him."

"Of course you do. But that doesn't mean you have to inflict this on yourself now." She glanced at the bracelet. The weapon was powering up, she observed. In a moment it would be ready for use.

"I do, Ilia. I do. This isn't some whim, you realise. I have planned this moment for much longer than you can conceive. Through all our conversations, it was always my intention to end myself."

"You could have done it while I was down on Resurgam. Why now?"

"Why now?" She heard what could almost have been a laugh. It was a horrid, gallows laugh, if that was the case. "Isn't it obvious, Ilia? What good is an act of justice if there isn't a witness to see it executed?"

Her bracelet informed her that the weapon had reached attack readiness. "You wanted me to see this happen?"

"Of course. You were always special, Ilia. My best friend; the only one who talked to me when I was ill. The only one who understood."

"I also made you what you are."

"It was necessary. I don't blame you for that, I really don't."

"Please don't do this. You'll be hurting more than just yourself." She knew that she had to make this good; that what she said now could be crucial. "Captain, we need you. We need the weapons you carry, and we need you to help evacuate Resurgam. If you kill yourself now, you'll be killing two hundred thousand people. You'll be committing a far greater crime than the one you feel the need to atone for."

"But that would only be a sin of omission, Ilia."

"Captain, I'm begging you . . . don't do this."

"Steer your shuttle away, please, Ilia. I don't want you to be harmed by what is about to happen. That was never my intention. I only wanted you as a witness, someone who would understand."

"I already understand! Isn't that enough?"

"No, Ilia."

The weapon activated. The beam that emerged from its muzzle was invisible until it touched the hull. Then, in a gale of escaping air and ionised armour, it revealed itself flickeringly: a metre-thick shaft of scything destructive quintessence force, chewing inexorably through the ship. This, weapon thirty-one, was not one of the most devastating tools in her arsenal, but it had immense range. That was why she had selected it for use in the attack against the Inhibitors. The quintessence beam ghosted right through the ship, emerging in a similar gale on the far side. The weapon began to track, gnawing down the length of the hull.

"Captain . . . "

His voice came back. "I'm sorry, Ilia . . . I can't stop now."

He sounded in pain. It was hardly surprising, she thought. His nerve endings reached into every part of *Nostalgia for Infinity*. He was feeling the beam slice through him just as agonisingly as if she had begun to saw off her own arm. Again, Volyova understood. It had to be much more than just a quick, clean suicide. That would not be sufficient recompense for his crime. It had to be slow, protracted, excruciating. A martial execution, with a diligent witness who would appreciate and remember what he had inflicted upon himself.

The beam had chewed a hundred-metre-long furrow in the hull. The Captain was haemorrhaging air and fluids in the wake of the cutting beam.

"Stop," she said. "Please, for God's sake, stop!"

"Let me finish this, Ilia. Please forgive me."

"No. I won't allow it."

She did not give herself time to think about what had to be done. If she had, she doubted that she would have had the courage to act. She had never considered herself a brave person, and most certainly not someone given to self-sacrifice.

Ilia Volyova steered her shuttle towards the beam, placing herself between the weapon and the fatal gash it was knifing into *Nostalgia for Infinity*.

"No!" she heard the Captain call.

But it was too late. He could not shut down the weapon in less than a second, nor steer it fast enough to bring her out of the line of fire. The shuttle collided glancingly with the beam—her aim had not been dead on—and the edge of the beam obliterated the entire right side of the shuttle. Armour, insulation, interior reinforcement, pressure membrane—everything wafted away in an instant of ruthless annihilation. Volyova had a moment to realise that she had missed the precise centre of the beam, and another instant to realise that it did not really matter.

She was going to die anyway.

Her vision fogged. There was a shocking, sudden cold in her windpipe, as if someone had poured liquid helium down her throat. She attempted to take a breath and the cold rammed into her lungs. There was an awful feeling of granite solidity in her chest. Her interior organs were shock freezing.

She opened her mouth, attempting to speak, to make one final utterance. It seemed the appropriate thing to do.

THIRTY-ONE

"Why, Wolf?" Felka asked.

They were meeting alone on the same iron-grey, silver-skied expanse of rockpools where she had, at Skade's insistence, already encountered the Wolf. Now she was dreaming lucidly; she was back on Clavain's ship and Skade was dead, and yet the Wolf seemed no less real than it had before. The Wolf's shape lingered just beyond clarity, like a column of smoke that occasionally fell into a mocking approximation of human form.

"Why what?"

"Why do you hate life so much?"

"I don't. We don't. We only do what we must."

Felka kneeled on the rock, surrounded by animal parts. She understood that the presence of the wolves explained one of the great cosmic mysteries, a paradox that had haunted human minds since the dawn of spaceflight. The galaxy teemed with stars, and around many of those stars were worlds. It was true that not all of those worlds were the right distance from their suns to kindle life, and not all had the right fractions of metals to allow complex carbon chemistry. Sometimes the stars were not stable enough for life to gain a toehold. But none of that mattered, since there were hundreds of billions of stars. Only a tiny fraction had to be habitable for there to be a shocking abundance of life in the galaxy.

But there was no evidence that intelligent life had ever spread from star to star, despite the fact that it was relatively easy to do. Looking out into the night sky, human philosophers had concluded that intelligent life must be vanishingly rare; that perhaps the human species was the only sentient culture in the galaxy.

They were wrong, but they did not discover this until the dawn of interstellar society. Then, expeditions started finding evidence of fallen cultures, ruined worlds, extinct species. There were an uncomfortably large number of them.

It was not that intelligent life was rare, it seemed, but that intelligent life was very, very prone to becoming extinct. Almost as if something was deliberately wiping it out.

The wolves were the missing element in the puzzle, the agency responsible for the extinctions. Implacable, infinitely patient machines, they homed in on the signs of intelligence and enacted a terrible, crushing penalty. Hence, a lonely, silent galaxy, patrolled only by watchful machine sentries.

That was the answer. But it did not explain why they did it.

"But why?" she asked the Wolf. "It doesn't make any sense to act the way you do. If you hate life so much, why not end it once and for all?"

"For good?" The Wolf appeared amused, curious about her speculations.

"You could poison every world in the galaxy or smash every world apart. It's as if you don't have the courage to finally finish life for good."

There was a slow, avalanche-like sigh of pebbles. "It isn't about ending intelligent life," the Wolf said.

"No?"

"It is about the exact opposite, Felka. It is about life's preservation. We are life's keepers, steering life through its greatest crisis."

"But you murder. You kill entire cultures."

The Wolf shifted in and out of vision. Its voice, when it answered, was tauntingly similar to Galiana's. "Sometimes you have to be cruel to be kind, Felka."

No one saw much of Clavain after Galiana's death. There was an unspoken understanding amongst his crew, one that percolated right down through to the lowliest ranks of Scorpio's army, that he was not to be disturbed by anything except the gravest of problems: matters of extreme shipwide urgency, nothing less. It remained unclear whether this edict had come from Clavain himself, or was simply something that had been assumed by his immediate deputies. Very probably it was a combination of the two. He became a shadowy figure, occasionally seen but seldom heard, a ghost stalking *Zodiacal*

Light's corridors in the hours when the rest of the ship was asleep. Occasionally, when the ship was under high gravity, they heard the rhythmic thump, thump, thump of his exoskeleton on the deck plates as he traversed a corridor above them. But Clavain himself was an elusive figure.

It was said that he spent long hours in the observation cupola, staring into the blackness behind them, transfixed by the starless wake. Those who saw him remarked that he looked much older than at the start of the voyage, as if in some way he remained anchored to the faster flow of world-time, rather than the dilated time that passed aboard the ship. It was said that he looked like a man who had given up on the living, and was now only going through the burdensome motions of completing some final duty.

It was recognised, without the details necessarily being understood, that Clavain had been forced into making a dreadful personal decision. Some of the crewmembers grasped that Galiana had already "died" long before, and that what had happened now was only the drawing of a line beneath that event. But it was, as others appreciated, much worse than that. Galiana's earlier death had only ever been provisional. The Conjoiners had kept her frozen, thinking that she could at some point be cleansed of the Wolf. The likelihood of that happening must have been small, but at the back of Clavain's mind there must have remained the ghost of a hope that the Galiana he had loved since that ancient meeting on Mars could be brought back to him, healed and renewed. But now he had personally removed that possibility for ever. It was said that a large factor in his decision had been Felka's persuasion, but it was still Clavain who had made the final choice; it was he who carried the blood of that merciful execution on his hands.

Clavain's withdrawal was less serious to ship affairs than it might have appeared; he had already abrogated much of the responsibility to others, so that the battle preparations continued smoothly and efficiently without his day-to-day intervention. Mechanical production lines were now running at full capacity, spewing out weapons and armour. *Zodiacal Light*'s hull bristled with antiship armaments. As training regimes honed the battalions of Scorpio's army into savagely efficient units, they began to realise how much their previous successes had been down to good fortune, but that would certainly not be the case in the future. They might fail, but it would not be because of any lack of tactical preparation or discipline.

With Skade's ship destroyed, they had less need to worry about an attack while they were *en route*. Deep-look scans confirmed that there were other Conjoiner ships behind them, but they could only match *Zodiacal Light*'s acceleration, not exceed it. It appeared that no one was willing to attempt another state-four transition after what had happened to *Nightshade*.

Halfway to Resurgam, the ship had switched into deceleration mode, thrusting in the direction of flight, which immediately made it a harder target for the pursuing craft since they no longer had a relativistically boosted exhaust beam to lock on to. The risk of attack had dropped even further, leaving the crew free to concentrate on the mission's primary objective. Data from the approaching system became steadily more comprehensive, too, focusing minds on the specifics of the recovery operation.

It was clear that something very odd was happening around Delta Pavonis. Scans of the planetary system showed the inexplicable omission of three moderately large terrestrial bodies, as if they had simply been deleted from existence. More worrying still was what had replaced the system's major gas giant: only a remnant of the giant's metallic core now remained, enveloped in a skein of liberated matter many dozens of times wider than the original planet. There were hints of an immense mechanism that had been used to spin the planet apart: arcs and cusps and coils that were in the process of being dismantled and retransformed into new machinery. And at the heart of the cloud was something even larger than those subsidiary components: a two-thousand-kilometre-wide engine that could not possibly be of human origin.

Remontoire had helped Clavain build sensors to pick up the neutrino signatures of the hell-class weapons. As they had neared the system they had established that thirty-three of the weapons were in essentially the same place, while six more were dormant, waiting in a wide orbit around the neutron star Hades. One weapon was unaccounted for, but Clavain had known about that before he left the Mother Nest. More detailed scans, which became possible only when they had slowed to within a quarter of a light-year of their destination, showed that the thirty-three weapons were almost certainly aboard a ship of the same basic type as *Zodiacal Light,* probably stuffed into a major storage bay. The ship—it had to be the Triumvir's vessel, *Nostalgia for Infinity*—hovered in interplanetary space, orbiting Delta Pavonis at the Lagrange point between the star and Resurgam.

Now, finally, they had some measure of their adversary. But what of Resurgam itself? There was no radio or other EM-band traffic coming from the system's sole inhabited planet, but the colony had clearly not failed. Analysis of the atmosphere's constituent gases revealed ongoing terraforming activity, with sizeable expanses of water now visible on the surface. The icecaps had withered back towards the poles. The air was warmer and wetter than it had been in nearly a million years. The infra-red signatures of surface flora matched the patterns expected from terran genestock, modified for cold, dry, low-oxygen survivability. Hot thermal blotches showed the sites of large brute-force atmospheric reprocessors. Refined metals indicated intense surface industrialisation. At extreme magnification, there were even the suggestions of roads or pipelines, and the occasional moving echo of a fat transatmospheric cargo vehicle, like a dirigible. The planet was certainly inhabited, even now. But whoever was down there was not much interested in communicating with the outside world.

"It doesn't matter," Scorpio told Clavain. "You came here to take the weapons, that's all. There's no need to make this any more complicated than it has to be."

Clavain had been alone until the pig had visited him. "Just deal with the starship, is that it?"

"We can start negotiations immediately if we transmit a beta-level proxy. They can have the weapons ready for us when we arrive. Nice quick turnaround and we're away. The other ships won't even have reached the system."

"Nothing's ever that easy, Scorp." Clavain spoke with morose resignation, his eyes focused on the starfield beyond the window.

"You don't think negotiation will work? Fine. We'll skip it and just come in with all guns blazing."

"In which case we'd better hope they don't know how to use the hell-class weapons. Because if it comes to a straight fight, we won't have a snowball's chance."

"I thought that Volyova turning the weapons against us wasn't going to be a problem."

Clavain turned from the window. "Remontoire can't promise me that our pacification codes will work. And if we test them too soon we give Volyova time to find a workaround. If such a thing exists, I'm pretty sure she'll find it."

"Then we keep trying negotiation," Scorpio said. "Send the proxy, Clavain. It will buy us time and cost us nothing."

The man did not answer him directly. "Do you think they understand what's happening to their system, Scorpio?"

Scorpio blinked. Sometimes he had difficulty following the swerves and evasions of Clavain's moods. The man was far more ambivalent and complex than any human he had known since his time aboard the yacht.

"Understand?"

"That the machines are already there, already busy. If they look into the sky, surely they can't miss what is happening. Surely they must realise that it isn't good news."

"What else can they do, Clavain? You've read the intelligence summaries. They probably don't have a single shuttle down there. What can they do but pretend it isn't happening?"

"I don't know," Clavain said.

"Let us transmit the proxy," Scorpio said. "Just to the ship, tight-beam only."

Clavain said nothing for at least a minute. He had turned his attention back to the window, staring out into space. Scorpio wondered what he hoped to see out there. Did he imagine that he could unmake that glint of light, the one that had signalled Galiana's end, if he tried hard enough? He had not known Clavain as long as some of the others, but he viewed Clavain as a rational man. But he supposed grief, the kind of howling, remorse-filled grief Clavain was experiencing, could smash rationality to shards. The impact of so familiar an emotion as sadness on the flow of history had never been properly accounted for, Scorpio thought. Grief and remorse, loss and pain, sadness and sorrow were at least as powerful shapers of events as anger, greed and retribution.

"Clavain . . . ?" he prompted.

"I never thought there'd be choices this hard," the man said. "But H was right. The hard choices are the only ones that matter. I thought defecting was the hardest thing I had ever done. I thought I would never see Felka again. But I didn't realise how wrong I was, how trivial that decision was. It was nothing compared with what I had to do later. I killed Galiana, Scorpio. And the worst thing is that I did it willingly."

"But you got Felka back again. There are always consolations."

"Yes," Clavain said, sounding like a man grasping for the last crumb of comfort. "I got Felka back. Or at least I got someone back. But she isn't the way I left her. She carries the Wolf herself now, just a shadow of it, it's true, but when I speak to her I can't be sure whether it's Felka answering or the Wolf. No matter what happens now, I don't think I'll ever be able to take anything she says at face value."

"You cared for her enough to risk your life rescuing her. That was a difficult choice as well. But it doesn't make you unique." Scorpio scratched at the upraised snout of his nose. "We've all made difficult choices around here. Look at Antoinette. I know her story, Clavain. Set out to do a good deed—burying her father the way he wanted—and she ends up entangled in a battle for the entire future of the species. Pigs, humans . . . everything. I bet she didn't have that in mind when she set out to salve her conscience. But we can't guess where things will take us, or the harder questions that will follow on from one choice. You thought defecting would be an act in and of itself, but it was just the start of something much larger."

Clavain sighed. Perhaps it was imagination, but Scorpio thought that he detected the slightest lightening of the man's mood. His voice was softer when he spoke. "What about you, Scorpio? Did you have choices to make as well?"

"Yeah. Whether I threw my weight in with you human sons of bitches."

"And the consequences?"

"Some of you are still sons of bitches that deserve to die in the most painful and slow way I can envisage. But not all of you."

"I'll take that as a compliment."

"Take it while you can. I might change my mind tomorrow."

Clavain sighed again, scratched his beard and then said, "All right. Do it. Transmit a beta-level proxy."

"We'll need a statement to accompany it," Scorpio said. "A laying-down of terms, if you like."

"Whatever it takes, Scorp. Whatever the hell it takes."

In their long, crushing reign, the Inhibitors had learned of fifteen distinct ways to murder a dwarf star.

Doubtless, the overseer thought to itself, there were other methods, more or less efficient, which might turn out to have been invented or used at various epochs in galactic history. The galaxy was very large, very old, and the Inhibitors' knowledge of it was far from comprehensive. But it was a fact that no new technique for starcide had been added to their repository for four hundred and forty million years. The galaxy had finished two rotations since that last methodological update. Even by the Inhibitors' glacial reckoning, it was quite a worryingly long time during which not to learn any new tricks.

Singing a star apart was the most recent method to be entered into the Inhibitor library of xenocide techniques, and though it had achieved that status four hundred and forty million years earlier, the overseer could not help view it with a trace of bemused curiosity. It was the way an aged butcher might view some newfangled apparatus designed to improve the productivity of an abbatoir. The current cleansing operation would provide a useful testbed for the technique, a chance to fully evaluate it. If the overseer was not satisfied, it would leave a record in the archive recommending that future cleansing operations employ one of the fourteen older methods of starcide. But for now it would place its faith in the efficacy of the singer.

All stars already sang to themselves. The outer layers of every star rang constantly at a multitude of frequencies, like an eternally chiming bell. The great seismic modes tracked oscillations that plunged deep into the star, down to the caustic surface just above its fusing core. Those oscillations were modest in a star of dwarf type, like Delta Pavonis. But the singer tuned itself to them, swinging around the star in its equatorial rotation frame, pumping gravitational energy into the star at precisely the right resonant frequencies to enhance the oscillations. The singer was what the mammals would have called a graver, a gravitational laser.

In the heart of the singer a microscopic closed cosmic string, a tiny relic of the rapidly cooling early universe, had been tugged out of the seething foam of the quantum vacuum. The string was barely a scratch compared with the largest cosmic flaws, but it would suffice for the singer's purposes. It was tugged and elongated like a loop of toffee, inflated with the same vacuum phase energy that the singer tapped for all its needs, until it had macroscopic size and macroscopic mass-energy density. Then the string was deftly knotted into a figure-of-eight configuration and plucked, generating a narrow cone of throbbing gravitational waves.

The oscillations increased in amplitude, slowly but surely. At the same time, chirping gravitational pulses with precision and elegance, the singer sculpted the patterns themselves, causing new vibrational modes to spring into play, enhancing some and suppressing others. The star's rotation had already destroyed any spherical symmetry in the original oscillation modes, but the modes had still been symmetric with respect to the star's axis of spin. Yet now the singer worked to instil more profoundly asymmetric modes in the star, focusing its efforts on a single equatorial point immediately between the singer and the star's centre of mass. It increased its power and focus, the closed cosmic string oscillating even more vigorously. Immediately below the singer, on the outer envelope of the star, mass flows were pinched and reflected, heating and compressing surface hydrogen to near-fusion conditions. Fusion did indeed erupt in three or four concentric rings of stellar matter, but that was incidental. What mattered, what the singer intended, was that the star's spherical envelope should begin to pucker and distort. Something like a navel was appearing in the star's seething hot surface, an inward dimple wide enough to swallow a whole rocky world. Concentric rings of fusion, circles of searing brightness, spread out from the dimple, squalling X-rays and neutrinos into space. Still the singer continued pulsing the star with gravitational energy, the timing surgically acute, and still the dimple sank deeper, as if an invisible finger were pushing against the pliant skin of a balloon. Around the dimple the star was bulging higher into space as matter was redistributed. The matter had to go somewhere, for the singer was excavating a hole deep into the star's interior.

It would continue until it had reached the star's nuclear-burning core.

* * *

It was a fifteen-hour trip from Resurgam orbit to *Nostalgia for Infinity* and Khouri spent every minute of it in a state of extreme apprehension. It was not simply the strange and worrying thing that had started to happen to Delta Pavonis, although that was certainly a significant part of it. She had seen the Inhibitor weapon start its work, pointing like a great flared bugle at the surface of the star, and she had seen the star respond by growing a furious hot eye on its surface. Magnification showed the eye to be a zone of fusion, several zones, in fact, which surrounded a deepening pit in the star's envelope. It was in the face of the star that was turned towards Resurgam, which did not seem likely to be accidental. And whatever the weapon was doing, it was doing it with astonishing speed. The weapon had taken so long to reach readiness that Khouri had mistakenly assumed that the final destruction of Delta Pavonis would take place on the same leisurely timescale. This was clearly not going to be the case. She would have been better thinking of an elaborate build-up to an execution, with many legal hurdles and delays, but which would conclude in a single bullet shot or killing surge of electrical current. That was how it was going to be with the star: a long, grave preparation followed by an extremely swift execution.

And they had still evacuated only two thousand people—in fact, it was far worse: they had transported two thousand people from the surface of Resurgam, but none of those had yet seen *Nostalgia for Infinity,* or had any idea of what they were going to find when they stepped aboard it. Khouri hoped that none of her nervousness was apparent, since the passengers were volatile enough already.

It was not simply the fact that the transfer craft was designed to take far fewer occupants, and so they were forced to endure the journey in cramped, prisonlike conditions, with the environmental systems strained to the limit just to provide sufficient air, water and refrigeration. These people were taking a tremendous risk, putting their faith in forces utterly beyond their control. The only thing holding them together was Thorn, and even Thorn appeared on the edge of nervous exhaustion. There were constant squabbles and minor crises breaking out all over the ship, and whenever they happened Thorn was there, soothing and reassuring, only to dash off somewhere else as soon as the trouble had been allayed. His charisma was being stretched butter-thin. He had not only been awake for the entire trip, but also for the day before the lift-off of the final shuttle flight and the six hours it had taken to find places for the five hundred new arrivals.

It was taking too long; Khouri could see that. There would have to be another ninety-nine flights like this before the evacuation operation was done, ninety-nine further opportunities for all hell to break loose. It might get easier once word got back to Resurgam that there was a starship at the end of the journey, rather than some diabolical government trap. On the other hand, when the precise nature of the starship became clearer things might get an awful lot worse. And there was every likelihood that the weapon would soon finish whatever it had initiated around Delta Pavonis. When that happened, every other problem would suddenly look very slight indeed.

But at least they were nearly home and dry with this trip.

The transfer ship was not designed for transatmospheric flight. She was a graceless sphere with a cluster of motors at one pole and the dimple of a flight deck at the other. The first five hundred passengers had spent many days aboard, exploring every grubby cranny of her austere interior. But at least they had had some room to spare. When the next load came up, things became a little more difficult. Food and water had to be rationed and each passenger assigned a specific cubbyhole. But it was still tolerable. Children had still been able to run around and make nuisances of themselves, and adults had still been able to find a little privacy when they needed it. Then the next shipment had come up—another five hundred—and the whole tone of the ship had changed subtly, and for the worse. Rules had to be enforced rather than politely suggested. Something very close to a miniature police state had been created aboard the ship, with a harsh scale of penalties for various crimes. So far there had been only minor infringements of the draconian new laws, but Khouri doubted that every trip would run as smoothly. Sooner or later she would probably be required to make an example of someone, for the benefit of the others.

The final five hundred had been the greatest headache. Slotting them in had resembled a fiendish puzzle: no matter how many permutations they tried, there were always fifty people still waiting on the shuttle, glumly aware that they had been reduced to irksome surplus units in a problem that would have been a great deal more tractable had they not existed.

And yet, finally, a way had been found to get everyone

aboard. That part at least would be simpler next time, but the rule of discipline might have to be even stricter. The people could be allowed no rights aboard the transfer craft.

Thirteen hours out, a kind of exhausted calm fell across the ship. She met Thorn by a porthole, just out of earshot of the nearest huddle of passengers. Ashen light made his face statue-like. He looked utterly dejected, sapped of any joy in what they had achieved.

"We've done it," she said. "No matter what happens now, we've saved two thousand lives."

"Have we?" he asked, keeping his voice low.

"They're not going back to Resurgam, Thorn."

They spoke like business associates, avoiding physical contact. Thorn was still a "guest" of the government and there must not appear to be any ulterior motive behind his co-operation. Because of that necessary distance, an act that had to be maintained at all times aboard the shuttle, she felt the urge to sleep with him more strongly than she had ever done before. She knew that they had come very close aboard the ship after the encounter with the Inhibitor cubes in Roc's atmosphere. But they had not done it then, and nor had they when they were on Resurgam. The erotic tension that had existed between them ever since had been thrilling and painful at the same time. Her attraction to him had never been stronger, and she knew that he wanted her at least as much. It would happen, she knew. It was just a question of accepting what she had long known she had to accept, which was that one life was over and another must begin. It was about making the choice to discard her past, and accepting—forcing herself to believe—that she was not dishonouring her husband by that act of disavowal. She just hoped that wherever he was, alive or dead now, Fazil Khouri had come to the same realisation and had found the strength to close the chapter on the part of his life that had included Ana Khouri. They had been in love, desperately in love, but the universe cared nothing for the vicissitudes of the human heart. Now they both had to follow their own paths.

Thorn touched her hand gently, the gesture hidden in the shadows that hung between them. "No," he said. "We're not taking them back to Resurgam. But can we honestly say we're taking them to a better place? What if all we're doing is taking them to a different place to die?"

"It's a starship, Thorn."

"Yes, one which isn't going anywhere in a hurry."

"Yet," she said.

"I sincerely hope you're right."

"Ilia made progress with the Captain," she said. "He began to come out of his shell. If she managed to persuade him to deploy the cache weapons, she can talk him into moving."

He turned from the porthole, harsh shadows emphasising his face. "And then?"

"Another system. It doesn't matter which one. We'll take our pick. Anything's got to be better than staying here, hasn't it?"

"For a while, perhaps. But shouldn't we at least investigate what Sylveste can do for us?"

She took her hand from his and said guardedly, "Sylveste? Are you serious?"

"He took an interest in our affairs inside Roc. At the very least, something did. You recognised it as Sylveste, or a copy of his personality. And the object, whatever it was, returned to Hades."

"What are you suggesting?"

"That we consider the unthinkable, Ana: seeking his help. You told me that the Hades matrix is older than the Inhibitors. It may be something stronger than them. That certainly appeared the case inside Roc. Shouldn't we see what Sylveste has to say on the matter? He might not be able to help us directly, but he might have information we can use. He's been in there for subjective aeons, and he's had access to the archive of an entire starfaring culture."

"You don't understand, Thorn. I thought I told you, but obviously it didn't sink in. There's no easy way into the Hades matrix."

"No, I remember that. But there is a way, even if it involves dying, isn't there?"

"There was another way, but there's no guarantee it still works. Dying is the only way I know. And I'm not going there again, not in this life or the next."

Thorn looked down, his face a mask that she found difficult to read. Was he disappointed or understanding? He had no idea what it had been like to fall towards Hades knowing that certain death awaited her. She had been resurrected once, after meeting Sylveste and Pascale, but there had been no promises that they would repeat the favour. The act itself had consumed a considerable fraction of the computational resources of the Hades object, and they—whoever were the agents that directed its endless calculations—might not sanction the same thing again. It was easy for Thorn; he had no idea what it had been like.

"Thorn . . . " she began.

But at that moment pink and blue light stammered across the side of his face.

Khouri frowned. "What was that?"

Thorn turned back towards space. "Lights. Flashing lights, like distant lightning. I've been watching them every time I walk past a porthole. They seem to lie near to the ecliptic plane, in the same half of the sky as the Inhibitor machine. They weren't there when we left orbit. Whatever it is must have started in the last twelve hours. I don't think it's anything to do with the weapon itself."

"Then it must be our weapons," Khouri said. "Ilia must have started using them already."

"She said she'd give us a period of grace."

It was true; Ilia Volyova had promised them that she would not deploy any of the cache weapons for thirty days, and that she would review her decision based on the success of the evacuation operation.

"Something must have happened," Khouri said.

"Or she lied," Thorn said quietly. In the shadows he took her hand again, and with one finger traced a line from her wrist to the conjunction of her middle and forefingers.

"No. She wouldn't have lied. Something's happened, Thorn. There's been a change of plan."

It came out of the darkness two hours later. There was nothing that could be done to prevent some of the occupants of the transfer craft from seeing *Nostalgia for Infinity* from the outside, so all Khouri and Thorn could do was wait and hope that the reaction was not too extreme. Khouri had wanted to slide baffles across the portholes—the ship was of too old a design for the portholes to be simply sphinctered out of existence—but Thorn had warned her that she should do nothing that implied that the view was in any way odd or troublesome.

He whispered, "It may not be as bad as you expect. You know what a lighthugger's meant to look like, and so the ship disturbs you because the Captain's transformations have turned it into something monstrous. But most of the people we're carrying were born on Resurgam. Most of them haven't ever seen a starship, or even any images of what one should look like. They have a very vague idea based on the old records and the space operas they've been fed by Broadcasting House. *Nostalgia for Infinity* may strike them as a bit . . . unusual . . . but they won't necessarily jump to the conclusion that she's a plague ship."

"And when they get aboard?" Khouri asked.

"Now that might be a different story."

Thorn, however, turned out to be more or less correct. The shocking excrescences and architectural flourishes of the ship's mutated exterior looked pathological to Khouri, but she knew more about the plague than anyone on Resurgam. It turned out that relatively few of the passengers were as disturbed as she had expected. Most were prepared to accept that the flourishes of diseased design served some obscure military function. This, after all, was the ship that they believed had wiped out an entire surface colony. They had few preconceptions about what it should look like, other than that it was, by its very nature, evil.

"They're relieved that there's a ship here at all," Thorn told her. "And most of them can't get anywhere near a porthole anyway. They're taking what they're hearing with a large pinch of salt, or they just don't care."

"How can they not care when they've thrown away their lives to come this far?"

"They're tired," Thorn told her. "Tired and past caring about anything except getting off this ship."

The transfer craft executed a slow pass down the side of *Infinity*'s hull. Khouri had seen the approach enough times to view the prospect with only mild interest. But now something made her frown again.

"That wasn't there before," she said.

"What?"

She kept her voice low and refrained from pointing. "That . . . scar. Do you see it?"

"That thing? I can't miss it."

The scar was a meandering gash that wandered along the hull for several hundred metres. It appeared to be deep, very deep, in fact, gouging far into the ship, and it had every sign of being recent: the edges were sharp and there were no traces of any attempts at repair. Something squirmed in Khouri's stomach.

"It's new," she said.

THIRTY-TWO

The transfer shuttle slid alongside the larger spacecraft, a single bubble drifting down the flank of a great scarred whale. Khouri and Thorn made their way to the rarely used flight deck, sealed the door behind them and then ordered some floodlights to be deployed. Fingers of light clawed along the hull, throwing the topology into exaggerated relief. The baroque transformations were queasily apparent—folds and whorls and acres of lizard-like scales—but there was no sign of any further damage.

"Well?" Thorn whispered. "What's your assessment?"

"I don't know," she said. "But one thing's for sure. Normally we'd have heard from Ilia by now."

Thorn nodded. "You think something catastrophic happened here, don't you?"

"We saw a battle, Thorn, or what looked like one. I can't help jumping to conclusions."

"It was a long way off."

"You can be certain of that, can you?"

"Fairly, yes. The flashes weren't spread randomly around the sky. They were clustered, and they all lay close to the plane of the ecliptic. That means that whatever we saw was distant—tens of light-minutes, maybe even whole light-hours from here. If this ship was in the thick of it, we'd have seen a much larger spatial extent to the flashes."

"Good. You'll excuse me if I don't sound too relieved."

"The damage we're seeing here can't be related, Ana. If those flashes really were on the far side of the system, then the energy being unleashed was fearsome. This ship looks as if it took a hit of some kind, but it can't have been a direct hit from the same weapons or there wouldn't be a ship here."

"So it got hit by shrapnel or something."

"Not very likely . . . "

"Thorn, something sure as fuck happened."

There was a shiver of activity from the console displays. Neither of them had done anything. Khouri leaned over and queried the shuttle, biting her lip.

"What is it?" Thorn asked.

"We're being invited to dock," she told him. "Normal approach vector. It's as if nothing unusual's happened. But if that's the case, why isn't Ilia speaking to us?"

"We've got two thousand people in our care. We'd better be sure we're not walking into a trap."

"I do realise that." She skated a finger across the console, skipping through commands and queries, occasionally tapping a response into the system.

"So what are you doing?" Thorn asked.

"Landing us. If the ship wanted to do something nasty, it's had enough chances."

Thorn pulled a face but offered no counter-argument. There was a tug of microgravity as the transfer shuttle inserted itself into the docking approach, moving under direct control of the larger ship. The hull loomed and then opened to reveal the docking bay. Khouri closed her eyes—the transfer shuttle only just appeared to fit through the aperture—but there was no collision, and then they were inside. The shuttle wheeled and then nudged itself into a berthing cradle. There was a tiny shove of thrust at the last moment, then a faint, faint tremor of contact. And then the console altered again, signifying that the shuttle had established umbilical linkage with the bay. Everything was absolutely normal.

"I don't like it," Khouri said. "It's not like Ilia."

"She wasn't exactly in a forgiving mood the last time we met. Maybe she's just having a very long sulk."

"Not her style," Khouri said, snapping her response and then immediately regretting it. "Something's wrong. I just don't know what."

"What about the passengers?" he asked.

"We keep 'em here until we know what's going on. After fifteen hours, they can stand one or two more."

"They won't like it."

"They'll have to. One of your people can cook up an excuse, can't they?"

"I suppose one more lie at this point won't make much difference, will it? I'll think of something—an atmospheric pressure mismatch, maybe."

"That'll do. It doesn't have to be a show stopper. Just a plausible reason to keep them aboard for a few hours."

Thorn went back to arrange matters with his aides. It would not be too difficult, Khouri thought: the majority of the passengers would not expect to be unloaded for several hours anyway, and so would not instantly realise anything was amiss. Provided word did not spread around the ship that no one was being let out, a riot could be held off for a while.

She waited for Thorn to return.

"What now?" he asked. "We can't leave by the main airlock or people will get suspicious if we don't come back."

"There's a secondary lock here," Khouri said, nodding at an armoured door set in one wall of the flight deck. "I've requested a connecting tube to be fed across from the bay. We can get on and off the ship without anyone knowing we're away."

The tube clanged against the side of the hull. So far, the larger ship was being very obliging. Khouri and Thorn donned spacesuits from the emergency locker even though the indications were that the air in the connecting tube was normal in mix and pressure. They propelled themselves to the door, opened it and crammed into the chamber on the other side. The outer door opened almost immediately since there was no pressure imbalance to be adjusted.

Something waited in the tunnel.

Khouri flinched and sensed Thorn do likewise. Her soldiering years had given her a deep-seated dislike for robots. On Sky's Edge a robot was often the last thing you saw. She had learned to suppress that phobia since moving in other cultures, but she still retained the capacity to be startled when she encountered one unexpectedly.

Yet the servitor was not one she recognised. It was human-shaped, but at the same time utterly non-human in form. It was largely hollow, a lacy scaffold of wire-thin joints and struts containing almost no solid parts. Alloyed mechanisms, whirring sensors and arterial feedlines hovered within the skeletal form. The servitor spanned the corridor with limbs outstretched, waiting for them.

"This doesn't look good," Khouri said.

"Hello," the servitor said, barking at them with a crudely synthesised voice.

"Where's Ilia?" Khouri asked.

"Indisposed. Would you mind authorising your suits to interpret the ambient data field, full visual and audio realisation? It will make matters a great deal easier."

"What's it talking about?" Thorn asked.

"It wants us to let it manipulate what we see through our suits."

"Can it do that?"

"Anything on the ship can, if we let it. Most of the Ultras have implants to achieve the same effect."

"And you?"

"I had mine removed before I came down to Resurgam. Didn't want anyone to be able to trace me back here in a hurry."

"Sensible," Thorn said.

The servitor spoke again. "I assure you that there won't be any trickery. As you can see, I'm actually rather harmless. Ilia chose this body for me intentionally, so that I wouldn't be able to do any damage."

"Ilia chose it?"

The servitor nodded its wire-frame approximation of a skull. Something bobbed within the openwork cage: a stub of white wedged between two wires. It almost looked like a cigarette.

"Yes. She invited me aboard. I am a beta-level simulation of Nevil Clavain. Now, I'm no oil painting, but I'm reasonably certain that I don't look like this. If you want to see me as I really am, however . . ." The servitor gestured invitingly with one hand.

"Be careful," Thorn whispered.

Khouri issued the subvocal commands that told her suit to accept and interpret ambient data fields. The change was subtle. The servitor faded away, processed out of her visual field. Her suit was filling in the gaps where it would have been, using educated guesswork and its own thorough knowledge of the three-dimensional environment. All the safeguards remained in place.

If the servitor moved quickly or did anything that the suit decided was suspicious, it would be edited back into Khouri's visual field.

Now the solid figure of a man appeared where the servitor had been. There was a slight mismatch between the man and his surroundings—he was too sharply in focus, too bright, and the shadows did not fall upon him quite as they should have done—but those errors were deliberate. The suit could have made the man appear absolutely realistic, but it was considered wise to degrade the image slightly. That way the viewer could never lapse into forgetting that they were dealing with a machine.

"That's better," the figure said.

Khouri saw an old man, frail, white-bearded and white-haired. "Are you Nevil . . . what did you say your name was?"

"Nevil Clavain. You'd be Ana Khouri, I think." His voice was nearly human now. Only a tiny edge of artificiality remained, again quite deliberately.

"I've never heard of you." She looked at Thorn.

"Me neither," he said.

"You wouldn't have," Clavain said. "I've just arrived, you see. Or rather I'm in the process of arriving."

Khouri could hear the details later. "What's happened to Ilia?"

His face tightened. "It isn't good news, I'm afraid. You'd best come with me." Clavain turned around with only a modicum of stiffness. He began to make his way back down the tunnel, clearly expecting to be followed.

Khouri looked at Thorn. Her companion nodded, without saying a word.

They set off after Clavain.

He led them through the catacombs of *Nostalgia for Infinity*. Khouri kept telling herself that the servitor could do nothing to harm her, nothing at least that Ilia had not already sanctioned. If Ilia had installed a beta-level, she would only have given it a limited set of permissions, its possible actions tightly constrained. The beta-level was only driving the servitor, anyway; the software itself—and that was all it was, she reminded herself, very clever software—was executing on one of the ship's remaining networks.

"Tell me what happened, Clavain," she said. "You said you were arriving. What did you mean by that?"

"My ship's on its final deceleration phase," he said. "She's called *Zodiacal Light*. She'll be in this system shortly, braking to a stop near this vessel. My physical counterpart is aboard it. I invited Ilia to install this beta-level, since light-lag prohibited us from having anything resembling meaningful negotiations. Ilia obliged . . . and so here I am."

"So where is Ilia?"

"I can tell you where she is," Clavain said. "But I'm not totally sure what happened. She turned me off, you see."

"She must have turned you on again," Thorn said.

They were walking—or rather wading—through knee-deep ship slime the colour of bile. Ever since leaving the ship bay they had moved through portions of the vessel that were spun for gravity, although the effect varied depending on the exact route they followed.

"Actually, she didn't switch me on," Clavain said. "That's the unusual thing. I came around, I suppose you'd say, and found . . . well, I'm getting ahead of myself."

"Is she dead, Clavain?"

"No," he said, answering Khouri with a degree of emphasis. "No, she isn't dead. But she isn't well, either. It's good that you came now. I take it you have passengers on that shuttle?"

There seemed little point in lying. "Two thousand of them," Khouri said.

"Ilia said that you'd need to make around a hundred trips in total. This is just the first round-trip, isn't it?"

"Give us time and we'll manage all hundred," Thorn said.

"Time may well be the one thing you no longer have," Clavain replied. "I'm sorry, but that's just the way it is."

"You mentioned negotiations," Khouri said. "What the fuck is there to negotiate?"

A sympathetic smile creased Clavain's aged face. "Quite a lot, I fear. You have something that my counterpart wants very badly, you see."

The servitor knew its way around the ship. Clavain led them through a labyrinth of corridors and shafts, ramps and ducts, chambers and antechambers, traversing many districts of which Khouri had only sketchy knowledge. There were regions of the ship that had not been visited for decades of worldtime, places into which even Ilia had shown a marked reluctance to stray. The ship had always been vast and intricate, its topology as unfathomable as the abandoned subway system of a deserted metropolis. It had been a ship haunted by many ghosts, not all of which were necessarily cybernetic or imaginary. Winds had sighed up and down its kilometres of empty corridors. It was infested with rats, stalked by machines and madmen. It had moods and fevers, like an old house.

And yet now it was subtly different. It was entirely possible that the ship still retained all its old hauntings, all its places of menace. Now, however, there was a single encompassing spirit, a sentient presence that permeated every cubic inch of the vessel and could not be meaningfully localised to any specific point within the ship. Wherever they walked, they were surrounded by the Captain. He sensed them and they sensed him, even if it was only a tingling of the neck hairs, a keen sense of being scrutinised. It made the entire ship seem both more and less threatening than it had before. It all depended on whose side the Captain was on.

Khouri didn't know. She didn't even think Ilia had ever been entirely sure.

Gradually, Khouri began to recognise a district. It was one of the regions of the ship that had changed only slightly since the Captain's transformation. The walls were the sepia of old manuscripts, the corridors pervaded by a cloisterlike gloom relieved only by ochre lights flickering within sconces, like candles. Clavain was leading them to the medical bay.

The room that he led them into was low ceilinged and windowless. Medical servitors were crouched hunks of machinery backed well into the corners, as if they were unlikely to be needed. A single bed was positioned near the room's centre, attended by a small huddle of squat monitoring devices. A woman was lying on her back in the bed, her arms folded across her chest and her eyes shut. Biomedical traces rippled above her like aurorae.

Khouri stepped closer to the bed. It was Volyova; there was no doubt about that. But she looked like a version of her friend who had been subjected to some appalling experiment in accelerated ageing, something involving drugs to suck the flesh back to the bone and more drugs to reduce the skin to the merest glaze. She looked astonishingly delicate, as if liable to splinter into dust at any moment. It was not the first time Khouri had seen Volyova here, in the medical bay. There had been the time after the gunfight on the surface of Resurgam, when they were capturing Sylveste. Volyova had been injured then, but there had never been any question of her dying. Now it took close examination to tell that she was not already dead. Volyova looked desiccated.

Khouri turned to the beta-level, horrified. "What happened?"

"I still don't really know. Before she put me to sleep there was nothing the matter with her. Then I came back around and found myself here, in this room. She was in the bed. The machines had stabilised her, but that was about the best they could do. In the long term, she was still dying." Clavain nodded at the displays looming above Volyova. "I've seen these kinds of injuries before, during wartime. She breathed vacuum without any kind of protection against internal moisture loss. Decompression must have been rapid, but not quite quick enough to kill her instantly. Most of the damage is in her lungs—scarring of the alveoli, where ice crystals formed. She's blind in both eyes, and there is some damage to brain function. I don't think it's cognitive. There's tracheal damage as well, which makes it difficult for her to speak."

"She's an Ultra," Thorn said with a touch of desperation. "Ultras don't die just because they swallow a little vacuum."

"She isn't much like the other Ultras I've met," Clavain said. "There were no implants in her. If there had been, she might have walked it off. At the very least, the medichines could have buffered her brain. But she had none. I understand she was repulsed by the idea of anything invading her."

Khouri looked at the beta-level. "What have you done, Clavain?"

"What it took. It was requested that I do what I could. The obvious thing was to inject a dose of medichines."

"Wait." Khouri raised a hand. "Who requested what?"

Clavain scratched his beard. "I'm not sure. I just felt an obligation to do it. You have to understand that I'm just software. I wouldn't claim otherwise. It's entirely possible that something booted me up and intervened in my execution, forcing me to act in a certain manner."

Khouri and Thorn exchanged glances. They were both thinking the same thing, Khouri knew. The only agency that could have switched Clavain back on and made him help Volyova was the Captain.

Khouri felt cold, intensely aware that she was being observed. "Clavain," she said. "Listen to me. I don't know what you are, really. But you have to understand: she would sooner have died than have you do what you've just done."

"I know," Clavain said, extending his palms in a gesture of helplessness. "But I had to do it. It's what I would have done had I been here."

"Ignored her deepest wish, is that what you mean?"

"Yes, if you want to put it like that. Because someone once did the same for me. I was in the same position as her, you see. Injured—dying, in fact. I'd been wounded, but I definitely didn't want any stinking machines in my skull. I'd have rather died than that. But someone put them in there anyway. And now I'm grateful. She gave me four hundred years of life I wouldn't have had any other way."

Khouri looked at the bed, at the woman lying in it, and then back to the man who had, if not saved her life, at the very least postponed her moment of death.

"Clavain . . . " she said. "Who the hell are you?"

"Clavain is a Conjoiner," said a voice as thin as smoke. "You should listen to him very carefully, because he means what he says."

Volyova had spoken, yet there had been no movement from the figure on the bed. The only indication that she was now conscious, which had not been the case when they arrived, was a shift in the biomedical traces hovering above her.

Khouri wrenched her helmet off. Clavain's apparition vanished, replaced by the skeletal machine. She placed the helmet on the floor and knelt by the bed. "Ilia?"

"Yes, it's me." The voice was like sandpaper. Khouri observed the tiniest movement of Volyova's lips as she formed the words, but the sound came from above her.

"What happened?"

"There was an incident."

"We saw the damage to the hull when we arrived. Is . . . "

"Yes. It was my fault, really. Like everything. Always my fault. *Always my damned fault.*"

Khouri glanced back at Thorn. "Your fault?"

"I was tricked." The lips parted in what might almost have been a smile. "By the Captain. I thought he had finally come around to my way of thinking. That we should use the cache weapons against the Inhibitors."

Khouri could almost imagine what must have happened. "How did he trick . . . "

"I deployed eight of the weapons beyond the hull. There was a malfunction. I thought it was genuine, but it was really just a way to get me outside the ship."

Khouri lowered her voice. It was an absurd gesture—there was nothing that could be hidden from the Captain now—but she could not help it. "He wanted to kill you?"

"No," Volyova said, hissing her answer. "He wanted to kill himself, not me. But I had to be there to see it. Had to be a witness."

"Why?"

"To understand his remorse. To understand that it was deliberate, and not an accident."

Thorn joined them. He too had removed his helmet, tucking it respectfully under one arm. "But the ship's still here. What happened, Ilia?"

Again that weary half-smile. "I drove my shuttle into the beam. I thought it might make him stop."

"Seems as if it did."

"I didn't expect to survive. But my aim wasn't quite right."

The servitor strode towards the bed. Unclothed of Clavain's image, its motions appeared automatically more machinelike and threatening.

"They know that I injected medichines into your head," it said, its voice no longer humanoid. "And now they know that *you* know."

"Clavain . . . the beta-level . . . had no choice," Volyova said before either of her two human visitors could speak. "Without the medichines I'd be dead now. Do they horrify me? Yes. Utterly, to the absolute core of my being. I am racked with revulsion at the thought of them crawling inside my skull like so many spiders and snakes. At the same time, I accept the necessity of them. They are the tools I have always worked with, after all. And I am fully aware that they cannot work miracles. Too much damage has been done. I am not amenable to repair."

"We'll find a way, Ilia," Khouri said. "Your injuries can't be . . ."

Volyova's whisper of a voice cut her off. "Forget me. I don't matter. Only the weapons matter now. They are my children, spiteful and wicked as they may be, and I won't have them falling into the wrong hands."

"Now we seem to be getting to the crux of things," Thorn said.

"Clavain—the real Clavain—wants the weapons," Volyova said. "By his own estimation he has the means to take them from us." Her voice grew louder. "Isn't that so, Clavain?"

The servitor bowed. "I'd much rather negotiate their hand-over, Ilia, as you know, especially now that I've invested time in your welfare. But make no mistake. My counterpart is capable of a great deal of ruthlessness in pursuit of a just cause. He believes he has right on his side. And men who think they have right on their side are always the most dangerous sort."

"Why are you telling us that?" Khouri said.

"It's in his—our—best interests," the servitor said amiably. "I'd far rather convince you to give up the weapons without a fight. At the very least we'd avoid any risk of damaging the damned things."

"You don't seem like a monster to me," Khouri said.

"I'm not," the servitor replied. "And nor is my counterpart. He'll always choose the path of least bloodshed. But if *some* bloodshed is required . . . well, my counterpart won't flinch from a little surgical butchery. Especially not now."

The servitor said the last with such emphasis that Thorn asked, "Why not now?"

"Because of what he has had to do to get this far." The servitor paused, its openwork head scanning each of them. "He betrayed everything that he had believed in for four hundred years. That wasn't done lightly, I assure you. He lied to his friends and left behind his loved ones, knowing that it was the only way to get this done. And lately he took a terrible decision. He destroyed something that he loved very much. It cost him a great deal of pain. In that sense, I am not an accurate copy of the real Clavain. My personality was shaped before that dreadful act."

Volyova's voice rasped out again, instantly commanding their attention. "The real Clavain isn't like you?"

"I'm a sketch taken before a terrible darkness fell across his life, Ilia. I can only speculate on the extent to which we differ. But I would not like to trifle with my counterpart in his current state of mind."

"Psychological warfare," she hissed.

"I beg your pardon?"

"That is why you've come, isn't it? Not to help us negotiate a sensible settlement, but to put the fear of God into us."

The servitor bowed again, with something of the same mechanical modesty. "If I were to achieve that," Clavain said, "I would consider my work well done. The path of least bloodshed, remember?"

"You want bloodshed," Ilia Volyova said, "you've come to the right woman."

Shortly afterwards she fell into a different state of consciousness, something perhaps not too far from sleep. The displays relaxed, sine waves and Fourier harmonic histograms reflecting a seismic shift in major neural activity. Her visitors observed her in that state for several minutes, wondering to themselves whether she was dreaming or scheming, or if the distinction even mattered.

The next six hours went by quickly. Thorn and Khouri returned to the transfer shuttle and conferred with their immediate underlings. They were gratified to hear that no crises had occurred while they were visiting Volyova. There had been some minor flare-ups, but for the most part the two thousand passengers had accepted the cover story about a problem with the atmospheric compatibility of the two ships. Now the passengers were assured that the technical difficulty had been resolved—it had been a sensor malfunction all along—and that disembarkation could commence in the orderly fashion that had already been agreed. A large holding area had been prepared a few hundred metres from the parking bay, just into the spun part of the ship. It was a region that was relatively unafflicted by the Captain's plague transformations, and Khouri and Volyova had worked hard to disguise the most overtly disturbing parts of the area that the plague had affected.

The holding area was cold and dank, and though they had done their best to make it comfortable, it still had the atmosphere of a crypt. Interior partitions had been put up to divide the space into smaller chambers which were each capable of containing a hundred passengers, and those chambers were in turn equipped with partitions to allow some privacy for family units. The holding area could accommodate ten thousand passengers—four further arrivals of the transfer shuttle—but by the time the sixth flight arrived, they would have to begin dispersing passengers into the main body of the ship. And then, inevitably, the truth would dawn: that they had been brought not only aboard a ship which was carrying the feared Melding Plague, but aboard a ship which had been subsumed and reshaped by its own Captain; that they were, in every sense that mattered, now inside that selfsame Captain.

Khouri expected panic and terror to accompany that realisation. Very likely it would be necessary to enforce a state of martial emergency even more stringent than that now operating on Resurgam. There would be deaths, and there would probably have to be more executions, to make a point.

And yet none of that would matter a damn when the real truth got out, which was that Ilia Volyova, the hated Triumvir, was still alive, and that she had orchestrated this very evacuation.

Only then would the real trouble start.

Khouri watched the transfer shuttle undock and begin its return trip to Resurgam. Thirty hours of flight time, she calculated, plus—if they were lucky—no more than half that in turnaround at the other end. In two days Thorn would be back. If she could hold things together until then, she would already feel as if she had climbed a mountain.

But there would still be ninety-eight further flights to bring aboard after that . . .

One step at a time, she thought. That was what they had taught her in her soldiering days: break a problem down into doable units. Then, no matter how stupendous the problem seemed, you could tackle it piece by piece. Focus on the details and worry about the bigger picture later.

Outside, the distant space battle continued to rage. The flashes resembled the random firing of synapses in a splayed-out brain. She was certain that Volyova knew something about what was going on, and perhaps Clavain's beta-level did, too. But Volyova was sleeping and Khouri did not trust the servitor to tell her anything except subtle lies. That left the Captain, who probably knew something as well.

Khouri made her way through the ship alone. She took the dilapidated elevator system down to the cache chamber, just as she had done hundreds of times before in Volyova's company. She felt an odd sense of mischief to be making the journey unaccompanied.

The chamber was as weightless and dark as it had been on their recent visits. Khouri halted the elevator on the lock level, and then shrugged on a spacesuit and propulsion pack. In a few breathless moments she was inside the chamber, floating into darkness. She jetted from the wall, doing her best to ignore the sense of unease she always felt in the presence of the cache weapons. She keyed on the suit's navigation system and waited for it to align itself with the chamber's transponder beacons. Annotated grey-green forms hoved on to her faceplate, at distances ranging from tens to hundreds of metres. The spidery lattice of the monorail system was a series of harder lines transecting the chamber at various angles. There were still weapons in the chamber. But not as many as she had expected.

There had been thirty-three before she had left for Resurgam. Volyova had deployed eight of them before the Captain tried to destroy himself. But just from the paucity of hovering shapes, Khouri could see that there were a lot fewer than twenty-five weapons left here. She counted the hovering shapes and then counted again, steering her suit deeper into the chamber just in case there was a problem with the transponder. But her first suspicion had been correct. There were only thirteen weapons left aboard *Nostalgia for Infinity*. Twenty of the damned things were unaccounted for.

Except she knew exactly where they were, didn't she? Eight were outside somewhere, and so—presumably—were the other twelve that had gone missing. And, very probably, they were halfway across the system, responsible for at least some of the glints and flashes she had seen from the shuttle.

Volyova—or someone, anyway—had thrown twenty cache weapons into battle against the Inhibitors.

And it was anyone's guess who was winning.

Know thine enemy, Clavain thought.

Except he didn't know his enemy at all.

He was alone on the bridge of *Zodiacal Light,* sitting in rapt concentration. With his eyes nearly closed and his forehead creased by habitual worry lines, he resembled a chess master about to make the most vital move of his career. Beyond the steeple of his fingers hung a projected form: a deeply nested composite view of the lighthugger that held the long-lost weapons.

He recalled what Skade had told him, back in the Mother Nest. The evidence trail pointed to this ship being *Nostalgia for Infinity*; her commander most likely a woman named Ilia Volyova. He could even remember the picture of the woman that Skade had shown him. But even if that evidence trail was correct, and he really would be dealing with Volyova, it told him almost nothing. The only thing he could trust was what he learned with his own extended senses, in the present.

The image before him composited all salient tactical knowledge of the enemy craft. Its details were constantly shifting and re-layering as *Zodiacal Light's* intelligence-gathering systems improved their guesswork. Long baseline interferometry teased out the electromagnetic profile of the ship across the entire spectrum from soft gamma rays to low-frequency radio. At all wavelengths the backscatter of radiation was perplexing, making the interpretive software crash or come up with nonsensical guesses. Clavain had to intervene every time the software threw up another absurd interpretation. For some reason the software kept insisting that the vessel resembled some weird fusion of ship, cathedral and sea urchin. Clavain could see the underlying form of a plausible spacecraft, and had to constantly nudge the software away from its more outlandish solution minima. He could only imagine that the lighthugger had cloaked itself in a shell of confusing material, like the obfuscatory clouds that Rust Belt habitats occasionally employed.

The alternative—that the software was correct, and that he was merely enforcing his own expectations on it—was too unnerving to consider.

There was a knock against the frame of the door.

He turned around with a stiff whirr of his exoskeleton. "Yes?"

Antoinette Bax stalked into the room, followed by Xavier. They both wore exoskeletons as well, though they had ornamented theirs with swirls of luminous paint and welded-on baroquework. Clavain had observed a lot of that amongst his crew, especially amongst Scorpio's army, and had seen no reason to enforce a more disciplined regime. Privately, he welcomed anything that instilled a sense of camaraderie and purpose.

"What is it, Antoinette?" Clavain asked.

"There's something we wanted to discuss, Clavain."

"It's about the attack," Xavier Liu added.

Clavain nodded and made the effort of a smile. "If we are very lucky, there won't be one. The crew will see reason and hand over the weapons, and we can go home without firing a shot."

Of course, that outcome was looking less likely by the hour. He had already learned from the weapon traces that twenty of them had been dispersed from the ship, leaving only thirteen aboard. Worse than that, the specific diagnostic patterns suggested that some of the weapons had actually been activated. Three of the patterns had even vanished in the last eight hours of shiptime. He didn't know what to make of that, but he had a nasty feeling that he knew exactly what it meant.

"And if they don't hand them over?" Antoinette asked, easing into a seat.

"Then some force may be in order," Clavain said.

Xavier nodded. "That's what we figured."

"I hope it will be brief and decisive," Clavain said. "And I have every expectation that it will be. Scorpio's preparations have been thorough. Remontoire's technical assistance has been invaluable. We have a well-trained assault force and the weapons to back them up."

"But you haven't asked for our help," Xavier said.

Clavain turned back to the image of the ship, examining it to see if there had been any changes in the last few minutes. To his annoyance, the software had started building up scablike accretions and spirelike spines along one flank of the hull. He swore under his breath. The ship looked like nothing so much as one of the plague-stricken buildings in Chasm City. The thought hovered in his mind, worryingly.

"You were saying?" he said, his attention drifting back to the youngsters.

"We want to help," Antoinette said.

"You've already helped," Clavain told her. "Without you we probably wouldn't have seized this ship in the first place. Not to mention the fact that you helped me to defect."

"That was then. Now we're talking about helping in the attack," Xavier said.

"Ah." Clavain scratched his beard. "You mean *really* help, in a military sense?"

"*Storm Bird*'s hull can take more weapons," Antoinette said. "And she's fast and manoeuvrable. Had to be, to make a profit back home."

"She's armoured, too," Xavier said. "You saw the damage she did when we busted out of Carousel New Copenhagen. And there's a lot of room inside her. She could probably carry half of Scorpio's army, with space to spare."

"I don't doubt it."

"Then what's your objection?" Antoinette asked.

"This isn't your fight. You helped me, and I'm grateful for that. But if I know Ultras, and I think I do, they won't give up anything without some trouble. There's been enough bloodshed already, Antoinette. Let me handle the rest of it."

The two youngsters—he wondered if they had really seemed so young to him before—exchanged coded looks. He had the sense that they were privy to a script he had not been shown.

"You'd be making a mistake, Clavain," Xavier said.

Clavain looked into his eyes. "Thought this through, have you, Xavier?"

"Of course . . ."

"I really don't think you have." Clavain returned his attention to the hovering image of the lighthugger. "Now, if you don't mind . . . I'm a little on the busy side."

THIRTY-THREE

"Ilia. Wake up."

Khouri stood by Ilia's bedside, watching the neural diagnostics for a sign that Volyova was returning to consciousness. The possibility that she might have died could not be dismissed—

there was certainly very little visual indication that she was alive—but the diagnostics looked very much as they had before Khouri had taken her trip to the cache chamber.

"May I help?"

Khouri turned around, startled and ashamed at the same time. The skeletal servitor had just spoken to her again.

"Clavain . . . " she said. "I didn't think you were still switched on."

"I wasn't until a moment ago." The servitor advanced out of the shadows, coming to a halt on the opposite side of the bed from Khouri. It moved to one of the squat hunks of machinery attending the bed and made a series of adjustments to the controls.

"What are you doing?" Khouri asked.

"Elevating her to consciousness. Isn't that what you wanted?"

"I . . . I'm not sure if I should trust you or smash you apart," she said.

The servitor stepped back from its handiwork. "You should certainly not trust me, Ana. My primary goal is to convince you to turn over the weapons. I can't use force, but I can use persuasion and disinformation." Then it reached down beneath the bed and tossed something to her with a lithe sweep of one limb.

Khouri caught a pair of goggles equipped with an earpiece. They appeared to be perfectly normal shipboard issue, scuffed and discoloured. She slipped them on and watched Clavain's human form cloak itself over the skeletal frame of the servitor. His voice came through the earpiece with human timbre and inflection.

"That's better," he said.

"Who's running you, Clavain?"

"Ilia told me a little about your Captain," the servitor said. "I haven't seen or heard from him, but I think he must be using me. He switched me on when Ilia was injured, and I was able to help her. But I'm just a beta-level simulation. I have Clavain's expertise, and Clavain has detailed medical training, but then I imagine the Captain must be able to draw on many other sources for that kind of thing, including his own memories. My only conclusion is that the Captain does not wish to intervene directly, so he has elected to use me as an intermediary. I'm his puppet, more or less."

Khouri felt an urge to disagree with him, but nothing in Clavain's manner suggested that he was lying or aware of a more plausible explanation. The Captain had only emerged from his isolation in order to orchestrate his suicide, but now that the attempt had failed, and Ilia had been hurt in the process, he had retreated into some even darker psychosis. She wondered whether that made Clavain the Captain's puppet or his weapon.

"What *can* I trust you to do, in that case?" Khouri looked from Clavain to Volyova. "Could you kill her?"

"No." He shook his head vigorously. "Your ship, or your Captain, wouldn't allow me to do it. I'm certain of that. And I wouldn't *think* of doing it anyway—I'm not a cold-blooded murderer, Ana."

"You're just software," she said. "Software's capable of anything."

"I won't kill her, I assure you. I want those weapons because I believe in humanity. I've never believed that the ends justify the means. Not in this war, not in any damned war I've ever served in. If I have to kill to get what I want, I will. But not before I've done all that I can to avoid it. Otherwise I'm no better than the other Conjoiners."

Without warning, Ilia Volyova spoke from her bed. "Why do you want them, Clavain?"

"I could ask you the same question."

"They're my damned weapons."

Khouri studied Volyova's figure, but she appeared no more awake than she had five minutes earlier.

"Actually, they don't belong to you," Clavain said. "They're still Conjoiner property."

"Taken your damned time reclaiming them, haven't you?"

"It isn't me who's doing the reclaiming, Ilia. I'm the nice man who's come to take them off your hands before the really nasty people arrive. Then they'll be my worry, not yours. And when I say nasty, I mean it. Deal with me and you'll be dealing with someone reasonable. But the Conjoiners won't even bother negotiating. They'll just take the weapons without asking."

"I still find this defection story a little hard to believe, Clavain."

"Ilia . . . " Khouri leaned closer to the bed. "Ilia, never mind Clavain for now. There's something I need to know. What have you done with the cache weapons? I only counted thirteen in the chamber."

Volyova clucked before answering. Khouri thought she sounded amused at her own cleverness. "I dispersed them. Killed two birds with one stone. Put them out of Clavain's easy reach, strewn across the system. I also let them go into autonomous firing mode against the Inhibitor machinery. How are my little beauties doing, Khouri? Are the fireworks impressive tonight?"

"There are fireworks, Ilia, but I haven't got a fucking clue who's winning."

"At least the battle is still continuing, then. That has to be a good sign, doesn't it?" She did nothing visibly, but a flattened globe popped into existence above her head, looking for all the world like a cartoon thought-bubble. Though she had been blinded in the attack by the cache weapon, she now wore slender grey goggles that communicated with the implants Clavain's proxy had installed in her head. In some respects she was now better sighted than she had been before, Khouri thought. She could see in all the wavelength and non-EM bands offered by the goggles, and she could tap into machine-generated fields with far greater clarity than had been possible before. For all that, however, she must have been quietly repulsed by the presence of the foreign machines inside her skull. Such things had always revolted her, and she would accept them now only out of necessity.

The projected globe was a mutual hallucination rather than a hologram. It was gridded with the green lines of an equatorial coordinate system, bulging at the equator and narrowing at the poles. The system's ecliptic was a milky disc spanning the bubble from side to side, dotted with many annotated symbols. In the middle was the hard orange eye of the star, Delta Pavonis. A vermilion smudge was the ruined corpse of Roc, with a harder, offset core of red indicating the bugle-shaped vastness of the Inhibitor weapon, now locked in rotational phase with the star. The star was itself gridded with glowing lilac contour lines. The spot on the surface of the star immediately below the weapon was shown to be bulging inwards for an eighth of the star's diameter, a quarter of the way to the nuclear-burning core. Furious violet-white rings of fusing matter radiated out from the depression, frozen like ripples on a lake, but those hotspots of fusion were mere sparks compared with the powerhouse of the core itself. And yet, as disturbing as these transformations were, the star was not the immediate centre of attention. Khouri counted twenty black triangles in the same approximate quadrant of the ecliptic as the Inhibitor weapon, and judged that those were the cache weapons.

"This is the state of play," Volyova said. "A real-time battle display. Aren't you jealous of my toys, Clavain?"

"You have no idea of the importance of those weapons," the servitor replied.

"Don't I?"

"They mean the difference between the extinction or survival of the entire human species. We know about the Inhibitors as well, Ilia, and we know what they can do. We've seen it in messages from the future, the human race on the brink of extinction, almost totally wiped out by Inhibitor machines. We called them the wolves, but there's no doubt that we're talking about the same enemy. That's why you can't squander the weapons here."

"Squander them? I am *not* squandering them." She sounded mortally affronted. "I am using them tactically to delay the Inhibitor processes. I'm buying valuable time for Resurgam."

Clavain's voice became probing. "How many weapons have you lost since you started the campaign?"

"Precisely none."

The servitor arched over her. "Ilia . . . listen to me very carefully. How many weapons have you lost?"

"What do you mean, 'lost'? Three weapons malfunctioned. So much for Conjoiner engineering, in that case. Another two were only designed to be used once. I hardly call those 'losses,' Clavain."

"So no weapons have been destroyed by return fire from the Inhibitors?"

"Two weapons have suffered some damage."

"They were destroyed entirely, weren't they?"

"I'm still receiving telemetry from their harnesses. I won't know the extent of the damage until I examine the scene of the battle."

Clavain's image stepped back from the bed. He had turned, if that was possible, a shade paler than before. He closed his eyes and muttered something under his breath, something that might almost have been a prayer.

"You had forty weapons to begin with. Now you have lost nine of them, by my reckoning. How many more, Ilia?"

"As many as it takes."

"You can't save Resurgam. You're dealing with forces beyond your comprehension. All you're doing is wasting the weapons. We need to keep them back until we can use them properly, in a way that will really make a difference. This is just an advance guard of wolves, but there'll be many more. Yet if we can examine the weapons perhaps we can make more like them; thousands more."

She smiled again; Khouri was certain of it. "So all that fine talk just now, Clavain, about how the ends don't justify the means—did you believe a word of it?"

"All I know is that if you squander the weapons, everyone on Resurgam will still die. The only difference is that they'll die later, and their deaths will be outnumbered by millions more. But hand over the weapons now, and there'll still be time to make a difference."

"And let two hundred thousand people die so millions can live in the future?"

"Not millions, Ilia. Billions."

"You had me going for a minute there, Clavain. I was almost starting to think you might be someone I could do business with." She smiled, as if it was the last time she would ever smile in her life. "I was wrong, wasn't I?"

"I'm not a bad man, Ilia. I'm just someone who knows exactly what needs to be done."

"Like you said, always the most dangerous sort."

"Please don't underestimate me. I will take those weapons."

"You're weeks away, Clavain. By the time you arrive, I'll be more than ready for you."

Clavain's figure said nothing. Khouri had no idea what to read into that lack of response, but it troubled her greatly.

Her ship towered over her, barely contained by its prison of repair scaffolding. *Storm Bird*'s internal lights were on, and in the upper row of flight deck windows Antoinette saw Xavier's silhouetted form hard at work. He had a compad in one hand and a stylus gripped between his teeth, and he was flicking ancient toggle switches above his head, taking typically diligent notes. *Always the bookkeeper,* she thought.

Antoinette eased her exoskeleton into a standing position. Now and then Clavain allowed the crew a few hours under conditions of normal gravity and inertia, but this was not one of those periods. The exoskeleton gave her dozens of permanent sores where the support pads and haptic motion sensors touched her skin. In a perverse way, she was almost looking forward to arriving around Delta Pavonis, since they would then be able to discard the skeletons.

She took a good long look at *Storm Bird*. She had not seen it since the time she had walked away, refusing to enter what no longer felt like her own territory. It felt like months ago, and some of the anger—though not all of it—had abated.

She was still pretty pissed off.

Her ship was certainly ready for the fight. To the untrained eye, there had been no drastic alteration in *Storm Bird*'s external appearance. The extra weapons that had been grafted on, in addition to the deterrents already present, merely amounted to a few more bulges, spines and asymmetries to add to those that were already present. With the manufactories churning out armaments by the tonne, it had been an easy enough matter to divert some of that output her way, and Scorpio had been perfectly willing to turn a blind eye. Remontoire and Xavier had even worked together to couple the more exotic weapons into *Storm Bird*'s control net.

For a time, she had wondered why she felt the urge to fight. She did not consider herself given to violence or heroic gestures. Pointless, stupid gestures—such as burying her father in a gas giant—were another thing entirely.

She climbed up through the ship until she reached the flight deck. Xavier carried on working after she had entered. He was too engrossed in what he was doing, and he must have become used to her never visiting *Storm Bird*.

She sat in the seat next to him, waiting for him to notice her and look up from his work. When he did he just nodded, giving her the space and time to say what she needed to. She appreciated that.

"Beast?" Antoinette said quietly.

The pause before Lyle Merrick replied was probably no

longer than usual, but it felt like an eternity. "Yes, Antoinette?"

"I'm back."

"Yes . . . I gathered." There was another long intermission. "I'm pleased that you've returned."

The voice had the same tonal quality as ever, but *something* had changed. She supposed that Lyle was no longer obliged to mimic the old subpersona, the one that he had replaced sixteen years before.

"Why?" she asked sharply. "Did you miss me?"

"Yes," Merrick said. "Yes, I did."

"I don't think I can ever forgive you, Lyle."

"I wouldn't ever want or expect your forgiveness, Antoinette. I certainly wouldn't deserve it."

"No, you wouldn't."

"But you understand that I made a promise to your father?"

"That's what Xavier said."

"Your father was a good man, Antoinette. He only wanted the best for you."

"The best for you as well, Lyle."

"I'm in his debt. I wouldn't argue with that."

"How do you live with what you did?"

There was something that might have been a laugh, or even a self-deprecating snigger. "The part of me that mattered the most isn't greatly troubled by that question, you know. The flesh-and-blood me was executed. I'm just a shadow, the only shadow that the eraserheads missed."

"A shadow with a highly evolved sense of self-preservation."

"Again, that's nothing I'd deny."

"I want to hate you, Lyle."

"Go ahead," he said. "Millions already do."

She sighed. "But I can't afford to. This is still my ship. You are still running it whether I like it or not. True, Lyle?"

"I was already a pilot, Little . . . I mean Antoinette. I already had an intimate knowledge of spacecraft operations before my small mishap. It hasn't been difficult for me to integrate myself with *Storm Bird*. I doubt that a real subpersona would ever prove an adequate replacement."

She sneered. "Oh, don't worry. I'm not going to replace you."

"You're not?"

"No," she said. "But my reasons are pragmatic. I can't afford to, not without seriously fucking up my ship's performance. I don't want to go through the learning curve of integrating a new gamma-level, especially not now."

"That's reason enough for me."

"I'm not finished. My father made a deal with you. That means you made a deal with the Bax family. I can't renege on that, even if I wanted to. It wouldn't be good for business."

"We're a little far from any business opportunities now, Antoinette."

"Well, maybe. But there's one other thing. Are you listening?"

"Of course."

"We're going into battle. You're going to help me. And by that I mean you're going to fly this ship and make it do whatever the fuck I ask of it. Understood? I mean *everything*. No matter how much danger it puts me in."

"Vowing to protect you was also part of the arrangement I made with your father, Antoinette."

She shrugged. "That was between you and him, not me. From now on I take my own risks, even if they're the kind that might get me killed. Got that?"

"Yes . . . Antoinette."

She stood up from her seat. "Oh, and one other thing."

"Yes?"

"No more 'Little Miss.' "

Khouri was down in the reception bay, showing her face and generally doing her best to reassure the evacuees that they had not been forgotten, when she felt the entire ship lurch to one side. The movement was sudden and violent, enough to knock her off her feet and send her crashing bruisingly into the nearest wall. Khouri swore, a thousand possibilities flashing through her mind, but her thoughts were immediately drowned under the vast roar of panic that emanated from the two thousand passengers. She heard screams and shouts, and it was many seconds before the sound began to die down to a general rumble of disquiet. The motion had not repeated itself, but any illusions they had that the ship was a solid and unchanging thing had just been annihilated.

Khouri snapped into damage-limitation mode. She made her way through the maze of partitions that divided the chamber, offering nothing more than a reassuring wave to the families and individuals who tried to stop her to ask what was going on. At that point she was still trying to work it out for herself.

It had already been agreed that her immediate deputies would assemble together in the event of anything unexpected happening. She found a dozen of them waiting for her, all looking only slightly less panicked than the people in their care.

"Vuilleumier . . . " they said, in near unison, on her arrival.

"What the hell just happened?" one asked. "We've got broken bones, fractures, people scared shitless. Shouldn't someone have warned us?"

"Collision avoidance," she said. "The ship detected a piece of debris heading towards it. Didn't have time to shoot it away, so it moved itself." It was a lie, and it did not even sound convincing to her, but it was at least a stab at a rational explanation. "That's why there was no warning," she added, by way of an afterthought. "It's good, really: it means the safety subsystems are still working."

"You never said they wouldn't be," the man told her.

"Well, now we know for sure, don't we?" And with that she told them to spread the word that the sudden movement had been nothing to worry about, and to make sure that the injured got the care they needed.

Fortunately, no one had been killed, and the broken bones and fractures turned out to be clean breaks that could be attended to with simple procedures, without the need to take anyone beyond the chamber to the medical bay. An hour passed, and then two, and a nervous calm descended. Her explanation, it appeared, had been accepted by the majority of the evacuees.

Great, she thought. *Now all I have to do is convince myself.*

But an hour later the ship moved again.

This time it was less violent than before, and the only effect was to make Khouri sway and reach hastily for a support. She swore, but now it was less out of surprise than annoyance. She had no idea what she was going to tell the passengers next, and her last explanation was going to start looking less than convincing. She decided, for the time being, not to offer any explanation at all, and to let her underlings figure out what had happened. Give them time and they might come up with something better than she was capable of.

She made her way back to Ilia Volyova, thinking all the

while that something was wrong, experiencing a sense of dislocation that she could not quite put her finger on. It was as if every vertical surface in the ship was minutely askew. The floor was no longer perfectly level, so that the liquid effluent in the flooded zones built up more on one side of the corridor than the other. Where it dripped from the walls it no longer fell vertically, but at a pronounced angle. By the time she reached Volyova's bed, she could not ignore the changes. It was an effort to walk upright, and she found it easier and safer to move along one wall at a time.

"Ilia."

She was, mercifully, awake, engrossed in the swollen bauble of her battle display. Clavain's beta-level was by her side, the servitor's fingers forming a contemplative steeple beneath its nose as it viewed the same abstract realisation.

"What is it, Khouri?" came Volyova's scratch of a voice.

"Something's happening to the ship."

"Yes, I know. I felt it as well. So did Clavain."

Khouri slipped her goggles on and viewed the two of them properly: the ailing woman and the elderly white-haired man who stood patiently at her bedside. They looked as if they had known each other all their lives.

"I think we're moving," Khouri said.

"More than just moving, I'd say," Clavain replied. "Accelerating, aren't we? The local vertical is shifting."

He was right. When the ship was parked in orbit somewhere it generated gravity for itself by spinning sections of its interior. The occupants felt themselves being flung outwards, away from the ship's long axis. But when *Nostalgia for Infinity* was under thrust, the acceleration created another source of false gravity exactly at right angles to the spin-generated pseudo-force. The two vectors combined to give a force that acted at an angle between them.

"About a tenth of a gee," Clavain added, "or thereabouts. Enough to distort local vertical by five or six degrees."

"No one asked the ship to move," Khouri said.

"I think it decided to move itself," Volyova said. "I imagine that was why we experienced some jolts earlier on. Our host's fine control is a little rusty. Isn't it, Captain?"

But the Captain did not answer her.

"Why are we moving?" Khouri asked.

"I think *that* might have something to do with it," Volyova said.

The squashed bauble of the battle realisation swelled larger. At first glance it looked much as it had before. The remaining cache weapons were still displayed, together with the Inhibitor device. But there was something new: an icon that she did not remember being displayed before. It was arrowing into the arena of battle from an oblique angle to the ecliptic, exactly as if it had come in from interstellar space. Next to it was a flickering cluster of numbers and symbols.

"Clavain's ship?" Khouri asked. "But that isn't possible. We weren't expecting to see it for weeks . . . "

"Seems we were wrong," Volyova said. "Weren't we, Clavain?"

"I can't possibly speculate."

"His blue shift was falling too swiftly," Volyova said. "But I didn't believe the evidence of my sensors. Nothing capable of interstellar flight could decelerate as hard as Clavain's ship appeared to be slowing. And yet . . . "

Khouri finished the sentence for her. "It has."

"Yes. And instead of being a *month* out, he was two or three days out, maybe fewer. Clever, Clavain, I'll give you that. How do you manage that little trick, might I ask?"

The beta-level shook its head. "I don't know. That particular piece of intelligence was edited from my personality before I was transmitted here. But I can speculate as well as you can, Ilia. Either my counterpart has a more powerful drive than anything known to the Conjoiners, or he has something worryingly close to inertia-suppression technology. Take your pick. Either way, I'd say it wasn't exactly good news, wouldn't you?"

"Are you saying the Captain saw the other ship coming in?" Khouri asked.

"You can be certain of it," Volyova said. "Everything I see, he sees."

"So why are we moving? Doesn't he *want* to die?"

"Not here, it would seem," Clavain said. "And not now. This trajectory will bring us back into local Resurgam space, won't it?"

"In about twelve days," Volyova confirmed. "Which strikes me as too long to be of any use. Of course, that's assuming he sticks to one-tenth of a gee . . . he has no need to, ultimately. At a gee he could reach Resurgam in two days, ahead of Clavain."

"What good will it do?" Khouri asked. "We're just as vulnerable there as here. Clavain can reach us wherever we move to."

"We're not remotely vulnerable," Volyova said. "We still have thirteen damned cache weapons and the will to use them. I can't guess at the Captain's deeper motive for moving us, but I know one thing: it makes the evacuation operation a good deal easier, doesn't it?"

"You think he's trying to help, finally?"

"I don't know, Khouri. I'll admit it is a distinct theoretical possibility, that is all. You'd better tell Thorn, anyway."

"Tell him what?"

"To start accelerating things. The bottleneck may be about to change."

THIRTY-FOUR

A figure grew to flickering solidity within *Zodiacal Light*'s imaging tank. Clavain, Remontoire, Scorpio, Blood, Cruz and Felka sat in a rough semicircle around the device as the man's form sharpened and then took on animation.

"Well," Clavain's beta-level said. "I'm back."

Clavain had the uneasy sense that he was looking at his own reflection flipped left-to-right, all the subtle asymmetries of his face thrown into exaggerated relief. He did not like beta-levels, especially not of himself. The whole idea of being mimicked rankled him, and the more accurate the mimicry the less he liked it. *Am I supposed to be flattered,* he thought, *that my essence is so easily captured by an assemblage of mindless algorithms?*

"You've been hacked," Clavain told his image.

"I'm sorry?"

Remontoire leaned towards the tank and spoke. "Volyova stripped out large portions of you. We can see her handiwork, the damage she left, but we can't tell exactly what she did. Very probably all she managed was to delete sensitive memory blocks, but since we can't know for sure, we'll have to treat you as potentially viral. That means that you'll be quarantined once this debriefing is over. Your memories won't be neurally merged with Clavain's, since there's too much risk of contamination. You'll be frozen on to a solid-state memory substrate and archived. Effectively, you'll be dead."

Clavain's image shrugged apologetically. "Let's just hope I can be of some service before then, shall we?"

"Did you learn anything?" Scorpio asked.

"I learned a lot, I think. Of course, I can't be sure which of my memories are genuine, and which are plants."

"We'll worry about that," Clavain said. "Just tell us what you found out. Is the commander of the ship really Volyova?"

The image nodded keenly. "Yes, it's her."

"And does she know about the weapons?" asked Blood.

"Yes, she does."

Clavain looked at his fellows, then back to the tank. "Right, then. Is she going to hand them over without a fight?"

"I don't think you can count on that, no. As a matter of fact, I think you'd better assume she's going to make matters a little on the awkward side."

Felka spoke now. "What does she know about the weapons' origin?"

"Not much, I think. She might have some vague inkling, but I don't think it is a great interest of hers. She does know a little about the wolves, however."

Felka frowned. "How so?"

"I don't know. We never got that chatty. We'd better just assume that Volyova has already had some tangential involvement with them—and survived, as I need hardly point out. That makes her at least worthy of our respect, I think. She calls them the Inhibitors, incidentally. I never got to the bottom of *why*."

"I know why," Felka said quietly.

"She may not have had any direct involvement with them," Remontoire said. "There is already wolf activity in this system, and must have been for some time. Very probably all she's done is make some shrewd deductions."

"I think her experience goes a little deeper than that," Clavain's beta-level answered, but made no further elaboration.

"I agree," Felka said.

Now they all looked at her for a moment.

"Did you impress on her our seriousness?" Clavain asked, turning his attention back to the beta-level. "Did you let her know that she would be much better off dealing with us than the rest of the Conjoiners?"

"I think she got the message, yes."

"And?"

"Thanks, but no thanks, was the general idea."

"She's a very foolish woman, this Volyova," Remontoire said. "That's a shame. It would be so much easier if we could proceed in a cordial manner, without all this unfortunate need to use aggressive force."

"There's another matter," the simulated Clavain said. "There's some kind of evacuation operation in progress. You've already seen what the wolf machine is doing to the star, gnawing into it with some kind of focused gravity-wave probe. Soon it will reach the nuclear-burning core, releasing the energy at the heart of the star. It will be like drilling a hole into the base of a dam, unleashing water under tremendous pressure. Except it won't be water. It will be fusing hydrogen, at stellar-core pressure and temperature. My guess is that it will convert the star into a form of flame-thrower. The core's energy will be bled away very rapidly once the drill has reached it, and the star will die—or at least become a much dimmer and cooler star in the process. But at the same time I imagine the star itself will become a weapon capable of incinerating any planet within a few light-hours of Delta Pavonis, simply by dousing that arterial spray of fusion fire across the face of a world. I imagine it would strip the atmosphere from a gas giant and smelt a rocky world to metallic lava. They don't necessarily know what will happen on Resurgam, but you can be certain that they wish to get away from there as soon as possible. There are already people aboard the ship, airlifted from the surface. A few thousand, at the very least."

"And you have evidence of this, do you?" asked Scorpio.

"Nothing I can prove, no."

"Then we'll assume that they don't exist. It's obviously a crude attempt at convincing us not to attack."

Thorn stood on the surface of Resurgam, his coat buttoned high against the harsh polar wind that scraped and scoured every exposed inch of his skin. It was not quite what they would once have called a razorstorm, but it was unpleasant enough when there was no nearby shelter. He adjusted flimsy dust goggles, squinting into starlight, looking for the tiny moving star of the transfer ship.

It was dusk. The sky overhead was a deep velvet purple which shaded to black at the southern horizon. Only the brightest stars were visible through his goggles, and now and then even these would appear to dim as his eyes readjusted to the sudden flash of one of the warring weapons. To the north, and reaching some way to east and west, soft pink auroral curtains trembled in invisible wind. The lightshow was only beautiful if one had no idea what was causing it, and therefore no grasp of how portentous it was. The aurorae were fuelled by ionised particles that were being clawed and gouged off the surface of the star by the Inhibitor weapon. The inwards bulge, the tunnel that the weapon was boring into the star, now reached halfway to the nuclear-burning core. Around the walls of the tunnel, propped apart by standing waves of pumped gravitational energy, the interior structure of the star had undergone a series of drastic changes as the normal convective processes struggled to adjust to the weapon's assault. Already the core was beginning to change its shape as the overlying mass density shifted. The song of neutrinos streaming out from the star's heart had changed tune, signifying the imminence of the core breakthrough. There was still no clear idea about exactly what would happen when the weapon finished its work, but in Thorn's view the best they could do was not hang around to find out.

He was waiting for the last of the day's shuttle flights to finish boarding. The elegant craft was parked below him, surrounded by a throbbing insectile mass of potential evacuees. Fights broke out constantly as people struggled to jump the queue for the next departure. The mob revolted him, even though he felt nothing but admiration and sympathy for its individual elements. In all his years of agitation he had only ever had to deal with small numbers of trusted people, but he had always known it would come to this. The mob was an emergent property of crowds, and as such he had to take credit for bringing this particular mob into being. But he did not have to like what he had done.

Enough, Thorn thought. Now was not the time to start despising the people he had saved simply because they allowed their fears to surface. Had he been amongst them, he doubted that he would have behaved with any great saintliness. He would have wanted to get his family off the planet, and if that meant stamping on someone else's escape plans, so be it.

But he wasn't in the mob, was he? He was the one who had actually found a way off the planet. He was the one who had actually made it possible.

He supposed that had to count for something.

There—sliding overhead. The transfer ship crossed his zenith and then dove into shadow. He felt a flicker of relief that it was still there. Its orbit was tightly proscribed, for any deviation was likely to trigger an attack from the surface-to-orbit defence system. Although Khouri and Volyova had dug their claws into many branches of government, there were still certain departments that they had only been able to influence indirectly. The Office of Civil Defence was one, and it was also one of the most worrying, entrusted as it was with the defences to prevent a recurrence of the Volyova incident. The Office had rapid-response surface-to-orbit missiles equipped with hot-dust warheads, designed to take out an orbiting starship before it became a threat to the colony as a whole. The Ultras' smaller ships had been able to duck and dive under the radar nets, but the transfer shuttle was too large for such subterfuge. So there had been brokering and behind-the-scenes leverage and the result was that the Office's missiles would be held in their bunkers provided that the transfer ship or any of the transatmospheric shuttles did not deviate from rigidly defined flight corridors. Thorn knew this, and was confident that the various ships' avionics systems knew it too, but he still felt an irrational moment of relief every time the transfer ship came into view again.

His portable telephone chimed. Thorn fished the bulky item from his coat pocket, fiddling with the controls through thick-fingered gloves. "Thorn." He recognised the voice of one of the Inquisition House operators.

"Recorded message from *Nostalgia for Infinity,* sir. Shall I put it through to you, or will you take the call when you are in orbit?"

"Put it through, please." He waited a moment, hearing the faint chatter of electromechanical relays and the hiss of analogue tape, imagining the dark telephonic machinery of Inquisition House moving to serve him.

"Thorn, it's Vuilleumier. Listen carefully. There's been a slight change of plan. It's a long story, but we're moving closer to Resurgam. I'll have updated navigation coordinates for the transfer ship, so you won't have to worry about that. But now we may be looking at much less than thirty hours' round trip. We might even be able to get close enough that we don't need to use the transfer ship at all, just bring them straight aboard *Infinity*. That means we can accelerate the surface-to-orbit flights. We only need five hundred rounds of shuttle flights and we've evacuated the entire planet. Thorn, suddenly it seems as if we might have a chance. Can you arrange things at your end?"

Thorn looked down at the brewing mob. Khouri appeared to be waiting for him to reply. "Operator, record and transmit this, will you?" He waited a decent interval before responding. "This is Thorn. Message understood. I'll do what I can to speed up the evacuation process when I know that it makes sense to do so. But in the meantime, might I inject a note of caution? If you can reduce the thirty hours' round trip, great. I endorse that wholeheartedly. But you can't bring the starship too close to Resurgam. Even if you don't succeed in scaring half the planet out of their skins, you'll have the Office of Civil Defence to worry about. And I mean worry. We'll speak later, Ana. I have work to do, I'm afraid." He looked down at the mob, noting a disturbance where all had been quiet a minute earlier. "Perhaps a little more than I feared."

Thorn told the operator to send the message and alert him if a reply was forthcoming. He slipped the phone back into his pocket, where it lay as heavy and inert as a truncheon. Then he began to scramble and skid his way back down towards the mob, kicking up dust as he descended.

"Clear of *Zodiacal Light,* Antoinette."

"Good," she said. "I think I can start breathing again."

Through the flight deck windows the lighthugger still loomed enormously large, extending in either direction like a great dark cliff, chiselled here and there with strangely mechanistic outcrops, defiles and prominences. The docking bay *Storm Bird* had just cleared was a diminishing rectangle of gold light in the nearest part of the cliff, the huge toothed doors already sliding towards each other. Yet even though the doors were sealing, there was still adequate room for smaller vessels to make their departures. She saw them with her own eyes and on the various tactical displays and radar spheres that packed the flight deck. As the armoured jaws slid towards closure, small skeletal attack ships, little more than armoured trikes, were able to slip between the teeth. They zipped out, riding agile high-burn antimatter-catalysed fusion rockets. They made Antoinette think of the mouth-cleaning parasites of some enormous underwater monster. By comparison, *Storm Bird* was a sizeable fish in its own right.

The departure had been the most technically difficult she had ever known. Clavain's surprise attack demanded that *Zodiacal Light* sustain a deceleration of three gees until its arrival within ten light-seconds of *Nostalgia for Infinity*. All the attack ships in the current wave had been forced to make their departures under the same three gees of thrust. Exiting any spacecraft bay was a technically demanding operation, most especially when the departing ships were armed and fuel-heavy. But doing it under sustained thrust was an order of magnitude more difficult again. Antoinette would have considered it a white-knuckle job if Clavain had demanded that they exit at a half-gee, the way rim pilots arrived and departed from Carousel New Copenhagen. But three gees? That was just being sadistic.

But she had made it. Now she had clear space for hundreds of metres in any direction, and a lot more than that in most.

"Cut in tokamak on my mark, Ship. Five . . . four . . . three . . . two . . . and *mark*." Through years of conditioning she tensed, anticipating the tiny thump in the seat of her pants that always signified the switch from nuclear rockets to pure fusion.

It never came.

"Fusion burn sustained and steady. Green across the board. Three gees, Antoinette."

She raised an eyebrow and nodded. "Damn, but that was smooth."

"You can thank Xavier for that, and perhaps Clavain. They found a glitch in one of the oldest drive-management subroutines. It was responsible for a slight mismatch in thrust during the switch between thrust modes."

She switched to a lower-magnification view of the lighthugger, one that showed the entire length of the hull. Streams of makeshift attack craft—mostly trike-sized, but up to small shuttles—were emerging from five different bays along the hull. Many of the craft were decoys, and not all of the decoys had enough fuel to get within a light-second of *Nostalgia for Infinity*. But even knowing that it still looked impressive. The huge ship appeared to be bleeding streams of light.

"And you had nothing to do with it?"

"One always tries one's best."

"I never thought otherwise, Ship."

"I'm sorry about what happened, Antoinette . . . "

"I'm over it, Ship."

She couldn't call it Beast any more. And she certainly couldn't bring herself to call it Lyle Merrick.

Ship would have to do.

She switched to an even lower magnification, calling up an overlay that boxed the numerous attack craft, tagging them with numeric codes according to type, range, crew and armament, and plotted their vectors. Some idea of the scale of the assault now became apparent. There were around a hundred ships in total. Sixty or so of the hundred were trikes, and about thirty of the trikes actually carried assault-squad members—usually one heavily armoured pig, although there were one or two tandem trikes for specialist operations. All of the crewed trikes carried some form of armament, ranging from single-use grasers to gigawatt-yield Breitenbach bosers. The crew all wore servo armour; most carried firearms, or would be able to disengage and carry their trike's weapon when they reached the enemy ship.

There were about thirty intermediate-sized craft: two- or three-seater closed-hull shuttles. They were all of civilian design, either adapted from the ships that had already been present in *Zodiacal Light*'s holds when she was captured, or supplied by H from his own raiding fleets. They were equipped with a similar spectrum of armaments as the trikes, but also carried the heavier equipment: missile racks and specialised hard-docking gear. And then there were nine medium-to-large shuttles or corvettes, all capable of holding at least twenty armoured crew and with hulls long enough to carry the smallest kind of railgun slug-launchers. Three of these craft carried inertia-suppressors, extending their acceleration ceiling from four to eight gees. Their blocky hulls and asymmetric designs marked them as non-atmospheric ships, but this would be no handicap in the anticipated sphere of combat.

Storm Bird was much larger than the other ships, large enough that its own hold now contained three shuttles and a dozen trikes, along with their associated crews. It had no inertia-suppression machinery—the technology had proven impossible to replicate *en masse,* especially under the conditions aboard *Zodiacal Light*—but by way of compensation, Antoinette's ship carried more armaments and more armour than any other ship in the assault fleet. It wasn't a freighter now, she thought. It was a warship, and she had better start getting used to the idea.

"Little . . . I mean, Antoinette?"

"Yes?" she asked, gritting her teeth.

"I just wanted to say . . . now . . . before it's too late . . . "

She hit the switch that disabled the voice, then eased out of her seat and into her exoskeleton. "Later, Ship. I've got to inspect the troops."

Alone, with his hands clasped tightly behind his back, Clavain stood in the stiff embrace of his exoskeleton, watching the departure of the attack ships from an observation cupola.

The drones, decoys, trikes and ships gyred and wheeled as they left *Zodiacal Light,* falling into designated squadrons. The cupola's smart glass protected his eyes against the savage glare of the exhausts, smudging the core of each flame with black so that he saw only the violet extremities. In the distance, far beyond the swarm of departing ships, was the brown-grey crescent face of Resurgam, the whole planet as small as a marble held at arm's length. His implants indicated the position of Volyova's lighthugger, though the other ship was much too distant to see with the naked eye. Yet a single neural command made the cupola selectively magnify that part of the image so that a reasonably sharp view of *Nostalgia for Infinity* swelled out of darkness. The Triumvir's ship was nearly ten light-seconds away, but it was also very large; the four-kilometre-long hull subtended an angle of a third of an arc-second, which was well within the resolving capabilities of *Zodiacal Light*'s smallest optical telescopes. The downside was that the Triumvir would have at least as good a view of his own ship. Provided she was paying attention, she would not be able to miss the departure of the attack fleet.

Clavain knew now that the baroque augmentations he had seen before and dismissed as phantoms added by the processing software were quite real; that something astonishing and strange had happened to Volyova's ship. The ship had remade itself into a festering gothic caricature of what a starship ought to look like. Clavain could only speculate that the Melding Plague must have had something to do with it. The only other place he had seen transformations that even approximated what he was seeing now was in the warped, phantasmagorical architecture of Chasm City. He had heard of ships being infected with the plague, and he had heard that sometimes the plague reached the repair-and-redesign machinery which allowed ships to evolve, but he had never heard of a ship becoming so thoroughly *perverted* as this one while still, so far as he could tell, being able to continue functioning as a ship. It made his skin crawl just to look it. He hoped that no one living had been caught up in those transformations.

The sphere of battle would encompass the ten light-seconds between *Zodiacal Light* and the other ship, although its focus would be determined by Volyova's movements. It was a good volume for a war, Clavain thought. Tactically, it was not the scale that mattered so much as the typical crossing times for various craft and weapons.

At three gees, the sphere could be crossed in four hours; a little over two hours for the fastest ships in the fleet. A hyperfast missile would take fewer than forty minutes to span the sphere. Clavain had already dug through his memories of previous battle campaigns, searching for tactical parallels. The Battle of Britain—an obscure aerial dispute from one of the early transnational wars, fought with subsonic piston-engined aircraft—had encompassed a similar volume from the point of view of crossing times, although the three-dimensional element had been much less important. The twenty-first century's global wars were less relevant; with sub-orbital waverider drones, no point on the planet had been more than forty minutes away from annihilation. But the solar system wars of the latter half of that century offered more useful parallels. Clavain thought of the Earth-Moon secession crisis, or the battle for Mercury, noting victories and failures and the reasons for each. He thought of Mars, too, of the battle against the Conjoiners at the end of the twenty-second century. The sphere of combat had reached far above the orbits of Phobos and Deimos, so that the effective crossing time for the fastest single-person fighters had been three or four hours. There had been timelag problems, too, with line-of-sight communications blocked by huge clouds of silvered chaff.

There had been other campaigns, other wars. It was not necessary to bring them all to mind. The salient lessons were there already. He knew the mistakes that others had made; he knew also the mistakes he had made in the earlier engagements of his career. They had never been significant errors, he thought, or he would not be standing here now. But no lesson was valueless.

A pale reflection moved across the cupola's glass.

"Clavain."

He snapped around with a whirr of his exoskeleton. He had imagined himself to be alone until then.

"Felka . . . " he said, surprised.

"I came to watch it happen," she said.

Her own exoskeleton propelled her towards him with a stiff, marching gait, like someone being escorted by invisible guards. Together they watched the dregs of the attack squadron fall into space.

"If you didn't know it was war . . . " he began.

" . . . it would almost be beautiful," she said. "Yes. I agree."

"I'm doing the right thing, aren't I?" Clavain asked.

"Why do you ask me?"

"You're the closest thing I have left to a conscience, Felka. I keep asking myself what Galiana would do, if she were here now . . . "

Felka interrupted him. "She would worry, just as you worry. It's the people who don't worry—those who never have any doubts that what they're doing is good and right—they're the ones that cause the problems. People like Skade."

He remembered the searing flash when he had destroyed *Nightshade*. "I'm sorry about what happened."

"I told you to do it, Clavain. I know it was what Galiana wanted."

"That I should kill her?"

"She died years ago. She just didn't . . . end. All you've done is close the book."

"I removed any possibility of her ever living again," he said.

Felka held his age-spotted hand. "She would have done the same to you, Clavain. I know it."

"Perhaps. But you still haven't told me if you agree with *this*."

"I agree that it will serve our short-term interests if we possess the weapons. Beyond that, I'm not sure."

Clavain looked at her carefully. "We need those weapons, Felka."

"I know. But what if she—the Triumvir—needs them as well? Your proxy said she was trying to evacuate Resurgam."

He chose his words. "That's . . . not my immediate concern. If she is engaged in evacuating the planet, and I've no evidence that she is, then she has all the more reason to give me what I want so that I don't interfere with the evacuation."

"And it wouldn't cross your mind to think for a moment about helping her?"

"I'm here to get those weapons, Felka. Everything else, no matter how well intentioned, is just a detail."

"That's what I thought," Felka said.

Clavain knew that it was better that he say nothing in answer.

In silence, they watched the violet flames of the attack ships fall towards Resurgam, and the Triumvir's starship.

When Khouri had finished responding to Thorn's latest message she arrived at a troubling conclusion. Walking was even harder than it had been before, the apparent slope of the floor even more severe. It was exactly as Ilia Volyova had predicted: the Captain had increased his rate of thrust, no longer satisfied with a mere tenth of a gee. By Khouri's estimation, and the Clavain beta-level agreed with her, the rate was now double that and probably climbing. Previously horizontal surfaces now felt as if they were sloping at twelve degrees, enough to make some of the more slippery passages difficult to traverse. But that was not what was concerning her.

"Ilia, listen to me. We have a serious fucking problem."

Volyova emerged from contemplation of her battlescape.

The icons floated within the squashed sphere of the projection like dozens of bright frozen fish. The view had changed since the last time she had seen it, Khouri was certain.

"What is it, child?"

"It's the holding bay, where we have the newcomers."

"Continue."

"It's not designed to deal with the ship moving under thrust. We built it as a temporary holding bay, to be used while we were parked. It's spun for gravity so that the force acts radially, away from the ship's long axis. But now that's changing. The Captain's applying thrust, so we've got a new source acting along the axis. It's only a fifth of a gee at the moment, but you can bet it's going to get worse. We can turn off the spin, but that won't change things. The walls are becoming floors."

"This is a lighthugger, Khouri. This is a normal transition to starflight mode."

"You don't understand, Ilia. We've got two thousand people crammed into one chamber, and they can't stay there. They're already freaking out because the floor is sloping so much. They feel as if they're on the deck of a sinking ship, and no one is telling them anything's wrong." She paused; she was a little out of breath. "Ilia, here's the deal. You were right about the bottleneck. I told Thorn to get things moving faster at the Resurgam end. That means we're going to be getting thousands of people arriving very soon indeed. We always knew we'd have to start emptying the holding bay. Now we'll just have to start doing it a bit sooner."

"But that would mean . . . " Volyova appeared unable to complete the thought.

"Yes, Ilia. They're going to have to get the tour of the ship. Whether they like it or not."

"This could turn out very badly, Khouri. Very badly indeed."

Khouri looked down at her old mentor. "You know what I like about you, Ilia? You're such a frigging optimist."

"Shut up and take a look at the battle display, Khouri. We are under attack—or we will be very shortly."

"Clavain?"

The merest hint of a nod. "*Zodiacal Light* has released squadrons of attack craft, around a hundred in total. They're headed here, most of them at three gees. They won't take more than four hours to reach us, no matter what we do."

"Clavain can't have those weapons, Ilia."

The Triumvir, who now looked far older and frailer than Khouri ever remembered, shook her head by the barest degree. "He isn't going to get them. Not without a fight."

They exchanged ultimatums. Clavain gave Ilia Volyova one last chance to surrender the hell-class weapons; if she complied he would recall his attack fleet. Volyova told Clavain that if he did not recall his fleet immediately, she would turn the thirteen remaining weapons against him.

Clavain readied his response. "Sorry. Unacceptable. I need those weapons very badly."

He transmitted it and was only slightly startled when the Triumvir's answer came back three seconds later. It was identical to his own. There had not been enough time for her to see his response.

THIRTY-FIVE

Volyova watched five of the thirteen remaining cache weapons assume attack positions beyond *Nostalgia for Infinity*. Their coloured icons floated above her bed like the kinds of bauble that were used to amuse infants in cots. Volyova raised a hand and poked it through the ghostly representation, pushing against the icons, adjusting the positions of the weapons relative to her ship, using its hull for camouflage wherever possible. The icons moved stubbornly, reflecting the sluggish real-time movements of the weapons themselves.

"Are you going to use them immediately?" Khouri asked.

Volyova glanced at the woman. "No. Not yet. Not until he forces my hand. I don't want the Inhibitors to know that there are more cache weapons than the twenty they already know about."

"You'll have to use them eventually."

"Unless Clavain sees sense and realises he can't possibly win. Maybe he will. It isn't too late."

"But we don't know anything about the kinds of weapons he has," Khouri said. "What if he has something equally powerful?"

"It won't make a blind bit of difference if he has, Khouri. He wants something from me, understand? I want nothing from him. That gives me a distinct advantage over Clavain."

"I don't . . . "

Volyova sighed, disappointed that it was necessary to spell this out. "His strike against us has to be surgical. He can't risk damaging the weapons he so badly wants. In crude terms, you don't rob someone by dropping a crustbuster on them. But I'm bound by no such constraint. Clavain has nothing that I want."

Well, Volyova admitted to herself, *almost nothing*. She had a vague curiosity concerning whatever it was that had allowed him to decelerate so savagely. Even if it was nothing as exotic as inertia-suppression technology . . . but no. It was nothing she needed desperately. That meant she could use all the force in her arsenal against him. She could wipe him out of existence, and her only loss would be something she was not even sure had ever existed.

But something still troubled her. Clavain, surely, could see all that for himself? Especially if she was dealing with *the* Clavain, the real Butcher of Tharsis. He had not lived through four hundred or more dangerous years of human history by making tragically simple errors.

What if Clavain knew something she didn't?

She moved her fingers through the projection, nervously reconfiguring her pieces, wondering which of them she should use first, thinking also that, given Clavain's limitations, it would be more interesting to let the battle escalate rather than taking his main ship out instantly.

"Any news from Thorn?" she asked.

"He's *en route* from Resurgam with another two thousand passengers."

"And does he know about our little difficulty with Clavain?"

"I told him we were moving closer to Resurgam. I didn't see any sense in giving him anything more to worry about."

"No," Volyova said, agreeing with her for once. "The people are at least as safe in space as they'd be on Resurgam. At least once they're off the planet they've got a hope of survival. Not much of one, but . . . "

"Are you certain you won't use the cache weapons?"

"I *will* use them Khouri, but not a moment sooner than I have to. Haven't you ever heard of the expression 'whites of their eyes'? Perhaps not; it's the sort of thing only a soldier would be likely to know."

"I've forgotten more about soldiering than you'll ever know, Ilia."

"Just trust me. Is it so much to ask?"

Twenty-two minutes later the battle began. Clavain's opening salvo was almost insultingly inadequate. She had detected the signatures of railgun launchers, ripples of electromagnetic energy designed to slam a small dense slug up to one or two thousand kilometres per second. The slugs took an hour to reach her from their launch points near *Zodiacal Light*. At the very limit of her resolution she could make out the skeletal cruciform shapes of the launchers themselves, and then watch the pulse of sequenced matter-antimatter explosions that drove the slugs up to their terminal velocities, gobbling up the railguns in the process. Clavain did not have enough railguns to saturate the immediate volume of space around her ship, so she could avoid being hit simply by making sure she—or rather the Captain—kept *Nostalgia for Infinity* in a constant random-walk pattern, never entering the volume of space where it had been an hour earlier, which was where any arriving railgun slug would have been aimed.

At first, that was exactly what happened. She did not even have to ask it of the Captain. He was privy to the same tactical information as Volyova, and appeared capable of arriving at the same conclusions. She felt the faint yawing and pitching, as if her bed was adrift on a raft on a mildly choppy sea, as *Nostalgia for Infinity* moved, shifting with short, thunderous bursts of the many station-keeping thrusters which dotted the hull.

But she could do better than that.

With the long-range grabs of the railguns and the electromagnetic launch signatures, she could determine the precise direction in which a particular slug had been aimed. There was a margin of error, but it was not large, and it amused Volyova to remain exactly where she was until the last possible moment, only then moving her ship. She ran simulations in the tactical display, showing the Captain the projected impact point of each new slug launch, and was gratified when the Captain revised his strategy. She liked it better this way. It was far more elegant and fuel-efficient, and she hoped that the lesson was not lost on Clavain.

She wanted him to become cleverer, so that she could become cleverer still.

Clavain watched as the last of his railguns fired and launched, destroying itself in a cascade of quick, bright explosions.

It was an hour since he had begun the attack, and he had never seriously expected that it would do more than occupy the Triumvir's time, diverting her attention away from the other elements of the attack. If one of the slugs had hit her ship it would have delivered about a kilotonne of kinetic energy on impact; enough to cripple the lighthugger, perhaps even to rip it open, but not enough to destroy it entirely. There remained a chance of success—four slugs were still on their way—but the Triumvir had already shown every indication that she could deal with this particular threat. Clavain felt little in the way of regret; more a sense of quiet relief that they were past the negotiating stage and into the infinitely more honest arena of actual battle. He suspected that the Triumvir felt likewise.

Felka and Remontoire were floating next to him in the observation cupola, which was decoupled from the spinning part of the ship. Now that *Zodiacal Light* had slowed to a halt on the edge of the battle volume they no longer had need of their exoskeletons, and Clavain felt oddly vulnerable without his.

"Disappointed, Clavain?" asked Remontoire.

"No. As a matter of fact I'm reassured. If anything feels too easy, I start looking for a trap."

Remontoire nodded. "She's no fool, that's for certain, no matter what she's done to her ship. You still don't believe that story about an evacuation attempt, I take it?"

"There's more reason to believe it now than there was before," Felka said. "Isn't that right, Clavain? We've seen shuttles moving between surface and orbit."

"That's all we've seen," Clavain said.

"And a larger ship moving between orbit and the lighthugger," she continued. "What more evidence do we need that she's sincere?"

"It doesn't necessarily indicate an evacuation programme," Clavain said through gritted teeth. "It could be many things."

"So give her the benefit of the doubt," Felka said.

Clavain turned to her, brimming with sudden fury but hoping that it did not show. "It's her choice. She has the weapons. They're all I want."

"The weapons won't make any difference in the long run."

Now he made no attempt to hide his anger. "What the hell is that supposed to mean?"

"Exactly what I said. I know, Clavain. I know that everything that is happening here, everything that means so much to you, to us, means precisely nothing in the long run."

"And this pearl of wisdom came from the Wolf, did it?"

"You know I brought a part of it back from Skade's ship."

"Yes," he said. "And that means I have all the more reason to disregard anything you say, Felka."

She hauled herself to one side of the cupola and disappeared through the exit hole, back into the main body of the ship. Clavain opened his mouth to call after her, to say something in apology. Nothing came.

"Clavain?"

He looked at Remontoire. "What, Rem?"

"The first hyperfast missiles will be arriving in a minute."

Antoinette saw the first wave of hyperfast missiles streak past, overtaking *Storm Bird* with a velocity differential of nearly a thousand kilometres per second. There had been four missiles in the spread, and although they passed around her ship on all four sides, they converged ahead an instant later, the flares of their exhausts meeting like the lines in a perspective sketch.

Two minutes later another wave passed to starboard, and then a third slipped by to port, much further out, three minutes after that.

"Holy shit," she whispered. "We're not just playing war, are we?"

"Scared?" Xavier asked, pressed into the seat beside hers.

"More than scared." She had already been back into the

body of *Storm Bird,* inspecting the ferociously armoured assault squad she carried in her ship's cargo bay. "But that's good. Dad always said . . ."

"Be scared if you aren't scared. Yeah." Xavier nodded. "That was one of his."

"Actually . . ."

They both looked at the console.

"What, Ship?" asked Antoinette.

"Actually, that was one of mine. But your father liked it enough to steal it from me. I took that as a compliment."

"So Lyle Merrick actually said . . ." Xavier began.

"Yes."

"No shit?" Antoinette said.

"No shit, Little Miss."

The last wave of slugs was still on its way when Clavain escalated to the next level of his attack against Volyova. Again, there was no element of surprise. But there almost never was in space war, where hiding places and opportunities for camouflage were so few and far between. One could plan, and strategise, and hope that the enemy missed the obvious or subtle traps buried in the placement of one's forces, but in every other respect war in space was a game of total transparency. It was war between enemies who could safely each assume the other to be omniscient. Like a game of chess, the outcome could often be guessed after only a few moves had been made, especially if the opponents were unevenly matched.

Volyova tracked the trajectories of the hyperfast missiles as they streaked across space from the launchers deployed by *Zodiacal Light*. They accelerated at a hundred gees, sustaining that thrust for forty minutes before becoming purely ballistic. Then they were moving at slightly less than one per cent of the speed of light—formidable targets, but still within the capabilities of *Nostalgia for Infinity*'s autonomic hull defences. Any starship had to be able to track and destroy rapidly moving objects as a normal part of its collision-avoidance procedures, so Volyova had barely had to upgrade the existing safeguards to make full-scale weapons.

It was a question of numbers. Each missile occupied a certain fraction of her available hull weapons, and there was always a small statistical chance that too many missiles would arrive at the same time for her—or the Captain, who was doing all the actual defending—to deal with.

But it never happened. She ran an analysis on the missile spread and concluded that Clavain was not trying to hit her. It was within his capability to do so; he had some control over the missiles until the moment they stopped accelerating, enough to correct for any small changes in *Infinity*'s position. And a direct hit from a hyperfast, even one with a dummy warhead, would have taken out the entire ship in a flash. Yet the missiles were all on trajectories that stood only a small chance of actually hitting her ship. They slammed past with tens of kilometres to spare, while roughly one in twenty went on to detonate slightly closer to Resurgam. The blast signatures suggested small matter-antimatter explosions: either residual fuel, or pinhead-sized warheads. The other nineteen missiles were effectively dummies.

A close blast would certainly damage *Infinity,* she thought. The five deployed cache weapons were robust enough not to worry her, but a close matter-antimatter blast could well incapacitate her hull armaments, leaving her wide open to a more concerted assault. Not that she was going to let it happen, but she would have to expend a good fraction of her resources in preventing it. And the annoying thing was that most of the missiles she had to destroy posed no actual threat; they were neither on intercept trajectories nor armed.

She did not go so far as to congratulate Clavain. All he had done was adopt a textbook saturation-attack approach, tying up her defences with a low probability/high consequence threat. It was neither clever nor original, but it was, more or less, exactly what she would have done under the same circumstances. She would give him that, at least: he had certainly not disappointed her.

Volyova decided to give him one last chance before ending his fun.

"Clavain?" she asked, broadcasting on the same frequency she had already used for her ultimatum. "Clavain, are you listening to me?"

Twenty seconds passed, and then she heard his voice. "I'm listening, Triumvir. I take it this isn't an offer of surrender?"

"I'm offering you a chance, Clavain, before I end this. A chance for you to walk away and fight on another day, against a more enthusiastic adversary."

She waited for his reply to crawl back to her. The delay could be artificial, but it almost certainly meant he was still aboard *Zodiacal Light*.

"Why would you want to cut me any slack, Triumvir?"

"You're not a bad man, Clavain. Just . . . misguided. You think you need the weapons more than I do, but you're wrong, mistaken. I won't hold it against you. No serious harm has yet been done. Turn your forces around and we'll call it a misunderstanding."

"You speak as someone who thinks they hold the upper hand, Ilia. I wouldn't be so certain, if I were you."

"I *have* the weapons, Clavain." She found herself smiling and frowning at the same time. "That makes rather a lot of difference, don't you think?"

"I'm sorry, Ilia, but I think one ultimatum is enough for anyone, don't you?"

"You're a fool, Clavain. The sad thing is that you'll never know how much of a fool."

He did not respond.

"Well, Ilia?" Khouri asked.

"I gave the bastard his chance. Now it's time to stop playing games." She raised her voice. "Captain? Can you hear me? I want you to give me full control of cache weapon seventeen. Are you willing to do that?"

There was no answer. The moment stretched. The back of her neck crawled with anticipation. If the Captain was not prepared to let her actually use the five deployed weapons, then all her plans crumbled to dust and Clavain would suddenly seem a lot less foolish than he had a minute earlier.

Then she noticed the subtle change in the weapon's icon status, signifying that she now had full military control of cache weapon seventeen.

"Thank you, Captain," Volyova said sweetly. Then she addressed the weapon. "Hello, Seventeen. Nice to be doing business with you again."

She pushed her hand into the projection, pinching the floating icon of the weapon between her fingers. Again the icon responded sluggishly, reflecting the dead weight of the weapon as it was brought out from the sensor shadow of *Infinity*'s hull. As it moved it was aligning itself, bringing its long killing axis to bear on the distant, but not really so distant, target of *Zodiacal Light*. At any time, Volyova's knowledge of the position of Clavain's ship was twenty seconds out of date, but that was only a minor annoyance. In the unlikely event that he suddenly moved, she was still guaranteed a kill. She would sweep his volume of possible occupancy with the weapon, knowing that she was sure to hit him at some point. She would know when she did; the detonation of his Conjoiner drives would light up the entire system. If anything was guaranteed to prick the interest of the Inhibitors, it would be that.

Still, she had to do it.

Yet Volyova trembled on the verge of execution. It felt wrong: too final; too abrupt; too—and this surprised her—unsporting. She felt she owed him a last chance to back down; that some final, direly urgent warning should be given. He had come such a long way, after all. And he had clearly imagined himself to be in with a chance of gaining the weapons.

Clavain . . . Clavain . . . she thought to herself. It should not have been like this . . .

But it was, and that was that.

She tapped the icon, like a baby poking a bauble.

"Goodbye," Volyova whispered.

The moment passed. The status indices and symbols next to the cache weapon's icon changed, signifying a profound alteration in the weapon's condition. She looked at the real-time image of Clavain's ship, mentally counting down the twenty seconds it would take before the ship was torn apart by the beam from weapon seventeen. The beam would chew a canyon-sized wound in Clavain's ship, assuming it did not trigger an immediate and fatal Conjoiner-drive detonation.

After ten seconds he had not moved. She knew then that her aim had been good, that the impact would be precise and devastating. Clavain would know nothing of his own death, nothing of the oblivion that was coming.

She waited out the remaining ten seconds, anticipating the bitter sense of triumph that would accompany the kill.

The time elapsed. Involuntarily, she flinched against the coming brightness, like a child waiting for the biggest and best firework.

Twenty seconds became twenty-one . . . twenty-one became twenty-five . . . thirty. Half a minute passed. Then a minute.

Clavain's ship remained in view.

Nothing had happened.

THIRTY-SIX

She heard his voice again. It was calm, polite, almost apologetic.

"I know what you just tried, Ilia. But don't you think I'd already have considered the possibility of you turning the weapons against me?"

She stammered an answer. "What . . . did . . . you . . . do?"

Twenty seconds stretched to an eternity.

"Nothing, really," Clavain said. "I just told the weapon not to fire. They're our property, Ilia, not yours. Didn't it occur to you for one moment that we might have a way to protect ourselves against them?"

"You're lying," she said.

Clavain sounded amused, as if he had secretly hoped she would demand more proof. "I can show it to you again, if you like."

He told her to turn her attention to the other cache weapons, the ones that she had already thrown against the Inhibitors.

"Now concentrate on the weapon closest to the remains of Roc, will you? You're about to see it stop firing."

It was a different kind of war after that. Within an hour the first waves of Clavain's assault force were reaching the immediate volume of space around *Nostalgia for Infinity*. He watched it at the dead remove of ten light-seconds, feeling as distant from the battle he had initiated as some antiquated hill-top general gazing at his armies through field glasses, the din and fury of combat too far away to hear.

"It was a good trick," Volyova told him.

"It wasn't any trick. Just a precaution you should never have assumed we wouldn't have taken. Our own weapons, Ilia? Be serious."

"A signal, Clavain?"

"A coded neutrino burst. You can't block it or jam it, so don't even think of trying. It won't work."

She came back with a question he had not been expecting, one that reminded him not to underestimate her for an instant.

"Fair enough. But I would have thought, assuming you have the means to stop them from working, that you'd also have the means to destroy them."

Despite the timelag he knew he only had a second or so to concoct an answer. "What good would that do me, Ilia? I'd be destroying the very things I've come to collect."

Volyova's response snapped back twenty seconds later. "Not necessarily, Clavain. You could just threaten to destroy them. I presume the destruction of a cache weapon would be fairly spectacular no matter which way you went about it? Actually, I don't need to presume anything. I've already seen it happen, and yes, it was spectacular. Why not threaten to detonate one of the weapons still inside my ship and see where that takes you?"

"You shouldn't give me ideas," he told her.

"Why not? Because you might do it? I don't think you can, Clavain. I don't think you have the means to do anything but stop the weapons from firing."

She had led him into a trap by then. He could do nothing but follow her. "I do . . . "

"Then prove it. Send a destruction signal to one of the other weapons, one of those across the system. Why not destroy the one you've already stopped?"

"It would be silly to destroy an irreplaceable weapon just to make a point, wouldn't it?"

"That would very much depend on the point you wanted to make, Clavain."

He realised that he gained nothing more by lying to her. He sighed, feeling a tremendous weight lift off his shoulders. "I can't destroy any of the weapons."

"Good . . . " she purred. "Negotiation is all about transparency, you see. Tell me, can the weapons *ever* be destroyed remotely, Clavain?"

"Yes," he said. "There is a code, unique to each weapon."

"And?"

"I don't know those codes. But I am searching for them, trying permutations."

"So you might get there eventually?"

Clavain scratched his beard. "Theoretically. But don't hold your breath."

"You'll keep searching, though?"

"I'd like to know what they are, wouldn't you?"

"I don't have to, Clavain. I have my own self-destruct systems grafted to each weapon, entirely independent of anything your own people might have installed at root level."

"You strike me as a prudent woman, Ilia."

"I take my work very seriously, Clavain. But then so do you."

"Yes," he said.

"So what happens now? I'm still not going to give you the things, you know. I still have *other* weapons."

Clavain watched the battle on extreme magnification, glints of light peppering the space around the Triumvir's ship. The first fatalities had already been recorded. Fifteen of Scorpio's pigs were dead, killed by Volyova's hull defences before they got within thirty kilometres of the ship. Other assault teams were reportedly closer—one team might even have reached the hull—but whatever the outcome, it no longer stood any chance of being a bloodless campaign.

"I know," Clavain said, before ending the conversation.

He placed Remontoire in complete control of *Zodiacal Light,* and then assigned himself one of the last remaining spacecraft in the ship's bay. The ex-civilian shuttle was one of H's; he recognised the luminous arcs and slashes of the banshee war markings as they stammered into life. The wasp-waisted ship was small and lightly armoured, but it carried the last functioning inertia-suppression device and that was why he had kept it back until now. On some subconscious level he must have always known he would want to join the battle, and this ship would get him there in little more than an hour.

Clavain was suited-up, cycling through the airlock connection that allowed access to the berthed ship, when she caught up with him.

"Clavain."

He turned around, his helmet tucked under his arm. "Felka," he said.

"You didn't tell me you were leaving."

"I didn't have the nerve."

She nodded. "I'd have tried talking you out of it. But I understand. This is something you have to do."

He nodded without saying anything.

"Clavain . . . "

"Felka, I'm so sorry about what I . . . "

"It doesn't matter," she said, taking a step closer. "I mean, it does matter—of course it matters—but we can talk about it later. On the way."

"On the way where?" he said stupidly.

"To battle, Clavain. I'm coming with you."

It was only then that he realised that she was carrying a suit herself, bundled under one arm, the helmet dangling from her fist like an overripe fruit.

"Why?"

"Because if you die, I want to die as well. It's as simple as that, Clavain."

They fell away from *Zodiacal Light*. Clavain watched the ship recede, wondering if he would ever set foot in it again. "This won't be comfortable," he warned as he gunned the thrust up to its ceiling. The inertia-suppression bubble swallowed four-fifths of the banshee craft's mass, but the bubble's effective radius did not encompass the flight deck. Clavain and Felka felt the full crush of eight gees building up like a series of weights being placed on their chests.

"I can take it," she told him.

"It's not too late to turn back."

"I'm coming with you. There's a lot we need to discuss."

Clavain called a battle realisation into view, appraising any changes that had taken place since he had gone to fetch his spacesuit. His ships swarmed around *Nostalgia for Infinity* like enraged hornets, arcing tighter with each loop. Twenty-three members of Scorpio's army were now dead, most of them pigs, but the closest of the attack swarm were now within kilometres of the great ship's hull; at such close range they became very difficult targets for Volyova's medium-range defences. *Storm Bird,* identified by its own fat icon, was now approaching the edge of the combat swarm. The Triumvir had pulled all but one of her hell-class weapons back within cover of the lighthugger. Elsewhere, on the general system-wide view, the wolf weapon continued to sink its single gravitational fang into the meat of the star. Clavain contracted the displays until they were just large enough to view, and then turned to Felka. "I'm afraid talking isn't going to be too easy."

[Then we won't talk, will we?]

He looked at her, startled that she had spoken to him in the Conjoiner fashion, opening a window between their heads, pushing words and much more than words into his skull. *Felka . . .*

[It's all right, Clavain. Just because I didn't do this very often doesn't mean I couldn't . . .]

I never thought you couldn't . . . it's just . . . They were close enough for Conjoined thought, he realised, even though there was no Conjoiner machinery in the ship itself. The fields generated by their implants were strong enough to influence each other without intermediate amplification, provided they were no more than a few metres apart.

[You're right. Normally I didn't want to. But you aren't just anyone.]

You don't have to if you don't . . .

[Clavain: a word of warning. You can look all the way into my head. There are no barriers, no partitions, no mnemonic blockades. Not to you, at least. But don't look too deeply. It's not that you'd see anything private, or anything I'm ashamed of . . . it's just . . .]

I might not be able to take it?

[Sometimes I can't take it, Clavain, and I've lived with it since I was born.]

I understand.

He could see into the surface layers of her personality, feel the surface traffic of her thoughts. The data was calm. There was nothing that he could not examine; no sensory experience or memory that he could not unravel and open as if it were one of his own. But beneath that calm surface layer, glimpsed like something rushing behind smoked glass, there lay a howling storm of consciousness. It was frantic and ceaseless, like a machine always on the point of ripping itself apart, but one that would never find respite in its own destruction.

He pulled back, terrified that he might fall in.

[You see what I mean?]

I always knew you lived with something like that. I just didn't . . .

[It isn't your fault. It isn't anyone's fault, not even Galiana's. It's just the way I am.]

He understood then, perhaps more thoroughly than at any point since he had known her, just what Felka's craving was like. Games, complex games, sated that howling machine, gave it something to work on, slowed it to something less furious. When she had been a child, the Wall had been all that she needed, but the Wall had been taken from her. After that, nothing had ever been enough. Perhaps the machine would have evolved as Felka grew. Or perhaps the Wall would always have turned out to be inadequate. All that mattered now was that she find surrogates for it: games or puzzles, labyrinths or riddles, which the machine could process and thereby give her the tiniest degree of inner calm.

Now I understand why you think the Jugglers might be able to help.

[Even if they can't change me—and I'm not even sure I want them to change me—they might at least give me something to think about, Clavain. So many alien minds have been imprinted in their seas, so many patterns stored. I might even be able to make sense of something that the other swimmers haven't. I might even be valuable.]

I always said I'd do what I could. But it hasn't got any easier. You understand that, don't you?

[Of course.]

Felka . . .

She must have read enough of his mind to see what he was about to ask. [I lied, Clavain. I lied to save you, to get you to turn around.]

He already knew; Skade had told him. But until now he had never entirely dismissed the possibility that Skade herself might have been lying; that Felka was indeed his daughter. *It would have been a white lie, in that case. I've been responsible for enough of those in my time.*

[It was still a lie. But I didn't want Skade to kill you. It seemed better not to tell the truth . . .]

You must have known that I'd always wondered . . .

[It was natural for you to wonder, Clavain. There was always a bond between us, after you saved my life. And you were Galiana's prisoner before I was born. It would have been easy for her to harvest genetic material . . .] Her thoughts became hazy. [Clavain . . . do you mind if I ask you something?]

There aren't any secrets between us, Felka.

[Did you make love with Galiana, when you were her prisoner?]

He answered with a calm clarity of mind that surprised even himself. *I don't know. I think so. I remember it. But then what do memories mean, after four hundred years? Maybe I'm just remembering a memory. I hope that isn't the case. But afterwards . . . when I had become one of the Conjoined . . .*

[Yes?]

We did make love. Early on, we made love often. The other Conjoiners didn't like it, I think—they saw it as an animal act, a primitive throwback to baseline humanity. Galiana didn't agree, of course. She was always the sensual one, the one who revelled in the realm of the senses. That was what her enemies never truly understood about her—that she honestly loved humanity more than they did. It was why she made the Conjoined. Not to be something better than humanity, but as a gift, a promise of what humanity could be if we only realised our potential. Instead, they painted her as some coldly reductionist monster. They were so terribly wrong. Galiana didn't think of love as some ancient Darwinian trick of brain chemistry that had to be eradicated from the human mind. She saw it as something that had to be brought to its culmination, like a seed that needed to be nurtured as it grew. But they never understood that part. And the trouble was you had to be Conjoined before you appreciated what it was that she had achieved.

Clavain paused, taking a moment to review the disposition of his forces around the Triumvir's ship. There had been two more deaths in the last minute, but the steady encroachment of his forces continued. *Yes, we did make love, back in my first days amongst the Conjoined. But there came a time when it was no longer necessary, except as a nostalgic act. It felt like something that children do: not wrong, not primitive, not even dull, just no longer of any interest. It wasn't that we had stopped loving each other, or had lost our thirst for sensory experience. It was simply that there were so many more rewarding ways of achieving that same kind of intimacy. Once you've touched someone else's mind, walked through their dreams, seen the world through their eyes, felt the world through their skin . . . well . . . there never seemed to be any real need to go back to the old way. And I was never much one for nostalgia. It was as if we had stepped into a more adult world, crammed with its own pleasures and enticements. We had no reason to look back at what we were missing.*

She did not respond immediately. The ship flew on. Clavain eyed the read-outs and tactical summaries again. For a moment, a terrible, yawning moment, he felt that he had said far too much. But then she spoke, and he knew that she had understood everything.

[I think I need to tell you about the wolves.]

THIRTY-SEVEN

When Volyova had made the decision, she felt a rush of strength, enabling her to rip the medical probes and shunts from her body, flinging them aside with wicked abandon. She retained only the goggles which substituted for her blinded eyes, while doing her best not to think of the vile machinery now floating in her skull. Other than that, she felt quite hale and hearty. She knew that it was an illusion, that she would pay for this burst of energy later, and that almost certainly she would pay for it with her life. But she felt no fear at the prospect, only a quiet satisfaction that she might at least do something with the time that remained to her. It was all very well lying here, directing distant affairs like some bed-ridden pontiff, but it was not the way she was meant to be. She was Triumvir Ilia Volyova, and she had certain standards to uphold.

"Ilia . . . " Khouri began, when she saw what was happening.

"Khouri," she said, her voice still a croak, but finally imbued with something resembling the old fire. "Khouri . . . do this for me, and never once stop to question me or talk me out of it. Understood?"

"Understood . . . I think."

Volyova clicked her fingers at the nearest servitor. It scuttled towards her, dodging between the squawking medical monitors. "Captain . . . have the servitor assist me to the spacecraft bay, will you? I will expect a suit and a shuttle to be waiting for me."

Khouri steadied her, holding her in a sitting position. "Ilia, what are you planning?"

"I'm going outside. I need to have a word—a serious word—with weapon seventeen."

"You're in no state . . . "

Volyova cut her off with a chop of one frail hand. "Khouri, I may have a weak and feeble body, but give me weightlessness, a suit and possibly a weapon or two and you'll find I can still do some damage. Understood?"

"You haven't given up, have you?"

The servitor helped her to the floor. "Given up, Khouri? It's not in my dictionary."

Khouri helped her as well, taking the Triumvir's other arm.

On the edge of the combat swarm, though still within range of potentially damaging weapons, Antoinette disengaged the evasive pattern she had been running and throttled *Storm Bird* down to one gee. Through *Storm Bird*'s windows she could see the elongated shape of the Triumvir's lighthugger, visible at a distance of two thousand kilometres as a tiny scratch of light. Most of the time it was dark enough that she did not see the ship at all, but two or three times a minute a major explosion—some detonating mine, warhead, drive-unit or weapons-trigger—threw light against the hull, momentarily picking it out the way a lighthouse might glance against a jagged pinnacle rising from the depths of a storm-racked ocean. But there was never any doubt about where the ship was. Sparks of flame were swarming around it, so bright that they smeared across her retina, etching dying pink arcs and helices against the stellar backdrop, the trails reminding her of the fiery sticks children had played with during fireworks shows in the old carousel. Pinpricks of light within the swarm signified smaller armaments detonating, and very occasionally Antoinette saw the hard red or green line of a laser precursor beam, caught in outgassing air or propellant from one or other of the ships. Absently, cursing her mind's ability to focus on the most trivial of things at the wrong time, she realised that this was a detail that they always got wrong in the space opera holo-dramas, where laser beams were invisible, the sinister element of invisibility adding to the drama. But a real close-range space battle was a far messier affair, with gas clouds and chaff shards erupting all over the place, ready to reflect and disperse any beam weapon.

The swarm was tighter towards the middle, thinning out through dozens of kilometres. Though she was on the edge of it, she was aware of how tempting a target *Storm Bird* must present. The Triumvir's defences were preoccupied with the closer attack elements, but Antoinette knew that she could not afford to count on that continuing.

Xavier's voice came over the intercom. "Antoinette? Scorpio's ready for departure. Says you can open the bay door any time you like."

"We're not close enough," she said.

Scorpio's voice cut over the intercom. She no longer had any difficulty distinguishing his voice from those of the other pigs. "Antoinette? This is close enough. We have the fuel to cross from here. There's no need for you to risk *Storm Bird* by taking us any closer."

"But the closer I take you, the more fuel you'll have in reserve. Isn't that true?"

"I can't argue with that. Take us five hundred kilometres closer, then. And Antoinette? That really will be close enough."

She magnified the battle view, tapping into the telemetry stream from the many cameras that now whipped around the Triumvir's ship. The image data had been seamlessly merged and then processed to remove the motion, and while there were occasional snags and dropouts as the view was refreshed, the impression was as if she were hovering in space only two or three kilometres beyond the ship itself. The silence was one thing that the holo-dramas got right, she realised, but she had never realised how terribly, profoundly wrong that silence would be when accompanying an actual battle. It was an abject void into which her imagination projected endless screams. What did not help was the way that the Triumvir's ship loomed out of darkness in random, fitful flashes of light, never lingering long enough for her to comprehend the form of the ship in its entirety. What she saw of the ship's perverted architecture was nonetheless adequately disturbing.

Now she saw something that she had not seen before: a rectangle of light, like a golden door, opened somewhere along the wrinkled complexity of *Nostalgia for Infinity*'s hull. It was open for only a moment, but that was long enough for something to slip through. The glare from the engine of the shuttle that had emerged caught the stepped spinal edge of a flying buttress, and as the ship gyred, orientating itself with strobing flashes of thrust, the black shadow of the buttress crawled across an acre of hull material that had the scaled texture of lizardskin.

What about the wolves, Felka?

[Everything, Clavain. At least, everything that I learned. Everything that the Wolf was prepared to let me know.]

It may not be all of the picture, Felka. It may not even be part of it.

[I know. But I still think I should tell you.]

It was not simply about the war against intelligence, she told Clavain. *That was only part of it; only one detail in their vast, faltering program of cosmic stewardship. Despite all evidence to the contrary the wolves were not trying to rid the galaxy of intelligence altogether. What they were striving to do was akin to pruning a forest back to a few saplings rather than incinerating or defoliating completely; or reducing a fire to a few carefully managed flickering flames rather than extinguishing it utterly.*

Think about it, Felka told him. *The existence of the wolves solved one cosmic riddle: the killing machines explained why it was that humanity found itself largely alone in the universe; why the Galaxy appeared barren of other intelligent cultures. It might have been that humanity was just a statistical quirk in an otherwise lifeless cosmos; that the emergence of intelligent, tool-using life was astonishingly rare and that the universe had to be a certain number of billion years old before there was a chance of such a culture arising. This possibility had lingered on until the dawn of the starfaring era, when human explorers began to pick through the ruins of other cultures around nearby stars. Far from being rare, it looked as if tool-using technological life was actually rather common. But for some reason, these cultures had all become extinct.*

The evidence suggested that the extinction events happened on a short timescale compared with the evolutionary development cycles of species: perhaps no more than a few centuries.

The extinctions also seemed to happen at around the time each culture attempted to make a serious expansion into interstellar space.

In other words, at around the development point that humanity—fractured, squabbling, but still essentially one species—now found itself.

Given that premise, she said, it was not too surprising to find that something like the wolves—or the Inhibitors, as some of their victims called them—existed; they were almost inevitable given the pattern of extinctions: remorseless droves of killer machines lurking between the stars, waiting patiently across the aeons for the signs of emergent intelligence . . .

Except that didn't make any real sense, Felka continued. *If intelligence was worth wiping out, for whatever reason, why not do it at source? Intelligence sprang from life; life—except in very rare and exotic niches—sprang from a common brew of chemicals and preconditions. So if intelligence were the enemy, why not intervene earlier in the development cycle?*

There were a thousand ways it might have been done, especially if you were working on a timescale of billions of years. You could interfere in the formation processes of planets themselves, delicately perturbing the swirling clouds of accreting matter that gathered around young stars. You could make it happen that no planets formed in the right orbits for water to occur, or that only very heavy or very light worlds were formed. You could fling worlds into interstellar cold or dash them into the roiling faces of their mother stars.

Or you could poison planets, subtly disturbing the stew of elements in their crusts, oceans and atmospheres so that certain kinds of organic carbon chemistry became unfavourable. Or you could ensure that the planets never settled down into the kind of stable middle age that allowed complex multicellular life to arise. You could keep ramming comets into their crusts so that they shuddered and convulsed under an eternity of bombardment, locked in permanent winters.

Or you could tamper with their stars so that the worlds were periodically doused in flame from massive coronal flares, or thrown into terrible deep ice ages.

Even if you were late, even if you had to accept that complex life had arisen and had perhaps even achieved intelligence and technology, there were ways . . .

Of course there were ways.

A single determined culture could wipe out all life in the Galaxy by the deft manipulation of superdense stellar corpses. Neutron stars could be nudged together until they annihilated each other in sterilising storms of gamma rays. The jets from binary stars could be engineered into directed-energy weapons: flame-throwers reaching a thousand light-years . . .

And even if that were not feasible, or desirable, life could be wiped out by sheer force. A single machine culture could dominate the entire Galaxy in less than a million years, crushing organic life out of existence.

But that's not what they are here for, Felka told him.

Why, then? he asked.

There's a crisis, she told him. *A crisis in the deep galactic future, three billion years from now. Except it wasn't really "deep" at all.*

Thirteen turns of the Galactic spiral, that was all. Before the glaciers had rolled in, you could have walked on to a beach on Earth and picked up a sedimentary rock that was older than three billion years.

Thirteen turns of the wheel? It was nothing in cosmic terms. It was almost upon them.

What crisis? Clavain asked.

A collision, Felka told him.

THIRTY-EIGHT

When she was five hundred kilometres closer to the battle, Antoinette left the bridge unattended, trusting the ship to take care of itself for three or four minutes while she said goodbye to Scorpio and his squad. By the time she reached the huge depressurised bay where the pigs were waiting, the exterior door had eased open and the first of the three shuttles had already launched. She saw the blue spark of its exhaust flame veering towards the glittering nest of light that was the core of the battle. Two trikes followed immediately behind it, and then the second shuttle was jacked forward, pushed by the squat hydraulic rams that were normally used for moving bulky cargo pallets.

Scorpio was already buckling himself into his trike alongside the third shuttle. Since the trikes aboard *Storm Bird* had not needed to make the journey all the way from *Zodiacal Light,* they carried far more armour and weaponry than the other units. Scorpio's own armour was an eye-wrenching combination of luminous colour and reflective patches. The frame of his trike was almost impossible to make out behind the layers of armour and the flanged and muzzled shapes of projectile and beam weapons. Xavier was helping him with his final systems checks, disconnecting a compad from a diagnostics port under the saddle of the trike. He gave a thumbs-up sign and patted Scorpio's armour.

"Looks like you're ready," Antoinette said through her suit's general comm channel.

"You didn't have to risk your ship," Scorpio said. "But since you did, I'll make the extra fuel count."

"I don't envy you this, Scorpio. I know you've already lost quite a few of your soldiers."

"They're our soldiers, Antoinette, not just mine." He made the control fascia of his trike light up with displays, luminous dials and targeting grids, while beyond him the second shuttle departed from the bay, shoved into empty space by the loading rams. The ignition of its drive painted a hard blue radiance against Scorpio's armour. "Listen," he said. "There's something you ought to appreciate. If you knew what the life expectancy of a pig in the Mulch was, nothing that's happened today would seem quite so tragic. Most of my army would have died years ago if they hadn't signed up for Clavain's crusade. I figure they owe Clavain, not the other way round."

"It doesn't mean they should die today."

"And most of them won't. Clavain always knew we'd have to accept some losses, and my pigs knew it as well. We never took a block of Chasm City without spilling some pig blood. But most of us will make it back, and we'll make it with the weapons. We're already winning, Antoinette. Once Clavain used the pacification code, Volyova's war was over." Scorpio tugged down his flash visor with one stubby gauntlet. "We're not even fighting the war now. This is just a mopping-up operation."

"Can I still wish you good luck?"

"You can wish me what the hell you like. It won't make any difference. If it did, it would mean I hadn't prepared well enough."

"Good luck, Scorpio. Good luck to you and all your army."

The third shuttle was being pushed forwards to the departure point. She watched it depart along with the remaining trikes—along with Scorpio—and then told her ship to seal up and head away from the battle.

Volyova reached weapon seventeen unscathed. Though the battle for her ship continued to rage around her, Clavain was evidently taking great pains to ensure that the prizes remained unharmed. Before departing she had studied the attack pattern of his trikes, shuttles and corvettes and concluded that her own ship could reach weapon seventeen with only a fifteen per cent chance of being fired upon. Ordinarily the odds would have struck her as unacceptably poor, but now, somewhat to her horror, she considered them rather favourable.

Weapon seventeen was the only one of the five that she had not withdrawn back into the safety and seclusion of *Nostalgia for Infinity*. She parked her shuttle next to it, moored close enough that there would be no chance of attacking the shuttle without harming the weapon. Then she depressurised the entire cabin, not wishing to go through the time-consuming rigmarole of cycling through the airlock. The powered suit assisted her movements, giving her a false sense of strength and vitality. But perhaps not all of that was down to the suit.

Volyova hauled herself from the shuttle's open lock, and for a moment she was poised midway between the ship and the looming side of weapon seventeen. She felt terribly vulnerable, but the spectacle of the battle was hypnotic. In every direction she looked, all she saw was rushing ships, the dancing sparks of exhaust flames and the brief blue-edged flowers of nuclear and matter-antimatter explosions. Her radio crackled with constant interference. Her suit's radiation sensor was chirping off the scale. She killed them both, preferring peace and quiet.

Volyova had parked the shuttle directly over the hatch in the side of weapon seventeen. Her fingers felt clumsy as they tapped the commands into the thick studs of her suit bracelet, but she worked slowly and made no mistakes. Given the shutdown order Clavain had transmitted to the weapon, she did not necessarily expect that any of her commands would be acted upon.

But the hatch slid open, sickly green light spewing out.

"Thank you," Ilia Volyova said, to no one in particular.

Headfirst, she sunk into the green well. All evidence of the war vanished like a bad dream. Above her, Volyova could see only the armoured belly lock of her shuttle, and all around her she could make out only the interior machinery of the weapon, bathed in the same insipid green glow.

She worked through the procedure she had gone through before, at every step expecting failure, but knowing that she had absolutely nothing to lose. The weapon's fear generators were still firing at full tilt, but this time she found the anxiety reassuring rather than disturbing. It meant that critical weapon functions were still active, and that Clavain had only stunned rather than killed weapon seventeen. She had never seriously thought otherwise, but there had always been a trace of doubt in her mind. What if Clavain himself had not properly understood the code?

But the weapon was not dead, just sleeping.

And then it happened, just as it had happened that first time. The hatch snapped closed, the interior of the weapon began to shift alarmingly and she sensed something approaching, an unspeakable malevolence rushing towards her. She steeled herself. The knowledge that all she was dealing with was a sophisticated subpersona did not make the experience any less unsettling.

There it was. The presence oozed behind her, a shadow that always hovered just on the very edge of her peripheral vision. Once again, she was paralysed, and as before the fear was ten times worse than what she had just been experiencing.

[There's no rest for the wicked, is there, Ilia?]

She remembered that the weapon could read her thoughts. *I thought I'd just drop by to see how you were doing, Seventeen. You don't mind, do you?*

[Then that's all this is? A social call?]

Well, actually it's a bit more than that.

[I thought it might be. You only ever come when you want something, don't you?]

You don't exactly go out of your way to make me feel welcome, Seventeen.

[What, the enforced paralysis and the sense of creeping terror? You mean you don't like that?]

I don't think I was ever meant to like it, Seventeen.

She detected the tiniest hint of a sulk in the weapon's reply. [Perhaps.]

Seventeen . . . there's a matter we need to talk about, if you don't mind . . .

[I'm not going anywhere. You're not either.]

No. I don't suppose I am. Are you aware of the difficulty, Seventeen? The code that won't allow you to fire?

Now the sulk—if that was what it had been—shifted to something closer to indignation. [How could I not know about it?]

I was just checking, that's all. About this code, Seventeen . . .

[Yes?]

I don't suppose there's any chance of you ignoring it, is there?

[Ignore the code?]

Something along those lines, yes. You having a certain degree of free will and all that, I thought it might just be worth raising, as—shall we say—a matter for debate, if nothing else . . . Of course, I know it's unreasonable to expect you to be capable of such a thing . . .

[Unreasonable, Ilia?]

Well, you're bound to have your limitations. And if, as Clavain says, this code is causing a system interrupt at root level . . . well, there's not a lot I can expect you to do about it, is there?

[What would Clavain know?]

Rather a lot more than you or I, I suspect . . .

[Don't be silly, Ilia.]

Then might it be possible . . . ?

There was a pause before the weapon deigned to reply. She thought for that moment that she might have succeeded. Even the degree of fear lessened, becoming nothing much more than acute screaming hysteria.

But then the weapon etched its response into her head. [I know what you're trying to do, Ilia.]

Yes?

[And it won't work. You don't seriously imagine I'm that easily manipulated, do you? That pliant? That ridiculously childlike?]

I don't know. I thought for a moment I detected a trace of myself in you, Seventeen. That was all.

[You're dying, aren't you?]

That shocked her. *How would you know?*

[I can tell a lot more about you than you can about me, Ilia.]

I am dying, yes. What difference does that make? You're just a machine, Seventeen. You don't understand what it's like at all.

[I won't help you.]

No?

[I can't. You're right. The code is at root level. There's nothing I can do about it.]

Then all that talk of free will . . . ?

The paralysis ended in an instant, without warning. The fear remained, but it was not as extreme as it had been before. And around her the weapon was shifting itself again, the door into space opening above her, revealing the belly of the shuttle.

[It was nothing. Just talk.]

Then I'll be on my way. Goodbye, Seventeen. I've a feeling we won't be talking again.

She reached the shuttle. She had just pushed herself through the airlock into the airless cabin when she saw movement outside. Ponderously, like a great compass needle seeking north, the cache weapon was re-aiming itself, sparks of flame erupting from the thruster nodes on the weapon's harness. Volyova sighted down the long axis of the weapon, looking for a reference point, anything in the sphere of battle that would tell her where weapon seventeen was pointing. But the view was too confusing, and there was no time to call up a tactical display on the shuttle's console.

The weapon came to a halt, stopping abruptly. Now she thought of the iron hand of some titanic clock striking the hour.

And then a line of searing brightness ripped from the maw of the weapon, into space.

Seventeen was firing.

It happens in three billion years, she told him.

Two galaxies collide: ours and its nearest spiral neighbour, the Andromeda galaxy. At the moment the galaxies are more than two million light-years apart, but are cruising towards each other with unstoppable momentum, dead set on cosmic destruction.

Clavain asked her what would happen when the galaxies met each other and she explained that there were two scenarios, two possible futures. *In one, the wolves—the Inhibitors or, more accurately, their remote machine descendants—steered life through that crisis, ensuring that intelligence came out on the other side, where it could be allowed to flourish and expand unchecked. It was not possible to prevent the collision,* Felka said. *Even a galaxy-spanning, super-organised machine culture did not have the necessary resources to stop it from happening completely. But it could be managed; the worst effects could be avoided.*

It would happen on many levels. The wolves knew of several techniques for moving entire solar systems, so that they could be steered out of harm's way. The methods had not been employed in recent galactic history, but most had been tried and tested in the past, during local emergencies or vast cultural segregation programmes. Simple machinery, necessitating the demolition of only one or two worlds per system, could be shackled around the belly of a star. The star's atmosphere could be squeezed and flexed by rippling magnetic fields, coaxing matter to fly off the surface. The starstuff could be manipulated and forced to flow in one direction only, acting like a huge rocket exhaust. It had to be done delicately, so that the star continued to burn in a stable manner, and also so that the remaining planets did not tumble out of their orbits when the star started moving. It took a long time, but that was usually not a problem; normally they had tens of millions years' warning before a system had to be moved.

There were other techniques, too: a star could be partially enshrouded in a shell of mirrors, so that the pressure of its own radiation imparted momentum. Less tested or trusted methods employed large-scale manipulation of inertia. Those techniques were the easiest when they worked well, but there had been dire accidents when they went wrong, catastrophes in which whole systems had been suddenly ejected from the galaxy at near lightspeed, hurled into intergalactic space with no hope of return.

The slower, older approaches were often better than newfangled gimmicks, the wolves had learned.

The great work encompassed more than just the movement of stars, of course. Even if the two galaxies only grazed past each other rather than ramming head-on, there would be still be incandescent fireworks as walls of gas and dust hit each other. As shockwaves rebounded through the galaxies, furious new cycles of stellar birth would be kickstarted. A generation of supermassive hot stars would live and die in a cosmic eyeblink, dying in equally convulsive cycles of supernovae. Although individual stars and their solar systems might pass through the event unscathed, vast tracts of the galaxy would still be sterilised by these catastrophic explosions. It would be a million times worse if the collision was head-on, of course, but it was still something that had to be contained and minimised. For another billion years, the machines would toil to suppress not the emergence of life but the creation of hot stars. Those that slipped through the net would be ushered to the edge of space by the star-moving machinery so that their dying explosions did not threaten the newly flourishing cultures.

The great work would not soon be over.

But that was only one future. There was another, Felka said. *It was the future in which intelligence slipped through the net here and now, the future in which the Inhibitors lost their grip on the galaxy.*

In that future, she said, *the time of great flourishing was imminent in cosmic terms; it would happen within the next few million years. In a heartbeat, the galaxy would run amok with life, becoming a teeming, packed oasis of sentience. It would be a time of wonder and miracles.*

And yet it was doomed.

Organic intelligence, Felka said, *could not achieve the necessary organisation to steer itself through the collision. Species co-operation was just not possible on that scale. Short of xenocide, one species wiping out all the others, the galactic cultures would never become sufficiently united to engage in such a massive and protracted programme as the collision-avoidance operation. It was not that they would fail to see that something had to be done, but that every species would have its own strategy, its own preferred solution to the problem. There would be disputes over policy as violent as the Dawn War.*

Too many hands on the cosmic wheel, Felka said.

The collision would happen, and the results—from the colli-

son and the wars that would accompany it—would be utterly catastrophic. Life in the Milky Way would not end immediately; a few flickering flames of sentience would struggle on for another couple of billion years, but because of the measures they had taken to survive in the first place, they would be little more than machines themselves. Nothing resembling the pre-collision societies would ever arise again.

Almost as soon as she had registered the fact that the weapon was firing, the beam shut down, leaving weapon seventeen exactly as she found it. By Volyova's estimation, the weapon had broken free of Clavain's control for perhaps half a second. It might even have been less than that.

She fumbled her suit-radio on. Khouri's voice was there immediately. "Ilia . . . ? Ilia . . . ? Can you—"

"I can hear you, Khouri. Is something the matter?"

"Nothing's the matter, Ilia. It's just that you seem to have done whatever it was you set out to do. The cache weapon landed a direct hit on *Zodiacal Light*."

She closed her eyes, tasting the moment, wondering why it felt far less like victory than she had imagined it would. "A direct hit?"

"Yes."

"It can't have been. I didn't see the flash as the Conjoiner drives went up."

"I said it was a direct hit. I didn't say it was a fatal hit."

By then Volyova had managed to call up a long-range grab of *Zodiacal Light* on the shuttle's console. She piped it through to her helmet faceplate, studying the damage with awed fascination. The beam had sliced through the hull of Clavain's ship like a knife through bread, snipping off perhaps a third of its length. The needle-nosed prow, glittering with carved facets of diamond-threaded ice, was buckling away from the rest of the hull in ghastly slow motion, like some toppling spire. The wound that the beam had excavated was still shining a livid shade of red, and there were explosions on either side of the severed hull. It was the most heart-wrenchingly beautiful thing she had seen in some time. It was just a shame she was not seeing it with her own eyes.

That was when the shuttle jarred to one side. Volyova thumped against one wall, for she had not had time to buckle herself back into the control seat. What had happened? Had the weapon adjusted its direction of aim, shoving her shuttle in the process? She steadied herself and directed her goggles to the window, but the weapon was in the same orientation as it had been when it had stopped firing. Again the shuttle jarred to one side, and this time she felt, through the tactile-transmitting fabric of her gloves, the shrill scrape of metal against metal. It was exactly as if another ship were brushing against her own.

She arrived at this conclusion only a moment before the first figure came through the still open airlock door. She cursed herself for not closing the lock behind her, but she had been lulled into a false sense of security by the fact that she was wearing a suit. She should have been thinking about intruders rather than her own life-support needs. It was exactly the kind of mistake she would never have made had she been well, but she supposed she could allow herself one or two errors this late in the game. She had, after all, delivered something of a winning move against Clavain's ship. The broken hull was drifting away now, trailing intricate strands of mechanical gore.

"Triumvir?" The figure was speaking, his voice buzzing in her helmet. She studied the intruder's armour, noting baroque ornamentation and dazzling juxtapositions of luminous paint and mirrored surface.

"You have that pleasure," she said.

The figure had a wide-muzzled weapon pointed at her. Behind, two more similarly armoured specimens had squeezed into the cabin. The first tugged up a black flash visor; through the thick dark glass of his helmet she caught the not-quite-human facial anatomy of a hyperpig.

"My name is Scorpio," the pig informed her. "I'm here to accept your surrender, Triumvir."

She clucked in surprise. "My surrender?"

"Yes, Triumvir."

"Have you looked out of the window lately, Scorpio? I really think you ought to."

There was a moment while her intruders conferred amongst themselves. She sensed to the second the moment when they became aware of what had just happened. There was the minutest lowering of the gun muzzle, a flicker of hesitation in Scorpio's eyes.

"You're still our prisoner," he said, but with a good deal less conviction than before.

Volyova smiled indulgently. "Well, that's very interesting. Where do you think we should complete the formalities? Your ship or mine?"

So that's it? That's the choice I'm given? That even if we win, even if we beat the wolves, it won't mean a damn in the long term? That the best thing we could do in the interests of the preservation of life itself, taking the long view, is to curl up and die now? That what we should be doing is surrendering to the wolves, not preparing to fight them?

[I don't know, Clavain.]

It could be a lie. It could be propaganda that the Wolf showed you, self-justifying rhetoric. Maybe there is no higher cause. Maybe all they're really doing is wiping out intelligence for no other reason than that's what they do. And even if what they showed you is true, that doesn't begin to make it right. The cause might be just, Felka, but history's littered with atrocities committed in the name of righteousness. Trust me on this. You can't excuse the murder of billions of sentient individuals because of some remote utopian dream, no matter what the alternative.

[But you know precisely what the alternative is, Clavain. Absolute extinction.]

Yes. Or so they say. But what if it isn't that simple? If what they told you is true, then the entire future history of the galaxy has been biased by the presence of the wolves. We'll never know what would have happened if the wolves hadn't emerged to steer life through the crisis. The experiment has changed. And there's a new factor now: the wolves' own weakness, the fact that they're slowly failing. Maybe they were never meant to be this brutal, Felka—have you considered that? That they might once have been more like shepherds and less like poachers? Perhaps that was the first failure, so long ago that no one remembers it. The wolves kept following the rules they had been instructed to enforce, but with less and less wisdom; less and less mercy. What started as gentle containment became xenocide. What started as authority became tyranny, self-perpetuating and self-reinforcing. Consider it, Felka. There might be a higher cause to what they're doing, but it doesn't have to be right.

[I only know what it showed me. It's not my job to choose, Clavain. Not my job to show you what you should do. I just thought you ought to be told.]

I know. I'm not blaming you for it.

[What are you going to do, Clavain?]

He thought of the cruel balance of things: equating vistas of cosmic strife—millennia-long battles thrumming across the face of the galaxy—against infinitely grander vistas of cosmic silence. He thought of worlds and moons spinning, their days uncounted, their seasons unremembered. He thought of stars living and dying in the absence of sentient observers, flaring into mindless darknesss until the end of time itself, not a single conscious thought to disturb the icy calm between here and eternity. Machines might still stalk those cosmic steppes, and they might in some sense continue to process and interpret data, but there would be no recognition, no love, no hate, no loss, no pain, only analysis, until the last flicker of power faded from the last circuit, leaving a final stalled algorithm half-executed.

He was being hopelessly anthropomorphic, of course. This entire drama concerned only the local group of galaxies. Out there—not just tens, but hundreds of millions of light-years away—there were other such groups, clumps of one or two dozen galaxies bound together in darkness by their mutual self-gravity. Too far to imagine reaching, but they were there all the same. They were ominously silent—but that didn't mean they were necessarily devoid of sentience. Perhaps they had learned the value of silence. The grand story of life in the Milky Way—across the entire local group—might just be one thread in something humblingly vast. Perhaps, after all, it didn't actually matter what happened here. Blindly executing whatever instructions they had been given in the remote galactic past, the wolves might strangle sentience out of existence now, or they might guard a thread of it through its gravest crisis. And perhaps neither outcome really mattered, any more than a local cluster of extinctions on a single island would make any significant difference when set against the rich, swarming ebb and flow of life on an entire world.

Or perhaps it mattered more than anything.

Clavain saw it all with sudden, heart-stopping clarity: all that mattered *was* the here and now. All that mattered was survival. Sentience that bowed down and accepted its own extinction—no matter what the long-term arguments, no matter how good the greater cause—was not the kind of sentience he was interested in preserving.

Nor was it the kind he was interested in serving. Like all the hard choices he had ever made, the heart of the problem was childishly simple: he could concede the weapons and accept his complicity in humanity's coming extinction, while knowing that he had done his part for sentient life's ultimate destiny. Or he could take the weapons now—or as many of them as he could get his hands on—and make some kind of stand against tyranny.

It might be pointless. It might just be postponing the inevitable. But if that was the case, what was the harm in trying?

[Clavain . . .]

He felt a vast, searing, calm. All was clear now. He was about to tell her that he had made his mind up to take the weapons and make a stand, future history be damned. He was Nevil Clavain and he had never surrendered in his life.

But suddenly something else merited his immediate attention. *Zodiacal Light* had been hit. The great ship was breaking in two.

THIRTY-NINE

"Hello, Clavain," Ilia Volyova said, her voice a fine papery rasp that he had to struggle to understand. "It's good to see you, finally. Come closer, will you?"

He walked to the side of her bed, unwilling to believe that this was the Triumvir. She looked dreadfully ill, and yet at the same time he could feel a profound calm about the woman. Her expression, as well as he could read it, for her eyes were hidden behind blank grey goggles, spoke of quiet accomplishment, of the weary elation that came with the concluding of a lengthy and difficult business.

"It's good to meet you, Ilia," he said. He shook her hand as gently as he could. She had already been injured, he knew, and had then gone back into space, into the battle. Unprotected, she had received the kind of radiation dose that even broad-spectrum medichines could not remedy.

She was going to die, and she was going to die sooner rather than later.

"You are very like your proxy, Clavain," she said in that quiet rasp. "And different, too. You have a gravitas that the machine lacked. Or perhaps it is simply that I know you better now as an adversary. I am not at all sure I respected you before."

"And now?"

"You have given me pause for thought, I will certainly say that much."

There were nine of them present. Next to Volyova's bed was Khouri, the woman Clavain took to be her deputy. Clavain, in turn, was accompanied by Felka, Scorpio, two of Scorpio's pig soldiers, Antoinette Bax and Xavier Liu. Clavain's shuttle had docked with *Nostalgia for Infinity* after the immediate declaration of cease-fire, with *Storm Bird* following shortly after.

"Have you considered my proposal?" Clavain asked, delicately.

"Your proposal?" she said, with a sniff of disdain.

"My *revised* proposal, then. The one that didn't involve your unilateral surrender."

"You're hardly in a position to be putting proposals to anyone, Clavain. The last time I looked, you only had half a ship left."

She was right. Remontoire and most of the remaining crew were still alive, but the damage to the ship was acute. It was a minor miracle that the Conjoiner drives had not detonated.

"By proposal I meant . . . suggestion. A mutual arrangement, to the benefit of both of us."

"Refresh my memory, will you, Clavain?"

He turned to Bax. "Antoinette, introduce yourself, will you?"

She came closer to the bed with something of the same trepidation that Clavain had shown. "Ilia . . . "

"It's Triumvir Volyova, young lady. At least until we're better acquainted."

"What I meant to say is . . . I've got this ship . . . this freighter . . . "

Volyova glared at Clavain. He knew what she meant. She was acutely conscious that she did not have a great deal of time left, and what she did not need was indirection.

"Bax has a freighter," Clavain said urgently. "It's docked with us now. It has limited transatmospheric capability—not the best, but it can cope."

"And your point, Clavain?"

"My point is that it has large pressurised cargo holds. It can take passengers, a great many passengers. Not in anything you'd call luxury, but . . ."

Volyova gestured for Bax to come closer. "How many?"

"Four thousand, easily. Maybe even five. The thing's crying out to be used as an ark, Triumvir."

Clavain nodded. "Think of it, Ilia. I know you've got an evacuation plan going here. I thought it was a ruse before, but now I've seen the evidence. But you haven't made a dent in the planet's population."

"We've done what we could," Khouri said, with a trace of defensiveness.

Clavain held up a hand. "I know. Given your constraints, you did well to get as many off the surface as you've managed to. But that doesn't mean we can't do a lot better now. The wolf weapon—the Inhibitor device—has nearly bored its way through to the heart of Delta Pavonis. There simply isn't time for any other plan. With *Storm Bird* we'd need only fifty return trips. Maybe fewer, as Antoinette says. Forty, perhaps. She's right—it's an ark. And it's a fast one."

Volyova let out a sigh as old as time. "If only it were that simple, Clavain."

"What do you mean?"

"We aren't simply moving faceless units off the surface of Resurgam. We're moving people. Frightened, desperate people." The grey goggles tilted a fraction. "Aren't we, Khouri?"

"She's right. It's a mess down there. The administration . . ."

"Before, there were just two of you," Clavain said. "You had to work with the government. But now we have an army, and the means to enforce our will. Don't we, Scorpio?"

"We can take Cuvier," the pig said. "I've already looked into it. It's no worse than taking a single block of Chasm City. Or this ship, for that matter."

"You never did take my ship," Volyova reminded him. "So

don't overestimate your capabilities." She turned her attention to Clavain and her voice became sharper, more probing than it had been upon his arrival. "Would you seriously consider a forced takeover?"

"If that's the only way to get those people off the planet, then yes, that's exactly what I'd consider."

Volyova looked at him craftily. "You've changed your tune, Clavain. Since when was evacuating Resurgam your highest priority?"

He looked at Felka. "I realised that the possession of the weapons was not quite the clear-cut issue I'd been led to believe. There were choices to be made, harder choices than I would have liked, and I realised that I had been neglecting them because of their very difficulty."

Volyova said, "Then you don't want the weapons, is that it?"

Clavain smiled. "Actually, I still do. And so do you. But I think we can come to an agreement, can't we?"

"We have a job to do here, Clavain. I'm not just talking about the evacuation of Resurgam. Do you honestly think I'd leave the Inhibitors to get on with their business?"

He shook his head. "No. As a matter of fact, I already had my suspicions."

"I'm dying, Clavain. I have no future. With the right intervention I might survive a few more weeks, no more than that. I suppose they might be able to do something for me on another world, assuming anyone still retains a pre-plague technology, but that would entail the tedious business of being frozen, something I have had quite enough of for one existence. So I am calling it a day." She raised a bird-boned wrist and thumped the bed. "I bequeath you this damned monstrosity of a ship. You can take it and the evacuees away from here once we're done airlifting them from Resurgam. Here, I give it to you. It's yours." She raised her voice, an effort that must have cost her more than he could even begin to imagine. "Are you listening, Captain? It's Clavain's ship now. I hereby resign as Triumvir."

"Captain . . . ?" Clavain ventured.

She smiled. "You'll find out, don't you worry."

"I'll take care of the evacuees," Clavain said, moved at what had just happened. He nodded at Khouri as well. "You have my word on that. I promise you I will not let you down, Triumvir."

Volyova dismissed him with one weary wave of her hand. "I

believe you. You appear to be a man who gets things done, Clavain."

He scratched his beard. "Then there's just one other thing."

"The weapons? Who gets them in the end? Well, don't worry. I've already thought of that."

He waited, studying the series of abstract grey curves that was the Triumvir's bed-ridden form.

"Here's my proposal," she said, her voice as thin as the wind. "It happens to be non-negotiable." Then her attention flicked to Antoinette again. "You. What did you say your name was?"

"Bax," Antoinette said, almost stuttering on her answer.

"Mm." The Triumvir sounded as if this was the least interesting thing she had heard in her life. "And this ship of yours . . . this freighter . . . is it really as large and fast as is claimed?"

She shrugged. "I suppose so."

"Then I'll take it as well. You won't need it once we've finished evacuating the planet. You'd just better make sure you get the job done before I die."

Clavain looked at Bax, and then back to the Triumvir. "What do you want her ship for, Ilia?"

"Glory," Volyova said dismissively. "Glory and redemption. What else did you imagine?"

Antoinette Bax sat alone on the bridge of her ship, the ship that had been hers and her father's before that, the ship that she had loved once and hated once, the ship that was as much a part of her as her own flesh, and knew that this would be the last time. For better or for worse, nothing would be the same from this moment on. It was time to finish the process that had begun with that trip from Carousel New Copenhagen to honour a ridiculous and stupid childhood vow. For all its foolishness it had been a vow born out of kindness and love, and it had taken her into the heart of the war and into the great crushing machine of history itself. Had she known—had she had the merest inkling of what would happen, of how she would become embroiled in Clavain's story, a story that had been running for centuries before her birth and which would see her yanked out of her own environment and flung light-years from home and decades into the future—then perhaps she might have quailed. Perhaps. But she might also have stared into the face of fear and been filled with an even more stubborn determination to do what she had promised herself all those years ago. It was, Antoinette thought, entirely possible that she would have done just that. Once a stubborn bitch, always a stubborn bitch—and if that wasn't her personal motto, it was about time she adopted it. Her father might not have approved, but she was sure that in his heart of hearts he would have agreed and perhaps even admired her for it.

"Ship?"

"Yes, Antoinette?"

"It's all right, you know. I don't mind. You can still call me Little Miss."

"It was only ever an act." Beast—or Lyle Merrick, more properly—paused. "I did it rather well, wouldn't you say?"

"Dad was right to trust you. You did look after me, didn't you?"

"As well as I was able to. Which wasn't as well as I hoped. But then again, you didn't exactly make it easy. I suppose that was inevitable, given the family connection. Your father was not exactly the most cautious of individuals, and you are very much a chip off the old block."

"We came through, Ship," Antoinette said. "We still came through. That has to count for something, doesn't it?"

"I suppose so."

"Ship . . . Lyle . . . "

"Antoinette?"

"You know what the Triumvir wants, don't you?"

Merrick did not answer her for several seconds. All her life she had imagined that the pauses were inserted cosmetically into the subpersona's conversation, but she knew now that they had been quite real. Merrick's simulation experienced consciousness at a rate very close to normal human thought, so his pauses indicated genuine introspection.

"Xavier did inform me, yes."

Antoinette was glad at least that she did not have to reveal that particular piece of the arrangement. "When the evacuation is done, when we've got as many people away from the planet as we can, then the Triumvir wants to use *Storm Bird* for herself. She says it's for glory and redemption. It sounds like a suicide mission, Lyle."

"I more or less came to the same conclusion as well, Antoinette." Merrick's synthesised voice was quite unnervingly calm. "She's dying, so I gather, so I suppose it isn't suicide in the old sense . . . but that's a fairly pointless distinction. I gather she wishes to make amends for her past."

"Khouri, the other woman, says she isn't the monster the people on the planet make out." Antoinette struggled to keep her own voice as level and collected as Merrick's. They were skirting around something dreadful, orbiting an absence neither wished to acknowledge. "But I guess she must have done some bad stuff in the past anyway."

"Then I suppose that makes two of us," Merrick said. "Yes, Antoinette, I know what you are concerned about. But you mustn't worry about me."

"She thinks you're just a ship, Lyle. And no one will tell her the truth because they need her co-operation so badly. Not that it would make any difference if they did . . . " Antoinette trailed off, hating herself for feeling so sad. "You'll die, won't you? Finally, the way it would have happened all those years ago if Dad and Xavier hadn't helped you."

"I deserved it, Antoinette. I did a terrible thing, and I escaped justice."

"But Lyle . . . " Her eyes were stinging. She could feel tears welling inside her, stupid irrational tears that she despised herself for. She had loved her ship, then hated it—hated it because of the lie in which it had implicated her father, the lie that she had been told; and then she had come to love it again, because the ship, and the ghost of Lyle Merrick that haunted it, were both tangible links back to her father. And now that she had come to that accommodation, the knife was twisting again. What she had learned to love was being taken away from her, the last link back to her father snatched from her hands by that bitch Volyova . . .

Why was it never easy? All she had wanted to do was keep a vow.

"Antoinette?"

"We could remove you," she said. "Take you out of the ship and replace you with an ordinary subpersona. Volyova wouldn't have to know, would she?"

"No, Antoinette. It's my time as well. If she wants glory and redemption, then why can't I take a little of that for myself?"

"You've already made a difference. There isn't any need for a larger sacrifice."

"But this is still what I choose to do. You can't begrudge me that, can you?"

"No," she said, her voice breaking up. "No, I can't. And I wouldn't."

"Promise me something, Antoinette?"

She rubbed her eyes, ashamed at her tears and yet oddly exultant at the same time. "What, Lyle?"

"That you will continue to take good care of yourself, no matter what happens from here on in."

She nodded. "I will. I promise."

"That's good. There's one other thing I want to say, and then I think we should go our separate ways. I can continue with the evacuation unaided. In fact, I positively refuse to let you put yourself in further danger by continuing to fly aboard me. How does that sound for an order? Impressed, aren't you? You didn't think I was capable of that, did you?"

"No, Ship. I didn't." She smiled despite herself.

"One final thing, Antoinette. It was a pleasure to serve under you. A pleasure and an honour. Now, please go away and find another ship—preferably something bigger and better—to captain. I am sure you will make an excellent job of it."

She stood up from the seat. "I'll do my best, I promise."

"Of that I have no doubt."

She stepped towards the door, hesitating on the threshold. "Goodbye Lyle," she said.

"Goodbye, Little Miss."

FORTY

They pulled him shivering from the open womb of the casket. He felt like a man who had been rescued from drowning in winter. The faces of the people around him sharpened into focus, but he did not recognise any of them immediately. Someone threw a quilted thermal blanket around the narrow frame of his shoulders. They eyed him without speaking, guessing that he was in no mood for conversation and would wish instead to orientate himself by his own efforts.

Clavain sat on the edge of the casket for several minutes until he had enough strength in his legs to hobble across the chamber. He stumbled at the last moment and yet made the fall appear graceful, as if he had intended to lean suddenly against the support of the porthole's armoured frame. He peered through the glass. He could see nothing beyond except blackness, with his own ghastly reflection hovering in the foreground. He appeared strangely eyeless, his sockets crammed with shadows which were the precise black of the background vacuum. He felt a savage jolt of *déjà vu,* the feeling that he had been here before, contemplating his own masklike face. He tugged and nagged at the thread of memory until it spooled free, recalling a last-minute diplomatic mission, a shuttle falling towards occupied Mars, an imminent confrontation with an old enemy and friend called Galiana . . . and he remembered that even then, four hundred years ago—though it was more now, he thought—he had felt too old for the world, too old for the role it forced upon him. Had he known what lay before him then, he would have either laughed or gone insane. It had felt like the end of his life, and yet it had been only a moment from its beginning, barely separable in his memories now from his childhood.

He looked back at the people who had brought him around and then up at the ceiling.

"Dim the lights," someone said.

His reflection disappeared. Now he could see something other than blackness. It was a swarm of stars, squashed into one hemisphere of the sky. Reds and blues and golds and frigid whites. Some were brighter than others, though he saw no familiar constellations. But the clumping of the stars, stirred into one part of the sky, meant only one thing. They were still moving relativistically, still skimming near the speed of light.

Clavain turned back to the small huddle of people. "Has the battle taken place?"

A pale dark-haired woman spoke for the group. "Yes, Clavain." She spoke warmly, but not with the absolute assurance Clavain had expected. "Yes, it's over. We engaged the trio of Conjoiner ships, destroying one and damaging the other two."

"Only damaged?"

"The simulations didn't get it quite right," said the woman. She moved to Clavain's side and pushed a beaker of brown fluid under his nose. He looked at her face and hair. There was something familiar about the way she wore it, something that sparked the same ancient memories that had been stirred by his reflection in the porthole. "Here, drink this. Recuperative medichines from Ilia's arsenal. It'll do you the world of good."

Clavain took the beaker from the woman's hand and sniffed at the broth. It smelt of chocolate when he had expected tea. He tipped some down his throat. "Thank you," he said. "Do you mind if I ask your name?"

"Not at all," the woman said. "I'm Felka. You know me quite well."

He looked at her and shrugged. "You seem familiar . . . "

"Drink up. I think you need it."

His memory came back in swathes, like a city recovering from a power failure: block by random block, utilities stuttering and flickering before normal service was resumed. Even when he felt all right, there came other medichine therapies, each of which dealt with specific areas of brain function, each of which was administered in doses more carefully tuned than the last, while Clavain grimaced and cooperated with the minimum of good grace. By the end of it he did not want to see another thimbleful of chocolate in his life.

After several hours he was deemed to be neurologically sound. There were still things that he did not recall with great precision, but he was told this was within the error margins of the usual amnesia that accompanied reefersleep fugue, and did not indicate any untoward lapses. They gave him a lightweight bio-monitor tabard, assigned a spindly bronze servitor to him and told him he was free to move around as he pleased.

"Shouldn't I be asking why you've woken me?" he said.

"We'll get to that later," said Scorpio, who seemed to be in charge. "There's no immediate hurry, Clavain."

"But I take it there's a decision that needs to be made?"

Scorpio glanced at one of the other leaders, the woman called Antoinette Bax. She had wide eyes and a freckled nose and he felt that there were memories of her that he had yet to unearth. She nodded back, almost imperceptibly.

"We wouldn't have woken you for the view, Clavain," Scorpio said. "It's a piece of crap even with the lights out."

Somewhere in the heart of the immense vessel was a place that felt like it belonged in some entirely different part of the universe. It was a glade, a place of grass and trees and synthetic blue skies. There were holographic birds in the air: parrots and hornbills and suchlike, skimming from tree to tree in cometlike flashes of bright primary colour, and there was a waterfall in the distance which looked suspiciously real, hazed in a swirling talcum-blue mist where it emptied into a small dark lake.

Felka escorted Clavain on to a flat apron of cool glistening grass. She wore a long black dress, her feet lost under the black spillage of the hem. She did not seem to mind it dragging through the dew-laden grass. They sat down facing each other, resting on tree stumps whose tops had been polished to mirrored smoothness. They had the place to themselves, except for the birds.

Clavain looked around. He felt much better now and his memory was nearly whole, but he did not remember this place at all. "Did you create this, Felka?"

"No," she said cautiously, "but why do you ask?"

"Because it reminds me a little of the forest at the core of the Mother Nest, I suppose. Where you had your atelier. Except it has gravity, of course, which your atelier didn't."

"So you do remember, then."

He scratched at the stubble on his chin. Someone had thoughtfully shaved off his beard when he was asleep. "Dribs and drabs. Not as much of what happened before I went under as I'd like."

"What do you remember, exactly?"

"Remontoire leaving to make contact with Sylveste. You almost going with him, and then deciding not to. Not much else. Volyova's dead, isn't she?"

Felka nodded. "We got the planet evacuated. You and Volyova agreed to split the remaining hell-class weapons. She took *Storm Bird,* loaded as many weapons on to it as she could manage and rode it straight into the heart of the Inhibitor machine."

Clavain pursed his lips and whistled quietly. "Did she make much difference?"

"None at all. But she went out with a bang."

Clavain smiled. "I never expected anything less of her. And what else?"

"Khouri and Thorn—you remember them? They joined Remontoire's expedition to Hades. They have shuttles, and they've initiated *Zodiacal Light*'s self-repair systems. All they have to do is keep supplying it with raw material and it will repair itself. But it will take a little while, time enough for them to make contact with Sylveste, Khouri thinks."

"I didn't know quite what to make of her claim to have already been into Hades," Clavain said, picking blades of grass from the area around his feet. He crushed them and sniffed the pulpy green residue that stained his fingers. "But the Triumvir seemed to think it was true."

"We'll find out sooner or later," Felka said. "After they've made contact—however long that takes—they'll take *Zodiacal Light* out of the system and follow our trajectory. As for us, well, it's still your ship, Clavain, but day-to-day affairs are handled by a Triumvirate. Triumvirs Blood, Cruz and Scorpio, by popular vote. Khouri would be one of them, of course, if she hadn't chosen to stay behind after the evacuation."

"My memory says they rescued one hundred and sixty thousand people," Clavain said. "Is that shockingly wide of the mark?"

"No, it's about right. Which sounds pretty impressive until you realise that we didn't manage to save forty thousand others . . ."

"We were the thing that went wrong, weren't we? If we hadn't intervened . . ."

"No, Clavain." Her voice was admonitionary, as if he was an old man who had committed some awful *faux pas* in polite company. "No. You mustn't think like that. Look, it was like this, understand?" They were close enough for Conjoined thought. She piped images into his head, pictures from the death of Resurgam. He saw the last hours as the wolf machine—that was what they were now all calling the Inhibitor weapon—bored its gravitation sinkhole into the very heart of the star, stabbing an invisible curette deep into the nuclear-burning core. The tunnel that it had opened was exceedingly narrow, no more than a few kilometres wide at its deepest point—and though the star was being drained of blood, the process was no uncontrolled haemorrhage. Instead the fusing matter in the nuclear-burning core was allowed to squirt out in a fine jetting arc, a column of expanding, cooling hellfire that speared from the star's surface at half the speed of light. Constrained and guided by pulses of the same gravitational energy that had cored the star in the first place, the spike was bent in a lazy parabola that caused it to douse against the dayside of Resurgam. By the time it impacted, the starfire flame was a thousand kilometres across. The effect was catastrophic and practically instantaneous. The atmosphere was boiled away in a searing flash, the icecaps and the few areas of open water following instants later. Arid and airless, the crust under the beam became molten, the spike gouging a cherry-red scar across the face of the planet. Hundreds of vertical kilometres of the planet's surface were incinerated, gouting into space in a hot cloud of boiled rock. Shockwaves from the initial impact reached around the world and destroyed all life on the nightside: every human being, every organism that humans had brought to Resurgam. And yet they would have died soon enough without that shockwave. Within hours, the nightside had turned to face the sun. The spike continued to boil, the well of the energy at the heart of the star barely tapped. Resurgam's crust burned away, and still the beam continued to chew into the planet's mantle.

It took three weeks to reduce the planet to a smoking red-hot cinder, four-fifths of its previous size. Then the beam flicked to another target, another world, and began the same murderous sweep. The depletion of matter from the star's heart would eventually bleed Delta Pavonis down to a cool husk of itself, until so much matter had been removed that fusion came to an abrupt halt. It had not happened yet, Felka said—at least not according to the lightsignals that were catching up with them from the system—but when it did, it stood every chance of being a violent event.

"So you see," Felka said, "we were actually lucky to rescue as many as we did. It wasn't our fault that more died. We just did what was right under the circumstances. There's no sense feeling guilty about it. If we hadn't shown up, a thousand other things could have gone wrong. Skade's fleet would still have arrived, and she wouldn't have been any more inclined to negotiate than you were."

Clavain remembered the vile flash of a dying starship, and

remembered also the ultimate death of Galiana that he had sanctioned with the decision to destroy *Nightshade*. Even now the thought of that was painful.

"Skade died, didn't she? I killed her, in interstellar space. The other elements of her fleet were acting autonomously, even when we engaged them."

"Everything was autonomous," Felka said, with curious evasion.

Clavain watched a macaw orbit from tree to tree. "I don't mind being consulted on strategic matters, but I'm not seeking a position of authority on this ship. It isn't *mine,* for a start, no matter what Volyova might have thought. I'm too old to take command. And besides, what would the ship need with me anyway? It already has its own Captain."

Felka's voice was low. "So you remember the Captain?"

"I remember what Volyova told us. I don't remember ever talking with the Captain himself. Is he still running things, the way she said he would?"

Her voice remained guarded. "Depends what you mean by running things. His infrastructure is still intact, but there's been no sign of him as a conscious entity since we left Delta Pavonis."

"Then the Captain's dead, is that it?"

"No, that can't be it either. He had fingers in too many aspects of routine shipwide functioning, so Volyova said. When he used to go into one of his catatonic states, it was like pulling the plug on the entire ship. That hasn't happened. The ship's still taking care of itself, keeping itself ticking over, indulging in self-repair and the occasional upgrade."

Clavain nodded. "Then it's as if the Captain's still functioning on an involuntary level, but there's no sentience there any more? Like a patient who still has enough brain function to breathe, but not much else?"

"That's our best guess. But we can't be totally sure. Sometimes there are little glimmers of intelligence, things that the ship does to itself without asking anyone. Flashes of creativity. It's more as if the Captain's still there, but buried more deeply than was ever the case before."

"Or perhaps he just left behind a ghost of himself," Clavain said. "A mindless shell, pottering through the same behavioural patterns."

"Whatever it was, he redeemed himself," Felka said. "He did something terrible, but in the end he also saved one hundred and sixty thousand lives."

"So did Lyle Merrick," Clavain said, remembering for the first time since he had awakened the secret within Antoinette's ship and the necessary sacrifice the man had made. "Two redemptions for the price of one? I suppose it's a start." Clavain picked at a stray splinter of wood that had embedded itself in his palm, torn from the very edge of the tree stump. "So what *did* happen, Felka? Why have I been awakened when everyone knew it might kill me?"

"I'll show you," she said. She looked in the direction of the waterfall. Startled, for he had been certain that they were alone, Clavain saw a figure standing on the very edge of the lake immediately before the waterfall. The mist ebbed and swirled around the figure's extremities.

But he recognised her.

"Skade," he said.

"Clavain," she answered. But she did not step closer. Her voice had been hollow, the acoustics all wrong for the environment. Clavain realised, with a jolt of irritation at how easily he had been fooled, that he was being addressed by a simulation.

"She's a beta-level, isn't she," he said, talking only to Felka. "The Master of Works would have retained a good enough working memory of Skade to put a beta-level aboard any of the other ships."

"She's a beta-level, yes," Felka said. "But that isn't how it happened. Is it, Skade?"

The figure was crested and armoured. It nodded. "This beta-level is a recent version, Clavain. My physical counterpart transmitted it to you during the engagement."

"Sorry," Clavain said, shaking his head, "my memory may not be what it was, but I remember killing your counterpart. I destroyed *Nightshade* shortly after I rescued Felka."

"That's what you remember. It's almost what happened, too."

"You can't have survived, Skade." He said it with numb insistence, despite the evidence of his eyes.

"I saved my head, Clavain. I feared that you would destroy *Nightshade* once I gave you back Felka, even though I didn't think you would have the courage to do it when you knew I had Galiana aboard . . . " She smiled, her expression strangely close to admiration. "I was wrong about that, wasn't I? You were a far more ruthless adversary than I had ever imagined, even after you did this to me."

"You had Galiana's body, not Galiana." Clavain held his voice steady. "All I did was give her the peace she should have had when she died all those years ago."

"But you don't really believe that, do you? You always knew she was not really dead, but merely in a state of deadlock with the Wolf."

"That was as good as death."

"But there was always the chance the Wolf could be removed, Clavain . . . " Her voice became soft. "You believed that, too. You believed there was a chance you could have her back one day."

"I did what I had to do," he said.

"It was ruthlessness, Clavain. I admire you for it. You're more of a spider than any of us."

He stood up from the stump and made his way to the water's edge until he was only a few metres from Skade. She hovered in the mist, neither fully solid nor fully anchored to the ground. "I did what I had to do," he repeated. "It was all I ever did. It wasn't ruthlessness, Skade. Ruthlessness implies that I felt no pain when I did it."

"And did you?"

"It was the worst thing I have ever done. I removed her love from the universe."

"I feel sorry for you, Clavain."

"How did you survive, Skade?"

She reached up and fingered the curious collar where armour joined flesh. "After you left with Felka, I detached my head and placed it inside a small warhead casing. My brain tissue was buffered by interglial medichines to withstand rapid deceleration. The warhead was ejected backwards from *Nightshade*, back towards the other elements of the fleet. You never noticed because you were concerned only with the prospect of an attack against yourselves. The warhead fell through space silently until it was well beyond your detection sphere. Then it activated a focused homing pulse. One element of the fleet was delegated to change velocity until an intercept was feasible. The warhead was captured and brought aboard the other ship." She smiled and closed her eyes. "The late Doctor

Delmar was aboard another fleet vessel. Unfortunately it happened to be the ship you destroyed. But before his death he was able to finish the cloning of my new body. Neural reintegration was surprisingly easy, Clavain. You should try it one day."

Clavain almost stumbled on his words. "Then . . . you are whole again?"

"Yes." She said it tartly, as if the subject was a matter for mild regret. "Yes. I am whole again now."

"Then why do you choose to manifest this way?"

"As a reminder, Clavain, of what you made of me. I am still out there, you see. My ship survived the engagement. There was damage, yes—just as there was damage to your ship. But I haven't given up. I want what you have stolen from us."

He turned back to Felka, who was still watching patiently from her wooden stump. "Is this true? Is Skade still out there?"

"We can't know for sure," she said. "All we know is what this beta-level tells us. It could be lying, trying to destabilise us. But in that case Skade must have shown astonishing foresight to create it in the first place."

"And the surviving ships?"

"That's sort of why we woke you. They are out there. We have fixes on their flames even now." And then she told him that the three Conjoiner ships had streaked past at half the speed of light relative to *Nostalgia for Infinity*, just as the simulations had predicted. Weapons had been deployed, their activation sequences as carefully choreographed as the individual explosions in a fireworks performance. The Conjoiners had used particle beams and heavy relativistic railguns for the most part. *Infinity* had fired back with lighter versions of the same armaments, while also deploying two of the salvaged cache weapons. Both sides made much use of decoys and feints, and in the most critical phase of the engagement savage accelerations were endured as the ships tried to deviate from predicted flight-paths.

Neither side had been able to claim victory. One Conjoiner ship had been destroyed and damage wrought on the other two, but Clavain considered this almost as close to failure as having inflicted no damage at all. Two enemies were almost as dangerous as three.

And yet the outcome could have been so much worse. *Nostalgia for Infinity* had sustained some damage, but not enough to prevent it from making it to another solar system. None of the occupants had been hurt and none of the critical systems had been taken out.

"But we're not home and dry," Felka told him.

Clavain turned from Skade's image. "We're not?"

"The two ships that survived? They're turning around. Slowly but surely, they're sweeping back around to chase us."

Clavain let out a laugh. "But it'll take them light-years to make the turn."

"It wouldn't if they had inertia-suppression technology. But the machinery must have been damaged during the engagement. That doesn't mean they can't repair it again, however." She looked at Skade, but the image made no reaction. It was as if she had become a statue poised at the water's edge, a slightly macabre decorative feature of the glade.

"If they can, they will," Clavain said.

Felka agreed. "The Triumvirate ran simulations. Under certain assumptions, we can always outrun the pursuing ships—at least in our reference frame—for as long as you care to specify. We just have to keep crawling closer and closer to the speed of light. But that isn't much of a solution in my book."

"It isn't in mine either."

"Anyway, it doesn't happen to be practical. We do need to stop to make repairs, and sooner rather than later. *That's* why we woke you, Clavain."

Clavain walked back to the tree stumps. He lowered himself on to his with a crick of leg joints. "If there's a decision to be taken, there must be some choices on the table. Is that the case?"

"Yes."

He waited patiently, listening to the soothing white-noise hiss of the waterfall. "Well?"

Felka spoke with a reverent hush. "We're a long way out, Clavain. The Resurgam system is nine light-years behind us and there isn't another settled colony for fifteen light-years in any direction. But there's a solar system dead ahead of us. Two cool stars. It's a wide binary, but one of the stars has formed planets in stable orbits. They're mature, at least three billion years old. There's one world in the habitable zone that has a couple of small moons. Indications are that it has an oxygen atmosphere and a lot of water. There are even chlorophyll bands in the atmosphere."

Clavain asked, "Human terraforming?"

"No. There's no sign of human presence ever having established itself around these stars. Which leaves only one possibility, I think."

"The Pattern Jugglers."

She was evidently pleased that it did not need to be spelled out. "We always knew we'd stumble on more juggler worlds as we moved further out into the galaxy. We shouldn't be surprised to find one now."

"Dead ahead, just like that?"

"It isn't dead ahead, but it's close enough. We can slow down and reach it. If it's anything like the other Juggler worlds there may even be dry land; enough to take a few settlers."

"How many is a few?"

Felka smiled. "We won't know until we get there, will we?"

Clavain made his decision—it was, in truth, little more than a blessing on the obvious choice—and then returned to sleep. There were few medics amongst his crew, and almost none of them had received formal training beyond a few hasty memory uploads. But he trusted them when they said that he could not expect to survive more than one or two further cycles of freezing and thawing.

"But I'm an old man," he told them. "If I stay warm, I probably won't survive that way either."

"It'll have to be your choice," they told him, unhelpfully.

He was getting old, that was all. His genes were very antiquated, and though he had been through several rejuvenation programmes since leaving Mars, they had only reset a clock which then proceeded to start ticking again. Back on the Mother Nest they could have given him another half-century of virtual youth, had he wished . . . but he had never taken that final rejuvenation. The will had never been there after Galiana's strange return and her even stranger half-death.

He did not even know if he regretted it now. If they had been able to limp to a fully equipped colony world, somewhere that hadn't yet been ravaged by the Melding Plague, there might have been hope for him. But what difference would it have made? Galiana was still gone. He was still old inside his skull, still seeing the world through eyes that were yellow and weary with four hundred years of war. He had done what he could, and the emotional burden had cost him terribly, and he did not think he had the energy to do it one more time. It was enough that he had not totally failed this time.

And so he submitted to the reefersleep casket for the final time.

Just before he went under, he authorised a tight-beam laser transmission back to the dying Resurgam system. The message was one-time-pad coded for *Zodiacal Light*. If the other ship hadn't been totally destroyed, there was a chance it would intercept and decode the signal. It would never be seen by the other Conjoiner ships, and even if Skade's forces had somehow managed to sow receivers through Resurgam space, they would not be able to crack the encryption.

The message was very simple. It told Remontoire, Khouri, Thorn and the others that had gone with them that they were to slow and stop in the Pattern Juggler system; they would wait there for twenty years. That was enough time to allow *Zodiacal Light* to rendezvous with them; it was also enough time to establish a self-sustaining colony of a few tens of thousands of people, a hedge against any future catastrophe that might befall the ship.

Knowing this, feeling that in some small but significant way he had put his affairs in order, Clavain slept.

He woke to find that *Nostalgia for Infinity* had changed itself without consulting anyone.

No one knew why.

The changes were not at all apparent from within; it was only from the outside—seen from an inspection shuttle—that they became manifest. The changes had happened during the slow-down phase as the great ship was decelerating into the new system. With the inching speed of land erosion, the rear of the ship's conic hull, normally a smaller inverted cone in its own right, had become flattened, like the base of a chess piece. No control over this transformation had been possible, and indeed, much of it had already taken place before anyone had noticed. There were vaults of the great ship that were only visited by humans once or twice a century, and much of the rear of the hull fell into that category. The machinery that lurked there had been surreptitiously dismantled or relocated further up the hull, in other disused spaces. Ilia Volyova might have noticed sooner than anyone—not much had ever escaped Ilia Volyova—but she was gone now, and the ship had new tenants who were not yet as devoutly familiar with its territory.

The changes were neither life-threatening nor injurious to the ship's performance, but they remained puzzling, and further evidence—if any were needed—that the Captain's psyche had not completely vanished, and could be expected to surprise them still further at times in the future. There appeared little doubt that the Captain had played some role in the reshaping of the ship he had become. The question of whether the reshaping had been consciously driven, or had merely sprung from some irrational dreamlike whim, was much harder to answer.

So for the time being, because there were other things to worry about, they ignored it. *Nostalgia for Infinity* fell into tight orbit around the watery world and probes were sent arcing into the atmosphere and the vast turquoise oceans that nearly enclosed the world from pole to pole. Creamy cloud patterns had been dabbed on it in messy, exuberant swirls. There were no large landmasses; the visible ocean was unmarred except for a few carelessly tossed archipelagos of islands, splashes of ochre paint against corneal blue-green. The closer they had come, the more nearly certain it became that this was a Juggler World, and the indications turned out to be correct. Continental rafts of living biomass stained swathes of the ocean grey-green. The atmosphere could be breathed by humans, and there were enough trace elements in the soils and bedrocks of the islands to support self-sustaining colonies.

It wasn't perfect, by any means. Islands on Juggler worlds had a habit of vanishing under tsunamis mediated by the great semi-sentient biomass of the oceans themselves. But for twenty years, it would suffice. If the colonists wanted to stay, they'd have time to build pontoon cities floating on the sea itself.

A chain of islands—northerly, cold, but predicted to be tectonically stable—was selected.

"Why there, in particular?" Clavain asked. "There are other islands at the same latitude, and they can't be any less stable."

"There's something down there," Scorpio told him. "We keep getting a faint signal from it."

Clavain frowned. "A signal? But no one's ever supposed to have been here."

"It's just a radio pulse, very weak," Felka said. "But the modulation is interesting. It's Conjoiner code."

"We put a beacon down here?"

"We must have, at some point. But there's no record of any Conjoiner ship ever coming here. Except . . . " She paused, unwilling to say what had to be said.

"Well?"

"It probably doesn't mean anything, Clavain. But Galiana *could* have come here. It's not impossible, and we know she would have investigated any Juggler worlds she came across. Of course, we don't know where her ship went before the wolves found her, and by the time she made it back to the Mother Nest all on-board records were lost or corrupted. But who else could have left a Conjoiner beacon?"

"Anyone who was operating covertly. We don't know everything that the Closed Council got up to, even now."

"I thought it was worth mentioning, that's all."

He nodded. He had felt a great crescendo of hope, and then a wave of sadness that was made all the deeper by what had preceded it. Of course she had not been here. It was stupid of him even to entertain the thought. But there was something down below that merited investigation, and it was sensible to locate their settlement near the item of interest. He had no problem with that.

Detailed plans for settlement were quickly drawn up. Tentative surface camps were established a month after their arrival.

And that was when it happened. Slowly, unhurriedly, as if this were the most natural thing in the world for a four-kilometre-long space vessel, *Nostalgia for Infinity* began to lower its orbit, spiralling down into the thin upper reaches of the atmosphere. By then it had slowed itself, too, braking to sub-orbital velocity so that the friction of re-entry did not scald away the outer layer of its hull. There was panic aboard from some quarters, for the ship was acting outside of human control. But there was also a more general feeling of quiet, calm resignation about whatever was about to happen. Clavain and the Triumvirate did not understand their ship's intentions, but it was unlikely that it meant them harm, not now.

And so it proved. As the great ship fell out of orbit it tilted, bringing its long axis into line with the vertical defined by the planet's gravitational field. Nothing else was possible; the ship would have snapped its spine had it come in obliquely. But provided it did descend vertically, lowering down through the clouds like the detached spire of a cathedral, it would suffer no more structural stress than was imposed by normal one-gee starflight. Aboard, it even felt normal. There was only the dull roar of the motors, normally unheard, but now transmitted back through the hull via the surrounding medium of air, a ceaseless, distant thunder that became louder as the ship approached the ground.

But there was no ground below. Though the landing site it had selected was close to the target archipelago where the first camps had already been sited, the ship was lowering itself towards the sea.

My God, Clavain thought. Suddenly he understood why the ship had remade itself. It—or whatever part of the Captain remained in charge—must have had this descent in mind from the moment the nature of the watery planet became clear. It had flattened the spike of its tail to allow itself to rest on the seabed. Down below, the sea began to boil away under the assault of the drive flames. The ship descended through mountains of steam, billowing tens of kilometres into the stratosphere. The sea was a kilometre deep under the touchdown point, for the bed sloped sharply away from the archipelago's edge. But that kilometre hardly mattered. When Clavain felt the ship keel, coming to rest with a tremendous deep groan, most of it was still above the surface of the roiling waves.

On a nameless waterlogged world on the ragged edge of human space, under dual suns, *Nostalgia for Infinity* had landed.

EPILOGUE

For days after the landing the hull creaked and echoed from the lower depths as it adjusted to the external pressure of the ocean. Now and then, without human bidding, servitors scurried into the bilges to repair hull leaks where the seawater was surging in. The ship rocked ominously from time to time, but gradually anchored itself until it began to feel less like a temporary addition to the landscape than a weirdly hollowed-out geological feature: a sliver-thin stack of morbidly weathered pumice or obsidian; an ancient natural sea-tower wormed with man-made tunnels and caverns. Overhead, silver-grey clouds only occasionally ripped apart to reveal pastel-blue skies.

It was a week before anyone left the ship. For days, shuttles wheeled around it, circling it like nervous seabirds. Although not all the docking bays had been submerged, no one was yet willing to attempt a landing. Contact was however reestablished with the teams who had already landed on the Juggler world, and who had made the descent from the surface. Makeshift boats were sent across the water from the nearest island—a distance of fifteen kilometres only—until they kissed against the sheer-sided cliff of the ship. Depending on tidal conditions it was possible to reach a small human-only airlock.

Clavain and Felka were in the first boat to make it back to the island. They said nothing during the crossing as they slid through wet grey mist. Clavain felt cold and despondent as he watched the black wall of the ship fall back into the fog. The sea here was soup-thick with floating micro-organisms—they were on the very fringes of a major Juggler biomass focus—and the organisms had already begun to plaster themselves against the side of the ship above the waterline. There was a scabby green accretion, a little like verdigris, which made the ship look like it had been here for centuries. He wondered what would happen if they could not persuade *Nostalgia for Infinity* to take off again. They had twenty years to talk it into leaving, but if the ship had already made up its mind that it wanted to stay rooted here, he doubted very much that they would be able to persuade it otherwise. Perhaps it wanted a final resting place, where it could become a memorial to its crime and the redemptive act that had followed.

"Clavain . . . " Felka said.

He looked at her. "I'm all right."

"You look tired. But we need you, Clavain. We haven't even begun the struggle yet. Don't you understand? All that's happened so far is only the beginning. We have the weapons now . . . "

"A handful of them. And Skade still wants them."

"Then she'll have to fight us for them, won't she? She won't find that as easy as she imagines."

Clavain looked back, but the ship was hidden. "If we're still here, there won't be a lot we can do to stop her."

"We'll have the weapons themselves. But Remontoire will have returned by then, I'm sure of it. And he'll have *Zodiacal Light* with him. The damage wasn't fatal; a ship like that can repair itself."

Clavain tightened his lips and agreed. "I suppose so."

She held his hand as if to warm it. "What's wrong, Clavain? You brought us so far. We followed you. You can't give up now."

"I'm not giving up," he said. "I'm just . . . tired. It's time to let someone else carry on the fight. I've been a soldier too long, Felka."

"Then become something else."

"That's not quite what I meant." He tried to force some cheer into his voice. "Look, I'm not going to die tomorrow, or next week. I owe it to everyone to get this settlement off the ground. I just don't think I'll necessarily be here when Remontoire makes it back. But who knows? Time has a nasty way of surprising me. God knows I've learned that often enough."

They continued in silence. The crossing was choppy, and now and then the boat had to steer itself past huge seaweedlike concentrations of ropy biomass, which shifted and reacted to the boat's presence in an unnervingly purposeful way. Presently Clavain sighted land, and shortly after that the boat skidded to a halt in a few feet of water, bottoming out on rock.

They had to get out and wade the rest of the way to dry land. Clavain was shivering by the time he squelched out of the last inch of water. The boat looked a long way away, and *Nostalgia for Infinity* was nowhere to be seen at all.

Antoinette Bax came to meet them, picking her way carefully across a field of rockpools that gleamed like a tessellation of perfect grey mirrors. Behind her, on a higher rising slope of land, was the first encampment: a hamlet of bubbletents stapled into rock.

Clavain wondered how it would look in twenty years.

More than one hundred and sixty thousand people were aboard *Nostalgia for Infinity,* far too many to place on one island. There would be a chain of settlements, instead—as many as fifty, with a few hubs on the larger, drier nubs of land. Once those settlements were established, work could begin on the floating colonies that would provide long-term shelter. There would be enough work here to keep anyone busy. He felt an obligation to be part of it, but no sense that it was anything he had been born to do.

He felt, in fact, that he had *done* what he was born to do.

"Antoinette," he said, knowing that Felka would not have recognised the woman without his help, "how are things on dry land?"

"There's shit brewing already, Clavain."

He kept his eyes on the ground, for fear of tripping. "Do tell."

"A lot of people aren't happy with the idea of staying here. They bought into Thorn's exodus because they wanted to go home, back to Yellowstone. Being stuck on an uninhabited pissball for twenty years wasn't quite what they had in mind."

Clavain nodded patiently. He steadied himself against Felka, using her as a walking stick. "And did you impress on these people the fact that they'd be dead if they hadn't come with us?"

"Yes, but you know what it's like. No pleasing some people, is there?" She shrugged. "Well, just thought I'd cheer you up with that, in case you thought it was all going to be plain sailing from now on."

"For some reason, that thought never crossed my mind. Now, can someone show us around the island?"

Felka helped him pick his way on to smoother ground. "Antoinette, we're cold and wet. Is there somewhere we can get warm and dry?"

"Just follow me. We've even got tea on the go."

"Tea?" Felka asked suspiciously.

"Seaweed tea. Local. But don't worry. No one's died of it yet, and you do eventually get used to the taste."

"I suppose we'd better make a start," Clavain said.

They followed Antoinette into the huddle of tents. People were at work outside, putting up new tents and plumbing-in snakelike power cables from turtle-shaped generators. She led them into one enclosure, sealing the flap behind them. It was warmer inside, and drier, but this served only to make Clavain feel more damp and cold than he had a moment before.

Twenty years in a place like this, he thought. They'd be busy staying alive, yes, but what kind of a life was one of pure struggle for existence? The Jugglers might prove endlessly fascinating, awash with eternally old mysteries of cosmic provenance, or they might not wish to communicate with the humans at all. Although lines of rapport had been established between humans and Pattern Jugglers on the other Juggler worlds, it had sometimes taken decades of study before the key was found to unlock the aliens. Until then, they were little more than sluggish vegetative masses, evidencing the work of intelligence without in any way revealing it themselves. What if this turned out to be the first group of Jugglers that did not wish to drink human neural patterns? It would be a lonely and bleak place to stay, shunned by the very things one had imagined might make it tolerable. Staying with Remontoire, Khouri and Thorn, plunging into the intricate structure of the living neutron star, might begin to seem like the more attractive option.

Well, in twenty years they'd find out whether *that* had been the case.

Antoinette pushed a mug of green-coloured tea in front of him. "Drink up, Clavain."

He sipped at it, wrinkling his nose against the miasma of pungent, briny fumes that hovered above the drink. "What if I'm drinking a Pattern Juggler?"

"Felka says you won't be. She should know, I think—I gather she's been itching to meet these bastards for quite a while, so she knows a thing or two about them."

Clavain gave the tea another go. "Yes, that's true, isn't . . . "

But Felka had gone. She had been in the tent a moment ago, but now she wasn't.

"Why does she want to meet them so badly?" Antoinette asked.

"Because of what she hopes they'll give her," Clavain said. "Once, when she lived on Mars, she was at the core of something very complex—a vast, living machine she had to keep alive with her own willpower and intellect. It was what gave her a reason to live. Then people—my people, as a matter of fact—took the machine away from her. She nearly died then, if she had ever truly been alive. And yet she didn't. She made it back to something like normal life. But everything that has followed, everything that she has done since, has been a way to find something else that she can use and that will use her in the same way; something so intricate that she can't understand all its secrets in a single intuitive flash, and something that, in its own way, might be able to exploit her as well."

"The Jugglers."

Still clasping the tea—and it wasn't so bad, really, he noted—he said, "Yes, the Jugglers. Well, I hope she finds what she's looking for, that's all."

Antoinette reached beneath the table and hefted something up from the floor. She placed it between them: a corroded metal cylinder covered in a lacy froth of calcified micro-organisms.

"This is the beacon. They found it yesterday, a mile down. There must have been a tsunami which washed it into the sea."

He leaned over and examined the hunk of metal. It was squashed and dented, like an old rations tin that had been stepped on. "It could be Conjoiner," he said. "But I'm not sure. There aren't any markings which have survived."

"I thought the code was Conjoiner?"

"It was: it's a simple in-system transponder beacon. It's not meant to be detected over much more than a few hundred million kilometres. But that doesn't mean it was put here by Conjoiners. Ultras could have stolen it from one of our ships, perhaps. We'll know a little more when we dismantle it, but that has to be done carefully." He rapped the rough metal husk with his knuckles. "There is anti-matter in here, or it wouldn't be transmitting. Not much, maybe, but enough to make a dent in this island if we don't open it properly."

"Rather you than me."

"Clavain . . . "

He looked around; Felka had returned. She looked even wetter than when they had arrived. Her hair was glued to her face in lank ribbons, and the black fabric of her dress was tight against one side of her body. She should have been pale and shivering, by Clavain's estimation. But she was flushed red, and she looked excited.

"Clavain," she repeated.

He put down the tea. "What is it?"

"You have to come outside and see this."

He stepped out of the tent. He had warmed up just enough to feel a sudden spike of cold as he did so, but something in Felka's manner made him ignore it, just as he had long ago learned to selectively suppress pain or discomfort in the heat of battle. It did not matter for now; it could, like most things in life, be dealt with later, or not at all.

Felka was looking out to sea.

"What is it?" he asked again.

"Look. Do you see?" She stood by him and directed his gaze. "Look. Look hard, where the mist thins out."

"I'm not sure if—"

"Now."

And he did see it, if only fleetingly. The local wind direction must have changed since they had arrived in the tent, enough to push the fog around into a different configuration and allow brief openings that reached far out to sea. He saw the mosaic of sharp-edged rockpools, and beyond that the boat they had come in on, and beyond that a horizontal stroke of slate-grey water which turned fainter as his eye skidded toward the horizon, becoming the pale milky grey of the sky itself. And there, for an instant, was the upright spire of *Nostalgia for Infinity,* a tapering finger of slightly darker grey rising from just below the horizon line itself.

"It's the ship," Clavain said mildly, determined not to disappoint Felka.

"Yes," she said. "It's the ship. But you don't understand. It's more than that. It's much, much more."

Now he was beginning to feel slightly worried. "It is?"

"Yes. Because I've seen it before."

"Before?"

"Long before we ever came here, I saw it." She turned to him, peeling hair from her eyes, squinting against the sting of the spray. "It was the Wolf, Clavain. It showed me this view when Skade coupled us together. At the time I didn't know what to make of it. But now I understand. It wasn't really the Wolf at all. It was Galiana, getting through to me even though the Wolf *thought* it was in control."

Clavain knew what had happened aboard Skade's ship while Felka was her hostage. He had been told about the experiments, and the times when Felka had glimpsed the Wolf's mind. But she had never mentioned this before.

"It must be a coincidence," he said. "Even if you did get a message from Galiana, how could she have known what was going to happen here?"

"I don't know, but there must have been a way. Information has already reached the past, or none of this would have happened. All we know now is that somehow, our memories of this place—whether they're yours or mine—*will reach the past*. More than that, they *will* reach Galiana." Felka leaned down and touched the rock beneath her. "Somehow this is the crux, Clavain. We haven't just stumbled on this place. We've been led here by Galiana because she knows that it matters that we find it."

Clavain thought back to the beacon he had just been shown. "If she had been here . . . "

Felka completed the thought. "If she came here, she would have attempted communion with the Pattern Jugglers. She would have tried swimming with them. Now, she may not have succeeded . . . but just supposing she did, what would have happened?"

The mist had closed in completely now; there was no sign of the looming sea-tower.

"Her neural patterns would have been remembered," Clavain said, as if speaking in a dream. "The ocean would have recorded her essence, her personality, her memories. Everything that she was. She'd have left it physically, but also left behind a holographic copy of herself, in the sea, ready to be imprinted on another sentience, another mind."

Felka nodded emphatically. "Because that's what they do, Clavain. Pattern Jugglers store all who swim in their oceans."

Clavain looked out, hoping to glimpse the ship again. "Then she'd still be here."

"And we can reach her ourselves if we swim as well. That's what she knew, Clavain. That's the message she slipped past the Wolf."

His eyes were stinging as well. "She's a clever one, that Galiana. What if we're wrong?"

"We'll know. Not necessarily the first time, but we'll know. All we have to do is swim and open our minds. If she's in the sea, in their collective memory, the Jugglers will bring her to us."

"I don't think I could stand for this to be wrong, Felka."

She took his hand and squeezed it tighter. "We won't be wrong, Clavain. We won't be wrong."

He hoped against hope that she was right. She tugged his hand harder, and the two of them took the first tentative steps towards the sea.

NOW AVAILABLE IN HARDCOVER

THE PREFECT

By Alastair Reynolds

Tom Dreyfus is a Prefect—a law enforcement officer with the Panoply. His beat is the multifaceted utopian society of the Glitter Band, a vast swirl of space habitats.

His current case: investigating a murderous attack against one of the habitats. But then his investigation uncovers something even more potentially dangerous . . .

"Absorbing . . . a fine, provocative portrait of utopia on the brink."
—*Locus*

"Highly recommended."
—*Darker Matter*

penguin.com

M237T0108

Chosen by *Locus* and *Science Fiction Chronicle* as

ONE OF THE BEST SCIENCE FICTION NOVELS OF THE YEAR

Alastair Reynolds

CHASM CITY

"DEEP, COMPLEX . . . A NEW WORLD OF WONDER."

—*Denver Post*

In a city overrun by a virus that attacks both man and machine, an agent pursues a lowlife postmortal—and uncovers a centuries-old atrocity that history would rather forget.

"POWRFUL . . . CONFIRMS REYNOLDS AS THE MOST EXCITING SPACE OPERA WRITER WORKING TODAY."

—*Locus*

"SPACE OPERA AT ITS FANTASTIC BEST."

—*BookBrowser*

penguin.com

M119T0907